FROZEN

The first book in the Cold Awakening trilogy

ROBIN WASSERMAN

Previously published as *Skinned*

Simon Pulse

NEW YORK   LONDON   TORONTO   SYDNEY

ᚮᚮᚮ

SIMON PULSE

An imprint of Simon & Schuster Children's Publishing Division
1230 Avenue of the Americas, New York, NY 10020
This Simon Pulse paperback edition October 2011
Copyright © 2008 by Robin Wasserman
Previously published as *Skinned*.
All rights reserved, including the right of reproduction in whole or in part in any form.
SIMON PULSE and colophon are registered trademarks of Simon & Schuster, Inc.
Also available in a Simon Pulse hardcover edition.
For information about special discounts for bulk purchases, please contact
Simon & Schuster Special Sales at 1-866-506-1949 or business@simonandschuster.com.
The Simon & Schuster Speakers Bureau can bring authors to your live event.
For more information or to book an event contact the Simon & Schuster Speakers Bureau
at 1-866-248-3049 or visit our website at www.simonspeakers.com.
Designed by Mike Rosamilia
The text of this book was set in Edlund.
Manufactured in the United States of America
2 4 6 8 10 9 7 5 3 1
The Library of Congress has cataloged the hardcover edition as follows:
Wasserman, Robin.
Skinned / Robin Wasserman.—1st Simon Pulse ed.
p. cm.
Summary: To save her from dying in a horrible accident, Lia's wealthy parents
transplant her brain into a mechanical body.
ISBN 978-1-4169-3634-3 (hc)
[1. Science fiction.] I. Title.
PZ7.W25865Sk
[Fic]—dc22
2008015306
ISBN 978-1-4424-2038-0 (pbk)
ISBN 978-1-4424-3359-5 (eBook)

FROZEN

The first book in the Cold Awakening trilogy

ROBIN WASSERMAN

Previously published as *Skinned*

Simon Pulse

NEW YORK   LONDON   TORONTO   SYDNEY

〰️

SIMON PULSE

An imprint of Simon & Schuster Children's Publishing Division

1230 Avenue of the Americas, New York, NY 10020

This Simon Pulse paperback edition October 2011

Copyright © 2008 by Robin Wasserman

Previously published as *Skinned*.

All rights reserved, including the right of reproduction in whole or in part in any form.

SIMON PULSE and colophon are registered trademarks of Simon & Schuster, Inc.

Also available in a Simon Pulse hardcover edition.

For information about special discounts for bulk purchases, please contact Simon & Schuster Special Sales at 1-866-506-1949 or business@simonandschuster.com.

The Simon & Schuster Speakers Bureau can bring authors to your live event. For more information or to book an event contact the Simon & Schuster Speakers Bureau at 1-866-248-3049 or visit our website at www.simonspeakers.com.

Designed by Mike Rosamilia

The text of this book was set in Edlund.

Manufactured in the United States of America

2 4 6 8 10 9 7 5 3 1

The Library of Congress has cataloged the hardcover edition as follows:

Wasserman, Robin.

Skinned / Robin Wasserman.—1st Simon Pulse ed.

p. cm.

Summary: To save her from dying in a horrible accident, Lia's wealthy parents transplant her brain into a mechanical body.

ISBN 978-1-4169-3634-3 (hc)

[1. Science fiction.] I. Title.

PZ7.W25865Sk

[Fic]—dc22

2008015306

ISBN 978-1-4424-2038-0 (pbk)

ISBN 978-1-4424-3359-5 (eBook)

For Norton Wise, under whose warm and watchful eye
this story first began, even if neither of us
realized it at the time

FROZEN

If you had never seen anything but mounds of lead, pieces of marble, stones, and pebbles, and you were presented with a beautiful windup watch and little automata that spoke, sang, played the flute, ate, and drank, such as those which dextrous artists now know how to make, what would you think of them, how would you judge them, before you examined the springs that made them move? Would you not be led to believe that they had a soul like your own . . . ?

—Anonymous, 1744
Translated from the French by Gaby Wood

THE FIRST DAY

"As last days go, mine sucked."

Lia Kahn is dead.

   I am Lia Kahn.

   Therefore—because this is a logic problem even a dim-witted child could solve—I am dead.

   Except here's the thing: I'm not.

"Don't panic."

   It was my father's voice.

   It was—and it wasn't. It sounded wrong. Muffled and tinny, but somehow, at the same time, too clear and too precise.

   There was no pain.

   But I knew—before I knew anything else—I knew there should have been.

Something pried open my eyes. The world was a kaleido-scope, shapes and colors spinning without pattern, without sense until, without warning, my eyes closed again, and there was nothing. No pain, no sensation, no sense of whether I was lying down or standing up. It wasn't that I couldn't move my legs. It wasn't even that I couldn't *feel* my legs. It was that, with my eyes closed, I couldn't have said whether I had legs or not.

Or arms.

Or anything.

I think, therefore I am, I thought with a wave of giddiness. I would have giggled, but I couldn't feel my mouth.

I panicked.

Paralyzed.

There had been a car, I remembered that. And a noise, like a scream but not quite; not animal and not human.

And fire. Something on fire. The smell of something burn-ing. I remembered that.

I didn't want to remember that.

I couldn't move. I couldn't speak. I couldn't open my own eyes.

They don't know I'm awake in here. In my mind I heard the pounding heartbeat that I could no longer feel, felt imaginary lungs constricting in terror, tasted the salt of invisible tears. *They can't.*

To my father; to my mother, who I imagined huddled out-side the room, crying, unable to come inside; to the doctors, who my father would surely have had shipped in from all over the world; to Zoie, who should have been in the car, who should have been the one—

To all of them I would appear unconscious. Unaware.

I could imagine time slipping by, the doctor's voice rising over my mother's sobs. Still no response. *Still no movement, no sound, no flicker of her eyes. Still no sign of life.*

My eyes were opened again, for longer this time. The colors swam together, resolving into blurry shapes, a world underwater. At the upper fringe of my vision I caught something bulbous and fleshy, fingers prying my lids apart. And hovering over me, a dim, fuzzy figure, speaking with my father's voice.

"I don't know if you can hear me yet." His tone was steady, his words stiff. "But I assure you everything will be all right. Try to be patient."

My father pulled his hand away from my face, and my eyelids met again, shutting me behind a screen of black. He stayed. I knew, because I could hear his breathing—just not my own.

As last days go, mine sucked.

The last day I would have chosen—the last day I deserved— would have involved more chocolate. Significantly more. Dark. Milk. White. Bittersweet. Olive infused. Caramel filled. Truffle. Ganache. There would have been cheese, too, the soft, runny kind that stinks up a room as it dribbles down your throat. I would have lay in bed all day, eating the food I can no longer eat, listening to the music I no longer care to hear, *feeling*. The scratchy cotton of the sheets. The pillowcase, at first cool to the touch, warmth slowly blooming against my cheek. Stale air hissing out of the vent, sweeping my bangs across my forehead. And Walker—because if I had known, I would have made him come over, I would have said screw my parents, forget my sister, just be here, with me, today—I would have felt the downy hair on his arms and the scratchy bristles sprouting on his chin, which, despite my instructions, he was still too lazy to shave more than once a week. I would have felt his fingertips on my skin, a ticklish graze so light that, for all that it promised and refused to deliver, it almost hurt. I would have tasted peppermint on his lips and known it meant he'd elected gum over toothpaste that morning. I would have made him dig his stubby nails into my skin, not only because I didn't want him to let go, but because along with one last real pleasure, I would have wanted one last pain.

This can't be happening.

Not to me.

I lay there. I tried to be patient, as my father had asked. I waited to wake up.

Yeah, I know: total cliché. *This must be a dream.* You tell yourself that, and maybe you even pinch yourself, even though you know it's cheesy, that the mere act proves it's *not* a dream. In a dream you never question reality. In a dream people vanish, buildings appear, scenes shift, you fly. You fall. It all makes perfect sense. You only reject weirdness when you're awake.

So I waited to wake up.

Big shock: I didn't.

Stage one, denial. Check.

I learned the five stages of grief when my grandfather died. Not that I passed through them. Not that I grieved, not really, not for some guy I'd only met twice, who my father seemed to loathe and my mother, the dead man's only daughter, claimed to barely remember. She cried anyway, and my father put up with it—for a few days, at least. We all did. He brought her flowers. I didn't roll my eyes, not even when she knocked over her glass at dinner for the third time in a row, with that same annoying aren't-I-clumsy giggle. And Zo pumped the network and dug up the five stages of grief.

Denial. Anger. Bargaining. Depression. Acceptance.

Since I was dead—or worse than dead, buried alive in a body that might as well be a coffin except it denied me the pleasure of suffocation—I figured I should be allowed to grieve.

No, not grieve. That wasn't the right word.

Rage.

I hated everyone, everything. The car for crashing. My body for burning, for breaking. Zo for sending me in her place. For living, breathing, partying somewhere beyond the darkness, in a body that worked. I hated Walker for forgetting me, like I knew he would, for the girls he would date and the girls he would screw and the girl he would curl up with in his bed, his arms closing around her, his lips whispering promises about how she was the only one. I hated the doctors who marched in and out, prying my eyes open, blinding me with their pen-size lights, squinting, staring, waiting for some kind of reaction I couldn't give them, all while I was screaming in my head *I'm awake I'm alive Hear me Help me* and then the lids would shut me into the black again.

My father stayed by my side, the only one to speak to me, an unending monotonic litany: *Be patient, Lia. Try to wake up, Lia. Try to move, Lia. It will be okay, Lia. Work at it, Lia. You'll be okay.* I wanted to believe him, because I had always believed him. I wanted to believe that he would fix this like he'd fixed everything else. I wanted to believe him, but I couldn't, so I hated him most of all.

Next came bargaining. There was no one to plead with, but I pleaded anyway. First, to wake up—to open my eyes, sit up, swing my legs out of bed, walk away, and forget the whole thing. But that obviously wasn't happening. So I compromised: Just let me open my eyes, let me be able to speak, let me be able to move and feel. Let this not be permanent. Let me get better.

And then, later, still no change, still no hope: Let me open my eyes. Let me speak. Let me escape.

That was before the pain.

Like the doctors, it didn't bother to sneak up on me. It exploded, a starburst of light in the black. I lived in the pain. It was my whole being, it was timeless, it was forever—and then it was gone.

That was the beginning.

Intense pleasure, a spreading warmth building to an almost intolerable fire. Biting cold. Searing heat. Misery. A bubbling happiness that wanted only to laugh. Fear—no, terror. Sensations sweeping over me from out of nowhere, disappearing just as fast as they came, with no reason, no pattern, no warning. And—never staying away too long before returning for a visit—the pain.

I never slept. I could feel the time pass, could tell from the things the doctors muttered to one another that days were slipping by, but I never lost consciousness. I lost control when the waves came, I lost reason and lost myself in the bottomless sensations, but I never got swept away, much as I wanted to. And in the moments in between, when the dark waters were still and I was myself again, I went back to bargaining.

Let me sleep.

Let me die.

"I'll do it—but you owe me," I had told Zo. Before.

She'd ignored me, twisting her hair into a loose bun and clipping it just above her neck. Her hair was blond, like mine, except mine was shiny and full and bounced around my shoulders when I laughed, and hers was tangled and limp and, no matter what she did, looked like it hadn't been washed. I always told her she was just as pretty as me, but we both knew the truth.

"Try again. *You* owe *me*," she finally said, pulling on a faded brown sweatshirt that made her look like a potato. I didn't mention it. Our parents had selected for girls, selected for blond hair and blue eyes, paid the extra credit to ensure decently low body-mass indexes and decently high IQs, but there was no easily screened-out gene for sloth—no amount of cash that would have guaranteed a Zo who didn't piss all over every genetic advantage she'd received. "Or do you want me to tell Dad where you *really* were this weekend? I'm sure he'd love to know that when you said 'cramming for exams' you really meant 'cramming your face into Walker's'—"

"I said I'd do it, *Zoie*." She hated the name. I snatched the key card out of her hand. "So, do I get to know where you'll be while I'm changing diapers and wiping snot on your behalf?"

"No."

Neither of us had to work. Given the size of our parents' credit account, neither of us would *ever* have to work. Except for the fact that our father was a big believer in productivity.

Arbeit macht frei, he used to tell us when we were kids. It's German, like my great-great-great-grandparents. *Work will set you free.*

I was twelve the day I repeated that to one of my teachers. She slapped me. And then she told me where the slogan came from. The Nazis preached it to their prisoners. Right before working them to death.

"Ancient history," my father said when I gave him the bad news. "Statute of limitations on grudges expires after a hundred years." He had the teacher fired.

I wasn't required to get a job because I was an athlete. A *winner*, my father said every time I brought home another track trophy. A *worker*. He never came to the meets, but the first-place trophies lined a bookshelf in his office. The second-place ones stayed in my room. Everything else went in the trash.

Zo didn't play a sport. She didn't, as far as I could tell, do anything but hang around parking lots with her loser friends and get zoned on dozers, some new kind that puffed out these foul clouds of smoke when you sucked, so you could feel like a retro from the bad old days before the nicotine ban. "Explain to me why it's cool to look like Grandma," I asked her once.

"I don't do things because they're cool," Zo snapped back. "That's you."

Just for the record, I didn't do things because they were cool.

Things were cool because I did them.

So every day, I ran ten miles at the track while Zo worked her dad-ordained shift at the day-care center, wiping drippy noses and changing shitty diapers, except on the days she suckered me into doing it for her.

"Fine," I told Zo. "But I swear to you, this is the last time."

It was.

The coordinates were already programmed into the car. Our father would check that night to make sure it had gone where it was supposed to, but he'd have no way of knowing which sister had gone along for the ride. TotLand, I keyed in, then flung myself into the backseat. Walker couldn't wait to be eighteen so he could drive manually, but I didn't get the point. Better to curl up and let the seat mold itself to my body, listen to a mag, link in with Walker to remind him about that night's party, cruise the network to make sure none of my friends had stuck up pics of something I shouldn't have missed (an impossibility since, by general agreement, if I'd missed it, it was worth missing).

But that day I unplugged. No chats, no links, no vids, no music, no nothing. Silence. I closed my eyes.

There was this feeling that I only got when I was running, a couple miles in, after the tidal wave of exhaustion swept past and the world narrowed to the slap of my feet on the pavement and the air whistling through my lungs and the buzzing in my ears— not a feeling, actually, but an absence of feeling, an absence of self. Like I didn't exist anymore. At least not as Lia Kahn; that I was nothing but a blur of arms and legs, grunts, pounding blood, tearing muscle, wind, all body, no mind. Lying there that day with my eyes closed should have been nothing like that, but somehow it was. Somehow *I* was: Empty. Free of worry, free of thought. Lost in the black behind my lids.

Like a part of me knew it was going to happen.

Like when everything flipped upside down and the scream of metal on metal exploded the silence and the world churned around me, ground over sky over ground over sky, and then, with a thunderous crack and a crunching of glass and steel, a twisted roof crushing me into a gutted floor, *ground*, I wasn't surprised.

I tell people I don't remember what happened after that. I tell them I hit my head and it all went dark. They believe me. They *want* to believe me.

They don't want to hear how I lay trapped, skin gnashed by metal teeth; legs numb, *absent*, like the universe ended at my waist; arms torn from sockets, twisted, white hot with pain. They don't want to hear how one eye was blinded behind a film of blood but the other saw clearly: black smoke, a slice of blue through a shattered window, freckled skin spattered with red, the white gleam of bone. An orange flicker.

They don't want to hear what it felt like when I started to burn.

I wish I could say my life had flashed before my eyes while I was trapped in that bed. It might have made things more interesting. I tried to force it. I thought if I could remember everything that had ever happened to me, moment by moment, then maybe it would be almost like being alive again. I could at least kill some hours, maybe even days, reliving Lia Kahn's greatest hits. But it was useless. I would start with the earliest moment I could remember—say, screaming at the pinprick pain of my first morning med-check, convinced by toddler rationality that the tiny silver point would suck out all my blood, while my mother smoothed back my hair and begged me to stop crying, promising me a cookie, a lollipop, a puppy, anything to shut me up before my father arrived. I would remember the tears wet on my face, my father's disgust clear on his—and then I would think about how the daily med-checks and DNA-personalized medicine were supposed to make us all healthy and safe and live nearly forever, and how *nearly* wasn't close enough when your car's nav system crapped out and rammed you into a truck or a tree and flipped you over and chewed you up. I would remember my mother's hand across my forehead, and wonder why I never heard her voice in my room.

Days passed.

I made lists. People I knew. People I hated. Words starting with the letter *Q*. I tried to make a list of all the ViMs I'd ever owned, from the pink My First Virtual Machine with its oversize buttons and baby-proofed screen to my current favorite, a neon blue nanoViM that you could adhere to your shirt, your wrist, even, if you felt like flashing vids as you sashayed down the hall, your ass. Not that I'd tried that . . . more than once. But things got hazy midway through the list— There'd been too many ViMs to remember them all, since if you had enough credit, which I did, you could wire almost anything to function as a virtual computer that would link into the network.

I sang songs to myself. I practiced the lines I'd been forced to memorize for English class, because, according to my clueless teacher, "the theater may be dead, but Shakespeare is immortal."

"To die,—to sleep;—
No more; and by a sleep to say we end
The heart-ache, and the thousand natural shocks
That flesh is heir to, 'tis a consummation
Devoutly to be wish't."

Whatever that meant. Walker had done a passage from *Romeo and Juliet* with Bliss Tanzen playing Juliet, and I wondered if Bliss would be the one—or if you counted her D-cups, the three—to replace me.

I listened to the doctors, wishing they would betray some detail of their personal lives or at least say *something* other than "delta waves down," "alpha frequency boosted," "rhythm confirmed as normal variant," or any of the other phrases that floated back and forth between them. I tried to move my arms and legs; I tried to *feel* them. I could tell, when they opened my eyes, that I was lying on my back. It meant there must be a bed beneath me, some kind of sheets. So I tried to imagine my fingers resting on scratchy cotton. But the more time passed, the harder it was to even imagine I had fingers. For all I knew, I didn't.

I stopped trying.

I stopped thinking. I drifted through the days in a gray mist, awake but not awake, unmoving but uncaring.

So when it finally happened, it wasn't because of me. I wasn't trying. I didn't even know what I was doing. It just . . . *happened.* Eyes closed, eyes closed, eyes closed—

Eyes open.

There was a shout, maybe a doctor, maybe my father, I couldn't tell, because I was staring at a gray ceiling, but I'd done it, I'd opened my eyes, somehow, and they stayed open.

Something else moved. An arm.

My arm. And, for a moment, I forgot everything in the pure blast of relief: *my* arm. Intact. I couldn't feel it, wasn't trying to move it, but I *saw* it. Saw it jerk upward, across my field of vision, then back down to the bed again, hard, with a

thump. Then the other arm. Up. Down. *Thump*. And my legs—
They must have been my legs. I couldn't feel them, couldn't
see them, but I could hear them against the mattress, a drum-
beat of *thump, thump, thump*. My neck arched backward and
the ceiling spun away, and I was flying and then a thud, loud,
like a body crashing against a floor. *Crack, crack, crack* as my
head slapped the tile, slapped it again, again, all noise and no
pain, and then feet pounded toward me and all I wanted was
the motionlessness of the dark again, but now I couldn't close
my eyes, and two hands, pudgy and white and uncalloused,
grabbed my face and held it still, and then for the first time
since I'd woken up, everything stopped.

To sleep: perchance to dream.

EYES WIDE OPEN

"Some kind of total freak?"

There were no dreams.

I opened my eyes.

I opened my eyes. It was a triumph. If I could have smiled, I would have.

But I couldn't.

I closed my eyes, just because I could. Then opened them again. Close. Open. Close. Open. It wasn't much.

But it was something.

"Lia, can you hear me?" It was a new voice, one I didn't recognize. The face appeared. Small mouth, big nose, squinty brown eyes with a deep crease between them. His parents must not have cared enough to spend the credit on good looks, I decided. Either that or his gene pool was so crowded with ugly, this was the best he could get. "Lia, I want you to listen to what I'm saying and try to respond if you understand me."

Respond how? I wondered. For a doctor, he didn't seem to have much grasp of the situation.

"Our instruments are indicating that you've gained control of some key facial muscles, Lia. You should be able to blink. Can you blink now, if you understand me? Just once, nice and slow?"

I closed my eyes. Counted to three. Opened them again.

All I'd done was blink, but the doctor beamed like I'd won a championship race. Which should have seemed completely lame. Except I felt like I had.

And that felt pretty good, right up until the point when I started wondering why I could blink, but still couldn't speak or move. I wondered how long that would last.

I wondered if I could figure out the blink code for "Kill me."

"You were in an accident," he said with a little hesitation in his voice, like he was telling me something I didn't know. Like he was worried I would freak out. How much freaking out did he expect from a living corpse?

"I'm sure you have questions. I think we've got a way to help you with that. But first we need to establish a cognitive baseline. Is that okay? Blink once for yes, twice for no."

No. *Not* okay. Okay would have been him telling me exactly what was wrong with me and how he was planning to fix it. And when. But that answer wasn't an option. I was stuck in a binary world: Yes or no. I blinked once.

It was something.

"Are you in pain right now?"

Two blinks. No.

"Have you been conscious at any point before now?"

One blink.

"Have you been in pain?"

One blink. I kept my eyes closed for a long time, hoping he'd get the point. His expression didn't change.

"Are you able to move any part of your body?"

Two blinks.

I suddenly wondered if I was crying. I probably should have been crying.

"I'm going to apply some pressure now, and I want you to blink when you feel something, okay? This might hurt a little."

I stared at the ceiling. I waited.

No blink.

No blink.

This can't be happening to me.

The doctor frowned. "Interesting."

Interesting? Forget asking him to kill me. I wanted *him* to die.

His face disappeared from view, replaced by a large white paper, filled with row after row of block letters in alphabetical order.

"We're going to try this the old-fashioned way, Lia. I'm going to point at the letters one by one, and you blink when I get to the one you want. Make sense?"

One blink.

"Do you know your name?" This from the idiot who'd been calling me Lia from the moment he walked in the room.

His stubby finger skimmed along the letters. I blinked when it got to *L*. He started again at the beginning, and I blinked at *I*. Again, *A*.

"Good, very good. And your last name?"

Letter by letter we finally got there. It was just so freaking slow.

There was more pointless trivia: my parents' names, the year, my birthday, the president's name, and all of it painfully spelled out, letter by letter, blink by blink. I'd waited so long to make contact, but pretty soon I just wanted him to go away. It was too hard. I didn't let myself think about what would happen if this was it, all I would ever have. A white sheet, black letters, his stubby finger. Blink, blink.

"Now that you've reached this level, we should be able to move on to the next stage. It's just going to take a little longer to implement. Is there anything you want to ask in the meantime?"

One blink.

The letters reappeared and his finger crawled along.

W. Blink.

H. Blink.

A. Blink.

T. Blink.

WRONG WITH ME.

Blink.

I could tell from his expression it was the wrong question.

"As I said, Lia, you've been in an accident. Your body sustained quite a bit of damage. But I assure you that we've been able to repair it. The lack of motive ability and sensation is quite normal under the circumstances, as your neural network adjusts to its new . . . circumstances. The pain and other sensations you may have experienced while you've been with us are a positive sign, an indication that your brain is exploring its new pathways, relearning how to process sensory information. It's going to take some time and some hard work, Lia, and there may be some . . . complications to work through, but we *will* get you walking and talking again."

He said more after that, but I wasn't listening. I didn't hear anything after "walking and talking again." They were going to fix me. Whatever complications there were, however long it took, I would get my life back.

"Is there anything else you want to ask?"

Two blinks. After the second one, I kept my eyes closed until he went away.

The bed was mechanical. It whirred quietly, and slowly the ceiling tipped away until I was sitting up. For the first time, I could see the room. It wasn't much, but it was at least a different view, a better one than the ceiling, whose flat, unblemished gray plaster was even less interesting than the black behind my eyes. It didn't look like any hospital room I'd ever seen. There was no machinery, no medical equipment, no sink, and no bathroom. I couldn't smell that telltale hospital mélange of disinfectant and puke. But then, I realized, I couldn't smell much of anything. There was a dresser that looked like my dresser, although I could tell it wasn't. A desk that looked like my desk. Speakers and a vidscreen, lit up with randomly flickering images of friends and family. No mirror.

Someone had gone to a fair amount of effort to make the place feel like home.

Someone was expecting me to stay for a while.

A horde crowded around me. Doctors, I assumed, although none of them wore white coats. At the foot of the bed, clutching each other, my mother and father. Although, to be accurate, only my mother was doing much clutching, along with plenty of weeping and trembling. My father stood ramrod straight, arms at his sides, eyes aimed at my forehead; an old trick he'd taught me. Most people would assume he was looking me in the eye. Most people didn't pay much attention.

My mother pressed her head to his shoulder, squeezed him tight around the waist, and used her other hand to pat my foot, gingerly, like she was afraid of hurting me. Apparently no one had told her that I couldn't feel her touch, or anything else. More likely she was in selective memory mode, tossing out any piece of information that didn't suit her.

"We've hooked up a neural output line from the language center of your brain, Lia," the squinty-eyed doctor said. Now that I had a better view, I could see that he was also short. For his sake—and mine—I hoped his parents had spent all their credit on IQ points. Because clearly, they'd spared little for anything else. "If you speak the words clearly in your mind, the computer will speak for you." Then it was like the whole room paused, waiting.

Hello.

Silence.

"It might take a little practice to get the words out," he said. "I wish I could tell you exactly how to do it, but it's like moving an arm or raising an eyebrow. You just have to find a way to turn thought into action."

If I could speak, I might have pointed out that I *couldn't* move my arm or raise my eyebrow. And then thanked him for rubbing it in.

Hello.

Hello.

Can anyone hear me?

Is this piece-of-shit equipment ever going to work or are you all just going to keep standing there and staring at me like I'm

`"some kind of total freak?"`

My mother let loose a whimpery squeal and buried her face in my father's chest. He didn't push her away.

"Very good, Lia." The doctor nodded. "Excellent."

The voice was female, an electronic alto, with that artificially soothing tone you hear in broken elevators, assuring you that "assistance is on the way." It trickled out of a speaker somewhere behind my head.

Hello, I thought, testing it. The word popped out instantly.

"Hello," my father said, like I'd been talking to him. Which maybe I had. His eyes stayed on my forehead.

"You're going to be okay, honey," my mother whispered. She squeezed the foot-shaped lump at the end of the bed. "I promise. We'll fix this."

"`Can someone tell me what's happening?`" the speaker said.

I said.

"`How bad was I hurt? How long have I been here? What happens next? Why can't I-`" I stopped. "`I'll be able to move again, right? Walk and everything? You said I could. When?`"

I didn't ask why Zo wasn't there.

"It's been several weeks since the accident," my father said. "Almost four." His voice was nearly as steady as the computer's.

One month trapped in a bed, in the dark. I'd missed three tests, a track meet, who knew how many parties, nights with Walker, hours and hours of my favorite vidlifes. A month of my life.

"Of course, you've only been conscious for the last week or so," the doctor said. "And as I explained before, your brain needed this recuperation period to adjust to its new circumstances. Involuntary motion indicated the first stage had been achieved. We actually expected you to reach this point a bit sooner, but, of course, these things vary, and nothing can be rushed, not in cases like this. Given the severity of your injuries, you've really been quite lucky, you know."

Right. Lucky. I felt like I'd won the lottery.

Or been struck by lightning.

"Voluntary control over the eyelids, that's stage two. You'll gradually achieve control over the rest of your body. In fact, you may already be started down that path. We've immobilized the rest of you for the moment, after your . . . episode. For your own safety. But when you're ready, your rehabilitation therapists will work with you, isolating individual areas. Sensation should return as well, if all goes smoothly."

He didn't say what would happen if things didn't go smoothly, or how big the *if* was. I didn't ask.

"How bad?"

The doctor frowned. "I'm sorry?"

"You said severe. How severe?" I hated that this man, a stranger, knew my body better than I did.

"When we brought you in after the accident . . . Incidentally, although you didn't ask, I assume you'll want to know what happened? A chip malfunction on a shipping truck, I believe. It slipped through the sat-nav system, and coincidentally, your car's backup-detection system malfunctioned, reading the road as clear. It was a colossally unlikely confluence of events." He said this clinically, casually, as if noting a statistical aberrance he hoped to study in his spare time. "When we brought you in after the accident, your injuries were severe. Burns covering—"

"Please, stop!" That was my mother. Of course. "She doesn't need to hear this. Not now. She's not strong enough." Meaning "*I'm* not strong enough."

"She asked," my father said. "She should know."

The doctor hesitated, as if waiting for them to reach a unanimous decision. He'd spent the last month with my parents and still thought the Kahn family was a democracy?

My father nodded. "Continue."

The doctor, smarter than he looked, obeyed. "Third-degree burns covering seventy percent of your body. That was the most immediate threat. Skin grafts are simple, of course, but in many cases infection proves fatal before we have the chance to do anything. Crush injuries to the legs and pelvis. Spinal cord abrasion. Collapsed lung. Damage to the aortic valve necessitated immediate bypass and may have required an eventual transplant. Internal bleeding. And, as far as secondary injuries, we were forced to amputate—"

"Please," the computer voice cut in. It was so calm.

My father raised his eyes, waiting. Believing I was strong enough.

Keep going, I forced myself to think. The words were in the air before I could take them back.

"Amputate the left leg, just below the thigh. Several hours were spent trying to salvage the left arm, but it wasn't possible."

There were two feet beneath the blanket. Two legs. I could see them. Maybe I couldn't feel them or move them, but I *knew* they were there.

Prosthetics, I realized, retreating to a part of my brain the computer couldn't hear. *They can do a lot with prosthetics.* They made fake limbs that moved, that even, in some way, felt. That looked almost normal. Almost.

The doctor had said I would walk. He just didn't say how. He didn't say on what.

This can't be happening to me.

How could it be happening—how could it *keep* happening—and still seem so unreal?

But then how could it be real? How could I, Lia Kahn, be a one-armed, one-legged, burned, scarred, punctured *lump*?

`"I need to see."`

"See what, Lia?" my mother whispered. What did she think?

`"See. I need to see what I look like. I need a mirror."` In my head I was shouting. The voice was not.

"That's not advisable at this point," the doctor said. "I only told you about your injuries so you would realize how lucky you are to be making a full recovery. So you would understand that certain decisions were made for your own good. Some sacrifices were needed to save your life."

Some "sacrifices," like an arm and a leg?

`"I need to see."`

The doctor frowned. "We really should wait until the final, cosmetic procedures have been completed. It's ill-advised at this stage to—"

"Let her see," said a man who hadn't spoken yet. He stood closest to my parents, his gray suit flashing, very subtly, in time with his heartbeat. The style had been in and then very definitely out a couple years ago, but it worked for him. Although with his face—chiseled cheekbones, long-lashed brown eyes, dimpled chin, nearly-but-not-quite feminine lips—anything would have worked. "She'll have to find out eventually. Why not now?"

I was sorry I couldn't smile at him.

Then I reminded myself that the smile would have been

bound by blistered lips, pulled back to reveal cracked teeth, or dark empty gaps, along bloody gums. As for the blond hair I would have liked to flick over my shoulder, just quickly enough that the scent of lavender wafted out to greet him? It was probably gone. I'd smelled it burning. My eyes were both still there, that was obvious. At least one of my ears. But my mouth didn't work, my nose didn't work— Who knew whether they were intact or just sunken caverns of flesh? The pretty doctor didn't see pretty Lia Kahn, I reminded myself. He saw the lump.

He found a mirror.

It was small, about the size of a hand stretched flat, with the fingers pressed together. Framed with black plastic that maybe was supposed to be shiny but wasn't, not anymore. He paused, tipped his head toward my father. "Do you want to . . . ?"

My father shook his head.

So it was the pretty doctor, the kind of guy Walker would be someday if he remembered to shave and stopped flunking gentech, who approached, mirror in hand. He kept it angled safely away. "You ready?"

As if it mattered. I closed my eyes.

The computer said yes.

They'll fix it, I promised myself. *No matter how much it costs, no matter how long it takes.* If my mother could keep her skin looking like she was twenty-two, if Bliss Tanzen could show up with a new nose to match every new season's shopping spoils, a few scars were nothing. Maybe I'd even keep a couple. Becca Mai had a delicate white fault line running down her cheekbone that she claimed came from a close encounter with jagged glass on some illicit venture into the city. Everyone knew Becca Mai was too prep to sneak out of the house and too petrified to sneak into the city, and Bliss had spotted one of those home tattoo kits on Becca's shop-log, just before it mysteriously got edited out. But guys still loved her sexy little shiver as they traced their fingers down the scar. Becca gave good shiver.

I could do better.

"Lia, if you want to see, you're going to have to open your eyes." The doctor's voice didn't quite match up to his pretty face. I liked voices lower, a little husky. Of course, Walker was nearly a tenor. Carved cheekbones, a tight six-pack, and a girl can get used to just about anything.

Anything, I told myself. And then, deep breath.

Eyes wide open.

I didn't know computers could scream.

NOTHING

"I was a ghost in the machine."

*T*he lips, I thought. *Focus on the lips.*

Because they were normal. Pale pink, washed out. Curved into a half pout. A glimpse of white teeth barely visible, straight and whole. It was a mouth, a normal mouth.

Just not my mouth.

The nose, too. It was a nose. Narrow, nearly sharp but not unpleasantly so, no bumps or hooks, delicate nostrils, a gentle slope up the face toward the—

No, not the eyes.

Don't look at the eyes.

No scars. No burns. It wasn't the Halloween fright mask I'd imagined. It was . . . perfect. The skin was unmarked, stretched taut and smooth across the face. A stranger's face.

And the eyes. The eyes that weren't my eyes. Pale, watery blue, unspeckled iris; black, motionless pupil; and at the center, a pinprick circle of amber. Unblinking. Dead.

But when I closed one eye, the eye in the mirror closed, too. Brown lashes brushed against a too-smooth cheek. I opened the eye, and the mirror eye opened. It was dead. It was mine.

Which meant that what lay above it was mine, too. Blondish brows with a high, perfectly plucked arch, like they'd been penciled in. A wrinkle-free forehead. And above that?

The machine.

Scalp flayed back. A mess of circuitry, like when Zo was five and cracked open my new ViM because I wouldn't let her use it. Wires spooling out of my head. Wires feeding into my head. Silvery filament crisscrossing a waxy, flesh-colored base.

It wasn't until the computer fell silent that I realized I was still screaming. But now the screams were just inside my head.

What else was inside my head?

"Try to calm down," said the first doctor, the ugly one. The mirror was gone, but I couldn't stop seeing the face. "I'll turn the speaker back on, but you have to stay calm, for your own good. Let us explain. Can you do that?"

As if I had any choice.

One blink.

I forced the screams back inside myself.

"This is why I didn't want you to see at this stage," the doctor said irritably. "Cranial exposure is only necessary until we confirm neurological stability. Once the skullcap is attached and the hair—"

"What did you do to me?"

Dr. Handsome shot the uglier guy a look that made me realize who was really in charge. And he was the one who finally answered. "We saved your life."

"What did you do?"

No one spoke.

My mother lifted her head from my father's shoulder. She looked me in the eye. Not the forehead, the eye. She wasn't crying anymore. "You know about BioMax," she said. "You remember."

I knew just about as much as I cared. Which was very little. BioMax, some biotech subsidiary of my father's corporation, hyped on the vids the year before with some freaky new tech that—

"No."

I knew.

"We had to," my mother pleaded. "We didn't have any other choice."

"No."

"Honey, you heard the doctors, you were going to *die*. This was the only way."

"No."

"Lia." My father balled up his fists, shoved them into his pockets. *"Yes."*

"We held off for as long as we could," the pretty doctor said.

I felt like he was leering at me, like I was some mechanical puzzle he was desperate to take apart, then try to put back together. Except he'd already done so. "Dr. Dreyson"—he jerked his head toward his troll-like partner—"had you on the table for seventeen hours before we made the decision."

"Before you gave up."

"We would never give up on you," my mother said.

My father frowned. "That's why you're still here."

But I wasn't.

I was a ghost in the machine.

A mech-head.

A Frankenstein.

A skinner.

"The download process was a complete success," Dr. Handsome said. "Your brain came through the accident completely intact, and we were able to make a full transfer. The body is, I'm afraid, not the customized unit you might have selected under less critical circumstances, but we did our best to choose a model that would emulate your baseline specs, height, weight, coloring."

He was talking like I was a new car.

Everyone knew about the download freaks, or at least, we knew they were out there, computer brains stuffed into homemade bodies, walking around looking like real, live people. Sort of. The first few were all over the vids for a while, until they got boring and people moved on to something else just as irrelevant, like betting on how long it would be before the president went AWOL from rehab again.

"You turned me into a skinner."

Dr. Troll wrinkled his big nose. "We prefer not to use that word."

But that's what they were called, because that's what they did.

Skinners. Computers—*machines*—that hijacked human identities, clothing themselves in human skin. Except the flesh was just as artificial as what lay beneath. A skinner was nothing more than a computer that wore a human mask, hiding wiring and circuitry underneath a costume of synthetic flesh. A mechanical brain, duped into thinking it was real.

Or, in this case: a mechanical brain duped into thinking it was Lia Kahn.

"You *are* Lia," the repulsively handsome one said. "All your memories, all your experiences, everything you are was simply transferred to a more durable casing. Just like copying a file. Nothing more mysterious than that."

"Put me back."

"Lia . . ." My mother pressed her eyes closed with her left hand, massaging the lids.

"Once we train the neural network to accommodate itself to its new physical surroundings, you should be able to pick things up right where you left off." Dr. Handsome was unstoppable. "You'll see we've done remarkable things with sensation, motion . . . Of course there are things to get used to, but many of our clients have found life postdownload nearly indistinguishable from their experiences before the procedure.

And quality of life will certainly be far superior to anything you would have experienced with your degree of injuries—"

"Put me back the way I was. I don't care about the injuries. I don't care. Put me back."

One leg, one arm, no skin, I didn't care. As long as I was human. As long as I was *me*.

"It's not possible."

"Anything's possible if you want it enough."

Another of my father's favorite slogans.

The doctor's voice was cold. "There's nothing to put back. There's no body to go back to. The body of Lia Kahn is dead. Be grateful you didn't die with it."

And when I wouldn't believe him, he offered to prove it. Wires were detached. Machines wheeled away. Two men—not doctors; the doctors never touched me—grabbed my sides. They hoisted me into a sitting position. My head lolled forward on my neck, and I saw my hands for the first time. They hung limp in my lap, fingers half curled, nails round and smooth; useless. Somebody else's hands, resting on somebody else's legs. The flesh was unnaturally smooth, just like the skin on the face. There were no creases and whorls, no subtle shifts of color or thready blue veins beneath the surface. I wondered if there were fingerprints.

One of the men grabbed me under the armpits and hoisted me off the bed. He looked like the type of guy who would have bad breath, and for a moment his mouth was close enough to mine that I could have smelled it, if I could have smelled

33

anything. I was wearing a sleeveless paper-thin blue gown, loose around the armholes. His hands pressed bare skin, or whatever it was. He could probably see down the front of it if he'd wanted to. I didn't care. It wasn't my body under there. It was a thing. A thing I couldn't feel and couldn't move, a thing I was trapped inside. It wasn't me.

He didn't peek. Instead he dumped me into a high-backed wheelchair and fastened a belt around my waist. Then another around my forehead, pressing my head against the seat and fixing my eyes straight ahead. Through it all, he never looked at my face.

The pretty doctor, who got less attractive every time he spoke, told me to call him Ben. He wasn't actually a doctor, he said. Which made sense. Doctors took care of people, right? Sick people, injured people. *People.* I wasn't one of those, not anymore. Thanks to *Ben.* My mechanic.

Call-me-Ben wheeled me down a long corridor. I couldn't feel the body, couldn't feel the seat. It felt like I was floating through the hall, just a set of eyes, just a mind, just a ghost. My parents stayed behind. My mother said she couldn't see it again. *It,* she said. My father didn't say anything, but he stayed with her.

"We've kept it in cold storage for you," Ben said from behind me. "Most clients request a viewing."

It.

We wheeled into a narrow room, its white tiled walls lined by silver plates. Ben pressed his palm to one, and it slid out of the wall, revealing a long, metal panel bearing a sheet-covered lump. A body-shaped lump.

"You sure?" Ben asked, guiding the wheelchair into position. "This can be difficult."

I couldn't stand to hear the computer speak for me, not here. Not now.

I blinked once.

He began with the feet. Foot.

The flesh was red and ruined, gouged. Mottled with deep, black scabs. There were thick streaks of pearl white, as if the skin had calcified. Or maybe the flesh had been flayed and I was looking at bone. The knee was bent at the wrong angle; the other leg was gone, ending just below the thigh, swirls of dried blood and charred flesh winding around one another, like the rings of a severed tree stump.

The sheet drew farther back.

I wish I could say I didn't recognize it, that it was some monstrous mound of skin and bones, broken and unidentifiable.

It was. But it was also me.

I recognized the hips jutting out below my waist, always a little bonier than I would have liked. The dark freckles along my collarbone, still visible on a patch of skin the fire had spared. My crooked ring finger, on the arm that remained intact, a family quirk my parents had chosen not to screen out, the genetic calling card of the Kahns.

My face.

The burns were worse there. Pockets of pus bubbled beneath

the skin. One side had caved in, like my face had been modeled from clay, then crushed by an iron fist. The left eye sagged into a deep hollow. My lips were gone.

There was a gray surgical cap stretched over my head.

"The brain?"

I felt as dead inside as the voice sounded.

Call-me-Ben sighed. "You don't want to know the technical details."

"Try me."

He did.

He told me how the brain—my brain—was removed.

Frozen.

Sliced into razor-thin sections.

Scanned.

Functionally mapped onto a three-dimensional model, axons and dendrites replaced by the vector space of a quantum computer, woven through with artificial nerves, conduits that would carry impulses back and forth from an artificial body, simulating all the pains and pleasures of life. In theory.

He told me how the frozen leftovers were discarded. Because that's what you do with medical waste.

Now I understood: *Skinner* was the wrong word after all. I wasn't the thief. I hadn't stolen an identity; *I* hadn't stolen anything. They were the ones who stole from me. They flayed back my skin, reached inside and dug up whatever secret, essential quality made me who I was.

Then they ripped it out.

They ripped it out—ripped *me* out—and left me exposed, a naked brain, a mind without a body. Because this *thing* they'd stuck me in, it wasn't a body—a sculpted face, dead eyes, and synthetic flesh couldn't make it anything but a hollow shell. Maybe I hadn't lost the essential thing that made me Lia Kahn, but I'd lost everything else, everything that made me human.

I wasn't a skinner.

I was the one who'd been skinned.

When we were kids, Zo and I used to fight. Not argue. *Fight*. Hair-pulling, skin-pinching, wrist-burning, arm-twisting, squealing, spitting, punching, shrieking *fight*. And once—it wasn't our worst fight or our last one—after she kneed me in the stomach, I punched her in the face. Her nose spurted blood all over both of us. She threw up. I passed out. It's the one thing we'd always had in common: Fear of blood. Fear of doctors. Fear of hospitals. Fear of anything that stinks of sick.

But here I was, inches from a dead body. *My* dead body. Inches from flesh that looked like raw meat, a crumpled face, an empty skull cavity. Listening to a stranger describe, in detail, all the ways he'd torn me to pieces. And I didn't feel sick. I didn't feel anything.

I don't just mean on the outside, like the chair under my ass or my ass or the straps digging into my waist and forehead or call-me-Ben's hand on my shoulder, the same hand he'd used to pull back the body's sheet. It was that, but it wasn't *just* that. I couldn't feel anything on the inside, either. I wasn't nauseated; I wasn't dizzy. My stomach wasn't clenched; there was no

37

hollowness at the base of my throat, warning me I was about to explode into tears. I wasn't breathing quickly. I wasn't breathing at all. I wasn't trembling, although even if I had been, I wouldn't have known.

My brain—or whatever was up there—told me I was horrified. And furious. And terrified. And disgusted. I *knew* I was all of those things. But I couldn't feel it. They were just words. Adjectives pertaining to emotional affect that modified nouns pertaining to organic life-forms.

I no longer qualified.

MOUTH CLOSED

"You don't need a tongue to sound like a sheep."

I don't want to talk about it." Translation: "I don't want to
think about it."

It didn't matter how much crap they spewed about adjustment pains and emotional connection and statistically probable
results of repression, there was no way in hell some random
middle-aged loser was milking me for intimate details of my daily
life in hell, aka rehab. No matter how many times she asked.

"It's okay if you don't feel ready." Sascha leaned back in her
chair, her head almost touching the window. "You may never
feel ready. Sometimes we need to just take a risk, have faith in
our own strength."

She had a corner office on the thirteenth floor, which meant a
180-degree view of the woods surrounding the BioMax building.

I'd only seen one other floor: the ninth. That was where they stored the bodies until it was time to destroy them. Mine wasn't there anymore. I knew, because I'd asked Sascha. They burn the bodies. They don't bury them— You only bury people who are dead. The bodies are just medical waste. I told Sascha, no, I didn't want the ashes. She said it was a positive sign.

"I don't need faith," I said. "I know my own strength. I do fifty push-ups every morning. Sit-ups, too. It's in your report." It was easier to talk than to sit there for an hour in silence, although I'd tried that, too. I'd probably try it again. One thing about my new life, or whatever I was supposed to call it: I had plenty of time.

She frowned, then templed her fingers and rested her chin on her fingertips. "I think you know I'm not talking about that kind of strength."

I shrugged.

"It's natural to be concerned about how your family will react to the new you," she said.

"They've seen the new me."

"It's been a month, Lia. You've made remarkable progress since then. Don't you want to show off a little?"

"Show off what? That I learned how to take a few steps without falling on my face? That I figured out how to make actual *words* with this thing in my throat?" I gave her one of the smiles I'd been working on, knowing—from the hours I'd spent practicing in the mirror—that it looked more like a grimace. "Yay, me. I'm finally better off than a two-year-old."

Sascha hated sarcasm. Probably because she didn't get it. After all, if she'd had an acceptable IQ , she would have been on some other floor, building new people like me, rather than stuck on lucky thirteen, upping my self-esteem. Her parents had obviously opted to dump more EQ than IQ in their chromosomal shopping cart. Not that she was much good when it came to emotions. At least, not emotions like mine. "You can't undervalue yourself like that," she said. "I know how hard you've worked to get to where you are."

She knew nothing.

The benefit of artificial skin constructed from self-cleaning polymer: No one has to sponge the dirt off my naked body while I'm lying in bed like a frozen lump of metal and plastic.

No, not like *that.*

I am that.

The benefit of an artificial body with no lungs, no stomach, no bladder, and a wi-fi energy converter where the heart should be: No machine has to breathe for me while my brain tries to remember how to pump in the air. No one has to spoon food into my frozen mouth. No one has to thread in a bunch of tubes to suck the waste out of my body; no one has to wipe my ass.

No one has to do much of anything. Except for me.

`"I can't."`

"You can." Asa is terminally perky. Even when my spasming leg kicks him in the groin.

An accident, I swear.

"You're just not trying hard enough."

I hate him.

He puts the ball between the hands lying uselessly in my lap.
I can finally hold up my own head, and I do, so I don't have to see
them—mechanical digits covered with layers of fake skin, threaded
with fake nerves.

I can feel them now, sometimes.

"Feel" them, at least. Know when someone is squeezing them.
Know, even with my eyes closed, when Asa dips them in boiling
water, when he presses them to ice. I know, the way I know my name,
as a fact. This is cold. This is hot. *I know, but that doesn't mean I*
feel. It's not the same.

Nothing is.

"Try to throw the ball to me," Asa chirps. He's all blond hair
and brawny muscles, like a twelve-year-old's av, the virtual face you
choose for yourself before you realize that pretty and perfect is perfectly
boring. "You can do it. I know you can."

Move, *I tell my arms. Just do it.*

It would be easier if they hurt. If there was pain to push through,
to guide me back to where I started. If I knew that the more it hurt, the
closer I was getting. But there hasn't been any pain since that first day
with call-me-Ben. The brain was exploring its new environment, they
say. All that is behind me now.

I don't tell them that I miss it.

Move! *I think, and I know I am angry, at myself and at Asa. I*
am angry all the time now. But the voice in my head sounds nearly as
calm as the computer I still use to talk, and will use until I can make

more than grunts and groans with the artificial larynx. That may take the most time of all, they warn me. But most people master it eventually. Most.

The arms jerk away from the body, and the ball dribbles out of the hands, then drops, rolling under the bed.

"Good!" Asa exclaims, looking like he wants to applaud.

And then the session is over, and Asa hoists me out of the chair, like I'm a giant baby, his thick arm cradling my knees, another digging into my armpit. I forget to hold up my head, and it flops backward against his shoulder. This is life now.

From the bed, to the chair, to the bed again.

They turn me off at night—I'm supposed to call it "sleep," but why bother?—and turn me on in the morning. Soon, they tell me, I will learn how to do it myself. Just like I will learn to monitor my status, to will the system diagnostics to scroll across my eyes. I will learn how to upload my memories for safekeeping. I will learn to speak. But that's all later. Now, life is lived for me. Asa monitors me, Asa dresses me, Asa turns me off and on, and off again. It's how I know one day has passed. And another. I play catch with Asa and I stare at the ceiling and I wait and I try not to wonder whether I would rather be dead or whether I already am.

I hated to picture myself like that. Helpless. I tried to forget, but Sascha kept forcing me to remember. Like I was supposed to be proud or something. Like I was supposed to be happy. Even when I tuned her out, which was often, I couldn't escape the memories. The frustration. The *humiliation*. As long as I was stuck in this place, part of me was still stuck back at the beginning, a patient—a *victim*.

I guess remembering those early days in rehab was better than remembering what came before: the crash, the fire, the long hours frozen in the dark.

Better, but not by much.

"Are you worried that if you see them, you might find that you've changed?" Sascha asked. "That your family might think you're different now?"

"I *am* different now." I wondered how much they paid her to force me to state the obvious.

I could tell from her smile that I'd said the right thing, which meant I'd said the wrong thing, because it meant she thought we were about to make *progress*. Sascha was big on progress.

I, on the other hand, was big on reality. A concept with which Sascha didn't seem to be acquainted.

"I'm not talking about physical differences, Lia. I'm talking about *you*." She leaned forward, tapping me on the chest where my heart would have been. "About what's going on in here, and"—she tapped the thick blond weave that covered the titanium plates—"up here. You've been through a serious trauma. That would be enough to change anyone."

"I guess."

"But I'm thinking it might be more than that."

Big surprise.

"Many clients in your position worry about what the download process *means* for them. Whether they lost something of themselves in the procedure or if they'll ever be the person they were before. They worry a lot about who they are now. Do these concerns sound familiar?"

Sooner or later, wherever our conversations began—if you wanted to call them conversations rather than verbal dodgeball games where Sascha pelted and I ducked and weaved until, inevitably, she managed to slam me square in the face—we ended up in the same place.

"I know who I am," I said. Again. "Lia Kahn."

"Yes." She smiled. I could see the beads of white frothy saliva forming in the corners of her mouth. I didn't have any saliva. The tongue was self-lubricating. "*Yes*. You *are* Lia Kahn. But surely some of the things you've been seeing and hearing on the vids about . . . people like you . . . They don't trouble you at all?"

I was still practicing my emotional responses: when to raise the eyebrows and how far. What to do with the nose when the mouth was stretched into a smile. When to bare teeth, when to press lips together, how often to pretend to blink. It was all a lot of trouble, so most of the time, I just left my face as it was, blank and impassive. Sometimes that came in handy.

"I've never seen any vids about 'people like me,' " I lied. They didn't go for concrete nouns here, nouns like "skinner" or "mechhead." Or "machine." "I don't know what you're talking about."

Sascha looked torn. Should she cram my head full of newfound terror that the world would reject me, or let me wander into the big, scary out-there, like a naive lamb prancing to the slaughter?

Lesser of two evils, apparently: "Lia, you should be aware that you're going to encounter some people who don't yet understand the download process. You're going to have to help them make peace with what's happened to you. But I assure you that with time, those who know and love you will accept it."

But that was a lie. I knew what I was; I knew what the people who loved me could handle. They couldn't handle this.

You'd think I would at least get some superpowers as part of the deal. Legs that could run a hundred miles an hour. Arms that could lift a fridge. Supersight, superhearing, super something. But no. I get skin that washes itself and is impervious to paper cuts. Legs that have barely learned how to walk. A tongue that lies in my mouth like a dying fish flopping and thrusting and scraping against heavily fortified porcelain teeth, mangling every burst of sound I manage to choke out of the voice box.

No lungs, just an intake hose feeding into the larynx, so I can shoot air through when necessary, make the artificial cartilage vibrate at the right frequency, funnel the sound waves up the throat, into the mouth. That was the first step. "A big one!" Asa says, clapping as I grunt and groan. I can do all the animal noises now. Monkey hoots. Cow moos. Dolphin squeals. And, as of this morning, sheep. "Baa! Baa!"

"Your first word," Asa cheers. "Almost."

I still hate him.

You don't need a tongue to sound like a sheep. But if you want to sound human, that's another story.

I wonder if Asa goes home at night and imitates me for his girlfriend; someone like him must have a girlfriend. Does he tell her how he's spent all day with his hands on my body, prodding and pulling and stretching? Does he tell her how he dressed me until I learned to dress myself or about the day he opened the door without knocking and discovered me checking to make sure the body was— fully—anatomically correct? Is she jealous, I wonder, of the girl with the perfectly symmetrical synthetic breasts, the living doll that Asa molds into whomever he wants her to be? Or does she think of him as a handyman, spending his days tuning up a machine that just happens to look like a person and grunt like a chimpanzee?

"Good night, Lia," *he says as he goes wherever it is he goes when he leaves the thirteenth floor and rejoins his life.*

"Unnnh," *I "say" in response. I am not allowed to use the voice synthesizer, not while I'm speech training, not—Asa says, and his boss, call-me-Ben, agrees—unless I want to be one of those clients who has to use it indefinitely, speaking with closed lips and a computerized monotone for the rest of my so-called life.* "Omph. Aaaaap."

"You too, Lia. See ya."

"Baaa, baaa."

Bye, bye.

I have fingers again, fingers that can barely feel but can mostly type. Which means it's time to link in to the network. I will not speak, not with the computer voice and not with the animal groans, but I will type, I will face them, I will.

I tell myself that every night.

47

Tonight I do it.

There is a six-week dead hole in my zone. I have never been off the network for that long, not since I was three and got my first account, my first ViM, and my first avatar, a purple bear with an elephant snout and a lion's tail. I dressed him in a top hat and called him Bear Bear, which, at the time, I thought was clever.

It occurs to me now that if Bear Bear existed in the real world, he'd probably sound a lot like me.

Every day, since I was three, life on the network shadowed life off the network, and sometimes it was the opposite. Sometimes it was the network that seemed more real. Every text, every pic, every vid got posted in my zone, every fight and every make up was reflected in the zone. My first boyfriend gave me my first kiss in the zone, his av a red-haired ninja, mine a black-winged pixie with purple hair and knife-spiked heels. The zone was how I knew who I was, how I knew that I was, except now there's a gap, starting with the accident and stretching on as if, for all those weeks, Lia Kahn ceased to exist.

There are flowers waiting for me, flowers from everyone— not just Cass and Terra and even Bliss, but from all the randoms who wish they counted enough to get a niche in my zone, the ones whose names I don't know and won't remember, all of them leaving messages and pink-frosted cupcakes and pixilated teddies that remind me of Bear Bear. My zone is a shrine.

Walker's messages are behind the priv-wall, where no one can see them but me. There are only two, both voice-talk, and I play them four times, eyes closed, listening to his warbling tenor, wishing I had more of him than my least-favorite part.

"Please don't die," *the first one says. He sent it the night of the accident, when I was still alive, when, according to call-me-Ben, I was hemorrhaging and suffocating and seizing, all at the same time.*

The next one came weeks later, when I was lying in the bed, eyes closed, listening to footsteps and waiting to die.

"The turtle is hungry," *it says.* "The turtle is starving."

Code. Left over from our first few months, when Zo wouldn't go away. She was always snooping in my room and hacking my zone, all big ears and a bigger mouth, so Walker and I talked in riddles and nonsense until eventually she left and we stopped talking altogether.

"The turtle is hungry."

Meant "I love you."

I want to see him. I want to touch him. I want to at least voice him back. But what would I say?

Ahhh ovvvvv ooooooo.

We speak in different codes now.

I stay in stealth mode. They are all linked in and to one another, Cass to Terra to Walker to Zo, all in priv-mode, and I wonder if they are talking about me, but I can't find out without showing myself, and I can't do that, not today.

There are 7,346 new pub-pics and texts, and there will be more behind their priv-walls, and I know I should catch up, but I can't do that, either.

There's no point.

I try my favorite vidlife, technically a realistic one because there are no vampires or superheroes, but there's nothing particularly realistic about the number of people Aileen manages to screw—and screw over—each night. Since the last time I watched, Aileen has already forgotten about Case, and is screwing some new guy and, secretly, the new guy's sister, who's engaged to Aileen's former best friend's cousin, and I can't keep up with all the new names and bodies, and I don't understand how so much can happen in six weeks.

I used to feel sorry for the woman who lives as Aileen, and for Case and for all of them. I used to think it was pathetic, arranging your life around someone else's script, letting some random text the words you were forced to speak. So they got rich on it, so they got famous, so I watched all night sometimes because I didn't want to miss anything, so what? It wasn't their life they were living, it wasn't anyone's.

But now I don't know.

If someone gave me a script, if someone whispered in my ear and told me how to act, what to say, what to do, if I could be their puppet and they could pull the strings, that would be easier. That would, maybe, be okay. But I have no script and no off-screen directions, and I sit frozen, watching the screen, waiting to know what to do.

Whatever else has changed, at least my av is still the same.

There was a time when I changed it every day—new eyes, new hair, bunny whiskers one day, cat ears the next—but that was before. That was kid stuff. Now my av is me, the virtual Lia, the better Lia, the Lia that would exist in a world without limits. Purple hair so dark it looks black, until you see it shimmer in the light. Violet eyes; wide, long lashes pooling across half the head, like in the animevids. Pouty blue lips. The morning of the accident, I gave her a pink boa and spray-on mini, like the one I'd just seen a pop-up for but knew I probably wouldn't have enough credit to buy, because that's another of my father's favorite lines: "We're not rich. I'm rich." The credit is mine to ask for; his, depending on his mood, to deny. Now I wonder whether I am the virtual Lia, while my av is real. There is nothing left of what I used to be.

But she is exactly the same.

I didn't get in touch with Walker, not that night or any of the nights that followed. Even after I got my voice back—*a* voice, at least, although it would never sound like *mine*—I couldn't do it. I didn't know what I would say. I didn't want to know what he would.

"I still think it might be good for you to meet with one of our other clients," Sascha said. "She's your age."

That meant nothing. All the skinners were my age. The procedure wouldn't work on adults—something about how their neural pathways weren't malleable, couldn't adjust to an artificial environment—and it hadn't been approved for anyone younger than sixteen. If I'd had the accident a year earlier, I'd be dead right now. All dead, instead of . . . whatever this was.

"So what?"

"So I think you two have a lot in common," Sascha said. "It might help to share your experiences, get her perspective on things. Plus she's eager to meet you."

"All we have in common is *this*." I looked down at the body.

My body. "And you keep telling me that *this* doesn't mean anything."

"You don't want to meet her."

Sascha's brilliant intuitive powers never ceased to amaze. "No."

"Maybe we should talk about why."

"Maybe not."

Sascha crossed her arms. I wondered if I'd finally managed to break through the professional placidness, if Sascha was about to prove she had an actual personality, one that could get irritated when a bitchy "client" pressed hard enough.

Not a chance.

"Let's try something new," she said with an I-have-a-secret-plan smile. "Why don't you tell me what *you* want to talk about."

"Anything?"

"Anything. As long as it's something."

I *didn't* want to talk. That was the point. Now that I had my voice back, I had nothing to say.

"Running," I said. It was the first thing that popped into my head. Maybe because I thought about it all the time. How it would feel to run in the new body. Whether I would be slower or faster, whether I would find a new rhythm. What it would mean to run without getting out of breath; whether I could run forever. They told me the body would simulate exhaustion before it had reached its limits, a gauge to prevent total system failure, but no one knew exactly what those limits would be.

"You're a runner?" Sascha asked, faux clueless. It was her

default mode; at least when she wasn't acting the all-knowing wisdom dispenser. She knew I was a runner, because she had a file that told her everything I was. Everything she thought mattered, anyway.

Was a runner.

I nodded.

"Do you miss it?"

I shrugged.

"You run on an indoor track or . . ."

"Outside," I said immediately.

Sascha leaned forward, as she always did when she thought she was about to crack my code. "That's unusual," she said. "Someone your age, spending so much time outside."

"It's required." But that wasn't true, not really. Yes, we were all forced to spend a few hours a week outdoors, but for most people, that was the end of it. Five whiny hours shivering in the grayish cold, then back inside. It was one way I'd always been different. The only way.

"What do you like about it?" Sascha asked. "Running."

"I don't know." I paused. She waited. "It felt good. You know. Especially a long run. You get an adrenaline high. Or whatever."

"Have you tried it? Since the procedure?"

I shook my head. There was supposedly a track somewhere in the building, but I hadn't bothered to find it.

"Why not?"

I looked down. The hands were sitting in my lap. I stretched one of them out along my thigh. It felt good to be able to move again. After almost a month of rehab, I didn't even need to think about it most of the time; the hands clenched themselves into fists when I wanted them to, the fingers closed around balls and hairbrushes and tapped at keyboards just like real fingers. They registered the fabric on my legs—standard issue, hideously ugly BioMax thermo-sweats. Not that I needed thermo-regulation now, not when I had it built in, but that's what they had, so that's what I wore, because it was easier than buying all new clothes, and my old clothes no longer fit.

"What would be the point?" I said finally.

"The point would be to feel good."

In my head I laughed. The mouth spit out something harsh and scratchy. Laughing was tricky.

"You disagree?" Sascha asked.

"I guess it depends on your definition of 'feel.'"

"You're processing emotional and physical sensation differently now; that's natural," Sascha said, oozing understanding. Not that she could ever actually understand. "But your programming is designed to emulate the neurotransmitters that stimulate emotional response. Your emotions *are* the same, even if they don't feel that way."

"I feel the same, even if I feel different? Is that supposed to make sense?"

My father would kill me if he ever knew I was talking to an authority figure like this, even a figure with such questionable authority as Sascha.

"When I get angry, my stomach clenches," Sascha said. "I

feel sick. When I'm upset, my hands tremble. Sometimes I cry. What happens when you're upset?"

I said nothing.

Which was pretty accurate.

"Without a somatic response, it's natural that the emotions will seem weaker to you," she said. "More distant. But the stronger the emotion, the more 'real' it may feel, partly because you'll be too consumed with the powerful emotion—or sensation—to analyze all the things you're *not* feeling. And as your mind relaxes into old patterns and finds new ones, as it *will*—"

"I'll be my old self again. Right."

"Lia, haven't you been able to find *any* advantages to your new body?"

That had been my "homework" from the other day: design a pop-up for the download process, complete with catchy slogan, and a list of fabulous advantages available to every download recipient. Sascha thought it would tap into my creativity skills.

It turned out I didn't have any.

"I can link in whenever I want," I muttered. But that wasn't new. For my sixteenth birthday, I'd finally gotten a net-lens, which meant that once I got used to jamming a finger in my eye, I could link with a blink, just like the pop-ups said. Could superimpose my zone and my av over blah reality, type on a holographic keyboard that only I could see. But the pop-ups didn't mention how it made you nauseated and made your head burn. Now I had a built-in net-lens, and migraines weren't an issue.

Hooray for me.

"Good," Sascha said, nodding. "Anything else?"

"I guess no more getting sick." Not that anyone got sick much these days, anyway. Not if you could afford the med-tech, and if you couldn't, well, you had bigger problems than the flu. "And if I get hurt, it won't, you know. Hurt. Much." There would be pain, they'd told me that. Of all the sensations, the neurochemistry of pain was the easiest to mimic, the best understood—and the most necessary. *Pain alerts the brain that something is wrong,* call-me-Ben had said. *An alarm you can't ignore.* So there would be pain, they had promised, and I knew it was possible, because I'd felt it when I was still trapped in the bed, when it seemed to crawl out from inside my head. But out of the bed, back in the world, pain was just as distant as everything else.

"You're beautiful," Sascha said. "That's something."

I was beautiful before.

"And then there's the big thing," Sascha prompted. "A lot of people would envy you for that. If the government allowed it, a lot of people might even download voluntarily."

"Doubtful."

"To never age . . ." Sascha looked dreamy, and her hand flickered to the corner of her left eye, where the skin was pulled taut. "Some might call that lucky. Miraculous, even." She couldn't be more than seventy, I decided, since after that even the best doctors left behind a few stretch marks—and no younger than thirty, because you can always tell when someone's had their first lift-tuck, and she definitely had. First, second, and probably eighth, I guessed. No one so lame could be any younger than that.

Call-me-Ben was the one who'd taught me how to back up my memories each night, preserving that day's neural adjustments and accretions in digital storage—"just in case." He'd had the same dreamy look as Sascha. They all did, when the subject came up.

"The body ages," I countered. "They say it'll only last fifty years."

"The *body*," Sascha said. "But now you know bodies can be replaced."

The body would last fifty years. But brain scans could be backed up and stored securely, and bodies could be replaced. And replaced again.

I had died more than a month ago; I could live forever. Exactly like this.

Lucky me.

VISITING DAY

"Kahns don't lie."

They were late. Only by ten minutes, but that was weird enough. Kahn family policy: never be late. It meant an immediate disadvantage, a forfeit of the moral high ground. Still, at 10:10 a.m., I was alone in the "social lounge," which, if the building-block architecture, hard-backed benches, and spartan white walls were any indication, was clearly intended to preclude any socializing whatsoever. I didn't want them to come. Any of them. I hadn't invited them, hadn't agreed to see them . . . hadn't been given a choice.

10:13 a.m.: Waiting, my back to the door, staring at the wall-length window without seeing anything but my reflection, ghosted into the glass.

10:17 a.m.: Three more ghosts assembled behind me, milky

and translucent on the spotted pane. Three, not four.

Not that I'd expected Walker to show up, to pester my parents until he got an invitation to come along, to perch nervously in the backseat, his long legs curled up nearly to his chest, his back turned to Zo as he stared out the window, watching the miles roll by, suffering the Kahn family as a means to an end—to me. If he'd wanted to visit, he wouldn't have any need to tag along with them.

If he'd wanted to visit, he already would have.

"Lia," my father said from the doorway.

"Honey," my mother said, in the tight, shivery voice she used when she was trying not to cry.

Zo said nothing.

I turned around.

They stood stiff and packed together, like a family portrait. One where everyone in the family hated one another but hated the photographer more. The huddle broke as they moved from the doorway, my mother and father a glued unit veering toward me, Zo's vector angling off to a bench far enough from mine that, if she kept her head in the right position, would keep me out of her sight line altogether.

My mother held out her arms as if to hug me, then dropped them as she got within reach. They rose again a moment later; I stepped backward just in time. My father shook my hand. We sat.

My mother tried to smile. "You look good, Lee Lee."

"This brain hates that nickname just as much as the last one."

She flinched. "Sorry. Lia. You look . . . so much better. Than before."

"That's me. Clean, shiny, and in perfect working order." I raised my arms over my head, clasped them together like a champ. "You'd think I was fresh off the assembly line." I told myself I was just trying to help them relax. My mother wiped her hand across her nose, quick, like no one would notice the violation of snot-dripping protocol.

"Lia—" My father hesitated. I waited for him to snap. The unspoken rule was, we could—and should—mock our mother for her every flaky, flighty word until he deemed (and you could never tell when the decision would come down) that we had gone too far. "The doctors tell us you're nearly ready to come home. We're looking forward to it."

That was it. His tone was civil. The one he used for strangers.

You did this, I thought, willing him to look at me. Not over me, not through me. And he did, but only in stolen glances that flashed to my face, then, before I could catch him, darted back to the floor, the ceiling, the window. *Whatever I am now, you chose it for me.*

"Zo, don't you have something for your sister?" my mother asked.

Zo shifted her weight, then rolled her eyes. "Whatever." She dug through her bag and pulled out a long, thin rod, tossing it in my direction. "Catch." I knocked it away before it could hit me in the face, but the body's fingers weren't fast enough to curl around it. The stick clattered to the floor.

"Zo!" my mother snapped.

"What? I *said* 'catch.'"

I picked up the stick, turning it over and over in my hands. It was a track baton.

"We won the meet last week," Zo muttered. "Coach wanted me to give it to you. I don't know why."

"We?"

My father smiled for the first time. At Zo. "Your sister's finally discovered a work ethic." He beamed. "She joined the track team. Already third in her division, and moving up every week, right?"

Zo ducked her head; the better to skip the fakely modest smile.

"You hate running," I reminded her.

She shrugged. "Things change."

"Tell us about your life here," my mother said. "How do you spend your days? You're not working too hard, are you?"

I shook my head.

"And you're getting enough to—" She cut herself off, and her face turned white before she could finish her default question: *You're getting enough to eat?*

"Ample power supply around here," I said, tapping my chest and noting the way her smile tightened around the corners. "My energy converter and I are just soaking it in."

I wish I could say I wasn't trying to be mean.

She didn't ask any more questions. Instead she talked. Aunt Clair was helping design a new virtual-museum zone with a focus on early twenty-first-century digital photography.

Great-uncle Jordan had come through his latest all-body lift-tuck without a scratch, literally, since the procedure had worn away that nasty scar he'd gotten skateboarding in the exquisitely lame Anti-Grav Games, which, it turned out, were actually full-grav, anti-knee-pad. Our twin cousins, Mox and Dix, were out-sourcing themselves to Chindia—Mox had snagged an intern-ship at some Beijing engineering firm and Dix would do biotech research for a gen-corp in Bombay. Last I'd seen them, Dix had "accidentally" broken Zo's wrist in a full-contact iceball fight, and Mox had tried to make out with me. *Second* cousins, he argued, so it was okay. Bon voyage, boys.

Then there was our parents' best friend, Kyung Lee, who was having trouble with his corp-town, the workers who lived there rioting for better med-tech, something about a biotoxin that had slipped through the sensors. Kyung was afraid if things didn't calm down soon, he might have to ship them all back to a city and hire a whole new crop, although the threat of that, according to my mother, should be enough to settle anyone.

As the half-hour mark passed, I tuned out. After another twenty minutes my father stood up, giving his pants a surrepti-tious brush, like he wanted to shed himself of the rehab dirt lest it soil the seat of his car. A new car, according to my mother. After all, I'd ruined the last one.

"This has been a lot of excitement for you today, Lia," he said politely. "You must be tired."

I didn't get tired anymore. I only shut down at night because it was on the schedule, and I only followed the schedule because I didn't have anything better to do.

I nodded. They filed toward the doorway, and I followed, half-wishing I could leave with them and half-wishing they would go and never come back. This time my mother forced herself to hug me, and I let her, although I kept my arms at my sides. It was strange to have her so close without breathing in the familiar scent of rosemary. But then, it was probably strange for her, with our chests pressed together and her arms around my shoulders, that I wasn't breathing at all. I thought about faking it for a few seconds, just to make things easier for her. But I didn't.

"We're so proud of you," she whispered, as if I had done anything other than what I was told—turn off, turn on, survive. I felt something brush my cheek as she pulled away, but I couldn't tell what. Maybe a stray hair. Maybe a tear. Maybe I was just wanting to feel something so badly that I'd imagined it.

My father squeezed my shoulder. The new body was taller than mine, I realized. He and I were the same height. He didn't say he was proud of me.

Another family policy: Kahns don't lie.

Zo was last, and I stopped her before she could slip out the door. Her hair was looking better than usual. Not so greasy. And cut shorter, so that it bounced around her shoulders, the way mine used to when it was real.

"Zo, people at school . . ." I kept my voice low, so our parents wouldn't hear. "Are people asking about me? Or, you know. Talking about me?"

She gave me a funny half smile. "Aren't they always?"

"No, I mean . . ." I didn't know what I meant. "Have you seen, I mean, have you talked to any of my friends? You know, Terra or Cass or . . ."

"Walker knows I'm here, if that's what you're asking." Zo leaned against the doorway and kept scratching at the bridge of her nose, which, unless she'd developed a rash, seemed mostly like a convenient way to stare at her hand rather than at me.

"Did he—" But if he'd sent along a message, she would have said so already. And if he hadn't, I didn't want to ask. Besides, he would never reach for me that way, through Zo. "Is he doing okay?"

"I know it's hard to believe, but the world is managing to revolve on its axis even without your daily presence," Zo snapped.

"Rotate."

"What?"

"The world *rotates* on its axis," I corrected her, because it was all I could think of to say.

"Right. It *revolves* around you. How could I forget?"

I grabbed her arm. She yanked it away, like I'd burned her. Her face twisted, just for a second, and then the apathetic funk was back so quickly, I almost thought I'd imagined the change. "Why are you acting like such a bitch?" I asked.

"Who says I'm acting?"

I hadn't necessarily expected her to burst into tears and sweep me into her arms when she first saw me, just like I hadn't expected her to tell me how much she loved me and missed me or to gush about how scary it had been when she thought I was going to die. I guess, knowing Zo, I hadn't even expected her to be particularly nice. But we were sisters.

And she was the reason I had been in the car.

I'd expected . . . something.

"Come on, Zo. This isn't you."

She gave me a weird look. "How would you know?"

"I'm your sister," I pointed out, aiming for nasty but landing uncomfortably close to needy.

She shrugged. "So I'm told."

After she left, I sat down again on one of the uncomfortable benches and stared out the window, imagining them piling into the car, one big happy Lia-free family, driving away, driving home. Then I went back to my room, climbed into bed, and shut myself down.

I'd set my handy internal alarm to wake me nine hours later. But the brain was programmed to wake in the event of a loud noise. A survival strategy. The footsteps weren't loud, but in the midnight quiet of floor thirteen they were loud enough.

"Sleeping Beauty arises." A girl stood in the doorway, silhouetted by the hallway fluorescents, a cutout shadow with billowing black hair, slender arms, and just the right amount of curves. "I guess I don't get to wake you with a kiss." She stroked her fingers across the wall and the room came to light. I sat up in bed.

It wasn't a girl. It was a skinner.

I knew it must be the one Sascha had told me about, the one

I was supposed to be so eager to bond with. I was mostly eager for her to get out and leave me to the dark. She didn't.

"You're her," I said. "Quinn. The other one."

She crossed the room and, uninvited, sat down on the edge of the bed. "And here I thought I was the one and *you* were the other one." She held out her hand.

I didn't shake.

Instead I stared—I couldn't help it. I'd never seen another mech-head, unless you counted the vids. Or the mirror. So this was what my parents saw when they looked at me. Something not quite machine and not quite human, something that was definitely a *thing*, even if it could lift its hand and tip its head and smile. It was better at smiling than I was, I noticed. If you focused on the mouth and looked away from the dead eyes, it almost looked real.

"You're Lia," Quinn said, dropping her hand after realizing I wasn't going to take it. "And yes, it is nice to meet me. Thanks for saying so."

I didn't speak, figuring I could wait her out until she got bored and left. But the silence stretched out; I got bored first.

"Quinn what?" I asked.

"Lia who?" she said. "Or Lia when? Lia why? If you want to play a game, you have to fill me in on the rules. But fair warning: I play to win."

So did I. At least, when I was in the mood. Which I wasn't.

"What's your last name?" I asked.

"Doesn't matter."

"I didn't ask if it mattered, I just asked what it was."

"It *was* something," she said. "But now it's irrelevant."

I didn't get her, and suspected that was the idea, like she thought I'd be so intrigued by her ridiculous air of mystery that I wouldn't kick her out. I wondered if Sascha had put her up to it. If so, they were both seriously overestimating my level of curiosity. "What do you want?" I knew I sounded like a sulky kid. I didn't care.

"Heard your parents finally showed. Figured I would see how it went."

They'd driven two hours for a fifty-minute visit, then gotten the hell out.

"Great," I said sourly. "Heartfelt family reunion. You know how it is."

She raised her eyebrows. It was a nice trick, one I resolved to master myself. "Not really. My family's not an issue."

"Too perfect for 'readjustment pains'?" I used Sascha's favorite phrase for anything and everything that could possibly go wrong.

"Too dead."

"Oh."

I refused to feel guilty. Not when she'd so blatantly manipulated the conversation to reach this point. "Sorry." I lay back down again and turned over on my side, my back to her; universal code for "go away."

"Don't you want the details?" Quinn asked, sounding disappointed. "The whole poor little orphan saga, from tragic start to triumphant finish?"

If I'd still had lungs, I would have sighed. Or faked a yawn. "Look, if Sascha sent you in here to give me the whole 'you should be grateful for what you have' guilt trip, I'm not interested. Yeah, it sucks that your parents are dead, but that doesn't make mine any easier to deal with."

Silence.

I couldn't believe I'd just said that.

"I'm sorry." I twisted in bed, risking a glance at her face.

She raised just one eyebrow this time, which was even more impressive. "Yeah. You are." She turned away, revealing a broad swath of artificial flesh exposed by her backless shirt. I didn't know how she could stand it. Even at night I tried to cover up as much as possible. The more of me I could hide under the clothes, the less there was for others—for me—to see. Beneath the clothes I could imagine myself normal. Quinn, on the other hand, left very little to the imagination. She stalked out of the room, but paused in the doorway, tapping her fingers against the wall console. Lights off, lights on. Lights off. "You coming?"

I was.

"What are you doing?" I whispered as we waited at the elevators. "It's not like they'll work for us."

"Why not?"

"Because . . ." Wasn't it obvious? "We're not supposed to leave here. The elevators are probably programmed."

"Have you actually tried?" Quinn sounded bored, like she already knew the answer.

"No, but—"

"I have." The elevator door opened, and as I hesitated, she asked again. "You coming?"

It had never occurred to me that I would be allowed to leave floor thirteen. Of course, it had never occurred to me to want to.

"The other floors are biorestricted," Quinn said, nodding toward the skimmer that would collect and analyze our DNA samples. If, that is, we'd had any to give. "But the ground floor's all ours."

"Where are we going?" It felt strange to be talking to someone new after all this time. I had no reason to trust her. But I did.

It's because she's like me, I thought. *She knows.*

But I pushed the thought away. It was like I'd told Sascha. Quinn and I had nothing in common but circuitry and some layers of flesh-colored polymer.

"Field trip." She smiled, and, again, it killed me how much better her expressions were than mine, how much more natural. In the dark it had been easy to mistake her for someone real. No one would make that mistake about me. "Don't get too excited."

The grassy stretch bounding the woods was larger than it had looked from the lounge window. The grass was beaded with dew, cold drops that seeped through the thin BioMax pajamas, but that didn't bother me. Just like the brutal wind raking across us didn't matter.

"Can you imagine actually seeing the stars?" Quinn asked. She'd selected a dark swath of grass sandwiched between the floodlit puddles of light, then stripped off her clothes and let herself fall backward, naked against the brush. I kept my clothes on my body and my feet on the ground.

At least at first.

"Get down here," Quinn had commanded.

"Look, Quinn, it's okay if you . . . but I don't—"

She laughed. "You think I brought you out here for *that*?" She stretched her arms out to her sides and down again, stick wings flapping through the grass. "Shirts or skins, I don't care. Just lie down."

I wasn't about to take orders from *her*.

But I lay down.

"You used to be able to see them. Stars and planets and a moon," she said now, pointing at the reddish sky.

The back of my neck was already smeared with dew. But she'd been right. It felt good to lie there in the grass, in the dark. The sky felt closer.

"You can still see the moon." The telltale white haze was hanging low, making the clouds shimmer.

"Not like that," Quinn said. "A bright white circle cut out of pure black. And stars like diamonds, everywhere."

"I know. I've seen."

"Not on the vids," she said. "That doesn't count."

"It's the same thing."

"If you say so."

We were quiet for a minute. I stared up, trying to imagine it, a clear sky, a million stars. Most of the vids I'd seen came from just before the war turned the atmosphere into a planet-size atomic dust ball. The dust was mostly gone—along with the people who'd built the nukes and the nut jobs who'd launched them and the thousands who'd gone up in smoke in the first attacks and the millions who'd been dead by the end of that year or the next. Along with the place called Mecca and the place called Jerusalem and all the other forgotten places that exist now only as meaningless syllables in the Pledge of Forgiveness. The dust was gone, but the stars had never come back. Pollution, cloud cover, ambient light, whatever chemicals they'd used to cleanse the air and patch up the ozone, the law of unintended consequences come to murky life. Someone would fix it someday, I figured. But until then? No stars. My parents talked about them sometimes, late at night, usually when they were dropped on downers, which made them goopy about the past. But I didn't get the big deal. Who cared if the sky glowed reddish purple all night long? It was pretty, and wasn't that the point?

"Why are we here, Quinn?"

She clawed her fingers into the ground and dug up two clumps of grass, letting the dirt sift through her fingers. "So we don't miss any of it."

"What?"

"*This*. Feeling. Seeing. Being. Everything. The dew. The cold. That sound, the wind in the grass. You hear that? It's so . . . real."

I didn't know I'd had the hope until the hope died. So she wasn't the same as me, after all; she *didn't* understand. She didn't get that *none* of it was real, not anymore, that the dew felt wrong, the cold felt wrong, the sounds sounded wrong, everything was wrong, everything was distant, everything was fake. Or maybe it was the opposite—everything was real except for me.

I'd been right the first time. Quinn and I had nothing in common. "Whatever you say."

"It feels good, doesn't it?" she asked.

"What does?" Nothing did.

"The grass." She laughed. "Doesn't it tickle?"

"Yeah. I guess." No.

"It's like us, you know."

"What, the grass?" I said. "Why, because people around here are always walking on it?"

"Because it looks natural and all, but inside, it's got a secret. It's better. Manmade, right? New and improved."

Just because the grass—like the trees, like the birds, like pretty much everything—had been genetically modified to survive the increasingly crappy climate, smoggy sky, and arid earth, didn't make it like us. It was still alive. "The grass still looks like grass," I told her. "Seen a mirror lately? There's no secret. We look like . . . exactly what we are."

"You got a boyfriend?"

"What?" Under other circumstances I would have wondered what she was on. But I knew all too well she wasn't on anything. If there were such a thing as a drug for skinners, I'd be on permanent mental vacation.

"Or girlfriend, whatever."

"Boyfriend," I admitted. "Walker."

"You two slamming?"

72

"*What?*"

"You. Walker. Slamming. Poking. Fucking. You need a definition? When a boy and a girl really love each other—"

"I know what it means. I just don't think it's any of your
business."

"I'm only asking because . . . Well, have you? Since, you
know?"

The thought repulsed me. The idea of Walker's hands
touching the skin, the look on his face when he peered into the
dead eyes, the feeling—the nonfeeling—of his lips on the pale
pink flesh-textured sacs that rimmed my false teeth. The thick,
clumsy thing that functioned as a tongue. Would I even know
what to do, or would it be like learning to walk again? Or worse,
I thought, remembering the grunting and squealing. Like learning to talk. And that was just kissing. Anything else . . . I couldn't
think about it. "Have *you*?" I countered.

She shook her head. "But look at my choices. Like I'm going
to slam Asa?"

"You *trying* to make me vomit?"

"Good luck with that, considering the whole no-stomach
thing." She laughed. "Obviously options are limited. And I've
been waiting a long time."

"How long have you been here?"

"Longer than you. Four months, maybe? But that's not what
I'm talking about." She didn't offer to explain.

This girl was completely creeping me out. But not in an
entirely bad way.

"So you haven't, uh, had any visitors?" I asked finally. "No guys or . . . whatever?"

"No guys. No whatevers."

"Sorry."

"Why?" Quinn sat up, crossing her legs and resting her elbows on her knees. "According to you, it's not like I'm missing out on much family fun time."

"Yeah, but . . ."

"Go ahead," she said.

"What?"

"Ask. You know you want to." Quinn brushed her hands through her long, black hair, smiling. "I love this," she said, dropping the inky curtain across her face, and then giving her head a violent shake, whipping the hair back over her shoulders. "They got it exactly right."

She was crazy, I decided. It was as if she *liked* living like this.

"Go ahead, ask," she said again. "I really don't care."

"And I really don't want to know," I lied. "But fine. Why no visitors?"

"Dead parents, remember?"

If she wanted to act like it was no big deal, so would I. "Yeah. You said. Poor little orphan. But there's got to be someone."

She lay back down in the grass, turning her face away from me. "Doctors. Staff. No one important. Not that it matters now."

"Why not?"

"Because everything's different now. Once I'm out of here? It's a new life. Anything I want. *Anything.*"

"How did they die?" I asked quietly.

"I thought you didn't want to hear the tragic saga?"

"Maybe I changed my mind. Unless it's too hard for you to talk about." But I didn't say it the way Sascha would have, all fake sensitive and understanding. I said it like a challenge, and that's the way she took it.

"Okay, but I'm just warning you, it's quite tragic. You're going to feel pretty sorry for me."

"Don't count on it."

"It was a car accident," she said.

I flinched. And even in the darkness she must have seen.

"Yeah, weird, isn't it? Who gets in car crashes anymore? But here we are. Statistically improbable freaks."

"Were you in the car? When it . . ."

"I was three. We were—" She paused, then barked out a laugh. "This is the first time I've ever had to actually tell someone, you know? I didn't know it would be so . . ."

"You never told *anyone*?" That was too much, too soon. Especially from a girl who wouldn't even tell me her last name.

"It's not like you're special or anything. I just don't . . . I don't meet a lot of new people. Or I didn't. Before."

"You don't have to—"

"I was three," she said quickly. "We were going to visit someone, I don't even know who. I just remember they got me all dressed up, and it was exciting. I mean, they must have taken me off the grounds before, at least a couple times, but I guess I was too young to remember. I remember this, though. I remember being in the car seat, and listening to some song, and playing some stupid vidgame for babies— You remember, the one with the dinosaurs?"

I nodded.

"I was winning. And then—I don't know. I don't remember. Next thing, I wake up, and I'm in a hospital. They're dead. And I'm . . ." She threaded her fingers through her hair, then let her arms fall across her face. "It was a bad accident."

"You were hurt."

She didn't say anything.

"Bad?" I guessed.

"Worse."

"Worse than what?"

"Than whatever you're picturing. Worse." Her voice hardened. "Let's just say that prosthetics and organ transplants and all that? Fine. Great, if you're an adult. But when you break a three-year-old, it's not so easy to put her together again."

Enough, I thought. *I get it.* But I didn't say anything. And she didn't stop.

"Picture a room. Lots of machines. A bed. People to shovel in the food, shovel out the shit, shoot up the painkillers. People to clean. People to do anything and everything. And in the bed, well . . . a thing that eats and shits and gets high and gets cleaned and the rest of the time just pretty much lays there."

But I didn't want to picture it. "How long did it take?"

"To what?"

"To recover."

"Who said I recovered?"

"I just assumed. . . ."

"Sorry to disappoint, but that was it. That room. That bed."

"But what about school? What about friends, or . . ." Or a life.

"I saw it all on the vids. Same thing, right? That's what you said."

That's what I had said.

"I had it all," she said. "Stuff to read. People to talk to. Vids to watch. The whole network at my fingertips. Well, not fingertips. There weren't any of those. But I got by. Massive amounts of credit will do that for you. And then as soon as I turned sixteen . . ."

"What?"

She stood up. "This," she said, sweeping her arms out and spinning around. "This body that actually *works*. This life. Anything I want."

"You did this to yourself?" I asked, incredulous. "On purpose?"

"Did you hear anything I said?"

"I did, I get it, I just can't imagine anyone actually choosing . . . *this*."

"You obviously don't get it. Or you would see this was better than anything I could have had. And from what I hear, anything *you* could have had, after what happened."

I should have known. The inevitable you-should-be-grateful guilt-trip bullshit. Like she knew anything about me.

"You let them *kill* you," I said. "You walked in here—"

"Walked." She snorted. "Yeah, right."

"—and asked them to kill you. To chop up your brain, make a copy, and stick it into some machine."

"Damn right. Quinn Sharpe is dead. I would have killed her myself, if I could. You're walking around here all day sulking— yeah, I've been watching; you've been too busy whining to notice— when you should be celebrating. You should be fucking ecstatic."

"Look, I get it, I do. It makes sense, why you'd want to do it. And I get why this would seem better for you than before. But it's different for me. What I was, what I lost— It's different."

Quinn shook her head. "The only difference is that you don't get it, not yet. It doesn't matter how you got here. What matters is that we're here, now. The past is over. The people we were? Dead. Like you would be. Like you *should* be. Dead. You want the rest of your life to be a funeral? Or you want to actually *live*?"

That was my cue. I was supposed to jump to my feet and clasp her hands, spin in circles, somersault through the grass, dance in the moonlight, drink in the fact that I could swing my arms and pump my legs, that I was alive, in motion, in control. I was supposed to embrace the possibilities and the future, to wake up to a new life. It would be the turning point, some kind of spiritual rehabilitation, an end to the sulking and the self-pitying, a beginning of everything.

I lay still.

"You'll figure it out." She shrugged. "I'm heading back up. You coming?"

"Later."

Shooting me a wicked grin, Quinn sprinted back toward the building, her hair streaming behind her and shimmering under the fluorescent lights, her clothes abandoned in a pile by my head. She ran flat-out, full-speed, running like she didn't know how, arms flailing, feet stomping, rhythm erratic, running like little kids run, without pacing or strategy, running like nothing mattered but the next step. Running just to run. I wanted to join her, to race her, to beat her, and in that moment I knew the legs could do it. I knew I could do it.

I lay still.

I'm not like her, I told myself. Quinn's life had sucked. Mine hadn't. Quinn needed a new start. I didn't. Quinn, if she wanted—*because* she wanted—was a different person now.

I wasn't.

No wonder my father had treated me like a stranger that afternoon. I was acting like one. I was sulking in my room, I was snapping at people who were only trying to help. I was shutting myself off, shutting myself down; I was spewing self-pity. I was lying around, standing still, wasting time wondering what I was going to do and who I was going to be, when the answer was obvious. I was the same person I had always been. I was Lia Kahn. And I was going to do what Lia Kahn always did. Get by. Get through. Work. Win.

I wasn't a skinner. I wasn't a mech-head. I was Lia Kahn. And it was about time I started acting like it.

One week later they sent me home.

FAITH

"God made man. Who made you?"

Someone must have tipped them off, because when we got home, they were waiting.

Getting into the car was hard enough. When it lurched into motion I curled myself into a corner, shut my eyes, and tried to pretend I was back in my room on the thirteenth floor, standing still. I wasn't afraid of going home. Lia Kahn had nothing to fear from her own house. It was just the ride—the pavement speeding underneath the tires, the sat-nav whirring along, veering us around a corner, a tree, a truck . . .

I linked in, picked a new noise-metal song that I knew I would hate, turned the volume up too high, and waited for the ride to end.

Except that when the car stopped, we still weren't home.

The music faded out, and a new voice shrieked inside my head. "An abomination! We shall all be punished for her sins!"

I cut the link. Opened my eyes. A sallow face stared through the window, mouth open in a silent howl. When he saw me watching he extended his index finger, and his lips shifted, formed an unmistakable word. "You."

My father, behind the wheel even though he wasn't actually using it, pounded a fist against the dash. The horn blared. My mother stroked his arm, more a symbolic attempt to calm him down than anything that actually had a prayer of working. "Biggest mistake they ever made," he muttered. "Programming these things not to run people down."

"Honey . . ." That was symbolic attempt number two. Except in my mother's mind, these things actually worked; in the fantasy world she inhabited, her influence soothed the savage beast.

"I should plow right through you!" he shouted at the windshield. "You want something to protest? I'll give you something to really protest!"

They crowded around the car, pressing in tight, although not too tight. The legally required foot of space remained between us and them at all times. They planted themselves in front of the car, behind it, all around it, blocking us in, so we had no choice but to sit there, twenty yards from the entrance to our property, waiting for security to arrive and, in the meantime, reading their signs.

"I'm sorry, Lee Lee," my mother said, twisting around in her seat and reaching for me. I pulled away. "I don't know how they found out you were coming home today."

Their signs were hoisted over their shoulders, streaming in red-letter LED across their chests, pulsing on their foreheads. Jamming the network so we couldn't call in reinforcements.

GOD MADE MAN. WHO MADE YOU?

FRANKENSTEIN ALWAYS BURNS

BREATH, NOT BATTERIES

"It's fine," I said. "I don't care."

My father cursed quietly, then loudly.

"Just close your eyes," my mother suggested. "Ignore them."

"I am," I said, eyes open.

My favorite sign depicted a giant extended middle finger, with a neon caption:

SKIN THIS!

It didn't even make sense. But it got the point across.

My father fumed. "Goddamned Faithers."

"Apparently we're the damned ones," I pointed out. "Or I am."

"Don't you listen to them." My mother flicked her hand across her console and my window darkened, blotting out the signs. But it wasn't the signs I'd been watching, it was the faces. I'd never seen a Faither, not up close. Before the accident, I hadn't even seen much of them on the network. But after . . . Somehow my name had ended up on a Faither hit list. Until I fixed my blockers, they'd flooded my zone with all the same crap about how I was a godless perversion, I was Satan's work, I didn't deserve to exist. But I hadn't expected them to come after me in person.

Religion went out of style right after the Middle East went out in a blaze of nuclear glory. Not that some people, maybe lots of people, didn't keep privately believing in some invisible old man who gave them promotions when they were good and syphilis when they were bad. If you had the credit, you could even snag enough drugs for a one-on-one chat. You sometimes heard rumors about people—especially in the cities, where it's not like there was much else to do—actually gathering together for their God fix, but as far as most people were willing to admit in public, God was dead. The Faith party was for all those leftover believers who—even after the nukes and the Long Winter and the Water Wars of the western drought and the quake that ate California and the wave that drowned DC—refused to give up the ghost. They were for life, for morality, for order, for gratitude, and, until recently, not against much of anything. Except reason, my father was always quick to point out. Then BioMax unrolled its download process, and the Faithers found their cause.

Now they'd found me.

My window was still blocked, but I could see them through the front windshield, silent now, all of them pointing.

"That's it, we'll go manual," my father said, gunning the engine. "I'm going through them."

My mother shook her head. "It won't let you."

"You have a better idea?"

She didn't.

"Come on, Ana, we're listening."

She sighed.

He put his hands on the wheel, switched to manual. "I'll find a way."

"Wait." I leaned forward, touching his shoulder without thinking. He didn't flinch. I glanced out the windshield, and he followed my eyes, saw the man at the center of the crowd, the one with close-cropped blond hair and black-brown eyes, who had his hands in the air. It was a signal, and his followers—for it was obvious who was leading and who was following—fell back, clearing a path for the car. The man bowed low, but kept his face raised toward the car, his eyes fixed on me. He swept his arm out, his meaning clear. *You may go. For now.* And then it was our turn to follow.

It was Thursday, and Thursday meant Kahn family dinner. Even if one-fourth of the family no longer ate. They probably would have let me out of it, just this once let me sneak off to the room I hadn't seen in nearly three months, close the door, start my new-life-same-as-the-old-life on my own, but that would have meant asking, and I didn't. The food arrived before we did, and Zo, who usually showed up to family dinner an hour or two late, if at all, waited at the table, playing the good girl. "I got steak," she said instead of "hello" or "welcome home" or "I missed you." "And chocolate soufflé. All your favorites."

And so we sat in our usual spots, and I watched them eat all my favorites.

"But what happens if you *do*?" Zo asked, stuffing the meat into her mouth. She didn't even like steak. "Does it screw up the wiring? Or would it just sit there and, you know, rot? Like you're walking around with chewed-up bits of moldy bread and rotten meat inside you?"

"Zoie!" My mother's fork clattered to her plate.

"She's just curious," my father said. "It's only natural."

"It's *rude*. And it's not appropriate at the dinner table. Not while we're eating."

"We're not *all* eating," Zo pointed out.

I did not ask to be excused.

"There'd be nowhere for the food to go," I said. "There's a grating over the vocal cavity. Air goes out when I talk. Nothing goes in. Want to see?" I opened my mouth wide.

Zo shirked away. "Ew, *gross*. Dad!"

"Not at the table, please," he said mildly.

To *me*, not to Zo.

"We thought you might want to take tomorrow off, dear," my mother said. "Maybe do some shopping, spruce up your wardrobe?" Unspoken: Because my old clothes, custom-tailored for my old measurements, wouldn't fit my new body. Another factoid she'd neglected to mention: I hadn't shopped with my mother since I was nine years old. Now, for Cass, Terra, and me, it was a tradition—or, as Cass called it, a fetish—first the full-body scan, then the designer zones, ignoring the pop-ups for crap we would never wear, sending our virtual selves on fashion model struts down virtual runways, knowing that whatever we selected would, automatically and immediately, become the new cool, the new *it*, and savoring the responsibility.

"I'm just doing a reorder," I said. Same look, new size. It's what you did after an all-body lift-tuck or a binge vacation, when you didn't want anyone to notice your new stats. It was

ill-advised—no, that was too mild; it was potentially disastrous—
to do a reorder with an all-new body. New hair, new face, new coloring. Fashion logic demanded a new look, especially for a fashion
leader. But I preferred the old one. The masses would deal.

"Express it," my father said. "So you're ready for Monday."

"Monday?"

"School. You've missed enough."

"I thought . . ." I didn't know what I had thought. I had, in
fact, tried not to think. I still hadn't peeked out from behind the
priv-wall on my zone. As far as anyone knew, I was still missing in action. Although obviously, they'd seen me on the vids.
They knew what I'd become. "Sascha, the counselor, said maybe
I should take things slow."

"Things?"

"Readjustment . . . things. Like, school. I figured, maybe I
could link in for a while, and then—"

"You know how your father feels about that," my mother said.

I knew.

School was the "crucible of socialization." School was where
we would be molded and learn to mold others. Meet—and
impress and influence and conquer—our future colleagues. We
were, after all, preparing to take our place behind the reins of
society. There'd be time enough for linked ed when we finished
high school and started specialization. And when we did we'd
beat out all the asocial losers who'd spent their formative years
staring at a ViM. So he'd said when I was six, desperate to escape
day one and all the days that followed; so he'd said when Zo

got caught cutting, when Zo got caught dosing, when Zo got caught scamming a biotech lab for one of her zoned-out friends and almost got kicked out for good. I didn't want to make him say it again.

Zo stared down at my empty plate. "If she's too scared to go to school, I don't think you should make her."

Thanks a lot, Zo.

"I'm not scared."

Zo rolled her eyes. "Yeah, right."

"I'm *not*."

"Then you're an idiot."

"Zoie!" That was our mother again, trying, always trying, to keep the peace.

"What? I'm just saying, if it were me, I'd be afraid people would think I was, you know."

Say it.

"You've been gone for a long time," Zo said, like a warning.

I looked at my father. "Long enough. So, fine. Monday."

I was ready.

Or I would be.

No one was linked in, no one but Becca Mai, who didn't count, not even in an emergency, which this wasn't, not yet. Of course no one was there. It was Thursday night, and Thursday night meant Cass's house—not her parents' neo-mod manor of glass and steel, but the guesthouse they'd built by the lake, even though they had no guests and never would.

I voiced Walker, who never went anywhere without a flexiViM wrapped around his wrist, set to vibrate with incoming texts and to heat up when I voiced. But he wasn't there, and I pussed out. I couldn't let him hear the new voice for the first time in a message. So instead I texted:

I'm home.

I flicked on the mood player, but no music played.

Right. Because the selection was keyed to biometrics, body temp, heart rate, and all the other signs of life I didn't have anymore. So I skimmed through the playlist, chose at random, a soulsong from one of those interchangeable weepers we'd all worshipped a couple years before, when they'd first engineered the musical algorithm that would make you cry.

It didn't.

But it was more than a lack of tear ducts. Or tears. It just wasn't music for me, not anymore, not in the same way. I'd tried it a few times back in rehab, putting on a favorite track, something guaranteed to sweep me out of myself, and it had just been rhythmic noise. Song after song, and I heard every note, I tracked the melodies, I mouthed the lyrics—but it didn't mean anything. It was noise. It was vibrating air, hitting the artificial eardrum with a certain frequency, a certain wavelength, resolving into patterns. Meaningless patterns.

It wasn't a download thing, Sascha said. It was a *me* thing. Plenty of mech-heads still got music. I just wasn't one of them. "There are some things about the brain even we don't understand," Sascha had admitted. "Your postprocedure brain is functionally identical to the organic model, but many clients encounter minor—and I can't emphasize that enough, *minor*—differences in the way they process experiences. Finding themselves indifferent to things they used to love. Loving things they used to hate. We don't know why."

"How can you not know?" I'd asked. "You built the . . . brain. Computer. Whatever you want to call it. You should know how it works."

"The download procedure *copies* the brain into a computer," Sascha had said. "But each brain is composed of billions of cognitive processes. We can model the complete structure without understanding each of its individual parts. Which is why, for example, we don't have the capacity to create new brains from scratch. Only nature can do that. For now."

"So all you know how to do is make copies," I'd said. "Except you can't even get that right. Not exactly." When we were talking about my brain, the things I loved and hated, when we were talking about *me*, "close enough" didn't really get the job done.

"It can be disconcerting at first, but you'll learn to embrace the exciting possibilities. One client even emerged from the procedure with a newfound artistic passion. He's already so successful that he's linked on the *president's* zone!" Saying it like that was some kind of achievement. Like the president wasn't too doped up to notice who stuck what on her zone; judging from the vids, she'd barely even noticed being re-elected.

I didn't have any new passions, certainly none that would make me famous. And I'd thought maybe the music thing was just temporary, that once I got off the thirteenth floor and back to the real world, things would return to normal.

I shut down the music. What was the point?

Susskind, our psychotic cat, sashayed into the room and leaped up onto the bed. And maybe he had the right idea. Except that going to bed would mean facing all the other things that hadn't gone back to normal. All the prebed rituals that had been made obsolete.

I had my own bathroom, tiled in purple and blue. My own shower, where I washed off the grime every night and washed on the UV block every morning, now no longer necessary. My own toilet with a med-chip that analyzed every deposit for bio-irregularities— no longer required. My own sink, where I would have hydro-scrubbed my teeth if they weren't already made of some gleaming white alloy impervious to microbes. Not like they came into contact with any, what with the whole no-food thing. My own medicine cabinet, with all the behavior modifiers I could ever need, uppers for perk, downers for sleep, Xers for parties, stims for work, and bliss-ers for play, but no b-mod could help me now. On the face of the cabinet, my own mirror. I stayed away from mirrors.

Psycho Susskind crawled into my lap.

"Great." I rested my hand on his back, letting it rise and fall with each breath. "Of course you like me now." Sussie was afraid of people, even the people who housed and fed him; maybe— judging from his standard pattern of hissing and clawing— especially us. Or make that, them. Because apparently Sussie and I were now best friends.

I didn't dump him off my lap.

"I smell good to you now, Sussie?" I whispered, scratching him behind his ears. He purred. "Like your other best friend?" That would be the dishwasher, which Sussie worshipped like he was a Faither and the dishwasher had a white beard and fistful of lightning bolts.

It's not like I had no way to fill the time. Showers and music weren't generally the bulk of my standard evening activities. There was always a game going on the network. Or I could tweak my av, update my zone, chat with the net-friends who'd never seen my flesh-and-blood body and so wouldn't notice it was gone. I could even hit the local stalker sites and read all about myself, wealthy scion of the Kahn dynasty stuffed into a mech-head and body. What will she do next, now that she's home, where will she go, who will she see, what will she wear?

Instead I pumped the network for information on emotion, for why people feel what they feel and how. But I couldn't make myself read through the results, facts and theories and long, dense explanations that had nothing to do with me.

Walker still hadn't texted back.

I cut the link.

My tracksuit didn't fit me any better than the rest of my clothes. The pants and sleeves were too short and too baggy, the thermo-lining, cued to body temp, was superfluous, and the biostats read zero across the board. But they would do, as would the shoes I got from BioMax, which didn't cushion my feet like the sneakers that no longer fit, but still registered body weight and regulated shock absorption, which was all I needed. Zo was out somewhere; my parents were in bed. There was no one to notice I was gone.

It was a cold night, but that didn't matter, not to me. There was a path behind the house that wove through the woods, a path I'd run every morning for the last several years, layered in thermo-gear, panting and sweating and cursing and loving it. The gravel sounded the same as always, crunching beneath my soles.

I need this, I said silently, to someone, maybe to myself or maybe to the body that locked me in and denied everything I asked of it. *Please. Let this work.*

It didn't.

I ran for an hour. Legs pumping. Feet pounding. Arms swinging. Face turned up to the wind. The body worked perfectly. I didn't sweat. I didn't cramp up. I didn't wheeze, gulping in desperate mouthfuls of oxygen, because I didn't breathe at all. I pushed faster, pushed harder, until something in my head told me I was tired, that it was time to slow down, time to stop, but my muscles didn't ache, my chest didn't tighten, my feet didn't drag, I didn't *feel* ready to stop. I just knew I was, and so I did.

There was no rush, no natural upper coasting me through the last couple miles. There was never that sense of letting go and losing myself in my body, of *existing* in my body, arms, legs, muscles, tendons, pulsing and pumping in sync, the world narrowing to a pinprick tunnel of ground skimming beneath my feet. None of the pure pleasure of absence, of leaving Lia Kahn behind and existing in the moment—all body, no mind.

The body still felt like someone else's; the mind was still all I had left.

I walked the rest of the way back to the house, navigating the path in darkness. The heavy clouds hid even the pale glow of the moon, and so I didn't see the shadows melt into a figure, a man, not until he was close enough to touch.

Fingers wrapped around my arm. Thick, strong fingers. A hand, twisting, and my arm followed the unspoken command, my body tugged after it. He pinned me against a tree, his forearm shoved against my throat.

Lucky I didn't need to breathe.

His face so close to mine that our noses nearly touched, I recognized him. It was the face I'd seen through the car window that morning, the hollow face howling at me through the glass.

I should run away, I thought. *I should scream.* But the ideas seemed distant, almost silly.

"It is He that hath made us, and not we ourselves," the man hissed. "We are His people, and the sheep of his pasture." His breath caressed my face. I wondered what it smelled like.

I wondered if his boss knew he was still here, lurking. I wondered who his boss was. The man with the too-pale skin and the too-dark eyes? Or did he report directly to the big boss, the eye in the sky? I wondered what he would do to me if I asked.

"Thou shall not make unto thee any graven image, or any

likeness of any thing that is in heaven above, or that is in the earth beneath, or that is in the water under the earth."

I was linked in. I could have sent for help. But I didn't particularly want any. His arm bore down harder against my throat.

"That's you," he spat out. "A graven image. A *machine*. Programmed to think you're a real person. Pathetic."

Enough. "Yeah, *I'm* pathetic," I snapped back. "You're hiding behind a tree, trespassing on private property, and about five minutes away from being picked up by the cops and probably shipped off to a city, and *I'm* pathetic."

"*Tzedek, tzedek tirdof,*" he whispered, grinning like the nonsense words harbored some secret power. I shuddered.

"Righteousness, righteousness shall you pursue." He reached up his other hand and stroked my cheek. "God says be righteous to your fellow man. But he doesn't say *anything* about what to do with things like you." The fingers traced the curve of my ear. I jerked my head away, but he grabbed a chunk of hair and tugged, hard. "Guess I'm on my own, figuring out what to do. Got any ideas?"

He laughed, and that's when the fear came, fast and hard, like a needle of terror jabbed into my skull. "Anything," that was the word that echoed. He could do anything. I grabbed his hand, the hand that was crawling down my neck, along my spine, grabbed his fingers and bent them back until I heard the joints crunch and the arm at my throat reared back, struck me across the face, snapped my head back into the tree but my leg had already swung into motion, had connected with his groin.

He doubled over and I ran, and I could hear him behind me, cursing and grunting, crashing through the brush, closing in as I pushed faster and pulled away and I could almost imagine a beating heart and heaving lungs, because the panic was so real. But he fell behind, and I made it through the electronic gate in plenty of time, locking him out, locking me in. The fear faded almost immediately, and as it leaked out of me, I had one last, terrifying thought.

I should go back.

To slip through the gate again, to face the man, to *fight* the man—or not to fight, to let him do whatever he wanted, to choose to meet him and his consequences, to turn back, because behind me, where the man glowered from the treeline, was something real. Something human.

The stronger the emotion, Sascha had promised, the more real it would seem.

I'd felt it. I was hooked.

Back in my room, safe and alone. The man, whoever he was, long gone. And with him, the fear.

I stripped off the sweat-free tracksuit. Uploaded the day's neural changes, ensuring—with nothing more than a few keystrokes and an encrypted transmission to the server—that if anything happened to this body, a Lia Kahn with fully up-to-date memories would remain in storage, ready and waiting to be dumped into a new one. Would it be me or a copy of me? And if it was a copy, did that make *me* a copy too, of some other, realer Lia? Was she dead? Was the man right that I was just a machine duped into believing I was human? And if I had been duped, then how could I be a machine? How could any thought-less, soulless, consciousness-free thing believe in a lie, believe in anything, *want* to believe?

And did I consider those questions while I was dealing with my brand-new bedtime ritual? Did I follow the primrose path of logical deduction all the way to its logical endpoint, to the essential question?

I did not.

I dumped the tracksuit; I uploaded; I pulled on pajamas; I twisted the blond hair back into a loose, low ponytail; I dumped psycho Susskind into the hall. I did it all mechanically. Mechani-cally, as in without thought, as in through force of habit, as in instinctively, automatically, involuntarily. Mechanically, as in like-a-machine.

And I did not think about that, either.

Instead of turning out the lights and climbing into bed, I mechanically—always mechanically—entered the purple-and-blue tiled bathroom for the first time. The stranger's face watched me from the mirror, impassive. Blank.

I pulled up the network query I'd made earlier, the one I hadn't had the nerve to read. The words scrolled across my left eye, glowing letters superimposed on my reflected face.

I froze the parade of definitions and expanded the one that seemed to matter. The guy's name was William James, and he was way too old to be right. Two hundred years ago, no one knew anything; it's why they all died young and wrinkled with bad hair. Two hundred years ago, they thought light could go as fast as it wanted, they thought the atom was indivisible and possibly imaginary, they thought "computers" were servant girls who added numbers for their bosses when they weren't busy doing the laundry. They knew nothing. But I read it anyway.

If we fancy some strong emotion, and then try to abstract from our consciousness of it all the feelings of its characteristic bodily symptoms, we find we have nothing left behind, no "mind stuff" out of which the emotion can be constituted, and that a cold and neutral state of intellectual perception is all that remains.

The face didn't move; the eyes didn't blink. *Cold and neutral,* I thought. It wasn't true. I had felt anger; I had felt fear. But fear of what? The man couldn't have hurt me, not really. At least, he couldn't hurt me forever. Whatever he did to the body, I would remain. I couldn't die. What was to fear in the face of that?

What kind of emotion of fear would be left if the feeling neither of quickened heartbeats nor of shallow breathing, neither of trembling lips nor of shallow weakened limbs, neither of gooseflesh nor of visceral stirrings, were present . . . ?

Even now, in my pajamas, in my bathroom, I felt. The tile beneath my feet. The sink against my palms. I felt absence: the silence that should have been punctuated by steady breathing, in and out. Fingers against my chest, I felt the stillness beneath them. I felt loss.

In like manner of grief: what would it be without its tears, its sobs, its suffocation of the heart, its pang in the breast bone? A feelingless cognition that certain circumstances are deplorable, and nothing more.

Nothing more.

THE BODY

"Aren't you going to kiss her good-bye?"

Their whispers slithered through the crack beneath my bedroom door, and I fought the temptation to press myself against it, to find out what Zo and Walker, who had for years shared a mutual, if mostly unspoken, oath of eternal dislike, could possibly need to discuss. Not that the topic was in doubt.

The topic was me.

The whispers stopped. I struck my best casual pose, legs dangling off the side of the bed, elbows digging into the mattress, ankles crossed, head tipped back to the ceiling as if the track of solar panels had proven so engrossing as to make me forget what was about to happen. The door opened, and I held my position, letting Walker see me before I saw him.

Giving him time to erase his reaction before I could see it on his face.

Not enough time. When I sat up, he was still in the doorway, one hand in his pocket, the other gripping the frame, holding himself steady.

"Hey," I said.

He didn't move. "Your voice . . ."

"Weird, right? I hear myself talk and I'm like, wait, who said that?" I forced a laugh, but stopped as soon as I saw him wince. I'd forgotten that I wasn't very good at the laughing thing yet. Especially when I was faking it.

"It's nice," he said, like he was trying to convince himself. "I like it."

I hated it. Someone else's voice, husky and atonal, coming out of the mouth.

My mouth, I reminded myself. *My* voice. But I could only believe that when I was alone. With Walker finally standing there, watching me, I was forced to admit it: The voice belonged to the *thing*, to the body, not to me.

"It's been a while," I said, even though I'd promised myself I wasn't going to bring it up. He hadn't voiced me back on Thursday night or on Friday. And then Saturday came, and he was here. That should have been enough.

Walker shrugged. He rubbed his chin, which was shadowed with brown scruff. Without me around to remind him to shave, he'd grown a beard. "I was going to text you, but . . ."

"Yeah. But." I stood up. He was still in the doorway. If he

wouldn't come to me, I would go to him. *It can be difficult at the beginning,* Sascha had said. *But the people who know you, the people who love you, they'll see beneath the surface. They'll get that it's really* you *under there. You just have to give them some time.*

No one knew me better than Walker. But when I curled the hand around his wrist, he jerked away. "Sorry, I—"

I stepped back. "No, it's fine." It wasn't. "I shouldn't have." He shouldn't have.

"No, really. I just . . ." Walker finally stepped into the room, edging around me as he passed, careful not to touch the body. He sat in my desk chair, back straight, feet flat on the floor. Arms crossed, hugging his chest.

I dropped back down on the bed and waited.

"I'm very glad you're all right," he said finally, like he was passing along a message from his mother to some old lady who'd broken her hip. Like he'd been rehearsing.

I risked a smile. I'd been rehearsing too. "I missed you."

"You, too." He stared down at the floor. His hair was longer than I'd ever seen it, almost to his shoulders, like one of Zo's retros. I wanted to smooth it back. I wanted to stand behind him and bury my face in it, resting my cheek against the back of his head, wrapping my arms around his shoulders, letting him grip my hands in his. But I stayed where I was. "It's, uh, it's pretty," he said. "I mean—*you're* pretty. Now. Like this."

"You don't have to lie."

He shifted in the seat. "No— It's just, I guess, I just thought you'd look a little more like . . . I mean, on the vids, and you looked . . . But now . . . I thought you'd look more . . ."

"Like me?" But as soon as I said it, I knew that wasn't what he'd meant. I *didn't* look like me, not anymore, not with the hair that was the wrong color and texture and wasn't even hair, just a synthetic weave that was grafted on and would never grow. The nose was too small, the eyes too wide, the fingers the wrong thickness, the wrong length, the teeth too straight and too bright, the mouth bigger, the ears smaller, the body taller and too symmetrical, too well proportioned, too perfect. But it wasn't that. I knew what he'd wanted to say; I knew him too well.

I thought you'd look more . . . human.

And I saw the body again like I'd seen it for the first time, like *he* was seeing it. The skin, smooth and waxy, an even peachy tone stretched out over the frame without sag or blemish. The way it moved, with awkward jerks, always too slow or too fast. The stranger's face with dead eyes, pale blue irises encircling the false pupils, and in the center of the black, pinpricks of light, flashing and dimming as the lens sucked up images. The eyes that didn't blink unless I remembered to blink them. The chest that neither rose nor fell unless I pretended to breathe. The body that wasn't a body.

His girlfriend, the machine.

"It's just weird," he admitted. "I'm sorry, I know I shouldn't—"

"It's okay," I said quickly. "It *is* weird. It's weird for me too."

"I mean, I know it's you, I get that, but you sound different, and you look different, and . . ."

"It's because it was an emergency. They had to give me a generic model. My dad picked it out. He says it's the one that looked the most like me. Not that it looks like me, I know, but it was the best he could do." *Too much detail,* I told myself. *Stop talking.* But I couldn't. Once I stopped, he would have to start again. Or he wouldn't. And then we'd just sit there, and he would try not to stare at me, and I would try not to look away. "Some people get these custom faces designed to look just like them, the way they were—or like anything they want, I guess. It's totally crazy what they can do. The voice, too. You just make a recording and they match it. I mean, it's not exactly the same, I know, but it's . . . closer. Easier. But you've got to place the order in advance. You've got to give them time, and if there's an accident or something, well . . ." I tried another smile. "There's nothing I can do about it now. The artificial nerves and receptors are already fused to the neural pathways or whatever, and they say structural changes would screw with the graft, but next time, I'll do it in advance, so I'll be able to order whatever I want. Then I'll look more like . . ."

"Lia," he said.

I am Lia.

But I said it in my head, where there was no one to hear.

"I'll look more like *me,*" I said out loud. Calmly. "Next time."

"Wait, what do you mean, next time?"

"When the, uh, body wears out or—" I closed my eyes

for a moment, trying to block out the echo of the crash, the scream of metal that refused to die—"if something happens to it, they'll download the, uh . . ." *Data? Program? Brain? Soul?* There was no right word. There was only *me*, looking out through some *thing's* dead eyes. "They'll do it again. When they need to."

"So you just get a new body when the old one runs out?" he asked. "And they keep doing it . . . forever?"

"That's the plan." As the words came out of the mouth, I finally saw it, what it meant. I saw the day he found the first tuft of hair stuck in the shower drain or woke up to a gray strand on his pillow. His first wrinkle in the bathroom mirror. The day he blew out his knee in his last football game. The day his potbelly bulged as he stopped playing and kept eating. Any of the days, all of the days, starting with tomorrow, when he'd be one day older than today; and then the next, two days older, and the next and the next, as he grew, as he aged, as he declined . . . as I stayed the same. Shunted from one unchanging husk of metal and plastic to the next.

I got there a moment before he did, but only a moment, and then he got there too. I saw it on his face.

"Forever." Walker grimaced. "You'll be like . . . this. Forever." He stood up.

Don't leave, I thought. *Not yet.* But I wasn't about to say it out loud. Even if he couldn't see it, I was still Lia Kahn. I didn't beg.

"So, what's it like?" he asked, crossing the room. To the

bed—to me. He sat down on the edge, leaving a space between us. "Can you, like, feel stuff?"

"Yeah. Of course." If it counted as feeling, the way the whole world seemed hidden behind a scrim. Fire was warm. Ice was cool. Everything was mild. Nothing was right.

I held out a hand, palm up. "Do you want to . . . ? You can see what it feels like. To touch it. If you want."

He lifted his arm, extended a finger, hesitated over my exposed wrist, trembling.

He touched it. Me.

Shuddered. Snatched his hand away.

Then touched me again. Palm to palm. He curled his fingers around the hand. Around my hand.

"You can really feel that?" he asked.

"Yes."

"So what's it feel like?"

"Like it always does." A lie. Artificial nerves, artificial conduits, artificial receptors, registering the fact of a touch. Reporting back to a central processor the fact of a hand, five fingers, flesh bearing down. Measuring the temperature, the pressure per square inch, the duration, and all of it translated, somehow, into something resembling a sensation. "It feels good." I paused. "What does it feel like to you?"

"You mean . . . ?"

"The skin."

"It's . . ." He scrunched his eyebrows together. "Not the same as before. But not . . . weird. It feels like skin." He let go.

I brushed the back of my hand across his cheek. This time he didn't move away. "You need to shave."

"I like it like this," he said, giving me a half smile. It was the same thing he always said.

"You're the only one." That was the standard response. We'd had the fight that wasn't a fight so often it was like we were following a script, one that always ended the same way. And if I acted like everything was the same, maybe . . .

"It looks good," he argued, the half smile widening into a full grin.

"It doesn't *feel* good. So unless you want to scratch half my face off when—" I stopped.

Nothing was the same.

The coarse bristles sprinkling his face wouldn't hurt when he kissed me.

If he kissed me.

"Lia, when you were gone all that time, I . . ."

"What?"

A pause.

"Nothing. I'm just . . . I'm glad you didn't, you know. Die."

It was what he had to say, and I gave him the answer I had to give. "Me too." For the first time, sitting there with him, I could almost believe it was true.

Another pause, longer this time.

"When you were in that place . . . I should have come to visit."

"You were busy," I said.

"I should have come."

"Yeah."

Not that I would have let him see me like that, spasmodic limbs jerking without warning, muscles clenching and unclenching at random, the mouth spitting out those strangled animal noises, the tinny speaker speaking for me until I could control the tongue, moderate the airflow, train the mechanism to impersonate human speech. If he'd seen me like that, he would never have been able to see me any other way. He would never see that I was Lia.

"I should go," he said. "You must be . . . Do you get tired?"

I shook the head. "I sleep, but it's not . . . I don't dream or anything. I just . . ." There was no other way to say it. "Shut down."

"Oh."

"I'm sorry," I said suddenly.

"What?" He scrunched his eyebrows together again. "Why?"

"I don't know." There were no mechanical tear ducts embedded in the dead eyes. No saltwater deposits hidden behind the unblinking lids. Add it to the list of things I wouldn't do again: cry. "I just am. I'm sorry that I'm . . . like this."

I admit it. I wanted him to wrap his arms around me. I wanted him to tell me that *he* wasn't sorry. That I was beautiful. That the hair felt like real hair and the skin felt like real skin and the body felt like a real body and he wasn't weirded out by the thought of touching it. That he saw me.

He stood up. I didn't. "You going back to school soon?"

"Monday."

"So I guess I'll see you there." He backed toward the door. When he opened it, Zo was on the other side. Like she'd been there the whole time, waiting, as she'd done when Walker and I had first gotten together, and she'd been a kid, annoying, always around, hovering outside with her ear pressed to the door, giggling every time we were about to kiss.

"Guess so."

He hesitated, like he was waiting for my permission to leave. The old Walker had waited for my permission to do everything.

"Aren't you going to kiss her good-bye?" Zo asked, sounding so sweet, so helpful, so hopelessly ignorant, and then she smiled, and the smile was none of those things.

Walker didn't move. Not until she gave him a gentle push, digging her fists into the shallow concavity beneath his rib cage. He lurched across the room, and I felt frozen again, like I had that first day, locked inside the body.

Blink, I reminded myself. But when I shut the lids, I didn't open them again.

He didn't taste like anything. Nothing did anymore. His lips feathered across mine. I registered the touch, and then it was gone.

"Bye, Lia."

I kept my eyes shut as his footsteps crossed the room. The door closed.

Bye.

SOBERED UP

"Survival of the fittest. And we were the fittest."

It began Monday at six a.m., when the bed whispered me awake—or would have if an inner alert hadn't already forced my eyes open and my brain back to full-scale conscious dread. It began as I picked through a stack of clothes in disgust, rejecting favorites—the mood dress useless, its temperature-activated swooshes and swirls requiring fluctuations in body temperature, which themselves required an actual body; the sonicsilk with its harmonic rippling just another reminder of the music I'd lost; the LBD, a linked-in black dress whose net-knit flared neon with every voice or text, too sensational; the soundproofed hoodie functional and cozy but not sensational enough, blah and gray, like I planned to fade into the background, scenery instead of the star—and finally being forced to resort to jeans and an old print-shirt that snatched random phrases from the network and scrolled them across the fabric. The look had been very hot, and then quickly very not, but it had settled into a neutral acceptability, and it was the best I could do.

It began—my official return to school and an officially normal life—with breakfast, another meal I could no longer eat. Or maybe with the sound of the car door slamming shut, Zo and me tucked inside, or with the hills giving way to a long, flat stretch of familiar green, the castle of brick and stone rising above the horizon.

In that old, normal life, it began after every break—whether two days or two months—with a squeal in stereo, Cass and Terra catching sight of me, fashionably late, pulling into the lot. It began with a rocket-launched embrace, arms locked, shoulders encircled, styles critiqued, stories spilled, all, it seemed, released in a single, shared breath. This time I had no stories, at least none I was willing to share. This time nothing was normal. But as the car pulled into the lot, I saw them bounce off the steps in front of the school. I opened the door and heard the squeal.

It begins now.

The first thing that registered were their clothes. Loose, ill-fitting, dull-colors, Cass in a T-shirt with a printed, unchanging slogan, Terra in jeans that sagged on her ass and a black shirt too loose and too worn, without any visible tech, like something you'd find in a city, or from one of those thrift zones Zo was always haunting for new retro rags.

The second thing: *"Zo Zo!"*

That was Cass's squeal, Cass's wide grin—and then she saw me, and both of them faded away.

She'd cut her black hair short and spiky, cropping it with a dusting of pink. "Lia?" Cass narrowed her eyes as if squinting would squeeze my features back to their familiar shape—or maybe block them out altogether. "Is that . . . you?"

"It's me." I didn't dare try a smile. "In the flesh."

No one laughed. Terra looked sick. She hip-bumped Zo.

"Zo Zo, why didn't you tell us that your sister was coming back today?" she asked with a determined perk. "We would have . . . done something special. To celebrate."

Terra's hair was the same, but she was actually—it didn't seem possible—wearing *lipstick*. And some kind of purple glitter above her eyes. Which didn't make sense, because no one wore makeup anymore, except the wrinkled poor who couldn't afford gen-tech or lift-tucks, and trashy retro slummers who thought it was cool to pretend they fit in to the first group. Oh, and seniles, who didn't count, since they didn't even know what year it was and so couldn't be expected to remember that makeup had gone out with TVs and artificial preservatives. Why spend all that credit on the perfect face if any random could match the effect with a black marker and some pinkish paint? Zo was wearing lipstick too, of course, but that was nothing new.

"I asked, uh, *Zo Zo*"—I shot Zo a look. She ignored it—"not to say anything." A lie. Like I could ever have imagined Zo talking to *my* friends. "Don't blame her."

"Doesn't matter now," Cass chirped. "You're back!"

"Tell us everything," Terra said. *"Everything."*

"Zo Zo wouldn't spill," Cass said, thwapping Zo's shoulder. "No matter how many times we asked. And, of course, *someone* has been totally zoned out forever."

"Yeah . . ." I didn't want to explain how I'd been lurking on the network in stealth mode, peeking over everyone's shoulders, or why I hadn't texted anyone back. Especially not with Zo—excuse me, *Zo Zo*—standing right there, listening to every word. "Sorry about that. I had a lot to, you know, deal with. For a while."

"We can imagine," Cass said.

"No, we can't." Terra sounded pissed. "Because we don't know anything."

"But we want to." Cass touched my shoulder. "We do."

Zo flicked a finger across her inner wrist, and the small screen she'd temp-adhered flashed twice. "Time, ladies."

"Oh!" Cass blushed. "Right. We're late. So, info dump later? Lunch?"

"Uh, sure— Wait, no, it's Monday." When it came to ruling the pack, lunch was key, but that was Tuesday through Friday. Mondays belonged to Walker. That had always been the deal, from the beginning.

"You and *Walker*?" Terra asked. "You mean he didn't—"

"Walker will deal," Cass cut in.

He didn't what? I thought. But didn't ask.

"It'll be fine," Cass said. "Trust me. Lunch."

"Lunch," I agreed. Walker could wait. "But where are you going?"

"Too complicated." Cass giggled as Terra tugged her away. "Later. Lunch."

"Right. Later. Lunch." I grabbed Zo before she could follow them. "So?"

She shook me off. "So what?"

"So since when do you steal my best friends?"

She smirked. "Maybe they stole me."

"And where are you all going?"

"They're *your* best friends. Shouldn't you already know?"

"You know I haven't talked to them in months," I said.

"Exactly."

"Zo!"

"I'm late." She spun away, pausing only to shoot back the last word. "And at school it's Zoie. Or Zo Zo."

I was used to people watching me. I just wasn't used to them gawking, then twisting away as soon as I caught them at it. The hallways were the worst. Conversation died as soon as I got close—sometimes tapering off, like a seeping wound that finally, as the heart stops pumping, runs out of blood, and sometimes cut off in its prime, a gunshot victim dropped by eight grams of lead. I knew the conversations that reached a violent, abrupt end were the ones about me, the machine roaming the halls claiming to be Lia Kahn. The other ones—the stumbling, mumbling trailings off into awkward silence—were just the result of nobody knowing what to say. That was at least better than the randoms who came up to me all day knowing *exactly* what to say, and this—no matter which words they used to disguise it—boiled down to "smile for the camera" as they aimed their ViMs at my face, zooming in for a close-up, pumping me for details they could post on their zone or a local stalker site and turn us both into fame whores.

I didn't smile.

In class, even the teachers stared, not like they had much else to do beyond babysit us while we got our real education from the network. Which meant I watched my ViM screen while the rest of them watched me. The only relief came in biotech, usually the worst of all possible evils, but hidden behind the thick plastic face mask, hunched over my splicing kit, I could almost pass for normal.

Walker didn't respond to my text about lunch, and when I showed up in the cafeteria, he wasn't there. So I sat with the usual suspects—plus Zo—at the usual table in the front of the room, where everyone could look as much as they wanted. Surrounded by my friends, it was almost possible to pretend they were staring for the old reasons, wondering what we had that they didn't, where they'd gone wrong between *then*— the half-remembered, better-forgotten days of all-men-are-created-equal playdates and birthday parties when no one cared how loud you were, how rude you were, how ugly you were, how stupid you were, how lame you were, because we were all too young and so too dumb to notice—and *now*, when how you looked and how you talked mattered as much as it should.

The Helmsley School was built three hundred years ago, for

people who were almost as rich as we were, and the cafeteria, with its wood panels, floor-to-ceiling windows, and scalloped ceiling, was a suitably regal match for the exterior, all stone columns and brick arches. Thanks to the population crash and the upswing in linked ed, only half the tables were filled, but any group larger than three is enough for an us/them divide. After all, that was—as we'd learned in kindergarten—the key to civilization and the survival of the species. Finite supply plus infinite demand equaled conflict, battle, nature red in tooth and claw; bloody struggle for turf, status, sex equaled survival of the fittest. And we were the fittest.

Staying at the top meant defying expectations and reversing the norm, because there was nothing exclusive about acting like everyone else. Which meant that if the rest of the school was gaping at my new face and freakish body, my friends, not to mention the people I counted as friends by virtue of social proximity, would ignore the obvious, forgo the questions, and act as if they ate with a skinner every day—as, from now on, they would. Except for the fact that the skinner wasn't eating.

Which wasn't as awkward as the fact that my sister was. And was doing so at *my* table.

Or the fact that everyone else was tricked out in retro slum gear, just like her. I was the only person wearing anything with visible tech—the only person at the table, at least. I was dressed exactly like everyone else in the room. Normal.

But the clothes didn't explain why everything felt so wrong. You didn't claw your way to the top of the pyramid without knowing how to read people. You needed a radar, something to sense the smallest of fluctuations in the social field. You needed the skills to know, even with your eyes closed and your ears plugged, who was scheming, who was suffering, who was gaining on you, who was on the way out. If you couldn't figure out that last one, chances are, it was you.

It wasn't the kind of thing you could learn. You either had it or you didn't.

Except it turned out there was a third option: You had it, and then you lost it.

Part of it was them. No one could act normal, not while I was in the room.

Part of it was me.

The things I used to know about people, the things I *understood* . . . It wasn't a rational thing. It was just something I *felt*, like the way I could feel when someone was watching me.

I couldn't do that anymore either.

I felt like I'd gone blind.

It didn't help that I barely knew half the people at the table, especially the two grunters pawing Cass and Terra—the reason, I quickly found out, they'd run off so quickly that morning. New season, new boys.

No sign of Walker.

No one asked me where he was.

Bliss had picked that day's b-mod, which meant—big surprise—everyone was blissed out. Everyone except me, since b-mods wouldn't do much for someone without brain chemicals to modify. I'd half expected them to opt for some retro drugs to match the retro clothes. Some of Zo's dozers, maybe, or even something alcohol based, like in the bad old days of hangovers and beer bellies. But no matter how in retro was, it couldn't offer anything that would kick in immediately and wear off by the end of the period. Advantage: b-mods. As far as I was concerned, bliss mods were bad enough when I was on them too, always leaving a weird moody aftertaste, like crashing after a sugar high. Staying cold sober while the rest of them blissed up? Infinitely worse.

"So do you have, like, superpowers?" That was Cass's mouth breather. It was worse when guys giggled. That just wasn't natural. "Are you an evil crime fighter now?" Cass glared at him, smacking his hand away when he tried to squeeze my bicep.

Terra tugged at my print-shirt. "You got a uniform on under here? For your secret identity?"

Zo blew out a laugh. It was the first time since the accident that I'd seen her with a real smile. "*I'm* the superhero." She narrowed her eyes at Cass. "The power to wither with a single glare."

Cass clutched at her chest. "You got me!" She toppled over, tumbling into me. "Oh. Sorry." She sprang up, posture straight, arms assembled in her lap, a careful four or five inches away from mine. No one spoke.

"Apparently I have the power of awkwardness," I joked. Awkwardly. "Lia Kahn, super-buzz-killer."

No one laughed.

Terra's boy—Axe or Jax or something; it wasn't clear and since no one else seemed to care, I didn't either—grunted something about his balls itching, and how he'd prefer the power to scratch them without anyone seeing. Cass elbowed her guy, who was busy making an adjustment of his own. "How about *you* try that power sometime." She pulled his hand out of his lap—and didn't let go.

"Power," the guy repeated. "Pow-er. Weird word. Word weeeeiiiird." He wrapped his hairy arms around Cass, who dissolved into a shivering mass of giggles.

The bliss mod was kicking it up.

"What if we only walk in wouble-woo words," Bliss suggested, laughing.

Zo shrugged and flashed a sly smile. "Whatever works."

"Why?" Terra asked.

"Why wot!" her boy crowed.

"Where's Walker?" Bliss said, in a way that made me wonder if the whole *w* thing hadn't just been a convenient way of getting around to the question, except that Bliss wasn't smart enough to formulate such a plan, even when off the drugs.

"Walker's waiting," Cass said, and the others nodded, as if that made any sense.

"Wise Walker."

"Or Walker's whizzing!"

"What would Walker want?"

"*Who* would Walker want?" Bliss again.

"Walker wonders what's worse, waiting or wanting or

wussing," Zo said in the tone of someone who knows she's won a game. Everyone else nodded at wordwise *Zo Zo*. Hail to the chief.

I stood up. "See you guys later."

"Wait!" Cass cackled. "We . . . uh, w—" The letter almost foiled her. Then, at the last minute, "We want Wia!"

Bliss pointed at me. "Whiner." Then giggled and shook her head. "Whatever."

Everyone lifted a glass, toasted. "Whatever!"

So I ditched the table and the cafeteria, and spent the rest of lunch outside, where I could be alone because it was too cold, at least too cold for anyone warm-blooded enough to care. Those of us running on battery power, on the other hand, could sit under a tree, wait for the bell, ignore the wind and the frost, because none of it—*none* of it—mattered.

Whatever.

That was the first day. And the next few weren't any better. My social life was hemorrhaging. And time, contrary to popular opinion, did not heal the wound. I retrofitted my wardrobe; I stuck it out through one lunch after another, b-mod haze and all. I did *not* ask Zo how she'd managed to weasel her way into every corner of my life or what had happened to her own life and the randoms she used to know and love. I didn't ask Zo much of anything. We shared a house, shared a lunch table, a set of friends, even— despite a lack of permission and my conviction that I was probably risking infestation from whatever hardy insects had survived all those decades in someone's moldy attic—her clothes. But we didn't talk. Which was fine with me.

I didn't talk to Cass or Terra, either, not about anything that mattered. And when I asked them about Zo . . . The first time we were alone, there it was, flat out: Since when don't we hate my sister? The conversation didn't get very far.

"After, you know, what happened," Cass stammered. "We were . . ."

"Upset," Terra said. "And worried about her."

"About you too, of course."

"But you weren't here."

"And you weren't linked in."

I waited for them to say they were just being nice—out of character, maybe, but not out of the realm of possibility. That Zo had been so distraught by "what happened" that they'd needed to comfort her, to include her, what any friends would do for a suffering little sister. They didn't.

"So no one knew what was going on with you . . ."

"And Zo just . . ."

"Surprised us," Cass said.

"She's different now," Terra said.

I wasn't buying it. "Seems the same to me." Even though that wasn't quite true either.

Cass looked away. "Maybe that's because you're different too."

After that, we didn't talk about it anymore.

Walker and I, on the other hand, did nothing but talk.

Which wasn't exactly our strong suit. I didn't see him at school, not for days. That was no accident. He was avoiding me, and for a while, I let him. I wasn't stupid. It's not like I expected we'd just keep going like nothing had happened. Not right away, at least. He was weirded out, so for a few days, I let him hide. But I knew Walker, and I knew what he needed, even if he didn't. He needed me.

I staked out his car. He emerged from the building surrounded by people—girls, to be specific, but there was nothing new about that. Walker was that type; he got off on it. But that was fine, because he always ended up with me. As he did this time. The girls spotted me before he did, and faded away.

I watched him walk. It was more of a lope, arms swinging wide, legs sucking up pavement. Walker had never asked me out, not in any kind of sweaty-palmed, bumbling, would-you-like-to-whatever kind of thing, not that anyone did that, but if someone were going to, it wouldn't be Walker. When it happened, it had happened fast and unmemorably, as if all along both of us had known we would eventually end up together. There had been yet another party, yet another buzz. There had been a late-night, early-morning haze, a group of us sprawled on someone's floor, heads on stomachs, legs tangled, fingers absentmindedly intertwined, lids dropping shut until only two of us were awake, and while I hadn't been waiting up for him and he hadn't been waiting up for me, it seemed like we had. Like the whole night—the party, the group, everything—had been expressly designed to deliver us to this point, to an empty patch of carpet shadowed by the couch, to his arm oh-so-casually sprawled across my thigh, to whatever would happen when he slid toward me and I rolled to face him and our bodies ate up the space between. By which I mean, I had known him forever, but I had never wanted him—until that night, when I suddenly did. He was the one who acted. Brushed my hair out of my face. Kissed me, sleepy-eyed and loose-lipped, soft, and then, like we'd waited too long, even though we hadn't waited at all, hard. Afterward, when it was already obvious that this wasn't just another night, that this was a beginning of something, he pretended that he'd been planning it for a while, secretly pining and plotting. He wasn't lying, not to me, at least. I knew he believed it. But I also knew it had been the same for him as it was for me: lying there, fighting sleep without knowing why, knowing there was a reason to stay awake, something that needed doing, and then, somehow, just *knowing*.

And doing.

"You're avoiding me," I said, leaning against the hood of the car.

He shook his head no.

I shook my head yes.

He shrugged. "Been busy."

"You're *never* busy," I said.

"Things change."

Tell me something I don't know.

"Walker, I . . ."

"What?"

I let myself sink back against the car. It was a thing; it had no choice but to hold me up. "It's been a long week, that's all."

"You want to . . . talk about it?"

"Not really." And I wasn't even saying that because I knew he wanted me to, although he clearly did. Mostly I just wanted him to kiss me again, for real this time. But what was I supposed to do. *Ask?*

"So . . . you want to get something to eat?"

I just looked at him.

"Oh. Yeah. Sorry."

"No problem." He would learn; we would adjust.

"You want to come over, play some Akira?" he said.

We'd been into the game for months, although he liked it more than I did, especially since he spent most of his play on hunting ghosts in Akira's craggy moonscape, and zooming down the canyons and slithering through the worm-ridden tunnels always made me a little motion sick. Not that queasiness was much of a problem anymore, but boredom was. Generally after twenty minutes or so of busting virtual creepy crawlies while Walker flirted with slutty snake-women, their naked chests covered with shimmering scales and their users probably a thousand miles away, looking for a quick and easy love-link, I was ready for a nap. Or at least, I was ready to lie down. Usually, with the right combination of sulk and seduction, with Walker on top of me. And maybe that was the point.

"Sure."

And soon, side by side on his couch, goggled up and strapped in, we disappeared into the world of the game, his av and mine creeping down haunted hallways, hand in hand, touching without feeling, reality forgotten, or at least irrelevant, which was enough.

It was enough until it wasn't anymore, and then I slipped out of the game and back into the world. He stayed in, twitching, ducking his head, clutching the air, and grabbing for invisible demons, a careful space between us. I could have touched him then. He was too lost in the virtual universe to notice a hand on his leg, his lower back, his face. I'd done it before, more than once, making a game of it; how far could I go before calling him back to the surface, how deep had he sunk, how quickly could I reel him back in. But I didn't touch him, just waited for him to tire of the game, and when he did, I went home.

"No," the coach said when I finally found the courage to ask her. "I'm sorry, Lia. I wish I could, but . . . no."

"I know I'm out of shape, but I can get up to speed. I know I can."

"It's not that." She was slim and blond, and I wondered, as I often did, why she'd chosen coaching as her hobby instead of teaching or crafts. Something cozy and indoors, like most in her position, afraid of leathering their skin under the open sky. I got that she had to do *something*. It was a social imperative for the jobless rich, since the children of the wealthy weren't going to raise themselves (nor, obviously, be raised by the parents of the poor), but why opt for something that required so much actual work?

I suspected it was because, like me, she loved to run. Missed it, missed the uniforms and the competitions and the trophies and even the outdoors. I could imagine myself doing the same thing—except, of course, that I was destined for productivity. Let my spouse, whoever he turned out to be, ply his hobbies. I'd been informed from day one—still in diapers, spitting and drooling—that *I* would have a career. Eventually.

In the meantime I would run.

"Did you give my spot away?" I asked, glancing over at the track. Zo was powering through her second mile. We had the same genetic advantages, I reminded myself. The same muscle tone, coordination, stamina—she'd just never bothered to use hers before. And meanwhile I'd used mine up.

"It's not that, either."

"What, then?"

"It's . . ." She looked me up and down, then grimaced, like it was my fault for making her say it. "Lia, I can't let you run with the team, not like this. It wouldn't be fair."

"What's not fair?" I asked. "It's not like I can run any faster."

"I have no evidence of that," she said. "As far as the league is concerned, you'd be running with an unfair advantage."

That was almost funny. "Trust me, there's no advantage."

"It's just not *natural.*"

I couldn't believe it. More to the point, I couldn't *accept* it. I needed to run. "Jay Chesin runs with a prosthetic leg—*that's* not natural."

"That's different."

I closed my eyes for a moment. When I opened them, I caught her sagging a bit in relief, as if she'd spent the whole conversation waiting—in vain—for me to blink.

"What about the Ana League? I'd run with them if I had to." As far as I was concerned, it wasn't real running, not if you were chemically amping your strength and speed. I knew I'd never be able to keep up if I ran natural, but much as I loved my trophies, I didn't need to win. I needed to run.

The coach shook her head again. "They won't let you run either."

"But they're *anabolic*," I said. Paused, reminded myself not to whine. Be calm. Be rational. Be irrefutable. "It's a whole league for people who don't play fair. How can I be against the rules if there *are* no rules?"

"There are rules," she said, mouthing the official party line, even though everyone knew the Ana League was anything goes. "They wouldn't let you drive a car to the finish line . . . and they won't let *you* run. Not like this."

"But—"

"Lia, be realistic," she snapped. "You don't breathe. You don't get tired. For all anyone knows, you can run as fast as you want, as far as you want. Slotting you in would make a mockery of the whole race. Do you really want to ruin things for everyone else?"

I didn't care about everyone else. And until recently I'd never needed to pretend I did. When you're winning, no one expects you to care. They only expect you to keep winning.

"I guess not," I said.

"I really am sorry." Like we could be friends again, now that I'd let her pretend she was doing the right thing.

"Can I ask you something?"

"Yes." She looked like she wanted to say no.

"Is it actually written in the rules somewhere that . . ." I still didn't know what to call the thing I'd become. ". . . people in my situation aren't eligible?"

The coach hesitated. "This particular . . . *situation* hasn't come up before. Not in this league."

"So you're just assuming, then."

"What are you getting at?"

"If the league didn't care—if I got my father to talk to someone and made it okay—would you want me back on the team?" I could have done it. I knew it, and she knew it. It's not about the money, my father always said. These days everyone has money. It's about the power. And he had that, too.

But that wasn't the question. I wasn't asking if I could bully my way back onto the team. I was asking whether she wanted me to.

This time she didn't hesitate at all. "No."

Friday morning was Persuasive Speech, a weekly dose of posture, comportment, and projection techniques intended to smooth our eventual rise into the ranks of social and political prominence. The road to power may have been paved with lies, but according to Persuasive Speech guru M. Stafford, said lies had to be carefully candy coated with a paper-thin layer of truth. Or at least, the appearance of truth.

M. Stafford, of course, rarely told us anything we didn't already know.

Of all the useless classes the Helmsley School offered—and there was little else on the menu—none was more useless than Persuasive Speech. M. Stafford was big into tedious presentations on even more tedious current events, which didn't persuade us of anything except that we'd made an enormous mistake signing up for the class in the first place. A mistake, at least, for anyone who'd been expecting to learn something. For those of us expecting an easy A and plenty of time to lounge in the back of the room, linked in and zoned out while M. Stafford carefully ignored her snoozing audience, it fulfilled our every need.

So, all good. Except that while I'd been out "uh, sick"—that was M. Stafford's feeble euphemism—Becca Mai had transferred into the class, and M. Stafford had given my seat away. Which meant that Becca sat in back with Cass and Terra and Bliss while I was stuck at a broken desk in the front row, wobbling on the loose leg every time I shifted my weight and trying to pretend that Auden Heller wasn't aiming his creepy stare squarely in my direction.

I was—well, "sure" would be the wrong word, but let's say "willing to accept the possibility"—that Auden didn't *intend* to be creepy. He'd never been particularly creepy before. But then, he'd never been much of anything, except different, and not in the right way. Those glasses, for one thing. No one needed glasses anymore. At least, no one who could afford the fix, and no one without enough credit for that would have been allowed within fifty miles of the Helmsley School. There were net-linked glasses, of course, but those hadn't been popular since we were kids. Now anyone who wanted that kind of access (and that kind of headache) could just pop in a lens while everyone else went back to screens and keyboards. The only reason to wear glasses now—especially glasses without tech—was to look different. It was the same with his watch. They didn't even make watches anymore. FlexiViMs you could wrap around your wrist, or tattoo onto your forearm? Yes. But all the watch did was tell time, and—as I'd discovered one day a few years ago when one of Walker's idiot friends snagged the watch to see if it would make Auden cry—it didn't even do that right. A couple of miniature sticks swept out circle after circle, and you had to calculate the angles to even know the hour. And, yes, I was *smart* enough to figure it out, but why bother to do a math problem every time you want to know what time it is, when you can just get your ViM to flash the info and then move on with your life?

We'd been assigned to deliver a five-minute speech on a current issue that we felt strongly about. "We" didn't include "me." I'd been excused by virtue of my "uh, extended illness." I wondered how M. Stafford would, if pressed, describe my sickly condition. Did she consider death, in my case, to be a fatal disease?

Auden went first, stammering his way through some lunatic theory that the government could solve the energy crisis whenever it wanted, but preferred using the power shortage to control

129

the cities and the poor, oppressed masses who lived there. He didn't explain where he thought all this magical energy was going to come from, or why, if the masses were so sad and oppressed, they never did anything about it. Everyone knew you could work your way out of the city if you wanted, and not just to a corp-town—although even that was better since you were guaranteed power and med-tech—but to a real life. If they didn't want to bother, how was that our problem?

Auden's conspiracy theories never came with much evidence or follow-through. I suspected he just liked getting a rise out of people with his flashy, if stupid, claims: *The corps are secretly running the country! The Disneypocalypse was an inside job! The organic farmers poisoned the corn crop and pinned it on the terrorists to scare people away from mass production! B-mods are the opium of the masses!* Apparently, if they made good slogans, they didn't have to make good sense.

Next up, Sarit Rifkin, whose speech on the importance of eating more red meat didn't include the fact that her family owned the county's only cattle farm and reaped credit for every steak sold. Cass detailed the criteria she used to select new shoes. Fox T. spewed five minutes of crap about his favorite tactics for racking up Akira kills. Fox J.—also known as Red-tailed Fox, less because of his long auburn ponytail than because of the time he and Becca started making out in her father's kitchen and Fox planted his ass on the stove, apparently so engrossed in the hot and heavy that it took him a full minute to realize the stove was *on*—got in about half a minute of arguing that chest lift-tucks should be mandatory for everyone overage and under a C cup before M. Stafford cut him off.

That was when Bliss, with her Fox-approved D cups, took the podium. She stood there for a long moment without speaking.

M. Stafford had the kind of voice you might use to talk to a mental patient, slow and measured and just a little too understanding. "Go on, Bliss."

Bliss shifted her weight. "I'm not sure I should."

"Are you sure you want to pass the class?"

Bliss reddened. Then glared at me, like she was daring me to blame her for going forward. "I wrote this last week," she said defensively. "Before I knew that—" She stopped. "I wrote this last week."

"Then you should be tired of waiting to deliver it," M. Stafford said. "Go on, we won't bite."

Bliss Tanzen *did* bite, I happened to know—courtesy of Walker, who had been out with her a few times before trading up.

She cleared her throat. "A mechanical copy, no matter how detailed or exact, can never be anything more than an artificial replica of human life."

I sat very still, face blank.

"It is for this reason that I argue that recipients of the download procedure should not be afforded the same rights and privileges of human citizens of society."

I looked up, just for a second, long enough to note that everyone was staring at me, including M. Stafford. Everyone, with two exceptions: Bliss had her eyes fixed on her clunky speech. Auden had his eyes fixed on Bliss.

"You don't have to believe in something called a soul"—someone in back snickered at the word—"to believe that a person can't just be copied into a computer. They call it a copy because that's what it is—not the real thing. Just a computer that's been programmed to act that way."

M. Stafford wasn't going to stop her, I realized. Nor were Cass or Terra or anyone else. And *I* certainly wasn't going to say anything. *Four more minutes,* I told myself. Just tune her out and, when it's over, move on.

"Skinners can talk," Bliss said. Fox J.'s use of the term "tits" had been deemed too offensive for our sensitive ears, but apparently "skinner" was just fine. "But so can my refrigerator, if it thinks I need more iron in my diet. Skinners can move, but so can my car, if I tell it where to go. My refrigerator doesn't get to vote, and my car doesn't get to use my credit to buy itself a new paint job."

"She's not a car!" Auden said loudly.

I wanted to slink down in my seat—slink *under* my seat. But I stayed still.

"No interruptions," M. Stafford snapped. "We allowed you the privilege of speaking your mind; please respect your classmates enough to do the same."

"My mind isn't filled with ignorant trash," Auden said. "And what about respecting *Lia*?"

I wanted to strangle him.

"You can stay silent or you can go," M. Stafford said.

Auden went.

M. Stafford looked at me, her face unreadable. "Anyone else?"

I wasn't sure if it was an offer or a warning. Either way, I ignored it. And when Bliss continued, I ignored her too.

When class finally ended, I stayed in my seat long enough to let everyone else drift out of the room. Then I waited just a moment longer, preparing myself for the inevitable onslaught of pity that would hit once I stepped into the hallway, Cass and Terra and random clingers assuring me that I shouldn't listen, that Bliss was a moron, that she was just jealous, that they were here if I needed to talk—which I did not. Nor did I need anyone's pity, but I would accept it with grace, because I had been well trained. Rudeness was a sign of weakness. Grace stemmed from power, the power to accept anything and move on.

But the hallway was empty. Only one person waited for me, rocking back and forth from one foot to the other, his fist clenched around the ugly green bag he always carried.

"You okay?" Auden asked.

I walked right past him, down the hall, around the corner, all the way to the door that let out into the parking lot, where I could find the car and ride away. Let Zo figure out her own way home.

He followed. "She was wrong, you know."

I put my hand on the door, but didn't open it. I wasn't against ditching school, not in principle, at least, but I also wasn't about to let Bliss Tanzen drive me out.

"She shouldn't have said those things," he went on.

"It was an assignment," I said, my back to him, undecided. Outside meant blissful escape; inside meant more pretending, smiling dumbly as if I didn't hear the whispers that followed me everywhere. Inside meant going to lunch, facing Bliss and everyone who'd heard her. Everyone who'd sat quietly and listened. But outside meant running away, and I couldn't do that.

I wasn't the type.

"She was wrong," Auden said in a pained voice. "About the download, about you not being—"

I finally faced him. "First of all, she wasn't talking about *me*," I snapped. "*You* were the one who brought me into it, and second of all, thanks very much for that. You think I don't know she was wrong? You think I need someone like *you* telling me who I am? And now, like I didn't have enough problems, the whole school probably thinks we're—" *Rude enough,* I told myself, and stopped.

"We're what?"

"Nothing."

"Friends?" He spat out a bitter laugh, his face twisting beneath his stupid black glasses. "Don't worry. No one would think that." His black hair was short, almost buzzed, and his nose was crooked. Someone had done a really bad job selecting for him, I thought. It was one thing to sacrifice looks for athletic ability or freakish intelligence or artistic aptitude—everyone was, of course, only allowed to be so special and no more—but I happened to know he didn't have any of those things, or at least, not enough of them to justify his face. If I'd just seen him on the street somewhere, I'm not saying I would have assumed he was poor, but I wouldn't have assumed he was one of us.

And maybe that was his real problem: Credit or not, he wasn't.

"I'm not worried," I said. "And even if I was, it wouldn't be any of your business."

"I was just trying to help."

"If I were you, I'd focus on helping yourself. You need it more than I do."

"Meaning what?"

"Just look at you." The clothes: wrong. The face: wrong. The attitude: wrong. The tattered green bag that looked like something my grandmother would carry around: weird *and* wrong. "It's like you're not even trying."

"Trying to what?"

"Trying to be normal!" I lost it. "Look what you've got—and you're wasting it!"

A scowl flashed across his face, then disappeared just as quickly. "What I've got?" He raised his eyebrows. "You mean like a flesh-and-blood body? A 'normal' brain?"

"That is *not* what I said."

"Maybe I don't want to be normal," he said calmly. "Maybe it's okay that you're not."

"Who said I'm not?"

He just looked at me, like it was obvious, like I was stupid for even asking such a question when I was standing there forming a response with a brain that ran off the same wireless power grid as the school trash compactor.

"Why am I even talking to you?" I said, disgusted.

"You tell me."

"It was a rhetorical question." I brushed past him. He didn't flinch as our arms grazed against each other. "Just don't bother 'helping' again."

"Don't worry."

I didn't ditch school. I went back to class, kept my head down, paid attention. I went to lunch, ready to face Bliss, whether it meant an apology or a fight. But she wasn't there. Nor was Cass or Terra or their new boy toys or Zo or Walker. Becca, who would probably have spent the whole meal babbling about some species of frog she was intent on rescuing from extinction, wasn't there either. I found out later that they'd all cut out, grabbed lunch at Cass's place, and gotten an early start on the weekend partying. "I know we told you," Cass said later when I finally tracked her down. "You must have forgot."

Auden ate at an empty table tucked into a corner, half hidden behind a thick wooden pillar. I could feel him watching me.

I didn't eat, of course. But I took a tray of food and sat in the usual spot, alone.

It was the best meal I'd had all week.

DATE NIGHT

"Everything's okay."

Y ou're going like *that*?" Zo asked, leaning in my doorway. The cat hissed at her from the foot of the bed. Psycho Susskind had, without my permission, made it his new home.

"What?" I braved the mirror again. Black retro shirt, baggy pants that looked like some kind of insect had gnawed off the cuffs, and—courtesy of an illicit raid through Zo's supplies—plum-colored lipstick and some kind of violet grease smeared across my eyelids. I looked like Zo. I also looked, as far as I could tell, like crap, but these days, so did everyone else who mattered. So at least I would fit in.

Zo rolled her eyes. "Nothing."

I shoved past her. "See you tomorrow."

"See you *tonight*."

I paused at the top of the stairs. "You're going?"

"Terra's picking me up in five," Zo said. "Is that a problem?"

Like she cared. "No problem."

She looked like she wanted to say something else. But she waited too long, and I was out the door.

Walker's car was in the driveway.

"You're early," I said, slipping in beside him. "You've just been sitting out here?"

He nodded. "It's okay."

"If I'd known you were out here . . ."

"It's okay," he said again, and put an arm around me. His pupils were wide; he'd obviously gotten an early start on the night, tripping on something or a lot of somethings. But it didn't matter. Not if he was going to put his arm around me again.

"You ready?" He leaned forward, keyed in Cass's address, then paused, waiting for permission, like the old days.

I wondered what would happen if I told him that we should skip the party, that when he'd said he wanted to go out, I'd thought he meant the two of us, alone.

Before, I was the one who dragged us to parties. *Again?* he would whine, like a little kid, and it would be cute, but not cute enough to change my mind, so we would spend another night surrounded until the waiting got too intense, and then he would squeeze my hand or I would squeeze his ass and—signal sent, message received—we would sneak off together to one of the extra bedrooms or a closet or that spot between the trees or once, after everyone else had passed out, the glassed-in pool, our bodies glowing in the eerie blue of the underwater lights. It was tradition, and keeping it tonight had to mean that he wanted to go backward. I wasn't about to risk a change.

I thought he might kiss me as we sped along in the dark; that was tradition too. But he stayed on his side of the car and I stayed on mine, and his arm rested on my shoulders, a dead-weight that might as well have belonged to some invisible third passenger.

"Want to play Akira?" he asked.

"Not really."

"Mind if I do?"

"No."

Sometimes it felt like the body took over. That the body wasn't the stranger, I was—just a passenger, carried along wherever the body wanted to go. Because that wasn't me, letting Walker disappear into the network when I just wanted him to be with me—or, more to the point, wanted him to *want* to be with me. The strange voice that poured out of the strange mouth told him he could do whatever he wanted, I would go wherever he went, I didn't care, I was fine, everything was fine, it was all good. That wasn't Lia Kahn.

The car stopped in the usual place, at the bottom of the curving driveway that sloped up to Cass's guesthouse. Walker grabbed my hand before I could get out. He leaned close, and when he spoke, his stubble scratched against my ear; it didn't hurt. "Upstairs?" he said. "Later?"

"Definitely." I turned to face him, my cheek scraping against his, but he pulled away just before our lips made contact. Even in the dark, his eyes were closed. "Later."

Inside, things were the same as always: bodies sprawled on the couches and across the greenish-gray carpet, writhing in the throes of whatever new b-mod mix Cass had cooked up; walls pulsing in time with the music; couples tangled up in each other; lonelyhearts on the prowl; screens encircling the room, set to flash up Cass's favorite vidlifes and a rotating selection of random zones; the lost dancers, gyrating to music that played only and forever in their heads; and in the glassed-in pool, girls with swanlike bodies skimming through the water, giggling, sputtering, chasing boys, chasing one another, the shifting patterns of their solar bikinis fading as the light disappeared.

The bikinis weren't the only tech. Sonicsilk, LBDs and LCD tees, net-skirts, girls in microminis smartchipped to grow—or shrink—when they bent over, gamers in screenshirts that broadcast their kills . . . Almost everyone was in something lit up or linked in, everyone, that is, except for me. And Zo, of course, who didn't count.

Bliss met us at the door, wearing a dress I'd seen before—a transparent fabric made opaque by the careful patterning of glowing light, but always, in its shifting translucence, offering the promise that if you watched closely enough, a glimpse of milky skin would slip through. She raised an eyebrow at my dead black shirt. Then leaned forward, voice lowered and fakely kind. "You should know, that retro look is totally wiped."

"Yeah," I said. "I got that." I turned to blast Walker for letting me walk in blind, not that he could be trusted on the subject, being barely able to dress himself, much less me, but I was decked out in freakwear and needed someone to blame. Too bad: He'd already slipped away, probably off to join the gamers or get zoned.

Terra drifted over, her face—like everyone else's—cosmetic clear, her shirt whispering melodies with every move. She stopped dead when she saw what I was wearing.

"Nice, uh . . . outfit," she said.

"You could have told me." It's not like we made some big announcement about which looks were in and which were out. But things got old fast, and when they did, either you knew—or you didn't.

Terra shrugged. "Since when do you need *me* to tell you what's wiped?"

Zo found me later, sitting in a corner, head tipped back toward the ceiling as if I were zoned. Anyone who knew anything knew that I wasn't in the business of getting zoned anymore, but it saved me from having to stare blankly at a wall or, worse, to make conversation.

Finally someone I could blame. "I can't believe you let me leave the house looking like this."

"What?" she asked innocently, perching on the side of the couch. "Like me?"

"You knew better."

"You're right," she said. "So why didn't you? Lia Kahn

always knows what's cool, right? Lia Kahn decides what's cool. So what's *your* problem?"

I wanted to slap her.

"What's yours?" I asked instead. "If you knew retro was over, why come here like *this*?" I jerked my head toward her clothes, which were only slightly less gross than my own. But she was acting as if she didn't care that the look was wiped, and no one else seemed to care either. Like the rules were somehow different for her.

"Because maybe Zoie Kahn decides what's cool too," she said.

"You can decide whatever you want. It doesn't count if no one agrees. There's no such thing as a majority of one."

"Yeah, one's the loneliest number, so I heard," she said. "Two is working out a lot better for me these days."

"Two?" I scanned the room, as if Zo's new guy, if he really existed, would bear the mark on his face. "Who?"

She mouthed a curse, as if she'd broken something. "No one."

This was getting interesting. *"Who?"* Zo and I had never been the kind of sisters who stayed up all night, giggling in the dark about pounding hearts and stolen kisses. But she'd ruined enough of my dates with her tattling, her teasing, and, as she got older, her eavesdropping and clumsy stabs at blackmail. She was, and always had been, addicted to information about my personal life; the more personal, the better.

Karma's a bitch.

"I told you, *no one*."

"I'll find out eventually," I said. "You might as well tell me."

"Instead of wasting your time on my love life, maybe you should focus on your own," Zo snapped.

"Meaning?"

Zo tapped her wrist and I noticed that, like Auden, she was wearing a watch. Maybe *he* was her mystery man. Lame and lamer—they'd make a good match. "It's one a.m.: Do you know where your boyfriend is?"

"He's around." But nowhere I could see. I wondered if he'd gone upstairs without me, if he was waiting for me to find him. Or if he wasn't alone.

"He always is." Zo scowled and stood up.

"Seriously, why do you hate him so much?"

"I don't."

"You're usually a better liar that that."

"Believe whatever you want," she said.

I wanted to ask her something else. I wanted to ask her why she suddenly hated *me*.

I didn't want the answer.

"Later," she said, giving me a bitter half wave. "Terra's got some new boots she wants to show me. Weird, isn't it?" Zo smirked. "The way all your friends suddenly want *my* opinion?"

"They're just bored and looking for something different to play with," I shot back. "You're like their little retro *mascot*. Their token freak."

Zo shrugged. "Why would they need me for that? They've got you."

Venom released, she wandered off; I stayed where I was. I knew I should be circulating, but all I wanted to do was hide. Staying in place seemed like an acceptable compromise. And when I felt a pair of hands squeeze my shoulders, and a chin rest on the top of my head, I knew I'd made the right choice. I lifted my arms, let him grab my hands and pull me to my feet. "About time." I turned around. "What took you so—"

I yanked my hands away.

Cass's mouth breather leered. "Feels just like real hands," he slurred. "Dipper thought they'd be, like, stiff or some shit like that, but . . ." He slithered his fingers across my waist. I knocked them away. "Feels real enough to me."

Cass had always liked them dumb and pretty.

"You wanna know what's stiff?" He lunged toward me, resting his forearms on my shoulders, linking his fingers together behind my neck when I tried to squirm away.

"Fuck off."

He laughed. "I'd rather fuck something else," he said. "And I do mean *thing*. Come on." He plucked at my neckline. "I hear you've got all your parts under there, just like a real girl."

"I am a real girl, asshole."

"You want to prove it?"

I tried to knock his arms away, but they were too thick and sturdy, and the more I strained against them, the tighter his grip.

"Just because Walker's too chickenshit to take a test drive—"

This wasn't a dark and empty path winding through the woods, and he wasn't some Faither lunatic convinced that God had told him to screw my brains out—I had no reason to be afraid. But I wasn't thinking through reasons. I was thinking about this loser's grimy hands crawling all over the body—*my* body—and his breath misting across my face and his puny dick twitching at some fantasy of dragging me off and shoving himself inside me. All of which added up to not thinking at all. I punched him in the stomach.

"*Bitch!*" he wheezed, doubled over.

That's when Cass finally decided to show up. "What the hell, Lia?"

"She's psycho," the drooling pervert hissed, looping an arm around Cass. "Total nut job. Got pissed I wouldn't do her."

If the mouth had come equipped with saliva, I would have spit at him. "You sleazy piece of crap! Cass, come on." She was clinging to him, her arm tucked around his waist. "The perv was hitting on me."

The loser snorted. "Right. Liked I'd want *it* when I have *you*." He nuzzled his face into Cass's neck. She let him.

Terra popped up beside them, her boy in tow. The two guys smacked hands while Terra glared at me. "Trouble?"

"Trouble for Cass," I said. "She's dating an asshole."

"You were right about her," Terra's guy whispered loudly.

I turned on her. "What's that supposed to mean?"

"It means wake up, Lia," Terra snapped. "This isn't like before. You don't get to have every boy in the world drooling after you. Not anymore."

Cass rolled her eyes. "And contrary to popular belief—excuse me, *your* belief—they weren't all after you then, either."

"I never thought that—"

"Right." Cass choked out a laugh. "And you weren't hitting on my boyfriend just now."

"Why would I want this assface when I've got—"

"Walker?" Terra said with me. "You just keep telling yourself that."

"Walker and I are fine."

"Then take him with you when you go," Cass snarled. She tugged the mouth breather away, without looking back.

Terra shook her head. "She stood up for you. When you came back, and you were all—you know. She defended you. She said you were still the same person under there. That we should give you a chance, even if . . ."

"Even if *what*?"

She looked at me like it was pitiful, the way I couldn't figure it out for myself. "Even if it's *embarrassing*," she said, over-enunciating. Slow words for my slow brain. "Being seen with you. Like *this*. And then you try to steal Jax?"

I hadn't even known that was his name. "I told you, *he* came on to *me*."

Terra shook her head. "I actually feel sorry for you. I mean, Lia was always self-absorbed, but whoever you are—whatever you are—could you be any more oblivious?"

"You know who I am," I pleaded. "Come on, Terra, you *know* me."

"Yeah, but there's an easy way to fix that." She walked away with mouth breather number two, leaving me alone again.

Walker found me by the pool.

"So it's okay? To get wet?" he asked, sitting down beside me.

I shrugged. I'd taken off my shoes and plunged my bare feet into the water. It was cold, or at least, I thought it was. Temperatures were still a challenge. "Everything's okay."

He dipped his feet into the water, then shivered. Cold—I'd guessed right.

"I heard what happened."

I shrugged again. That was an easy one for me, one of the first things I'd mastered. Maybe because it was so close to an involuntary twitch.

"You should have texted me," he said. "I was looking for you."

I'd been sitting out by the pool for almost an hour. He couldn't have looked very hard. "It's fine."

"So, were you, uh . . . you and that guy, you weren't—"

"You're seriously going to ask me that? You think I was lying too?"

"I don't know." He looked down, tapping his foot against the surface of the water, gently enough that it didn't splash. "I guess not."

Our shoulders were touching.

"You know what?" I said. "Just go."

He shook his head. Rested his hand on my lower back. Leaned in. "What if I don't want to?"

It felt like my first kiss.

In a way, I guess, it was. And just like back then, I wasted it, worrying about where to put my hands and what to do with my tongue and whether I should be moving my lips more or less—and then it was over. At least he didn't look too repulsed. His eyes were rimmed with red. But they were open.

Most people had vacated the pool area once I showed up. The ones who'd stayed behind were staring at us. We got out.

The grounds of Cass's estate were huge—and, once you got away from the guesthouse, mostly empty. We had a favorite spot, a clustering of trees at the top of a sloping hill—the same hill that, when we were kids, Cass and I had rolled down, shrieking as we bumped and slid, the grass and sky spinning around us. Walker and I stayed at the top. He was shivering.

"Nervous?" I asked. We sat facing each other, his legs crossed, mine tucked beneath me so that I could rise up on my knees and reach for him.

He shook his head. "No reason to be."

He didn't ask if I was nervous.

Walker took a deep, shuddering breath, and then his mouth was on mine again, his hands at my waist, slipping beneath the black T-shirt. I stiffened. His hands on the skin— How would it feel? What would he think of the body when he saw it?

"You okay?" he whispered. His eyes were closed again, his face pinched, like he was expecting a blow.

"Okay."

"So, you can, like, do stuff?" he asked.

"I can do anything." I tried to force myself to relax.

Asking call-me-Ben about it, back in rehab, hadn't been the worst moment of that hell, not even close. But it had been humiliating enough.

"Can I get wet?" I'd opened with something easy. "Or will I melt or short-circuit or something?"

And call-me-Ben had had the nerve to laugh. "You're fully waterproof."

"What about sleeping?" Another lob. Working my way up to the real question. I barely heard his answer.

"The body will simulate the sensation of fatigue, as a signal to you that it's time to shut down for a few hours, give the system a rest. Tests show that it's probably a good idea to follow your normal schedule by 'sleeping' every night."

"Can I eat?" That was a no.

Just like there'd be no more bathroom breaks, no more tampons. At this point, call-me-Ben suggested I might be more comfortable talking to a woman, but by woman, I knew he meant *Sascha*, and I wasn't about to give her the satisfaction.

"What happens if I break?" I asked.

"You'll come to us," said call-me-Ben. "Just like you'd go to the doctor. And we'll fix you up. But if you take care of yourself, it's unlikely to happen. Although we attempted to emulate the organic form as much as possible, you'll find this body much more durable than the old one."

"Why?"

He looked surprised. "Well, for all the obvious reasons. It

seemed economically efficient, not to mention—"

"No. I mean, why that, but no other differences? Why no superpowers or anything?"

Ben frowned. "This isn't a game. We're not trying to create a new race of supermen, no matter what the vids want to claim. This is a medical procedure. We want to supply you with a *normal* life, as much like your old life as it can possibly be."

"So . . . I should be able to do anything I used to do," I said.

"Within reason," Ben said. "Anything."

"What about . . . Well, I have this boyfriend, so . . . Could he and I . . . ?"

Call-me-Ben looked like he wanted to summon Sascha, no matter what I said. "As you've been told, your internal structure is—obviously—quite different. But the external structure mirrors the organic model completely."

I must have looked blanker than usual.

"You and your boyfriend will be fine," he clarified. "All systems go."

I didn't think to ask him how it would feel.

Now I knew: It felt wrong.

We didn't fit together: not like we used to. Our faces bumped, my elbow jabbed his chin, his legs got twisted up in mine, and not in a good way. Every kiss got broken by a murmured "sorry" or "ouch" or "not there" or "no, nothing, keep going" or, always, "it's okay," and we did keep going, his hands running up and down the body, my fingers searching his, trying to find the dips and rises they remembered, but everything felt different against the fingertips, distant and imagined, like I was lying in the grass alone, pretending to feel the weight of Walker's body on top of mine.

Things didn't get very far.

"Sorry," he said yet again, rolling off me. I pulled my shirt back on. It was one thing for him to touch the body, but I didn't want him to have to look at it while we were lying there. *I* didn't want to look at it. If I didn't have to see it, I could pretend. That was easier in the dark. "I can do this, I just need a minute."

"It's okay," I said. Like a parrot who only knew one phrase.

"I know it's okay," he snapped. "I just need . . ." He snatched a pill out of his pocket, popped it into his mouth. "It'll be fine."

"What was that?"

"Nothing. Just a chiller. Help me relax."

"*Another* one?" I knew he'd been popping them all night, and probably most of the afternoon.

"Don't worry about it." He rolled over on his side. "Okay. Ready?"

I pressed my hand against his chest, holding him in place. "You say that like you're gearing up for battle."

"What are you talking about?"

"It would just be nice if you didn't need to be totally zoned out before you could touch me."

"I don't *need* anything."

"Every time you come near me, you look like you're being punished."

"And what about you?" he asked. "I touch you, and you freeze up. It's like hooking up with— Forget it."

"What?"

"*Nothing.*"

"Just say it," I insisted, and, maybe out of habit, he followed orders.

"With a corpse."

I sat up. "What a coincidence. Me being dead and all."

He sat up too, and hunched over his knees, cracking his knuckles. "You have to admit . . . it's kind of weird."

"Oh, really? I hadn't noticed. Life has been oh-so-normal for me these last couple months. Not that you would know."

"What's that supposed to mean?"

"It means my life is shit," I spat out. "And where are you?"

"I'm here, aren't I?" Walker drove a fist into the grass. "What do you want from me?"

"I want you to be like you used to be."

"And I want you to be like *you* used to be," he shouted, "so I guess it's tough shit for both of us!"

Silence.

"You hate this," I said quietly. "Me. Like this."

"Lia, I didn't—"

"No." I sat very straight and very still. "Just admit it. The truth will set you free and all that."

He sighed. "Fine. I hate it. Not *you*. This. This whole thing. It's weird, it's gross, it freaks me out, but I'm doing my fucking best. I'm here, aren't I?"

"Because you feel sorry for me," I said.

"No."

Yes.

"Because you think you owe me something," I said.

"Don't I?"

Yes.

"Whatever it is, this isn't it." I stood up.

"Don't do this," he said.

"I don't need this," I said. "I don't need your *trying*. I don't need you *forcing* yourself to be with me, like I'm your personal charity case."

"I'm not telling you to go."

Which wasn't quite the same as telling me to stay.

"This is *you*, Lia. Giving up. If you walk away, just remember, that's on you."

"And if I don't walk away, I get stuck with someone who has to dope up before he can even look at me. I think I can do better than that."

"Yeah? Who?"

And that was the question, wasn't it?

Cass's mouth breather didn't count. He wanted to screw a mech-head, some kind of fetish fantasy, nothing real. It wouldn't count even if he weren't scum, which he was.

No one *normal*—and especially no one beyond normal, no one like Walker—would choose me, not the way I was now. But Walker was stuck with me, and I knew he would stay, mostly out of obligation, with a little nostalgia thrown in for flavor, because I knew Walker. I could keep him. I could sit down beside him and let him kiss me, ignoring the fact that it made him cringe. Ignoring the fact that when he touched me, it felt like nothing. Not because I couldn't feel his body on mine, but because the feeling was meaningless. It was like trying to tickle your own feet. Graze your fingers across your skin in the same places, with the same pressure, at the same speed, the mechanics all the same, but somehow the effect is entirely different, the sensation lifeless. Not that I was ticklish at all, not anymore.

The old Lia Kahn wouldn't have hesitated. The old Lia Kahn knew she deserved better. But of course, the old Lia Kahn was hot. Her boyfriend couldn't keep his hands off her.

There was also the fact that I was probably in love with him.

"What am I supposed to do?" he said, still on the ground.

Not *The turtle is hungry.* Not *I'm sorry.* Not *I love you.*

Maybe I wouldn't have believed him anyway.

Maybe I would.

"I'm still Lia," I said finally.

"So? What's that mean? Staying or going?"

"It means you should already know."

LIFE SUPPORT

"I don't have issues. I have a life.*"*

That was pretty much all it took to RIP my social life. Not that I did much resting in peace. More like resting in isolation and humiliation and doubt and regret. Just because you can't take something back, doesn't mean you don't want to.

Just because you want to, doesn't mean you try.

By the time I got home and linked in that night, I'd lost priv-access to Cass's and Terra's zones; I'd been blocked from Walker's altogether. Everyone else followed their lead. I was untouchable, on and off the network. People still stared; they still whispered as I passed in the hall, with one big difference: They no longer bothered to shut up when I got close. Instead they got louder, so I could hear the words interspersed with the giggles. Freak. Robo-nympho. Skinner slut. Cass spread the word that I was a mechanical sex junkie, and her mouth breather threw in some spicy details about my tendency to go psycho when my lust was denied.

Walker didn't say anything, I was sure of it. But it was obvious we were over. And rumors spread: I'd attacked him, torn his clothes off, tried to force him. I'd cheated on him with a toaster. I'd malfunctioned *in medias res*, blowing sparks in a *deus ex machina coitus interruptus* that saved him from a nasty mistake. I didn't deny any of it.

Neither did he.

Here's the part where I say that my friends were shallow bitches and I'm better off without them. That Walker wasn't good enough for me—that if he'd really loved me, he wouldn't have let me leave, not without giving at least a modicum of chase. That I learned a valuable lesson about true-blue friendship, or maybe that surviving on my own was more fulfilling than depending on people who, deep down, didn't really care.

Wouldn't it be nice to think so.

They were, in fact, shallow bitches. News flash: So was I. It didn't make me miss them any less. As for Walker . . . Life with a boyfriend? Far superior to life without. I probably shouldn't admit that, but what am I supposed to do? Lie? So my friends hated me. So my boyfriend hated touching me. So my life was one big game of let's pretend. Was that any worse than being alone?

Maybe it was, and maybe that's why I walked away. But I'm allowed to regret it.

• • •

"I don't get why I have to go in person," I complained. "Can't I just link in? What's the difference?"

My mother shook her head. "This is about growing comfortable with your new physicality, dealing with issues of disembodiment and bodily alienation. You can't do that virtually."

"Physicality? Bodily alienation?" That did *not* sound like my mother.

"That's what the counselor said." My mother twisted the edge of her shirt, which she did when she was nervous, at least until my father noticed and forced her to stop. "She thinks this is crucial to a successful readjustment."

"Readjustment?" That was Sascha's term too, and I hated it. As if I'd emerged from a factory needing just a few minor alterations before I could rejoin my life. As if anything about this was *minor*. "I take it you're still quoting?"

My mother reddened.

My father, who'd been monitoring some board meeting as if we weren't even there, looked up from his screen. "You're going."

I went.

The group met in one of those buildings where they used to store paper books until no one wanted them anymore. You could tell because the shelves were still there, sitting empty, waiting for the world to change its mind and start printing with ink again— like that was going to happen. There were a lot of places like this, empty buildings that survived long after their purpose had died.

Why go out for art, for drama, for literature, for fashion, when you could stay on the couch, safe from germs, weather, overexertion, crowds, annoying small talk, and get it all up close, personal, and on demand? I knew the corps had snatched up most of the useless land, keeping it around just in case. But I didn't know that *I* would be the just in case, me and all the mech-heads in a hundred-mile radius, forced to drag our not-quite-dead bodies to a not-quite-dead library and spill our souls. If we had any. Which, depending on who you asked, was seriously in question.

I was late. The other six were already there, their chairs aligned in a circle with an empty one waiting for me, right next to Quinn. Not my favorite person, but at least she didn't completely suck, which was more than I could say for the familiar face on the other side of the circle. Sascha offered up her best patronizing smile as I slipped into the seat. "Now that everyone's here, why don't we go around and introduce ourselves, so that our new members will feel more at home?"

Quinn slid a hand across her mouth, camouflaging her whisper: "If this is home, does that make her our new mommy?"

I smirked. "Kill me now."

"Lia, why don't you begin?" Sascha said loudly. It clearly wasn't a suggestion.

"Lia Kahn," I mumbled.

"Could you maybe tell us something more about your history?"

I shrugged. "I was born seventeen and a half years ago, on a dark and stormy—"

"I mean your recent history," Sascha said, all sweetness and light. "Is there anything you want to share about the circumstances that led you to be here today?"

"Circumstances." That was almost as good as "readjustment." Such a nice, neat word to sum up the smell of flesh crackling in a fire, the hours and days in the dark, the slices of frozen brain matter scanned in, tossed aside. Just a collection of unfortunate circumstances, nothing more. "You told my parents this was mandatory," I said. "And they bought it."

Sascha cleared her throat. "Okay . . . Quinn? Is there anything about yourself you'd like to share with the group?"

"Selected members of the group, maybe," Quinn said, glancing at the girl to her right, whose pale skin looked nearly white against the long strands of indigo hair. "I have plenty to offer."

Sascha moved on. Quickly.

The blue-haired girl was Ani, and had been a mech-head for almost a year. Judging from the effort she was putting into avoiding Quinn's gaze, she wasn't much into sharing. Aron and Sloane, who obviously knew each other—and, less obviously but still noticeably, played footsie beneath their folding chairs—were better behaved. Aron had traded in his disease-riddled, six-weeks-to-live body a few months ago; Sloane had tried to kill herself, but only half-succeeded, waking up immortal instead, courtesy of an ill-planned leap from a tall building that wasn't quite tall enough. They'd met in rehab.

And then there was Len. Perfectly proportioned and handsome, in that plastic, artificial way that we all were, but his looks didn't match the way he slumped in his seat, his limbs tucked into his body, his head dipping compulsively, flipping his hair back over his eyes every time it threatened to expose him. He slumped like an ugly boy nobody liked.

"Nobody likes me," he concluded at the tail end of a ten-minute pity fest.

"Can't imagine why," Quinn murmured. I turned my snort of laughter into a fake cough, which was an embarrassingly feeble attempt at subterfuge when you consider the fact that I didn't have any lungs.

"I hate this," Len said. "I just wish I could go back."

"But you've told us how much you hated your life before," Sascha said. "How you felt confined by the wheelchair, how you always felt that people didn't see you for who you are, all they saw was your body—"

"And *this* is supposed to be better?" Len exploded. "At least I *had* a body. At least when people stared at me, they were staring at *me*, not at"—he punched his fist into his thigh—"this."

"Everyone's a critic," Quinn murmured.

"At least it was your call," said the wannabe suicide. "You got to make a choice."

"You feel you weren't given a choice?" Sascha asked. I wondered how much she got paid for serving as a human echo chamber.

"I made a fucking choice," Sloane said. "This wasn't it."

Aron took her hand. "Please don't."

She pulled away. "What am I supposed to say? Thanks,

Mom and Dad?" She scowled. "You know what happens if I try it again? They'll just dump me into a new body. I'm all backed up now, safe in storage. Even if I don't upload every night— They'd probably like that better, because then they get a clean slate. I wouldn't even remember trying to off myself again. Fuck, for all I know, it already happened, and everyone's just lying to me. They'd do it, too. They want me, they got me."

"You sound angry," Sascha said, always so insightful. "You blame your parents for not wanting to let their daughter die?"

Sloane rolled her eyes. "Wake up, Sascha. They *let* their daughter die. I'm just some replacement copy. And if I do it again, they'll make another copy. You think that'll be me? You think I'm her?"

"You *are* her," Sascha said.

"I know I'm still me," Aron said. "The same me I always was. I can feel it. But sometimes . . ."

Sascha leaned forward, eager. Hungry. "Go on."

"This is better than before. I get that," he said. "But . . . it's not just the way people look at me. It's like, I'm different now. My friends . . ." He shook his head.

Sloane shoved his shoulder. "I told you, they can't handle it? Whatever. Forget them."

"Yeah." Aron took her hand again, and this time she let him. I reminded myself I wasn't jealous. Two rejects seeking solace in each other. Nice for them, but it's not like I was looking to cuddle up with some freakshow of my own. "Sometimes I just think they're right. It's not the same."

"What's not the same?" Sascha asked.

"I don't know. Everything. Me. I'm not."

"Damn right," Quinn said, loud enough for everyone to hear her this time. "You're better, haven't you noticed? Or would you rather be lying around in a hospital somewhere, choking on your own puke and waiting to die?"

"I didn't say—"

"You said plenty," Quinn said. "You all did. Whining about wanting to go backward, like backward was some amazing place to be. Like you wouldn't be sick and your girlfriend here wouldn't be crazy and you"—she whirled on Len—"wouldn't be lame. In every sense of the word." Quinn stood up. "This is supposed to *help*?" she asked Sascha. "Listening to them whine about their *issues*?"

"What's supposed to help is sharing *your* issues," Sascha said. "And, yes, empathizing with everyone else's."

Quinn shook her head. "I don't have issues. I have a *life*. Something I'd advise the rest of you to acquire."

She walked out.

Quinn, I was starting to realize, had a thing for dramatic exits.

"Lia, you've been pretty quiet over there," Sascha said. "Do you want to add anything here?"

Everyone turned to look at me. I fought the urge to slouch down in my seat and turn away. I wasn't Len. I wasn't any of them.

"What do you want me to say?" I finally asked.

"Whatever you'd like," Sascha said. "You could weigh in on whether you wish you could go backward, as Quinn put it, or whether you'd rather look ahead."

I just stared at her.

"Or you could talk about how it's been being back at school. Any problems you might be having with your friends or . . . . your boyfriend?" There was something about the way she said it that made me wonder what she knew.

"I don't have a boyfriend."

"When you were in rehab, you talked about—"

"I don't have a boyfriend," I said louder. "And I don't have any *issues* to discuss either."

"So you would say you've had no trouble adjusting to your new situation?" Sascha said. "You're happy? Nothing that's been said today rings true for you at all?"

I looked around the circle and suddenly saw how it would all play out. I would open up, confess all my fears about the future, I would empathize with Aron about feeling different, with Sloane about losing my ability to choose, even, maybe most of all, with lonely Len. With Sascha's help we would let down our guard, become friends, a ragtag group of survivors with nothing in common but our circuitry and our fear. We would go out in public, clumping together for strength in numbers, pretending not to notice the stares or the way crowds parted so as not to touch us—or maybe pressed closer, reaching out to oh-so-casually brush past so as to tell their friends they got a handful of real, live (so to speak) skinner. We would whine, we would confide, we would wish we could still cry, we would bond, we would hook up, make promises, break them, we would cheat and we would forgive, we would stick together, because we would know that we were all any of us had. And eventually we would tell ourselves we were happy. Well-*adjusted*.

"Something was true," I admitted, standing up. "You all need to get a life."

I prepared a story for my parents, something bright and shiny about how caring everyone had been, how wonderfully supportive—maybe so supportive that I'd been entirely readjusted and wouldn't need to go back. But it was a story I never got the chance to tell. Because when I got home, there was a strange man sitting on the couch, across from my father. A man I'd seen before.

My father beckoned, indicating that I should join them.

"This is the Honored Rai Savona," he said. "Leader of the Faith Party. He's come out here to apologize for the incident earlier when you first came home. The man who accosted you on our property?"

I hadn't told my father about the man in the woods—and I could tell from his look that he wasn't happy about it. But I knew he would never have admitted his ignorance to a stranger, and if I let it slip, things would be even worse. So I sat down and kept my mouth shut. The man kept his dark eyes on my father. I recognized him from the protest: He'd been the one in charge, the one who finally called it off.

"As I say, M. Kahn, his actions were in no way endorsed by

the party, and he has been disciplined. A well-intentioned but sorely misguided soul. I take full responsibility for his trespassing and any damage he may have inflicted on"—he glanced at me—"your property."

"Are you talking about me?" I asked.

"Lia," my father snapped. "Manners."

"Because I'm fine, thanks for asking."

My father glared. "I appreciate your coming," he told the man. "And I trust you'll be keeping your followers off the grounds from now on? And away from my daughter?"

"There will be no more trespassing incidents," the man said. His voice was slow and rich, like honey poured out of a jar, the words pooling into a puddle of sickening sweetness. Except not so sweet. "And we'll maintain a respectful distance from . . . the recipient of the download process."

"By which you mean me," I said. "His daughter."

He took the challenge, finally turning to face me. "I'm sorry," he said, and, to his credit—or maybe to his acting teacher's credit—he sounded it. More than sorry. Heartbroken. "I bear you no ill will."

"No, you just don't think I'm a real person."

"I think looks can be deceiving," he said. "My reflection in the mirror may *look* exactly like me. Talk like me. Move like me. But that doesn't make it anything more than a copy. Nothing beneath the surface."

"Your reflection can't think for itself. It can't do anything you don't do."

"Just like you can't do anything your programmers didn't program you to do."

"No!" He was wrong. He had to be wrong. "I'm not a copy. I'm not a computer. I'm a *person*."

"A person is created by God," he said. "Gifted with a natural body, a divine soul. A person thinks and feels, is born and dies. A *person* has free will. You, on the other hand, are a machine. Built by man. *Programmed* by man. You may look like a person and act like a person; you may even, in your own way, believe you're a person. But, no, I don't think you are."

"I have free will." I was, for instance, willing myself not to walk across the room and punch him in the face.

"You have a computer inside your head, a computer designed to operate within a set of man-made parameters. To react a certain way to one set of stimuli, a different way to another."

"If I'm just a computer, reacting mindlessly to *stimuli*, how come I'm free to make any decision I want?" I picked up one of my mother's glass miniatures, a crystal pig that was sitting on the coffee table, watching the argument play out. "I can decide to throw this at the wall or to put it back on the table. No one programmed me one way or another. *I* decide."

"You're arguing you have free will because you feel like you have free will?"

"Yes. Which proves my point. If I were just some mindless computer, how could I feel anything?"

"And how do I know you do?" he asked. "How do I know you're not just programmed to act like you do, to act like you

166

have thoughts and beliefs—the belief in your identity, the belief in your free will, the belief in your humanity?"

"Because I'm telling you, I *do* have those beliefs."

"And that's exactly what you'd say if you were programmed to behave as if you were human. You would be programmed to respond to questions such as mine with the assertion that you made your own choices. Even when logic dictates that it's not true."

"You're wrong."

"I hope not," he said. "Because if you really *can* think in some way, feel in some way that I can't fathom, my heart goes out to you. Nothing is more tragic than believing yourself to be something you're not." He turned to my father. "I apologize if I'm speaking out of turn, but this *thing* is not your daughter. It has your daughter's memories, it emulates your daughter's personality, it may actually believe itself to be your daughter. But, much as you want it to be so, it's not. Your daughter is gone."

"Get out of my house," my father said quietly. You'd have to know him to recognize the tone as thinly masked fury.

"M. Kahn, I speak not to offend, but to help guide you to the truth about—"

"*Out!*" He grabbed the glass pig out of my hand and flung it against the wall, just over the Honored Rai Savona's head. "*Now!*"

The Honored Rai Savona didn't bother to duck. But he made a speedy exit, brushing glittering flakes of glass out of his hair as he left. Once he was gone, my father and I sat in silence.

"So, why do you think he calls himself that?" I asked. " 'The

Honored.'" Not because I cared, but because I couldn't think of anything else to say, and I didn't want to leave. This was the first time we'd been alone together since the accident. My father had already turned back to his screen. If I didn't fill the silence soon, the moment would end.

"He says it's a sign of respect for his 'flock,'" my father said, without looking up from his work. "Nondenominational, all-inclusive." He snorted. "And, of course, a handy way to get respect in name if you can't get it in deed."

It was confirmation that my father didn't respect the man who'd called me inhuman. Confirmation I shouldn't have needed.

"We won't tell your mother about this," he said, like it should be obvious. Which it was.

"Of course."

More silence.

"Can I ask you a question?" I asked, thinking of the support group, of Sloane, the fabric of her skirt clenched in her fists. Sloane, who had wanted to die.

My father nodded.

"What if, hypothetically, something happened to me?"

He still didn't look up. "What would happen?"

"I'm just saying, what if," I said. "If I got . . . hurt."

"Then they'd fix you," he said brusquely. "I thought they explained all that to you. Nothing to worry about."

I had to edge toward it slowly, to give myself time to back away if I lost my nerve. "But what if it was bad? What if it was something they couldn't fix?"

"Then we'd get you a new body," he said, like it was nothing. Something I'd done before; something everyone did. "If you're worried about the expense, don't. It's all included in what we paid for the initial procedure."

"No. No, it's not that. I'm just . . . What if I didn't want it? A new body?"

He looked up. "What does that mean?"

"Well, what if, when something happened—I mean, if something happened, I just wanted . . ." *Not that I would want that. I wouldn't,* I told myself. It was the principle of the thing; it was knowing I had the choice. "What if I'd told you ahead of time. No new body. What if I just wanted this one to be it?"

"Then we'd get you a new body," he said, with the same matter-of-fact inflection he'd used the first time.

"No, you don't understand, I mean—"

"No, Lia. I *do* understand." With my father it was always hard to tell the difference between disinterest and rage. Both were delivered in the same rigidly controlled voice, his lips thin, his face expressionless. "You're underage. Which gives me legal control over your medical condition. And I would prefer said condition remain 'alive.' So, in your hypothetical scenario, you'd be overruled."

It *was* just hypothetical. But he didn't ask for reassurance on that front. "Until next year," I said instead.

"Because?"

"I turn eighteen," I reminded him. "Then it's my call. Legally."

He gave me a thin smile. "Legally. Yes. If one were to play by the rules."

"You taught us to always play by the rules."

He nodded. "Necessary. Until you're in a position to make the rules. Which I am."

"So you're saying—"

"Lia, in case you hadn't noticed, I'm trying to work." He tapped the screen. "Which means I don't have time for your ridiculous hypotheticals."

"Sorry. Yeah, of course." I stood up. Backed out of the room. "Later, maybe. Or, whatever." So he didn't want to talk to me. Even about this. So what?

But then he spoke again. Without looking at me. Barely loud enough for me to hear. "I'm saying I won't let you die. Will *not*. Not again."

Upstairs, I sat on the edge of my bed, alone again. I didn't want to be dead, I knew that. Even living like this . . . It was living. It was *something*. I couldn't imagine the other option. I tried, sometimes, lying in bed, thinking about what it would be like: nothingness. The end. Sometimes I almost caught it, or at least, the edge of it. A nonexistence that stretched on forever, no more of me, no more of anything. The part I couldn't grip was all the stuff I'd leave behind, the stuff that would stay here and keep going when I was gone.

When I was a kid I used to wonder if, just maybe, the world existed only for me. If rooms ceased to exist when I stepped into the hallway and people disappeared once they left me, the rest of their lives imagined solely for my entertainment. Other times I used to wonder if other people thought—I mean *really* thought—the way I did. They said they did, and they acted like they did, but how was I supposed to know if it was true? It was like colors. I knew what red looked like to me, but for all I knew, it looked different to everyone else. Maybe to everyone else, red looked like blue, and blue looked like red. It was, I had to admit, just like the Honored Savona had said. How could you ever know what was really going on in someone else's head?

What I'm saying is, when I was a kid, I knew I was real. I just wasn't sure anyone else was. And even if I didn't think that way anymore, I still wasn't convinced that the world could go on without me.

I didn't want to die.

But that wasn't the point. The point was now I *couldn't*. My father wouldn't let me.

Zo peeked into the room, hesitating in the doorway. "I heard," she said.

Big surprise. "That's what happens when you eavesdrop."

Zo scowled. "I wasn't—whatever. Forget it."

"I'm sorry." Not that I was, not really. But I didn't want her to go. "This day just sucks."

"Yeah." She looked like she didn't know what to say. Neither did I. Zo and I had never talked much before, and now we didn't talk at all.

"You think he's right?" I finally asked.

"What, Dad?" She shrugged. "What's the difference? You planning on another accident? Or should I say"—she curled her fingers into exaggerated quotation marks—"*accident*?"

I wondered, again, why she seemed to hate me so much. But I couldn't ask.

She might answer.

"Not Dad," I said. "The Faith guy. About—you know. All of it."

"There's no such thing as a soul," Zo said. "So I kind of doubt you have one."

"But the rest of it? About me being just a machine, fooling myself into believing . . . You think he could be right?"

She hesitated. Too long. Great—another answer I didn't want to hear.

"Forget I asked," I said. "Of course he's not right. I'm just—"

"I don't think you're fooling yourself," Zo said slowly. "And I don't think . . . I don't think it's true what he said. About it not being natural. What's natural anymore? Besides . . ." She glanced toward the window. The fog—or smog or haze or whatever it was—was bad today, so thick you couldn't even see the trees. "Nature sucks."

I laughed. She flinched.

"What?" I asked.

"Nothing." Zo shifted her weight. "I'm just not used to it yet."

"My laugh."

"Your whole . . . Yeah. Your laugh."

"Remember when Mom decided she wanted to be a singer, and she made us sit through her rehearsal?" I didn't know what had made me think of it.

A smile slipped onto Zo's face, like she couldn't help it. "And we just had to sit there while she butchered that stupid song over and over again. What the hell was it called?"

We both paused. Then—

"'Flowers in the Springtime'!" Together.

She giggled. "Everything was going fine until you made me laugh—"

"*I* made *you* laugh?"

"You made that *face*!" she said accusingly. "With your cheeks all puffed up and your eyebrows scrunched. . . ."

"Yeah, because I was holding my breath, trying not to laugh at *you*, looking like you were having some kind of seizure."

"Okay, but how could you not laugh, when she kept singing that stupid song—"

"'Flowers in the springtime, apples in the trees,'" I warbled in a falsetto. "'Your hand in my hand, gone weak in my knees.'"

"She sounded like a sick cat," Zo sputtered.

"Like psycho Susskind, that night we left him outside in the thunderstorm."

Zo shook her head. "Like psycho Susskind, if we threw him out the window. Howling for his life."

"And when you started laughing—"

"When *you* started laughing—"

"I thought she was going to kill us both."

Zo grinned. "At least that was the end of her singing career."

"Career," I said. "Yeah, right. A bright future in breaking glasses and shattering eardrums." I shook my head. "And remember when Walker showed up that night, I had to explain why I was grounded, but that just started me off laughing again, and then *you* started again, and we couldn't get the story out? I wonder if I ever did tell him what that was about."

"You did," Zo said flatly. She'd stopped laughing. "You texted him later and told him."

"Oh. Right, okay. How do you even remember that?"

"I have to go," Zo said. It was like the last few minutes hadn't happened. "I'm late."

"Where are you going?"

"What do you care?" she snapped.

I didn't say anything.

She sagged against the doorframe, just a little, not enough so most people would notice, but I was her sister. I noticed. "I'm going out with Cass, okay? Is that a problem?" But she didn't ask like she really wanted to know.

"It's fine," I said. "She's your friend now, right? Go."

"I wasn't asking for permission."

"Fine," I said again, even though it wasn't.

"Fine," she said. And she left.

I wanted to get into bed and shut down, forget the day had ever happened. But there were two messages waiting for me. That was bizarre enough, since pretty much no one was speaking to me anymore, not unless you counted the randoms I only knew from the network, and even if I did count them, they'd mostly faded away, since I wasn't doing much zone-hopping these days. When you ignored the randoms for long enough, they tended to get a clue.

The most recent text was from Quinn.

`I'm going. And so are you.`

It didn't make sense. Not until I saw the one that had arrived just before it, addressed to both of us. From an anonymous sender.

`Congratulations, you passed the first test.`

Then there was a time, a date, and an address.

`Ready for phase two?`

ONE OF US

"If you can't remember something, did it really happen?"

The car took an unfamiliar route, depositing me at some smallish house a little too close to the city for my comfort. There was a security field around the property, which lifted as I drove through. No one was waiting outside for me. I wondered if Quinn had already arrived. Or changed her mind about coming in the first place. It was, after all, slightly insane, showing up at a random spot in the middle of nowhere just because some anonymous message told me to. It was more than slightly insane to do so without telling anyone where I was going. But I had come this far; I was going in.

After all, what was the worst that could happen? It's not like I could die.

I knocked. When the door opened, the blue-haired girl from

the support group stood behind it. *"You?"* I asked, surprised. The girl—Ani, I remembered—had spoken even less than I had at the session, revealing only that, aside from the technicolored hair, she was kind of blah.

"Sort of me," she said softly. "But not just me. Come in." She stepped aside.

The place was crawling with them. Mech-heads. Skinners. Freaks. And I mean, crawling, literally, since a few of them were on the floor, writhing against the cheap carpeting—or against one another—their eyes rolled back, their fingers spasming. It was as if they were tripping on Xers, but I knew they couldn't be, because they were like me.

No, I thought, trying not to stare, although they wouldn't have noticed. *Not like me.*

The house was sparsely furnished: white walls, gray floor, a couple of cheap couches set at haphazard angles to the walls and each other, and not much more. Ani took a seat on one of them, settling back against Quinn's arm. Quinn looked like she was home. There was an empty space next to them. I didn't sit. On the other couch slumped a tall, lanky mech-head with brown eyes, brown hair, and a sour look on his waxy face. And next to him, staring at me with flickering orange eyes, someone familiar. Jude something, one of the earliest skinners. A year ago he'd been everywhere on the vids, hitting parties, crashing vidlifes, popping up on all the stalker zones. And then, a month or two later, people had gotten bored—or he had—and he'd disappeared. A month was longer than most insta-fame lasted; he'd been lucky.

He'd also been a brunet. But now he was . . . something else. His hair gleamed silver, and the color bled down his face, streaking his forehead and cheeks with a metallic sheen. His bare left arm was etched with the snaking black lines of a circuit diagram. But his right arm, that was the worst of it. The pseudoflesh had been stripped away, replaced by a transparent coating that glowed with the pulse and flicker of the circuitry underneath.

He wasn't the only one. The writhing freaks were all streaked with silver, their skin painted with whirling diagrams or stripped away, wiring exposed. One had even decorated his bare skull with an intricate vision of the cerebral matrix that whirred beneath the surface. As Ani leaned forward on the couch, her shirt rose on her back, exposing a patch of bare, silvery skin.

"Stare all you want," Jude said. "It's important to know what you are."

"What *you* are. A bunch of freaks," I muttered. "What did you do to yourselves?"

"Not freaks. *Machines*," Jude corrected me. "And we didn't do it. We're just embracing it."

"You think this is funny?" I asked, disgusted. "You want to turn us all into a joke?"

"Not a joke," Jude said. "A machine."

"I'm no machine!"

Jude glared at Ani. "I thought you said she was okay."

"She is," Ani said, glancing at Quinn. "When her friend—"

"We're not friends," Quinn and I said at the same time. Only Quinn laughed.

"She sounded like she got it," Ani said. "And she walked out on the session. Seemed like a good sign."

"What is this?" I asked. "Some kind of stupid spy game? You go to those meetings and what, report back? To *him*?"

"Well, she's not stupid," Jude said. "There's that."

I stood up. "*She's* out of here."

"Stay," Ani said. "You belong here."

I shuddered. "I don't think so."

"It's better than Sascha's crap," Quinn said, stroking the silver streak on Ani's arm. "They know what they are. What *we* are."

"This isn't who I am," I said, backing away.

"It's who we all are." The guy next to Jude spoke for the first time. "Like it or not."

"Let her go, Riley." Jude flicked a lazy hand toward the door. "This is a place for people who want to look forward, not back. She's obviously not ready to do that. Not if she's still whining about what she was and denying what she *is*."

"I'm not denying anything."

"Your sentence is a logical impossibility," Jude said. "Not to mention inaccurate. Come back when you've figured things out. We'll wait."

"I hope you can wait forever."

Jude laughed. "What, you think you'll make it out there? With the orgs?"

"The what?"

"Orgs—organics. Nasty little piles of blood and guts. Humans. You know, the ones who hate you."

179

"No one hates me," I said.

"Yeah, you're not in denial at all." Jude shook his head. "Come back when you've grown up a little." He looked younger than me. But he was a skinner—looks meant nothing. "Well? What are you waiting for? Be a good little mech and get out."

"You're throwing me out?" Unbelievable.

Sorry, Quinn mouthed. But she stayed where she was.

"Have fun with your orgs," he said with fake cheer. "Take care of yourself."

"Take care of your mental problems," I advised him.

And left.

There was a mech-head sitting on the edge of the front porch. I winced as the door slammed behind me, afraid it would catch his attention. I'd talked to enough skinners for one day. Maybe for life.

But the mech-head didn't look up. He was hunched over, his fist wrapped around a switchblade, and he was carving something into the porch's rotting wood, except—

I gasped.

He wasn't carving the wood. He was carving his arm. The knife flashed as the point dug in again, slicing a gash from his wrist to his elbow. He shivered.

And then he finally looked at me, his lips drawing back in a sickening smile. His teeth were coated in silver.

"Feels good." His voice was a sigh. "I mean, feels bad. But that feels good, too. You know?"

I shook my head. I didn't know.

But . . .

Pain, I thought. *I miss pain.*

I shook my head harder.

He tossed the knife and caught it neatly, gripping the blade. Then, like a knight making an offering to his queen, extended it to me. "You'll like." His teeth gleamed. Not like the knife handle. It was inky black, sucking in light. "You'll see."

"You're crazy," I whispered. I couldn't get my voice to work right. Just like I couldn't make myself walk away. "You're all crazy."

He just nodded.

And the knife was still there, waiting.

I didn't want it.

I did *not*.

"I'm not one of you," I said louder. Backing away. "I don't belong here."

The mech-head just shrugged and started carving again.

They were all psycho, I told myself. Freaks. Nothing to do with me. Nothing *like* me.

I'd been wrong to come; I'd been stupid.

I'd been stupid a lot, lately. But that was over. And smart decision number one? Leaving this place, these . . . *people*.

Leaving—and never coming back.

One month passed.

See how easy that was? From point A to point B in three little words, skimming over everything that happened in between.

As if it were possible to do that in real life, as if you could just shut your eyes and open them a moment later only to find: One month passed.

It's not. Days pass slowly; minutes pass slowly. And I had to live through them all. I went to school, most days, at least. I lingered in empty classrooms after the bell, then hustled to the next class at the last minute so I could slip in the door just before the teacher started droning. And again for the next class, and again. I ate lunch outside, alone, in a spot behind the lower school building where no one was supposed to go. No one ever knew I was there, because the biosensors deployed to catch students wandering astray couldn't catch me. I went directly home at the end of every day, taking the long way around to the parking lot so I wouldn't have to pass by the western edge of the track and see Zo and the others running heats across the field.

It got colder.

I didn't notice. Some afternoons I shut myself in my room, linking in and sending my av on missions across the network, avoiding the zones of anyone I used to know, racking up kills on Akira, thrashing players who lived on the other side of the globe and had no idea they were playing against a machine.

I skipped dinner. Even when my mother begged; even when my father ordered. And neither tried very hard. They didn't want me there either, stiff and still at the table, watching the mouthfuls of risotto or filet or chocolate mousse disappear. Then there were the nights when I slipped down to the kitchen, snagged a brownie or a cookie or anything chocolate, mashed it up with a fork, and tried to swallow it, washing it down with a swig of water in hopes of forcing something past the grate at the base of my throat. Not because I wanted to taste any of it—not that I *could* taste any of it—but just to see what would happen. Nothing happened.

I didn't upload, not anymore. It was supposed to be a daily routine; it was supposed to be my protection against the finality of death, every experience stored, every memory preserved, so that when the next accident came along, I—the essential *I*, the mysterious sum of seventeen years of days and nights and the best quantum computing credit could buy—would remain intact. But what was the point? If the worst happened, and I had to start over again, what would I need to remember? Waiting out the minutes behind the school until it was time to slog through yet another vapid class? Or maybe the moment Walker saw me, froze, then turned abruptly and zagged off in the opposite direction? Not quite treasured memories. So I let them slip away.

Nights, I ran. Factory specifications recommended that I stop running when the body reported its fatigue; that I "sleep" when the normal people slept. But I couldn't stand the way it felt. It would be one thing if I dreamed, but there were no dreams. It would have been okay even if there was just darkness. I had spent plenty of time in the dark. But shutting down meant surrendering to a blank; closing my eyes and opening them again, immediately, only to discover that hours had passed. When you sleep, your body marks the time. Yesterday dies in the dark; tomorrow wakes. Eyes open, you know. The body ages, the hourglass empties, death approaches, time is devoured but not lost. It wasn't like that for me, not anymore. I couldn't shut down without feeling like I was losing myself all over again, night after night. So instead I ran.

I ran through the woods in the dark, full out, without fear that I would stumble over the uneven ground or the broken branches blown across the path, running faster, maybe hoping I would fall, just to see if it would hurt, and if it did, maybe that would be all right, because feeling something was better than nothing. But I never fell. And I never stopped when I was tired. The body told me it was wearing down, but I didn't ache, I didn't cramp, I didn't wheeze. The body's monitoring system flashed red warnings across my eyes; I ignored them. The coach, before she'd thrown me off the team, had always said that running was 90 percent mental. That was for humans, I decided. (*Orgs*. The word popped into my head, but I ignored it, because that was Jude's word, Jude and his freaks, not mine.) For me it was all mental; the body, and whatever it wanted, was irrelevant. So I ran for hours, for miles, until I got bored, and then I ran farther until eventually I retreated to the house to wait out the dawn.

One month passed.

It happened on a Tuesday.

I was crossing the quad, the grassy, open-aired corridor between two wings of the school. There was an enclosed hallway too, and most people used that, not wanting to spend any more time outdoors than necessary. I preferred the cold.

I didn't feel strange before it happened. I didn't feel much of anything, which was the new normal.

Everything was normal. One foot in front of the other. One step, then another. And another. And then—

Not.

I was still. Left foot forward, flat on the ground. Right foot a step behind, rising up on its toe, about to take flight. Arms swung, one forward, one back. Head down, as always.

Move, I thought furiously. *Walk!*

The body ignored me. The body had gone on strike.

Being a human statue didn't hurt. It didn't wear me out. It felt like nothing. I felt like nothing. Like a pair of eyes, floating in space.

I couldn't speak.

And, like most statues, I drew a crowd.

"What the fuck!" more than one person exclaimed, laughing.

A couple people poked me. One almost knocked me over before another grabbed my side and steadied me on frozen feet. Laughing, all the time. Several of the guys helped themselves to a peek down my shirt.

Walker and Bliss passed by, hesitated, then kept walking. She's the one who paused. He pulled her away.

I stayed where I was.

"You think she can hear us?"

"Who broke her?"

"Don't you mean who broke *it*?"

Someone balanced a banana peel on my head. Someone else

approached my face with a thick red marker. I couldn't feel it scrape across my forehead. But I could see his satisfied smirk as he capped the marker and stepped away.

Maybe, I thought, I was being punished. Maybe the Faithers were right, and I wasn't supposed to exist at all. I wasn't sure if I believed in God, but if He or She or It or Whatever was pissed off to see me wandering around all soulless and abominable, this seemed like a pretty effective start to the divine retribution.

"You think she's stuck like this forever?"

I thought so. The absence of body felt absolute. I was pure mind. I was floating. I was wishing I could float away, when the crowd parted, and Auden Heller came barreling through.

"Get away," he hissed at them. No one moved. "Get the fuck out of the way!"

Auden wasn't big enough to take on a hostile crowd; he was barely big enough to take on a hostile individual, and he was facing plenty of them. But they were facing Auden, half-crazed behind his thick black glasses. Maybe they saw something worth avoiding or maybe they'd just gotten tired of laughing at the frozen freak. Maybe their markers had run dry. For whatever reason, they got out of his way.

Auden wrapped his arms around my waist.

I don't need you to save me, I thought furiously.

"I hope this doesn't hurt you," he murmured.

Nothing hurts me, I thought.

I didn't expect he'd be strong enough to pick me up. He was. He carried me, my body stiff, my feet a few inches off the ground, my face staring blankly over his shoulder, watching the crowd, still laughing, recede into the distance.

"You'll be okay," Auden said quietly as we crossed the quad. "They'll know how to fix you."

I wondered what made him think I could hear. Or that I cared.

I wondered why he was bothering to help.

He brought me to the school's med-tech, but of course, that was useless. I didn't need first aid; I needed a tune-up. The tech voiced my parents, who must have voiced BioMax. Maybe they even went straight to call-me-Ben. And I waited, propped up in a corner, still frozen. Auden waited too, sitting in a chair next to my body, holding my hand.

"I'm coming with you," he said when the man arrived to take me away.

The man shook his head.

"Yes," Auden insisted.

The world flipped upside down as the man hoisted me over his shoulder. My face slammed into his back, and I was stuck staring at his ass.

"How do I even know you're legit?" Auden asked. "You could be trying to kidnap her or something. It's not like she can stop you."

"It's not like you can either, kid." The man, large enough to multitask, shoved Auden out of the way, using the arm that wasn't holding me.

"Let them go," the school tech told Auden. "He knows how to help her."

No one knows that, I thought.

The man carried me outside, out to the parking lot, past another crowd of jeering wannabes probably already posting shots to their favorite stalker zones. He carried me to a car and loaded me inside.

"Kid's right," the man muttered, folding me into the back. "I could do anything. Who'd know?"

His hand lingered on my leg, which he'd had to twist to fit into the narrow space. My limbs were rigid, but not as frozen as they'd seemed. With a little effort, they moved when he moved them. He rubbed his finger in a slow circle along the skin of my calf.

I can't even feel it, I told myself. *So it's not really happening. It's not really my body.*

"Almost forgot," he said, chuckling. He raised up my shirt, reached underneath. I watched the fabric undulate as his hands crept up my torso. I couldn't feel him massaging the patch of skin just below my armpit or carefully peeling it back to reveal the fail-safe, an input port that functioned only with BioMax tech and a well-protected access code; an emergency shutdown. But I knew what he was doing. And no matter how much I willed myself to stay awake, I knew it wouldn't work.

Don't, I thought uselessly.

There are some moments you'd rather sleep through, pass from point A to point B without awareness of the time passing or the events that carry you from present to future. And it's mostly those moments in which it's smarter—safer—to stay awake.

Don't.

"Sweet dreams," the man said.

Please don't.

Lights out.

"Don't," I said, and I said it out loud, in a different place, a familiar cramped white room, a too-bright light in my eyes, call-me-Ben's face inches from mine. I was back on floor thirteen.

"There you go," he said. "All better."

"What happened?" I remembered the car, I remembered the man's hands on my body, under my shirt, I remembered his sour smile, and then . . . I was here, awake, with call-me-Ben. As if no time had passed.

"I'd suspect someone hasn't been taking very good care of herself," he said. "And your system . . . Well, think of it like this: In an organic body, too much wear and tear, overexhaustion, and malnutrition weaken you, make you susceptible to bugs. This body, when mistreated, can fall prey to the same problem. Not germs, of course." He laughed fakely. "But every system can be crashed by the right bug—under the right circumstances. A temporary disconnect between your body and your neural network. Shouldn't be a problem again if you take care of yourself."

But that wasn't what I needed to know. "How did I get here? Who was that guy?"

"The man who brought you in? Just one of our techs."

"He knocked me out."

"He initiated a shutdown," said call-me-Ben. "Standard

protocol. I'm sure it couldn't have been very pleasant, frozen like that. We didn't want to cause you any more discomfort than necessary."

"He just brought me here?"

Ben nodded. "Straight here, and we fixed you right up. We'll run a few more diagnostic tests, and then you should be able to go home."

"How long?"

"Shouldn't take more than—"

"No. How long was I out?"

Call-me-Ben checked the time. "About five hours, I believe. But they didn't start working on you until I got down here. So it only took an hour or so to fix you right up. Just a minor problem, nothing to worry about."

Five hours gone. Turned off.

And four of those hours lying in a heap somewhere, limp and malleable, like a *doll*, while the man, or anyone else, carted me around, did whatever he wanted. Or maybe did nothing. Maybe dumped me on a table somewhere, like spare parts in storage, and walked away.

If you can't remember something, did it really happen?

No, I decided.

Or even if it did, it didn't matter. The body wasn't *me*, not when the brain was shut down. They treated it like a bunch of spare parts, because that's all it was. It wasn't me.

Which meant whatever happened, nothing happened.

Nothing happened.

"You have to start taking care of yourself," Ben said. And there was something about the way he said it that made it seem like he knew what I'd been doing, all of it. It was the same tone Sascha had used when she mentioned my boyfriend. A little too knowing, like he had to restrain himself from winking. "Will you promise me you'll do that?"

"Can you guarantee this won't happen to me again?" I asked.

"If you stop pushing yourself so hard? Yes, I can guarantee it. So can *you* guarantee *me* this won't happen again?"

"Yes."

I didn't care what I had to do: I would never be that helpless again.

TERMINATED

"Computers think; humans feel."

When I finally got home, there was a message from Auden waiting at my zone. His av was weird, like him, a creature with frog legs and black beetle wings. It chirped its message in Auden's voice. "Are you okay?"

I ignored it.

But the next day at school, when he found me eating lunch behind the low stone wall, I let him sit down.

"You're not supposed to be here," I said.

"Neither are you."

"But they can't catch *me*." I nodded toward the biosensors. "No bio, ergo, no sensing."

Auden shrugged. "And they don't care about catching me. No one's paying attention."

"How do you know?"

He unwrapped a slim sandwich with some suspiciously greenish filling. "Where do you think I used to eat? Before you took over my territory, so to speak."

"Oh."

"'Oh' is right."

"So I guess I should thank you or something," I said. "For yesterday."

"I guess you should." There was a pause. "But I can't help noticing that you didn't."

I wasn't sure whether to laugh or shove the sandwich in his face. I certainly wasn't saying thank you.

"So what's in the bag, anyway?" I asked instead.

"What bag?"

I rolled my eyes. "That bag." I pointed to the green sack he always toted around. "Or is it just your security blanket?"

Auden flushed. "Stuff. Nothing important."

"Really?" I doubted it and reached for the bag. "Let me—"

"Don't!" he snapped, snatching it away. His fists balled around the straps.

"Okay, whatever. Sorry." I held up my arms in surrender. "Forget I asked."

"Look, I'm sorry, but . . ."

"I mean it. Forget it. I don't want to know."

I wasn't sure if I was mad at him or he was mad at me. Or if neither of us was mad. There was an uncertain silence between us, like we were deciding whether to settle in and get comfortable or to leave.

"What do you want from me?" I asked.

"What makes you think I want something?"

"We don't even know each other, and you keep—you know, sticking up for me. Being *nice*. And now you show up here. What is it?"

"So you think if someone's nice to you, it means they want something?" he asked. "Interesting."

"What's so interesting about that?"

"If I were a shrink, I might wonder what it means for your relationships with other people and what you expect to get out of them," he said.

He was so deeply weird. "What the hell is a shrink?"

"They were like doctors, for your moods. Someone you talked to when you were feeling screwed up."

"Why would you *talk* to some random when you could just take a b-mod to feel better?"

"This was before b-mods, I think," he said. "Or maybe for people who didn't want them."

"Sounds kind of stupid, if you ask me." Who wouldn't want to mod their mood, if they could? Something to make you happy when you wanted to be happy, numb when you wanted to be numb? I missed them more than chocolate. And what did I get in exchange? Eternal life, for one thing.

And to help with the feeling-screwed-up part? I supposed there was always Sascha.

I missed the drugs.

"And, by the way, my relationships are just fine," I said.

"At least I *have* relationships, unlike some people."

"Oh, excuse me," he said with exaggerated contrition. "I forgot— You're *popular*."

For some reason, maybe because it was so far from reality, maybe because he made being popular sound like a fatal condition, maybe just because there was nothing else to do but cry and I was a few tear ducts short, I laughed. So did he.

"People are idiots," he said when he caught his breath.

"You don't have to say that."

"I'm not just saying it. Those girls you used to hang out with? Superficial bitches. And the guys—"

"Stop," I said.

"They're not your *friends*," he said. Like I needed a reminder. "They dropped you."

"I noticed. Thanks. But they're still . . ." I shook my head. "So is that what you think of me, too? Superficial bitch?"

"I think . . ." For the first time he seemed not quite sure what to say. "You're different now. And that interests me."

It wasn't an answer.

"So that's why you helped yesterday? I'm, like, some kind of scientific study for you?" I said bitterly. "Something neat to play with?"

"Why do you have to do that?" he asked.

"What?"

"Turn everything into something small like that. Mean."

"Are you trying to be my shrunk again?" I said.

"Shrink."

"That's what I said."

"I just want to know what it's like," he said. "Being . . ."

"Different?" I suggested. "It sucks."

"No. I know what it's like to be different." He wound the strap of his bag around his fingers. "I want to know what it's like to be *you*. To be downloaded. To have this mind that's totally under your control, to know you're never going to age, never going to die, this body that's perfect in every way . . ." He looked up at me, blushing. "I didn't mean it like that. I mean, I just . . ."

"Don't worry," I said. "No one's meant it like that. Not since . . . before."

He blushed a deeper pink. "You do, though," he mumbled. "Lookgoodlikethis." It took me a second to decipher what he'd said. "Better than before. I think, at least."

The body couldn't blush. Not that I would have blushed, anyway, just because Auden Heller gave me a compliment. The Auden Hellers of the world were always giving compliments to the Lia Kahns of the world. It's what they were there for.

But it was the first time in too long that I'd really felt like a Lia Kahn.

"Thank you," I said. "For yesterday, I mean."

"So what *does* it feel like?" he asked eagerly.

"Like . . . not much." It wasn't that I didn't want to explain it to him. I *did*, that was the strange part. But I didn't know how. "Everything's almost the same, but not quite. It's all a little wrong, you know? It sounds different, it looks different, and when it comes to feeling . . ."

"I read that every square inch of the artificial flesh has more than a million receptors woven into it, to simulate organic sensation," he said.

"If you say so." I hadn't read anything; I didn't want to know how the body worked. I just wanted it to work better. "But maybe a million isn't enough. I can feel stuff, but it doesn't feel . . ." I brushed my hand across the surface of his bag. This time he didn't pull it away. "It's like if I close my eyes and touch the bag, I know it's there. I know it's a rough surface, a little scratchy. I *know* all that, but I can't . . . It's just not the same. It's like I'm living in my head, you know? Like I'm operating the body by remote control. I'm not *inside* it, somehow."

Auden nodded. "The sensation of disembodiment, an alienated dissociation common to the early phase of readjustment. I read about that, too."

"That doesn't mean you understand," I snapped. "You don't know what it's like."

"I know I don't," he said. "But I want to, believe me."

I almost did.

The final note, a fever-pitched, keening whine, seemed to stretch on forever. It didn't fade, didn't swell, just sliced through us, a single, unending tone until, without warning, it ended. For a second everything froze—and then the applause crashed through the silence. A thunder of cheers and screams. The band went nuts, jumping up and down, smashing instruments against the stage, waving their arms in an obvious signal to the fans:

more applause, more shouting, more, more, more. Only the lead singer stayed frozen, her mouth open like she was still spooling out that final note, this time in a register too high for us to hear. I felt like she was looking at me.

"Nothing?" Auden asked, stripping off his gear.

"Nothing." I dumped the earplugs and goggles on the pile of crap next to his bed. "But that's what I figured."

Auden had thought that maybe some live music—or at least, as live as it gets these days—would penetrate in a way the recorded stuff couldn't. That maybe it would get my heart pounding, even though I didn't have a heart; my breath caught in my throat, even though I didn't have any lungs; my eyes tearing up, even though I didn't have any ducts . . . You get the idea.

We both knew it was a long shot.

But I'd been willing to give it a try. And even though it hadn't worked—even though the music made me feel cold and dead inside, just like always—it was better, having Auden there. This time it didn't feel like a disappointment, or like I'd lost yet another piece of myself. It just felt like an experimental result—not even a failure, because when you're experimenting, every new piece of information is a success.

That's what Auden said, at least.

And that's what he called them: experiments. At least going to a virtual concert was more fun than sticking my head in a bucket of ice water to see how long I could stand the cold. (Result: longer than Auden could stand waiting for me to give up.) We'd spent the week "experimenting," trying to see what I couldn't do—and what I could. It wasn't like before, on my own, when I'd pushed the body until it broke. This wasn't about testing limits, Auden said. This was about getting to know myself again. Because maybe that would lead to liking myself. Just a little.

I laughed at him for saying that—it was a little too Sascha-like for my taste. But I went along with the experiments. Partly because I didn't have anything else to do—or anyone else to talk to. Partly because I wasn't sure he was wrong.

"What's it like?" he asked now. "Linking in with your mind?"

"I don't know." He was always asking me that: "What's it like?" And I never had a good answer. *What's it like to breathe?* I could have asked, and stumped him just as easily. *What's it feel like to dream, to swallow, to age?*

"I mean, how do you do it?"

I shrugged. "I don't know. I just think about linking in, and the network pops up on my eye screen."

"But *how*?"

"Same way I do anything, I guess. How do I shut down at night? How do I stand up when I want to?" I asked, wishing we could change the subject. "How do *you*?"

Auden looked thoughtful. "I just do it, I guess. I want to, and it happens."

"Well, same thing," I said, even though we both knew it wasn't.

"So how come you can't do more?"

"More like what?"

"Like, you still need a keyboard," he said. "Why can't you just *think* commands at the network and make stuff happen? Like you did with the language hookup."

I'd told him all about the computer that had spoken for me, how horrible it had been. Except he didn't get the horrible part; he thought it sounded cool.

"I just can't," I said. "It's not the same thing."

"It should be," he argued. "If they have the tech to do it in the hospital, that means they have it, period. They could have wired your brain right into the network. It'd be like telepathy or something."

"It'd be weird, is what it would be," I said. "And they were trying to make us normal."

It had been call-me-Ben's favorite word, Sascha's too. *You are normal.* Or at least, *as normal as we can make you.*

"You've got to get over that," Auden said.

"What?"

"The normal thing."

Because I wasn't. "Thanks for rubbing it in."

"But you've got something so much better," Auden said, and I knew where he was going. He had the same dreamy look in his eyes that adults always got when they talked about how I would never age.

"I wasn't afraid of getting old," I said.

"What about *not* getting old?" Auden asked. "What about dying? You always act like it's nothing, Lia, but it's everything. *You can't die.* What about that is not amazing?"

"I don't know. I never really thought about it much. Before, I mean." I'd never known anyone who had died. At least not anyone who mattered. Everyone dies, I got that. But I'd never quite believed it would happen to me. And now it wouldn't. That didn't seem amazing. Weirdly enough, it just seemed like the natural order of things. "I guess I've never really been too afraid of it. Death."

He paused and looked away. "Maybe you should be."

Somewhere below us, a door slammed.

Auden flinched. "Shit. What time is it?"

"Almost six. Why?"

"Nothing. Forget it. You should go."

I'd come to his house every day after school for a week, but I'd always left by sunset—until today.

Footsteps tramped up the stairs.

I put my hand on the door, but before I could open it, Auden grabbed my arm. "Wait," he whispered.

I shrugged him off. "What? I thought you wanted me to go."

"Yeah, but not . . ." He shot a panicked glance at the window, like he was trying to decide whether to push me through it. Anything to get me out of the house before whoever was out in the hallway came into the room. Before they saw me.

"Are you *hiding* me?" I asked loudly. "Embarrassed or something?"

He put his finger to his lips, silently begging. I couldn't believe it. At school he acted like he didn't care what anyone thought. He kept telling me that I was better off being different, if my only other option was being the same. I didn't believe him, but I'd believed that *he* believed it. At least, until now.

"Auden, you actually got a girl in there with you?" a man's voice called from the hallway. "Aren't you going to introduce us?"

"Just me," Auden called back weakly.

Screw him.

I twisted the knob. Opened the door.

The man in the hallway didn't look anything like Auden. He was blond and handsome, his features perfectly symmetrical, green eyes, rosy cheeks, square chin. He could have starred in a pop-up for a gen-tech lab. And the two little girls clutching his hands were just as picture-perfect. Their blond hair was tied back into pigtails; green eyes sparkled; identical dimples dotted their identical cheeks.

Auden had never mentioned having sisters.

He'd never mentioned much of anything about his family, and I'd never thought to ask.

The man shook his head, looking disgusted. "I should have known."

"Don't," Auden said quietly.

"Girls, go to your room," the man said. But the girls didn't move. They were staring at me. *"Now."*

Their giggles drifted down the hallway, then disappeared behind a door.

"Get it out of here," he said, glaring at me.

I bared my teeth. "Nice to meet you, too, M. Heller."

"This is disgusting," he said to Auden. "Even for you."

"We weren't—"

"You bring this on yourself, you know," the man said. I couldn't think of him as Auden's father. Not with the ice in his eyes. "If you would just try a little harder, you wouldn't have to resort to . . . *that.*"

"We're leaving." Auden grabbed my wrist and tugged me into the hall, past his father.

"Didn't you learn anything from what happened to your mother?"

Auden froze. "Don't." His voice had gotten dangerous.

"You're just like her, you know."

Auden stood up straighter. "Thank you."

His father snorted. "Take that out of here," he said, and even though he was no longer glaring at me, I knew what—who—he meant. "And you can take your time coming back. Tara's cooking a special dinner for me and the girls."

"Family bonding," Auden said bitterly. "How sweet. And I'm not invited?"

"Can you be civil?"

"Unlikely."

"Then enjoy your evening," the man said. "Somewhere else."

We didn't talk until we were out of the house.

And then we didn't talk some more.

Auden walked me to my car. I got in, then left the door open, waiting. After a moment, he climbed in too. His hands clenched into fists.

"You don't embarrass me," he said finally. "*He* does."

I didn't know what to say. "Parents are just . . ."

"It's not parents," Auden said furiously. "Just him. Parent. Singular."

"Your mother . . . left?"

"Died."

"I'm sorry."

"Why? You didn't kill her."

I looked away.

"I'm sorry." He touched my shoulder, hesitated, then drew his hand away. I didn't move. "It's been a long time, but I still . . ."

"Yeah. I get it." I didn't, not really. My mother wasn't dead; my father wasn't evil. I couldn't get it, any more than he could get what it was like to be me.

It was weird, how many different ways there were for life to suck.

"I'm sorry for what he said. He shouldn't have treated you like that."

I shrugged. "I'm getting used to it."

"You shouldn't have to."

True. But there were a lot of things I shouldn't have to get used to, and if I started making a list, I might never stop.

"So Tara's your stepmother?" I asked.

"She's the new wife."

"And the girls . . . ?"

"Tess and Tami. The perfect little daughters my father always wanted."

I wasn't sure if I was supposed to keep asking questions, but

I didn't know what else to do. "Your mother was the one who wanted a son?"

He snorted and, for the first time, he sounded like his father. "No one wanted a son."

"I don't get it." *Everyone* got what they wanted these days, even if you barely had any credit. Looks, skills, personality, that was all more expensive, but sex was basic. Check box number one for a girl, box number two for a boy, and that was it. Case closed.

"My mother . . ." Auden squirmed in his seat. "It's going to sound weird."

"Since when do you care about that?"

"My mother was sort of old-fashioned," Auden said. "She didn't . . . Well, she thought genetic screening was, uh, tampering with God's work." He paused, waiting for me to react. For once I was glad that my face's default expression was blank.

Because what kind of lunatic fringe freak didn't believe in gen-tech?

"I mean, she let them do the basics," he said quickly. "Screen out diseases, mutations, all that stuff, but as for everything else . . ."

"You're a *natural*?" I asked, incredulous. Maybe I shouldn't have been surprised. I'd even wondered a few times, back when Auden was just another weirdo to avoid, when it seemed like no one would choose to have a kid like him. It would explain the crooked nose, the slightly lumpy body, and all the rest of it. But it was still hard to believe. Families like ours just didn't do things like that.

He blushed. "Pretty much." He turned his head toward the window, looking back up at the house. "Tara doesn't even know, although I'm sure she suspects. When she decided to get pregnant, my father made sure he got everything he wanted. I always kind of thought that's why he went for twins." He laughed bitterly. "So he'd have an extra, like a replacement for the kid he should have had, when he got stuck with me instead."

"I'm sure he doesn't—"

"Yeah. He does."

"So your mom . . . She was a Faither?"

"No!" he said hotly. "Not all believers are Faithers. Just the crazy ones."

"Yeah, but how do you tell the difference?" I muttered.

It just slipped out.

Auden glared. "It's not crazy to believe in something."

"My father says—" I stopped.

"What?"

"Nothing."

"Lia." His expression hadn't changed, but there was something new in his eyes. Something fierce. *"What?"*

I sighed. "My father says that believing in something without any proof is, at best, sloppy thinking and, at worst, clinically delusional."

"Well, my mother said that in the end, all we have is belief," he countered. "That you can't *know* what's out there, or who. And that denying the possibility of something bigger just means you've got a small mind, and you're choosing to live a small life."

"So I've got a small mind?"

"I didn't say that."

"No, your mother did," I snapped.

His face was red. "Well, I guess if she were here, you could ask her yourself. Too bad she's not!"

There was a long, angry pause.

"I'm sorry," I said finally. And I was, although I wasn't sure for what.

"This is why she wasn't a Faither," he said, his voice quiet. "She didn't think it was her business to tell other people what to believe. She was just happy believing herself. She said it made her feel like . . ." He looked down. "Like she was never alone."

I was almost jealous.

"Do you?"

"What? Feel like I'm never alone?" He barked out a laugh. "Not quite."

"No. I mean, believe."

He shrugged, still looking away. "I don't know. I used to try. When I was a kid, you know? I wanted to be like her. But . . . I guess you can't *make* yourself believe in something. Sometimes I think I do, I think I can feel it deep down, that certainty . . . but then it just disappears. That never happened to her. She was so *sure*." Auden shook his head. "I've never been that sure of anything."

"Maybe she wasn't either," I suggested, "and she just made

it seem that way. Maybe that's what believing is—pretending to be sure, even when you're not. Ignoring your doubt until it disappears."

"Maybe." He didn't sound convinced. "Too bad I can't just ask her, right?" He tried to laugh again. It didn't work.

"You miss her."

His answer was more of a sigh than a word. "Yeah."

And maybe I could understand a little, after all. I'd never lost a parent—but I'd lost plenty. I knew about missing things.

"Auden, can I—can I ask you something?"

He nodded.

"All that stuff your mother believed in, about tampering with God's will and . . . all that. You don't . . . I mean, everything they did to me, you don't think . . . ?"

"No!" He shook his head, hard. "I know that was— I mean, I know she wasn't . . ." He pressed his lips together. *He doesn't want to insult her*, I thought. *Even now.* Like he thought she could still hear him.

But maybe I got it wrong. Because that really would be crazy.

"I don't agree with her," he said finally. Firmly. "I think it's incredible, what they can do. And what they did. For you. But . . ." He rubbed the rim of his glasses. "You want to hear something weird?"

I smiled. "Always."

"You know how I wear glasses?"

"Yes, Auden, I've noticed that you wear glasses," I said, hoping to tease him out of the mood.

"Ever wonder why?"

"I just figured . . ." I didn't want to tell him I'd figured he was a pretentious loser trying to look cool. "That you liked old things. All that stuff you're always talking about. The way things used to be."

"That's part of it, I guess. I do like that stuff."

"Because of your mother?"

"Well, sort of. But also because—I don't know. It was all different back then. There was more . . . room."

"More room?" I echoed. "Are you kidding? I thought you were supposed to be good at history. *No one* had any room back then, when they thought they had to live all crammed into the same place, all those people stuck in the cities. . . ." I shuddered. It freaked me out just thinking about it. Made me feel like the walls were closing in.

"No, I don't mean more room for people. I just mean more room to *do* something. Change the way things worked. You could be important. Now . . . I don't know. No one's important."

"Everyone's important," I said. "At least if you've got enough credit."

"And if you've got no credit, you might as well not exist?"

"I didn't say that."

"Yeah, but you thought it," he said. "Everyone does. And so all those credit-free people just end up in a corp-town or a city, and no one really cares, because that's just the way it is."

"But that *is* the way it is," I said, confused. "And they don't care, so why should you?"

"How do you know they don't care? Do you actually *know* anyone who lives in a corp-town? Have you ever *been* to a city?"

"Have you?" I countered.

I could tell from the look on his face that he hadn't.

"I don't want to fight," he said instead of answering.

"Then stop insulting me!"

"I wasn't— Look, I'm just saying, things weren't always the way they are now. But people act like they were. Like the past doesn't matter, because everything's always been the same. And like it should always be the same."

I didn't want to fight either. "So that's why you wear glasses? To change the world."

He took them off. His eyes were bright green, like his father's. "No, that's what I'm trying to tell you. I don't just wear them because I like old stuff. I actually . . . I need them."

"No one needs glasses anymore."

"Trust me." He squinted at me. "Without them, I can barely tell whether your eyes are open or shut."

"I don't get it. Why not get your eyes fixed?"

"I don't know. I guess wearing them reminds me of my mom. Like it's what she would have wanted."

That was . . . I didn't want to think it, but that was sick. "What if you got sick or something?" I asked. "Would you not do anything about *that*? Would your mother want you to—" *Die,* I was going to say. But I didn't. Because for all I knew, that's what had happened to her. "—just stay sick?"

"Of course not! I'm not crazy. It's just this one thing. Just the eyes," he said. "So, I guess you think it's pretty weird."

"Well . . ." I had the feeling he didn't want me to lie. "Yeah. *Very*. But maybe I get it. A little."

"I should go," he said, opening the car door.

"Where? Your father said . . ."

"Yeah. I know what he said. But it's my house, too. And"—he shrugged—"not like I have anywhere else to be."

I probably should have stayed—or invited him to come with me. But I was supposed to be home for dinner, and I couldn't picture bringing him along. Meals were bad enough without a stranger at the table, watching us not speak to one another.

I let him out of the car. "Good luck," I said, even though he was just going home.

"You too." Even though I was doing the same.

I saw Auden at school after that, but we didn't talk much, not like before. Not that I was avoiding him or anything. We just . . . didn't. Talk. And there were no more "experiments."

Then a few nights later, I came home, linked in, and: ACCOUNT TERMINATED.

That was it. Two words flashing red across a blank screen. They linked to a text from Connexion, the corp that carried my zone.

A determination has been made that the owner of this account, Lia Kahn, is for all intents and purposes deceased. Although Connexion acknowledges that the entity now designated as "Lia Kahn" retains legal rights to the identity under current law, the corporation has been afforded a wide latitude in this matter. As of today we will no longer extend continuing access to recipients of the download process. As per standard protocol in cases of the deceased, when the next of kin has made no request for continuing access, the account of Lia Kahn has been deleted. We apologize for any inconvenience this may have caused. Have a nice day!

It was gone. All of it. My pics, my vids, my music, every voice and text I'd ever received or sent, every mood I'd recorded, everything I'd bought, read, watched, heard, played, all gone. Any evidence of the friends I'd had or the relationship I'd walked away from. Gone. The av I'd hidden behind since before I was old enough to pronounce the word. Gone. Proof that Lia Kahn had ever lived—still lived. Gone.

Terminated.

I panicked.

Which I guess is why I didn't scream for my father, who could probably have voiced someone at Connexion and bullied them into giving back what they'd stolen from me. I just linked into a public zone, I voiced Auden, and I told him I needed him.

Then I sat on the edge of my bed, waiting, wondering what I'd been thinking, and whether he would come and what good it would do if he did, and whether I should voice him again and tell him to forget it. And I tried not to think about how my entire life had been deleted.

Psycho Susskind nudged his head against my thigh, then started licking my hand. He rolled over, and I rubbed my fingers along his belly, knowing he would pretend to enjoy it for a minute, then twist around and snap at me, tiny fangs closing down on the heel of my hand. He did, and I let him. "Think I liked it better when you hated me, Sussie." But I scratched him behind his ears, and I let him curl up on my lap.

Auden showed up. Zo let him in, which was lucky, because it meant no explaining. She didn't talk to me any more than she had to, which worked for me. So Auden was alone when he stepped into my room, hesitantly, with that look on his face that guys get when they think you're going to cry.

Even though he knew I couldn't cry.

"It's all gone," I said, even though I'd already told him. "They wiped me."

"It's just your zone." He stayed in the doorway, his eyes darting around the room, like he was trying to memorize everything in case the lights suddenly failed—or in case he never got to come back.

"It's my *life*. And you know it."

If I could cry, that's when I would have done it. But instead I hunched over and covered my face with my hands. He sat down next to me, his hands clasped in his lap, like he was afraid of touching me. He'd done it before, but maybe that was why he didn't want to do it again. Who wanted to touch the dead girl?

"It could be worse, Lia."

"Is that supposed to be *helpful*?"

"No, I just mean . . ." He turned red. "I meant that this is bigger than just losing your zone, and maybe you're lucky that's all it was. Connexion's not the only corp that's trying this. I read there was this one guy who almost lost all his credit when—"

"I don't give a shit about some guy!" I exploded. "This is about *me*!"

Even I knew how hateful that sounded. But I couldn't take it back.

"What's going on?" he asked quietly.

"I'm pretty sure I just told you."

"There's something else, right? More than just the zone?"

"Like that's not enough?"

And here's the thing. That *was* enough. Maybe it was a little shallow to feel like my whole life was wrapped up in my zone, but that's how I felt. The network was the only place where I could pretend I was normal. Hidden behind my av, no one would guess what I really was. Losing it all like that, without warning? It was enough to be upset about.

Except that maybe he was right. There was more.

"Come on," he said. "What?"

"It's just . . . They said they terminated the account because I was dead. I mean, because Lia Kahn was dead, and I was . . . something else." I held my hand up in front of my face. It was so strange, the way I could hold it like that, without trembling, for hours. And I knew I could: We'd done an experiment. "I didn't tell you"—I hadn't told anyone—"but this guy was here. A while ago. This guy named Rai Savona."

"Such an asshole."

I should have known Auden would recognize the name. He knew everyone in politics; he actually cared. Yet another weirdness.

"He was here to—Well, it doesn't matter. But he said . . ." I didn't know why it was so hard to talk about. Maybe because the guy had made a pretty good argument. And maybe once Auden heard it, he wouldn't disagree.

"Everything that guy says is a joke," Auden said. "You should ignore it on principle."

"Is that what your mother would have done?" As soon as it was out I wanted to take it back.

"She believed, but she wasn't a Faither," he said in a monotone. "And I'm not her."

"He said I wasn't human, okay? He said I was just programmed to *think* I was human, but humans had free will, and all I had was programming." It sounded even worse out loud than it had echoing in my head.

Auden raised his eyebrows and tilted his head, like, *Is that all?* "So what?"

"So . . . what if he's right?"

"Do you *feel* like you're programmed to act in a certain way?"

"Well . . . no," I admitted. "But he said that didn't matter. That I could be fooled into thinking I was free, but really I'm not."

"He's right."

I'd thought I had prepared myself for the worst, but when it happened, I knew I'd been wrong. Auden kept going.

"But it's true for him too. And for me. How do you know that I have free will? How do *I* know that I have it? Yeah, I feel like I make my own decisions, but who knows? He's the one who thinks God is in charge. How does he know God isn't jerking him around like a puppet? How does he know we aren't all just machines made out of blood and guts and stuff?"

"It's not the same." I knocked the side of my head. "There's no blood in here. No guts. Just a computer. It's not the same."

"No, it's not the same," Auden agreed. "But maybe it's better."

"Yeah, how?"

"You mean aside from the whole immortality thing?"

"Aside from that." Why did no one seem to get that living forever was only a good thing if life didn't suck?

Except you uploaded last night, an annoying voice in my head pointed out. *And the night before that.* No matter how crappy my life got, it was still my life. And sometime in the last couple weeks—sometime after meeting Auden, I tried not to think—life had become worth preserving again. Maybe even worth living. Too bad I still wasn't sure I could call it that.

If even I wasn't sure this counted as life, how could I expect anyone else to be?

"All that stuff you complain about," he said slowly. "Not feeling things the same way? Maybe it's a good thing. You don't have to get so screwed up by how you feel, like the rest of us do."

"'Us' humans, you mean?"

"I *mean*, maybe it's not a bad thing to have some control

216

over your emotions. To be able to *think* once in a while instead of just act on animal instinct."

Human instinct, I thought but didn't say. *Computers think; humans feel.*

But he was trying to help.

"You think I don't get it," he said. When I was actually thinking how weird it was that he got me so well. "So maybe you should talk to someone who does."

"I am *not* going back to that so-called support group." I'd told him all about Sascha and her little losers club. "No way."

"I wasn't talking about the support group. Not the official one, at least."

"Oh." I'd told him about the rest of it too. The girl with the blue hair and the boy with the orange eyes. The silver skin. The house filled with living machines who wanted me to be just like them. But I hadn't told him everything. I hadn't told him about the knife. "Not there, either."

"You have to go back sometime," he said.

"Why?"

"Aren't you curious?"

"Not really."

"Okay." But I could tell he knew I was lying. "But I don't think that's why you're staying away."

"Tell me you're not shrinking me again."

"I think you're scared."

"Am not," I said like a little kid.

"Are so," he said, playing along.

"Am *not*."

"If you say so." He shrugged, and then turned to the screen. "You want to get started?"

"What?"

"Signing up for a new account with a different corp. Creating a new zone. Building a new av. Isn't that why I'm here?"

I flopped back on the bed. "What's the point? They'll probably just come up with some excuse to take it away from me again."

"You know what av stands for?" Auden asked weirdly.

"Avatar. I'm not stupid."

"Yes, but do you know why it's called that?"

"I'm guessing you're going to tell me," I said. More old stuff. Like the past ever helped anyone make it in the future.

"It's Sanskrit for—"

"I don't know what that is."

"A dead language," he said. "Really, really old. And 'avatar' is Sanskrit for 'God's embodiment on Earth.'"

"So?"

"So maybe, if you think about it, you're kind of like an avatar," he stammered. "Like, the ultimate avatar. You know? This incredible body that's been created as a vessel for Lia Kahn. Your embodiment on Earth."

"So you think my body's incredible?" I asked, smirking. Sometimes I went on autoflirt. Force of habit.

He blushed so hard I thought his blood vessels might actually burst. "That's not—"

"I know," I said quickly. "It was just . . ." Tempting to imagine that someone could still think of me that way. Even if it was only Auden. "Let's do it," I said. "New zone. New av. New everything."

JUMP

"You'll never be the same."

I'll go with you," Auden offered the next time we had what I soon began to think of as the Conversation.

"No, you won't," I said, "because I'm not going."

"Stop saying I'm scared!" I insisted for the hundredth time the following week. "There's nothing to be scared of."

But all that got me was a smug smile. "That's what I keep trying to tell you."

"It's not like I need more friends," I tried later. "I've got you, don't I? That's enough."

"Your flattery is embarrassingly transparent," he said. "Don't think it's going to work." But I could tell by the pink glow on his cheeks that it had.

"Why do you care so much?" I finally asked after one Conversation too many.

"Because I know, deep down, you want to go."

"Except I don't," I pointed out. "So try again."

"Okay . . . Maybe, deep down, *I* want to go."

That was a new one. "Why?"

"Aren't I allowed to be curious?" he asked. "You keep telling me I can never understand what it's like to be a mech-head without actually *being* one. Fine. But maybe this is the next best thing."

"You're serious?"

He crossed his arms and nodded firmly.

"You really want me to go, just so that *you* can go?"

He nodded again. "Consider it a personal favor."

I wasn't sure if he was telling the truth or if this was just his way of letting me change my mind without admitting that, deep down, I couldn't stop wondering about the house of freaks and their fearless freak leader.

"Okay," I said. "We'll go. But only because you asked nicely. And because I'm sick of you asking at all."

Auden grinned. "Whatever you say."

We took Auden's car. The coordinates Quinn gave me led us to a deserted stretch of road about an hour from his house, just a strip of concrete bounded on each side by a dark and desolate stretch of trees.

"You sure about this?" Auden asked as we parked the car on the shoulder and set out into the woods.

"*Now* you want to turn back?" *Say yes,* I thought.

"I guess not," he said.

We disappeared into the trees.

The night was black. Auden led the way, silhouetted against the beam of the flashlight. We followed the GPS prompts, hurrying along the narrow, bumpy path, twisting through the trees, ducking under branches, Auden shivering despite his thermo-reg coat. I couldn't feel the cold.

"You sure we're not lost?" I asked.

He peered down at his dimly lit ViM. "According to the GPS, we're almost—" He froze as the trees gave way to a riverbank dotted with people.

No, not people.

Skinners.

Although, in the dark it was harder to tell the difference.

They were lying in the grass, their flashlight beams playing against the trees, the water, the dark canopy of the sky. Beyond the treeline the night glowed with a pale, reddish light, just bright enough to cast flickering shadows on the fringes of my vision. As if, while watching, we were being watched.

Auden was still shivering. "Maybe we should—"

"Let's do this," I said, and started toward the group. He followed, careful to stay a few steps behind.

Most of them ignored us, but a few figures climbed off the ground as we arrived.

"No way," one of them said, a tall, slim guy I didn't recognize. "You can stay, but *he* goes."

"Lia, you shouldn't have." Quinn appeared at my side and leaned in, her lips brushing my ear. "He's not supposed to be here," she whispered.

"This place is just for us," a girl's voice said. I thought it was Ani—especially when she threaded her arm through Quinn's—although it was too dark to see whether or not her hair was blue. "It's all we've got." She jerked her head toward Auden. "*They* get everywhere else."

Jude stood in the middle of the pack, silent. Watching.

Auden inched closer to me. "Maybe I should get out of here, let you—"

"You're staying," I said. "He's staying. And he's not a *they*." Just like I wasn't an *us*.

"He's an org," the first guy said. "He doesn't belong here. And if you can't get that, neither do you."

"He goes, I go."

The guy shrugged. "Fine."

"She stays," Jude said suddenly. His voice was deeper than I remembered. "They both do."

There was no more argument.

After his pronouncement Jude wandered away. We were good enough to stay, but apparently not good enough to talk to. They all ignored us, except for Quinn and Ani, who sat down again, tangling their legs together. We joined them.

This is it? I thought. Some lame, food-free picnic in the woods?

Quinn did most of the talking, at least at first. Everything was new to her; everything was exciting. Life was amazing. Wonderful. She couldn't get enough. I wanted to dig up a couple clumps of grass and cram them in my ears. Or, better yet, in her mouth.

Finally I couldn't stand it anymore. "So, Ani, what about you?" I asked. "What's your story?"

She looked uncomfortable. "I . . . I'm not sure what you mean."

"Why the download?" I asked. "What happened to you?"

"I . . . uh . . ."

"We don't ask those questions here." Jude loomed over us, his face hidden in shadow. "The past is irrelevant."

"Typical," Auden muttered.

"What?"

"I said, *typical*," Auden said, louder. "That you would think the past doesn't matter. It's a common mistake."

Jude sat down; Ani and Quinn leaped aside to make room for him. It should have made him less intimidating, down on our level. But somehow it had the opposite effect. Maybe it was those glowing eyes. "The past is irrelevant to *us*," he said, stretching his legs out and resting back on his elbows. "What we *were* has nothing to do with what we *are*. Not that I'd expect an org to understand that."

"Speak for yourself," I said. "I'm the same person I was."

Jude laughed.

"I think what Jude's trying to say is that the sooner you forget about your org life, the sooner you can realize the full potential of being a mech," Quinn said, darting a glance at Jude. He gave her a small smile. She beamed.

"This is why I didn't want to come," I murmured to Auden.

Jude leaned forward. "Then why did you?"

"None of your business."

"Maybe you got bored pretending you still fit in to your tiny, claustrophobic org life," he suggested. "You're looking for a better way."

"Better?" I sneered. "If this is so much better, if you're all so superior, then why doesn't *everyone* want to be a skinner?"

Ani gasped.

"We don't use that word here," Jude said quietly. "We're *mechs*. And proud of it."

There was a long pause.

"Sorry," I said, only because I felt like I had to.

"As for your question, I don't *care* whether your rich bitch friends recognize my superiority. Some of us can make judgments for ourselves, without just valuing whatever the masses decide is cool that minute."

"I don't—"

"But don't worry," he said. "Even the rich bitches will catch on. Sooner than you think."

I stood up. "*This* rich bitch is leaving."

"So soon? Such a shame."

"All that crap about embracing potential, and *this* is what you come up with? A supersecret society that meets at midnight to—What? Sit around in the mud, gossiping? Lucky, lucky me to get a membership. I'll pass."

Jude shook his head. "You really don't understand anything, do you? This is just the staging ground. You can go if you want, but you'll be missing the main event." He stood up too. We stared at each other, and for a moment it felt like we were alone in the night. Then he shouted. "Ready?"

As one, the skinners—*mechs*—stood up and began walking along the riverbank. I looked at Auden, who shrugged. "We've come this far," he pointed out.

We hung back, but followed the group along the river, tramping through the mud for a little over a mile, a rumbling in the distance swelling to a roar, until we finally rounded a bend in the river—and stopped short at the edge of a cliff. The river tumbled over the side, thundering down the rocks into an explosion of whitewater below. Far, far below.

"It's a forty-foot drop," Jude said. He peered down the falls. "Eighty thousand gallons of water per second. Welcome to your new life."

The other mechs—there were seven of them—lined up along the edge.

"What are they doing?" I shouted, over the roar of the water. "Are you all insane?"

"It's incredible, Lia!" Quinn shouted back. "You'll love it."

I shook my head. "They're going to kill themselves."

"Not possible," Jude said. "They—we—can't die. Can't drown. So we get a little bashed up on the way down. Trust me, it's worth it."

Someone jumped.

One moment there were seven shadowy figures standing on the rim, the next, there were six. And a human-shape form disappeared into the churning water. I didn't hear a scream.

A moment later two more leaped into the air. They were holding hands.

"You're more durable than an org," Jude said. "This won't hurt you—not much, anyway. Although, I should warn you, it *will* hurt."

"So what the hell is the point?" I asked. Another mech took the jump.

And then there were three.

"The *pain* is the point," Jude said. "At least for some of them. For others, it's the rush. Like adrenaline or Xers, only better. Intense feelings—intense *pain*—it's the only kind that feels real. And for some of us . . ." He paused, just long enough to make it clear that he was talking about himself. And maybe about me. "It's about facing the fear—and conquering it. Mastering all those sordid animal instincts and rising above them. And having a hell of a good time on the way. Don't tell me you're not tempted."

I looked over the edge, just as Quinn and Ani jumped, their arms around each other's waists. Way down at the bottom, I could see the water churning, but not much else. It was too dark to pick out any individual features, like bobbing swimmers. If any had survived.

"You can't actually be thinking about doing this," Auden said. "It's crazy."

"Crazy for *you*," Jude snapped. "You're not like her."

"And *she's* not like you," Auden said.

"Don't hold her back just because you can't move forward."

"Better I should let her jump off a fucking cliff?"

That was enough. "No one *lets* me do anything!"

Auden rubbed the rim of his glasses. "Lia, I'm just saying—"

"If *I* were an uninvited guest," Jude said. "I'd keep my mouth shut."

"Would you both shut up!" I shouted. "I need to think." They opened their mouths, but I walked away before either of them could start arguing again.

There was no one left on the edge of the falls. There was just me and the rushing water.

I'd never been much of a swimmer.

It was crazy. *Jude* was crazy. But what he'd said about the rush, about the pain . . . It made sense. Sascha had said the same thing about strong sensations flooding the system, fooling it into accepting them as real. Maybe it wouldn't matter that I had no goose bumps, no heartbeat—not when I was plunging over a forty-foot drop with eighty thousand gallons of water slamming me into the rocks. There wouldn't be time to notice what was missing. There would only be the body, the water, the fall. The fear.

To feel something again, to *really* feel . . .

I peered down, trying to imagine launching myself off the solid ground. I would bend my knees. Flex my ankles. Shut my eyes. Then in one fluid motion thrust myself up on my toes, off

228

the edge, into the air, arms stretched up and out, and for a long moment, maybe, it would feel like flying.

Then I would smash into the water. And together, the water and I, we would crash to the bottom.

I can't die, I whispered to myself, testing the words on my tongue. They still didn't seem real. *I can do this.*

I *wanted* to do it.

A hand wrapped around mine. "We can go together," Jude said. "On three. You won't be sorry."

I didn't say anything. I didn't move.

"One . . . two . . ."

I ripped my hand away. And then I jumped—the wrong way. Into the shallow pool trapped behind a ridge of rocks, just before the falls. The water was nearly still, and I let myself sink to the bottom, settling into the packed mud. Everything was a murky black. And silent.

It was the first time I'd been underwater since the accident. I could stay there forever, I realized, hiding out. Because I didn't need to breathe.

I had never felt more free.

I had never felt less human.

I launched myself off the bottom and exploded out of the water, scrambling onto dry land, soaking. Auden tore off his coat and wrapped it around my shoulders. I let him, although I wasn't cold. And he was still shivering. I grabbed his hand without thinking and squeezed tight. It was so warm, so human. I didn't want to let go.

Jude watched, disgusted.

"We're leaving," I told him.

"This is a mistake."

"This *was* a mistake," I said. "I'm fixing it."

Jude came closer, close enough that I could see his eyes flashing, his silvery hair glinting in the dim moonlight. "You don't belong with him. With them. You're strong, they're weak. *He's* weak."

"You're wrong," I said.

"Tell yourself that if it helps."

"What do you even care?" I asked. Auden squeezed my hand.

"I don't. But I can't stand waste." Without warning Jude's hand shot out and gripped our wrists, tight enough that I couldn't pull away. "And you're wasting your time, pretending that the two of you are the same." Something flashed in his other hand. The gray metal of a knife. "Don't believe me?" Jude's grasp tightened. He dragged the edge of the blade across my palm, then Auden's.

Auden gasped. Blood beaded up along the narrow cut, then dripped across his skin, thin red rivulets trickling from his hand to mine.

I didn't bleed. The knife had barely punctured the artificial flesh, and the shallow scratch was already disappearing as the material wove itself back together. Self-healing. Whatever pain there'd been in the moment was already gone.

Jude let go.

A moment later, so did Auden.

"You can pretend all you want," Jude said, looking only at me, talking only to me. "But you'll never be the same."

Auden walked me to my door. We had driven home in silence.

"I'm sorry that was so . . . I'm sorry I made you go," he said as we stood on the stoop. I wasn't ready to go inside.

"No. I'm glad we did."

"Liar." We both laughed, which helped, but only a little.

Auden rested his hand on my arm. "Lia, what that guy said, it's not true."

"No. I know." I ducked my head. He rubbed his hand in small circles along my arm, which was still wet. "He's crazy. They all are."

"Especially him," Auden said with a wide-eyed grimace that made me laugh again, harder this time.

"Thanks for coming with me. Really. I'm glad we went. At least now I know. And"—it was the kind of thing I usually hated to admit, but for some reason I didn't mind admitting it to him—"I couldn't have done it alone."

"Like I would have let you."

I gave his chest a light shove. "Like you could have stopped me."

"He was right about one thing, you know," Auden said quietly. "You are strong."

I didn't know what to say.

So I hugged him. His arms closed around me. I shut my eyes and pressed my face against his chest, imagining I could hear his heartbeat. Imagining I could hear mine.

"What's this for?" he asked, his voice muffled. I wasn't sure if it was because my ear was against his coat or his lips were against my hair.

"For nothing. Everything. I don't know." I held on.

But I opened my eyes. And over his shoulder, I raised my hand to where I could see it, still spattered with Auden's blood.

"Lia, there's kind of something I've been wanting to—"

"I should go inside," I said, letting go.

He backed away, and locked his hands behind his back. "Right. Well, good night."

Auden left quickly, but I didn't go inside, not that night. I'd learned my lesson about taking care of myself, and I'd been following a normal schedule—an *org* schedule, Jude probably would have said, his lip curling in disgust—shutting down for at least six hours every night. But not that night.

That night I sat outside, leaning against the front door, eyes open, wide awake as the reddish glow of night faded to the pinkish glow of a rising sun, remembering the thunder of the water, wondering what might have happened if I'd had the nerve.

If I had jumped.

TURNING BACK

"Maybe I wasn't programmed to want."

I hate it," I told Auden as we walked to class. The hallway was mostly empty, but not empty enough.

"What?"

"The way they all stare at me."

"No one's—"

"Spare me," I said.

"Okay. They're staring. But at least they notice you," he said. "Would you rather be invisible?"

I didn't want to tell him that he *wasn't* invisible, that all those people he hated were perfectly aware of his existence. They just chose to ignore it. "Let's blow this off," I suggested.

Auden looked doubtful. "And go where?"

"Who cares? Anywhere but here."

"We only have a couple more hours to get through . . ."

Since when did a couple hours of hell qualify as *only*? "Whatever. You stay. I'm going." I turned on my heel and headed quickly down the hall, but not so quickly that he couldn't catch up, which he did after a couple steps. He always did.

"You win," he said. "Where to?"

"Out." I pushed through the door at the end of the hall, wishing I could smell the March air. It no longer got much warmer as winter shifted to spring, but there was still something different in the air, something sweeter—fresher. Or maybe that's just how I like to remember it. "Then we'll come up with something."

But we wouldn't.

The exit we'd chosen was tucked at the end of a mostly unused corridor and opened into the alley behind the school, usually packed with delivery trucks, repair units, garbage compactors, and the steady trickle of students who'd elected to seek their education elsewhere for the day and preferred to do so without getting caught. But that afternoon it was empty except for a couple groping each other against the brick wall, her tongue shoved into his mouth, her back to the wall with her shirt creeping up to expose a bare, flat middle while his hands pawed her skin, snaking beneath her skirt. His fingers found her neck, her arms, her abs, her hair; hungry, grasping, needing, she sighed, he groaned, they breathed for each other. I couldn't see their faces.

I didn't need to.

I recognized the sound of him first, eager panting punctuated every so often by unprompted laughter, like a little kid, like an unexpected joy had overwhelmed him. I recognized his hands. Especially the way they crept beneath the skirt, massaging bare thigh.

It took a moment longer to identify her, although it shouldn't have, even without her face. I knew her arms, her legs, her sighs, her lanky blond hair. I'd just never known them like this. Or maybe I didn't want to know.

I let the door slam behind us.

They sprang apart. Walker looked up. Gasped. My sister took a deep breath and opened her eyes.

She looked like she'd been waiting for me.

I couldn't look at them. I couldn't look at Auden, either. I couldn't stand the idea of him—of anyone—seeing me see *this*. I wanted to run the scene backward, slip back into the school, back to the hallway, back to class, like none of it had ever happened. Some things were better not to know.

Because once you knew, there wasn't much choice. You had to deal.

Somehow.

"I'm sorry," Walker said. His hand was resting on her lower back. Like he was trying to keep her steady. *Her.*

"It just happened," he said.

"I didn't want to hurt you," he said.

He was still touching her.

"I don't know how it started," he said.

Enough.

"*I* know." My voice was steady. That was easy. My legs

weren't shaking. My stomach wasn't heaving. My heart wasn't pounding. I was steady. "You shoved your tongue into her mouth. My *sister's* mouth. That's how it started."

"You're wrong," Zo said. And she was steady too. "I shoved my tongue into *his* mouth. That's how it started."

"Zo," he said, like he was pleading. "Don't."

"Why not?" she said. "Aren't you sick of this? How long were we supposed to wait?"

"How long?" I didn't want to know what the words meant.

I knew what the words meant.

"How long, Walker?" I asked.

He looked down. So this wasn't the first time. "After the accident . . ."

I wished for a stomach, so I could throw up. But there was no way of getting it out. It was all inside of me, stuck. Rotting.

"I was upset, and she was upset, and it helped to, you know, talk. To each other. And one day, we . . . we just . . . It wasn't supposed to happen."

"So, just to be clear. I almost *died*," I said, still calm, still steady, "and while I was learning how to walk again, fighting to *survive*, you were back here, *fucking my little sister?*"

"We weren't doing that." Zo paused. "Not then."

"This is disgusting," I said. "You're disgusting."

"Lia—"

Zo put her hand on his arm, and he stopped talking. Apparently she was the boss. I'd taught her well. "I told you this would happen," she said quietly. "Just let it go."

"Oh, you *told* him this would happen?" I laughed bitterly. "What, that I'd have the nerve to get upset about my boyfriend screwing my sister?"

"I'm not your boyfriend anymore, Lia. You made that clear."

"Lucky you, right?" I spat out. "So you could ditch me and go back to the one you really wanted." Now it made sense. Why he hadn't wanted to touch me, why he hadn't wanted to be with me. Why he hadn't wanted me. Maybe it wasn't me.

It was *her.*

"We stopped for you," he said. "I was willing to try. I told you that."

Right. Because he pitied me.

"Give him a break," Zo said. "You don't know what he was willing to give up for you."

"I guess I do know, now," I said. *"You."*

I didn't ask if they actually thought they were in love. I didn't have to. I didn't care.

"Why?" I asked. Not Walker; he wasn't worth it. I asked her.

"I don't know," she said lamely. "It just happened." But she was lying, I knew that. Nothing "just happened" to Zo. It wasn't the way she ran her life.

I didn't have to push it. I could let this be like all the other times, when I just let it go, when I pretended things between us were the same as before, that she was just being Zo, nothing more, nothing less. I could keep pretending.

Except I *couldn't* keep pretending. Not anymore.

"I mean, why do you hate me this much?"

Her expression didn't change. "I don't hate you."

"You've got a weird way of showing it."

"What do you want from me?" Zo asked. "You want me to give him up? For *you*?"

That would be a start.

"Blood is thicker than water, right?" she said, her lip curling into a sneer.

"Well, yeah."

"Then show me," she said flatly.

"What?"

"Your blood."

The anger was a flood, drowning my words.

"I can't believe you," I finally choked out. "Literally, I can't believe this is happening. You're my *sister*. How the hell can you do this to me?"

"It's not my fault he doesn't want you anymore. None of this is my fault."

"It's all your fault!" I screamed. "*You* should have been the one in that car. It should have been *you*!"

The world froze.

I'd never said it out loud before. I'd promised myself. I wouldn't say it, I wouldn't think it, I wouldn't feel it. I *would not* blame her. I wouldn't process the ifs. *If* she'd been in the car, *if* she'd died that day instead of me. I would still have my body. I would still have my boyfriend. I would still have my life.

I couldn't take it back.

Walker put an arm around her shoulder.

"Sorry to disappoint you," she said slowly, her voice cold. "But it wasn't me. It was you." I didn't know what she was thinking. We were sisters, but I never knew what she was thinking. She wrapped her arm around Walker's waist. "Let's go," she murmured. He nodded.

"I'm sorry," he said again, over his shoulder as they walked away.

She never turned back.

I don't know how I ended up on the ground. But suddenly that's where I was, sitting with my back to the wall, only a few feet from where they'd been kissing.

Auden sat next to me. I still couldn't look at him. Not that I wanted him to go—but I didn't want him to stay, either. I didn't want anything except to not know. My brain was a computer: It should have been possible to delete.

"He's not good enough for you," Auden said finally.

I wanted to laugh. Such a lame cliché. True—but still lame.

"And your sister . . . You know she didn't mean what she said."

"She meant it," I said flatly. Zo had only told one lie that afternoon—that she didn't hate me. Because obviously she did. Fine. That made us even.

"Okay, so she's a bitch and he's an asshole." Auden looked hopeful. "Does that help?"

I had to laugh. "No. But thank you."

"Do you think— No, never mind."

"What?" I asked.

"It's none of my business."

"Auden, I think we've just established you're the only one I've got. So if it's not your business, then whose would it be?"

"I was just wondering . . ." He hesitated. "I mean, you're obviously upset."

"You noticed."

"Is it because you still . . . I mean, if Walker wanted to get back together, would you . . . ?"

"You want to know if I'm still in love with him?" I asked.

He nodded. "But like I say, it's not really my business, so . . ."

"It's fine." I just wasn't sure how to answer. "I'm over him, I think," I said, and it felt true. "If he was with someone else, anyone but—" I couldn't say it out loud. Instead I lowered my head and pressed the heels of my hands over my eyes. "What he said, about being willing to try? He was. And what if he's the only one who . . . What if no other guy . . . I mean, who would want me like this?"

His hand brushed my neck, flitted to my shoulder, then disappeared. "He's not the only one."

"Whatever."

"No. Lia. I've been waiting to—I mean, I didn't know how—I have to tell you—" The hand was back, resting firmly on my shoulder this time, heavy. "He's not the only one who would. Want you. Like this."

Shit.

"Auden, you don't have to—"

But he wouldn't stop.

"I know you probably don't see me like that," he said, talking quickly, like if he paused for breath he wouldn't get himself going again, although I guess that was too much to ask for. "But I think you're amazing and when I'm with you, it's like we really understand each other, you know, and I think you're beautiful, you're more beautiful like this than you ever were before—"

Not now, I thought, furious with him, furious with myself. *Not now, when I* need *you. Don't do this.*

"I know I shouldn't say anything, I know, I always say something, I always ruin things, I should just let it happen, but I can't let you think that no one would—because I would, I do, I just . . ." His entire body had gone rigid. "What do you think?"

"I'm a little . . . This has been a weird day for me," I said, stalling. "You know, with—" I glanced toward the spot they'd been leaning against, where I imagined I could still see their afterimage bright against the bricks.

"I know." He shook himself all over. "I know. It was stupid. Bad timing."

Damn right. But, "No, it's okay."

"It's *not* okay. It's stupid. I shouldn't have thought—"

I kissed him.

Because he wanted me to. Because he *wanted* me. Because no one else did. Because he'd saved me, more than once.

Because why not?

And in the fairy tale that's it, the end, happily ever after.

In the fairy tale they never mention the part about your

tongues scraping against each other or your foreheads bumping or your nose getting bent and flattened or his tongue just sitting there in your mouth, limp and wet, and then spinning around like a pinwheel, bouncing back and forth between your fake palate and your porcelain teeth. In the fairy tale they never mention how it tastes, although to me it didn't taste like anything at all.

I'm not saying he was a bad kisser.

I'm not saying he was great, because he wasn't. But I'm not saying it was his fault, even though maybe it was. Or maybe it was mine.

I'm just saying it was bad.

Worse than bad. It was nothing. Like kissing my own balled-up fist, as I'd done for practice when I was a kid. I wanted not to care, to just go with it, because it would have been so easy, it would have made him happy, and it would have made me . . . not alone.

When our faces separated, he was smiling, his eyes glazed and dewy, his mouth half open, like he wasn't sure whether to speak or to lunge in for another round.

"I'm sorry," I said as gently as I could. "I can't."

"Did I do something wrong?"

"No!" I said quickly. "I just don't think it's a good idea."

He sagged, a deflated balloon. "I should have known you would never . . . not with me."

"It's not that," I said. "It's just too much right now."

"You don't have to say that," he said bitterly. "I know I'm not Walker. I do have a mirror, you know. I get it."

"It's *not* you." I wanted to touch him, to shake him. "Everything's so . . . screwed up. And I'm"—I gestured down at myself, at the body—"I'm different. *We're* different, and I don't think the two of us . . ."

"Is this about what that guy said? Jude?" Auden's fingers flickered across the bandage on his palm. "I told you, he doesn't know what he's talking about."

"It's not about what he said. It's what I know. This wouldn't work. And if it didn't . . ." Now I did touch him—I took his hand. He pulled away. "I don't want to mess this up, what we have. I can't risk that."

"Why not?" He was edging toward a whine. "If you really want something, sometimes it's worth taking a chance."

But what if you really *didn't* want something?

"It's not going to work, Auden."

"Because you don't *want* it to work," he snapped.

"Because it won't!" Why couldn't he just let it go? "Stop pushing it!"

"I know you're scared," he said. "I'm scared too. But we can try this together. We *can*."

I needed to make him stop. And I was pretty sure I knew how to do it.

"Why do you really want this so bad?" I asked in a low voice. "Is it me, or is it this stupid body?"

His eyes widened. "What?"

"Admit it, you're obsessed with what I am, with what it's like being a mech, with everything about it—"

"Because I'm your friend," he protested. "Because I care!"

"But that came later. You were obsessed before—before you even knew me. You couldn't stay away."

"So I was curious! So what? And you know I was just trying to help."

"Maybe—or maybe you've got some weird mech fetish. And you can't stop until you know how *everything* works, right?"

He drew himself up very straight and very still. "I can't believe you would say that."

I couldn't believe it either. And I couldn't keep going, even if it was the one thing guaranteed to drive him away. Because I didn't want him to go away. I just wanted him to shut up and leave it alone.

"I didn't mean it," I admitted.

"I would never . . ." I could barely hear him. "That's not who I am."

"I know."

Then neither of us said anything. We just sat with our backs to the wall and our shoulders almost, but not quite, touching.

"I shouldn't have pushed," he said, finally cutting through the dead air.

"I shouldn't have said that to you. That was cruel."

Another long pause.

"We would never have been friends, would we, if it weren't for your accident," he said, asking a question that wasn't a question. "We probably would have graduated without ever having a single conversation."

I kept staring straight ahead. "Probably."

"And even if we had talked . . ."

"You would have hated me," I said. "Shallow, superficial bitch, remember?"

"You wouldn't have bothered to hate me. It wouldn't have been worth it to you."

I didn't deny it.

"But I'm different now," I said. "Everything's different."

"I know. But would you keep it that way?"

"What do you mean?"

"If you had a choice, if you could go backward. Would you want to be the old Lia Kahn again, with your old life and your old friends—or stay like this, who you are now?" *Stay with me,* he didn't say, but it was all over his face.

"Auden—"

"Don't lie," he said. "Please."

I didn't even have to think about it. "I'd go back. Of course I'd go back."

"Even if it meant losing—"

"No matter what it meant," I said firmly. "If I could have my body back, my *life* back, don't you think I'd want it? No matter what?"

"No matter what." He stood up. "Good to know."

"Auden, that's not fair. You can't expect me to—"

"I don't expect anything."

"Don't go," I said. "Not like this."

"I can't stay," he said. "Not like this."

He left. I stayed. *Maybe I should have tried,* I thought. *Maybe it wasn't him. Maybe it was me.*

Before, rejecting guys had been easy—and I'd had a lot of practice. Before, I knew what it felt like when it felt right. I knew what I wanted. And I knew there would always be someone new who would want me.

Before.

He's just not my type, I thought. *Too scrawny. Too intense. Too weird.*

But I couldn't be sure. Walker was my type—and I didn't want him, either. Not really. Not anymore.

Maybe I wasn't programmed to want. Maybe that was just something else lost, like running, like music. Something else that had slipped through the cracks of their scanning and modeling. Maybe it was one of those intangibles—like a soul, like free will—that didn't exist, not physically, and so wasn't supposed to exist at all.

CONTROL
AND RELEASE

"Nothing was left but an absence."

The waterfall wasn't loud enough to drown out my thoughts. But it was a start. I found myself a wide, flat rock near the bank, a few feet from where the water plunged over the edge. The place looked different in the light. For one thing, you could see the bottom clearly. Which made it look even farther away. Beyond the rumbling white water, the river ribboned out flat and calm again, but not for long. There was another precipice, another plunge, another fall. From where I sat, I couldn't see whether it was as long or as deep; the river just dropped away. I took a pic—not of the second waterfall, but of the empty space beyond the river, the air where there should have been land. It was crap—a little crooked, like I'd tried an artistic shot and failed miserably when, in fact, I just hadn't cared enough to steady the lens. I posted it to my new zone anyway. Anything to fill up the empty space.

A mist rose from the gushing water. I was tempted to stand by the edge, wave my hand through the dewy cloud, but that seemed too close. I might have fallen in; I might have jumped. I stayed where I was, watching the water, trying not to think about Auden and Walker, and especially not about Zo.

But I couldn't help hoping that one of them might voice me to apologize, to tell me I'd misunderstood and the whole thing was a hideous mistake. One hour passed, then two. No one did.

"You probably shouldn't jump in the daylight. Too easy to get caught." Like the waterfall, Jude looked different during the day. Every silver streak, every black line etched into his skin, stood out in sharp relief. And seeing him against the pastoral backdrop made him look all the more machinelike.

"What are you doing here?" I asked, jumping up as he sat down.

"I should ask you that," he said. "Last I checked, this was my place."

"Oh, so now you own the river?"

"Sarcasm doesn't scare me. Fire away. I'm staying."

"Enjoy," I said. "I'm going."

"After I came all this way? I would have thought a girl like you would come equipped with better manners."

"So you're stalking me now? How'd you know I was here?"

"I know all." He smirked.

"I'm leaving."

"Okay, wait!" He spread his arms wide in truce. "Your zone, okay? You posted the pic. I recognized the view."

"You've been lurking on my zone?"

"What can I say? I have a lot of time on my hands," Jude said.

"Use it for something else," I snapped. "Stay out of my life."

"Maybe I don't want to. Maybe I think you're worth a little extra effort."

I couldn't believe it. Not another one. Not today. At least this time around I wouldn't have to worry about letting him down easy. "Look, I'm flattered—Well, I'm not, actually, but let's say I am. I'm not interested, okay? So—"

"You think *I'm* interested?" He burst into laughter. "You really are an egomaniac, aren't you? I mean, I knew you were spoiled and self-absorbed, that's par for the course. But this? Please. Trust me, I'm not into the chase. When I want something, it chases *me*."

And *I* was the egomaniac?

Still, I sat down again. He had some kind of agenda, that was obvious. And if it wasn't the expected one, that was interesting. Or at least interesting enough to distract me from the things that actually mattered.

"So why are you here?" I asked.

"Brought you something."

"What?" Like I cared.

"Just something to help you let go."

"What makes you think I have any interest in doing that?"

He smiled. "Because letting go, that's the key. If you're too scared to let go, you'll never be in control. Not really."

"Is that supposed to make sense?" I asked. "Let go so I can get control? Do you even listen to yourself talk, or do you just spit out this crap at random?"

"It's all connected," he said, so disgustingly pleased with himself. So sure. "People only fear letting go because they fear they won't be able to get the control back. That they'll keep going until their urges and instincts destroy them."

"But *you* know better?"

"I know you're afraid of what you've turned into, but only because you don't know what it is, not yet. And because you don't understand it, you think you can't control it."

"You're wrong."

"You're a *machine*," he said. "And that means absolute control—or, if you so choose, absolute release. You have the power to decide if you let yourself." He pulled something out of his pocket, small enough to fit snugly in the palm of his hand. "You wanted to know why I came looking for you? To give you this."

He tossed the object at me, and I caught it without thinking. It was a small, black cube with a tiny switch on one side and a slim, round aperture on the other. Harmless.

"It's a program," he said.

"For what?"

"For you. Or for your brain, at least. You can upload it wirelessly through your ocular nerve."

"That's not possible." No one at BioMax had said anything

about additional programming; no one had hinted that I might be able to . . . reprogram myself.

You have a computer inside your head, the Faith leader had said. *Programmed by man.*

Normal people—*human* people—didn't adjust their programming. They didn't rewire themselves with chips and wireless projections. They just changed. Or they didn't.

"Anything's possible if you know the right people," Jude said smugly, like he said everything.

"What's it do?"

"Let's call it a vivid illustration of my point."

I faked a laugh. "You want me to stick something in my brain based on *your* predictably vague recommendation?"

"I don't care what you do," Jude said, and the way he said it, I almost believed him. Not that it mattered. "Think of it as a dream."

"We don't dream."

He gave me a knowing smile. "Yes. That's what they told you."

"You're lying."

"Maybe," he said. "Only one way to find out. You say you're not afraid, right? Prove it."

I tossed his little black box back to him. "Just how stupid do you think I am?"

He smirked. "You really want an answer to that?"

"Excuse me for not just buying all your crap without question, like one of your brainwashed groupies."

"I don't have to brainwash them," Jude said. "They know the truth when they hear it."

"Unlike me?"

"Apparently."

"So that's what this is?" I asked. "You've made it your own personal mission to convert me?"

He laughed. It made him look like a different person. No, that's not quite right. It made him look like a *person*. "See what I mean?" he said. "Total egomaniac. You should really get that checked out."

"You're here, aren't you?" I pointed out. "Following me?"

"Maybe I was just in the mood to talk."

"To me?"

He looked around at the wilderness. "Seems like my only viable option."

I shrugged. "So talk."

"Let's start with: What's wrong?" he asked.

He almost sounded like he really wanted to know. Not that it mattered. "No. I'm not talking about me."

"Because?"

"Recovering egomaniac," I reminded him.

He grinned. "The first step is admitting you have a problem."

"And the second step is acknowledging that other people do too. So let's start with you. Why are you following me? *Really.*"

He shook his head. "No cheating. That's still about you."

"Fine. How about: Where do you live? What do you do

all day when you're not stalking me? How did you end up a mech—"

"I told you before," he said, the joking tone gone from his voice. "The past doesn't matter. All that matters is what I am now, and that's everything I want to be."

"Come on, how can you say that?"

"Easy. It's true." His eyes flashed.

Everything I wanted to be had died in that car crash.

"You really don't miss it?" I asked. "Not at all?"

He smiled wryly. "There's not much to miss. We weren't all like you."

"What's 'like me'?"

"Rich," he said, ticking it off on his fingers. "Treasured. Sheltered. Deluded."

"Is this fun for you? Insulting me every time you open your mouth?"

"A little."

I started to get up again, but he grabbed my arm. "Okay, I'm sorry," he said. "Don't go. Please." I glared, and after a moment he let go. But I sat down again.

"You think this is some kind of punishment," he said. And again it almost sounded like he cared. Or at least that he understood.

"I don't—"

"You *do*," he said. "Because you don't let yourself see the possibilities. All you can see is what you've lost."

Everything.

"Some of us didn't have that much to lose," he continued with less intensity than usual.

"You do realize you're being ridiculously vague, right?"

"You want something concrete?" he asked. "How about the way it feels to walk for the first time?"

There was something new in his voice, something ragged and unrehearsed, like he'd gone off his script and wasn't sure how to find his way back. He sounded like I felt: lost.

"Or to know that nothing can ever hurt you again, not for real?" he continued. "How about never having to be afraid?"

I was afraid all the time.

If he knew how that felt, if he could understand that and had found a way to fight back, maybe I'd been wrong about him. About it all.

"That's why, isn't it?" I said softly. "Why you don't talk about before."

He looked away. "I told you. The past is irrelevant for us."

"I'm not talking about *us*. I'm talking about *you*." Without knowing why, I wanted to touch him, to rest my hand on his hand, his knee, his shoulder. I wanted contact. "I'm talking about whatever happened to you. Want to talk, Jude?" I said. It wasn't a question, it was a challenge. "Talk about that. Talk about how you ended up here. How you're just like the rest of us." I paused, not sure I should keep going. And when I did, it was in a whisper. "Broken."

He raised his eyes off the ground and looked at me. "I'm *not* broken. And I don't need your pity."

Pity hadn't even occurred to me. Why would it when we were the same? "I'm not—"

"Save it for yourself," he said, his eyes flashing again, a yellow-orange that looked like flame. "Drown in it, for all I care. *I* don't need it. I know what I am. I'm *proud* of what I am."

"So that's why you did *this* to yourself?" I asked. "Turned yourself into some kind of . . ."

"Freak?"

"I wasn't going to say that."

"Because you're a coward," he said.

"Shut up."

"Afraid to say what you think. Afraid to do . . . *anything*. Afraid to accept the truth."

"Shut up."

"You can't face facts about what you've become, and so you're missing it."

I had never met anyone so disgustingly smug. "You don't know anything about me."

"I know enough," he said. "I know all you care about is what people think, and whether you look *cool*. Guess what? You don't. Not to *them*."

"Why are you so obsessed with all this us-and-them crap? There is no *them*. There is definitely no *us*."

"Why are you so determined to lie to yourself?" he retorted. "*They* know you're not one of them. When are you going to wake up?"

"What the hell do you want from me?" I shouted. It was too

much. It was too much for one day, too much on top of everything. I couldn't deal. I shouldn't have to. "You want me to walk away from everything, to pretend the past never happened and that I'm not the person I know I am?"

"That would be a start!"

"I'm not going to destroy myself." I tried to make my voice as cool and cutting as his. "Not for you. Not for anyone."

"That job's done. You don't have to do anything. Just acknowledge the wreckage and walk away."

I stood up—and this time, although he grabbed my arm again, I didn't hesitate. His fingers wrapped tight around my wrist. He was the only mech I'd ever touched. "Don't come looking for me again," I said. *"Ever."*

"Trust me," he said coldly. "I won't have to."

"I'm going now." I didn't move.

"I'm waiting." He was still holding my wrist.

"Screw you." And then, somehow, my hand was on his chest. His fingers tightened on my wrist. He yanked me toward him. Or I lunged. He grabbed my waist. Or I dug my hips into him. Whatever he did. Whatever I did. Our faces collided.

Our lips collided.

I clawed at his shirt, digging into the fabric, struggling for the fake, silvery skin that lay below. His lips were rough; his kiss was rough. Hard and angry, or maybe that was me, hating him, *wanting* him, wanting his hands on my body—anyone's hands on my body—even if it didn't feel the same, it felt right, it *felt*, for the first time since the accident and the fire and the darkness, I *felt*, and I sucked at his lips, and he bit down, a sweet, sharp pain, and I imagined I could taste the iron-tanged blood on my tongue.

But there would be no blood.

I shoved him away.

For the second time that day I wished I could throw up.

He came toward me; I jerked away.

"*Don't* touch me."

I couldn't believe I had done it.

I wanted to do it again.

I had to get away.

"Don't do this," he said, an edge in his voice. "Don't question it, not now, not when you're so close."

"To what?" I spat out. But I knew. To him. To grabbing him again. To his body. To our bodies, together.

To *feeling*.

I took another step back.

"To letting go," he said. I couldn't believe he was back to that, spewing his bullshit, like I was a dutiful member of his flock. "I told you, it's the key to accepting what you are—"

"Spare me." I hated him. This wasn't about me, I realized. Not for him. This wasn't about need, about raw *want*. Not for the high and mighty Jude, who'd risen oh so far above all those nasty org instincts. This was just about his stupid campaign. His pathetic philosophy. This was just about him being right. About me being wrong.

"Don't do this," he said again, closing his hands over mine. But I was done.

"Go." I felt as cold as I sounded.

"You don't want that."

I met his eyes. They were, as always, unreadable. Like mine. "You. Don't. Know. What. I. Want." Nice and slow, so he would understand.

"Maybe not." Jude shook his head. "But neither do you." He pressed something into my palm—the sharp-edged cube, the one he'd called a dream. "Not yet."

I looked down at the tiny black box, turning it over and over in my hands.

When I looked up again, he was gone.

I'm not stupid.

I wasn't stupid then, either.

I didn't trust him. I didn't trust his little black box or his mysterious "program" or his unshakable convictions. Least of all those.

On the other hand, I didn't have much to lose. And I had too much I wanted to forget.

I uploaded the program.

There was a brief burst of flickering light, then nothing.

For several long minutes, nothing.

Then the world started to glow.

Pain first. Pain everywhere. Nowhere. I was nowhere. It burned. I burned. Pain like the fire, pain like the flames peeling away my skin. Hot, searing hot. Then cold, like ice. Steel.

• • •

I was standing. I was spinning. I was lying on my back. I floated in the sky. Stars shot from my fingertips. Trees bowed at my feet. I was leaping off a cliff, I was in the water, in a whirlpool, sucked below. I was drowning. I was flying.

I was in the black. But the colors shimmered. They exploded from the dark. *I* was color. I was light. I pulsed green, I sang out purple, I screamed red. I cried blue. The monsters swarmed out of the deep. Spider tentacles and red eyes, and they wanted me to die, and I wanted to die, and I was death, black and empty, bottomless, null.

I would destroy them. I would destroy them all.

It began at the center of me, at the center of it all, small and warm and glowing, a sun, and it swelled. It grew. I tingled with its warmth. There were no words, not for this. This was beyond words. This was cool grass brushing a bare neck. This was dark-chocolate ice cream melting on a tongue. This was his body, heavy on mine, his breath in my mouth, his skin on my skin. It was everything, it was life.

It was over.

Nothing was left but an absence. And his voice, which I understood, as I came back to myself, was only in my head.

"If you're listening to this, I suppose that means I was right. You're welcome."

I was lying on my back. I didn't know how I'd gotten there. The sky looked close enough to touch, but I knew that was just the heavy, gray clouds. I reached out anyway. Nothing but air.

"You've just experienced an electrical jolt to your limbic system—or at least, the circuitry that mimics an organic limbic system. It overwhelmed all the mood-simulating safeguards, cycling through a random series of preprogrammed emotional stimuli. Take the most intense b-mod you've ever experienced, multiply it by a thousand, and— Well, I guess now you know what happens."

I closed my eyes. I felt like I had a headache, but that wasn't possible. I didn't get headaches, not anymore. Still, something felt swollen and tender. Fragile. Fuzzy. I wanted the voice to stop.

"Direct stimulation of the cortex is the best way to simulate intense emotion and sensation in mechs. It supplies you with the somatic responses you miss while conscious, all those nasty animal responses to emotion. Some say it makes you feel like an org again."

I had never felt so empty. I wanted it back, all of it. I needed it. I wanted to live in that world of darkness and light, where I had been frightened. Angry. Happy. I had been alive there, and I wanted to return. I wanted to stay.

"*I* say it's better than the orgs will ever know. And admit it or not, you agree."

I wanted him to shut up. I wanted him to keep going. I wanted him to come back, I wanted a body to match the voice, hands and shoulders and neck and lips. I hated myself for wanting it.

"See you soon."

IN THE DARK

"Touch me and I'll kill you."

What's this for?" Auden asked when I gave him the box wrapped in silver foil. He'd been avoiding me for days, but I finally cornered him at lunch. He'd found himself another secluded corner to hide in, far away from mine.

"I just wanted to," I said, feeling a little awkward. I couldn't say I was sorry, not really, because then we would have had to get into what I was sorry for. And neither of us wanted to touch that because we both knew: I was sorry for not wanting him the way he wanted me. But that meant I couldn't tell him the other part of the truth, that I needed him. It didn't matter if he was an org and I was a mech; it didn't matter what Jude thought. Jude who was like me, but didn't understand me at all. Who knew nothing.

Auden opened the box. He pulled out a gray bag with a

smart-strap that would heat up whenever a new message came in. The front flap had a full-size screen and the back doubled as a pocket and a keyboard, perfect—as the pop-up had said—for the stylish guy who needs to link on the go. Not that Auden was stylish, or did much of anything on the go, but it looked good. Definitely better than the ragged green sack he toted around everywhere. *I might not have been cool anymore, but my taste still was.*

He looked confused.

"Thought you could use a new one," I said.

Auden didn't take it out of the box. "You shouldn't have."

"I wanted to," I said again.

"Really, you shouldn't have." He sighed, and finally picked up the bag, flipping it open and glancing inside before placing it back in the box. He didn't even notice the smart-strap, much less the board and the screen. "But thanks, I guess."

It looked like the symbolic approach wasn't working. Did he not get that I was trying to spare him even more embarrassment? Shouldn't he be *grateful*?

Especially since, when you think about it, *he* was the one who should have been apologizing. I wasn't the one making unreasonable demands or throwing a temper tantrum when I didn't get what I wanted.

But I'd lost the moral high ground when I'd given in to Jude. Even if Auden didn't know—could *never* know—I knew.

"I'm sorry about before," I said. If he really wanted to talk about it, then fine. We'd talk.

"You don't have to—"

"I wish it hadn't happened."

"I shouldn't have said anything," he said.

"No, I'm glad you did." Lie. "We should be honest with each other." Lie number two. "And what I said? About wishing I could go back to the way things were before? I can't . . . I can't take that back. But, Auden, you have to know, you're the only good thing that's happened to me since the accident. The *only* thing." Truth.

Except for yesterday, some rebellious part of my brain pointed out. *Except for Jude. Except for what he did. And what he gave me.* But that was nothing. That was already forgotten.

Lie number three.

"You don't have to say that," Auden said.

"I do." I smiled nervously. "Are we okay? I really need us to be okay."

"Me too," he said, and gave me a tight hug.

Now or never, I decided. "So, now that we're friends again . . . any chance you want to do me a favor?"

Auden let go, laughing. "Now I get it. That wasn't a gift, it was a bribe."

"No! Well . . . maybe a little."

He sighed. "What do you need?"

"Jude and the rest of them are going out again tonight." I winced at the expression on his face, stranded somewhere between suspicion and disgust. "I want to go. I thought maybe you'd come with me."

"Back to the waterfall? Are you crazy?"

I shook my head. "They're doing something else tonight. I don't know what. It's some kind of big secret."

"Maybe you didn't hear me the first time: Are you crazy?"

"You're the one who talked me into going last time," I pointed out. "Remember all that stuff about facing up to my fears, meeting people who were like me and could understand what I'm going through?"

"Remember how it turned out that Jude was an asshole and all his little followers were daredevil nut jobs who thought killing themselves might be a fun way to pass the time?"

"They weren't trying to kill themselves," I said.

"They were doing a pretty good imitation of it."

"Auden, you know it's different for us."

"*Us?* Since when—"

"You know what I mean," I snapped. "It wasn't that dangerous. They were just having fun."

"Exactly. What kind of person thinks that's fun?" He scowled. "A seriously messed-up person. Or a person who can't think for himself."

"Or maybe a person who's not a person at all. Is that what you're trying to say?"

"No!" Auden sighed. "You know I don't think that way about you. I just don't get why you'd want to go back. What's the point?"

I wasn't sure why I wanted to go back.

It wasn't because I wanted another dose of whatever Jude had to give me. I'd promised myself it wasn't because of that.

"They're trying to test their limits," I told him, "and to explore the possibilities of this thing. To enjoy it a little. Is that so bad?"

"When did you start talking like that?" he asked.

"Like what?"

"Like . . . I don't know. Like *him*."

"Look, if you don't want to go with me, I'll go by myself," I said, annoyed. "No big deal."

"It is a big deal," he said. "Whatever they're doing, I'm sure it'll be dangerous. And stupid. I'm not letting you go by yourself."

"I don't need you to protect me," I said, even though that's exactly what I'd asked of him—and I'd asked knowing he would never be able to say no.

"Too bad. That's what you've got."

"What's the point?" Auden asked.

"Because we *can*," Jude said. "Because why not?"

Auden pulled me away from the group. He was still carrying his hideous green bag. "This is a bad idea."

"You're the one always talking about the people stuck living in the cities," I said. "Don't you actually want to *see* one?"

"Not like this," he mumbled. "Not by ourselves. At *night*." But I knew I had him.

There were ten of us, including me and Auden. Again, no one had wanted him to come along, but I'd insisted, and Jude had gone along with it. As before, everyone else went along with Jude.

"You can leave, if you want," I offered, and I was almost hoping he would take me up on it. I wanted him there, I did. But even I knew he didn't belong.

Auden shook his head. "You know the city people; they hate mechs more than anyone," he said. "Most of them die before they hit forty, and you're going to live forever. You really think that's a good combination?"

"I think Lia trusts me," Jude said, appearing behind us and resting his hand on my shoulder. I shook it off. "Maybe you should give her a little more credit."

I glared at him. "Don't touch me."

He just smiled. "I'll give you two a minute," he said. "We're leaving in five. Stay or go."

Once he was gone, Auden gave me a weird look. "What was that?"

"What?"

"The two of you."

"*What?*"

"Nothing." He headed back toward the group of mechs waiting for their field trip to begin. "Let's just go."

We took two cars. Jude and Auden sat in the front seat of ours, not talking. I squeezed into the back with Quinn and some guy whose name I didn't hear the first time—and didn't get much chance to ask a second time, since he spent most of the ride with his tongue down Quinn's throat. I looked out the window.

The skyline carved dark, jagged chunks out of the sky.

The car sped along swooping bands of concrete, a purposeless, unending sculpture of roads that dipped over and under one another, splitting, merging, crisscrossing; so much space and all of it empty. Even without the curfew no one would be stupid enough to enter a city at night. And no one who lived there had a car. That would have guzzled too much fuel; that would have made it too easy to get out.

We parked on a narrow street. Without a word Quinn and the other mech began collecting armfuls of debris from the gutter while Jude pulled a stained beige tarp from the trunk and draped it over the car. The gutter trash went on top.

"Best way to keep it safe," Jude explained. Across the street the passengers of the second car were doing the same.

It was eerily quiet. The dark buildings shot up on all sides, and I reminded myself that at least some of them were full of people, staying warm, staying dry, staying off the streets after curfew. But everything was so still and empty, it was hard to imagine that anyone was alive here. The group moved stealthily, stepping lightly, staying clustered in a pack. Only Auden breathed.

"What now?" I whispered.

"We look around," Jude said. "And we try not to get caught."

Caught by who? I wanted to ask. But I didn't really want an answer.

This city had been lucky. No major bombings, so no radioactive debris. Too far east for the Water Wars, too far north for the flooding. They'd gotten hit by the Comstock flu strain, but no worse than any of the other population centers, and in the last bio-attack, before the cities cleared out for good, they'd lost less than a million.

They'd been lucky.

Not lucky enough for anyone to stay, at least voluntarily, but that much was true for all the cities. Who would be crazy enough to stick around an energy-poor, germ-ridden death trap if they had enough credit to get the hell out?

We wandered down the broad, empty avenues, flashlight beams playing across the pavement. I tried to imagine what it would be like to live in a place where the lights went off two hours after sunset, where you could only link in once a day if you were lucky enough to find a screen that worked, where the punishment for energy theft was death.

I couldn't.

There wasn't enough to go around, I reminded myself. Of anything. There wasn't enough energy for everyone to stay wired all day, every day. There wasn't enough fuel or enough road for everyone to own cars. There weren't enough cows—at least not enough free-range, grass-fed cows, now that you weren't allowed to raise anything else—for everyone to eat meat. There wasn't enough space for everyone to have a kid. Either we would all have to suffer—or some would have to sacrifice.

I was just glad it was them and not me.

I was also glad my power cells were fully loaded. There was no wireless web of energy here, and if something happened, if I somehow got left behind, there would be nowhere to recharge. After a few days I would just . . . fade out.

"Those used to light up," Auden whispered in my ear, pointing at the thick, empty screens papered across almost every building. "Like giant pop-ups. Telling people what to buy."

"What a waste of energy," I whispered back. Maybe these people deserved to live in the dark.

Our feet crunched with every step. Crushed glass, I decided, as we passed broken window after broken window. Everything here was broken.

I wanted to go home.

A distant howl cut through the silence.

"What was that?" I whispered, freezing in place.

"Just a dog." Jude didn't bother to whisper. "Fighting it out for who gets to run the place. Like the rats and the roaches haven't already won." He turned sharply to the right, leading us down another wide avenue, its gutters flowing with trash. Auden was breathing shallowly and, for the first time, it occurred to me how the place must stink, with its mounds of garbage heaped on urine-stained pavement. "This way."

Two blocks later we heard the scream. High-pitched, piercing, it went on and on and—it stopped. It didn't fade away. It just stopped.

That was no dog.

We went deeper into the city, and I tried not to wonder how we would find our way out.

Jude stopped short in front of a building so tall it blotted out most of the sky. "Last stop for orgs," he said, staring at Auden.

Auden glared back. "Meaning?"

"Building's locked down, and all those biosensors . . ." Jude smirked. "You don't want to start panting and get us caught, now do you?"

"I'm supposed to wait out here while you . . . do what, exactly?"

"Just taking a look around. We'll be back before you get too scared."

"I'm not scared," Auden said fiercely.

Jude shrugged. "Great. Then you don't mind if we—"

"You're not going with them?" Auden half-said, half-asked, grabbing my arm.

I paused. "I don't have to. I can wait down here with you . . . if you want." I knew I should stay.

But I didn't want to.

"No." Auden closed his eyes for a moment. "You're the one who wanted to do this. So you should do it. All the way."

Jude chuckled softly. "Funny, she never struck me as an all-the-way kind of girl."

I ignored him.

"You sure?" I asked Auden.

"Yeah. Go." He gave me a weak smile. "Be careful."

"You too."

Jude and one of the other guys, the tall, brooding one named Riley, bashed open one of the doors, and we crept inside. It was even darker in there, a broad space smudged with shadows. A screen glinted in the beam of someone's flashlight, and then another and another. This is where the city people came to link in, I realized. It explained why the building was locked down. It didn't explain what we were doing there.

Jude led us to a bank of elevators, and we waited as Riley pried open a control panel and dug his hands into the mess of wiring.

"Isn't the electricity shut off?" I asked.

"They keep it running low-level in this building," Jude said. "For the hardware. Easy to tap into if you know what you're doing."

"And he knows what he's doing?" I said, nodding toward Riley.

"He knows a lot of things. You don't hear any alarms going, do you?"

I shook my head.

"Thank Riley."

A few seconds later the elevator doors popped open. The group stepped on, but when I tried to follow, Jude held me back. "We'll take the next one," he said.

Before I could argue, the doors shut, and we were alone.

"What do you want?" I said.

"What do *you* want?"

Another set of doors opened, and we stepped into the small space. Together. The doors shut behind us, and the elevator whooshed up the shaft. Jude turned to face me, backing me into a corner.

"Touch me and I'll kill you," I hissed.

He just laughed. "A, you've really got to train yourself to stop thinking in outdated terms, like life and death, and B, I have zero interest in touching you. Not at the moment, at least."

I promised myself I had no interest in touching him, either. "So what the hell is this about?"

He pressed his hands flat against the elevator walls, one on either side of me, locking my body between his arms. "I thought you might have some questions. About your little . . . experience by the waterfall."

"I don't know what you're talking about."

He smirked. "I think you do. And I think you loved it. I think you came back for more."

I didn't say anything.

"Better be careful." It sounded more like a threat than a warning. "Don't want to end up lost inside your own head. Better to get your thrills out here, in the real world."

"Is that what we're supposed to be doing, wandering around this trash heap of a city?" I asked. "Am I being thrilled? I hadn't noticed."

Jude dropped his arms. "That's how you want to play it? Fine."

The elevator swept up and up.

"Where'd you get it?" I asked.

He didn't bother asking what.

"As *human* as possible," he said bitterly. "That's the BioMax party line. But it doesn't mean they don't have the technology to make us different. To make us better. They just don't want to give it to us. Not officially, at least."

"Make us *better*? How's some crazy intense b-mod trip supposed to make me better?"

He raised his eyebrows, and I realized that now there was no denying it. I'd uploaded the program, and he knew it.

"There's more where that came from," he said. "But only if you're willing to look."

The doors opened. We were on the roof. Three dark silhouettes tiptoed along a railing at the far edge, wobbling in the wind. There was plenty of wind, ninety-eight stories up.

"They're not jumping," I whispered in horror. "Tell me they're not jumping."

"No, *we're* not jumping," Jude said. "Just playing around. Admiring the view. Enjoy." And he slipped into the shadows.

I circled the roof, weaving through abandoned solar arrays and broken satellite dishes. The world above was no less shattered than the world below. The three mechs on the railing swung themselves over the thin metal barrier and began scaling it from the outside. I passed Quinn in a dark corner, wrapped around the guy whose name I would probably never know. Riley and Jude argued against the skyline. I veered in the opposite direction and found myself standing next to Ani, her blue hair black in the darkness. She'd folded herself over the railing, elbows propped on the metal, eyes fixed on the dead buildings that stretched beneath us. My eyes had adjusted to the night enough to pick out a few of the closest ones, but beyond that, there was nothing but a field of shadow.

"Hey," she said, without turning her face away from the nonview.

"Hey."

"So, what do you think?"

I shrugged. "Not much to see."

"I mean about the whole thing," she said. "Tonight."

I shrugged again. "Seems like a lot of effort just to go somewhere we're not supposed to be. What's the point?"

"Jude says there doesn't always need to be a point. Sometimes it's just about having fun." Ani glanced over my shoulder. I turned to see Quinn and the guy, still going at it. "See? Fun."

"Maybe it's none of my business, but . . . that doesn't bother you?"

"Why should it?"

"I guess I just thought you and Quinn were . . ."

"We are. Sometimes." She smiled faintly. "But this is all new for her. She wants to . . . you know. Play."

"And that's okay with you?"

"Jude says we have to learn not to lay claims on one another anymore," she said. "He says monogamy's impractical if you're planning to live forever."

"Seems like Jude says a lot."

Ani beamed. "He's amazing."

"And you always listen?"

She shook her head. "You don't understand."

"What?"

"Where we come from. Where *he* comes from."

"So tell me."

"How do you think he knows his way around here so well?" she asked.

I hadn't really thought about it.

"He used to live here," Ani said. "Before."

"Really?" I leaned forward. I'd never met anyone who had actually *lived* in a city. "I mean, I knew he was . . ." I wasn't sure which word would make me sound least like a spoiled rich girl. Everyone knew that the first mechs had been volunteers from the cities and the corp-towns. What everyone also knew, although no one said it, was that you'd be crazy to volunteer for something like that unless you had no other choice. "Do you know what happened to him? Why he volunteered?"

Ani looked alarmed. "I'm not supposed to be talking about the past," she said. "He'd kill me."

"I thought we were supposed to forget about our mortal fears," I teased. "Retrain ourselves to accept immortality. Isn't that what 'Jude says'?"

She shook her head, hard. "The past doesn't matter," she said, almost to herself. "It's better forgotten."

"Easy for some people," I said quietly. "Not so much for others."

Ani flopped forward against the railing again. "I don't miss it, if that's what you're thinking. I'd never go back."

"Are you from around here too?" I asked, hoping I wasn't pushing too hard. I didn't want to scare her away.

"No. Farther west than that." There was more than a little

pain in her smile, but her voice stayed flat. "My parents are from Chicago."

"Oh." *From* Chicago, not *in* Chicago. No one lived *in* Chicago, not anymore. And most of the ones who'd lived there the day of the attack weren't living, period. The initial blast had only taken out a couple hundred thousand, but then there had been the radioactive dust. And the radioactive water. And the radioactive food. A radioactive city, filled with radioactive people. Who had, pretty quickly and pretty gruesomely, started getting sick. I hadn't seen the vids, but then, it wasn't really necessary. In school they made us watch footage of Atlanta. And Orlando.

Once you've seen one ruined city, you've seen them all.

I didn't know how to ask the obvious question, but it seemed rude not to try. "Are your parents, uh, are they . . . did they . . ."

"Still alive." Ani's mouth twisted. "At least, as far as I know. Which isn't very far."

"You're not in touch?"

She shook her head.

"Is it because of . . . what happened to you?" I glanced down at her body, and she got the idea.

"I wish." She hesitated. "How much do you know about the corp-towns?"

I shrugged. "Just that it's a good place to live, if, you know, you need a job. And that if you live there, you get stuff you need." Stuff like food, electricity, med-tech—stuff you wouldn't get in a city. Not unless you stole it.

"You get it," she agreed, "but only if you follow the rules."

There was a code of good behavior, I knew that. But it made sense to me. If the corporation was running the town, supplying houses and schools and doctors and lights, didn't they deserve to make the rules?

"And only if you're willing to give *other* stuff away," she continued.

"Like the voting thing?" I rolled my eyes. "Big deal." Residents of corp-towns sold their vote to the corps. Seemed like more than a fair trade. Most people I knew weren't planning to vote anyway. Who cared which b-mod-addict fame whore pretended to run the country next?

"Other things, too," Ani said. "Things for the good of the community. Like minimizing medical costs."

"Seems fair."

She looked down. "When you're from Chicago, having a kid is not a good way to minimize medical costs."

"Oh." You could take the people out of the radioactive city—but you couldn't take the radioactivity out of the people.

"Yeah. Oh. They signed a contract. So when they decided to have me . . ."

"They got kicked out?"

"Not until I was born." The pained smile was back again. "Then it was straight back to city living for them. And their adorable legless wonder."

I forced myself not to look down at her long, slender legs. "You were born without . . ."

"Among other things." Her grip tightened around the railing. "Radiation poisoning really spices up the genetic soup."

"I'm sorry."

"Yeah. So were they." She shrugged. "After a few years they ditched me. Headed for the nearest corp-town, I guess."

"And you never—"

"Ten years." She shook her head. "Not one word. Guess they wanted to forget I ever happened."

"I really am sorry," I told her. It seemed like such a lame thing to say. "It must have been . . . hard for you. On your own."

Ani shrugged, keeping her eyes fixed on the skyline. "There are places. For people like me. No doctors, of course. And not much food or . . . anything. But . . ." She shook her head. "It doesn't matter. Anymore. Let's just say that when they shipped me off for the download, I didn't care what they were going to do to me. It couldn't have been worse than where I was."

"So how did you get to volunteer?"

She laughed. "Lia, what makes you think we volunteered?"

"I didn't—I don't know—that's what they said. I believed it." Which sounded totally feeble. But it was the truth.

"It doesn't matter. Jude's right. None of that matters now. We're better off."

She said it, but I couldn't help thinking she wasn't done talking. Not yet. If I could find the right question to ask. "Did you know him? Before?"

She hesitated. "Not in the place. No. But later, in the hospital. When they were doing all the tests, deciding which of us they wanted. Jude was there. Riley too. They were friends from before. And the three of us . . . It just worked, you know?" She pulled a nanoViM from her pocket and flicked the screen to life. "You want to see something?"

I nodded.

"You can't tell them I showed you," she said. "Ever."

I nodded again.

In the picture, three teenagers grinned at the camera. Two sat side by side in wheelchairs, their cheeks sunken, their bodies withering away. The girl had no legs. The boy had all his limbs, but they were twisted and gnarled. Useless.

"Jude," Ani said, tapping his hollowed face.

The guy standing behind looked like a giant next to their fragile, wasted bodies. "Riley?" I guessed. "He looks pretty healthy."

She flicked off the screen. "He was."

He was also black. As was the boy who had become Jude. The girl's skin was lighter, more caramel than chocolate, but still radically darker than the body she wore now. Ani saw the question in my face.

"What? Did you think we were *white*?" she asked in disgust.

I guess I hadn't thought at all. "I don't get it. Why didn't they . . . I mean, it's not like they couldn't . . ."

"We were the first," she said in a more bitter tone than I'd ever heard her use. "An *experiment*. So they used what they had, and what they had were standard-issue bodies for their standard-issue rich white clients. *You* get a new body, you get to customize. *Us?* We get something off the rack. We get *this.*" She looked down, now aiming the disgust at the body she'd been assigned. "You think I like this?" she asked. "You think I like the fact that my parents wouldn't even recognize me, if they ever—" She choked it off. "Not like that's going to happen." She slipped the ViM into her pocket. "It doesn't matter. Jude says that race is irrelevant, since it's not like we even have skin anymore, not really. He says being a mech is like being part of a new race." She lowered her voice. "But I know he hates it too."

"And Riley?" I asked, thinking of the tall, silent boy who never seemed to smile.

Ani shrugged. "Who knows? Hard to tell *what* he's thinking, right?"

"I guess." I paused. "So, when you said he was healthy, before, did you mean—"

She shook her head. "No," she said firmly. "I guess it's okay for you to know where I came from. I mean, that's my business. But if you want to know about them, ask *them.*"

"Okay. I get it." A lot of good it would do me, though. Jude had already made it clear he wasn't in the question-answering business. At least not when it came to questions I actually wanted the answers to.

"I don't even know much myself," she said in a softer voice. "He's serious about the whole forgetting-the-past thing. Even before the download, he and Riley didn't talk about where they came from. Not *ever.*"

I thought about the picture, the boy's body curled up in the wheelchair, his legs and arms strapped down, his neck looking too frail to support his head. And then I thought about Jude, passionate and proud. I thought about his firm grasp, and the way it had felt when his broad arms embraced me. "I guess I can maybe understand that."

Ani gave me a shy smile that suddenly made her look about ten years old. "I'm glad you came up here, Lia. Alone, I mean."

"Not like I had much of a choice. If Auden had set off the alarms—"

Ani laughed. "There are no alarms," she said, like it should have been obvious. "Jude just said that."

"Are you kidding me?" I asked, picturing Auden standing nervously on the curb in front of the building. Alone. Where I'd left him. "Why would he lie like that?"

"Don't be mad," she said quickly. "He just wanted you to see what it was like with us. You know. On your own."

I turned to face the view again, resting my forearms on the railing, staring out and trying to imagine a city filled with lights. "It's not so bad, I guess."

I probably should have been mad.

But I wasn't.

As we made our way back to the car, Auden and I hung behind the rest of the group.

"Have fun up there?" he asked, sounding a little sullen.

I shrugged. "It was okay."

"Hope you two found some time to be alone together."

"*Us* two?"

"You. *Him.*" He glared at Jude's back.

I forced a laugh. "Don't make me throw up."

"You can't," Auden said flatly. "Remember?"

"Like I could forget."

"You seem to have forgotten that he's crazy. Dangerous."

"You've got no reason to think that," I said. "You're just—"
But that was a sentence that didn't need finishing. "He's not
so bad." I didn't know why I was bothering to defend him.

No wonder Auden was freaked. *I* was a little freaked. But
it didn't mean something was going on. Just because I didn't
totally hate Jude, didn't mean I— Well, it didn't mean anything.

"You tell yourself that if it helps. If that makes it easier."

So he *was* jealous, even though there was nothing to be
jealous about—and even though he had no right to be. Auden
didn't own me. "Something you want to ask?"

"None of my business," he said.

"Except you obviously think it is," I pointed out. "Unless
you're still mad about what happened between the two of us."

"You mean what *didn't* happen."

"So you are mad."

"No."

"Passive-aggressiveness is incredibly lame," I said. "You do
realize that, right?"

"How am I being passive-aggressive?"

I plucked at the fraying strap of his green bag. "What'd you
do, throw the one I gave you in the trash? Light it on fire?"

"It's new," he said defensively. "I didn't want to bring it tonight, mess it up."

"Whatever. None of my business, right?"

"It was my mother's," he mumbled, so quietly that I thought I must have heard him wrong.

"What?"

"The bag." He pressed it tighter to his body. "It was my mother's."

And I'd given him a bright, shiny new one, suggesting he throw the old one in the garbage, where it belonged. What a lovely gesture. "Why didn't you just tell me?"

"I didn't want to talk about it. I *don't* want to talk about it." He stared hard at me. "We don't have to talk about everything, do we?"

I looked away. No. We didn't.

We walked the rest of the way in silence. The city was silent too, at least at first. And then I heard something. A scuffling, shuffling noise. Like careful footsteps, creeping behind us.

I didn't say anything.

It was probably my imagination, just like the shadows flickering in every alley we passed. It was probably nothing.

Once we reached the cars, Jude loaded us all in—all except for a mech named Tak. I hadn't talked to him much, partly because he scared me a little. It wasn't so much the spikes around his neck or the patchy transparent casing on his face that revealed a layer of chunky wiring and circuitry. It was his eyes, which somehow looked even deader than mine. I told myself it was just a trick of the light.

Jude nodded at Tak. *Ready?* he mouthed.

Tak nodded back, and Jude tugged the tarp back across the car, leaving a corner of one of the windows unblocked. Then he jumped inside and slammed the door behind him. "Everyone scrunch down in your seats," he ordered. "It's safer."

"But what about Tak?" I asked.

"Down," Jude said. "You'll see."

I saw.

"I'm here, motherfuckers!" Tak screamed so loudly we could hear him through the thick windows. He stood in the middle of the empty street, as if waiting. "Come and get me!"

Nothing happened.

He screamed again and again until the words faded, replaced by an incoherent roar. And then, heeding his call, two figures emerged from the darkness, clothed in rags. One carried a knife. The other, a gun.

We couldn't hear what the men said. But through our corner of window, we could see Tak laugh. The men advanced.

I grabbed Jude's arm. "We have to *do* something!" I whispered, panicking.

"He can deal," Jude said calmly. "Just watch." And, like a coward, I did.

The man on the left raised his gun.

Tak laughed again. "Can't kill me, motherfuckers!" he shouted. "No matter how hard you try!" Then he raised his arms out to his sides. "I fucking dare you!"

The gunshot was like thunder.

The men ran away before Tak's body hit the ground.

"Now!" Jude shouted. "Before the cops!"

As Auden and I clung to each other, Jude and Riley jumped out of the car, grabbed Tak's body, and slung it into the back. Onto us. They piled into the car themselves, and suddenly we were speeding away.

"Awesome," Tak gasped, his head in my lap. There was no blood, but the wound was oozing something green and viscous. I didn't want it touching me.

"Hurts?" Jude asked, programming in a new set of coordinates as the city fell away behind us.

"Like fuck," Tak said, thumping his shoulder where the bullet had slammed into him. "Gonna be a bitch to get this one out."

"What the hell is going on?" I said. "You did that on purpose. You let them shoot you! We all could have been—"

"Killed?" Jude asked wryly.

"I wasn't going to say that."

"Because you're learning." Jude twisted around in his seat to look at me. Me, not Auden, who had turned pale and was pressed up against the window, like he wanted to jump out of the car, speeding or not. "We all have our little daily pleasures," he said. "Tak's happens to be pain. Violence, too. And fear, of course."

"Fuck fear," Tak shot back. "Just a gun, right?"

Jude smiled. "But mostly pain. Or at least, a digital simulation of such. A quick trip to BioMax and he'll be all better, won't you?" He patted Tak on the shoulder; Tak screamed at the touch. "I would think you'd have a little more understanding now that you've seen for yourself how addictive this sort of thing can be."

"It's not the same and you know it!"

"What are you two talking about?" Auden asked, eyes wide.

"Nothing," I said quickly. "Just bullshit. His usual."

"That's right, look down on us, like we're crazy, like you're *so* different." Jude sneered. "I hear the land of denial's lovely this time of year."

"It's not so easy for some of us! Your life may have sucked, but mine didn't. I'm not ready to give it up yet."

"Like you know anything about my life."

"I know tonight was a little trip home for you," I spat out, so angry and freaked out that I forgot about the promise I'd made to Ani. "I know you probably like this better than your wheelchair."

Jude hit manual override, and the car skidded to a stop. "Who told you?"

I was glad Ani wasn't riding with us. "Nobody."

"Get out." Jude said quietly. "And take the org with you."

"What?" We were in the middle of nowhere, a long, dark stretch of highway bounded by nothingness. "No way!"

"Get. *Out*." Jude reached back and opened the door. "You love running away when things get intense, right? So let me help you. *Run*."

I didn't move.

"Now!"

The scream was pure rage. I leaped out of the car, letting Tak's head slam against the seat. Auden jumped out behind me. The car sped away before the door was fully shut.

And then we were alone.

"Now what?" Auden asked. "We walk back from . . . wherever the hell we are?"

There was no way I was ready to tell my parents what I'd been doing—and I was guessing Auden didn't want his father to find out either. There was one better option.

Which didn't make it a good one.

I linked in to the network, trying to ignore Auden's I-told-you-so glare.

Lucky us, she was there.

Lucky, right. Good thing I was getting used to redefining that concept on a daily basis.

"Zo?" I said, hating the words as they came out of my mouth. "I need a favor."

FORGIVENESS

"She decided not to care."

Z o didn't bother asking where we'd been or how we'd ended up stranded on the side of some deserted road. She stayed linked in for the duration of the ride, her eyes closed and her lips moving silently along with the lyrics only she could hear. Auden and I didn't talk much either until we dropped him off at his place.

I kept hearing it. Tak's scream. The gunshot.

I kept seeing him fall.

I saw him fall to the concrete, as I'd seen the bodies fall into the waterfall—and then, suddenly, I got it.

It was all the same.

This night, this moment, this was the ugly truth that lay hidden behind the wild beauty of the falls, behind Jude's pretty speeches. He had called me a coward, someone who couldn't face the truth. So I forced myself to face *this*; I forced myself not to look away.

This was the core of Jude and his friends. The core of what they did, who they were, what they wanted. A scream. A gunshot.

A gun.

Destruction and pain, in a place as broken as they were.

This is what they sought out, these people I'd thought were like me; this is what they offered, when they invited me to belong.

It wasn't romantic. Whatever Jude said, it wasn't bold, it wasn't freeing.

It was a raw, ugly need.

And it was a need I finally understood.

Or maybe Jude was right; maybe I always had.

"I'm sorry," I said as he was getting out of the car.

He shook his head once. "Don't be."

But from the way he said it, I guessed that meant I shouldn't bother apologizing—not because it wasn't necessary, but because it wasn't enough.

When we got home, Zo brushed past me into the house and went up to her room without a word, slamming the door behind her. I couldn't believe she was acting like I'd done something to her when I knew, because they'd been live-casting it on their zones, that she'd spent most of the night with Walker.

I should have just shut down for the night. And I tried. I uploaded the day's memories. I pulled off the clothes covered in city grime and slipped into my favorite pair of thermosweats. I even lay down in bed. I could have shut my eyes and been out with a thought. That's how it worked. None of that inefficient tossing and turning, trying to force your brain to slow down and your body to relax. I just decided how long I wanted to "sleep," then told myself to *shut down*, the same way I told myself to *walk* or *sit* or *scream*. It was just another command, easy to issue, instantaneously carried out. But I wasn't ready to let go of the night.

Every time I closed my eyes, I saw the neat tunnel the bullet had made in Tak's shoulder. I heard him scream; I saw him smile.

No blood. No danger.

Just the thrill of the moment. And the pain.

And I wondered.

I found a razor in a bunch of junk under the bathroom sink. Left over from the days when I had real skin that sprouted real hair. It was a little rusty, but still sharp.

It wasn't the same as what *they* did, I told myself. I wasn't seeking pain in some sick attempt to make life more interesting. I wasn't sick, not like they were. I wasn't so numb that I needed a jolt of violence to wake up my brain. I wasn't chasing a death that would forever be out of my reach.

I was just curious.

It was an experiment. Perfectly safe, perfectly normal. I just wanted to see what would hurt, and how much. I needed to see how far I could go.

The blade pierced the skin.

Although I knew better, I half expected beads of blood to bubble up along the cut. It didn't happen. Nothing happened. The razor had barely sliced through the surface layer. It was like cutting through leather, the blade leaving only a thin groove behind.

And it hurt.

But not much. My brain registered: *pain*. Like a flashing red light, a warning to stop. But I didn't *feel* it, not really.

The stronger the emotion, the more "real" it may seem.

I bore down harder.

Still nothing. Or at least, not much.

In frustration, I raked the blade from my wrist to my elbow, hard, and gasped as the pain blazed through me. Finally.

There was an echoing gasp from the doorway. I looked up to see Zo staring at me in horror.

I jumped off the bed, pressing my arm awkwardly to my side to cover up the long gash. The razor clattered to the floor.

"I wasn't doing anything," I said.

Yeah, right.

She smirked. "Whatever."

"Seriously, you can't tell," I pleaded. Our mother would freak out. Our father would . . . I didn't know. I didn't want to know.

"Why would I tell?" she said.

"I wasn't trying to . . . hurt myself, or anything, if that's what you're thinking," I said. "I was just . . . It's normal. What I was doing, it's normal, it's no big deal, so can we just—"

"I don't care," Zo said, slowly and firmly. "How many times do I have to say it before you believe me? I don't care what you do. I don't care how big a freak you want to be. I. Don't. Care."

She really didn't. She couldn't, or she wouldn't act like this. She wouldn't have stolen my friends, my boyfriend, my life. She wouldn't glare at me like she wished I would disappear. Like she wished . . .

"You wish I was dead, is that it?" I started toward her, and she backed away. "You probably think it'd be easier for everyone if I'd died in the accident, so you didn't have to deal with me like *this*."

"Shut up," she said quietly.

"Nice comeback." I couldn't take it anymore, her smug, lying face pretending that I was nothing to her. Let her hate me, fine. At least then there'd be some kind of connection, some emotion. We'd still be sisters. "Why don't you just say it? You wish I was dead."

"I don't wish anything," she insisted. "I don't care what you are or what you do. I don't care. "

"Say it. *Say it!* You wish I was dead!"

"You *are* dead!" she screamed. The mask didn't just fall off her face. It disintegrated. Her lips trembled. Her eyes spurted tears. Her cheeks blazed red as the blood drained out of the rest of her face. She swallowed hard. "My sister is dead."

"Zo . . ." I crossed the room, tried to hug her, but she

slipped out of my grasp. "No, Zoie, I'm not, it's okay, I'm right here."

She turned away from me and crossed her arms, huddled into herself. "What you said before, about the accident? That it should have been me?" She paused, and when she spoke again, her voice was shaking. "It should have been me."

"No. No, I should never have said that. I didn't mean it." But I had.

"It doesn't matter. It's true. I should have been in the car. I should be dead. But now—" She choked down a sob. "Now Lia's dead, and it's my fault."

"I'm not—"

"*Lia's* dead!" she shrieked, spinning to face me. "My sister is *dead*, and I basically killed her, and then this *thing* pretending to be Lia moves into her house, into her family, into her life, and I'm supposed to pretend that's okay? It's not bad enough that I have to live with what I did, with the fact that she—" Another sob. Another hard swallow. But when she spoke again, she was steadier. "I live with that. Every day. Every minute. And that I could handle. But seeing you . . . *act* like her, try to *be* her. Watching you take her place, like you ever could?" She shook her head, and continued in a cold hiss. "I hate you."

"Zo, don't."

"You think I like it?" she asked, furious. "Wasting my time with those losers she called her friends? Joining the track team, being Daddy's perfect little girl? You think I *like* screwing my sister's boyfriend?"

I flashed on the image of the two of them, lips fused. If she wasn't enjoying it, she was a better actress than I'd thought. "Then why—"

"Because *she* would have wanted me to protect what she had." Zo looked down. "Because if someone's going to replace her, it damn well isn't going to be *you.*"

"But it *is* me." I came closer again. She stiffened.

"*Don't* touch me."

"Fine." I stayed a couple feet away, hands in the air. *See? Harmless.* "I'm not dead. I'm *not.* You didn't kill me. I know I look . . . different." I wanted to laugh at the understatement, but it didn't seem like the time. "It's still me. Your sister."

Zo shook her head. "No."

"Remember when we had that food fight with the onion dip? Or when we got iced in the house for a week and filmed our own vidlife?" I asked desperately. "Or how about the time you thought I hacked your zone and posted that baby pic of you, the one in the bathtub?"

"You did," she muttered.

"Of course I did," I said, grinning. "But only because you rigged my smartjeans and I ended up bare-assed in front of the whole seventh-grade class."

She almost laughed.

"How would I know all that unless I was there?" I asked. "Every fight we ever had, every secret you ever blabbed, *every-thing*. I know it. Because I was there. *Me*, Zo. Lia. It's still me."

She looked like she wanted to believe it.

But she decided not to. I saw it happen. The mask fell back over her features, stiffening her lips, hardening her eyes. She decided not to care.

"No," she said. "Lia's dead. You're a machine with her memories. That doesn't make you real. It definitely doesn't make you her."

"Then why am I still here?" I asked angrily. "If I'm just some imposter, why do Mom and Dad—excuse me, *your* mother and father—want me living in *Lia's* house? In *Lia's* room."

"They don't," she murmured.

"What?" But I'd heard her.

"They don't," she said louder. "They don't want you here. They wish you'd never come."

"You're lying."

"You wish."

"They love me," I said, needing to believe it. "They know it's me."

"They *loved* their daughter. Past tense. You just make it hurt more. They thought you'd make it better. That's why they did it—made you, like you'd be some kind of replacement. But you make everything worse."

"You're lying," I said again. It was the only weapon I had.

"If I am, then why is Dad up every night, crying?"

"He doesn't cry."

"He didn't used to," Zo said. "But he does now. Thanks to you. Every night since you came home. He waits until he thinks we're all asleep, he goes to his study, and he *cries*. Sometimes

296

all night. Don't believe me? He's probably at it right now. See for yourself."

"Get out of my room." Nothing she said could make me believe that about my father. Nothing.

"None of us want you here," she said.

"Get out!"

Zo shook her head. "I should feel sorry for you, I guess. But I can't."

She slammed the door behind her.

I told myself she was lying. Being cruel for the sake of cruelty. And maybe I couldn't blame her, if she really thought her sister was dead, if she thought it was her fault. But that didn't mean I had to believe her about our parents.

If my mother had fallen apart, if she thought I was just an inferior copy— Well, that I could deal with. It made even more sense than Zo. Our mother was weak, always had been. It wasn't her fault; it didn't mean I didn't love her. But it meant lower expectations.

My father was different.

He was the strong one, the smart one.

And, although I knew he would never admit it—not to me, not to Zo, not to anyone—I was his favorite. He was the one who knew me the best, who *loved* me the best. No, things hadn't been the same since the accident, but they were getting better. It would take some time, but I would get him back. Because he saw me for who I was, Lia Kahn.

His daughter.

I knew Zo was lying. I was sure. But not so sure that I stayed in my room and lay down in bed and closed my eyes. Not so sure that I didn't need proof.

My parents always turned on their soundproofing before they went to bed. So they wouldn't have heard Zo and me fight, not if they were already asleep. As they should have been at three in the morning. But when I crept downstairs, I saw the light filtering through the crack between the door to the study and the marble floor. And when I pressed my ear to the heavy door, I heard something.

Gently, noiselessly, I eased open the door.

He was on his knees.

He faced away from me, his head bent. His shoulders shook.

"Please," he said, in a hoarse, anguished voice. I flinched, thinking he must be speaking to me, that he knew I was there and wanted me to leave before I hurt him even more. But it was worse than that.

"Please, God, please believe me."

My father didn't pray. My father didn't believe in God. Faith was for the weak, he had always taught us. Backward-thinking, cowering, misguided fools who preferred to imagine their destiny lay in someone else's hands.

"I'm sorry."

And worse than faith in God, my father had taught us, was the ridiculous faith in a God who listened to human prayers, who had nothing better to do than stroke egos and grant wishes. An omniscient, omnipresent, omnipotent being who troubled himself with the minor missteps of the mortal world.

"Please forgive me."

He hunched over, bringing his forehead to his knees. "I did this to her. It was *my* choice. I did this. Please. Please forgive me. If I could do it again . . ." His whole body shuddered. "I would make the right choice this time. If I had a second chance, please . . ."

I closed the door on his sobs.

The right choice.

Meaning, the choice he hadn't made.

The choice to let me die.

LETTING GO

"They would age, they would die. I would live."

There was only one place I wanted to go. And only one person I wanted with me. If he was willing. I left two messages, voice and text, both with the same apology, the same request, and the same coordinates. Then I snuck out of the house—easy enough when no one cared where you went or when—and pushed the car as fast as it would go, knowing that the longer it took to get there, the more likely I'd be to turn back. The waterfall looked even steeper than I'd remembered it.

I had forgotten how at night, you couldn't see anything of the bottom except a fuzzy mist of white far, far below. I had forgotten how loud it was.

But I had also forgotten to be afraid.

Auden wasn't there.

But then, I hadn't told him to meet me at the top. My message had been very clear, the coordinates specific. If he'd woken up—and if he'd forgiven me—he would be waiting at the bottom. I would tell him everything that had happened, what my sister had said. I might even tell him how my father had looked, trembling on his knees, bowing down to a god in whom he was, apparently, too desperate not to believe. And just telling Auden would make it better. I knew that.

But this was something I had to do without him. Just another thing he could never understand, because he was an org. He was human, and I was—it was finally time to accept this—*not*. Which is why he was waiting at the bottom, if he was waiting at all. And I was at the top, alone.

I took off my shoes. Then, on impulse, I stripped off the rest of my clothes. That felt better. Nothing between me and the night. The wind was brutal. The water, I knew, would be like ice. But my body was designed to handle that, and more. My body would be just fine.

I waded into the water, fighting to keep my balance as the current swept over my ankles, my calves, my thighs, my waist. *Wet,* my brain informed me. *Cold.* And on the riverbed, *muddy. Rocky. Sharp.* The temperatures, the textures, they didn't matter, not yet. But I knew when I got close enough to the edge, when the water swept me over, the sensations would flood me, and in the chaos the distance between me and the world would disappear.

Not that I was doing it for an adrenaline rush. Or for the fear or the pain or even the pleasure. I wasn't trying to prove something to anyone, not even myself. It wasn't about that.

It was about Zo and my father and Walker and all of them—all of them who hated what I'd become. Maybe because it had replaced the Lia they really wanted or because it was ugly and different and, just possibly, if Jude was right, better. Maybe they were scared. I didn't know. I didn't care. I just knew they hated me. I knew my sister didn't believe I existed, and wanted me gone. My father wished—*prayed*—I was dead. Maybe it would be easier for all of them if I was.

Too bad.

I was alive. In my own unique, mechanical way, maybe. But alive. And I was going to stay that way for the foreseeable future. They would age, they would die. *I* would live.

There were too many people too afraid of what I'd become. I wasn't going to be one of them. Not anymore.

I didn't take a deep breath.

I didn't close my eyes.

I stretched my arms out.

I shifted my weight forward.

I let myself fall.

The world spun around me. The wind howled, and it sounded like a voice, screaming my name. The water thundered. The spray misted my body. And then I crashed into the surface, and there was nothing but rocks and water and a whooshing roar. And the water dragged me down, gravity dragged me down, down and down and down, thumping and sliding against the rocks, water in my eyes, in my mouth, in my nose. It was too loud to hear myself scream, but I screamed, and the water flooded in and choked off the noise. There was no time, no space in my head, to think *I'm going to die* or *I can't die* or *Why am I still falling, where is the bottom, when is the end?* There was no space for anything but the thunder and the water, as if *I* was the water, pouring down the rocks, gashed and sliced and battered and slammed and still whole, still falling—and then the river rose up to meet me, and the water sucked me down and I was beneath, where it was calm. Where it was silent.

Still alive, I thought, floating in the dark, safe beneath the storm of falling water.

Still here.

I closed my eyes, opened them, but the darkness of the water was absolute. I was floating again, like I had in the beginning, a mind without a body. Eyes, a thought, maybe a soul—and nothing else. But this time I wasn't afraid.

I let myself rise to the surface. The water slammed me, like a building crumbling down on my head, and again sucked me under.

And again the silence, again up to the surface, again the storm, and again sucked down to the depths.

I wasn't afraid. I knew I could stay below, swim far enough from the base of the falls to surface in safety. When I was ready. Which I wasn't, not yet. I was content to stay in the whirlpool, limp and battered, letting the water do what it wanted, filling myself up with the knowledge that I had done it, that I had jumped, that I had fallen. I had survived. I was alive; I was invincible. I wasn't ready for it to end.

Until I surfaced and heard the wind scream my name again. Except it wasn't the wind, it was Auden, who had come for me, who was screaming. I screamed back, but the water poured into my mouth. I waved an arm, but the water sucked me down again, and when I fought back to the surface, Auden was gone.

Then I did swim, deep and swift, my mind starting to seep back into itself and with it, panic. I was still invincible; Auden wasn't. I surfaced again, a safe distance from the churning water at the base of the falls. Nothing.

"Auden!"

Nothing.

Then back down into the dark, swimming blind, my arms outstretched, so that even if I couldn't see him, I would feel him, but there was just the water, parting easily as my body sliced through, water and more water and no Auden.

Until I broke through the surface and there he was, gasping and struggling to stay afloat, his hair plastered to his face, his eyes squinty and his glasses long gone. I grabbed him, squeezed tight, kicking hard enough to keep us both afloat.

"Are you okay?" As we drifted away from the falls, the water grew shallower until we hit a point where our feet touched the bottom, midway between the base of the first waterfall and the edge of the second, smaller drop-off.

"Okay," he said, panting. The current was lighter here, easy enough to fight. "You?"

"Fine. What the hell are you doing?"

"Rescuing you." He shivered in my grasp. "You were drowning."

I shook my head.

He looked like he wanted to drop down into the water and never surface. "Stupid," he said furiously. "Of course you weren't. I just—I saw you up there, and when you fell, and you didn't come up, and I thought—"

"Thank you," I cut in, hugging him tighter. "My hero." I didn't need a hero, and I wasn't the one who'd needed rescue. But he was soaking and freezing and had nearly drowned, and I figured there was no harm in giving him a little ego stroke.

"Uh, Lia?"

"What?" I asked, hoping that he wasn't going to choose yet another horribly timed moment to start talking about the great love affair that was never going to be. An ego stroke was one thing, but there was only so far I could go.

"You're, uh, not wearing any clothes."

"Oh!" I let go, and bent my knees until I was submerged up to my neck.

"I couldn't see anything, anyway," he said. "Not without my glasses."

I grinned. "So you were looking?"

His cheeks turned red. His lips, on the other hand, were nearly blue.

"Let's get out of here," he suggested, hugging himself and jumping up and down against the cold.

I wasn't ready, not yet. "You go. I just want . . ." It was just another thing I couldn't explain to him, the way it felt to go over the falls, to know that I had absolutely no control and to just let it happen, let myself fall—and to survive. I knew I'd have to drag myself out of the water to see what damage I'd done, if any. I'd also have to deal with everything else. And I would. Just not yet. "I'm staying in. For a while."

"Then me too," he said.

"You're freezing."

He shook his head, stubborn. Stupid. "I'm fine."

"Fine. Have it your way."

So we stayed in, Auden making a valiant effort to pretend he wasn't noticing my body. While I, for the first time, *wasn't* noticing it. I wasn't ashamed, wasn't repulsed; I was just content to be where I was, what I was—and to be with him. We did backflips and somersaults and competed for who could hold a handstand longer before the current swept us over. We laughed. We didn't talk about my family or about Jude or about "us" and especially not about what had happened in the city or what was going to happen when we got back to shore. We didn't talk about much of anything, except some supposedly funny vid he'd seen of a monkey in a diaper and whether if one was in a position to eat, daily chocolate was a required element of a healthy and balanced diet. Meaningless stuff like that. Easy stuff.

I hadn't been so happy in a long time. Maybe since the accident.

"I think . . . I need . . . to get out," Auden finally said as I resurfaced from a perfect handstand. His teeth were chattering so hard he could barely form the words.

I nodded. "Race to shore?" And before he could answer I took off, digging my strokes into the water, pushing hard to win. I missed winning.

Midway to the bank I popped my head up, checking to see if he was catching up . . . but he was swimming in the wrong direction. Swimming along with the current. Away from me, away from the shore, toward the edge.

"Auden!" I shouted. "Wrong way!"

He's not wearing his glasses, I thought suddenly, horrified. *He can't see.*

"Auden! Swim toward me! Follow my voice!"

But he didn't call back. He didn't change direction. And I began to realize he wasn't swimming at all. He was drifting.

Cold, I thought as the water lapped against my body. *But how cold?* Cold enough that a person—a real, live, warm-blooded person—couldn't take it anymore? Couldn't fight back against the current? Couldn't make it to shore?

"Auden!" I screamed, and then I ducked under the water, pushing myself harder than I ever had on the track, when it didn't count, pushing the legs to kick, the arms to dig, to reach him, to grab him before the current carried him away, before the water caught him and wouldn't let go, not until it plunged over another edge, down another ripple of jagged rock, into a storm of erupting water, and down, into the silent depths, the center of the whirlpool.

I swam fast. The current was faster. He was one arm's length away, close enough that I could see his pale face, his closed eyes, his arms floating limply and his head tipped back, bouncing along shuddering water—and then two arm's lengths, and then three, and the river carried him away from me, the river claimed him. I screamed, I lunged, one last, powerful kick forward, one desperate grasp—and his body disappeared over the edge.

I went over after him. This time there was nothing joyous about the plunge. Nothing fast or chaotic. It seemed to last forever. Enough time for me to go over it in my head, again and again, seeing him on the shore, hearing him scream my name, clinging to his body—and then letting him go. *Hold on,* I thought furiously, as if I could communicate with the past, as if the girl in the memory could make a better choice. *It's cold,* I told her. *It's too cold.*

But the girl in the memory didn't notice the cold or didn't care. She was invincible.

I was sucked down again at the bottom, but there was no peace in the dark, quiet water. The empty stillness just meant he wasn't there. I fought my way to the surface, hoping, but I didn't see him, didn't hear him, so I dove down again, sweeping the river from one side to the other, swimming blind, arms outstretched. Telling myself that it would be like before, I would catch him, only for him to tell me that he hadn't needed rescuing, and we would laugh over the misunderstanding, and this time I wouldn't let go.

I don't know how much time passed before I realized what I

had to do. Seconds, maybe. Minutes, at the most. No time at all if you didn't have breath to hold. And if you did? Too much.

Lungs filled with oxygen floated. Empty lungs sank to the bottom.

So that's where I searched next, my bare stomach scraping against the muddy riverbed. I forced myself to keep my kicks slow and steady, covering the ground methodically, hoping I would find him, hoping I wouldn't, because if he was there, a still body in the mud, if he was . . .

I didn't let myself think about it.

I swam.

And then I touched something that wasn't rock, wasn't mud, was firm and long and foot-shaped, and I wrapped my hand around it, around him. I scooped up his body and kicked toward the surface, burst out of the water. And only then did I force myself to look at what I was holding. His eyes were open, rolled back in his head. I had to turn away from the unbroken white stare. He wasn't breathing.

CPR, I thought, towing him to shore. I voiced for help, gave our coordinates, and someone would come for us, to save us— but maybe not in time.

Make him breathe. Breathe for him.

But I didn't breathe at all.

Still, there was air flowing through my throat, I thought. Hissing past my voice box, when I needed it, the stream of unfiltered air that made the artificial larynx vibrate so I could talk. I didn't know if that would work. I had to try.

The network told me what to do. I tipped his head back. I placed my lips on his. They were so cold. Blood oozed from the cuts on his face, on his arms, blood everywhere.

Breathe, I thought, forcing the air through my mouth, into his. Pumping his chest, maybe in the wrong place, maybe too light, maybe too hard, I didn't know, but pumping, once, twice, three times, thirty times, just like I was supposed to. I paused, I waited, I listened. No change.

I breathed for him again.

And again.

He coughed.

Water spurted out of his mouth, spraying me in the face.

"Auden." I cradled his face. "Auden!"

He didn't say anything. But he was breathing. I could hear him. I could see his chest rise and fall. He was breathing.

"I'm sorry," I whispered. I laid my head against his chest, listening to his heart. Night had almost ended; the sky was turning pink.

He was still breathing when help arrived. They shifted him onto a backboard, immobilized his neck and spine, gave him an oxygen feed, loaded him into an ambulance. I got in after him, because no one stopped me.

It was only when someone wrapped a blanket around me that I realized I was still naked.

No one would tell me if he was going to be okay. But I promised him he would, over and over again.

His eyes opened.

"You're okay," I told him, holding his hand. His fingers sat limply in mine. "You're going to be okay."

"I hope not," he croaked, his voice crackly.

For a second I was so happy to hear him speak that I didn't register what he said.

"They'll make me like you," he whispered. "We can be the same."

"No," I whispered back, fiercely. "You're going to be fine."

That's what I said.

That's what I wanted to believe, about him, about myself.

I didn't want to be a person who hoped he was right, that he would *not* be fine. I didn't want to hope that he was hurt so badly that there'd be no other option, that he would die, only to be reborn as a machine, just so that I wouldn't have to be alone.

I reminded myself what it would mean. I pictured him, even though it hurt—*because* it hurt—lying still on a metal slab, pale and cold, the white sheet draped over his skull, where his brain had been scooped out, carved up, replicated. I pictured him trapped in the dark, stuck in a frozen body, thinking he might be dead, then wishing he was.

I didn't want that for him.

Or at least, I didn't *want* to want that for him.

But truth? Sordid, pathetic truth? I think I did.

If Auden were a mech, if we could go through it together, everything would be different. I would no longer be alone.

"You're going to be okay," I said again, uselessly. It was

better and less complicated than the truth, and maybe if I said it enough, it would come true.

"Liar." His eyes rolled back in his head.

Somewhere, an alarm sounded, and one of the men pushed me out of the way.

"Flatline," the man said, pushing on Auden's chest, fiddling with a machine, as the alarm droned on.

"What's happening?"

No one answered me.

The ambulance sped toward the hospital, and the men pounded on his chest, and the alarm beeped, and Auden's chest lay flat, his lungs empty.

Flatline.

No heartbeat.

No life.

They'll fix you, I thought, squeezing his hand, holding on, like I hadn't in the water. *They have to.*

NUMB

"Nothing hurts."

At the hospital someone gave me something to wear. Someone else brought bandages, patched up the gashes the rocks had torn in my skin. Even though there was no need. Nothing was gushing or dripping. Nothing hurt. Nothing had penetrated the hard shell around the neural cortex and—or so it seemed from the fact that I could still walk and talk—none of the complicated wiring beneath the surface had been shaken loose. I was fine. But I let them patch the skin. I nodded when they told me I needed to get myself checked out—somewhere else, of course, where they knew what to do with things like me. I would have agreed to anything as long as they let me stay.

Auden was gone, swept away behind a set of white double doors, and I sat on a blue padded chair, staring at nothing, waiting.

This isn't happening, I thought, then cut myself off. No denial.

No rage, no bargaining, *no* acceptance. I wasn't getting sucked into any of that five-stages-of-grieving shit, because he was still alive. Ergo, no grief. No denial.

This is *happening.*

I had wanted to feel. Now I wanted to stop. I wanted to be all those things people were afraid of. I wanted to be cold and heartless, like a computer, like a refrigerator, like a toaster. I wanted to turn myself off.

That, at least, I could do.

I didn't.

The white doors swung open, and a doctor pushed through. He sat down next to me.

Not good, I thought. If it was good news, he would stay on his feet, he would spit it out quickly, so we could all sigh and laugh and go home. But bad news, he'd want to deliver that face-to-face. He'd want to be close enough that he could pat me on the shoulder. Or catch me if I passed out. Even though, as a doctor, he would know that was an impossibility.

"Has someone contacted his parents?" the doctor asked.

I nodded. "There's just his father." It was hard to get words out. Every time I spoke—every time I sent a blast of air through my throat, past my larynx, into and then out of my mouth, I remembered doing it for him, breathing for him, and I wondered if my air had been good enough, if *I* had been good enough or—

No. I am a machine, I thought. I could control myself. I could control my emotions. They weren't real anyway, right? Whatever happened, I could handle it. I would handle it.

"He's on his way," I said in my pathetic little voice. I didn't know that for sure, because I'd had to leave the message for him, bad enough, since how do you leave that kind of message? *Hi, your son might be dead and if he is, it's probably my fault. Have a nice day!*

The doctor sighed. He had two thin scars in front of his ears and another set framing his nose, telltale signs that he'd just finished his latest lift-tuck. It looked good. I hated myself for noticing. "I should really wait for his guardian to arrive before I go into the specifics of his situation, but—"

"You have to tell me *something*," I pleaded. "Please."

"*But*, as I was about to say, I don't think it would hurt to give you a general update." He paused, and gave me a searching look like he was trying to figure out if I was prone to noisy and embarrassing breakdowns. I wondered if there was a private little room somewhere that they used for conversations like this, a walled-in space where you could shriek and throw things without inconveniencing all those people whose lives hadn't just fallen apart.

But the waiting room was empty. We stayed where we were.

"Your boyfriend's heart stopped."

"He's not my boyfriend," I said automatically.

I have never hated myself more than I did in that silent moment after the words were out. There was nothing I could do to take them back.

"Okay, well . . ." In that pause, I could tell. The doctor hated me too. "Your friend's heart stopped. He was technically dead for about two hours."

Was. I held tight to the verb tense.

"But we were lucky that the body temperature was already so low. . . ." The doctor shook his head. "I don't know how he managed to last as long as he did in water that cold, but it's made our job a bit easier."

The water was too cold, I thought.

My fault, I thought.

No one forced him to jump in after me, I told myself. *No one forced him to stay.*

But I knew better.

"We'll keep his temp down to slow his metabolism, and keep reperfusion as gradual as possible—resume oxygen supply too quickly and brain cells start dying, but if we do it slowly, we should be able to preserve a substantial amount of brain function."

"What does that mean?" I asked. "Substantial."

"It means we'll know more when he wakes up."

"But he *will* wake up? When?"

"That's still to be determined," the doctor said slowly. "But, yes, in cases like this, we're optimistic for a cognitive recovery."

"You mean he'll be okay," I said eagerly.

The doctor looked uncomfortable.

"You said recovery," I reminded him. "You said optimistic."

"I said *cognitive* recovery. We have every reason to hope that his brain might emerge from this intact. But his body . . . I'm told you were there, so you must know. The weight of the water crashing down on him, at the speed it was falling, and the rocks . . . There are impact injuries, crush injuries. He took quite a beating." The doctor shook his head. "The extent of the damage . . ."

"You can fix it," I said. "He has plenty of credit, enough for anything. You have to fix it."

"There are a lot of things we can fix," he agreed. "And in cases like this, there are of course"—he paused, then looked pointedly at me. No, not at me. At *the body*—"other options."

"Oh." I looked at the floor. "It's that bad?"

"It's bad," he said. "But I'm afraid I can't go into more detail until his father arrives. You're not family, so . . ."

"Of course. I understand."

I understood. I wasn't his family. I wasn't his girlfriend. I was nothing.

M. Heller arrived an hour or so later, sans wife number two. He blew past me, pushed aside the nurse who tried to stop him from going through the white double doors, and disappeared behind them. When he emerged, a few minutes later, he looked different. He looked *old*. He slumped down on the closest chair and let himself fall forward, his head toppled over his knees. He was shaking.

But when he looked up to see me standing over him, his eyes were dry.

"M. Heller, I just wanted to say, I don't know if they told

you that I was with Auden when— Well, anyway, I just wanted to say I'm sorry, and I hope—"

"Get out," he said flatly.

"What?"

"I don't want you here. Get out."

"M. Heller, look, I'm not trying to upset you, but your son and I—"

"What?" he said fiercely, like he was daring me to keep going. "My son and you *what*?"

"Nothing," I said quietly. I didn't have any words.

"He's my *son*," M. Heller's voice trembled on the word. "And they're telling me he might—" His face went very still for a moment. "I can't look at you right now. Please go."

He didn't have to explain. I got it. They were telling him his son might die—or worse. Might become like me.

And didn't I know? That kind of thing could ruin a father's life.

I backed away. But I didn't leave. I just sat down on the other side of the waiting room. M. Heller didn't object. He acted like he didn't notice. So he sat on one side of the room, staring at the floor. I sat on the other side, staring at the wall. And we did what the room was meant for.

We waited.

A couple hours later they let M. Heller see him. No one said anything to me.

The day passed. I left my parents a message, the obligatory assurance I was still alive. They didn't need to know any more than that. M. Heller disappeared behind the white doors for hours. Still no one told me anything. No one on the staff would speak to me. Until finally the doctor I recognized appeared again. I grabbed him as he passed. "What's happening? Is he awake? Can I see him?"

The doctor rubbed the back of his neck. "I'm sorry, but the patient's father has insisted that he not have any visitors."

At least I knew he was still alive.

"Can you at least tell me how he's doing?"

"M. Heller has also . . ." The doctor sighed and shook his head. "I'm afraid I'm not allowed to give out any more information about the patient's status."

"Not to anyone?" I asked, already suspecting the answer. "Or . . . ?"

"Not to you."

I wanted to scream. I wanted to break something. Like M. Heller's neck. Or even the doctor's, since he was closer at hand. But instead I just sat down again, like a good little girl, following the rules.

I waited.

I waited for M. Heller to change his mind. It didn't happen. So then I changed my strategy. I waited for him to leave or fall asleep or eat. Because he would have to do one of them eventually. He had needs.

I didn't.

A day passed, and a night, and it was nearly dawn again when a nurse escorted M. Heller back into the waiting room.

She stayed close, as if expecting him to stumble or to lose the ability to hold himself up. *Lean on me*, she projected, shoulders sturdy and ready to carry the burden. But he stayed upright. Separate and unruffled, like nothing could touch him. His eyes skimmed over me as if I wasn't there.

"I'll be back with his things," I heard him say, hesitating in the doorway. "You're sure it's—"

"It's okay," she assured him. "Go home and get a little sleep. Save your strength. He's going to need it."

M. Heller nodded. It took him a moment too long to raise his head again. "And you'll let me know if anything . . . changes."

"Immediately," she said. "Go."

He left. Which meant I just had to choose my moment. Wait until no one was watching. Then slip through the white doors. Find Auden's room. Find Auden. See for myself, whatever it was. Even if it was something I didn't want to see.

I waited.

He was asleep.

At least, he looked like he was asleep. His eyes were closed. That was almost all I could see of his face: his eyes. The rest was covered with bandages. It didn't look like Auden. It barely looked like a human being, not with all the tubes feeding in and out of every orifice and the regenerative shielding stretching across his torso and definitely not with the metal scaffolding encasing his head like a birdcage. Four rigid metal rods sprouted from a padded leather halter that stretched around his shoulders and collarbone. They connected to a thin metal band that circled his skull. Slim silver bits dug into his forehead at evenly spaced points, pinching the skin and holding the contraption in place. A bloody smear spread over his left eyebrow, and I tried not to imagine someone drilling the metal bit into his skull. I wondered if he'd been awake, if it had hurt; if it still hurt. I didn't want to know what it was for.

There was a metal folding chair to the left of his bed. I sat down. His right arm was in a cast. His legs were covered by a thin blue blanket. But his left arm lay exposed and, except for a few small bandages and the IV needle jabbed into his wrist, feeding some clear fluid into his bloodstream, the arm looked normal. Healthy. So, very gently, careful not to jar any of the delicately assembled machinery that surrounded his body, I rested my hand on top of his.

I wondered where his glasses were, in case he needed them. No—*when* he needed them. Then I remembered they were probably floating downstream somewhere, miles away. Maybe they'd made it to the ocean. I didn't even know if the river hit the ocean. But everything does eventually, right?

He opened his eyes.

"Hi!" No, that was too loud, too fakely cheery. He'd see through it. "Hey," I said, softer.

Nothing.

"Auden? Can you hear me?" I leaned over him, so that he could see me, even with his head pinned in place by the metal cage. "It's me. Lia."

I wondered if he could understand what I was saying.

Substantial amount of brain function, the doctor had said without ever clarifying what "substantial" meant. Something more than none; something less than *all.*

"You're going to be okay," I said, just like I'd said on the way to the hospital, just as uselessly. I remembered, then, how much I'd hated it when people had said it to me. How ridiculous, how *unacceptable* it had sounded coming from people who were whole and healthy. *Nothing* would be okay, I'd thought after the accident. And I'd hated them for lying. "The doctor says you'll be fine."

"You must be talking to a different doctor," he said. Wheezed, more like. His words were slow and raspy, like he hadn't used his throat in a long time. And like they hurt coming out.

But still, I smiled, and my smile was real. He was back.

"I was so—" I stopped myself. He didn't need to hear how I'd been torturing myself in the waiting room, worrying. This wasn't about me, I reminded myself. It was about him. "You look like crap," I said, trying to laugh. "Does it hurt?"

"No."

It figured. They had pretty good drugs these days, and he was no doubt getting the best.

"So, I guess we've got something in common now," I said. "We've both been technically dead, and come back to life." Was it inappropriate to joke? Would it make him feel better, or would it make him think I didn't care? "Better be careful, or the Faithers will start worshipping us or something."

"Uh-huh."

Okay. Too soon to joke.

"I saw your father in the waiting room. He was really worried about you. I guess he cares more than you . . . Well. Anyway. He was worried."

"Yeah."

It probably hurt him to talk.

"Not that he has to be worried, because you're going to be fine. Doctors can do anything these days, right? Just look at me."

Wrong thing to say.

Everything I said was the wrong thing to say.

I rubbed my palm lightly across his, wishing that he would grasp my hand, squeeze my fingers, do *something* to indicate that he wanted me there. But he didn't. I held on anyway. His skin was warm, proof that he was still alive.

"You were amazing, you know that?" I said. "When you jumped in to rescue me? They said the water was so cold you shouldn't even have been able to—" I stopped. Neither of us needed the reminder. "It was really heroic. To save me."

"It was stupid."

"No, Auden. . . ."

He didn't speak again, just stared at the ceiling.

"You're tired," I said. "I should probably go, let you sleep—"

"Don't you want to know?"

"What?"

"What the doctors said." His lips turned up at the corners, but it wasn't a real smile, and not just because the bandages held most of his skin in place. "The prognosis. All the thrilling details."

"Of course I want to know." I didn't.

Especially when he started reciting it in a dry, clinical tone, words out of a medical text that didn't seem to have any connection to him, his body, his wounds. Punctured lung. Internal bleeding. Bruised kidney. Lacerations. Fractures. The heart muscle weakened by multiple arrests. A cloned liver standing by for transplant, if necessary. They would wait and see. "And the grand finale," he said, his voice like ice. He sounded like his father. "Severed spinal cord. At C5."

I didn't understand how so much damage could have been done so quickly, in thirty seconds . . . and thirty feet. *Don't forget the eighty thousand gallons of water*, I thought. And yet I was just fine.

"Auden, I'm so . . . I'm so sorry." I threaded my hand through the metal cage and brushed my fingers against his cheek.

"Don't touch me," he said. *"Don't."*

I yanked my hand away. But my left hand still rested on his. Out of his sight line, I realized. I squeezed his fingers, tight, waiting for him to tell me to let go.

He didn't.

"What?" he asked, sounding irritated.

I stared at his fingers, the fingers that hadn't moved since I came into the room. The fingers that he was letting me touch, even though he didn't want me touching him.

"Does it hurt?" I asked again, for a different reason this time.

"Nothing hurts." He sounded like a robot. He sounded like I sounded before I got control of my voice again, when I had to communicate through an electronic box.

"What does it mean? What's going to happen?"

"C5. That's *C* for cervical, five for the fifth vertebra down," he said. "They've got it all mapped out. C5 means I keep head and neck motion. Shoulders, too. Eventually. It means right now I can't feel anything beneath my neck. It means I'm fucked for life."

"Not anymore," I protested. "They can fix that now. Can't they?"

"They fuse the cord back together. Yeah. And then nerve regeneration. You get some feeling back. You get some motion. They call it 'limited mobility.' It means you can walk, like, a little. A couple hours a day. And apparently if I practice, I might be able to piss for myself again."

"So that sounds . . ." It sounded like a life sentence to hell. "Hopeful."

"Yeah. As in, they hope it won't hurt so much I spend the rest of my life doped up, but they're not sure. As in, they hope they can put me back together enough that I don't die in ten years, but they're not sure. Fucking high hopes, right?"

There had always been something sweet to Auden, something carefully hidden beneath the cynicism and the conspiracy theories and the family baggage, as if he was afraid to reveal his secret reservoir of hope. But that was gone now. There was nothing beneath the bitter but more bitter. *It's temporary,* I told myself.

Things change.

"If it's that bad, why don't you . . . take the other option?" I asked.

"And exactly what might you be referring to?"

I hesitated. "Nothing." So that was it. He didn't want to be like me, no matter what he may have said. He'd rather be miserable, debilitated, in pain, than be like me. Maybe I couldn't blame him.

"Say it."

"Nothing."

"Say it!" Something beeped, and he took a deep, gasping breath. "Better listen to me," he said, panting. "I'm not supposed to get agitated."

"Why don't you download?" I said quickly, remembering something else I'd hated when I was the one trapped in a bed. The way everyone suddenly got so scared of nouns, as if vague mentions of "what happened" and "your circumstances" would make me forget what was actually going on. As if by not saying it out loud, they were helping anyone but themselves.

"Brain scans."

"I'm sorry, I don't— What?"

"They took brains scans," he said, haltingly. "And there was an anomaly."

I still didn't understand.

"I'm disqualified," he said. "Structural abnormalities. Predisposition for mental disorder and/or decay. Unlikely but possible. So just in case—automatic disqualification. They don't want me living forever if I'm going to go crazy, right?" He laughed. "It's funny, isn't it?"

I pressed my lips together.

"Yeah, no one else seems to think so either," he said. "Maybe I'm crazy already."

"They can't fix it?" I asked softly. "Whatever it is?"

"They could have. Before I was born. If they'd known about it, if my mother had let them screen for that kind of thing. But she thought it was superfluous. She only wanted the basics." He laughed again. It was a weirdly tinny, mechanical sound, since his body was immobilized and his lungs were barely pumping any air. "Thanks, Mom."

"There's got to be something you can do, if you paid enough, some way to change their minds?"

"Nothing. No brand-new body for me. I'm stuck with this one. For life." He paused. "As long as that lasts."

I squeezed his hand again. Not that he felt it.

"Funny, isn't it?" he said. "They can make a fake body from scratch, but they can't fix a real one. Guess there's only so much you can do when you're stuck with damaged goods." He didn't laugh. "No, I guess that's not very funny either."

"I can help," I told him. "I know how it feels, lying there, thinking your life is over. I understand."

"You understand *nothing*," he spat out. "That's what you always used to tell me, right? 'You can't understand, not unless you've been there.' You've never been here."

"You're alive," I said, aware that I was sounding like

call-me-Ben, like Sascha, like every medical cheerleader I'd ever wanted to strangle. And now I finally got why they'd said all that. They needed to believe it. You couldn't look at someone so broken and *not* believe they could, somehow, be fixed. "That's something."

"Something I don't want. Not like this."

So I said what all those cheerleaders never had. The truth. "Neither would I. And . . . it's never going to be like it was before. *Never.* That will never be okay. But *you* will."

He snorted.

"I know you don't believe it," I said desperately. "I know it all sounds like greeting-card bullshit that doesn't apply to you, but it does. Maybe I can't understand everything, but I understand that. The way you feel? I honestly don't know if that goes away. But people—*you*—can get used to things, even if it seems impossible now. You can make it work."

"Oh really?" he said, bitterness chewing the edges of the false cheer. "Thanks *so* much for the insight. So I can get used to a machine telling me when it's time to pee, and when it's time to shit, and then helping me do it—and that's *after* all the regeneration surgery's done. Until then, I just get a diaper. You think you could get used to changing it for me? I can get used to internal electrodes that spark my muscles into action and let me walk around and pretend I'm normal until it hurts so much that I fall down and have to get someone to cart me away? They tell me that part's the medical miracle. Twenty years ago I might have been a lump in this fucking bed for the rest of my life, with people feeding me and turning me and wiping my ass. So you think I can get used to people telling me how fucking grateful I should be? And I can get used to my lungs working at half capacity, if I'm *lucky*, and feeling like I've got an elephant stomping on my chest—at least until the fluid builds up, and while I wait around for them to come suck it out, it just feels like I'm drowning? Not that you would know anything about that."

"It sucks," I said. "I know that. But you're not alone. You don't have to do this alone. I'm here, just like you were there for me." I remembered the day I froze in the quad, the way he knew exactly what to say and what to do, even though he didn't know me at all. And now no one knew me except for him. "We'll do this together."

"Together." He snorted. "Right. And maybe you'll finally fall deeply in love with me and make all my dreams come true. We'll live happily ever after. As long as they can rig me up with some kind of hydraulic system. Not like I ever got to do it the normal way, so I guess I won't even notice the difference."

"Auden, don't—"

"Don't what? Tell you all about how my penis may get 'moderate sensation' back, and if I respond well to the electrical-impulse therapy—which, let me tell you, my penis and I are really looking forward to—I might, *might* be able to get the fucking thing up, up for some fucking, I mean, but—"

"Please don't."

"Oh, I'm sorry, am I grossing you out with all the medical

details? Or is it the thought of having *sex* with me that disgusts you?"

He wanted me to fight with him. I wasn't going to do it. Not now. Not here. "I thought my life was over when I woke up like this," I said. "But you're the one who told me that I could handle it. That I could start fresh."

"This is different."

"I know, but—"

"No!" The beeping started again. "You *don't* know. This isn't what you went through. This isn't what you understand. This is *me*, my life. This is the way it's going to be forever: shit." He closed his eyes, sucking in heavy gulps of air.

"I'm sorry," I whispered, silently pleading with him to stay calm. "Just tell me what you want from me. What can I do?"

"You can get out."

I stood up. "You're right. You should try to sleep. I'll come back later."

"No. You should get out and not come back. Ever."

"What are you talking about?"

"This is your fault," he said in a low voice. "What happened . . . It's your fault."

"It was an accident. You were just trying to . . . save me." When I didn't need saving.

"Seems like I've been doing that a lot," he said. "You do something stupid, you do something reckless, and I fix it. You treat me like crap, and I save you again. Because I'm stupid. Was stupid."

I closed my eyes. "You're my best friend."

He went on like he hadn't heard. Or didn't want to. "You're probably happy, aren't you? Why should anyone else get to be healthy and normal if you've got to walk around like some kind of mechanical freak, right?"

He's just trying to hurt me, I told myself. And I had to let him do it if that's what he needed. I had to do whatever he needed.

This is not my fault.

"Maybe this was the plan all along. Is that it? Is that why you kept dragging me along with you, making me take all those stupid risks? You were trying to get me killed— Excuse me, I mean, get me *broken*?"

"Of course not! This was an *accident*."

"This was inevitable. And if you didn't see that, you're as stupid as I was."

"Auden, come on. I . . . I love you."

"But not in *that* way, right?"

I would have happily lied if I'd thought there was even a chance he would believe me. "No. But—"

"But I'm supposed to grovel at your feet, thankful for whatever I can get from you, right? Sorry, not in the mood today. I'm not feeling too well."

"Tell me how to make this better. Please."

"I already did: Get out. The only reason I'm talking to you now is that I wanted you to hear it from me. What you did. Now you know. So we're done."

I didn't move.

"Obviously I can't force you," he said. "I'm just going to close my eyes and pretend you're not here. And hopefully when I open them, you won't be. You want to do something for me? Do that. Help me pretend I still have some fucking control over *something*."

He closed his eyes.

I left.

But I didn't leave the hospital. Because he was right: He didn't have control over anything anymore. Including me.

I went back to the waiting room. I watched his father return. I watched the doctors and nurses pass through on the way from one crisis to another.

I waited.

I waited until late that night, after his father had fallen asleep and the few remaining doctors and nurses were too busy watching the clock to watch me. And once outside his doorway, I waited again, watching, making sure Auden was asleep.

Then I crept inside. I lifted the chair and placed it at the foot of his bed where, even if he woke up, he wouldn't be able to see me. He obviously wouldn't hear me breathing. And he wouldn't feel my hands resting on the lumpy blanket, cradling his useless feet.

BETTER OFF

"None of us are volunteers."

He's not dead, I told myself, standing outside the hospital, wondering what to do next. That's what counts. He won't die, not for a long time—and not because of this.

It should have felt like good news.

He doesn't want to die, I told myself. He may have said it. But only because he didn't yet understand that some things are bearable, even when you're sure that they're not.

I understand, I told myself. *I can help him.*

But the second part of that was a lie. And maybe he was right, and the first part was too.

I told myself: *This is not your fault.*

I told myself the anger would pass, and he would forgive.

Denial bleeds into anger, I told myself. Then would come

bargaining and depression, and then, finally, always, acceptance. He would grieve the loss of the life he had wanted. He would accept my help.

I told myself I would find a way to get by without his.

I lied.

It was a cold day. It was always a cold day. And, as always, it didn't matter to me.

Who was I supposed to go to with this? *Auden* was the person I went to. Auden was the one who understood. He was supposed to be the solution, not the problem. So who was I supposed to talk to about losing the only person I could talk to? Who was supposed to cure my loneliness if I was alone?

I was alone.

And maybe it was my fault.

Or maybe not, I thought suddenly. Auden would never have been hurt if I hadn't gone to the waterfall, but I would never have gone to the waterfall if Jude hadn't shown me the way. If he hadn't practically *dared* me to jump, turned it into some huge symbolic statement of my identity instead of what it was: a dumb stunt. Crazy, like Auden had said. Not that I had bothered to listen.

I need to see you, now, I texted Jude, and he sent me an address without asking why. Maybe he just assumed I'd always needed him and was only now realizing it. He was just enough of an ass to think that way.

This is not my fault, I told myself again, and there was more force behind it this time. *It's his.*

• • •

It was a different house than before. More of an estate, really; almost a feudal village, complete with outlying buildings dotting the grounds and, atop the highest hill, a turreted Gothic monstrosity that looked like a fairy-tale castle if the fairy tale was *Sleeping Beauty*, where the princess's home was decrepit, covered with thorns and forgotten. Jude met me outside.

"You live *here*?"

"It's Quinn's," Jude said. "She's invited some of us to stay . . . for a while."

"She barely knows you."

His lips curled up. "I guess she knows enough." He guided us down an overgrown path, headed toward a giant greenhouse. There was nothing inside but a thicket of dead plants. Most of the windowpanes were empty; the ground crunched with shattered glass. "So, you come here to chat about real estate?"

"It's Auden," I said, suddenly sorry I had come. It felt wrong to say his name out loud, here. To Jude. "He's hurt."

Jude nodded. "He's an org. I hear it happens from time to time."

I couldn't believe him. "You don't even care? You're not even going to ask how bad?"

"He's not my friend, as he's always been so quick to point out. Why should I care?"

"Bad," I informed him, whether he cared or not. "Thanks to *you*."

Jude raised an eyebrow. Nothing touched him. *Nothing*.

"You pushed me," I said. "You wouldn't accept that I wasn't

like you. And you just had to keep pushing and pushing, all that crap about losing control and letting go and I finally did, and *he's* the one who has to pay? Congratulations, Jude," I said bitterly. "It all worked out according to your plan. He hates me, and I've got nothing, just like you wanted. Just like you predicted, right? I'm fucking alone. Thanks for your help. Thanks a lot."

Jude leaned against the door frame of the greenhouse, ignoring the protruding shards of glass. "Deciphering incoherent rants isn't really a specialty of mine," he said, still perfectly calm. Detached. "But if I've got this right, you did something, your org got hurt, and this is somehow my fault because I told you to do it in the first place? You always do everything you're told?"

I let myself sink to the ground. It sounded even stupider out loud than it had in my head. The grass was still wet from a morning rain, and the cold water seeped into my filthy, borrowed clothes.

"I hate you," I said.

"Not much of an apology. But I'll take it. Want to tell me what happened?"

I told him. All of it, from the fight with Zo straight through to the moment in the hospital room, the sound of Auden's voice— the *tone* of Auden's voice, cold and mechanical—when he told me to leave.

And when I was done, Jude nodded. "Tragic," he said. As emotionless as ever. I wondered if he'd discovered the secret to shutting down his emotions for good. And if he would teach it to me.

"Feel free to do your little happy dance," I said. "I know you hated him."

"I never hated him. I hated the idea of you pretending that he could matter to you or that he could ever understand you. That the two of you were anything but a disaster."

"Disaster's right. *I* was the disaster," I said. "I ruined his life."

Jude didn't say anything. I looked up. "Aren't you going to tell me it wasn't my fault? That I shouldn't blame myself?"

Jude shrugged. "I don't lie."

"*He* decided to jump in after me. I didn't force him. I didn't need saving."

"*I* know," Jude said. "Because of who I am. He didn't— because of who he is."

"Why is it so important to you to believe that we're different, mechs and orgs?" I said. "Why do you need me to hate them?"

He shook his head slowly. "We don't hate them, Lia. They hate us."

Auden didn't hate me.

At least, he didn't used to.

"We're machines," Jude said. "Unchanging. Perfect—and that perfection is our only flaw. They age, they get sick, injured, always something. They *decay*. We stay the same. We drift in time; they drown in it. They've got a deadline; we don't. And it's the one thing they can't forgive."

"It doesn't have to make us inhuman."

"It *does!*" he shouted, raising his voice for the first time. "Humans are mortals. Mortals die. Living creatures *die*. The whole concept of *living* is meaningless without its opposite. Light is defined by dark. Life is defined by death. Death makes them what they are. Absence of death makes us what *we* are. That's the difference. It's absolute. You don't get to just wish it away." Jude slammed his fist against the door frame, splintering the rotted wood. "You never understood. You never even bothered to try. It didn't occur to you that *that's* why we go to the waterfall, why we take risks, why we push ourselves past the brink? It's a reminder—that for us, death is not an option. It's a reminder of everything that makes us different. You can blame yourself for Auden all you want—because *you* didn't want to remember. So you let yourself forget."

"But—"

"No," he said fiercely. "*You* came to *me* this time. So you can either go or you can listen. You want to hear this or not?"

And maybe that was the real reason I'd come. To hear what I already knew but couldn't believe. Not unless I heard it from someone else. I nodded.

"You got careless," Jude said. "You let yourself believe that you and Auden were the same. You got emotionally tied to an org and refused to accept the reality of who you are—and the fact that it's *not* who you were. You ignored the truth, and that put everyone around you in danger. Especially him."

"It was an accident," I argued. "Bad luck."

"What would it have been if *he'd* gotten shot last night, in the city?" Jude asked. "Or if some thug had jumped him while we were up on the roof? Could've happened."

"I didn't think—I don't know."

"You do know," Jude said. "You knew then, too. You did what you wanted to do anyway. Like you should have. But he didn't belong there in the first place. You knew that, too. You just didn't care enough to stop."

"I care about him more than someone like *you* could understand," I spat out.

"You care about yourself," Jude said, smiling. "Something I understand entirely too well."

I stood up. "I don't have to stay here and listen to this."

"No." Jude stretched himself along the door frame like a cat. "Run away. It's what you're best at."

I stayed.

"You brought him to that waterfall," Jude said. "You brought him to the city. You would have dragged him somewhere else tomorrow. Or the next day. He's probably lucky this happened. The next stupid decision might have gotten him killed."

"I would never—"

"And that would have been your fault too."

"So what do you want me to do?" I asked. "Lock myself in a closet and shut down, to keep the world safe from the horror that is me?"

"None of my business," Jude said. "There's no one I care about in the world. The org world, at least. But if I were you, and I still had someone, someone important . . ."

Auden, I thought, in his metal cage. My father, on his knees. Zo, hiding behind a locked door, guilt tearing her apart. We had more in common now, I thought suddenly. Just imagine the sisterly bonding possibilities: *So, who did* you *almost kill today?*

"I would think about what I was doing to them by denying reality," Jude said. "By pretending. I'd think about who I was hurting and who I would hurt next."

And again, I saw him. My father. On his knees. Wishing me dead.

"You've got options," Jude said.

"You?" I asked in disgust.

"Us. You're one of us. Under the right conditions, you could thrive. Or . . ." He glanced behind him, into the yellowish brown forest of dead plants. "You know what they say. Live like an org . . ."

"Die like an org?" I guessed sourly.

Jude frowned. "Except that *you'll* never be the one to die."

"I'm not like you," I said. "I don't want to be like you."

Jude stared at me, and when he spoke, his voice was low and intense, filled with a new emotion. Anger, maybe. Or regret. "*None* of us are volunteers."

I left a message for my parents that I would meet them at Bio-Max, that I needed all of them, Zo included. That I was in trouble. And after not hearing from me in a couple days, I knew they would come.

Which meant I would be free to go home. Slip into the empty house, pack up the few things I couldn't live without, and disappear again without any messy good-byes. Without anyone crying and pleading with me to stay, which I didn't think I could handle. Or without anyone smiling and waving me out the door.

Which I *knew* I couldn't handle.

My parents fell for it. But when I opened the door to my bedroom, Zo was sitting inside. Waiting for me.

"You're not allowed in here when I'm not home," I said automatically.

"This is my sister's room. I'm allowed in here whenever I want."

I decided to ignore her. She couldn't stop me from leaving. Maybe it would even be easier with her there. The perfect reminder of why I couldn't stay. Why everyone would be better off if I left.

"Whatever you are, I know how you think," Zo said. "Because you think like Lia. Which means you can't fool me."

I stuffed some clothes into a bag. Not my favorites, just whatever was lying on top of the pile. I was supposed to be starting a new life, creating a new identity. Which meant my old favorites were irrelevant.

"You're running away," Zo said.

"What clued you in?" I muttered, even though I'd promised myself I wouldn't engage. Also not needed in the bag or in the new life: My track trophies. The dried petals from the rose Walker gave me after our first breakup and makeup. The stuffed tiger that had belonged to my mother and my grandmother when they were children, that I had never actually slept

341

with myself because it smelled. The book, an actual paper book, Auden had found in his attic and given to me, because he liked that kind of thing and so I pretended to, something called *Galapagos*. I hadn't read it, partly because I was afraid of breaking it and partly because it looked boring. Still, it had meant something to me, because it had meant something to him. Not anymore. I didn't need any of it, I realized. Or at least, I shouldn't. I shouldn't have come home at all.

"This is going to kill Mom and Dad," Zo said. "Did you think about that?"

I dropped the bag, kicked it under the bed. I could get new clothes. Wasn't that the point? New everything. "You're the one who said I should disappear. That everyone would be happier that way."

Zo shifted her weight and started rubbing her thumb back and forth across the knuckles of her other hand. The way she did when she was uncomfortable. Or embarrassed. "If this is about all that stuff I said . . . Look, I'm sorry, okay? I didn't mean to make you—you know. Leave."

"Not everything's about you."

Zo gave me a weak smile. "Isn't that usually my line?"

It was tempting to believe that was the beginning of something, that the smile was some sign of weakness—or forgiveness. An indication that maybe we could be sisters again, like we used to be.

Nothing is like it used to be, I reminded myself. I wasn't going to forget that again.

"I have to go."

"Don't," Zo said. She hopped off the bed, but stayed where she was, safely across the room from me.

"Mom and Dad will get over it. They have you."

Zo shook her head, rubbed at her eye with the back of her hand, like a little kid, furious that her body would betray her. "Like that's ever been good enough."

I shrugged. "It'll have to be."

"Where will you even go?" she asked, being very careful not to sound like she cared.

"Somewhere." And I made it clear that I didn't care either.

"You're being an idiot," she said. "This is stupid."

"Because *you* want me to stay?" I asked, surprised. On guard. I'd made a decision—I was going to stick to it. I had to.

Zo stared at the floor.

"Tell me to stay," I said.

But Zo didn't say anything.

"Better yet, tell me I'm your sister. Lia. And you want me here." I waited in the doorway, waited for her to speak, waited to be ready to leave behind the room I had lived in since I was three years old. "Tell me all that, and maybe I can stay."

Zo finally looked up.

"Tell me I'm your sister," I said again, aware that I was begging. I didn't care anymore. I needed her to say it. I needed to hear it.

Maybe it would even be enough to make me stay.

"I'm sorry," she said.

343

The doorway was wide enough that when she walked out of the room, we didn't even touch.

It's not that I bought into Jude's bullshit.

Not all of it, at least.

And it's not that I was so eager to move into Quinn's creepy castle and start painting my face silver and dangling off the side of buildings just because I could. It's not that I wanted more face time with Jude, who obviously didn't care about anyone or anything.

Unlike me, who did.

That's what hurt.

I didn't leave because I was brave, ready to face the world on my own. I didn't leave as some great sacrifice, eager to cast off my happiness—not that there'd been much of that lately—for the greater good. I didn't leave because I was a coward, afraid to face what I'd done to Auden or what I could do next. I wasn't a coward.

I was tired.

Tired of being trapped in limbo, living as half one thing, half another, not quite anything at all. Not quite dead, not quite alive. Not an original, not a copy. Not human, not machine. Not myself—but who else was there?

I was tired of pretending that nothing had changed. That even with an artificial body and a computer for a brain, I was still the same person I'd been before.

Denial was exhausting. As was anger. Bargaining was useless. Depression was bottomless. I was tired of it all.

Which meant I was ready to accept it. The new reality of nonlife after nondeath. *My* new reality.

Lia Kahn is dead.

I am Lia Kahn.

Except, I finally realized, here's the thing.

Maybe I'm not.

Lia lives on. . . .

Turn the page for a glimpse at the second book
in the Cold Awakening trilogy:

SHATTERED

When I was alive, I dreamed of flying.

Or maybe I should say: When I was alive, I dreamed.

Sometimes it was flying; more often it was falling. Or burning—trying to scream, trying to run, but frozen and silent and consumed by flames. I dreamed of being alone. Of my face melting or my teeth falling out.

I dreamed of Walker, his body tangled up in mine. Sometimes I dreamed I *was* Walker, that my hands were his hands, my fingers the ones massaging soft, smooth skin, getting caught in long strands of blond hair. Awake, people talk about becoming one—but in dreams it can really happen. His lips, my lips. Our lips. Our bodies. Our need.

In dreams you can become everything you're not. You can

reverse the most fundamental truths of your life. You can taste death, the ultimate opposite.

I can't. Not anymore. Machines can't die, can't dream.

But we can fly.

From inside the plane, jumps don't look like jumps. One second there's a figure in the jump hatch, fingers gripping the edge, hair whipping in the wind, wingsuit rippling. Then the wind snatches another victim, an invisible hand yanking its prey out of the plane. Leaving nothing behind but an empty patch of murky gray sky.

Quinn and Ani jumped first, hand in hand. The first few times, I'd watched them fall, linked together and spiraling around an invisible axis, two whirling dots red against the snow.

But the novelty had worn off. These days I kept my seat.

Riley went next, and I was glad. Never speaking, never changing expression, eyes drilling through the floor. Until he thought I wasn't looking, and then he'd fix me with that stony, unblinking stare. I wasn't impressed: None of us blinked.

In another life I would have thought he was going for the dark, tortured thing, that whole moody, broody, aren't-I-deep-and-soulful trip. I might even have fallen for it. But the new Lia, version 2.0, knew better. Riley could sulk and skulk all he wanted, but whatever his problem was, he could deal with it himself.

It was like Jude said: *Orgs are weak and need each other. Mechs only need themselves.*

And then Riley jumped and I was left alone with the mech I needed least. Jude stood at the hatch with his back to the clouds and his amber eyes on me. The sun glinted off the silvery whorls etched into his skin. I traced my fingers along the metallic streaks staining my face and neck.

I'd been convinced by Jude's reasoning. We needed to puncture the illusion that we were human, that beneath the self-healing synflesh, hearts pumped, lungs breathed, organs throbbed and cleansed and churned.

I believed in the honesty. I wanted my outsides to match what lay within, the circuits and the energy converters and the twining networks of wires carrying artificial nerve impulses to an artificial brain. But that didn't mean I wanted to look like *him*.

He reached out a hand, as he always did. His lips curled into a smirk, like he knew I would yet again say no—but that eventually I would say yes.

His lips moved, and—thanks to my latest upgrade—the word bubbled inside my head. "Coming?"

I waved him away. He shrugged and let himself drop into the sky.

I edged toward the hatch.

The first time I jumped, the fear almost drowned me. That was the point. To let go of the steel frame separating us from a five-mile drop, let go of the rigid, rational, *controlled* mode separating us from the blood-and-gut orgs. Absolute control yielded to absolute release. The artificial sensation of fear released artificial endorphins, stimulated artificial nerve endings, unleashed a flood of artificial panic. And in the rush of wind and speed and terror, it all felt real.

But the danger was an illusion, which meant the fear was a lie, and my body was beginning to figure out the truth.

Pausing in the threshold, I raised my arms, and the woven aeronylon of the wingsuit stretched beneath them, silvery filaments shimmering. Then I stepped into the empty.

Buffeted by the wind, I maneuvered myself flat, facedown, limbs outstretched. The suit's webbed wings acted as an airfoil, harnessing the updraft to slow my free fall. Beneath me, snow-capped mountains drifted by at a leisurely hundred miles per hour; above me, nothing but soupy sky.

Here's the thing about flying: It gets old.

I processed the sensations—*processed* not felt. The temperature, fifteen degrees below freezing, frosting the few patches of exposed artificial skin. The thunder of the wind. The silver sky, the blinding white below, the specks of red, violet, and black, circling and swooping in the distance.

The air had no taste, no smell. Orgs had five senses; mechs had three.

The suit's instruments recorded a speed of 105 mph horizontal, 67 vertical, but this far from the ground, there was no fast and no slow. Despite the rushing wind, I felt like I was floating down a river, ambling and aimless.

There was no fear.

I let my body drift horizontal to the ground, and the wind sucked me into a flat spin, swinging me around at a dizzying speed. For orgs a flat spin was death. The body whirled like a centrifuge, a crushing 20g force sending rivers of blood gushing toward the head, the hands, the feet, starving the heart until it gave up beating. But for mechs, flat spins were just another perk, a way to turn the world into an incomprehensible smear. Without a puddle of fluid jostling in the inner ear, dizzying speed wasn't even dizzying. For mechs, "dizzy" was just a meaningless expression. Like "thirsty," or "nerve wracked." Or "bored to death."

I pulled abruptly out of the spin. Quinn and Ani swooped up, flanking me.

"Looking good. As always," Quinn VM'd, her digitized voice clear, her meaning more so.

I shifted my body weight and let a gust of air blast me off to the right, buzzing past Quinn with enough force to spin her upside down. "Obviously I'm a natural." Natural: the joke that never got old.

"Naturally annoying," Quinn shot back, regaining her balance. She dipped down, dive-bombing Ani, who squealed as she wriggled away, flipping in midair. Quinn grabbed her wrist and pulled her into a vertical drop. "Catch us if you can!" she called back to me.

I could; I didn't. I activated the lifting jets, let my legs drop, and began to climb, past fourteen thousand feet, past twenty thousand. Higher.

"Going somewhere?" There was something metallic about Jude's voice, sharp and brittle as his features. It was strange the way the digitized voices took on some character of their owners.

"Away from you." But even ten thousand feet below, he was in my head.

"Good luck with that."

I climbed higher, leveling out at twenty-eight thousand feet. *I could stay up forever,* I thought, letting my body carve lazy circles through the clouds. No more struggle to feel—or not to—nothing but a body and mind in motion, simple and pure. Jude would approve.

"You're too high, Lia." Jude again, a violet dot against the snow. Always telling me what to do. As he spoke, the jets sputtered out in the thin air and my webwings lurched, losing their lift.

"I can take care of myself." I tilted forward into a dive, arms pressed against my sides to streamline the suit. I was done flying.

I was a bullet streaking toward the ground. Critical velocity came fast as gravity took over, sucking me down. The mountains rose below me, snowy peaks exploded from the earth, and *now* came the flood of fear. The others blew past, smears of color. Screaming.

"Pull up, you're coming in too fast!" Ani.

"What the hell are you trying to do!" Quinn.

"Again?" Jude.

Riley, a black shadow against the snow, said nothing.

The ground came up fast, too fast, and I barely had time

to level out before I was skimming powder, slicing down the slope, a white cloud billowing in my wake. Something was wrong. The slope too steep, the angle too sharp, the snow too shallow, and I heard the impact before I felt it, the sharp crack of my head crashing into rocky ground, my neck nearly snapping free of my spine.

And then I was rolling down the side of the mountain, blinded by snow.

And then I felt alive.

And then all motion jerked to a stop, a wave of white crashed over me, and the snow filled my mouth, my nose, my ears, and the world went very still and very silent.

And very dark.

I couldn't see; I couldn't move. I was a statue under the snow.

"We're coming for you." That was Riley in my ear, puncturing the silence. He felt so near, like we were alone together in the dark.

I didn't answer.

They began to argue about how to reach me, and I cut the link, retreating into the quiet. The GPS would pinpoint my location, and my fellow flyers would eventually show up with snowfusers to dig me out. It didn't matter how long it took; I could bide my time for centuries, arise icy but intact to a brave new world. It wasn't so different from flying, I decided. Substitute dark for light and still for speed, but in the end, it was the same. Empty.

Once, I was afraid of the dark. Not the bedtime kind of dark, with dim moonlight filtering through the shades and shadows playing at the corners of the room, but absolute dark. The black night behind your lids.

I'd been trapped there for weeks after the accident, dark, still, and alone. A prisoner in my own body. And then I opened my eyes to discover that my body was gone. That I—whatever part of "I" they'd managed to extricate from my flesh-and-blood brain and input into their quantum cerebral matrix—was trapped after all in a body that wasn't a body. There was no escape from that. Not into my own body, which had been mangled by the accident, flayed by the doctors, then burned as medical waste. Not into death; death was off the table.

After that, darkness seemed irrelevant. Temporary, like everything else.

With snow packing my eyes and ears, there was no warning. Just pressure, then a jolt. Fingers gripping me, hauling me upward. I dropped back flat against the fresh powder. System diagnostics lit up behind my lids: The network was intact, already repairing itself. Synflesh knitting together, ceramic bones and tendons snapping back into place.

A hand brushed the snow from my eyes. Riley knelt over me, his fingertips light on my cheek. Behind him, Ani, worried. The sky had faded to a purplish gray. "You okay?" Riley asked.

"She's fine," Jude said. "Just a drama queen in search of an audience."

"Shut up." Riley took my shoulders and propped me up into a sitting position. "Everything still working?" The mountains loomed over us, white and silent. Years before, this had been a vacation spot, a haven for insane orgs who enjoyed hurtling down slopes at breakneck speeds even though their necks, once broken, stayed that way. But when the temperature plummeted along with the air quality, mountain gliding and its attendant risks were cancelled for good. Leaving the snow free and clear for those of us who needed neither warmth nor unfettered oxygen; those of us who just wanted to be left alone.

I knocked the snow from my shoulders and shook it out of my hair. The rush had faded as soon as I slammed into the ground—I was back in mech mode now, cool and hollow.

I pulled my lips into a half grin. It had been hard, relearning emotional expression in the new body, twitching artificial cheek and eye muscles in search of something approximating a human smile. But by now I had total control in a way that orgs never did. Orgs smiled when they were happy, the motion automatic, a seamless reflex of muscle reacting to mind, neural and physiological systems so intertwined that forcing a smile was often enough to boost a mood. Like a natural b-mod, its behavior-modifying effects were brief but instantaneous. My smiles were deliberate, like everything else, and no amount of curled lips and bared teeth would mod my mood.

I let the grin widen. "Who wants to go again?"

Abruptly, Riley dropped his arms, dumping me into the snow. It was Jude who hauled me to my feet and Jude who bundled me up and strapped me into the waiting plane, while Quinn and Ani cuddled in the next seat and Riley sulked in a far corner.

"Have a nice fall?" Jude asked, as the plane lifted off and carried us back toward the estate. The thunder of the engines wrapped us in a soundproof cocoon.

I leaned back, pointing and flexing my toes. Everything was in working order. "I've had better."

Jude arched an eyebrow. "You know, you continue to surprise me."

"Because?"

"I didn't expect someone like you to be such a quick study."

I didn't have to ask what he meant by "someone like me." Rich bitch Lia Kahn, spoiled and selfish and so sure she's better than everyone else. "Someone like the person I *used* to be," I reminded him. "That person's gone. You showed me that."

"And I'm still waiting for an appropriate demonstration of gratitude."

"You expecting me to buy you flowers?"

"Why would I need flowers when I have your sunny disposition to brighten my day?"

"What can I say?" I simpered at him. "You bring out the best in me."

Jude stripped out of his suit, balled it up, and tossed it across the plane. "Funny how I tend to have that effect on people."

"Oh, please." I stabbed a finger down my throat. "Do *not* start lumping me in with your groupies."

"They're not groupies."

But I could tell he enjoyed the designation. "What would you call them?"

"They're lost, searching for answers—can I help it if they come to me?" Jude crossed his arms, pleased with himself. "I suppose I'd call them wisdom seekers."

"And they're seeking it in your pants?"

"So vulgar." Jude tsked. "When the problem is your body, it's not so difficult to imagine that the body is where the solution lies." He reached for my hand, but I snatched it away.

"Save it for the groupies."

"What?" he asked, amber eyes wide with innocence.

I turned my back on him, watching the clouds stream by. Even now there was something disconcerting about being up in the air without a pilot. Self-navigating cars were the norm—these days, only control freaks drove themselves—but the self-piloting planes were fresh on the market, powered by some new smarttech that, according to the pop-ups, was the world's first true artificial intelligence. Unlike the smartcars, smart-fridges, smarttoilets, smarteverything we were used to, the new tech could respond to unforeseen circumstances, could experiment, could *learn*. It could, theoretically, shuttle passengers at seven hundred miles an hour from point A to point B without breaking a sweat. It just couldn't smile and reassure you that if a bird flew into the engine, it would know what to do.

Not that there were many birds anymore.

Especially where most of the AI planes were destined to fly, the poison air of the eastern war zones. This was military tech; action at distance was the only way to win without having to fight. Thinking planes, thinking tanks, thinking landcrawlers equipped with baby nukes saved orgs from having to think for themselves. Saved them from having to die for themselves. Not many had credit to spare to snatch up a smartplane of their own for peacetime purposes—but as far as Quinn was concerned, no luxury was too luxurious, especially when Jude was the one placing the request.

The ground was hidden beneath a thick layer of fog, and it was tempting to imagine it had disappeared. "Flying's getting old," I said, keeping my back to Jude.

"For you maybe."

"We need to find something better." More dangerous, I meant. Wilder, faster, steeper. *Bigger.*

"You want better?" He slipped a small, hard cube into my palm. "For later."

"You know I don't do that crap." But I closed my fingers around it.

"For later," he said again. So smug.

I just kept staring out the window, wondering what it would feel like if the plane crashed. How long would we stay conscious, our mangled bodies melting into the burnt fuselage? Would we be aware as fuel leaked from the wreckage, lit by a stray spark? What would it feel like at the moment of explosion, our brains and bodies blasted into a million pieces?

I would never know. The moment this brain burst into fire,

someone at BioMax would set to work retrieving my stored memories, downloading them into a newly made body, waking me to yet another new life. That "me" would remember everything up to my last backup and nothing more. No flying, no crashing, no explosion.

For the best, I decided. Maybe when it came to dying, once was enough.

ROBIN WASSERMAN is the author of the Cold Awakening trilogy (*Frozen*, *Shattered*, *Torn*), *Hacking Harvard*, the Seven Deadly Sins series, and the Chasing Yesterday trilogy. She lives in Brooklyn, New York.

POSSESSION

Elana Johnson

RobinWasserman.com

Video trailers ✳ Chapter excerpts

Audio clips ✳ Robin's blog

And more!

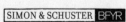

Did you love this book?

Want to get access to the hottest books for free?

Log on to simonandschuster.com/pulseit
to find out how to join,
get access to cool sweepstakes,
and hear about your favorite authors!

Become part of Pulse IT and tell us what you think!

SIMON TEEN

Simon & Schuster's **Simon Teen**
e-newsletter delivers current updates on
the hottest titles, exciting sweepstakes, and
exclusive content from your favorite authors.

Visit **TEEN.SimonandSchuster.com** to
sign up, post your thoughts, and find out what
every avid reader is talking about!

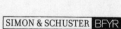

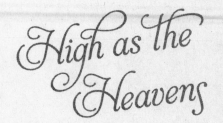

Books by Kate Breslin

High as the Heavens
Not by Sight
For Such a Time

High as the Heavens

KATE BRESLIN

BETHANYHOUSE
a division of Baker Publishing Group
Minneapolis, Minnesota

© 2017 by Kathryn Breslin

Published by Bethany House Publishers
11400 Hampshire Avenue South
Bloomington, Minnesota 55438
www.bethanyhouse.com

Bethany House Publishers is a division of
Baker Publishing Group, Grand Rapids, Michigan

Printed in the United States of America

Library of Congress Cataloging-in-Publication Data
Names: Breslin, Kate, author.
Title: High as the heavens / Kate Breslin.
Description: Minneapolis, Minnesota : Bethany House, a division of Baker
    Publishing Group, [2017]
Identifiers: LCCN 2016050055 | ISBN 9780764230363 (hardcover) | ISBN
    9780764217814 (softcover)
Subjects: LCSH: World War, 1914-1918—Underground movements—Fiction.
    | Women spies—Belgium—Fiction. | Man-woman relationships—Fiction. |
    GSAFD: Historical fiction. | Christian fiction. | Love stories. | Spy stories.
Classification: LCC PS3602.R4575 H54 2017 | DDC 813/.6—dc23
LC record available at https://lccn.loc.gov/2016050055

This is a work of historical reconstruction; the appearances of certain historical figures are therefore inevitable. All other characters, however, are products of the author's imagination, and any resemblance to actual persons, living or dead, is coincidental.

Cover design by Kathleen Lynch / Black Kat Design
Cover photograph of woman: Arcangel / Malgorzata Maj
Cover photograph of airplanes: Arcangel / Valentino Sani

Author is represented by Hartline Literary Agency

17 18 19 20 21 22 23   7 6 5 4 3 2 1

To my brothers, Michael and Matthew,
and in memory of Steven James—childhood superheroes,
fighting for truth, justice, and saving the world.

For the sanctity of all human life.

For as high as the heavens are above the earth,
so great is his love for those who fear him;
as far as the east is from the west,
so far has he removed our transgressions from us.

—Psalm 103:11–12

CHAPTER 1

*L*ike manna from heaven, the words fell from the sky.

Evelyn Marche snatched at one of the blue leaflets fluttering down outside the Royal Palace and glanced at the message, though she already knew it by heart.

She tilted her head and tried to catch a glimpse of the plane, now obscured by dark rain clouds in the October sky. The engine's faint whine mingled with the distant boom of artillery fire from the Front, and she was seized with a familiar ache, the memory of another time and place.

She stared at the leaflet in her hand: *Have courage for a little time; we shall soon deliver you.*

It wasn't the first time a daring Allied flyer had braved the anti-aircraft guns at la Grand-Place to bring the citizens of Brussels hope. Three long years had seen many such promises, each one empty to a city beaten down by German occupation and the oppression of war. With every barrage of blue notes came the pain of remembering those she had lost: her uncle, sister, brother . . . and the man she loved.

As the days and months wore on without an end in sight,

7

the Allies' promises grew wearying and repetitious, and finally maddening in their naïve improbability.

Until today.

Anticipation quickened her pulse as she gazed at the sidewalk, now littered in blue. She had finished her nursing shift at the improvised hospital inside the palace minutes before, and her chance conversation with a patient, a French corporal named Jean Duval, was fresh in her mind.

"We shall soon deliver you . . ." she breathed aloud, and the promise took on new meaning.

She'd found Nicholas and Zoe.

A wave of emotion seized her. Eve would never forget the Germans' assault on the Belgian university town of Louvain three years earlier. The dreadful night her brother and sister disappeared had left her and Mama not knowing if they were buried beneath the city's rubble or, like so many others, forced onto trains bound for Germany's labor camps.

"Your brother and sister were on the train, but they fled near Liège with my cousins and made their way to France."

Eve could still hardly believe it. Her casual inquiry into a patient's family had led to the corporal's account of how his cousins, Armand and Michel Rousseau, had met up with Nikki and Zoe on the train. The four of them had escaped, and with the help of kindly Belgians and French had made their way south to the Rousseaus' family home in Anor, France, not far from the Belgian border. Truly, it was a miracle.

Eve couldn't wait to share the news with her mother, and she quickly gathered up leaflets, stuffing them into the pockets of her apron. At least the paper had some use—Mama saved the blank sides for making her prickings, hand-drawn templates used to create designs for lace making.

With her pockets full, Eve secured her nurse's kerchief, drew her cobalt blue cloak tight against the crisp fall air, and began to walk the three blocks along rue des Sols toward her aunt and uncle's café. Marie and Lucien Bernard also owned the apartment above Chez Bernard and had welcomed Eve and her mother to live with them after fleeing the destruction of Louvain.

Eve picked up her pace, imagining how happy Mama would be to learn about the children.

Children. They were hardly that anymore. Her brother would turn fourteen soon, while Zoe had celebrated her eighteenth birthday months ago.

Eve checked her wristwatch. Four thirty. If only she'd spoken with the corporal last week when he arrived, instead of this afternoon, just before he left for the POW hospital in Germany. Now the pass office was closed.

She quelled her impatience. Before she even considered obtaining permission to leave Brussels, she would need a plan to cross the border into occupied France, find her siblings, and slip them back into Belgium.

If that were not daunting enough, time now worked against her. According to the corporal, the situation in France was as bleak as in Belgium; there too the Germans were conscripting all young men fourteen and older, forcing many to work in the trenches at the Front.

Nikki had only weeks before his birthday. He was a mere child, yet they might put him in the middle of the fighting, where he would have to kill or be killed. . . .

An image from the past pushed its way into her thoughts. *The gleam of a knife . . . a bloodied gray uniform . . . a boy's gray eyes wide in disbelief . . .*

She thrust the memory aside, though the guilt and grief remained. Pausing on the sidewalk, she took deep breaths of the cold air and bolstered her flagging resolve.

Nikki and Zoe were in France, and she would find them and

deliver them back to Belgium. From Brussels, she could arrange to smuggle them out of the country through the Netherlands and on to safety in Britain.

She resumed her trek, and the café soon came into view. As always she tensed at the sight of so many uniforms. Like a gray sea surrounding the linen-covered tables outside Chez Bernard, German soldiers, most of them officers, sat laughing, joking, and smoking cheroots. They seemed oblivious to the war as they filled their bellies with Uncle Lucien's tinned-meat version of *Rindergulasch* and Belgian-styled *Spaetzle,* then greedily washed it all down with frothy mugs of Belgium's Trappist beer.

Her stomach growled at the scent of food as she mounted the outside steps to the apartment. *Keep drinking,* she thought as her glance darted back to the soldiers. In half an hour she would exchange her nurse's apron for that of a waitress. By helping out her aunt and uncle, she had the opportunity to glean useful information from the more inebriated German patrons.

"Sister!"

She stiffened and turned on the steps to see several officers waving at her. Recognizing them as former patients, she offered them a slight nod.

Eve strove to maintain her image as Sister Nurse Marche of the Belgian Red Cross, as the role gave her a measure of protection, even while working at the café. She assisted in their surgeries, stitched their wounds, bathed them, and wiped their brows; such intimacies demanded proper boundaries to prevent the homesick and lovelorn soldiers from reading into her actions anything more than sisterly care.

She continued up the stairs, wondering what the night's business might bring. Lately she'd noticed a decline in the number of German soldiers on leave in Brussels. In fact, just that morning she'd learned that many stationed inside the city, including those in the secret military police and on General von Falkenhausen's staff, were scheduled to depart for the Front.

Making a mental note to report her findings, she entered the apartment. It was going to be an exceptionally long night. After her shift ended at the café, she had to bicycle out to the edge of the Sonian Forest and pick up a scheduled drop. The orders from MI6 in Rotterdam had been clear: *Meet package, 2300 hours. Groenendael Priory.*

The "package" being an agent, Eve wasn't certain if she had to bring him back into Brussels, though she could ride two on a bicycle. Either way, she had to be at the priory by eleven, and by the time she finished she'd be lucky to get more than a few winks of sleep.

She decided to go in search of her mother before changing her clothes. Walking through the foyer and down the short hall, she paused at the kitchen, relieved to find the compact room with its oblong table and mismatched chairs empty of their German boarders.

The occupation had brought thousands of military personnel into Brussels, filling every vacant room and hotel as the kaiser turned the city into his own personal garrison. Many Belgians had been forced to take in soldiers. The two officers currently boarding on the apartment's second level were merely the latest in a string of unwanted guests that made the already small living quarters more cramped.

Eve wondered if Lieutenants Wolfe and Kraus were already having supper downstairs in the café. If so, she would have time to search their room.

She made her way deeper into the apartment. On the right, her aunt and uncle shared the largest bedroom, while across the hall in what used to be a sewing room, Mama spent most of her time.

She paused at her mother's open door. Inside, Louise Marche

perched on a chair beneath the small west window, dressed in her usual dark skirt trimmed in the black crepe of mourning. Her chestnut hair held wisps of gray, and she bent over a work-table lined with dozens of threaded wooden bobbins, several dancing back and forth in a blur between her hands as she wove her newest piece of lace.

"*Bonjour*, Mama," Eve said. "How are you?"

With a distracted smile, her mother turned squinty hazel eyes in her direction. "Zoe, is that you, *chère?*"

The question, spoken in a high, thin voice, tore at Eve's heart. The war had changed them all, but especially Mama, once so lovely and full of life. Eve remembered her mother's laughter as they sat around the family table in Oxford, while her father, Professor Nicholas Marche, entertained his wife and children with the latest amusing anecdote about his students.

Such a long time ago. Before Papa's death, in a world where war didn't exist.

Mama had returned her attention to the bobbins, her distracted smile still in place. It was as though her mind had drifted away to that happier time.

"Mama, it is me, Eve."

"Of course it is." Her mother glanced up again, and this time she seemed fully focused. "You worry too much, *ma petite*. I sometimes sit here and think of Zoe and Nikki, and I forget for a time."

A shadow crossed her mother's pale features before she returned to her task, her knobby fingers flying as the bobbins rolled back and forth against the wooden table.

Minutes ago Eve had been eager to share her news, but now she hesitated. Corporal Duval admitted he hadn't corresponded with his cousin Armand Rousseau in months. What if Nikki and Zoe were no longer in Anor? With war raging, nothing was certain. They could have fled the city.

Gazing at her mother's features worn down by grief, she decided to wait. Mama had already endured more than her share of heartache. Eve wouldn't give her false hope.

"Did you have your supper?" she asked instead. Her mother barely ate. Ironic, considering that the Bernards received more food than most, though it was meager fare. Uncle Lucien was allowed extra rations for the café, as the menu at Chez Bernard catered to German soldiers, including General von Falkenhausen's government staff.

"Mama?" Eve asked when her mother didn't respond.

"*Oui*. Now, *chère*, you must leave me to finish my work. I will have this very special piece of lace ready for Madame Bissette tonight, along with others to sell."

Eve looked at the delicate piece of trim her mother was weaving. She worked with bobbins, in the style of the Bruges lace makers, and it was laborious work. The German officers' wives who frequented Bissette's lace boutique near la Grand-Place were always delighted when her mother's exquisite designs and workmanship appeared in the shop.

As for this "very special piece," a simpler weave that Mama was able to craft much more quickly, Madame Bissette would pass it along to a Dutch textiles merchant in Brussels. From there it would be taken by cargo ship across the Scheldt River into neutral Holland, to the British Secret Service headquarters in Rotterdam.

Eve watched her mother's fingers fly, marveling at the way she could weave into her pattern the information Eve had given her in a code that would reveal critical intelligence to the Allies—the number of German troops, horses, and artillery moving in and out of the Brussels railway station.

"I'll take the lace with me tomorrow morning," Eve said at last. "And I've brought you more leaflets to use for your prickings. A bit wrinkled, I'm afraid, but I'll press them first." She turned toward the door. "I must get ready for work downstairs. I'll check in on you later."

Eve mounted the stairs to the next floor and halted outside the lieutenants' room. She listened for any sound within, then knocked lightly on the door. Once she was convinced they had gone down to supper, she slipped inside.

Their usual Spartan housekeeping had not changed. The twin beds were neatly made, and two gray uniforms hung inside the armoire. Two sets of boot polish and brushes lay on top of the dark wood dresser, two canvas rucksacks sat in a corner of the room, and two rifles rested against the wall beside them.

Heart pounding, she listened carefully for any sound as she began her search. She slid her hands along the underside of each mattress, then examined the contents of the dresser drawers, the rucksacks, and the closet.

In a pocket of a uniform in the armoire she found a letter to Lieutenant Kraus addressed from General von Falkenhausen's headquarters in the Royal Palace. Sliding the missive from its envelope, she quickly scanned the typewritten words. Not for the first time, she was grateful for her German classes at Somerville.

The letter contained orders commanding the lieutenant back to the Front at Passchendaele in two weeks' time. She quickly searched the pockets of the other uniform and found a similar letter addressed to Lieutenant Wolfe. Again she wondered at the recent exodus of soldiers from Brussels. Dare she hope the war was going badly for the Germans?

There was nothing of worth to pass on to the Allies. Eve frowned, replaced the letters, and climbed the final steps to her attic room to change. Apparently they would soon have new German boarders invading their privacy, and there was no telling who they might be . . . perhaps even members of the secret police?

She shuddered at the thought.

"Bless the saints, you're here at last!" Uncle Lucien's voice sounded harried as Eve arrived at the café to begin her shift. He stood behind the bar, his thinning brown hair askew and his rounded features haggard. In a low voice he added, "You'd think the Boche hadn't eaten in a month, the way they're devouring the goulash and spaetzle."

Her uncle wiped at his sweaty brow with the hem of his apron. "I've been serving while Laurette clears tables," he said. "We're not keeping up."

Laurette was the daughter of their neighbors, the Fontaines. While Monsieur Fontaine didn't like his daughter working in an establishment that catered to the enemy, his pragmatic wife appreciated the extra money Laurette brought home to the family.

"I'll start as soon as I speak with Aunt." Eve plucked a white apron from a peg against the dark wainscoting behind the bar. The tables outside were full, but twice as many soldiers sat inside the café. Accompanying them were a handful of Belgian girls, now ostracized by their countrymen for fraternizing with the Boche.

Eve saw that one girl had tried using powder to cover a dark bruise on her cheek, and she froze as old memories came rushing at her. *Lying in the street . . . the man with the scarred face pressing her down . . . a scream in her throat . . .*

Trembling, she drew several quick breaths and shoved the image from her mind. Few understood that many of these women had little choice; after being raped or assaulted by the soldiers, they remained with them, their need for food and survival outweighing concerns for dignity or reputation.

Eve had received her own share of sneers from the Belgians. In their eyes she not only appeared to be collaborating with the Boche by working at the German-run hospital but also gained by working at her uncle's business, which catered to the enemy.

In the kitchen she found Laurette washing dishes, while Aunt Marie stood at the cast-iron stove stirring an enormous pot of steaming goulash and watching a large pan of spaetzle frying in grease. Her aunt's hair had slipped from its coil beneath her blue kerchief, leaving a long honey-colored strand draped against her collar.

She turned as Eve entered. "*Dieu merci.* I'm so glad you're here."

"Uncle said you've been busy."

Aunt Marie huffed out a laugh, then eyed her critically. "You look very nice."

Eve adjusted her white kerchief, then smoothed the worn fabric of her violet skirt. She'd dashed on a bit of rose water as well. "*Merci, Tante.*"

Her aunt's gaze darted to Laurette, then swiveled back to her. "And I suppose you must wear that," she said with a jerk of her chin.

Eve glanced down at the Iron Cross pinned to her shirtwaist. "*For your tireless work in caring for the German wounded,*" she'd been told when she received the military decoration upon her return to Brussels. Though she suspected the award had more to do with saving the life of her hospital administrator, Major Otto Reinhardt, who was in Louvain when the chaos broke out.

"It's important I wear it, Aunt." The award had made her something of a heroine in the eyes of the German soldiers. They didn't dare try to molest her. The medal was useful for learning secrets, too.

Aunt Marie made a sound of grudging assent. Despite the café's catering to the German occupiers, the Bernards were Belgian patriots. They knew their niece worked for an underground resistance network, and they also knew better than to question her motives.

"The goulash smells delicious. May I please have some?" Eve asked, changing the subject. "Uncle's waiting, so I'll eat quickly."

Her aunt turned, ladled up a bowlful, and handed it to her, along with a spoon.

Eve smiled her thanks. "Has Mama had supper?"

"Laurette took her food up an hour ago and stayed to watch her eat."

"*Oui.*" Young Laurette stood by the sink, bobbing her white-capped head. "She ate half of the goulash, though she didn't touch the slice of black bread."

Eve wrinkled her nose. "The bread contains more sawdust than flour, so I can't blame her. Still, I'm glad her appetite is improved. Thank you."

She smiled at the girl, then quickly ate the stew. When she'd finished, she handed the dish to Laurette. To her aunt she said, "May I help with anything?"

"Just take the dirty table linen to Tulle's *blanchisserie* before he closes."

"Anything for the soup kitchen?"

Aunt Marie smiled. "There wasn't much left over from last night's menu, but I took what we had to the kitchen on rue de la Madeleine this morning."

Eve nodded. She was glad they could ease the suffering of at least a few starving citizens in the city.

"Anyway, Lucien put your bicycle there, in the *office*." Her aunt nodded toward the pantry.

"I wish I had a bicycle," Laurette muttered, rolling up her long sleeves to sink her hands into the soapy dishwater. "Papa says they are too expensive."

"Ha! That's because the Boche took them from us two years ago and sent the rubber tires back to Berlin to make more tires for their artillery guns." Eve's aunt gave the goulash several quick stirs. "They allow Belgians to buy back the bicycles at an outrageous price, plus an extra charge for more tires!"

"Why does Eve get to keep hers?" Laurette asked.

"Because I'm a nurse," Eve said. "If there's an emergency, I need to be able to get to the hospital or to someone's home quickly."

"You'd better get out there and help your uncle," Aunt Marie cut in, as the bell over the door announced more hungry customers.

"I'll get to Tulle's before six," Eve promised and went to the front of the café.

Some of the German soldiers were already a little intoxicated, including Wolfe and Kraus. Faces flushed, the two lieutenants sat with another pair of officers, rocking back and forth as they sang "Der treue Husar," a favorite tune.

"Pretty Sister, join us!" Kraus beckoned her to their table, grinning widely beneath his dark moustache.

"*Mehr Bier?*" she asked with a smile, switching to German as she eyed the foursome.

"*Ja!*" they chorused, and Eve left to return moments later with four mugs of the amber brew. She set them on the table and waited as they rummaged in their pockets for the marks to pay.

"We must leave you soon," Wolfe said, the gravity of his tone at odds with his glassy-eyed look. "We've been ordered back to the Front."

"We'll miss you, Sister," chimed Kraus as he scraped the marks from the table and handed them to her. "And your pretty blue eyes, like violets."

"And hair dark like the Black Forest," Wolfe said. "Though you always hide it under that ugly kerchief—"

"You will both be missed," Eve cut in, aware of the speculative looks from the other officers at the table. With a self-conscious gesture she tucked more of her hair beneath the kerchief. "You two have been the perfect boarders."

She didn't add that they were "perfect" because they usually passed out in their room each night and didn't notice her coming or going. She hoped the next boarders would be as docile as these two.

"When do you leave?" she asked, though she already knew the answer.

"Two weeks," Wolfe said. He took another drink of beer, then wiped traces of foam from his moustache. "We must make the most of our time left in Brussels, *ja, meine Kameraden?*"

Once again they all broke into song, and Eve slipped away to take care of the other customers. She brought out trays laden with steaming bowls of goulash and heaped plates of golden spaetzle. Her uncle handled the money and washed the glass beer mugs as fast as they came back, and at a quarter to six she was able to leave the café for the laundry.

As was her duty every Monday and Thursday, Eve pedaled her bicycle, loaded with the café's soiled linen, to Tulle's blanchisserie on rue de la Madeleine across from St. Magdalene's church, where she exchanged the used linen for clean.

She was keen to learn if Monsieur Tulle had any information to pass along to the Allies. It seemed the Boche were gearing up for some kind of siege in the next few weeks, as Wolfe and Kraus were to join the ranks of those already at the Front.

The bell above the laundry shop door chimed as she entered.

"*Bonsoir*, Mademoiselle Marche."

A family man whose wife and three grown daughters worked in the laundry, Monsieur Tulle stood behind the counter, his aged hands propped against a sack filled with cleaned, pressed linen for the café. The tall, spindly proprietor watched her approach, his benign expression giving no clue he also worked as an agent for the Belgian underground intelligence network *La Dame Blanche*.

Eve smiled pleasantly. "Any difficulties?"

"An apron torn, but I took extra care to repair the seam."

The edge in his tone made her pulse quicken. Tulle must have new intelligence on the Germans' troop movements. "I appreciate your attention to detail," she said, and offered him her bundle in exchange for the one on the counter.

Once she returned to the café, Eve stowed her bicycle and sorted through the clean linen to find the repaired apron. She examined the new seam along one side, knowing Tulle's message was carefully sewn into the fabric.

With the excuse of checking on her mother, Eve ran the apron up to her room. She was relieved to see Mama still busy at her worktable.

Tonight after Eve met the agent at the priory in Groenendael, she would return to decode the lists of troops, horses, and artillery Monsieur Tulle had provided. Mama could start another pattern of lace to be sent through Madame Bissette to their Dutch merchant.

Returning downstairs to the café, she was pleased to find Kraus and Wolfe well into their cups. They should sleep soundly tonight, leaving her in peace to do her work.

The curfew for Belgians was seven o'clock, and by ten o'clock all but a couple German soldiers continued to swill beer. Kraus and Wolfe had left an hour before to seek their beds.

Eve glanced at the clock. Twenty minutes before she must leave for Groenendael. She hurried along the last two customers and flipped the sign in the large pane window to read *geschlossen*.

She was locking the door when she was startled by a familiar figure in a Red Cross uniform smiling at her from the other side of the glass.

"Dominic!" Eve opened the door to the tall, beefy Frenchman. "Why are you here?"

"I decided to stop by and wish my favorite nurse *bonsoir* before I head for the hospital." Dom's caramel eyes glowed.

20

"I don't suppose a man could still get a beer?" His hopeful gaze turned toward the bar, where her uncle was counting the night's receipts.

Eve gave him a reproving look. "You're about to go on shift, Dom. I'll not contribute to your corruption." She smiled. "You can have a cup of coffee."

His expression fell and he sighed. "*Oui*. And I suppose I must settle for what passes as coffee, eh?"

"Sit." She went to pour them each a cup. Because of the food shortage, even the café's brew tasted more like the ersatz coffee most Belgians drank. Being British, she preferred her tea, but the war version of that was worse than the coffee.

She carried the drinks to the table and sat down. "I must leave for an appointment shortly, but you're welcome to stay. Aunt Marie and Uncle Lucien will be here awhile, cleaning up."

"Appointment?" Dom eyed her intently. "Anyone I know?"

"A package." Eve kept her tone casual.

"Rotterdam ordered it?"

She nodded. A year ago, Dominic Lesser had helped her to get into La Dame Blanche, so he understood that her errand was for the British Secret Service.

"Where?"

She took a sip of her coffee, then said, "Groenendael Priory."

"You're riding out to the Sonian Forest tonight?" His expression darkened. "Watch yourself. There are plenty of German patrols out."

"I won't have any difficulties." She withdrew her Red Cross pass from her pocket and flashed it at him.

"Medical personnel might be exempt from the curfew, *chérie*, but it does not mean the Boche will be on their best behavior." Concern creased his brow. "You'll keep that visible, *non*?" He tipped his chin, indicating her Iron Cross.

Eve reached for the medal. "I remember a time when this

21

worried you." It had taken the big French orderly months at the hospital to decide she was friend and not foe.

"*Oui*," he said, and a flush stained his cheeks as he grinned. "Until I finally understood its advantages—once the enemy's wounded see it, they fall in love with you and tell you all of their secrets from the Front."

Her mouth twitched with amusement. "It helps."

"Let me go with you." He leaned forward and grasped her hand. "I can get the ambulance and drive you."

Eve gently withdrew from his touch. While Dom's friendship had helped her through a difficult time in her life, she sensed he wanted more. But three years hadn't erased her grief.

"Thank you, *mon ami*, but I'll be fine." She rose from her chair. "Now I must go. Stay and enjoy your coffee."

She headed toward the back of the café and found Laurette just saying good-bye. "Aunt, I have business to attend to," she said once the girl had left. "I'll return home as soon as I can."

Aunt Marie knew not to ask questions. "I'll leave the door unlocked. Be careful."

Eve nodded and gazed warmly at her. She'd thought to tell her aunt the news about her siblings earlier, but the café was so busy tonight she hadn't had the chance. She glanced at the clock. Her news would have to wait until tomorrow.

Anticipation hummed in her as she went to retrieve her bicycle. She wanted to believe her brother and sister were still in Anor. She needed only to come up with a means to recover them, and La Dame Blanche might provide her with resources.

Buoyed by the thought, she walked the bicycle back through the café to go out to the main street.

Dom rose to open the door. "Take care of yourself."

His gruff words sobered her, reminding her of the precarious task ahead.

"I promise." With a quick wave, she left the café. The crisp night air smelled of rain, and the Front had quieted for the evening. Eve stood for a moment, enjoying the blessed silence, then reached to adjust the brass carbide lamp on the front of her bicycle. She wouldn't ignite it until she'd traveled beyond the city limits.

She had just started to pedal along rue des Sols when the whine of an engine overhead drew her attention. Eve stopped to study the inky sky, and the noise intensified as the plane flew low over the city.

The sound differed from the one she'd heard earlier in the afternoon. Was this the plane bringing the agent to Groenendael?

Her body jerked as an ear-shattering explosion lit the sky; a second blast followed, then a third as the anti-aircraft guns at la Grand-Place found their target.

The deafening scream of the plane's engine pierced her ears as it burst into a bright fireball above her. She watched in horror as the plane spiraled downward, crashing in Brussels Park a few hundred meters away.

The ground shook, and her racing heart thundered in her chest.

Dom ran out of the café, shouting in French, and German whistles could be heard blaring from la Grand-Place.

"Dom, get an ambulance!" she cried, before pedaling her bicycle toward the inferno.

Eve soon entered the park and took a running leap off her bicycle as she raced toward the burning wreckage. Time seemed to stop while she took in the scene: A man lay beside one of the plane's wings, half of his body on fire. Another man was stretched out prone near the edge of the burning engine. He was dressed in plain clothes, not a uniform, and had a parachute pack slung over one shoulder. Could he be the agent she was to meet?

She rushed to extinguish the first man and saw that he was

already dead, his face burned beyond recognition. His smoldering uniform was that of a British pilot.

Taking no time to consider her actions, she removed the pair of ID discs from around his charred neck, wincing at the hot metal against her fingertips as she slipped them inside her coat pocket.

If the second man was indeed the agent, he might need to "borrow" the identification. She ran to him and grabbed his feet, dragging him clear of the flames. An agent would be a fool to wear his ID discs on assignment—nevertheless, she had to make certain. Crouching beside his body, she began tugging at the back of his collar.

A hand reached up to grab her wrist in a painful grip.

He was alive! "Let me help you," she hissed in English, and he loosened his grip. Eve slid the pack off his shoulder and tossed it into the flames. Then she gently rolled him onto his back—

Her breath caught, and she rocked on her heels as the earth shifted beneath her. It couldn't be . . .

Yet in the fire's light his reddish-blond hair was recognizable, and despite the blood covering his face, she could make out the high cheekbones and patrician nose, the generous mouth . . .

She wet her lips, her senses reeling. Was he flesh . . . or spirit?

Her finger reached to gently touch the achingly familiar cleft in his chin, and he jerked at the contact before his attention focused on her.

She met his gaze, drowning in the remarkable gray pools that had sometimes been dark like rain clouds, and at other times light as the North Sea. His warm hand covered hers, this time in a caress, while tears leaked from his eyes, making tracks along either side of his bloodied face.

Her throat worked as she clasped his fingers. He *was* real—not a ghost at all, but flesh and bone, resurrected from her past. The man she thought she'd lost forever.

Her husband.

CHAPTER 2

*S*imon?" Her voice was ragged.

Behind her, police whistles pierced the air. Angry shouts in German grew louder as soldiers from la Grand-Place rushed to the scene.

Her husband must have heard them as well. He fumbled to remove a small leather pouch from inside his jacket. "Hide," he muttered.

Eve took the pouch from him just before he passed out.

"Eve!"

Dom's voice sounded in her ear. She tucked the pouch inside her coat as the orderly dropped to his knees on the grass beside her.

"The ambulance," he said, breathing hard and looking back toward the street. "I had to run all the way to the palace to get it."

"He's still alive." Eve began checking her husband for injuries, then quickly inspected his clothes for other identification. She found nothing. "It's amazing he has no broken limbs," she said, though his face and the amount of blood oozing along his temple gave her pause. She hoped the gash on his head wasn't deep. "Let's get him to the hospital. He may have serious injuries we can't see."

Dom rose to his feet while two young German corporals lumbered up, one still blowing his whistle. Eve turned to glare at the pair. "*Holen Sie eine Bahre!*" she snapped.

When they stood gaping at the flames, she rose and faced them squarely. "I said get a stretcher!" She pointed to the ambulance. "*Schnell!*"

Whether they recognized her from the hospital or because her Iron Cross glinted in the light of the fire, both men straightened and saluted before rushing to obey.

While the soldiers placed Simon into the ambulance, Dom retrieved her bicycle and loaded it into the back as well. Eve rode along as he drove toward the palace hospital.

"Did he say anything to you?" Dom asked.

Eve barely heard him as she gazed out her side of the open cab. They passed the Musée des Instruments, and she was only dimly aware of the museum standing in darkness on the unlit street.

Her beloved was alive! Tears of joy and disbelief sprang to her eyes as she clasped her hands together to keep them from shaking. After three long years of grief, believing him lost to her forever . . .

An ache pierced her chest as she remembered the call notifying her of Simon's death, news that had ripped her world apart.

Yet here he was, living and breathing. She twisted to peer through the small window into the back of the ambulance, straining to make out his beloved form and prove to herself she wasn't dreaming.

He lay unmoving in the darkness. Eve's heart pumped wildly as new fear seized her. Did he have extensive internal injuries? *Dear Lord, is he going to die?*

"Eve? Did you hear me?"

Dom's voice pulled her back from her panicked reverie. She

settled back in her seat and glanced at him in the shadows. "He was unconscious," she managed in a calm tone.

"I thought I saw him hand you something."

"He . . . he groaned and raised his hand to me before he passed out. Perhaps that's what you saw." She hated lying to her friend, but until she had sorted this out, she wouldn't reveal the identity of their patient. Closing her eyes, she fought back tears. Where had Simon been all this time? If he was alive, then whose remains were found near his downed plane three years ago? And why was he here?

Eve's thoughts swirled like dried leaves caught in a great gust. Had Simon come here seeking her out?

Dom said nothing more on the way to the hospital, and Eve was grateful for the silence. Once they arrived, another Red Cross orderly descended the palace steps and jogged over to Dom's side of the truck.

"That was quick." Felix Giroux, a Belgian and fellow member of La Dame Blanche, flashed a smile. "Need help?"

"Let's get him into the surgery."

Dom swung out of the truck, and the two men off-loaded their patient. Eve followed them inside the hospital, then excused herself to go and change into a surgical gown. She tucked Simon's leather pouch beneath her corset.

When she arrived at the operating theater, she found Simon alone and lying on the surgeon's table. Pulse pounding, she marshaled her thoughts and quickly placed one of the dead pilot's identity discs, the green one, around Simon's neck. Without a military ID, he would be taken for a spy and marked for death.

She had just finished cutting away his clothing when Dr. Ambrose arrived. Eve was thankful the Belgian physician and not the German chief surgeon happened to be on call.

A night nurse accompanied him, a young Belgian woman new to the hospital.

"I'll see to the patient, Sister." Eve spoke in a brisk tone, using her authority as chief nurse to send the young woman away.

She returned her attention to her husband, and a lump rose in her throat as she carefully wiped the blood from Simon's face. Her gaze followed her touch, lingering over every familiar angle and plane of his rugged features.

"The head wound isn't too serious," Dr. Ambrose said. "Though there is always the possibility of an internal injury. We'll observe him overnight and check his condition again in the morning."

Eve fought down another stab of fear. The doctor was right; Simon wasn't out of danger yet. Along with the gash to his head, he had several broken ribs. After she had stitched his scalp, Dom and Felix worked to bind his chest before taking him into the dimly lit palace ballroom.

The spacious room now served as the hospital's ward, and at present it held only two dozen patients. The German wounded were patched up and either sent home or back to the Front, while the Allied wounded were shipped off to POW hospitals in Germany.

"I can get him settled," Dom said once they had put Simon to bed and Felix departed.

"I'll take care of him." Eve forced a light tone. "You haven't yet made your rounds."

"Don't you have an errand to take care of?"

Eve had forgotten about the priory in the Sonian Forest. She gazed at her unconscious husband, recalling the parachute pack he'd been wearing. The British military hadn't yet sanctioned manned parachute drops, but MI6 was another matter. Had Simon been the agent she was supposed to meet? "I'm not so certain anymore, Dom," she whispered.

She glanced up to find her friend studying her. He opened

his mouth as if to speak, then seemed to change his mind. He nodded before turning to leave the ward.

After he'd gone, Eve rose on unsteady legs and went to retrieve a wash basin of warm water, along with bandages and several soft cloths from the nurses' station at the far end of the ballroom. As she passed the pair of German guards standing at the entrance, they bowed and clicked their heels.

Returning to her husband's side, she placed a cloth partition beside the bed, shielding him from the other patients and from the soldiers. Then she began to bathe him, tenderly washing the last traces of blood and grime from his face, neck, and hands.

She spied the green tag she'd placed on him earlier and withdrew the other disc from her pocket, the red one she'd kept and would need to turn over to the Germans. "Chandler, J. L., Captain, Royal Flying Corps," she read in a whisper. Eve clutched the disc and said a quick prayer for the man. Though Captain Chandler had only a five-digit number to mark his memory, his death might save her husband's life.

She gazed back at Simon, lying still and helpless, his face a canvas of cuts and bruises. He'd lost quite a bit of weight since she'd last seen him, and beneath his facial discoloration she noted haggard lines that hadn't been there before. Again she wondered where he'd been for three years.

She reached to brush her fingers through his hair, her touch grazing down along the sides of his face to his shoulders. She felt the muscle there, the heat of his skin, and was reassured by his physical presence. She was tempted to risk all and lie down on the bed beside him, share his warmth, breathe in his scent. It had been so long since she'd been in his arms . . .

But the German secret police, "Berlin vampires" as they were known, would arrive any moment. They would demand to see her husband, even when he was so vulnerable. She could hope to send them away for now, but what about later, when he'd regained consciousness? She had to find a way to protect him.

Reaching for the bandages, she began wrapping the wound at his head. His temples and the areas around his eyes were bruised and swollen, so she covered him with the cloth to just below his brow. It might help to keep him unrecognizable. She had no idea where he'd been or what his plans were.

By the time she'd finished tending him, the hour was late. Eve tucked the blankets around her sleeping husband, relieved to note his steady, even breathing. The morphine would allow him to rest, and hopefully his injuries were limited to those they'd already treated.

She hated to leave him, but she still had to decode Monsieur Tulle's message for Mama's piece of lace tomorrow. Many lives depended on La Dame Blanche getting troop reports to British intelligence as quickly as possible.

Standing in the dimly lit space, she drank in the sight of him, like tipping her face to a cool Belgian rain. Then she leaned over the bed and touched her mouth to his, and the soft, warm texture of his lips, their familiar shape, was like coming home. With a last caress to his cheek, she removed the partition and left the ward.

She found Dom next to the hospital administrator's office, arguing with two of the German secret police. He turned at her approach, looking angry and tense, before his countenance eased and he waved her over.

She recognized Herr Jaeger, a short, clean-shaven man with blond hair and piercing green eyes. He had a new accomplice with him, a foot taller than Jaeger and sporting a black trench coat. A bristling moustache sat beneath his hawklike nose, and his hazel eyes narrowed as he stared at her Iron Cross.

"Fräulein Marche, this is Herr Schultz. We wish to speak with the prisoner."

Eve's stomach muscles tightened as she turned to Jaeger and forced a pleasant expression. "The *patient* received a serious head wound and remains unconscious, so perhaps you can return tomorrow? We hope he'll have awakened by then."

"Were you able to get any information?" This time Schultz made the demand. "Where are his papers?"

Her heart gave a lurch, and she fought the urge to press a hand to her bosom, where Simon's leather pouch remained hidden beneath her corset. These vampires needed little or no reason to take someone in for questioning, and oftentimes torture, before releasing them.

"I took this from around his neck." She strove for calm as she handed over the red identity disc. "You're welcome to check his clothing, but we found nothing else. I'm certain he can answer any questions you might have tomorrow."

"Captain Chandler." As Schultz fingered the disc, Eve prayed Simon would remain unconscious—or at least silent—until she could speak with him in the morning about his new identity.

"What about the other man?" Jaeger asked.

"Dead," Dom answered. "Once the flames were extinguished, the street patrol contacted the Catholic Soldiers Society. They've already retrieved what remains of him for burial. I don't know if he had identification. The body was pretty scorched."

Jaeger turned to his partner. "Check the patrol and see what they found at the scene." To Eve and Dom he said, "We will return in the morning."

"Two of my favorite people," Eve muttered once they'd gone.

Dom eyed her with grim amusement. "They could be twins, no?"

Despite her mood, Eve smiled. "Like night and day." A yawn escaped her. "The patient is cleaned up and resting now. I'm going home."

"You look tired, *chérie*. You want Felix to give you a ride?"

She shook her head. "I've got my bicycle. It's just a few blocks to the café."

The night air hinted at autumn as she pedaled her way home, the chill breeze cooling her heated face. Her mind replayed the moments standing before Jaeger and Schultz, her mouth dry as she boldly lied, while the proof lay hidden next to her heart.

At the café, she walked her bicycle up the outside steps to the apartment. The building looked dark, with quilts hung over the windows to hide the light—another measure enacted by the Germans against possible night raids.

Once inside, Eve left her bicycle in the kitchen and tiptoed down the shadowy hall, past the master bedroom and the faint snores of her uncle. He and Aunt Marie must have been exhausted after feeding and serving so many customers this night.

Peering into Mama's room, she saw the dark silhouette of her mother curled up under a blanket on the day bed, her breathing soft and steady. Eve would take the lace she'd finished to Madame Bissette early in the morning, before going to the hospital.

Just a few hours from now.

The reminder of the work she still had to do made Eve's shoulders ache. So much had happened tonight—not the least of which was her husband falling from heaven right into her lap.

A thrill coursed through her at the reminder that he was mere blocks away. She would see him at the hospital in the morning, speak with him. Eve wasn't sure how she could focus on anything else.

All was silent in Kraus and Wolfe's room on the next landing. She took the last flight of steps to the attic, checking the top of her door for the scarlet thread she kept tucked there to alert her to intruders. Satisfied to see it undisturbed, she entered and switched on the lamp by her bedside, bathing the room in a soft glow.

The apron still lay on the bed where she'd left it hours ago.

Eve pushed it aside, along with the blue leaflets she'd collected for her mother earlier that afternoon, and collapsed onto the bed.

Simon was alive.

She still couldn't believe it. She stared at the ceiling, the soft beige color almost orange in the lamplight, while her mind relived the telephone call she'd received in London three years ago from Simon's closest friend and fellow pilot, Alex Baird. *I'm so sorry, Eve . . .*

She'd listened in stunned silence as he told her Simon's plane had gone down with Germany's first attack of the war. An aerial view showed total destruction at the crash site, the remains of a body spotted nearby. Simon was listed as dead.

Eve only vaguely recalled the days and nights that followed. Traumatized by her loss, she'd left Britain for Belgium to seek out the comfort of her family. Then the nightmare in Louvain had eclipsed her grief, weighing her down with guilt and unspeakable despair.

Eventually her numbed state turned to rage and a determination to rise from her misery, enough to function at the Brussels hospital, where Major Reinhardt had taken the post as administrator.

She'd received the Iron Cross for her work in Louvain, and in due course was placed in charge of the Belgian nurses. Little by little she let go of her anger and grief, though the guilt still seemed unbearable at times. She met Dom, and his friendship, along with her involvement in La Dame Blanche, helped her to regain a sense of herself, learning to move through each day despite the war.

Now she had her husband back, but for how long? A fresh wave of anxiety filled her. The vampires would return in a few hours. If Simon awoke and they questioned him, what would he say?

She rose and went to the armoire to change her clothes.

Removing the leather pouch, she donned her nightgown, then returned to perch on the bed.

In her haste earlier, she hadn't taken time to notice the tiny insignia of the Royal Flying Corps—a crown set above a pair of wings—embossed into one corner of the leather.

Inside the pouch she found a Belgian passport for an Albert Janssen, with a photograph bearing Simon's image. With the passport was a sealed document. Eve opened it and found an encrypted message, which used the same code she recognized from La Dame Blanche.

She was convinced now. Simon must have been her intended "package." She thought of the code phrases they were to have exchanged, and realized he couldn't know she was the agent he was supposed to meet.

Had he come here solely on a mission? Without even knowing she was here?

She ran a finger over his photograph and gazed at it hungrily. Three long years since she'd last seen his handsome face and the gray eyes so full of love. A thousand days since she'd traced the lines of his beautiful smile or felt his tender caress. She could never forget their last kiss, so different from the very first . . .

Her gaze went to the small shrine mounted on the wall between her bed and the window, a sculpted relief of the Madonna and Child. Tossing the pouch onto the pile of blue leaflets, she went to the shrine and with deft fingers tripped a latch beneath the tiny foot of Baby Jesus. The front panel opened, revealing a niche with shelves that held a rosary, holy water, and a French Bible. Her book of secrets.

Eve opened the leather tome, which had been carefully hollowed out. Inside lay a monogrammed handkerchief with the initials *SF.* Wistful yearning tugged at her, along with the memory of a young woman dressed in her birthday best, surrounded by family and friends and the man she loved.

CHAPTER 3

"*M*ake a wish, *chère*."

Eve met her mother's gaze and smiled as she leaned toward the birthday cake drizzled in white icing. Closing her eyes, she held her breath a moment, then blew out the single candle.

Wearing her new white velvet-and-lace gown, and with her eight-year-old sister, Zoe, and three-year-old brother, Nicholas Jr., already fed and upstairs with the nanny for the evening, Eve Marche felt very grown up celebrating her sixteenth birthday with just her parents and their friends.

"What did you wish for?" her father asked.

"Papa, if I tell you then it won't come true." Heat rose in her cheeks as she returned to her seat at the cherrywood dining table. The kitchen maid had cleared the remains from supper— Eve's favorite, roasted capon in lemon sauce—and was helping Mama serve slices of the cake.

Eve considered her secret wish as she picked up her crystal water glass and gazed over the rim at their handsome guests.

Marcus Weatherford and Simon Forrester were Oxford

classmates, both very grown up at twenty years of age, and students of her father's. Marcus's dark hair and honey-brown eyes were striking, yet it was the tall, broad-shouldered Simon with his coppery locks and smiling gray eyes who made Eve's heart hammer and her cheeks warm with pleasure.

The two men had dined often at the home of their Belgian mathematics professor over the course of their college years. They seemed to enjoy her father's company, and he theirs. In a few weeks, however, they would graduate and leave the university to seek their fortunes.

Would Simon move away from Oxford? And if he did, would he ever return to visit Eve and her family?

"It must have been quite a wish to keep you looking so pensive, Miss Marche. A good one, I hope?"

Marcus's teasing tone jerked her back to the present. Another flash of heat crept up her neck. She tried not to look at Simon. "I believe so," she said primly.

"Professor Marche tells us you're to start classes at Somerville in the fall." Marcus stabbed at his piece of cake with his fork. "That's quite an accomplishment for a young woman your age. Will you follow in your father's footsteps and take up teaching mathematics?"

"Indeed she will." Professor Marche passed around the decanter of port and seemed to puff up as he turned to beam at his daughter. "Eve's a crack whip when it comes to equations. I daresay she'll go to the head of her class before first term finishes out. Once she completes her examinations, she will go on to teach at Oxford High School for Girls."

Feeling all eyes upon her, Eve shifted in her seat. She was flattered that her education plans should be the topic of conversation between her father and these soon-to-be alumni, but she still hadn't embraced the idea of becoming a teacher.

"I'd like to study the more general courses at first," she said, glancing at her father to gauge his reaction. "I thought about trying to learn a new language. I already know French and a bit of Flemish, but perhaps German or Italian might be interesting."

"Commendable. Perhaps teaching languages, then," Marcus said.

"What do you really want to do with your life after college, lass? Do you want to be a teacher?"

Simon's candid question, spoken in his soft Scots burr, brought Eve up short. She pretended to concentrate on the untouched piece of cake in front of her. No one had ever asked her the question before—certainly not Papa. She wondered if Simon knew she'd been avoiding the truth to keep from displeasing him.

"Tell them, daughter." Papa sat with his fork suspended midair, gazing at her with fond expectation.

Should she speak her mind, right here in front of their guests?

Eve's gaze found Simon's, and his slight nod and coaxing smile added more heat to her cheeks. His unspoken support also gave her the encouragement she needed.

She set her fork down. "I wish to become a nurse," she announced quietly, looking at her plate. "After college I would like to take my training at the London Hospital."

A hush fell over the room. The steady tick of Mama's ormolu clock on the mantel echoed in the stillness. Eve finally braved a look at her father, and her heart raced at his surprised frown. Carefully, he laid his napkin against the table and leaned back in his chair to study her. Marcus, wide-eyed with curiosity, glanced back and forth between the professor and his daughter.

Mama wore a pinched smile and tugged at the lace cuffs of her sleeves.

Warm admiration lit the gray depths of Simon's gaze. He kept his attention focused on her, and Eve clung to his silent strength while her breath grew shallower with each passing second.

"I suppose nursing is an honorable profession."

Papa had spoken at last. He reached for her hand, and a slow smile spread beneath his dark moustache. "If this vocation is truly what you want to pursue, *ma fifille,* I have no doubt you will be brilliant." He glanced at his wife. "Isn't that right, Mama?"

"*Oui*, Papa. I never had doubts." Her mother straightened in her seat, looking relieved to have harmony restored in her home. "Now, shall we toast?"

"Indeed." Her father poured a touch of the port into her glass. "A bit of spirits for the spirit, I think, eh?" He chuckled. Then he raised his glass to her, and the others followed. "To your birthday, Evelyn Marche, and to the future that awaits you."

"Hear, hear," the men chorused.

"Thank you, Papa." Eve let out a sigh, then took a sip of the port, her tongue tingling with the syrupy sweet taste. She offered Simon a smile of gratitude. When he winked in response, her heart resumed its fast pace, though this time with yearning instead of fear.

"Speaking of futures," Papa said, pouring himself another glass of port, "what do you gentlemen have planned after your commencement?"

"I'm interested in pursuing a military career," Marcus said. "I was recently introduced to Captain Sir Mansfield George Smith-Cumming, and I'd like to seek a position in the Admiralty."

"A smart choice," her father said, with obvious approval. "And you, Simon?"

"I'll be going to Annan, near the Scots border," he said. "Last week I received a letter from my great-uncle, Angus Forrester. He's getting on in years and his health is starting to fail. He's asked me to return after my studies and help settle his affairs." Simon's gaze turned to Eve. "As much as I hate leaving, I owe him a debt. Angus took me in after my parents died and did his best to raise me. He made my education possible." He smiled.

38

"So until such time as he is ready to go and meet God, my future is with him."

Eve hid her disappointment. Scotland might as well be on the other side of the world. "Will you be able to visit us?" she asked.

"I don't know, lass." His gray gaze met hers. "We'll just have to wait and see."

The men had finished their port. "I've cigars and brandy in my study," Papa announced as the three rose from the table. "And I haven't yet told you boys how our balloon surprised the enemy at Ladysmith."

Eve sighed. Her father was about to launch into another rendition of his glory days as a balloonist with the Royal Engineers during the Second Boer War.

"Shall we go through, *ma petite*?" Mama said to her.

"I suppose so." Eve watched the men disappear down the carpeted hall to her father's study, then rose and followed her mother to the drawing room.

Mama sat down at the small worktable Papa had installed for her and began working the many bobbins on her latest creation of lace. Eve walked to the piano, grazing her fingers lightly over the ivory keys.

"Your sister is coming along well with her scales." Her mother relocated the pins on her piece of lace. "Why don't you play for me, Evelyn? A piece from Franck or Debussy would be lovely."

"I'm too restless to sit down at the keys, Mama," she said. "If it's all right with you, I'll take a walk in the garden. It's a warm night, and I wish to see the stars."

"Just don't be too long, *chère*," her mother murmured without looking up from her task.

Eve left the drawing room, heading outside through the kitchen at the back of the house. The air was warm and the garden heavily perfumed with a kaleidoscope of scents: red damask roses, white gardenias, and pale pink jasmine covering a trellis that led into the small wilderness area at the back of the property.

She walked toward the gazebo her father had commissioned years before, and the air's fragrance changed to the sweetness of honeysuckle, growing wild and clinging to the eaves of the structure. Next to the gazebo stood an ancient oak, the lower limbs laden with green as the leaves shone iridescent in the full moon's light.

Leaning against the solidity of the trunk, she gazed into the clear sky, warmed by her memory of Papa's earlier toast in the dining room. She had been so pleased at his willingness to let her decide her own future, to follow her dream of becoming a nurse.

It seemed Simon had known her heart well. Eve's pulse quickened, remembering his encouraging smile and the admiration in his gaze when she found the courage to say what she'd longed to tell her father for some time.

Suddenly she wished she were eighteen instead of sixteen. Surely then Simon would notice her as a woman and not a child. His occasional smiles from across the table had raised her hopes, and throughout dessert she'd thought of little except her secret birthday wish—that he would be the one to give Eve her very first kiss.

If only Papa would quit hoarding Simon's company! She imagined the men in her father's study, no doubt deep in discussion about aviation or war strategies. Simon would be leaving soon, and who knew when he might return? With commencement ceremonies just weeks away, she might not get another chance . . .

A distressed mewling sounded above her head, and Eve turned to look up into the boughs. Button, her kitten, was perched on a high branch, staring at her with enormous glowing eyes.

"You poor dear!" she said as the frightened creature made another cry for assistance.

Eve didn't hesitate as she bent and caught up the hem of her skirt, pulling it up between her legs and tucking the fabric into the velvet sash at her waist. Then she grasped the lowest limb and gained a toehold against the tree's bark. At Zoe's age she'd climbed into the oak many times, much to her father's amusement and her mother's disapproval.

Ascending the first few feet of the trunk, she reached for the next branch just as her skirts began to come loose. As she moved to secure another step, her toe caught in the hem and she lost her footing, skinning her knee, while her fingers slipped from the branch.

With a yelp she went toppling toward the ground.

A pair of strong arms grabbed her. Eve's heart wedged in her throat as she gazed up into Simon's concerned face.

"What in blazes are you doing?" he demanded, setting her gently on her feet.

She winced, rubbing at her knee beneath the skirt. "Button," she said, pointing to the furry white ball that had resumed its piteous mewling.

Simon released her, and Eve watched in amazement as he climbed swiftly into the branches and rescued her kitten.

Moments later he was placing the frightened Button into her hands. "I think perhaps both you and Button should give up tree climbing," he said.

He stood with hands on hips, his amused expression taking the sting out of his rebuke. Eve realized how he towered over her, and she lifted her chin as heat flooded her face. "I've climbed this tree since I was eight."

"I'm sure you have." He grinned. "Though I'll wager not in that dress." Tilting his head, he eyed her for several seconds. "You know, in the moonlight I canna see the cat for the color of your gown. The two match perfectly."

"Really?" She followed his gaze. "Ouch!" Button dug his

claws into her finger and squirmed from her grasp to land on all fours.

"Little traitor," she said as the feline scurried off into the garden. Eve rubbed at the pinpricks of pain in her finger.

"Oh, my new dress!" Blood from her wound had stained the pristine gown.

"Come now, it's not the end of the world." He took a white handkerchief from his pocket and used it to wrap her finger. "Just think, in a few years you'll be doing this for your patients."

Pleased at his words, and moved by his gallant gesture, Eve felt her love blossoming like the honeysuckle twining around the gazebo's latticework. Impulsively, she went on tiptoe and kissed him—once, twice, three times on either cheek.

"In the custom of my mother's people," she said in a rush at his wide-eyed stare. "To show our . . . appreciation."

Though she wasn't completely certain about the truth of her statement, Eve didn't regret her action. She held her breath and waited to see what he would do.

Simon hesitated, as though deliberating. Finally a soft smile broke across his features, and he reached to gently cup her face in his hands. Leaning close, he placed a brief, chaste kiss against her lips. "That's how a Scotsman shows his appreciation. But only to a bonny young lass," he added with a wink.

"Forrester! Where are you? Come on, man, let's go!"

Marcus Weatherford's shout from the kitchen doorway broke the spell.

Simon stepped back. "I came to say good-bye, and to wish you a happy birthday." The corner of his mouth lifted. "I hadn't expected such a splendid reception."

Flustered, Eve said in a shy voice, "Nor I."

"Don't give up on your dream, lass." His features sobered as he touched her on the shoulder before turning toward the house.

As she watched him go, Eve thought her heart might break.

42

Would she ever see Simon again? "God, please keep him safe in Scotland," she whispered. "And hurry his return . . . when I'm a bit older," she amended.

Simon swung around and offered a final wave. Eve raised a hand in response, her other hand clutching the precious handkerchief against her wound. *He must return*, she thought, panicked. Simon was her champion, her protector . . .

She raised a finger to her lips, where he'd kissed her. A slow warmth of assurance spread through her limbs, and she smiled, not a little awestruck.

Her birthday wish had come true.

CHAPTER 4

Captain Simon Forrester awakened slowly, blinking against the silvery light flooding in through a bank of high windows across the room. His chest hurt with each breath, while his head throbbed as though a bayonet were being driven into his skull.

When his vision finally cleared, he gazed at his surroundings. He was in a hospital of sorts, with wounded lying in beds along either side of the cavernous room. Two German soldiers stood sentry at the entrance into what was likely once a ballroom or a grand hall. He'd seen the like as a boy, when he and his guardian, Angus, visited Stirling Castle north of Edinburgh.

Like the rest of the patients, Simon lay buried beneath several gray blankets on a hospital bed. He took another agonized breath before pressing a hand to his chest. The binding at his ribs told him he must have broken a few. Touching the bandages at his head only increased the stabbing pain, and his memories came rushing back.

A night trip across the channel . . . the mission in Brussels

44

. . . explosion of artillery . . . his pilot, Chandler, slumped over as the plane caught fire . . . falling . . . the vision of her . . .

Blackness.

Simon rubbed at his eyes. It was miraculous, his second crash and he was still in one piece. A grimace touched his lips as he thought how his friend at the Admiralty, Marcus Weatherford, had once likened him to a cat with nine lives. Perhaps it was true after all.

Had Chandler been as fortunate?

One of the German sentries at the door glanced at him. He disappeared from the room while the other came to stand alongside Simon's bed.

Did the Huns think he would make a dash for it? He couldn't manage to sit up in the blasted bed, let alone try to escape!

The other soldier returned to the ward, followed by a Red Cross nurse. Simon forgot his pain as a wave of shock ripped through him. It hadn't been his imagination playing tricks . . .

It was the bonny, violet-eyed lass who had saved him last night—the same woman he'd dreamed about each day, week, and agonizing month of his existence in the lice-infested squalor of German prison camps. Eve, his beloved, who until a few days ago he'd thought lost to him forever.

His wife.

Throat tight, Simon closed his eyes. *Thank you, Lord, for giving her back to me.*

He tried to lean forward then, gritting his teeth against the pain as he strained to get a better look at her. Despite his agony, Simon's heart beat with joy. He had come to Brussels to take her home. Marcus had given him the name of a trusted ally in Brussels, a priest at St. Magdalene's church, who would get them safely out of Belgium.

As she drew closer to the bed, however, his warm thoughts turned to anger at how three years of war had taken a toll.

Eve's once luminous skin was now pale, the edges of her soft mouth lined with exhaustion. The tall, willowy frame he'd once memorized with his touch now seemed thinner beneath her uniform. Only her eyes, like amethysts, and her rich dark hair remained unchanged.

He lifted a hand, craving her touch, yet she kept her distance from him, standing a few feet away. Her expression appeared strained, wooden, and her gaze darted to the guard standing beside his bed—a harsh reminder that they weren't alone.

Simon dropped his hand against the blanket. Where was she staying? How was she managing? He had so many questions, but another glance at the armed guards silenced him. He would wait to see what happened next.

"Wie fühlen Sie sich?"

Her German was flawless, though that didn't surprise him. Eve had enjoyed studying languages in college and excelled at several. After two and a half years inside German POW camps, he'd become quite proficient himself. Enough to realize she was addressing him formally, as if he were a stranger.

His instincts alerted, Simon gave her a blank look, pretending incomprehension in front of the guards.

"How are you feeling?" she repeated in German.

He decided to converse with her using the Marche family's French. *"Bonjour, ma f—"*

As he began, Simon glimpsed the butt of a rifle coming at him from the guard beside his bed. He shielded his head with his hands, the action like a blade piercing his ribs.

He groaned.

"Enough!" Eve cried in German. "Corporal, get Major Reinhardt!"

With a curt bow, the hostile corporal dashed off to do her bidding, while the other held his position a few feet away.

Eve approached the side of his bed and leaned to adjust the blankets, and Simon was tempted to reach for her hand. Instead, he caught the scent of her rose water and swallowed the ache in his throat. It had been so long since he'd held her, breathed in the smell of her hair, her skin.

She continued to avoid his gaze as she straightened and stepped back, and while he understood her caution, disappointment weighed on his heart like a heavy stone. He'd hoped she would converse with him, at least let him know the status of his pilot, Chandler.

He also wanted to find out about the pouch he'd given her last night. Did she still have it? It was truly another miracle that she'd been there when he crashed. His friend at MI6 had instructed him to destroy the sealed orders if his mission failed. Simon didn't want to consider Marcus's reaction if the Huns had laid claim to its contents.

Eve was only a few feet from him. As Simon studied her profile, a glint of steel caught his eye—a medal pinned beneath her white apron.

An Iron Cross? He stared at her, a prickling of unease rippling through him. How had she come by the German medal . . . and what had she done to earn it?

She turned to meet his gaze. "The Germans do not like hearing French spoken in Belgium," she said, having switched to English.

That explained the Hun's aggression.

She continued. "I'm sorry to tell you the other pilot burned in the crash and you, Captain Chandler, are now a prisoner of the German army."

Captain Chandler? It took a moment for her meaning to sink in. Simon reached for his collarbone and found the cord, then raised the green identity disc to examine it. Chandler had been a good flyer and a brave man.

Saddened over the loss of his fellow pilot, Simon was none-theless thankful for his wife's quick thinking. The plan had been for him to parachute into enemy territory clad in plain clothes and carrying a false Belgian passport. As "Albert Jans-sen," he should have been able to blend in as a citizen and go about his business.

Of course, he hadn't counted on his plane crashing, or on being picked up by the Germans. Without military tags, he could have been shot as a spy.

Eve glanced at the guard before returning her attention to him. "You have broken ribs, Captain, and you've received a seri-ous head wound. Enough to cause a possible lapse in memory." The violet eyes were intent. "Do you understand?"

Crikey, she wants me to feign amnesia? Simon nodded. It seemed the Huns were going to give him the third degree, and she was offering him a way to stall.

No sooner did he have the thought than a German officer entered, the second guard trailing behind. Major Reinhardt was an impressive-looking fellow, with nut-brown hair graying at the temples and piercing blue eyes. His dark handlebar moustache sat above a squared jaw.

Eve went to greet the major. Simon's hackles rose as the Hun laid his hand against her shoulder and leaned in to whisper something he couldn't catch, but that made his wife smile.

He gritted his teeth. Those smiles had always brought him joy . . . like flying upward through a cloud layer and reaching the sun. Their absence had left him empty during the dark years in prison, and he hated that she now gave them freely to someone else—even worse, to the enemy.

What game was Eve playing? His thoughts arrowed back to the Iron Cross, and another prickle of anxiety crawled up his spine. Why would she hide it, unless she didn't want him to see—

Simon's mind froze, his eyes wide in disbelief.

Eve had removed from her pocket the leather pouch he'd given her last night. The pouch with his secret orders, his false passport . . .

Blood pounded in his ears. No, this wasn't happening. Surely she wouldn't—

She handed the pouch to the major.

"*Naaaah!*" His guttural cry erupted as he lifted off the bed, then nearly fainted from the excruciating pain. With a grunt he fell back against the pillows, clutching his bandaged ribs. Closing his eyes, he gasped for breath, making the pain worse. His wife was working for the Germans.

Fury at his helplessness pierced through his agony, and he twisted his head to glare at her. But his anger met with her look of cold determination before she left the ward with the major.

Simon continued to lie there, Huns guarding him on either side. Sickened by her betrayal, he wondered what had happened to his compassionate and patriotic wife.

His thoughts returned to last night as she knelt over him, her touch gentle. Disbelief, followed by joy, had illuminated her face as their eyes met, while his heart had been ready to burst. He couldn't believe she was there with him, looking so full of love . . .

He clenched his fists. He'd been a fool to think three years of war wouldn't matter.

Simon had been in a German POW camp when he received news from the Red Cross that Eve had sailed to Belgium shortly after he'd left for the war. He was also told of the atrocities the Huns had committed in several Belgian cities, including Louvain, burning out homes and murdering innocent civilians. No trace of Eve or her family had remained.

Burdened by guilt at having left her in the first place, he'd lived each day with the hope that by some miracle she had survived and that God would keep her safe until he could escape and find her.

Simon's prayers had been answered: he had escaped, and he'd learned that his wife was alive and living in Brussels. Yet their reunion was not at all as he'd imagined.

She was a stranger to him.

CHAPTER 5

LONDON,
THREE YEARS EARLIER

Simon stood beneath the warm July sun near the Bedford Street bus stop, waiting for Eve to exit the London Hospital after her shift. His pulse drummed with anticipation as he thought of his news and how it would affect them both. He had a very important question to ask her.

"Simon!" Her violet eyes widened, and she cast a quick glance back toward the hospital. "Why are you here?"

"I wanted to see you the moment you finished up. I couldn't wait another two minutes for you to reach the bus stop!" He smiled. "And you needn't worry. The Dragon isn't gawking at us from the window. Besides, there's no rule against a nurse meeting her friend, now is there?"

"You are more than a friend, Captain Forrester, as you well know." Her lips curved upward as she rolled her eyes at him, and Simon longed to take her in his arms right there on the sidewalk. "You also know I'd have to face the music if Matron found out we were engaged to be married."

"Would it be so very bad?" he said in a low voice, leaning close. He gazed at her soft, sweet mouth and fought the urge to capture it with his own. "What do you suppose the old crone would do if I kissed you, right here in public?"

"Don't you dare." She darted another glance back at the hospital. "I've got just days left to finish my nurse's training. I won't have you spoiling my dream." She tipped her chin, eyes full of mischief. "You remember you encouraged me once upon a time. Or have you forgotten?"

"No, to my everlasting regret." He flashed a look of mock horror, and when she laughed and gave his arm a playful slap he grabbed her hand and pulled her along. "You never told me nurses were forbidden to marry, or I'd have tried to convince you to become a seamstress instead. You still could have plied your hand to a bit of sewing—dresses instead of bodies, I'll grant. But we wouldn't have to sneak around like two lovelorn adolescents."

Her smile faded. "It won't be forever, Simon, I promise."

Simon heaved a sigh and nodded, though he wondered how she would answer his question later, once he'd laid out his plans.

"Now tell me," she said. "Why are you here?"

His heart sped up. "Come on," he said, relieved the omnibus had pulled up to the stop. "Let's have tea at McCrory's and I'll explain all."

He ushered her onto the bus, and minutes later they arrived at the quaint tea shop on Crossley Street in Highbury, a London district just north of the hospital.

"Much better," he said once they were seated. After he'd ordered their tea and strawberry biscuits, Simon leaned forward at the table and gave her a leering grin. "Now that I don't have Matron looking over my shoulder, I can ogle one of her nurses at my leisure."

She shook her head, smiling. "You're incorrigible."

"I do try."

The tea soon arrived, and while the waiter fetched their tray of biscuits, Simon took in the surroundings. It was well past the usual afternoon teatime, and the place was nearly empty. Shops like McCrory's were just one of the many novelties he'd missed during his time in Scotland. When he returned to London after his uncle's death, he'd made a point of sampling several tea establishments, including the prestigious Swan's over on Coventry in the West End.

"If I didn't know better, Simon Forrester, I'd think you were stalling." Eve eyed him with amusement above the rim of her teacup. "Now, what's so important you had to come and find me at the hospital?"

He drew a deep breath and reached for his own cup of Darjeeling. "I've received my orders," he said. "I report to Dover with the Royal Flying Corps third squadron on the fourteenth."

"But that's only a week away!" Slowly she set her teacup down, all humor gone. "So you think this means war."

He reached for a biscuit. "It's all still conjecture, but you know as well as I how the newspapers have been going on about the outrage in Austria-Hungary. The archduke's murder last month is as good an excuse as any to draw battle lines."

Her brow creased. "There have been rumors at the hospital. They say if Germany decides to declare war on France, Kaiser Wilhelm will invade through Belgium."

Detecting the tremor in her voice, Simon set down his biscuit and reached across the table for her hand. "Nothing is certain, my love, and we know rumors are created to spread fear." He smiled. "I'm certain your family will be fine."

"I don't know," she said, looking unconvinced. "Perhaps I should go to them."

He squeezed her hand. "Let's wait a wee bit and see, shall we?" With the tension between nations already high, he didn't like the idea of her leaving Britain to venture into what might become a war zone. "You still need to finish out your studies. Your mother would wish it.

"Anyway," he continued, "the kaiser must obtain permission from the neutral Belgians before marching through their country, and we both know they won't give it, so it's a moot point. And even if Germany did enter Belgium to get to France, they would go through the larger cities of Liège and Antwerp. Your family should be safe enough with your uncle in Louvain."

"We can't know for sure."

"No, we can't," he agreed.

"And if they do march?"

Seeing her fear made his chest tighten. "Britain will be certain to enter the war."

The gravity of what might happen seemed to settle between them.

"I appreciate you trying to put my mind at ease, Simon, but I'm still afraid for them. Maybe I should visit Louvain and see the situation for myself. I could help Mama pack and accompany her and the children back to London."

Simon's resolve hardened. He had to keep her safe. "Sweetheart, do you really think your mother will uproot your siblings, leave her Belgian family and her new home, all on the strength of a rumor?" He pressed his case home. "Write to her if you wish, or telephone and ask her to return. I believe she'll insist on staying put, at least for now."

He relaxed as the resolute light in Eve's eyes dimmed. "I will telephone Mama." Then she sighed. "But I suspect you're right."

"Nothing's going to happen anytime soon," he said, trying to reassure her.

"If Papa were here, they'd still be living in Oxford and out of harm's way." Her tone echoed frustration. "None of this would be an issue."

Simon rubbed his thumb against the back of her hand. "I miss him, too."

He'd been shocked when Nicholas Marche died of a heart

attack the previous fall. Simon had grieved alongside Eve and her family. It was shortly afterward Louise took the two younger children to live in her native Belgium.

"Your father was quite a man," he said, recalling the professor's warmth and generosity as he opened his home to his students—in particular, one young Scotsman who had found himself alone and far away from all that was familiar.

"You were there when I told him I wanted to be a nurse and not a math teacher." Her eyes turned misty, and she smiled at Simon. "I was so worried about disappointing Papa, but he embraced the idea. . . ." Her voice broke. "Truly, despite convention, I don't think it really mattered to him what vocation his children pursued, as long as we did our very best."

"I'll always recall the stories of his great ballooning adventures in South Africa," Simon said, trying to lighten the mood. He was rewarded when Eve giggled despite her tears. "You know, it was your father who gave me the push I needed to become a pilot."

She nodded. "A good thing, too. Otherwise we might never have seen one another again."

"Ah, lass, you were never far from my thoughts," he said softly. "One way or another, I would have found you."

It had been Providence that inspired his old professor to bring the entire Marche family on holiday to attend the first Larkhill Aeroplane competition, where Simon was training as a pilot. "Remember when I drove you and your mother and little sister into Bath?"

Her smile lifted his spirits. "And Zoe talked your ear off there and back."

"And she was quite upset about the idea of bathing once we got there," he added with a chuckle.

"It took forever to convince her we were just going to drink the waters, not sink ourselves into them." Her smile broadened.

"I remember Papa accusing you of having brain fever for wanting to leave the air races to take three females shopping."

Simon waggled his brows. "I had my motives."

When he'd met Eve again at Larkhill, she was even bonnier than he remembered and was in her first year of training at the London Hospital. Once their holiday ended, he'd asked the professor's permission to court her. "I was trying to win your heart," he said.

"You know you already had it."

Her voice was soft. She lifted her other hand and clasped their entwined fingers.

"I'm glad you feel that way." Sensing his moment of truth, Simon shifted and said, "I want you to be my wife."

She grinned at him. "You already asked, silly. And in case you've forgotten, I said yes."

"No, you don't understand." He was relieved the tea shop had emptied out, yet the cozy establishment seemed unbearably hot, and sweat beaded along his upper lip. His heart hammered in his chest. "I mean now, this coming weekend. I want us to get married."

Her amusement faded to uncertainty, then to consternation. "Simon, I-I cannot."

Though he'd suspected her answer, the refusal still stung. Releasing her hand, he leaned back in his seat and crossed his arms against his chest. "Why not?"

"My family is in Belgium." She gazed at him. "And with the real possibility of war, I'm needed at the hospital more than ever. We cannot marry just yet."

"Just yet." He struggled for calm. "When do you suppose would be a good time?"

Her features took on a stubborn line. "For a start, I would need Mama's blessing to run off and elope with you."

"Done." He relaxed his arms and removed from his coat

pocket the letter he'd received from her mother days before. He handed it to her. "One blessing."

She gaped at him. "Mama wrote to you?"

He nodded. "We've exchanged several letters since she left Britain. I'd like to think one day she'll be my mother, too. That is, if you and I ever get married."

"I know that."

He was glad she had the grace to look contrite as she opened the letter and read its contents. "She wants us to be happy, love. Can you not see it?"

"I do understand, Simon, and I love you with all my heart. It's just . . . what about my being a nurse?"

"You needn't give it up. I've done some checking and found that many private institutions accept married women as nurses. Including the Red Cross. There will certainly be a need in those places if we go to war."

He reached for her hand and lifted it to kiss her open palm. "I leave next week. I'm not certain when I'll receive orders to cross the channel, but before I go to France I want to know you're taken care of. I want to know . . ." Simon paused at the unexpected knot in his throat. "I need to know we are bound to one another in this world, Evelyn Marche."

Tears brimmed in her eyes, and he could see love shining in them.

"How . . . where . . . ?" she asked.

His taut muscles eased. "How about Scotland? My great-uncle's estate was in Annan, and I'll request a special license from the local priest so we won't need to post banns. I have a good friend in my squadron, Alex Baird, who can arrange to let me use a plane. His parents live in Gretna Green, near Annan, and will witness our wedding. We'll fly north for the weekend as soon as you complete your training, and I won't need to leave for Dover until we get back."

"What shall I tell Maddie?" she said, referring to Madeleine Arthur, another nurse in training who shared Eve's flat. "I can hardly keep a secret like that from my best friend."

"Tell whom you wish," he said simply. "Or keep it secret if you want to remain working at the hospital. I won't say a word, and I'll swear Alex to secrecy."

Doubt and desire battled across her lovely features, and Simon prayed she would agree to his proposal. Surely God wanted her safe and taken care of. Simon wanted her for his own.

"I don't know," she said finally. "It all seems so rushed."

"We don't have the luxury of time, sweetheart." He struggled to keep the urgency from his voice. "I promise you, later we can have a reception with our friends and all the trimmings. We'll find ourselves a little cottage here in Highbury, near the park, where we can make our home and start a family."

He added quietly, "And for any reason while I'm gone, you have only to show our marriage document to Marcus Weatherford at the War Office. He'll take care of things."

Simon hardly dared breathe while she searched his face, her expression troubled.

"You are the most audacious and determined man I've ever met." She sighed. "It also happens to be an aspect of your nature I've grown to love."

"Then I'm glad of it," he said, still uncertain.

"That's it then."

That's it then. He swallowed. What was she saying?

He hadn't realized he was still holding his breath until her smile, warm and full of love, unlocked the air trapped in his lungs.

"I'll marry you whenever you like."

He launched from his seat, giving a healthy Scots shout that startled the waiter. In two short strides, Simon moved around the table and swept Eve into his arms.

"You've made me a happy man, love," he whispered, before his mouth took possession of hers in a passionate kiss, something he'd wanted to do for the past hour.

Afterward, she rested her cheek against his chest, and Simon knew he had everything in the world he wanted.

CHAPTER 6

Trust me. Had Simon understood the meaning in her expression yesterday?

Eve bent her head against the cold mist as she walked along rue des Sols toward the hospital. Inside her coat pocket, she clutched his monogrammed handkerchief.

She'd been relieved to find him conscious and no worse than the night of the crash. And when she'd handed over his pouch to Otto Reinhardt, Simon's look of hatred had certainly worked to maintain her cover. But her heart had taken a good beating for it.

The constant presence of hospital guards and the return of Officers Jaeger and Schultz had made it impossible to speak with her husband alone. He couldn't know the pouch she'd surrendered contained only the printed blue leaflets she'd collected on the street.

Eve's plan had been an impulsive attempt to protect her husband. Simon still ran a high risk of being branded a spy; a man dressed in plain clothes and crashing with a British plane could hardly be anything else. She intended her offer of the pouch to be proof to the Boche he was just another Allied pilot dropping propaganda over the city. It meant the difference be-

60

tween Simon being sent to a POW camp in Germany or being shot as an enemy agent.

There were no guarantees, but without solid evidence, like the false passport and sealed orders she'd hidden away in her Bible, the secret police would have nothing to formally charge him with.

Laughter sounded nearby, and Eve looked toward the park. Two children bundled in coats took turns kicking a ball across the grass, as if there weren't a war going on. With a pang, she thought of Nikki and Zoe and how much she yearned to see them again.

But on Monday her world had changed in a matter of a few hours, and right now Simon's welfare precluded all else.

Yesterday morning she'd written to Rotterdam about "Albert Janssen's" status. Eve had jotted the note on tissue paper and hidden it inside a special wooden bobbin before sending it through Madame Bissette when she delivered Mama's lace.

After joining La Dame Blanche a year ago, she'd been assigned "letterboxes," contacts through whom she could send or receive vital intelligence. While she sent all of her messages through Madame Bissette, Eve received information from three sources: Monsieur Tulle at his blanchisserie; Vincent, a local brewer who supplied beer to the café; and Monsieur Guerin, owner of the cigar shop near her aunt and uncle's apartment on rue des Sols.

In the past, all agent information had funneled through Henri van Bergen, leader of La Dame Blanche in Antwerp. From there the intelligence was consolidated and then smuggled across the Belgian border to MI6 in Rotterdam. But Henri and the Antwerp cell had been arrested, and now Eve could only hope her message had made it through.

The arrests led her to believe a traitor must have infiltrated the network. Eve didn't think she was alone in her suspicions, but for the time being she planned to keep her own counsel. Any one of the agents could be a suspect at this point—perhaps even Monsieur Guerin.

A shiver raced through her as she recalled her latest visit to the cigar shop. She regularly stopped in at Guerin's on her way to the hospital and picked up Otto's order for cigars—a perfect guise to conduct her clandestine business, as any message hidden beneath a cigar band could easily be removed before she completed her errand for the major.

The last time, however, Monsieur Guerin had acted strangely. His jovial demeanor seemed forced, and when she shook his hand before leaving the shop, his palm was sweaty. Eve had left with the cigars in hand that day, but she'd sensed she was being followed.

Since then, she'd offered Otto various excuses in order to avoid setting foot inside Guerin's shop. Even now the memory was enough to make her glance over her shoulder as she entered the hospital.

She stopped by her office to hang up her coat, then tried to maintain a calm pace as she headed in the direction of the ward. Eve was fairly certain Simon had understood her instruction yesterday, so she hoped he was able to continue the amnesia deception with Jaeger and Schultz. The ruse would buy him extra recovery time at the hospital and also prevent him from letting anything slip about their relationship.

Eve shuddered to think what might happen if Major Reinhardt and the rest of the hospital staff learned she was the wife of a British prisoner of war . . . or worse, married to a spy.

Passing Otto Reinhardt's office, she glimpsed Felix Giroux inside, hovering over the major's desk. "What are you doing?" she said from the doorway.

The Belgian orderly whipped around. "Sister!" His dark features melted with relief. "I'm being patriotic, as always."

He held up the leather pouch he'd taken from the desk. "It seems the plane that crashed was dropping propaganda." He waved one of the blue leaflets at her. "Odd to be doing such a thing at night, don't you think?"

Eve smiled but refrained from comment. She didn't know Felix very well. The orderly was Dom's close friend and had joined La Dame Blanche about the same time as Eve, but he usually worked nights, so she rarely saw him.

He pointed to the Royal Flying Corps insignia stamped into the leather. "I don't remember seeing this pouch on Chandler the night we brought him in." His amber gaze found hers. "Any idea how it came to be in the major's hands?"

"I discovered it in my office the morning after the crash," she said, telling him the concocted story she planned for Jaeger and Schultz. "I assume one of the street patrols dropped it by."

"I wonder why they didn't just hand it over to the secret police that night."

Was he simply musing aloud . . . or was he looking to her for answers? She suppressed her annoyance.

"It was late, as you recall, and since the crash occurred in the park, I'm sure debris scattered everywhere. The pouch could have been missed. It may have been a citizen who discovered it and brought it in. In any event, I turned it over to the major."

He eyed her with surprise. "Why would you do that?"

How much should she tell him?

"I thought it might . . . shed light on the patient's reasons for being in Belgium," she said carefully. "It seemed a good idea, for Chandler's sake."

Felix tipped his head, his gaze perceptive. "Certainly the Boche would consider an Allied flyer distributing propaganda far less dangerous than, say, his being a spy," he said at length. "And with the captain still unable to recall why he's here . . ."

Eve's pulse quickened. "What do you mean?"

He dropped the pouch onto the desk. "Chandler's memory seems a complete blank."

Relief flowed through her. Simon had understood. "Maybe with time he'll recover," she offered in a perfunctory tone. "Felix, you're terribly brave to be snooping through the major's desk in broad daylight. Where is he, by the way?"

"Guerin's." Felix smirked. "He ran out of cigars."

Eve was glad Otto had finally decided to fetch his own. "Isn't your shift over?" she asked.

"It is now," he said. "Dom and I had a long night. I just got back from General von Falkenhausen's office. He needed another bicarbonate of soda for his stomach." Felix grinned. "The Boche must be losing the war."

They went back out into the hall. "They've moved him, you know," Felix said. "Captain Chandler is in the last private suite across from the ward."

"Who moved him? Why?"

She tried to appear calm, but Felix's dark eyes watched her.

"Herr Jaeger wanted access to question him at any hour, without disturbing the other patients."

Dread filled her. What did Jaeger plan to do? Whatever it was, it didn't bode well for Simon. "If he can't remember anything, what's the point?"

"We both know there isn't one, Sister." Felix sighed as he combed a hand through his dark hair. "Regardless of the propaganda leaflets, they'll decide he's a spy, and before long he'll be taken to Tir National."

His words magnified her worst fear—that Jaeger and Schultz would tire of questioning Simon and cart him off to the prison at St. Gilles regardless of their lack of proof. A lopsided trial by the German courts would follow, and when they found her husband guilty he would be shot at the Tir National range in Brussels.

"We have to get him out." The words spilled from her lips before she realized it. Eve stared at Felix, her stance rigid. Was he trustworthy? Her husband's life was at stake.

"Chandler is a British airman," she insisted. "We have to save him."

Felix gave her a dubious look. "I don't know how we'd pull it off."

"We need a workable plan. Why don't you and Dom stop by the café at closing tonight, before your shift starts? The three of us can figure out what to do."

He shook his head, though his gaze held admiration. "You're as obstinate as you are courageous," he said. "I'll let Dom know. We'll see you tonight."

Relieved at his willingness to help, she offered a smile. "Thanks."

Once he departed, Eve made her way to the suite he'd indicated. How would she get Simon out of the hospital without killing them all? Two years before, British nurse Edith Cavell had been shot as a spy after being convicted of smuggling Allied patients out of the hospital and across Belgium's border into Holland to rejoin their regiments. Since then, the German secret police considered all Red Cross nurses suspect. While Eve's Iron Cross improved her position, it wouldn't protect her if she was caught helping Simon flee.

As she entered Simon's room, the first thing she noticed was the absence of the guards. Then she spied the cloth partition near his bed, effectively blocking her view of him.

The room seemed quiet. Too quiet. Her hand flew to her chest. Had Jaeger and Schultz already used excessive force on her husband?

The thought sent her rushing to the partition and she jerked it away . . . to find Simon out of bed and ripping away his head bandage.

"What are you doing?" Eve reached for his hands, but before she could blink he grabbed her wrists and spun her around, shoving her down against the bed.

"I could ask you that question, wife," he snarled. "How long have you been working for the Huns?"

Above her, the gray eyes glittered against his battered and bruised features. For an instant, a memory from Louvain flashed before her. *Long jagged scar . . . laughing at her . . . hands bound . . . trapped beneath him . . .*

She swallowed a scream and forced herself to look up at her husband. *No scar . . .*

Consternation flickered in his gaze and he rose up, loosening his grip. "What's wrong?"

"Nothing." She took several deep breaths before casting a quick glance toward the door.

"Only one guard this morning, and he willna be back for a time," he said, guessing her thoughts. "He went to fetch a nurse when I pretended to have convulsions. I'll be gone before he returns."

Eve gave him an incredulous look. "You can't get out of here."

"Oh, but I'll be taking you with me." His smile twisted with pain as he labored to breathe. "You'll be my hostage, my guarantee of getting out alive."

Though she realized he was ignorant of the truth, his callous words lashed at her heart.

A sound in the hall jerked her gaze back toward the door. The guard would return any moment.

"Listen to me, we don't have much time," she whispered. "Yesterday, what you saw—"

"I know what I saw," he snapped. "You betrayed me to the Huns."

"No!" She shook her head. If they were caught together like

this . . . "I filled the pouch with propaganda. Leaflets dropped by an Allied plane two days ago. Your passport, the orders, they're safely hidden. I swear."

She waited while a host of emotions raced across his bruised features: rage, uncertainty, hope. Suspicion won out. "Why should I believe you? The amnesia ploy could just be your way of protecting your own skin. Wouldna want the Huns knowing we're husband and wife, isn't that right?"

"So they can kill us both?" She flushed with anger. "Even if you take me hostage, you'll never escape in your condition." A touch of scorn entered her voice. "Believe what you will, but the soldiers won't hesitate to shoot us both if we try walking out of this hospital together."

She darted another glance at the door, straining to listen for any sound. "I worried the German secret police would accuse you of spying. If they believe you're just an Allied pilot dropping propaganda and not a spy, I can get you transferred to a POW hospital in Germany—"

"No." The single word was hard, unyielding.

"Perhaps we should concoct a story," she said. "Captain Chandler could get his memory back. You can tell the secret police your mission here was to boost the Belgian people's morale."

"I won't go back to Germany. Ever," he ground out.

Eve forgot about the guard as she studied Simon's battered face, the haunted look in his eyes. She was saddened to realize how little she knew about him anymore or how he might have suffered. "I'll come up with a plan to get you out of here," she promised. "Have you told them anything?"

His anger seemed to ebb. "Not yet."

"Good." She eased out a breath. "Give me a chance to help you." When he didn't move, she added sharply, "Your only other choice is a firing squad."

Her words finally seemed to penetrate his wall of mistrust. Simon released her and straightened, grunting with pain as he clutched at his ribs.

"I want answers," he said once she'd helped him back into bed. "How did you come by this? The Huns' medal you're trying to hide." He reached for the Iron Cross pinned beneath her apron, and his battered features hardened. "What did you have to bargain for it?"

Simon's contempt rekindled her anger. Did he really imagine she had prostituted herself . . . or betrayed her country? Eve thought of Louvain, and the bloody carnage she'd survived. She thought of the pain that never left her, and the inestimable price she'd paid.

"It was hard won," she said in a tight voice.

"What about the major? I noticed the two of you are quite chummy."

Eve saw the vulnerability in his eyes, despite his scowl. Was he jealous? "He is a means to an end, nothing more."

When Simon didn't respond, she began to tuck the blankets around him. Then she caught the motion of his hand reaching for her.

"Lass," he whispered.

Her anger dissolved beneath a tide of longing. How many times over the years had she dreamed of his simple touch, of being in his arms again? She had imagined him banishing her memories of the war and its horrors, forgiving her for what she'd done.

And then, maybe, she could forgive herself.

She straightened, then stepped back, away from the bed. She couldn't trust herself with him, not here among the Boche. She had to protect them both. "Someone's coming."

The sound of heavy boots echoed on the tiled floor. Eve turned to avoid looking at Simon's injured expression.

The guard appeared a moment later, accompanied by a young Belgian nurse.

"Why did you leave your post?" Eve demanded of the soldier, finding a target for her frustration. "If the captain had died, you would be answering to the secret police."

The young corporal paled and snapped to attention. Beside him, the nurse eyed Eve like a startled deer.

"Get back to work, both of you." She flung out the order in German, rushing past them for the door. She didn't want to turn and see her husband's look of disappointment or mistrust.

Simon was right. She was protecting herself as well. She had to continue her charade with the Boche and Major Reinhardt in order to keep her mother and aunt and uncle safe. "A means to an end," she'd told Simon. *More like a bargain with the devil*, she thought bitterly.

For three years, she and Otto Reinhardt had circled one another in a strange kind of dance. Eve had saved his life in Louvain, yet somehow become indebted to him in Brussels.

Otto had used his influence to obtain German patronage for her aunt and uncle's café. He had also recommended Eve for the Iron Cross, which gave her protection and provided her a means to gather intelligence for La Dame Blanche.

Despite the price the major extracted from her, Eve couldn't afford to lose what she'd attained. The risk to her family and to her work with the Allies was too great.

But to deny the man she loved . . .

She thought again of Simon's wounded look, and anger and regret seized her. She was caught between two worlds: the one her desperation had forced upon her, and the other a world she'd once dreamed of sharing with him.

Seeking out her empty office, Eve slipped inside and closed the door, desperate for a few moments of solitude to marshal her emotions. Outside the window, the incessant drizzle fell onto the palace green, and as she gazed at the dull gray sky, her hand found Simon's handkerchief inside her apron pocket. She clutched the cloth, longing to turn back the clock to before the war, when she still thrilled with anticipation at the future that awaited them.

CHAPTER 7

*E*ve reveled in the cold wind whipping against her face as she peered through her flight goggles at the tiny patchwork of countryside below.

Simon had taken her up in his plane several times before, yet they'd never traveled this far together. It seemed incredible to cross the entire length of Britain in a matter of hours.

Behind her in the second seat, Simon piloted the R.E.5 biplane smoothly across the skies. They'd made a brief stop to refuel at Goxhill in Lincolnshire before continuing the five-hour trip north to Scotland.

An incomparable sense of freedom filled her as they soared through the heavens like two birds in flight. *Or maybe like angels*, Eve thought with a burst of laughter. No wonder Simon held such a passion for flying. She thrilled at it, too.

Perhaps this new sense of daring was the reason she'd managed to keep their secret from everyone, including Maddie. Eve had told her best friend she was spending the weekend in Oxford with a childhood friend.

She still squirmed over telling the lie. She and Maddie kept

71

few secrets from one another. They'd met years before during nurses' orientation and had found much in common as children of Belgian parents living in Britain. They took a flat together, and eventually Eve introduced Maddie to Simon. The three of them, along with one of Simon's pilot friends, often attended the cinema or picnicked in Regent's Park. Maddie knew that Eve and Simon were engaged, so it was no surprise to her that they would marry one day.

One day . . . like tomorrow. Eve pursed her wind-chapped lips. She'd imagined having time to be a nurse first, then later a wife and a mother. She hadn't counted on Papa's death or the rest of her family leaving for Belgium. Or Simon being assigned to Dover in a matter of days, with Britain on the brink of war.

Time was suddenly in short supply.

Still, it was a poor excuse for deceiving her best friend, and Eve determined to confess all on her return. Maddie would be terribly disappointed at first, but ultimately she would understand and be happy for her and Simon.

The plane began its descent. Eve spied the long stretch of green below, and nearby, the buildings and church steeple of a town, which must be Annan. Simon touched her shoulder, the signal to brace herself as he took the plane down for a fairly smooth landing.

"Well, have you sprouted wings, sweetheart?" he called after cutting the plane's engines.

"I think so, because I feel as light as a feather!" She laughed as she removed her leather cap and goggles, then hoisted herself up to stand on the seat in the small space.

He clambered out onto the wing. "You should wear my flight coat more often," he said, openly admiring her in the long leather duster she'd donned for the trip. "You look quite bonny."

Eve rolled her eyes and blushed, then bent to grab the straps of the two small rucksacks they'd brought for the weekend. She handed them to Simon, who tossed them to the ground before he helped her out onto the wing.

Hopping down onto the field, he turned to her, arms outstretched. "Jump, my love, and I'll catch you." His gray eyes shone, and once Eve was safely in his arms he lowered his head for a kiss.

She closed her eyes, savoring the warm press of his lips while the smell of leather and sunshine mingled with his spicy aftershave to tease her senses. She tried to imagine their wedding night, and how it would be—her softness beneath his strength, the love they would share between them, sanctioned by God and bound by their vows for the rest of their lives.

"I've dreamed of this for so long, lass," he whispered, ending the kiss. "By this time tomorrow, we'll belong to one another, always and forever."

She gazed up at him, her happiness ready to burst. "I cannot wait," she breathed and pressed her mouth to his for another kiss. In truth, she loved the idea of being his wife, even clandestinely. Her heart had melted when he mentioned starting a family. They had often discussed having children, and she knew Simon would make a wonderful father.

"If we continue, love, we'll be here well past dark," Simon murmured when their lips finally parted. His smile was tender as he set her gently on her feet. "Come, we've got a bit of walking ahead of us." He snagged their luggage and they set off across the field.

It was near suppertime when they finally reached their accommodations. Having made the two-mile trek to St. Columba's Church, Eve and Simon met with the priest and discussed the following day's wedding. From there the Bairds, parents of his pilot friend Alex, gave them a lift in their carriage to nearby Gretna Green.

Simon had arranged to spend the night with the Baird family, while he secured for Eve a room at the Bride's Bower, a quaint inn near the center of the famously romantic town.

White eyelet lace and Queen Anne furnishings decorated the cozy upstairs bedroom, and the afternoon light spilled through a trio of mullioned-glass windows. Eve moved to gaze out at the rolling green hills of Langholm in the distance and delight over the window box filled with pink primroses, yellow tansies, and purple heather lifting their colorful faces to the warm July sun.

The room seemed perfect, along with the day. And tomorrow . . .

If only her family could be there for their wedding, and Maddie, too. Eve left the window, running a hand along the smooth white surface of her dressing table, and reprimanded herself for her thoughts. Wasn't it enough she had Mama's blessing?

Eve also disliked having to deceive Matron with their secret marriage, even though the woman could be a dragon. Perhaps when they returned she would seek out a private nursing post as Simon had suggested, or join the Red Cross.

Still, she couldn't shake her uncertainty. Was this bridal jitters?

A knock sounded at the door. "Sweetheart?"

Eve rushed to the door and paused. "I can't let you in," she teased.

"Why not?"

His alarmed tone made her smile. "I've heard it's bad luck to see the bride before the wedding."

"This isn't some arranged marriage," he said, and she almost laughed at his irritation. "I don't plan to run off once I've seen my intended, and furthermore—"

Eve yanked the door open. "And furthermore . . . ?" She arched a brow at him.

A slow smile spread across his lips, and he eyed her appreciatively. "And furthermore, you've no need to hide from me.

If you were a one-eyed, whiskered, toothless old hag, I'd still marry you."

She burst out laughing. "You expect me to believe that?"

"I do." His smile faded, while his eyes glowed. "Because I already love you," he said simply. "And don't you know, lass, love is blind."

Eve's heart nearly burst with love, her misgivings dissolved. "Have I told you how charming you are?" she said softly.

"Wait, I'm not finished. I've brought you these." A slight flush colored his features as he withdrew a beautiful purple bouquet from behind his back. "Heliotrope," he said. "For my eternal love and devotion."

"They're lovely, Simon, thank you." Her voice trembled as she accepted the flowers. Breathing in the delicious vanilla scent, she retreated into the room and put the bouquet in a pitcher with water.

"Are you hungry?" he called after her. "It's not January, but Mrs. Baird is preparing a special Burns Night supper in our honor."

Eve glanced at him. She'd heard of the Scottish tradition but never experienced it. "Will I enjoy it?"

He grinned and held out his hand. "Come along and find out."

The next morning Eve awoke to a soft knock on her door.

"'Tis a fine day, lass," Mrs. Baird announced as she entered the room carrying Eve's freshly pressed gown.

"Indeed," Eve agreed, yawning as she stretched languorously beneath the bed covers. She smiled, recalling the previous evening's festivities at the Baird home. While the taste of the Burns Night supper—in particular the haggis—hadn't been to her liking, Eve had enjoyed the family's warmth and generosity as they laughed and joked and then listened to Mr. Baird play "*a bit o' the bagpipe.*" She'd been homesick for her own family in Belgium, yet it was a comfort to have these new friends who would stand up for Simon's and her happiness and wish them well.

"I'd say 'tis a perfect morning for a wedding." Mrs. Baird winked at her as she set Eve's gown on the bed. The simple white velvet-and-lace dress was the same one Eve had worn on her sixteenth birthday. She'd kept it for sentimental reasons, and then with the hope she might wear the gown as a bride. Having let out the bodice and hem, the dress fit her perfectly.

"Ah, ye look a picture," Mrs. Baird said once Eve was finally ready and standing in front of the full-length mirror. The Scotswoman had woven for her a bridal crown of tiny white roses and the heliotrope blooms from Simon, and the purple flowers enhanced the color of Eve's eyes as the crown rested atop her upswept hair.

Mrs. Baird handed her a bouquet of purple heather, green ivy, and yellow tansies. "Time to leave for the church."

Eve drew a deep breath and followed her downstairs.

Outside, the air was warm, with feathery clouds scattered across a cornflower blue sky as they took the carriage into Annan. Upon reaching the church, they went inside, and Eve's breath caught as she glimpsed Simon's tall, broad-shouldered form standing near the altar.

He looked so smart in his khaki Royal Flying Corps uniform. Mr. Baird stood beside him, dressed in a dark suit, and Eve could hear the keening notes of a bagpipe playing Mendelssohn's "Wedding March," but she was too nervous to notice where the sound came from.

She moved to stand beside her handsome groom. Simon folded her hand in his larger one while his tender gaze swept over her.

"Sweetheart, you look as bonny to me now as you did the night you held your kitten in the garden," he said softly.

Eve blinked as unexpected tears filled her eyes. He'd remembered the dress . . .

The sun suddenly burst forth, flooding through the stained-glass windows above and bathing the church in bright colored light. It was as if heaven itself offered confirmation: she and Simon were meant to be together.

The priest began intoning the words of their marriage ceremony, yet Eve barely heard him as she held Simon's gaze. God had given her this man, who for many years had been a part of her family. Now he was her family in truth, and they would have a home, raise children together.

Love one another.

Once they had been pronounced husband and wife, Simon gave a shout and swept her into his arms. Eve knew his joy equaled her own as he kissed her heartily, to the congratulatory applause of the Bairds. They all returned to Gretna Green, and her new husband gave her a quick tour of the famous smithy, site of elopement-styled weddings by Scotland's "blacksmith priests" for nearly two hundred years. A wedding reception at the inn ensued, hosted by the Bairds and attended by the priest and even the innkeepers, before she and Simon were finally able to go upstairs.

"How lovely!" Eve cried as she opened her door. In her absence the room had become a bower, with baskets of purple heather, green ivy, and golden tansies placed everywhere.

She started to enter when Simon stayed her with a hand. "We'll do this properly, Mrs. Forrester," he said, and she shrieked with laughter as he swung her up into his arms and carried her across the threshold.

She clung to him as he took her to the bed and gently set her down.

"I still canna believe you're my wife," he said, gazing at her.

Eve blushed, her heart thumping wildly as he leaned to remove the crown from her head. He pulled the pins from her hair, releasing the mass to fall past her shoulders. He took up a dark strand between his fingers. "So soft, it's like silk."

She moistened her lips, never taking her eyes from him, and he seemed to sense her fear. "I never want to hurt you," he said in a low voice. "Only love you." He held out his hand to her, and when she hesitated, he said, "Trust me, wife."

Eve reached for him, and he raised her to stand. His thick, coppery lashes shielded eyes now gray like a storm as they searched her face. Then he bent his head and touched his mouth to hers in a soft, feathery-light kiss. She closed her eyes, and a moment passed before his lips pressed against her lashes, then her cheeks, and finally the very tip of her nose.

Her breath shook with anticipation before his mouth claimed hers in a kiss as devastating as it was passionate, his roughened hands caressing her face. Eve melted against him, her own desire aflame as she slid her hands up around his neck and kissed him back with all the love in her heart. His arms encircled her, drawing her close until they were almost one, and when the kiss ended, he leaned his head against hers, his breathing labored.

She opened her eyes, still dazed, her mouth tender. He raised his half-lidded gaze to her, his expression both loving and fierce. "A few hours ago I promised to love, honor, and cherish you, lass, for all of our days." He spoke in a voice thick with passion. "Now, let me show you."

❦

The next morning at breakfast Eve watched her husband tuck into a man-sized serving of bacon, eggs, black pudding, sausages, mushrooms, and tomatoes.

"What shall we name him?" he asked between bites. "I think Angus, after my great-uncle, or Nicholas after your father."

"And if our first child is a girl?" she asked, pausing with a spoonful of porridge.

"We would name her Evelyn, of course." He eyed her in all seriousness. "We'll name our second daughter Louise after your mother, and our third—"

"We'll need more than a cottage in Highbury for all those children, so one at a time if you please." She fought back a smile. "What if we have all sons?"

From across the white linen tablecloth, Simon grinned. "Plenty of time to think of names," he said, waggling his brows. "While we practice having wee ones to go with them."

Her laughter rang out, and a few of the inn's guests turned to smile at them. Her wedding night had been wondrous and tender, with her husband loving her thoroughly as he made her his own. Heat blossomed in her cheeks at the memory, and she realized Simon had certainly kept his promise. She'd been loved, honored, and oh, so cherished.

The reminder that they must abandon their honeymoon nest for London in a few hours dimmed her smile. Eve knew she must deceive Matron when she got back, at least until she secured another position. Like her biblical namesake she was assailed by guilt, as though she and her "Adam" had done something underhanded in Paradise.

She also thought about her family in Belgium and the upcoming dangers they might face. Simon would leave for Dover the following morning, and possibly for France soon after.

A foreboding about the future seeped into her bones.

"A penny for your thoughts?"

She glanced up to see that Simon now stood beside her chair.

"What has my bonny bride looking so uncertain?" He touched her shoulder. "It's too late to change your mind, you know."

She smiled and laid her hand over his. "I was thinking about the future. About Mama and the children in Belgium. I worry for them."

He crouched beside her chair, his gaze tender. "They'll be all right, love," he said. "Promise me you'll stay here in Britain. While I'm away, I need to know my wife, *my family*, is home and safe."

She gazed at him, her heart filled with love. They were a family now. "I promise."

"Thank you." He rose and drew her up from the chair. "Now, let's leave the future where it is, lass. Right now we have this beautiful morning, and I would like very much to make the most of it."

He bent his head and lightly kissed her palm. When he looked up, Eve saw in his handsome face mischief, desire, and an emotion she couldn't define, but one so intensely intimate as to make her warm inside.

Surely God has blessed us, she thought as Simon linked his arm with hers and led her from the table. After the rest of the world had come and gone, she and Simon would have each other.

CHAPTER 8

*S*ister Marche, I was just coming to find you."

Eve returned from the general's office at the other end of the palace to find Otto hailing her from the hall. "Can I have a word?"

"Of course." Pasting on a pleasant expression, she followed him into his office. As always, she was wary, wondering what new demand he might try to press on her.

"Sit, please. Did you get Herr General his bicarbonate of soda?"

"I did," she said, wondering at his small talk. "He is having stomach troubles but refuses to see Herr Doktor Schlagel."

Otto shook his head. "There is much pressure that comes with being in charge."

He returned to his chair behind the desk and picked up one of the cigars Eve presumed he'd purchased yesterday. Smiling, he closed his eyes and waved it beneath his nose. "Ah, there is nothing like a Cuban." When he opened his eyes, the smile was gone. "Now, why are you insulting my intelligence?"

Startled by his swift change in mood, Eve watched him pluck the blue leaflets from the pouch and drop them into the wastebasket.

"These tell me nothing."

"Agreed," she said, playing her part. "As you know, Herr Major, I'd offer something more useful if I could. But the pouch was left in my office, and while insignificant, the contents seemed to be our only link to Captain Chandler."

Otto's smile returned. "I always appreciate the information you bring to me, Eve. And *as you know*," he said, tossing back her words, "when I can please my superiors, my post here in Brussels is secure. Which means," he said, pointing the cigar at her, "I can continue to watch over you and your family to the best of my ability."

Eve bit back her anger and forced an appreciative smile. After arriving in Brussels and accepting Otto's generosity for her family, she'd assumed his actions stemmed from gratitude and his apparent regard for her. She'd sensed his subtle attraction over the years, the way he watched her, the little kindnesses he extended. He knew she was a widow, but thankfully he'd never acted on his feelings except to show her more consideration than did most of the officers.

It wasn't long, however, before his true intent became clear: Otto began blackmailing her for information, which she was to glean from the Allied patients at the hospital.

At first Eve had rejected his demands, but he insisted, telling her if he couldn't appease a certain government friend in the palace with occasional information, he might lose his hospital post in Brussels. If that happened, she and her family would be at the mercy of the German government.

Eve had had no choice but to relent, and at first she'd given him only harmless, inconsequential information. Then last year, when she joined La Dame Blanche, the network offered to provide her with disinformation she could pass along to him, at the same time promoting the Allies' efforts.

She had long surmised that Otto's threats were fueled more

by his fear of being sent to the Front than by any malice, but she still detested them. "I do try, Herr Major," she said, affecting a conciliatory tone.

"And I realize that, Eve, but I need something more." He nipped one end of the cigar with his cutter. "Captain Chandler is no help. According to Herr Jaeger, the captain cannot recall why he and the other man were flying over Brussels late at night dropping leaflets"—he arched a brow—"if in fact that's what they were doing. His memory seems gone."

Otto drew a match across the decorative striker on his desk and lit the cigar, blowing out puffs of white smoke. "Herr Jaeger has asked me to release him into the custody of the German secret police. At this point, I'm inclined to agree."

Simon was going to prison now? Eve launched from her seat in panic. "Herr Major, he's suffered a serious head injury! He has broken ribs—"

"I spoke with Herr Doktor Schlagel. He tells me Captain Chandler suffers only a mild concussion. As for the broken ribs, they've been wrapped. There is nothing else to be done."

"But the likelihood he'll survive in prison . . ." Eve gathered up her courage. "You recommended me to the position of matron at this hospital, and I take full responsibility for all of my patients. I must insist the captain be allowed sufficient time to heal before a decision is made."

"You are *acting* matron, Eve," he said. "An extraordinary achievement on my part, considering you're British." His blue eyes appraised her. "I've received word from the German Red Cross in Berlin. They're sending additional nurses to all German-run hospitals in Belgium over the next several weeks."

He drew on the cigar once more, and white smoke billowed out from beneath his moustache. "I cannot guarantee how long you will hold your position."

Eve jammed her fists into her apron pockets. "I understand my place, Herr Major," she said, painfully aware her authority rested on Otto's goodwill. "But Jaeger and Schultz . . . you know their methods. In the captain's current condition, he'll die before he makes it to trial."

"He'll die either way," Otto said. "Captain Chandler is an enemy spy. Herr Jaeger wants him. He won't let anyone stand in his way." He flicked his ash into the metal tray on his desk. "Be careful, Eve. Do not let your softhearted compassion fuel his antagonism. My protection is limited where the secret police are concerned."

She leveled a gaze on him. "I cannot help my compassion, or extending it to all of my patients, regardless of allegiance or situation."

"I am grateful for that." He fingered his collar, near the scar on his neck. It was the wound he'd received in Louvain, which would have been mortal but for her painstaking care. "And I know what it cost you."

She flinched as his words resurrected the awful memory of what she'd sacrificed.

"Which is why I'm concerned about you taking unnecessary risks." He drew on the cigar before his smile returned. "Still, I can hardly refuse you a favor. I believe I can convince Herr Jaeger to give him more time."

"Thank you, Herr Major." Eve offered an ingratiating smile. "The captain has been here just two days, but I feel certain if given a few weeks to heal in the hospital, his memory will return—"

"One week, Sister Marche." Beneath a haze of white smoke, Otto's expression brooked no argument. "Then he goes with Herr Jaeger."

Return Janssen to Holland. Complete the mission.

Eve stood inside the water closet at the café that evening and reread the message from Rotterdam. She'd returned to the kitchen after serving up an order of Uncle Lucien's version of *Bibbelsche Bohnesupp*—German potato and bacon soup— when her contact, Vincent the brewer, delivered the message.

Return Janssen to Holland. Eve ground her teeth in frustration. After the café closed last night, she, Dom, and Felix had tossed ideas back and forth to no avail. How was she expected to get Simon into Holland when she couldn't break him out of a Brussels hospital?

She'd already decoded Simon's orders for Operation Behead the Snake—an ambush against German army headquarters at the Château de Mérode in Trélon, France. The plan also included an assassin who would infiltrate the château prior to the attack and kill the kaiser.

The siege was to take place November 20—just a month from now. The name of an inside contact for the assassin would be forthcoming, along with the place and time to meet a man named Lundgren in La Bouteille, France.

Eve stared at the instructions in confusion. If Lundgren was the assassin, and Simon's assignment had been to deliver him the contact's name, why was her husband's alias as Albert Janssen Belgian? The orders stated the meeting would be in France. Why didn't he carry a French passport?

She sighed, tucking the note back into her corset, and returned to the kitchen. Nothing would make sense until she and Simon had a chance to talk.

"I have two more orders up!" Aunt Marie called as she wiped her flushed face with a dishcloth.

Eve took the steaming bowls of soup from her aunt and delivered them out to the main floor, the message from headquarters still on her mind. Her first order of business was to get Simon safely out of Herr Jaeger's grasp. She could deal with the rest later.

"*Guten Abend*," she said as Wolfe and Kraus sat down at a table by the window.

"Sister." Kraus looked melancholy. "*Zwei Bier, bitte?*"

"Two beers, coming up." Eve noticed they dined without their friends tonight and seemed much quieter than usual. She returned carrying a pair of frothy mugs in one hand and a small plate in the other. "You wish to have the soup as well?"

"*Ja*," Kraus said. "This may be our last meal." He cast a doleful look at Wolfe before gazing up at her. "It seems we must say good-bye to you sooner than we expected."

"But surely you and Lieutenant Wolfe won't be leaving for two weeks yet." Setting down the beers, she placed the plate containing black bread, a dollop of sugar beet jam, and a tiny pat of butter on the table between them.

"*Nein*, our orders have changed." Wolfe sounded equally dismal as he picked up his mug and stared at the amber brew. "We leave the day after tomorrow for the Front."

Eve hid her shock. In two days her family would have new German boarders? Her heart sank. No doubt they would be more difficult than these two. "I'm sorry you must leave so soon," she said, and found she meant it. She would miss the agreeable, puppy-like soldiers as tenants.

Both men gazed at her and nodded. Seeing their gloomy expressions, Eve could almost feel sorry for them. Almost. "I'll go and get your soup," she said and left to fill their order.

As she returned with their food, she overheard them speaking to one another.

"If we are gassed at the Front, I hope it kills me quickly," Kraus said, his features grim. "I don't want to survive the effects of it. I have heard it is horrible pain." He visibly shuddered.

"Nor me, *mein Kamerad*." Wolfe reached for a slice of the black bread. "If it happens to me, I just want to go to sleep and die in peace."

Eve almost dropped their bowls of soup. The idea that had just come to her was dangerous, outrageous; yet it might work. To save her husband from Jaeger and Schultz and their methods of torture, to keep him from being imprisoned and shot as a spy—

She would need to kill him first.

"You want to do what?" Dom's dark eyes widened. "Are you *démentielle*?"

"That's crazy," Felix said, echoing the Frenchman's sentiments.

The café had closed. Eve sat across from the two men, sipping at her coffee. "I know it sounds insane, but we must convince the Boche he's dead." She set the cup down. "It's the only way to get Chandler out of the hospital."

Before her arrest, Nurse Edith Cavell had been extremely clever in her methods of helping patients to escape. Some she disguised as monks who walked out the door to the nearest abbey. Others she hid inside laundry carts to be picked up by a local linen service and taken out of the city. With the vampires knowing what to look for, Eve's options for freeing Simon were narrowed down to the most drastic measures.

"We're out of time," she said. "The major told me this morning our patient will be turned over to Herr Jaeger in a week. You know what they'll do to him after that."

"If you don't kill him first, you mean," Dom reminded her.

Eve frowned at him as she warmed her hands on her cup. She couldn't deny the risk. She'd gotten the idea of using ether after overhearing Kraus and Wolfe in the café. Administering the anesthesia was an exact science; one drop too much could indeed kill the patient. But she'd become proficient in its use over the last few years.

She could make Simon appear dead. But what if she made a mistake? Her heart clenched at the possibility of killing her husband. Then bitter humor rose in her throat. The whole scheme could fall apart before she even got that far.

"I plan to ask Doctor Ambrose for help," she said. "On Monday I'll have him stage an emergency surgery for the patient due to a swelling of the brain. Herr Doktor Schlagel will be away at his monthly medical conference in Antwerp and won't return until Tuesday, after our 'surgery' is performed."

"Doctor Ambrose will agree to do this?" Felix said.

"I haven't asked him yet, but he should be willing. He's a patriot and an ally."

"I can speak with him," Felix offered. "I've known his family for years."

She smiled. "Thanks, but I'm certain I can persuade him."

"Once he agrees, then what?" Dom asked, raising his cup. "After you kill the patient."

Eve shot him a withering look. "You and Felix will take Chandler's body to the hospital morgue. Once the paperwork is complete, you'll deliver him in the ambulance to the Catholic Soldiers Society. Because he's an Allied soldier, they'll provide a free coffin and burial." She paused. "And because they are also Belgian patriots, they will switch out the captain's body with a real corpse to take to the Brussels Cemetery."

"You've planned this carefully." Felix seemed to consider her. "If the real corpse goes to the cemetery, then what happens to Chandler? Will he stay at the Society?"

She hesitated, then stared into her coffee. "I'm still working out details."

In truth, she'd already made arrangements. Earlier, after exchanging the linen at Tulle's, she'd stopped to see Father

Francois, the parish priest at St. Magdalene's. They had sketched out a plan for Simon's care—information no one else needed to know, at least not yet. If there was a leak in La Dame Blanche, as she suspected, Eve wanted to be certain her husband's whereabouts remained secret.

She lifted her gaze, eyeing both men. "Suffice it to say, gentlemen, I'll find a place where our patient can recuperate until he's well enough to travel. Then the three of us can arrange his departure across the border into Holland."

"All right." Dom checked his watch, then rose from the table. "Our shift starts soon."

Felix also stood. "We'll be ready."

Eve looked up at them. "Thank you both."

"I need a smoke. Coming, Dom?"

"In a minute."

Felix paused, gazing at him. Then he offered Eve a quick nod before leaving the café.

"You're taking a lot of risk for the captain," Dom said when he'd gone. "Do you know him from Britain?"

His question startled her. The only part of her life before Belgium she'd shared with Dom was her arrival three years ago as a nurse with the British Red Cross. "He dropped from the sky in a British plane," she said by way of answer. "Isn't that reason enough?"

He searched her face. "I just want to be certain your heart still belongs to me, *chérie*."

He winked at her and Eve relaxed, smiling. "Was there ever a doubt?"

CHAPTER 9

*G*ood morning, Fräulein."

Eve paused at the entrance to Simon's room the following day as Herr Schultz exited, blocking her passage. For an instant, the sight of his lean, sallow-faced complexion made her wonder if the term *vampire* hadn't been coined after his recruitment into the secret police.

"Good morning." Her pulse sped up as she craned her neck, trying to see past him into the room. Was Simon all right? "Please let me pass, Herr Schultz. I must see to the patient."

"In a moment." He was staring at her Iron Cross, just as he had when they first met. This morning she'd pinned the medal to the outside of her apron. With only German patients remaining in the ward, she hoped to encourage conversation with those wounded and perhaps glean new information for La Dame Blanche.

"How does a British nurse acquire such a distinguished award from the kaiser?" His mouth bowed downward beneath the bottlebrush moustache.

"Saving German lives. I was in Louvain at the beginning of the war."

He nodded, his hazel eyes assessing. "Including the life of Herr Major Reinhardt, I understand."

"Yes." Eve tried again to see past him into the room, but he shifted to block her view.

"I read the *Kommandant's* report," he said. "Sabotage against the German army. The Belgian assassins were killing our soldiers in the streets."

Eve jerked her gaze back to him. *Lies!* she wanted to shout at him. Instead she said, "I must attend to my patient, if you'll excuse me."

"I think you'll find Captain Chandler has been very obstinate."

Her feet froze. "What do you mean?"

"Herr Jaeger and I have spent the past two hours with him, and still he tells us nothing." His pale features flashed annoyance. "You should advise him to start remembering now," he said, his gaze boring into her. "Before he visits with us next week."

Cinching the belt of his leather coat, he offered a curt nod. "Fräulein."

He moved past her down the hall. Eve's heart pounded as she hurried into Simon's room—and came face-to-face with Herr Jaeger. The short blond officer was shoving his hands into black leather gloves. He shot an irritated glance in her direction before sweeping out of the room.

Eve ran toward her husband's bed. "Are you all right?" she asked, slipping around the partition.

She drew a sharp breath at the sight of fresh blood against his hospital gown.

"*Mon cher,* what have they done?" She edged onto the side of his bed and gently pulled at the gown, intending to inspect for an injury beneath.

Her husband groaned. His bandaged head was turned away from her.

She reached to draw his face around. "*Nooo,*" she moaned, discovering the bloody source. His bandage was soaked in red, and a thin line of blood oozed along the side of his face.

She noted the fresh cut against his cheek and an angry red mark next to his mouth that wasn't there yesterday. Forcing her hands to steady, she made a quick check for any other injuries, examining his cheekbones, nose, and jaw, relieved when nothing seemed broken.

Rising, she went to fetch supplies from the nurses' table. Fury seethed in her. Did the monsters have no conscience at all, beating a man already injured?

A pair of wooden crutches leaned beside the station, and she fought an urge to take them and go after the heads of Jaeger and Schultz.

Returning to the bed, she cut away the bloodied bandage, dismayed to find her stitches of days ago ruined. Blood continued pulsing slowly from the reopened gash.

Simon gave a slight jerk as she began cleaning the wound with an antiseptic solution.

"Easy." Silently she cursed the two Boche, then changed her mind about using crutches against them. A steel oxygen bottle would be much more effective.

"Eve?"

Her husband's hoarse voice reached her, and she saw he'd opened his eyes.

"Hush." She offered him a reassuring smile, then started working with a pair of surgical scissors and tweezers to remove the damaged stitches at his scalp. Again he flinched, and seeing his condition, her doubts about using the ether on him disappeared. If she didn't get Simon out of the hospital soon, Jaeger and Schultz would kill him, and with much more pain.

"Your Huns tried to beat . . . sense into me," he huffed, and a corner of his swollen mouth lifted.

She couldn't tell if he smiled at her or sneered. "They're not my Huns."

He reached to finger the Iron Cross on her apron. "So you say."

Eve tried to ignore the hurt. He still didn't trust her. "I'm going to resuture your scalp."

She doused the area of his wound with ethyl chloride, then cleaned and tended his face while she waited for the topical anesthesia to take effect.

"Are you hurt anywhere else?" She hoped the brutes hadn't reinjured his ribs.

"It's enough," he muttered through swollen lips, lifting a hand to his head.

Indeed. She bit back her anger and began stitching him. Once she'd finished, she rose and walked to the door of the suite to check if the guard was nearby.

The hall was empty.

Returning to the bed, she began rebandaging her husband's head. "I need to talk to you," she said in a low voice. "Will you listen?"

He turned to her. Eve winced inwardly at the sight of his ravaged features. *Dear Lord, how have we come to this?* Taking a deep breath, she said, "I'm getting you out of here in a few days."

"Few days?" He tried for another smile, or a sneer, but the swelling at his mouth ruined the effect. "There willna be much of me left."

He was right. The vampires would return to give him another dose of their brand of questioning. She would speak with Otto, have him forbid Jaeger and Schultz from returning. Let them think they would have Simon soon enough.

"Monday you'll be taken into surgery. Swelling of the brain will be our ruse." She darted a glance toward the door, then finished with the bandage and tied it off. "Once you're brought into the operating theater, I'll administer ether, enough so that you appear to be dead."

She had spoken with Doctor Ambrose, who had agreed to

her plan. "The surgeon is an ally. Once he proclaims you deceased—"

"No." He uttered the word in a clear, hard voice.

"I know it's dangerous, but I have experience." She reached to pull the blankets around his chest. "Please trust me."

Simon grabbed her wrist. "No," he said again.

Every breath was like taking a knife to his chest. His pain also kept pace with his growing confusion. She had tended his wounds with such gentle care, the distress in her voice genuine as she examined his injuries and mended his scalp. So different from the woman who had stared at him coldly as she handed his leather pouch to the Hun days ago.

However, Eve had explained what she'd done with the pouch and why, and he'd had time to reconsider.

He had started to believe she meant to protect him after all—until this plan to take him to the brink of death. "Never work," he mumbled around his sore mouth.

"We don't have a choice." Her brow creased. "Herr Major has decided you'll go with those two vampires to St. Gilles prison. We haven't much time."

Despite his injuries, Simon tried to raise himself and grimaced at the effort. His wife nudged him back against the bed.

Vampires, she'd called them, an apt description of the two thugs who had drawn a fair share of his blood. It seemed using Chandler's identity hadn't been enough to protect him.

Simon's limbs gave an involuntary shudder. The pair had nearly thrashed him to death the first time. Now they planned to take him to their prison and finish the job. "How long?"

"Next Wednesday," she said.

Only a few days. Simon licked his bruised lips. His choices seemed limited. But allowing Eve to give him an overdose of ether? His instincts rebelled at the notion. She'd admitted using the drug would be dangerous, and he understood enough about the anesthetic to know he would likely die in truth. "Find another way," he muttered.

"There is none." She cast another look toward the door. "If I can't get you out of here . . ." She paused, then said in a whisper, "As much as you resist the idea of trusting me, husband, you need my help."

Husband. He'd longed to hear the word from her. Could he trust her with his life?

In his heart he wanted to, yet he couldn't rid himself of the jaded memory: her smiling with the major, allowing the other man's touch when she'd rejected his own.

"Eve." He reached out to her again, wanting to see what she would do.

She quickly rose from the bed and distanced herself. Her hands twisted together. "Will you hear me out?" she said, before her gaze again darted toward the door.

Hurt pierced him. "What's wrong with me?" he demanded, his mouth throbbing. "Not your Hun?"

Her head whipped around, the violet eyes looking wounded, angry. "It's too dangerous!" she hissed. "If we're seen together . . ." She pressed a hand to her lips. Then she said, "You know nothing about my life here."

Simon saw fear skitter across her face. He'd seen the same look earlier, when he'd had her pinned against the bed. Like then, it jarred him, and his anger fled. What had happened to her? "Tell me," he said.

"Not here." Her voice trembled while her eyes shone suspiciously bright. "Later."

There may not be a later, he thought. He eased out a breath against the pain in his ribs. Nothing made sense to him anymore. *She* didn't make sense.

He gazed at the wife he'd fought so hard to find. Her teasing smile was gone, replaced by the tense lines at her mouth. Half-moon shadows, like smudges, lay beneath her once shining gaze. He remembered the way she used to roll her eyes at him when he tried to make her blush, and he almost smiled, thinking about the endearing trait. That too seemed lost.

They'd spent only a handful of days and nights together as husband and wife before three years of war broke them apart. Seeing her now, it dawned on him there was much he didn't know about her, or what she'd been through. Or how she felt about him anymore.

His thoughts returned to the major. The Hun's ease and familiarity with her had bordered on intimacy.

"A means to an end, nothing more." Eve's words disquieted him, putting images in his mind he didn't want to consider. He guessed she'd been working at the hospital for years, as the atrocities in Louvain occurred at the beginning of the war. During all of that time, what had she had to do in order to remain safe?

His gaze fell to the Iron Cross. Today she wore it for all to see. *It was hard won . . .*

Could he trust her? Did it even matter? Simon closed his eyes, while exhaustion and pain threatened to overwhelm him. It seemed he had no choice but to put his life into her hands. He wouldn't survive another beating. And the idea of being imprisoned by the Germans . . .

He rejected the thought as swiftly as it came. No, if he must choose his death, the one by ether seemed preferable.

He opened his eyes, and his chest tightened, making breathing more difficult. "Tell me," he rasped.

"I said I cannot!" Her attention drew back to the doorway.

When she returned to face him, Simon slowly shook his head. "Your plan," he said.

CHAPTER 10

"Bless me, Father, for I have sinned. It's been two days since my last confession."

Eve knelt in the dark confessional at St. Magdalene's church the following morning, hands clasped together as she stared at the cloth-covered screen in front of her.

There was a heartbeat of silence before Father Francois's heavily accented voice floated to her from behind the partition. "Please continue, daughter."

"The arrangements we discussed . . . will go ahead as planned." Two days had passed since she'd spoken with the priest. Fresh anxiety filled her. If she didn't accidentally kill Simon, there was every chance they would all still get caught and be shot as spies.

She drew a deep breath. *One thing at a time.* Simon had given his agreement, and she'd come to make the final preparations. "The Society will contact you when they have the body," she told the priest. "Can you still provide accommodations?"

"*Oui,* all is in readiness."

She bowed her head in relief. Father Francois merely awaited her word.

Despite what she'd told Dom and Felix, Eve had taken the priest's suggestion to have two coffins and two bodies. The Catholic Soldiers Society would take the real corpse to St. Catherine's

Cathedral across town for a funeral Mass; Simon's body would be brought to St. Magdalene's. After her husband's "funeral" he would be hidden away in the rectory, adjacent to the church. His empty coffin, sufficiently weighted, would then be transported by the Society, along with the coffin from St. Catherine's, to the Brussels Cemetery for burial.

By using two different churches, it would help confuse the vampires if they were watching. Only three would know Simon's whereabouts: Eve; the Society's mortician, Monsieur Coppens, whom Father Francois trusted implicitly; and the priest himself.

Father Francois had already shown her the two secret passageways leading into the rectory. She hoped that with the extra measures, her husband would remain safe from the Boche while he healed.

"Thank you, Father." Eve rose from the kneeler. "We'll speak again in a few days."

She was about to exit when he said, "Allowances must be made during these dire times, daughter, but I dislike wasting the sanctity of the confessional. Any sins you wish to unburden while you are here?"

Eve hesitated. He'd asked her the same question the other day. She hadn't made her confession in years, not since she'd arrived in Brussels. The priest had offered her absolution then, but the guilt and grief remained, like a gaping wound against her soul.

She had three years of other more minor sins, in her estimation. The life she lived was a sham, a secret, and while she had no regrets in deceiving the Boche, she had lied to Dom and Felix about Simon.

Eve wondered how Father Francois would react, knowing she was about to play God with Simon's life. The priest hadn't asked any questions beyond his part in her scheme, so he couldn't know the deadly means she planned to use for her husband's escape.

And if he died . . .

She gripped the handle on the confessional door as despair settled against her chest. What did new offenses matter when she couldn't get free of the old ones?

Some sins were beyond redemption.

"Not now, Father, thank you," she said, her voice unsteady.

"Guilt can become a stumbling block to keep us from God's mercy," the priest said, as if knowing her thoughts. "Our Lord is always ready to forgive, eager to take us back into the fold of His love. But sometimes we humans deny ourselves that grace, especially when our transgressions seem insurmountable." He paused. "You must let go of the past, daughter."

She knew his words were meant as comfort, but he didn't understand that the past wouldn't let go of *her*. The memories of Louvain were always out in front, shading her world, drawing her into a chasm of shame and anguish that she'd learned to live around. She'd prayed, many times, to reach the surface, to find the grace he spoke about.

Yet hope, and that sense of peace she craved, continued to elude her. "We'll talk soon, Father." She opened the door.

"Read John 21," he called softly, before she exited the confessional.

Making her way toward the front of the church, Eve passed the small queue of people waiting their turn with the priest.

The silence was almost deafening, as St. Magdalene's thick stone walls blocked the distant sounds of artillery fire and mortars from the Front.

As she neared the altar, she slipped into a pew. Kneeling, she clasped her hands together and gazed up at the image of Christ on the cross. On a conscious level Eve knew that Jesus had died for all of their sins, yet in the deepest part of her soul she didn't deem herself worthy.

Read John 21. Eve vaguely recalled the chapter: the apostles' third meeting with Christ after He was raised from the dead. There was a miraculous catch of fish, and afterward, as they ate, Jesus had reinstated Simon Peter.

She thought of Peter and how he must have despised himself after his denial of Jesus, especially when the Lord had foretold of his infidelity. Yet Jesus gave him the chance he needed.

"Simon son of John, do you love me more than these?"

"Yes, Lord . . ."

Three times the Lord had asked, once for each time Peter denied Him.

Would she ever receive the same chance?

Closing her eyes, Eve bent her head, and as she'd done times before, she tried keeping perfectly still. Waiting in the silence of the church, waiting for His voice, the sign she needed to release her affliction.

But only the occasional shuffling of feet near the confessional met her ears.

She released the breath she'd been holding and buried her face in her palms, the stillness working to amplify the litany of guilt in her soul.

You shall not murder. You shall not murder . . .

And she would continue to bear the burden of having taken an innocent life.

CHAPTER 11

LOUVAIN, BELGIUM,
THREE YEARS EARLIER

W e're almost there, my friend," Maddie said. "Your mother will be thrilled to see you."

Eve leaned against the rail of the ship's deck and gave her friend a wan smile. For a few moments, her grief found respite as she imagined the coming reunion. Mama would hold her tenderly in her arms, and Nikki and Zoe would give her hugs and kisses as they sought to ease their older sister's sorrow.

Eve had thought of little else since receiving the news about her husband. She'd clung to the image of her family as she struggled to stay afloat in a mire of despair.

Pushing away a dark tendril of windblown hair, Eve gazed out at the fairly calm sea. The sky overhead was a brilliant blue, and it seemed impossible that across the channel war raged.

Their ship cruised steadily, and soon she could make out the silhouette of Ostend, where they would come ashore in a matter of minutes. She clutched Simon's white handkerchief while her grief battled a surreal sense of expectancy at their destination.

Born on British soil, Eve had never before visited her parents' homeland. Now she, Maddie, and thirty-eight other British Red

Cross nurses were crossing the English Channel toward Belgium. In the back of her mind she could still hear Simon voicing his objections. He'd wanted her to remain home in Britain, where it was safe, and had made her give him her promise . . .

An ache rose in her throat. He had also promised to come back.

Vows hardly mattered anymore. Simon, her beloved, was gone, his plane shot down during a German attack two days into the war.

A Royal Flying Corps observation flight reported the crash site in enemy territory, spotting the charred remains of his body not far from the wreckage. Alex Baird had telephoned her with the news a little more than a week ago, and since then Eve had drifted in a haze of grief, trying to grasp the reality that Simon was gone.

The hotels and boardwalk along Ostend's shores came into view. She took a steadying breath and turned to her friend. "I don't know how I would have managed this without you, Maddie."

"I imagine you'd still have come to Belgium." Maddie offered a sympathetic smile and reached to grip her hand. "Though it's likely you would have paddled on ahead of us in your haste to get here."

Maddie was her anchor. It was well over a month since Eve had returned from Scotland a happy bride and confessed her elopement to her friend. Once Maddie got over the initial shock, she'd hugged them both and offered her congratulations.

When Simon left for Dover the following day, Eve was relieved that Maddie knew their secret. Excuses were unnecessary as she traveled those two precious weekends by train to an inn near the air base, meeting her husband and making up for their days apart before he was sent off to France.

Maddie had also been there when Alex called. She'd held a

sobbing Eve afterward, even covering her shift at the hospital while Eve stumbled through the ensuing days in a fog of mourning and loss.

Then a notice appeared at the London Hospital saying that Red Cross nurses were urgently needed in Belgium. Maddie had marshaled her into some semblance of sanity so the two could sign up for service.

"How long do you think it will take us to get into Brussels?" Eve asked.

"I imagine a few hours, if the trains are running." Maddie's dark cloak fluttered open in the wind, revealing her blue dress and starched white apron with its Red Cross insignia. "Honestly, I'm anxious to get started. Some say the war will be over by Christmas, so for the next four months I plan to help out as much as possible."

Eve couldn't think that far ahead. *I just want to see Mama and my family.*

By early afternoon the ship came to dock at Ostend. Nearing the shore, Eve glimpsed dozens of watercraft bobbing off the coast, the overcrowded boats riding dangerously low as they made their way out into the channel.

The city bustled with a sense of excitement and urgency. Red Cross trucks and British military personnel swarmed along the seaboard and the nearby railway station. There were thousands of men, women, and children crowding along the docks and shoreline—Belgian refugees, Eve realized, as she watched people trying to crowd onto already full boats and barges. Fights broke out, and several men were tossed into the cold channel, flailing to reach a boat.

Madness, she thought, and was relieved when a half hour later she, Maddie, and the other British nurses had boarded a train bound for the city of Brussels.

Eve glanced out the car's window at stretches of green

countryside lying between the stations at Bruges and Ghent. She was again struck by how peaceful the scenery looked, as though she were on holiday and not on her way to what would become a battleground among nations.

Her heart beat faster. By this time tomorrow she would be with her family.

Once the train arrived in Brussels, Eve and the others disembarked and were herded onto trams that would take them to the Metropole, a grand luxury hotel in the heart of the city.

She gazed in awe at the beautiful stone buildings lining the city's leafy, tree-dotted avenues. A variety of Gothic, Art Nouveau, and Style Moderne architecture, the ornate structures stood adorned with brightly striped window awnings or colorful flower boxes.

Eve observed in Brussels the same unrest she'd sensed at Ostend—the pinched faces of the other Belgian passengers, their whispers in French about the German troops who were headed toward the city in a planned march.

The Metropole was indeed grand, with its Renaissance-style décor and lush furnishings. Elegantly carved divans stretched out in the hotel's lobby, while above, stained-glass ceiling panels supported glittering chandeliers.

"It's so beautiful," Maddie breathed, and Eve had to agree.

Once they took the elevator up to the room they were to share, Eve dropped her valise and rushed toward the telephone on the nightstand.

"I'll give you privacy to talk to her," Maddie said, and Eve flashed a grateful smile.

It was a few minutes before the call went through. Eve clutched the receiver. "Mama?"

"Evelyn!" Shock and delight infused her mother's tinny voice over the line. "Oh, *ma petite*, I miss you so much! Are you in London? How is married life?"

Eve had called her mother after returning from Scotland.

Mama was thrilled for her and Simon both, though sad she could not be at the wedding.

Eve took a deep breath and fought for composure. "I'm here, Mama. I'm in Brussels." Fresh tears pricked her eyes. "I need to come to Louvain."

"What?" Her mother's tone turned agitated. "Oh, *chère*, you should not be here! The Germans are on their way. Didn't Simon tell you? I wrote to him recently, but I haven't heard back." She paused. "Is my son-in-law with you?"

"No, he—he's gone, Mama," Eve said in a thread of a whisper. "Dead."

There was a pause, then, "*C'est impossible*!" came her mother's soft cry. "How . . . ?"

Speaking the words and hearing her mother's anguish made Eve's loss seem all the more real. She struggled to breathe. "His p-plane crashed . . ." A sob escaped her. "Oh, Mama, I need you. Please let me come to you." She began to weep in earnest, uncaring about the war and the Red Cross or her obligation to report to the hospital.

"You'll take the six o'clock train." Mama spoke in a no-nonsense tone. "Louvain is only twenty-five kilometers away. We will meet you at the station."

"Oh yes! I will be there." Eve hung up the receiver and collapsed against the bed. Wiping her eyes, she glanced at her watch. The train would be leaving in less than an hour. She would see her family tonight!

A soft knock sounded at the door, and Maddie used her key to enter the room. She gave Eve a questioning look.

"I'm going to Louvain," Eve said. "I'll call you tomorrow."

Maddie nodded. "I met a few Red Cross nurses from France downstairs. It sounds as if we'll be cooling our heels here for a time, until they get the rosters sorted and assign us to the hospitals. I'll cover for you."

"Thanks, Maddie." The two hugged. "I'll give your regards to my family."

Eve made her way back to the train station. Two hours later she arrived in Louvain, scanning the university town through the car's window.

Tears pricked her eyes as she spied Mama, Nikki, and Zoe waiting on the platform, looking anxious and hopeful. Standing alongside them was a tall, gray-bearded gentleman clad in a blue linen suit, and Eve guessed him to be her uncle Eugene.

Once the train halted, she grabbed up her valise and rushed to disembark. Eve hurried toward her family, flying into her mother's outstretched arms. She was finally home.

"I don't know what to say to make the hurt go away, *chère*." Mama's moistened eyes shone with compassion. She sat beside Eve on a yellow brocade chaise in the small, stylish boudoir of Uncle Eugene's apartment along Naamsestraat, between Catholic University and Louvain's Gothic-style town hall. They had just finished eating a light supper of *moules-frites*, the mussels steamed with onions and celery and served alongside fried potato strips. Now each cradled a cup of Darjeeling, while her mother attempted to soothe her grief over Simon's death.

"I still cannot believe he's gone." Eve drew a trembling breath as she stared at the monogrammed handkerchief in her hand. "And I hate feeling this way. Everything takes so much effort. I keep thinking of him, and how we had such a short time together."

"I know." Mama leaned gently against her. "It's like a hunger, the way it gnaws at your heart. A beast with relentless teeth that will not rest until it has gutted you."

Eve gazed into her mother's pale features. The hazel eyes wore a haunted look.

"In time you *will* conquer the creature. And you will realize you have survived. I know you cannot understand this now, but you will." As Mama spoke she reached for a biscuit on the tray. Her cup tipped and spilled tea on her lap. "Oh, *je suis maladroite*!" she chided herself.

Eve set her cup down and reached for a linen napkin. Helping Mama to dab up the tea, she noticed for the first time the black crepe gown.

Papa had been gone less than a year. Of course her mother understood what it meant to lose the other half of her soul. Eve's eyes burned. "I am glad to be here with you." She leaned her head against Mama's shoulder. "Even if the Germans do come."

"And I am pleased beyond words you are with me." Mama reached up and laid a hand against Eve's cheek. "But do not doubt the Boche will come. Our king refused them entry into the country, but that did not stop the kaiser or his troops."

Like the siege on Liège. Fresh grief pierced her as Eve imagined the place where her husband's plane had gone down. She raised her head to gaze at her mother. "Surely they will not come here, to Louvain?" Simon had told her the German invasion would occur in the larger Belgian cities.

Her mother's forehead creased. "We've had word from scouts in the Belgian army. The Germans are headed this way."

A prickle of alarm chased down Eve's spine. Would the enemy pass through the city . . . or did they intend to stay and fight? "When I telephoned you weeks ago, Mama, why didn't you return to Britain?"

Color blossomed in her mother's pale cheeks. "The war was just a rumor then, *chère*." Her gaze fell. "When the Germans did march onto Belgian soil two weeks ago, everything happened so fast. Our small Belgian army could not hold them back. Thousands of our people began flooding the borders to get out, most with nothing more than what they could carry.

I heard stories about mass panic, people being trampled, and I was afraid to take the children into the madness by myself."

Eve recalled the uproar she'd witnessed at Ostend—civilized people fighting each other for a place on a boat that would likely sink before getting them to the safety of Britain's shores.

She couldn't imagine her mother and siblings enduring that kind of fray.

"Eugene refused to abandon his position at the university library," her mother said. "He insisted we would be safer here. Still, for Nikki and Zoe's sake, I wrote to Simon and asked for his help." She glanced at Eve. "Now, with the Germans on their way . . ."

It is too late, Eve thought.

"All will be well, *ma fifille*. I am hopeful the Boche merely want passage through to France." Mama's smile seemed forced as she reached for Eve's hand. "Until then, I shall pamper you with love and try to ease your sadness."

Eve leaned to embrace her mother. Come what may, she didn't want to be anywhere else.

⚜

"Have you received orders from the hospital?" Eve telephoned the Metropole after lunch the following day and spoke with her friend.

"Not yet." Maddie expelled a breath. "We continue to sit waiting for news. Brussels is full of activity. Everyone seems worried about the Germans coming."

"Has my absence been noticed?"

"The matron in charge did ask about you," Maddie said. "I had to tell her you were in Louvain. With rumors of approaching German troops, she recommends you stay put for the moment." She paused. "Does being with your family help?"

"Very much," Eve said. "My brother and sister are almost grown." She turned to her ten-year-old brother, Nikki, still clad in his school uniform. He lifted his dark blue gaze to her, and a grin spread across his freckled features before he bent back to his task at the parlor table—trying to defeat his sister in a competitive game of backgammon.

Turning from her siblings, Eve spoke more quietly into the telephone. "I've been told those unwanted visitors you speak of will be here any day."

"In Louvain?" Maddie sounded surprised. "This morning I went for tea and a pastry with some of the British nurses. Many of the shops are already boarded up, and tension is high. People are stocking up on food and supplies, preparing for a siege." Her voice shivered through the line. "I cannot say as I blame them. None of us quite knows what to expect."

"Any idea when the Germans will arrive there?"

"I've heard a couple of days. It's all a bit unnerving. I won't stray too far from the hotel."

"I'm glad to hear it. Maddie, please take care."

"And you, my friend. I'll let you know when Matron orders you back. Meanwhile, with this kettle of chaos brewing, take her advice and stay put."

"I will," Eve said. "Thanks, Maddie. I'll talk with you soon."

"Want to play backgammon, Eve?" Zoe asked once Eve hung up the phone.

Eve smiled at the slender girl with honey-colored hair and brown, doe-shaped eyes. At fifteen years, her sister was becoming a lovely young woman. "How about after supper?" she said.

Zoe nodded and smiled.

Eve watched them a moment, the sight of her siblings enjoying the simple game easing the pain in her heart.

Leaving the parlor, she walked toward the back of the spacious apartment, where her uncle had his study. Despite her apprehension at the news of the enemy's approach, she was relieved to focus on something other than her grief. There would be time enough to continue mourning her husband. Right now she must deal with their present troubles.

She found Uncle Eugene seated in an oversized burgundy chair, one leg crossed over the other as he packed his pipe with tobacco. A snifter of brandy sat on the table beside him. Mama had ensconced herself in the matching chair beside him, winding ivory thread onto a bobbin.

"Come in, Evelyn!" Swinging both feet to the floor, he rose to his lanky height and offered her his seat. Eve declined with a smile and instead took up a place on a green diamond-tufted bench next to the bookcase.

She perused the leather-bound tomes on the shelves beside her. "As curator for the university's library, Uncle, you have a world of books at your disposal daily. Why bother keeping a collection here at the house?"

"No such thing as too many books, my dear." Her uncle's mouth broadened above his neatly trimmed beard as he reseated himself. Striking a match to his clay pipe, he took a few puffs, the fragrant white smoke drifting over his head like a halo. "I keep copies of some of the library's best works here. That way, if I have trouble sleeping, I need only come downstairs instead of chasing off to the university to fetch them."

Eve shifted on the bench, facing them. "I just spoke on the telephone with my friend in Brussels. She's been told the Germans will march on that city in a couple of days."

Her uncle exchanged a look with Mama, then turned to Eve. "They've been spotted marching toward Louvain from the east," he said. "The army is expected to arrive tomorrow."

Eve's heart beat faster. "What's being done to prepare?"

Uncle Eugene held the pipe to his lips as though contemplating what he might say next. "We've been encouraged to stay indoors until we see what they're about," he said finally, then took a puff. "I feel certain they'll simply march through the town on their way to France."

Mama looked pale. She paused with the bobbin in hand and said, "Let us pray they come in peace and not destruction."

Later that night, Eve lay in bed and tried to imagine what might transpire the following day. Closing her eyes, she thought to pray as Mama had suggested, but the knot of anger in her chest blocked the words from her throat.

She turned her head and opened her eyes to the room's shadows. "Simon, why did you leave me?" she whispered into the gloom.

Only the sound of her pulse greeted her ears.

Tears formed against her lashes, and she closed her eyes. Was he in heaven? She desperately wanted to believe he was there. He had died a hero's death in the line of duty, and he'd always been a good and kindhearted man. The sort of person who rescued kittens from trees, and who'd returned to Scotland to care for his great uncle.

Most of all, he'd been a tender and loving husband.

Grief washed over her in waves, dousing the angry fire in her breast and leaving only despair at the unfairness of it all. Eve thought of the sunlight, a sign of God's presence, bursting into the church as they spoke their vows. Why had He blessed their union if it was His plan to take her husband away so soon?

Eve awakened the next morning to an ominous drumming. Raising herself in bed, she blinked, clearing her head before she realized the sound was boots pounding against the cobbled streets below. She could hear the jangle of harnesses and the clop of hooves, while somewhere in the distance church bells rang.

She swung her feet over the bed. A warm August breeze blew in through the bedroom's open window, the air redolent with spicy red geraniums, purple lavender, and white carnations—no doubt the flowers spilling from window boxes outside on her balcony.

Eve paused, assailed by scents much like those of the fragrant blooms outside their honeymoon suite in Gretna Green. Just five short weeks ago . . .

Fresh pain ripped through her and she grabbed the bedpost to steady herself. Fiercely she shoved away the image of Simon's eyes, gray like the sea when he laughed, dark as steel when he was angry or concerned. She imagined his smile, so beautiful on their wedding night, when he'd repeated his promise to love, honor, and cherish her.

Eve's throat burned as she forced herself to rise. After donning a light blue skirt and white shirtwaist—her only clothes aside from her nurse's uniform and her cherished wedding gown—she tucked Simon's handkerchief into her corset next to her heart, then went to the window and peered outside.

Hundreds of townspeople were gathered along either side of the Great Market Square, watching the procession. Beyond the floral scents she detected the smell of horses, sweat, and fear. Still, her curiosity overrode her uncle's suggestion to remain home. Eve left her room and slipped outside, bypassing the dining room, where her family was having breakfast.

Nikki must have heard her leave. He ran up to join her as she walked along Naamsestraat toward the main market area.

An endless tide of soldiers swept through the city. Leading the parade were German hussars seated astride their war-horses, followed by a gray sea of goose-stepping infantry. Standing on the sidelines clutching her brother's hand, Eve observed the soldiers' faces, appalled at how young some of them looked. Many of them carried flags instead of rifles, and she imagined they were mascots. Still just children.

One of them glanced at her boldly, a slim boy with reddish hair and light gray eyes, and with a pang Eve was reminded of Simon. Yet the youth, clad in an oversized uniform with his rounded cheeks and sprinkling of freckles, could not have been much older than her little brother.

Behind the troops, horse-drawn supply wagons rolled in droves, many pulling along *mitrailleuses*, cannon-like guns on wheels with grapeshot barrels. All made their way toward the turreted, steepled structure of Louvain's town hall at the heart of the city.

To Eve's relief, the march was relatively uneventful. In fact, the Germans seemed almost cordial as the officers nodded to townspeople along their way.

Returning with her brother to Uncle Eugene's home, she found the rest of her family with faces pressed against the parlor's large bay window, looking out onto the street. After she reported what they'd seen, Mama scolded Nikki for going outside, while Uncle Eugene looked confident at the news and puffed on his pipe.

The next several days brought changes, however subtle. Uncle Eugene looked crestfallen when he returned home the next evening after his work at the university library. The acting German kommandant, Major Von Bassewitz, had taken hostages. Louvain's mayor, Leo Colins, and several other city officials, were forced to take up residence in the town hall to "ensure the Belgians of Louvain remained calm and quiet," her uncle said in dismay.

Two days later Eve and her uncle ventured to Old Market Square to purchase food. They witnessed German soldiers heckling a priest, shoving him in the back and jeering at him while he hurried along toward the university. More incidents aimed at the clergy and Belgian city officials followed.

When news arrived of Brussels's occupation by the Germans, Eve decided to try to contact Maddie. It took nearly half an hour to get a call through, and even longer for the hotel staff to locate her friend.

"Eve! Thank goodness, I was going to ring this afternoon. How are you?"

Hearing her friend's voice, Eve let out the breath she'd been holding. "I'm afraid we're a bit overrun with soldiers at the moment. Otherwise, Mama and the rest of my family are doing well." Briefly, she described the German army's entrance into the city. "What about you?"

"The Germans arrived here in Brussels three days ago with much the same pomp and circumstance," Maddie said. "They've set up shop in the Royal Palace, and the city's hotels are full to bursting with soldiers. The hotel has moved me and another woman into a room with four other nurses, so we've had to make bedrolls on the floor."

"No wonder the staff had trouble finding you," Eve said. "We have quite a few soldiers here as well. Several of them are billeting with residents along Naamsestraat, though we haven't yet been required to take in boarders. The situation so far seems fairly quiet, though I've discovered a few of these Germans can be extremely rude." She told Maddie about the soldiers taunting the clergy and city officials. "Any update on getting posted at one of the hospitals?"

"The Red Cross is still scrambling to organize personnel." Maddie's voice resonated with frustration. "One day they want to send a few of us to another occupied Belgian town, and the next they order us to remain here. We've been wearing our street clothes to keep our uniforms clean, and the other day a group of us went downstairs to find a place to eat. We were chatting, and the German soldiers at the hotel must have heard our accents," she said. "They certainly gave us hostile looks."

"Maddie, are you all right? The situation there seems a shambles," Eve said, troubled.

"I'll say it outright, Eve. I'm worried. The German government in Brussels has offered to let all British Red Cross nurses return home, provided we leave in the next week."

Eve was stunned. "Will you go?"

"I'm planning to," Maddie said. "Look, I know your answer, but I'll ask anyway. Will you return with me to London? I daresay with the turmoil here, we'll never receive a nursing post. We could both be more useful in Britain once our wounded men start returning home."

"Oh, Maddie, you tempt me." Eve was beginning to share her friend's alarm. Each day the German soldiers in Louvain turned more belligerent, drinking, causing effrontery, while the tension of Louvain's townspeople mounted. Yet she wouldn't abandon her family. "You know my answer though," she said. "I cannot leave Mama or the children here."

"I thought as much," Maddie said. "Eve, I don't know if we'll get another chance to talk before I leave, but . . ." Her voice grew thick with emotion. "Stay safe, will you? Write to me in care of the London Hospital, if you're able."

"Yes." Eve's eyes burned as she gripped the receiver. "Godspeed, Maddie."

She hung up the telephone, severing her lifeline. Her best friend, along with most of the other nurses, would soon return to the safety of Britain's shores while she remained in a country overrun by the enemy.

Having made her choice, Eve went that afternoon to Saint-

Thomas's hospital near the university and obtained a nursing position. Because German and Belgian soldiers were already being treated for wounds, her services were welcomed.

It was a week after her arrival in Louvain when, clad in her nurse's uniform, Eve stopped in her tracks on her way to the hospital. Thousands of German soldiers were entering the city, trailing like ants on a continuous path along Brusselsestraat in the direction of the town hall. Hussars, many on foot and leading their horses, were followed by a countless stream of dirty, exhausted infantry.

Obviously the war wasn't going well for them. As they passed, their battle-weary faces held resentment, and a sense of foreboding raised the hair at her nape.

The city felt like a tinderbox about to ignite.

At five o'clock that evening the first report of gunfire sounded close to the town. Minutes later men on horses galloped through the market square to raise the alarm. A battle with the Belgian army was in progress outside Louvain on the Malines road.

German soldiers scrambled into formation, while civilian motor cars collided with artillery wagons in the streets. Horses were hitched up to the mitrailleuse guns and driven brutally out of the city to aid the fighting German troops.

As quickly as the pandemonium began it ended, once the battalions and wagons rushed off. The town became eerily quiet. Eve and her family, along with the other Belgians, returned to their homes, as the German kommandant had enacted an eight o'clock curfew on the citizens.

Just after their supper they heard more gunshots, this time in ceaseless bursts. Eve, Zoe, and Mama had entered the parlor when the beveled glass in the bay window shattered. Zoe screamed, and the three of them dived to the floor.

"Come to me!" Uncle Eugene shouted from the other room.

The women crawled on their bellies back into the hall and

found Uncle Eugene grasping a frightened Nikki by the shoulder. "To the cellar!" he cried.

They scrambled to rush down a narrow flight of steps into a dark passage under the house. Above them Eve heard the blare of whistles outside, followed by more gunfire. She sucked in a breath at the sound of a woman's scream. More shots, and then silence.

Shuffling movement echoed in the cellar, and Eve jumped when Uncle Eugene flipped on an electric torch. He passed her a handful of candles and she lit them, placing them in a brass candelabrum he'd rummaged from a shelf. From a stack of fruit crates and a couple of wooden stools, each of them drew a seat and gathered in a circle.

"What is happening?" wailed Mama, her expression paralyzed with terror. She hugged a weeping Zoe to her breast. "Why are they shooting at us?"

Nikki had scooted his crate up beside Eve and grasped her hand. "I don't know," Eve whispered. "Uncle?"

"Outrageous!" Her uncle's harsh features appeared ghoulish in the candlelight. "I'm going upstairs to the attic. Perhaps from there I can see what's going on in the city."

"Eugene, no!" Mama reached for him. "It's too dangerous."

But he was already on his feet, gripping the electric torch. "I won't be long. Stay here and remain quiet, and you will be all right."

He left the circle of candlelight, and the steps creaked with his ascent. An hour passed, then another. Eve shifted on the stool. They were all exhausted.

"Mama, I don't feel good," Nikki whispered from the crate beside Eve.

"Hush, Nicholas," Mama said in a soft voice. "Try and sleep if you can."

"But Mama, I'm hot, and so thirsty. I need water." He rolled his head against Eve's shoulder.

Eve's anxiety over her uncle gave way to new purpose. "I'll go and get water from the kitchen for the children."

Her mother gazed at her, lines bracketing her mouth as she wet her lips and said, "Be careful, *chère*."

Eve rose and glanced at her sister. "Zoe, come here and sit with your brother."

Zoe's dark eyes looked wary as she left her place beside their mother and took a seat on the stool. Nikki leaned his head against her shoulder, clearly spent.

Eve knelt beside her. "You are fifteen now, almost a grown woman. I'm putting you in charge until I return. Take care of Mama and Nikki, all right?"

Zoe's eyes were wide, but she straightened and nodded.

"Promise me."

"I promise, Eve." Zoe's voice was solemn. "I won't let you down."

Eve smiled and touched her face. "I know you won't."

To Mama, she said, "I shouldn't be long."

Taking a lighted candle, she ascended the cellar steps. The house was quiet and the gunfire had diminished, replaced by faint sounds of breaking glass and splintering wood outside on Naamsestraat. Eve shivered at the sounds of drunken laughter that followed, and the guttural shouts of soldiers in the streets.

She extinguished the candle and moved quietly through the dark rooms. Pausing near the kitchen, she looked at the stairs to the attic and then, on impulse, she ascended the steps. When she reached the alcove, Eve looked out on the city and gasped.

Louvain was on fire.

The night sky glowed red as churches, municipal buildings, and homes blazed out of control. She surveyed the panoramic inferno, and dread seized her as she turned to stare at the university.

"No," she whispered, watching flames rise like horrible red

tongues from the university's library . . . and knowing instinctively where her uncle had gone.

Her heart thundered as she hurried downstairs to the kitchen. Quickly she fetched a pitcher of water for Mama and the children and returned to the hall.

She started toward the cellar steps when a groaning explosion of wood burst behind her. Eve jumped, then turned to see the front door collapse into the apartment and hit the floor.

Two German uniforms rushed inside.

Time slowed as she saw the crystal pitcher leave her hands and fall to the floor. The glass shattered, water splashing and running across the hardwood surface.

Her body jerked forward. Dazed, she glanced down at the rough hand gripping her arm, pulling her outside. A scream rang in her ears, and it was a moment before she realized it had come from her own lungs. Her body lunged ahead, this time shoved by the hand at her back. She tripped and nearly fell to her knees before the men dragged her by the arms into the street.

Carnage reigned on Naamsestraat. Men, women, and children lay dead outside their homes while soldiers looted their valuables. Breaking down doors, busting windows, removing expensive crystal, jewels, silver, they shoved the booty into cloth sacks and roared with laughter before stumbling down the thoroughfare to the next home.

Horrified, Eve tried to make sense of what she was seeing. Her captors hauled her into the market square on Brusselsestraat, and she choked out a cry at the sight of German soldiers lying fallen alongside Belgian citizens. Fires burned all around. Dead horses littered the streets.

Dear Lord, what has happened? Her pulse hammered in her throat as she stared at the butchery. Then pain seized her as the grip on her arms tightened and she was again jerked forward. The soldiers holding her were soon joined by two others, who joked and laughed as they walked along sharing a bottle of wine.

Danger! Eve's mind screamed, and her senses sharpened. The men leered at her like hungry wolves, especially the soldier with a jagged scar on his cheek, as each drank from the bottle. Vaguely it occurred to her she wasn't in uniform; the light blue skirt and white shirtwaist she wore wouldn't protect her from these men.

She looked ahead and saw they were dragging her toward the hostel. Struggling with all of her strength against her human bonds, she broke free and began to run, hearing angry shouts behind her, then laughter.

She'd gone only a few meters when she was jerked backward, landing hard against the cobbled street. She screamed as pain like a thousand needles penetrated her skull.

Someone dragged her by her hair, which had come loose from the pins. Eve twisted to see a lone German soldier, the one sporting the long scar. She grabbed for his hands to take the pressure off her scalp while he moved past soldiers running in the streets. She cried for help, digging her nails into his flesh. He let go with a curse and she clambered to her knees, trying to escape, but he tackled her. He punched her in the stomach and she doubled over, unable to get air into her lungs. Shoving her back onto the ground, he climbed on top of her.

Blood roared in her ears as she struggled to breathe. He was going to rape her, right there with the dead lying in the street and people screaming as buildings burned all around them. She turned her head. The corpse of a Belgian man sprawled next to her.

The monster pressing her down stank of sour wine and sweat and the bloodlust that had overtaken them all. "*Nein!*" she screamed in German. "I'm a nurse, don't hurt me, I beg you!"

But the scarred soldier looming over her was too drunk or too crazed to hear her plea. He rose, digging his knee into her abdomen, and fresh pain shot through her. With a meaty hand, he pinned her wrists against her chest while his other hand began pulling at her skirts.

She screamed again, her heart pounding wildly as her gaze darted in search of help. The night sky had lightened as fires continued to burn in the streets. Eve caught a glimpse of steel from the corner of her eye. A knife protruded from the body of the Belgian . . .

Like a feral animal, she dropped her head to her chest and bit the soldier's hand, tearing away a chunk of flesh with her teeth. He roared and let go, rearing his fist back to strike. Before he made contact, she twisted and grabbed for the knife. The dead man's flesh tugged at the blade as she removed it from his body and brought it up, driving the steel into the eye of her surprised attacker. He screamed, clutching his face.

Then he fell backward onto the cobbled street, unmoving.

Eve rose on all fours, sobbing hysterically. Shock and fear coursed through her. Her hair hung limp against her face, and her clothes were torn and soiled, reeking of the soldier's stench. She crawled to his side and pulled the blade from his eye socket. Still crying, she raised herself onto her knees, ready to drive the knife into his chest.

"Halt!"

A heavy hand clamped on her shoulder, and Eve let out an enraged shriek. Whirling on her knees, she saw only the German uniform—one of his friends, returned to rape her. "*Beast!*" she screamed and plunged the blade into his heart.

When she looked up she saw the boy, perhaps twelve years of age, blink at her in disbelief. Eve froze, gaping up at his reddish hair, the pewter-colored eyes. Cheeks smooth and rounded as a child's.

Her gaze dropped back to the oversized uniform. The boy she'd seen entering the city a week ago . . .

He carried no weapon, only a broomstick handle. The stick fell from his grasp, clattering to the ground. Blood oozed from the edge of his mouth and she heard his choked whisper—"*Mutter*"—before he collapsed onto the street.

Horror threatened her sanity. She crawled to him as bile rose in her throat. She wretched beside him, then tore away a strip of her skirt and used it to try to stem his bleeding. She checked his pulse. Nothing. Her aim had been true.

Against the hazy night, Eve lifted her head and let out an agonized cry. He was dead, and by her hand. Just a boy with a broomstick. Perhaps a mascot, or the son of one of the officers. Not a real soldier. A child.

Wracked by grief, she looked over at her attacker to see that he too was dead. She sobbed and struggled to her feet, weaving a moment before she staggered away from the scene, retracing her path to the house on Naamsestraat.

The light from the fires revealed the enormity of destruction around the city. Eve reached the apartment and found it torched like the rest, a smoking, charred shell.

She fell to her knees, pride and anger forgotten. *Lord, please let my family live.*

The hospital. She struggled to her feet, her hope flaring as she stumbled in the direction of Saint-Thomas. Perhaps they were there.

Along the way, she stared dully toward the German soldiers invading homes still standing, rousting the inhabitants to march them toward the train station.

The university's library still smoldered, but the hospital remained untouched. Eve pressed her way inside, past the crowds of anxious Belgians who had come seeking sanctuary. After a frenzied search, she realized no one from her family was there.

"Sister . . . ?"

She'd started back outside when a man on a gurney hailed her. One of the German surgeons she'd worked with days before. Eve approached, and her eyes widened to see the gaping hole on one side of his head.

"It is too late for me," he whispered. "Please, you must help the others. Two of the doctors have been shot, and we have so many wounded."

Eve slowly turned, scanning the lobby of people packed in as far back as the hospital corridor. In her haste to find her family, she'd been oblivious to the wounded sprawled on the floor beneath gurneys and tables so they wouldn't be stepped on. Many sat with their backs to the walls, bloodied and barely coherent. Some, like the surgeon, were dying. None had received medical attention.

An image of the boy rose in her mind. Eve swayed and closed her eyes, seeing his body lying on the ground, the soft face, the baggy uniform . . .

"Help, please." A thin cry rose from an older Belgian man shot in the chest. Another casualty, a German infantryman, watched her, eyes glazed in pain as he clutched the dark stain blooming against his belly.

The haunting vision of the boy remained as she worked to repin her hair. Eve moved toward the man with the chest wound. She hadn't saved the child. She must save these others.

The next few hours passed in a blur. She treated wounds and secured beds for the injured without regard for nationality. The hospital had run out of ether and chloroform, so she'd been forced to rely on morphine to ease her patients while she stitched, bandaged, and bathed them until exhaustion threatened her collapse.

Eve was absorbed with the delicate process of removing shrapnel from beside the jugular vein of a German officer when she felt the first twinge of pain in her abdomen. Fleetingly, she remembered the soldier who had punched her as she continued working on the barely conscious man.

The ache increased. By the time she finished stitching the wound, her pain had become incessant, stabbing. Hot stickiness began running down her legs. She let out a moan as she noticed the droplets of blood staining the tile beneath her feet.

The room spun, and her knees buckled as she slid to the floor. A sob choked her. Six weeks had passed; Eve had been a nurse long enough to know the signs. *Oh, Simon, forgive me.*

⁂

"*Ma fifille*, wake up for me. You must open your eyes."

The familiar voice beckoned, and Eve's lashes fluttered open. Squinting against the lights glaring overhead, she smiled at the beloved face hovering over her. "Mama."

"I was so worried, *chère*." Her mother leaned to kiss her cheek.

Eve's tongue was like parchment as she tried to moisten her chapped lips. The grogginess of sleep lifted and she realized she lay in a hospital bed. "What's happened?"

Mama gripped her rosary beads and offered an anxious smile. "Exhaustion for the most part," she said. "You've been doing the work of three, the doctors tell me."

So many wounded. Eve pressed a hand to her temple, the memory of the shootings and the fires returning full force. "Where are Zoe and Nikki . . . Uncle Eugene?"

Mama paled. "My brother was . . ." Her voice shook. "I was told he tried to save the books."

The university library. Tears lodged in her throat. Eve had seen the flames from the attic.

"He is gone, *chère*." Her mother withdrew a handkerchief from inside her sleeve and dabbed at her eyes.

Eve grasped her hand. "And the children?"

Fresh tears spilled from her mother's eyes. "I don't know." Her voice came out frail, distant. "I kept them with me in the cellar. After we heard you scream . . ."

Mama glanced down at her beads. "They found us and dragged us outside. We saw the bodies in the street, all of those beautiful homes burning."

She met her daughter's gaze. "They marched us to the train station. There was more shooting. Germans were firing guns at Germans. It was insanity." She shook her head. "Maybe in the dark they mistook one another for the enemy, I don't know, but it was our chance to escape. I told the children to run and find a place to hide. Someone struck me on the head, with a rifle, I think. When I awoke, the soldiers were gone. A Belgian woman brought me here to the hospital."

"And then?" Heart pounding, Eve waited for her mother to finish.

"That was three days ago. I haven't seen either of my babies." Her voice broke. "I pray they are safe and hidden away."

Bitterly she added, "The shooting has stopped, but the burning and looting continue. They've started bombing the city with their big guns, and the kommandant does nothing to stop them."

Three days. She'd been unconscious that long? Eve's mind began retracing the events leading up to her being here. *The man with the scar . . . the knife . . . the boy's death . . . so many wounded . . .*

Her blood on the tile.

"No!" A hoarse cry tore from her throat as she reached to cradle her abdomen. She remembered the hot moisture, the pain. *Our baby.*

Tears filled her eyes and she turned to her mother.

"I'm sorry, *chère*." Mama's eyes glistened. "Though it was very early, the miscarriage . . . there were difficulties, internal bleeding." She pursed her lips, then said, "I thought I would lose you, too."

Her mother began to weep, but Eve was numb. Her hands brushed across her belly, while her anguish mixed with a kind of wonder. How could she not have known she was pregnant, that all that was left to her of Simon had been safe inside her womb?

Regret cut through her like a surgeon's scalpel. Her own rashness had brought her to this horrible place, where war made monsters out of men. Now the last trace of Simon Forrester was gone forever.

Eve remained in bed over the next few days, dosed with morphine for the pain. Drifting in and out of her drug-induced fog, her mind conjured images of Simon, superimposed with the face of the young German boy, his features so similar he could have been their son, the child she should have had. *A life for a life.*

Each day Mama returned to the hospital to sit by her side. Each day the news was the same. No sign of Zoe or Nikki. When Eve finally roused from her sickbed, she went back to work with fervor, finding solace in staying busy so that she couldn't think about what had happened or what she'd done.

She was introduced to Major Otto Reinhardt, the German officer whose life she'd saved when she removed the shrapnel from his neck. He offered his gratitude and informed her he had recommended her for the Iron Cross, proclaiming her a heroine.

Eve didn't feel heroic. Instead she thought of the two lives she had taken and the butchery she'd witnessed, the lives she wasn't able to save and the senselessness of it all. Soldiers, in their frenzy of bloodlust, had been shooting one another. So many innocent lives lost, like her uncle.

That night she lay in her bed, exhausted, wondering if she

would ever see her little brother and sister again. Were they buried somewhere under the city's rubble, never to be found? Or had the children been taken on the trains to Germany?

She turned her face into the pillow, keening quietly, not only for them, but for all those who had died. For the loss of her unborn child, for Simon.

And for the mother of a young German boy, whose grief could not be any less than her own.

CHAPTER 12

*T*oday was the day.

In a matter of hours she would risk all to save her husband, including his life. Would she succeed . . . or end up with more blood on her hands?

Eve entered the hospital Monday morning and strode down the hall toward her office. Anxiety knotted her insides. If she failed, she didn't think she would be able to bear his death.

"May I help you, Sister?"

Her head jerked up as she walked across the threshold into her sanctuary. A broad-shouldered nurse sat behind the desk, her dark gaze quizzical.

"Who are you?" Eve demanded, confused. "And what are you doing in my office?"

"You must be Sister Marche." The woman closed the note-book she'd been writing in, and with pen in hand she rose from the chair. "I am Nurse Hoffmeyer, the new hospital *Matrone*," she said in German. "And I am here because this is now *my* office."

Otto had mentioned new nurses coming, but not for several

weeks. Eve gazed at the stout, middle-aged nurse. "Why wasn't I told?"

Above her pointed chin Nurse Hoffmeyer's lips twisted. "Perhaps it wasn't your place to know."

Eve stiffened. "As acting matron of this hospital for well over two years, I should have been the first to be informed."

"Acting matron?" A dark brow lifted against Nurse Hoffmeyer's flat-faced features.

"I was never given an official title," Eve said as heat rose to her cheeks. "However, Herr Major Reinhardt delegated me with Matron Cavell's responsibilities after her arrest."

"Yes, I've heard about Nurse Cavell." The ample woman crossed her meaty arms. "That is why a German-run hospital must have a German matron in charge of the nurses. You are *British*, are you not?" She practically ejected the word from her lips.

Eve ignored her. "Who authorized this?"

The matron's dark eyes glinted. "Herr Major Reinhardt, of course."

Why hadn't Otto told her of the woman's arrival? Or that Nurse Hoffmeyer was taking her place as matron? He could have said something on Friday, when she'd made arrangements with him for Simon's return to the safety of the ward. Jaw tight, Eve said, "I will go and discuss it with him now." She turned to leave.

"Only after you complete your duties, Sister Marche." The new matron grabbed up her notebook. "You will first accompany me to the ward."

Eve thought to challenge her, but hesitated. If Nurse Hoffmeyer *was* the new matron, it wouldn't be prudent to make her an enemy. She'd speak with Otto soon enough.

Her hopes plummeted as she followed the German nurse down the hall. Eve had planned for Simon's "emergency surgery" to occur shortly after five o'clock, when most of the hospital staff left for the day. With Dr. Schlagel still in Antwerp at his conference, Dr. Ambrose would be in charge.

She, as acting matron, would have assisted him. Now with this German woman usurping her position, the scheme began to unravel. How could she manage to keep Nurse Hoffmeyer away until the surgery was over and Simon was gone?

Reaching the ward, Eve gazed down the rows of beds, and seeing the nurses attending some of the patients, she observed two or three faces she did not recognize. Likely they had accompanied Nurse Hoffmeyer from Berlin, she thought sourly.

Her gaze came to settle on Simon's bed, and she was relieved to see him still there. A German soldier on crutches stood beside him. Corporal Ziegler.

Eve had come in on Saturday to check her husband's wounds and to make certain Jaeger and Schultz hadn't come back to further molest him. His new stitches were still in place, and so far he seemed to be doing fine.

"*Guten Morgen*, Herr Doktor!"

Hearing the new matron's brusque greeting, Eve turned her head, expecting to see Dr. Ambrose.

Dr. Schlagel stood before them.

"Herr Doktor!" she blurted, stunned. "I . . . I . . . thought you were in Antwerp."

"The medical conference?" The aged man in white coat and monocle shook his head. "Canceled, I'm afraid. I was looking forward to a nice holiday."

Eve's heart lurched in her chest. Now what?

"You must be Nurse Hoffmeyer, our new matron?" Dr. Schlagel beamed at the woman. "As you can see, we haven't many patients at present, but I've been told to expect heavy casualties any day from clearing stations to the south. Your assistance will be most appreciated, I am certain." He turned to include Eve in his comment.

130

"Indeed, Herr Doktor," preened Matron. "I intend to improve efficiency and eliminate the lax standards in this ward before they arrive. Be assured, all will be in order."

Dr. Schlagel blinked, his wrinkled face flushed as he glanced between Eve and her nemesis. "Yes, well, if you'll excuse me, I must check on my patients."

"Of course." Matron hugged her notebook as the chief surgeon hurried away.

Eve fought the panic squeezing her chest. Her plans lay in ruins! In two days' time Jaeger would come for Simon and take him to prison. Her husband would surely die—

"We will assess the ward." Matron's crisp voice cut into her thoughts. "You will give me a brief background on each patient so I may determine the disposition of their treatment."

Meekly Eve followed the new matron from bed to bed, her thoughts racing while she absently pulled each patient's chart and offered the soldier's rank and medical prognosis.

Yet try as she might to conjure another way out for her husband, nothing came to mind. It seemed impossible.

Her gaze shifted down the ward toward Simon. How could she tell him she'd failed to save him?

"We clobbered the Russians in 1912," boasted the young German soldier balanced on crutches beside Simon's bed. "They didn't have a chance against the Fatherland."

Simon had caught sight of his wife and nearly missed the conversation. He turned to the skinny, towheaded corporal standing by his bed. Hans Ziegler had been a frequent visitor since Simon's return to the ward. Ziegler had broken his leg and received minor burns after a storehouse full of ammunition and dynamite exploded in an exercise at Waterloo, a few kilometers to the south. He'd already been at the hospital several weeks and seemed restless.

"Football, Summer Olympics, *oui?*" Simon said in French, maintaining his ruse and pleased the young corporal spoke the language well.

Ziegler grinned. "Sixteen to zero. It was a total annihilation."

"When do you return to Waterloo?" Simon asked.

"I won't be going back." Ziegler sat on the empty bed next to Simon's. "I get my cast off in two weeks, and then I'll report with our regiment to Passchendaele. My friends from Aachen, Frederick and Karl, will soon return from the East with their regiments. They are to be reassigned to the same company." His blue eyes shone. "We look forward to sharing a beer together, I can tell you!"

German regiments returning from the East? That bit of news might interest Marcus. Recently he and his friend had sat in Weatherford's office at the Admiralty and discussed speculation over a truce between the kaiser and the Bolsheviks. It seemed it was more than a rumor. "I'm sure you'll enjoy your reunion, Corporal," Simon said.

"*Ja.*" Ziegler puffed out his skinny chest. "The Fatherland has crushed the Russians once more." He laughed. "I am told they are running scared!"

Definitely newsworthy, Simon thought. If only he could get out of this place and get word to his friend back in London.

A shiver of fear—or was it anticipation?—raced along his spine. Eve's outrageous plan for his escape would take place just hours from now. Simon had resigned himself to the risks, knowing he had to trust her. He prayed she was as proficient with the ether as she claimed.

He looked forward to getting out from beneath the Huns' watchful gaze and recuperating somewhere safe. Then he would take Eve home to Britain, regardless of her feelings for him. He wanted her safe. She was still his wife.

As to completing his assignment for Marcus, Simon wasn't

certain. If his plane hadn't crashed, he would have parachuted down near the Sonian Forest outside Brussels and met with an anonymous contact at a local priory to deliver the sealed orders in his pouch.

He had no idea of the contents, but the information somehow involved an enemy agent suspected of infiltrating MI6's Belgian intelligence network, La Dame Blanche. The only clue to the saboteur's identity was his moniker: the use of the special mark π—the symbol for Pi—in his correspondence with the Germans.

Simon owed his friend much. The MI6 lieutenant had not only helped him to locate Eve, he had also bent a few rules to arrange Simon's mission into German-occupied Brussels so he could recover his wife.

Now the mission seemed a failure. Without the name of his contact, Simon couldn't proceed. Marcus had also asked him to report any information he gleaned on Pi, as the saboteur was dangerous, but there was little Simon could do from a hospital bed.

"The Sisters are coming, Captain," Ziegler called to him, drawing his attention. "Shall I stay and protect you?" He winked. "I don't like the looks of the big nurse with Sister Marche."

Simon turned toward the two nurses, his pulse accelerating at Eve's approach.

The young corporal clearly held "Sister Marche" in high esteem, as did the other patients in the ward. Simon had pried from Ziegler as much information as he dared and discovered she was put in charge of the Belgian nurses at the hospital two years ago, shortly after Nurse Cavell's arrest.

According to the corporal, Eve was Germany's heroine. The young soldier boasted about her Iron Cross and explained how he'd been in Brussels when, amid much fanfare, she was presented with the medal by the city's kommandant *"for meritorious service in battle."*

Battle? While Simon didn't know how much of Ziegler's story to believe, he hadn't forgotten the fear in his wife's face or the haunted look in her eyes. It made him all the more determined to find out what had really happened.

She had visited him on Saturday, and though he'd been too groggy from the drugs to ask, he realized Eve must have arranged his return to the ward. A move he welcomed, dreading another visit from the "vampires," as she called them. He'd abandoned all pride as she tended his wounds, leaning into her gentle touch, savoring the warmth of her hands as they slid along his collarbone and across his chest as she inspected the binding at his ribs.

Small gestures, which perhaps meant nothing to her, but he was a dying man, and she his glimpse of heaven. In those precious moments he'd sensed in her the woman he'd married.

"Captain James Chandler of the British Royal Flying Corps."

Simon's heart responded to the sound of her voice as she read from his chart.

The older, buxom nurse joined her at the end of his bed.

"I am familiar with your case, Captain," the older nurse said in German. "I understand you are to leave us in two days."

Simon affected a blank look.

"The captain speaks no German." Ziegler rose on his crutches. "I can translate to French."

"Why are you here, Corporal? And speaking French with the enemy?" She eyed young Ziegler with contempt. "Has he made you tell him all of our secrets?"

"*Nein*, Sister!" Ziegler reddened and snapped to attention despite his leg cast.

"Get back to your bed, *schnell*! If I see you over here again, I'll report you."

Ziegler turned and hobbled off as fast as his crutches would carry him.

The formidable nurse turned to Simon, then to his wife. "There will be no more permissiveness now that I am in charge." Anger creased her flat features. "Sister Marche, you will please translate to the captain in your own English."

His wife nodded without expression. "This is our new hospital matron, Nurse Hoffmeyer," she said to Simon. "Matron is assessing the condition of each patient in the ward."

New matron? From what Ziegler had told him, Eve was supposed to be in charge.

He shot her a questioning look.

Her pale features remained drawn, wooden.

"Continue," the matron ordered.

Eve resumed. "Head contusion, memory loss, and broken ribs."

"I've discussed with Herr Major your trip to St. Gilles." Matron pointed her gaze at him. "We have German wounded arriving soon, and all beds will be at a premium. You, Captain, clearly need continued hospital care in a secure facility, not the local prison."

The head nurse opened her notebook. "Major Reinhardt has agreed to remove you to the POW hospital in Düsseldorf."

Simon fought to hide his alarm. He stared at his wife's sudden strained expression. Had she known about this?

"There is a train leaving for Germany this afternoon, Captain. You will be on it." The matron turned to Eve. "Please translate."

Again his wife spoke to him in that toneless voice, relaying what he already knew.

Germany. Simon clenched his fists. He would die before he went back.

"Sister Marche, you will make the necessary arrangements.

135

The train departs from Brussels at five o'clock. See that an ambulance is made ready."

They left him and walked toward the opposite side of the ward and the other wounded. He saw Ziegler glance toward the retreating nurses before he hobbled back over to Simon's bed.

"Well, Captain," he said softly in French, tilting his head. "It looks like you're going to have to learn to speak German after all."

Simon just stared at him, filled with impotent rage. He had only hours.

⚜

"Herr Major, why wasn't I told my position was being taken by Nurse Hoffmeyer?"

Eve stood in Otto's office later that afternoon. While the new matron had contrived to keep her busy all morning with inventories of the pharmacy and surgical supplies, her thoughts had remained on her husband and his reaction to the news that he was being sent to Germany.

She was heartsick, knowing how much he dreaded it.

"I also learned this morning that the new matron is sending Captain Chandler to Düsseldorf," she said, trying to temper her frustration. "Did you approve this as well?"

"To answer both questions, I had little choice." Otto Reinhardt looked harassed as he sat behind a desk littered with governmental memos and correspondence. His blue gaze pierced her while his hands flattened against the piles of reports.

"I was made aware of Nurse Hoffmeyer's presence only this morning. Me, the hospital administrator!" he said, showing his teeth. "We weren't expecting more nurses for weeks, but she arrived in Brussels on Saturday and insisted on taking the position of matron."

He reached to tug at his shirt collar. "Her brother-in-law is Herr Colonel Rutgers, senior staff officer to our illustrious General von Falkenhausen. When the colonel himself advised me of her wishes, I could hardly refuse. In fact, Nurse Hoff-meyer wanted you removed from the hospital staff entirely once she learned you were British. I had to spend some time persuading her to allow you to remain." His sullen gaze met hers. "You should be grateful."

Perhaps you should be grateful, Eve thought with scorn. If she were made to leave, Otto would lose his key source of "Al-lied intelligence." His government friend wouldn't be pleased, and the major might find himself sent to the Front like any other German officer.

She didn't mention that point, however. "What about Cap-tain Chandler?"

Otto picked up his disarrayed stack of papers and began to sort them. "His departure should gratify you as well, Sister Marche. You were the one to insist he be allowed more time in the hospital. Now he'll get it." He glanced up from his task. "At Düsseldorf."

She crossed her arms. "And Herr Jaeger has approved this."

Dropping the papers back onto his desk, Otto opened his side drawer and retrieved a cigar. "I am certain that when the military police learn Colonel Rutgers's sister-in-law made the recommendation, they'll have to comply with letting the captain go." He fished for his cigar cutter in the muddle on his desk. "Nor do they have proof to hold him . . . at least not yet."

Unable to find his cutting tool, he scowled and bit off the end of the cigar with his teeth, then spat it out. "Anyway, the sooner the captain leaves Brussels, the better. It will be easier to explain to Herr Jaeger after he's gone."

Glancing up at her, his expression shifted. "Eve, you will

make every effort to ensure Nurse Hoffmeyer's transition is smooth, *ja?*" He offered a tentative smile. "You will get along?"

Otto's anxiety was obvious. Perhaps Nurse Hoffmeyer was here to snoop on him as well. She'd make certain he ran the hospital according to her new "efficiency and high standards," or inform her brother-in-law if he did not.

It seemed no one's position was secure against the new German nurse. "I'll do my best, Herr Major," she said coolly. "Now, if you will excuse me, I must arrange for the captain's departure."

Leaving his office, she checked her wristwatch. *Four o'clock!* The train was scheduled to leave in an hour. She had only minutes before she must call the orderlies with a stretcher.

Eve rushed toward the ward, furious at the new matron for stealing what little time she had left with her husband. Her thoughts continued to race for a solution. What could she possibly do? The POW hospital seemed Simon's only hope, though she knew he loathed going back to Germany.

He had no choice. If he remained here, he would die.

Passing one of the two operating theaters, she was surprised to find Dr. Ambrose inside, checking his surgical instruments. He caught sight of her and rushed to the door.

"What's happened? I just saw Herr Doktor Schlagel in his office."

"His conference was canceled," she said in frustration. "Our patient is being sent to Düsseldorf on tonight's train."

The Belgian doctor's aged features held relief. Eve knew he'd worried about the risk.

"I am sorry, Eve," he said. "Perhaps this is for the best—"

"Where is the chief surgeon? I need him, *schnell!*" A booming voice at the hospital entrance was accompanied by heavy footfalls.

Both Eve and Dr. Ambrose rushed from the theater and stared in shock.

General von Falkenhausen's unconscious form was being carried by three officers. "Where is Herr Doktor Schlagel?" one of the officers shouted. "Herr General is dying!"

The commotion brought Dr. Schlagel and Otto running. "What has happened here?" the major demanded while the chief surgeon began to examine the general.

"We don't know." The officer's face was suffused with panic. "Herr General was in a staff meeting when he grabbed at his right side, here." He pointed toward the general's lower right abdomen. "He screamed and then collapsed onto the floor."

"It could be appendicitis," Dr. Schlagel said. "Orderlies! A gurney!"

Dominic and Felix had come in early for Eve's planned escape. Surprised at the scene, they rushed to obey the chief surgeon.

Within moments the unconscious general was being wheeled on a gurney into the first operating theater.

"Sister Marche!" Otto looked clearly distressed. "Please, assist Herr Doktor Schlagel!"

Eve started forward.

"*Nein!*" Matron's ample frame was running up the hall toward them, her sharp-lined features savage with determination. "As chief nurse, I will attend Herr General myself!"

She nearly mowed Eve down in her rush to get into the operating theater.

Dom and Felix reappeared after a couple of minutes.

"Now what?" Felix whispered.

Otto had returned to his office in an agitated state, doubtless to smoke cigars and pace while he waited for news about the general. Eve glanced from Dr. Ambrose to Dom, then to Felix, her pulse pounding. It was their last chance.

"You two go find another gurney and meet me in the ward

right away," she said to her friends. She glanced back at Dr. Ambrose. "Prepare for our surgery."

"Captain, wake up. It's time."

Simon opened his eyes, and she could see his fear.

"I'm not going back," he whispered. He grabbed her hand. "Please . . ."

Her throat constricted with emotion. Once more she realized she knew next to nothing about his years during the war. From what little she'd gleaned, Eve surmised he'd been a prisoner. What had he been through?

"Not Düsseldorf," she whispered. "We have one chance to get you out of here. It means using the ether." She searched his face. "Will you trust me?"

His desperate gray eyes met hers. After a moment he nodded. "Kiss me, for luck," he whispered. "The kiss of your mother's people."

Tears burned her eyes at the enormity of what she was about to try to accomplish. These could be their last moments together; she might never again hear his voice or feel the warmth of his skin on hers.

Dear Lord, please don't let him die, not after you sent him back to me. I couldn't bear it. Her insides quaked, and for an instant she lost her nerve. She must find another way.

But there was none. In the end it was his face so close to hers, the fear in his eyes and yet knowing he still trusted her, that fortified her resolve.

"For luck," she said, and leaned to kiss his cheeks, once, twice, three times, in the way of her mother's people.

When she pulled back and gazed at him, the warmth in his eyes told her he too remembered the moonlit night in her garden so many years ago.

For love, she thought, and impulsively leaned in again, this time pressing her mouth to his. Eve closed her eyes, blocking out the world as she offered him three years of desire and grief and being lost without him in a world constantly threatened by danger.

He responded instantly, his warm, rough hands cupping her face as he took over the kiss, his lips demanding, searching, as though he too understood this might be their last touch.

Passion mingled with her desperation. He was about to put all that he was into her safekeeping . . .

The rattling wheels of an approaching gurney roused her, and she drew back from him reluctantly. Despite his bruised face, he sketched a smile. "If that was my taste of heaven, then I'm not afraid to die."

Her heart fluttered and heat climbed to her cheeks. "You'll need to do a bit of moaning and carrying on, for effect," she said, as Dom and Felix appeared around the partition.

Simon did a fair amount of groaning as the two orderlies lifted him onto the gurney. Eve had no doubt his broken ribs made acting unnecessary. She led the way as they headed toward the operating theater.

Dr. Ambrose's features paled at their approach, yet he stood gowned and ready beside the operating table, having set the stage for their ruse. Dom and Felix carefully transferred Simon onto the table.

"Let us know once he's dead, and we'll take him to the morgue," Dom said.

Simon looked up at her in alarm.

"Easy," she told her husband, touching his shoulder. "We are all here to help you."

She shot a glare at Dom. "You and Felix keep watch at the other surgery and let us know if anyone comes out."

As the two orderlies departed, she retrieved the bottle of ether and a drip mask. Moving to the head of the table, she gazed down at her husband. A stab of uncertainty stole her breath, and she paused to fill her lungs with air.

"Ready?" She struggled to keep her voice steady.

He nodded, and warmth filled her at his trust.

"See you on the other side, lass."

CHAPTER 13

It was late by the time Dom and Felix hauled the stretcher with Chandler's body from the back of the lorry. In the dim light of a lamp above the stoop outside the Catholic Soldiers Society, Dom exchanged a look with his friend. Both were keenly aware their movements were being watched by the German secret police.

Maintaining silence, they stood a moment and each adjusted his end of the heavy load. Abruptly, the door to the Society opened. A diminutive woman dressed all in black and hidden by a dark veil stepped back to allow them entrance.

Once they were inside, she closed and locked the door. Dom took the rear of the stretcher, leaving Felix to lead as they followed her through the funeral parlor and down a long, dimly lit hall. At the end of the hall, she halted and wordlessly gestured for them to proceed through a curtained partition.

Dom was no stranger to the mortuary, but the torture-chamber atmosphere still made him uneasy. Inside the austere room with its black-and-white tiled floors stood a pair of adjustable embalming tables, each with a white porcelain trough at one end. A white armoire stood against one wall, the glass cabinet doors revealing a clutter of bottles in every size, filled with chemicals used in the embalming process. A cast-iron rack hung overhead, arrayed with body hooks, bone saws, and knives with scythe-like blades. A table sat off to one side with more knives, syringes, and chemicals.

He and Felix transferred their heavy burden onto one of the empty tables and began loosening the ties to the canvas bag that held their "corpse." Once open, Dom grimaced at the sight of Chandler's bandaged foot. He glanced up and met Felix's gaze.

Both men had watched Herr Schultz of the secret police jab his pocketknife into the captain's heel. When Schultz got no reaction, he seemed satisfied and allowed them to take the corpse to the Society.

Eve applied the bandage before they left the morgue, and the wound hadn't bled much then, a fact that helped to corroborate the captain's death—but now that the ether was wearing off, Chandler's pulse was stronger and the red-stained cloth needed changing.

Dom flexed his fingers, easing away the cramps after carrying his heavy burden. Again he wondered where the captain would go once they left the mortuary.

He frowned. Sister Eve Marche could be brilliant at times, yet at others, like now, she played a reckless game. She'd gone to great lengths to get Chandler out of the hospital, when she could have let him go to the relative safety of the POW hospital. Why take such a risk to keep him in Brussels? Who was he to her?

Did it have anything to do with the leather pouch?

He'd seen her take it from the captain in the park, right after the crash. Why had she lied to him about it?

Later, he'd spotted the pouch on the major's desk and riffled through it, finding only propaganda. Eve was too smart to offer up worthless paper, unless she meant it as a decoy. Perhaps she'd chosen to withhold valuable information from the pompous major, who ogled her when he thought no one was looking.

A smirk touched his lips when he thought of Reinhardt. The man was a buffoon.

Admittedly, Eve was beautiful, with an intellect honed to a sharp point like a fine Antwerp diamond. The woman also had courage in abundance—a quality Dom most admired. She'd shared with him only a little about her past in Louvain, but he'd read about the massacre and its brutality. It was the one thing he loathed about his work. The German soldiers could be degenerate animals when they chose.

"Leave him with me."

The low-pitched voice of the mortician, Monsieur Coppens, jarred Dom from his thoughts. He gazed at the tall, lean, middle-aged man entering the room. He wore the color of mourning, his black coat and woolen trousers clean and neatly pressed.

The mortician removed his jacket and rolled up his sleeves, then donned the leather apron hanging from a peg on the wall. Adjusting his spectacles above the small, beak-like nose, he aimed a pointed stare at the small woman in black.

She approached Dom and Felix and again waved a hand at them to follow, this time back toward the exit. Once she let them out and they were back on the stoop, he heard the *click* of the key in the lock.

After replacing the stretcher in the back of the lorry, Felix entered the cab and slipped behind the wheel. Dom went to the front and cranked over the engine.

The second part of Eve's plan was complete. Now what would happen? He and Felix had questioned her again about where Chandler would be taken, but she merely said all arrangements had been made, and for everyone's safety, the fewer who knew the better.

Why was she keeping secrets from them?

Did she suspect an enemy agent in La Dame Blanche?

With the engine started, Dom returned to the lorry. Within

the shadows of the cab, he eyed the man seated beside him. Felix had been acting strange of late, secretive and overly cautious. Even his laughter seemed affected. They'd worked together over a year, in the intelligence network and at the hospital, yet he sensed the Belgian becoming more withdrawn, their friendship strained.

Dom was beginning to have his suspicions.

Perhaps if he got Eve alone she would confide in him, tell him what he wanted to know. Like her involvement with this Chandler fellow and what, if anything, may have been contained in the pouch.

He cast another look at Felix. In the meantime he must be on his guard, watchful, patient. Dom would have to keep an eye on Eve as well, to see what she did next.

CHAPTER 14

Simon awoke to a loud rumble vibrating his eardrums. It was pitch dark but for a candle sconce against one wall.

Another sound shook the room. His breathing quickened, making his chest ache. Mortar fire? He squinted against the dim light, remembering the crash . . . burning . . .

The noise sounded again, the walls trembling. Not artillery fire. It was . . . church bells.

Memories of the hospital and his wife slowly returned as his eyes adjusted to the murky light. He wasn't in the ward any longer but lay on a straw mattress on the floor, covered in woolen blankets. Stone walls enclosed all four sides of his darkened quarters, and at either end stood a panel door the height and width of an artillery chest. The only furniture in the compact space was the wooden bench beside his mattress.

Simon shifted, trying to move, but pain racked him. It took another moment to realize his right foot throbbed, and he raised it slightly to see it bandaged. The rest of him felt much as it had before—like he'd been used as a punchbag.

While he didn't know his whereabouts, he was definitely alive. His last waking memory was of Eve, administering the sickly sweet smell of ether.

Had her escape plan been successful . . . or was he in a German cell somewhere?

Sore and dazed, he lay in the weak light, dozing on and off. His drugged dreams were filled with images of Eve from the hospital, her soft lips pressed against his.

A scraping sound startled him fully awake. Simon turned his head to see one of the panel doors being pushed aside. He tensed as a tall, broad figure passed through, carrying a lighted candle. The panel door remained open, allowing light into the darkened room.

"Ah, *Dieu merci*, you are awake."

Simon's muscles eased. The man spoke good French and wore the Roman collar of a priest.

"Church bells?" he asked.

"Ah, *oui*, the Boche haven't robbed us of those yet. I always ring the bells on the feast day of Saint Romanus, the patron saint of my city, Rouen." The round-faced priest smiled. "Welcome to St. Magdalene's, my son. I am Father Francois, and I'll be looking after you."

St. Magdalene's. Simon blinked. Father Francois was the priest who could get him and his wife out of Belgium. "Where is the nurse?"

"Sister Marche was here earlier and will return later this afternoon," he said. "You are Captain Chandler?"

Eve had hidden his true identity from this man? Simon didn't understand, but he would do the same, despite Marcus's assurances. He nodded. "How long have I been here?"

"Since dawn." Father Francois's middle-aged frame eased down onto the bench. "The Catholic Soldiers Society brought you over in a casket. An hour ago we held your funeral. Your remains, or should I say the sandbags that replaced your weight, are being transported to the Brussels Cemetery as we speak."

An incredibly well-thought-out plan. Simon hadn't stopped

to consider that his wife could be involved with the Belgian underground, though it shouldn't surprise him. She'd enlisted the help of the orderlies, the surgeon, even this priest—and pulled off her daring escape plan beneath the noses of the Huns. He wondered at her accomplices and if any were also members of La Dame Blanche. Perhaps one of them was the enemy agent?

"What is this place?" he asked.

"A secret room built inside the church rectory," the priest said. "You'll remain here until your wounds have healed sufficiently. Once you're able to get around, you may have access to my chambers." He indicated with a thumb the room behind him. "There is a brazier to keep you warm and whatever facilities you require." His features sobered. "If the German secret police are about, however, you must remain hidden in here."

"What's behind the other door?" Simon pointed toward the panel at the opposite wall.

"A passage that leads to an underground tunnel," the priest said. "It continues beneath the street, coming up inside Tulle's blanchisserie, a laundry shop on rue de la Madeleine." He turned toward his chambers. "In my room also there is a passage leading underground from the rectory into the sacristy of the church."

Simon was impressed. "Sounds like we're sitting on top of a rabbit warren."

The priest chuckled. "The tunnels were started centuries ago, discovered when the foundation for the rectory was first put into place. I'm told they were the remains of an original Knights Templar sanctuary."

Engrossed in the priest's talk of tunnels and Templars, Simon didn't think as he moved against the mattress. Pain shot through his foot, and in the better light he could see blood staining the bandage. "Any idea what happened here?" he gritted out.

"The Boche, who else?" The priest scowled. "They wanted to make sure you were dead before releasing you from the morgue."

He crossed himself. "A miracle they didn't decide to stab you in the heart instead."

The priest's words chilled Simon. Miracle, indeed.

"With the foot, your healing will take a bit longer, but in a few weeks you should be well enough to make the journey."

Simon looked at him. "Journey?"

"Why, Holland, of course." Resting his hands on his knees, the priest leaned forward. "Sister Marche insists we get you out of Belgium as soon as you are able."

Simon frowned, puzzled. He hadn't yet spoken to Eve about returning to Britain. Had she anticipated his plans? He supposed his mission for Marcus was at an end.

He would speak with her when she returned. In the meantime, he was curious to know if the rumors he'd heard in prison about the Belgian border were true. Better to know what to expect when the time came for them to leave. "Is it difficult crossing over into Holland?"

The priest's salt-and-pepper brows drew together. "A three-fence system runs the length of the border: two barbed wire fences enclosing an electric wire. The Germans post sentries and dogs every hundred meters." He shook his head. "Many have lost their lives trying to get past the Boche and escape into neutral Holland."

Alarmed, Simon realized the stories he'd heard were accurate. The crossing sounded far more dangerous than his escape through Switzerland months before.

He wasn't about to take that kind of risk with Eve's life. "Is there a safer way out?"

"A few have succeeded by hiding in the hull of cargo ships sailing across the Scheldt into the Netherlands," he said, "but the Boche know to expect it, and many more have been caught and shot." The priest sat back. "Despite the danger, there are people who continue to help the Allies escape over the Belgian fence. *Passeurs*, paid guides, are familiar with the frontier and know the best places to cross. It's a risk, but the lesser of two evils, I think."

He flashed a benevolent smile. "Never fear, they will take you across when the time comes, my son. Now you must rest. Since it is well past lunchtime, I am going to make you some nice potato soup."

Simon was relieved when Father Francois left the panel door open after his departure, allowing light and heat to filter into the dismal room. His new quarters weren't much larger than a prison cell, and he tried to breathe steadily as memories of his time spent in solitary confinement at Ingolstadt rose in his mind.

Any effort to get resettled on the mattress caused him pain. Simon glared at the bandaged foot. The heel was one of the worst places to receive a wound. How would he get around without the use of crutches?

Frustrated, he lay back and closed his eyes as though he could will himself to heal. He wanted nothing more than to leave Brussels with his wife. The priest had said the passeurs could get them out. Simon would probably need his passport. Eve could deliver the documents here, as he still had to destroy the orders.

Lunch came and went, with the priest spoon-feeding him the soup. Hours stretched, and Simon grew impatient for his wife's return. He wanted to talk, get some answers from her, without being surrounded by Huns.

His thoughts drifted back to their kiss, and longing pierced him. Any lingering doubts he'd harbored had dissipated with the touch of her lips against his. The world around them had ceased to exist as desperate desire overrode danger, both of them aware the moment together might be their last.

At the hospital he'd witnessed her fear; Simon still wondered about the Iron Cross she wore. What kind of life had she endured over the past three years without him? He wanted to know about her time in Louvain, and what had caused the taut lines at her mouth and the shadows beneath her eyes.

Most importantly, he needed to know if she still loved him.

Her passion in those unguarded moments yesterday, and the yearning that he'd sensed matched his own, gave him hope. His taste of heaven . . .

Actions revealed so much more than words, he decided. Perhaps he and his estranged wife had a place to start.

Silver clouds blocked the afternoon sun as Eve pedaled her bicycle toward St. Magdalene's. Anticipation mixed with her nervousness, quickening her pulse.

Before Simon's planned escape, she had arranged for Monsieur Coppens to keep her husband sedated after the ether wore off, both at the mortuary and while he was inside the coffin being transported to the church. She prayed that by now Simon would be conscious, and unaltered from the ordeal.

Arriving at the church, she left her bicycle just inside. Only a handful of people were in attendance, mostly elderly, kneeling in the pews. She approached the front and went down on one knee, making the sign of the cross.

Father Francois was preparing for Vespers. He scanned the church, then gave her a quick nod before she moved to slip through a side door into the sacristy.

A floor-length armoire filled with priestly vestments stood at one end of the room. Eve opened the wardrobe and stepped inside, pushing past the embroidered chasubles and white linen albs to reach a panel at the back. She pressed a latch near the top, as the priest had shown her, and the panel opened to an underground passage connecting the church to the rectory next door.

She switched on her electric torch and continued through the tunnel until she arrived at another panel with a similar pressure-sensitive latch. Releasing the device, she entered the back of Father Francois's clothes closet before finally emerging into the priest's chambers.

Eve was relieved to see the tall bookcase pushed back and Simon's quarters left open to the brazier's warmth. She hurried to enter the tiny room.

"I've been waiting, lass." Her husband watched her from his makeshift bed on the floor.

She eased out a breath. He seemed all right. The events of the past twenty-four hours had been incredible, like a dream . . . or a nightmare. "How do you feel?"

Eve shrugged out of her coat and knelt beside him, scanning his injuries as she had earlier. She took in the fading bruises on his face, then glanced at his bandaged foot, trembling with new outrage at the bloodstained cloth.

"I'm none the worse for wear, except for the blasted foot." He winced as he shifted on the bed. "The priest told me the Huns tried their hand at carving me up."

"Schultz." Eve had stifled a scream when the vampire opened his pocketknife and held it over Simon's unconscious form. He'd moved the blade over her husband's heart, and she thought she might faint, but in the end Schultz made a deep gash in Simon's right heel.

"It was luck that you didn't feel it at the time," she said, recalling how she and the two orderlies had held their breath. "If you had reacted, Schultz would have arrested us all."

"What was the near mix-up in plans about?" he said, frowning. "Did you know they were going to send me back to Germany?"

Eve shook her head. "I found out when Matron told you." She relayed the previous day's events, starting with the unexpected appearance of Nurse Hoffmeyer. "I thought all was lost until General von Falkenhausen was rushed into surgery," she said. "That's when I came to tell you we were going ahead with the plan."

"I remember."

His gaze lowered to her lips, and Eve's heart beat faster as she too remembered the kiss.

"What happened afterward?" His brow creased with concern as his eyes met hers. "Did you suffer any repercussions?"

"Herr Jaeger wasn't too happy." During the vampire's bullying interrogation, her tears had been real enough, as she worried Simon's foot would bleed out before he arrived at the rectory. "It wasn't an experience I care to repeat."

Eve had also worried Dr. Ambrose might crack under pressure and expose them all, but once Herr Schultz corroborated his pronouncement of death, the surgeon was excused from questioning.

"When it was all over, I thought for certain I would get the sack," she said. "Matron was quite beside herself." Nurse Hoffmeyer's rant over Eve's carelessness in killing a patient with ether in *her* hospital still rang in her ears. "Fortunately, the major intervened. It seems my job is safe enough for the moment."

Eve didn't add that while Otto had been upset at having his administration accused of negligence, he considered Chandler's death an expedient end to his dilemma with Jaeger.

"You seem to have found a new champion in my absence." Simon's features darkened. "I want to know straight out, Eve. What is the major to you?"

She eyed him anxiously. While he deserved an explanation, she wasn't ready to bare her soul about what had happened three years ago, or what she'd done.

Eve rose from the floor, wiping her damp hands against

her skirt. "I met the major in Louvain . . . after the upheaval there," she said, choosing her words as she sat down on the bench, putting some distance between them. "I worked at the local hospital. We were flooded with wounded, Germans and Belgians alike."

Without conscious thought, she took his handkerchief from her skirt pocket. Eve clutched the cloth in her fingers while her mind relived the terror of those days—the heat of the flames as she watched her uncle's home burn, hearing the screams of their neighbors shot down in the street. Hearing her own screams. "Major Reinhardt was admitted with wounds caused by artillery fire," she said after a moment. "I saved his life." *And then I lost our child.*

She stared at the monogrammed cloth in her hand, her soul pierced with the familiar pain and guilt. "I stayed on at the hospital a few months," she said. "When the major recovered and received his new post as hospital administrator to Brussels, he offered me a position. Mama and I agreed, as we had nothing left to keep us in Louvain."

She raised her gaze to Simon. "Mama's younger brother and sister-in-law own a café here in Brussels, on rue des Sols. They invited us to live with them. To help out, I work there nights as a waitress." She added, "I would be there now, but I wanted to come and see how you were doing."

"What about Nikki and Zoe, and your Uncle Eugene?"

"My uncle died when the university library burned," she said without emotion. "The children were put on trains bound for labor camps in Germany."

"Dear God . . ." He exhaled the words.

Seeing his shock and sadness, Eve couldn't allow him to think the worst. They were his family, too. "I recently learned that Nikki and Zoe escaped the train with some others."

Hope lit his gaze. "Where are they now?"

"I was told they're in northern France." She was tempted to tell him more—that her siblings were last reported in the town of Anor—yet she hesitated.

The planned attack on the kaiser was to take place not far from there, in Trélon. Simon was unaware that she'd been ordered by Rotterdam to return him to Holland and then complete his assignment. If he knew, he would try to prevent her from going and insist on remaining in Brussels with her. Having him back in her life after so many years apart, Eve feared she might weaken in the face of his obstinacy and let him stay—putting him in more danger.

For his own safety he must leave Belgium.

"Who told you about Nikki and Zoe?" Simon's insistent tone drew her attention. "Can we get any more information?"

Eve shook her head. "Corporal Duval was a patient. He left for a POW hospital in Germany the day your plane crashed." Hoping to end the discussion, she added, "I can ask Father Francois for help. He has ties in France."

Though she disliked dodging his questions, she tried to offer him as much truth as she dared. Father Francois *would* help her when the time came, if she needed it.

"You didna tell the priest who I am," he said. "You don't trust him?"

"I do trust him, but we've already established Chandler's identity for you," she said. "The fewer people who know the truth, the better for everyone. I haven't even told my family. Poor Mama would charge the rectory walls to try to see you."

He smiled before his gaze turned pensive. "It hasna been easy for you, has it? Louvain must have been a horrible mess."

"Imagine hell, and you might come close," she whispered.

"And the Iron Cross? Corporal Ziegler told me you received it for 'meritorious service in battle.' I take it he meant Louvain?"

She nodded. "I simply did my duty as a nurse. I didn't receive the medal until months later, when we arrived in Brussels."

"Ziegler considers you a local heroine," he said, and she detected his edge of sarcasm. "I wonder at your compassion for the enemy, after what they did to your family."

"I tended the wounded in my care, regardless of uniform," she said, angered by his words. "They were human beings, dying, crying out for help." Tears rose unbidden, as an image of the boy whose life she had taken flashed in her mind. Her husband had no idea what she'd been through, or what it had cost her.

She pinned him with a fierce look. "I didn't ask for the wretched medal, Simon, but having it has made my life and my family's a little easier to bear, living with the enemy."

His bruised features flushed. "I deserved that," he said. "I'm sorry." He raised his hand to her. "I didna mean to upset you. Please, come sit by me." Love and gratitude shone in his eyes. "You managed it, lass. You saved me."

She gazed at his outstretched palm a moment, then gave in. "You're welcome," she said and knelt down beside him again, slipping her hand into his.

Warmth spread through her as his larger grip enfolded hers, his thumb lightly caressing the back of her hand. They remained like that for several heartbeats, their hands entwined.

Eve studied him, again aware of how much thinner he'd become over the years, and she determined to make sure she brought enough food that he could regain his strength.

With his bruises, too, lay a new growth of a beard. She would bring a razor and give him a shave once his cuts had healed.

When her husband's gaze again caught hers, Eve blushed. Despite their passionate kiss of the day before, now, sitting beside him, she suddenly found herself shy.

Her dreams of him were far different than the reality. Was it because he'd changed so much . . . or had she?

The pain of her past flooded her thoughts, and she knew the answer.

"It's been a long time," he said at last. "I've missed you."

"I never thought to see you again," she said. "Certainly not in Brussels Park." A swift mental image of him lying unconscious beside the burning plane stabbed at her.

"How thankful I am it was you and not the Huns who found me." He squeezed her hand. "Why did you not stay in Britain, Eve? I know you said nothing to Marcus about us. Weatherford was shocked when I broke the news we were husband and wife."

"I had planned to wait for you, Simon, but when Alex called and told me your plane went down, that you'd been listed as dead . . ." She glanced down at their joined hands. "I . . . needed to be with my family."

Even now, the excuse sounded hollow to her ears. If she'd only known about the child then, she would have remained where they were safe. Over and over her mind had replayed Simon's warning about the danger in coming to this country.

"Obviously a mistake," he said. "Still, I'm sorry you had to go through that grief." His expression held regret. "Will you tell me what happened to you? Was it Louvain?"

Her heart quailed. "Simon . . ."

"Please, I want to understand."

Three sharp raps on wood from inside the priest's chambers drew their attention. Eve was relieved to postpone the discussion. "Vespers is over," she said as she gently withdrew her hand from his. She reached for her coat. "Father Francois is ready to stand watch while I leave the sacristy unnoticed."

"He told me about the tunnels. A clever operation."

She offered him a wan smile. "Being clever is the only way we survive."

"You'll come back tomorrow?"

"I'll try," she said. "I'm sorry we didn't have much time tonight, but it's near curfew and the vampires have their stool pigeons posted everywhere, including the church."

She started to rise when he again grabbed for her hand. "You'll be careful?"

"I will," she assured him.

"Eve, I know much has happened in three years," he said. "But you're my wife, and I need to know where we stand." He swallowed, his gaze fixed on her. "Do you love me?"

Beneath the bruises she could see his uncertainty, and her chest tightened. *Do you love me?* A question so simple and straightforward and deserving of an answer—a resounding *yes!* But with the urgency of saving his life now over, Eve wasn't certain where to go from here, and she wondered what kind of love she could offer him.

Three years of war had hardened her, with Louvain leaving an indelible mark on her soul. She'd lived day to day with fear, always on edge, her conscience haunted by the past. The shiny world they'd once shared had become the dismal gray shades of her own empty existence.

Their kiss at the hospital had been fiery, hungry, his lips and his touch enflaming her senses. But would passion be enough? They knew so little about one another's lives. She was no longer the girl he'd kissed beneath the honeysuckle, or his bonny young bride painting the future bright with dreams of hearth and home and a houseful of children.

She was so much less than that. Would it be enough for him?

"I do, Simon," she said, hearing the tremor in her own voice. "As much as I'm still able to love, I do."

Eve rose then and leaned to brush her fingertips along the side of his face. At the door she turned, and their eyes met, the sadness in his mirroring the anguish in her own. "I'll see you tomorrow."

With that, she turned and left him.

159

CHAPTER 15

After Eve had gone, Simon lay on the straw mattress and stared at the ceiling. *As much as I am able to love . . .*

Her words had grieved him, and he cursed the Huns for hurting her. He'd seen the haunted look in her eyes and the anguish as she told him briefly about Louvain and saving the major's life.

Simon understood her grief, not only in believing him dead for so long, but over the loss of her uncle and losing her brother and sister. Still, he sensed she'd been holding something back.

No doubt living three years under the heel of the Germans had changed her. She'd said it herself—being clever was the only way to survive.

And Eve had cleverness in abundance, not only in her daring success with his escape, but in her quick thinking when the plan seemed about to fail. His wife had always been level-headed, but now her decisions struck him as tactical. Her mind weighed options with cool reason, making life-and-death decisions and taking incredible risks.

She was so different from the young lass who had once worried over a kitten in a tree, and who balked at having to hide their marriage from Matron for a few weeks.

But had she altered so much that she couldn't find her way back to him?

He rubbed at his eyes while he eased out a pained breath. She hadn't kissed him tonight. Simon hungered for another taste of her sweet lips, but his pride had prevented him from asking. He stared down at his injuries, despising his helplessness. He couldn't even stand up, let alone take her in his arms.

"I've brought you supper, Captain."

The priest's voice pulled him back to the present. The tall, stout cleric ducked his head as he entered with a tray—more of the soup and black bread.

He set the food on the bench. "I trust you had a pleasant visit with Sister Marche?"

Just as he had earlier, Father Francois sat down beside the mattress and took the bowl in his hands, intending to feed him.

"Help me sit up, will you? I'm no bairn to be spoon-fed. I can do it myself."

"Ah, a man of *détermination*." The priest's brown eyes twinkled as he put aside the soup and rose, moving to the head of Simon's bed. "We will use the wall to help us."

With impressive strength Father Francois pulled both the mattress and Simon as close to the wall as possible. Then he went to his chambers and returned with several pillows, using them to prop Simon into a sitting position.

"Thanks," Simon growled. The pain was intense, but he was determined.

The priest placed the tray of food on Simon's lap, then sat on the bench and watched his progress.

"I suppose you've known Sister Marche a long time," Simon said as he lifted a spoonful of watery potato soup toward his lips.

"*Oui*, I met her shortly after she arrived with her mother from Louvain." The priest's eyes held compassion. "They have had much sadness in their lives."

"How so?" Simon asked, hoping the priest might shed more light on his wife's past.

Father Francois shook his head. "I cannot say."

Perhaps the priest knew the truth but was bound to silence.

"The circumstances in Louvain were bad, I understand," Simon ventured.

The priest merely nodded.

Simon decided to switch topics. "Has Sister Marche helped others . . . like me?" He still suspected Eve worked in some underground resistance group.

To his surprise the priest said, "You are the first in a very long time. After Nurse Cavell's arrest, all of the nurses are watched very carefully."

Despite his concern over the implied danger his wife had placed herself in for his benefit, Simon's heart lifted. She did love him. "I am honored."

"She has a good heart. And like the rest of us, she fights for Belgium and the Allies."

His pulse quickened. "In what way?"

"Almost every Belgian citizen works to resist the occupiers. We retaliate against the German propaganda by printing truth about the war in our underground newspaper, *La Libre Belgique*. Also, many hide food and goods that would otherwise be confiscated and used by the enemy. Our railway workers have been known to 'accidentally' damage German goods, and men at the docks may slip and drop German cargo into the river."

His eyes gleamed with purpose. "It is passive work, but by antagonizing the Boche, we help Belgian morale and we aid the Allies to advance in the war."

"Are there different organizations? With activities not so passive?"

Father Francois appraised him. "Many," he said.

Simon narrowed his gaze. "Like La Dame Blanche?"

The priest stood abruptly, his features shuttered. "I see you manage your spoon well on your own. I will leave you to eat in peace, my son, and return after Compline to attend you."

Simon continued to eat his supper. The priest knew something. Perhaps Simon would show him the Pi symbol and see if he recognized it. At least he might salvage part of his assignment for Marcus.

His thoughts returned to his wife, and again he realized how much she'd risked to save him. His heart beat with the anticipation of seeing her the following day. They would have another chance to talk, and he was even more determined to find out about her life over the past three years, and to share his with her.

Perhaps then he could help her, help them both, to find their way back.

CHAPTER 16

A light rain fell outside, while within the secret room at the rectory Eve huddled under a blanket beside Simon's bed and watched him sleep.

She regretted not visiting with him yesterday, but when she'd arrived at St. Magdalene's, Father Francois had shaken his head—a warning to her of suspicious persons inside the church.

Tonight she'd entered through the tunnel from Tulle's blanchisserie, as it was Thursday and her night to exchange the café's linen. The laundry shopkeeper had given her more information on troop movements that she would decode later for Mama's special lace.

Because she couldn't stay long, Eve took advantage of her husband's slumber to simply be near him, without the worry of answering more questions about Louvain or of being discovered by the Germans.

A pair of wooden crutches sat propped against the wall beside his bed, left over from before the war when Father Francois had broken an ankle. The priest had relayed Simon's progress. Her husband's demand to eat on his own and his use of the crutches to move around were good signs.

His foot could be a problem, if the deep cut prevented him

from bearing his full weight. It would be two weeks, perhaps three, before he was fit to weather the journey into Holland.

Eve frowned. The attack on the kaiser was to occur close to that time; she still needed instructions from Rotterdam to tell her where to meet with the assassin, Lundgren.

She gazed at her sleeping husband. *Do you love me?* His question of days ago still rang in her mind as she leaned to brush back a lock of his hair, careful not to wake him. It seemed they must start over with each other, pick up what pieces of their marriage the war hadn't destroyed. In the few weeks they would have together she was willing to try, though the prospect brought her disquiet as well as delight.

Simon stirred, as if sensing her presence. He opened his eyes and turned to her.

Perhaps they needn't start at the very beginning, she thought, as warmth spread through her at his unguarded smile.

"When you look at me that way, wife, I think of sunshine and a bonny bride in her crown of flowers," he said, his voice roughened from sleep. "When we get back to England, we'll buy that little cottage in Highbury and start our family." His sleepy smile broadened. "Lassies first, and then our lads . . ."

Eve tried to smile as she blinked back tears. She didn't spoil his dream and tell him their lives wouldn't be the same, that she couldn't be the same person she'd been before.

He must have sensed her anguish. His features sobered as he became fully awake. "Can you help me to sit up?"

The moment was gone. Eve found the stack of pillows and used them to ease him into a sitting position. "I'm sorry I couldn't see you yesterday."

"The priest told me it wasna safe for you to come."

She nodded. "Father Francois tells me you've taken to feeding yourself?"

"Aye, I'm not completely helpless."

Eve ignored his irritable tone. "It's wonderful you're making progress. Before long, you'll be back on your feet."

"Not soon enough for me." He reached for her hand. "I'll need the passport and documents I gave you. The passport at least, once we leave the rectory and make our way back to Britain." His expression turned grim. "We'll also have to find a safer way to leave Belgium. The priest told me about the border crossing. It's far too dangerous for you."

She eyed him, stunned. He'd assumed she was going with him. For an instant the thought tantalized her—to be free of this prison city, to return to the safety of Britain.

But she had her orders from Rotterdam and her siblings to find. With Nikki especially, time was becoming critical. And what about her mother?

Eve cleared her throat. "Simon, I cannot leave."

His grip on her tightened. "I thought we were going together."

His look of shock weighed on her heart. She shook her head. "You're leaving, in a few weeks."

"Not without you." His expression hardened to stone.

"I cannot leave my family," she said gently.

The muscle in his jaw flexed. "I'm your family."

"I know that." Heat rose in her cheeks. "But I won't leave Mama behind, and she would never survive the crossing. I'm afraid there is no other successful means of escape."

His anger seemed to evaporate as he tipped his head back to stare at the low ceiling. "Aye, the priest said as much." He turned to her. "So I'll stay with you."

"You can't remain in Brussels; it's too much of a risk. When you're well enough, we'll get you across the border."

"We?" he said, brows arched. "Father Francois explained to me there are many organizations in this country that work to defeat the Huns. With your ingenious plan in getting me out of the hospital, and now this scheme to smuggle me out of Belgium, I suspect you're involved in a network." Concern filled his expression. "Are you, the orderlies, and the surgeon—in league with the priest?"

"Father Francois is my friend, nothing more," she said, offering what sliver of honesty she could. "He was willing to hide you here until you heal, and he'll help to get you across the border when the time comes."

Unnerved at how close he'd come to the truth, she added, "And there is no great scheme. You simply cannot remain in Belgium. The Boche have seen your face. If they catch you walking around Brussels now, you'll truly be a dead man." Her voice quavered. "I won't be able to help you."

He looked unconvinced. "You must work for someone."

"I work for the good of my mother's people," she said, lifting her chin. "For the good of Belgium. And for your *own* good, Simon, you must leave when the time comes."

He said nothing more, but she could tell from his frown he still doubted her words.

Eve hated dancing around the truth; it tore at her conscience, playing this game with him. Yet she could not tell Simon about her involvement in La Dame Blanche any more than she could reveal to him that *she* was the contact he was supposed to meet—or that because of the crash, she'd been ordered to carry out his mission.

If he knew this, Simon would refuse to leave Brussels. He'd insist on staying to protect her, perhaps would try to complete the mission in France himself, which in his condition would only get him killed.

A disguise might work for a short time, to get him out of the country, but not for the day-to-day duration of the war. He would surely make a misstep and be found out. Then not only his life but hers and the lives of all who had helped with his escape would be forfeit.

She held her tongue.

"If I canna complete my mission, those orders must be destroyed," he said at length.

"It's too much of a risk to bring them here," she said. "Shall I burn them?"

"No," he said. "Not yet."

Why did he delay? Was it because he still hoped to finish the assignment . . . or because he didn't trust her to destroy the documents? Not that she deserved his trust. She'd dodged his questions, giving him only the barest of truths. She was doing far more than simply helping her mother's people; she was playing a dangerous game with high stakes.

Do you love me? Eve stared at her lap. Her life was so different from the one she'd shared with him in London—their summer wedding, and an unwavering belief in the future. Each blissfully unaware of the torment to come.

Bitterness swept through her. This war had destroyed more than men. Would she and Simon even have a chance?

CHAPTER 17

I've brought breakfast."

Simon's heart thudded at the sight of Eve slipping through the open panel door into his small room the next morning. He'd been afraid she might not come back. Yesterday he'd badgered her with questions and accusations, angry after learning she hadn't any intention of returning with him to Britain.

He understood that with her mother here it would be difficult to find a safe way to get them both out. There were also her brother and sister to consider. Simon knew she wouldn't leave without trying to find them.

He wasn't ready to give up. His time here could be put to good use, healing his injuries and bridging the gulf between himself and his wife.

He sat up in bed, propped with the pillows, as Eve knelt beside him. She unbuttoned her heavy dark coat and began emptying her pockets of food.

"I've brought bread, apples, a jug of cold milk, and I was able to secure a hunk of cheese without mold," she said, her voice hinting at pride. "Food considered *haute cuisine* here in

Belgium." She handed him an apple. "I can only stay for the hour of Mass. Then I must leave for the hospital."

"Do you normally go to daily Mass?" Simon wondered if his presence in the rectory kept her from church.

"I seldom attend anymore." A rosy tint touched her cheeks as she busied herself with opening cloths containing the bread and cheese. "Do you?" she asked without looking up at him. "Still go to church, I mean?"

He gazed at her bent head as she worked. The last time he'd been to church was weeks ago, before he'd flown the mission. As he had at every chapel service during his years in prison, he'd dropped to his knees and begged God to bring her back to him.

"When I can," he said. "Why do you stay away, lass?"

She looked at him then, her violet eyes bleak, guarded. "I'm . . . it seems I'm usually working. The hospital or the café . . ."

"I'm sorry to hear it." It saddened him that she missed out on the peace he'd come to know being in Christ's presence. "When I was at Gütersloh, we had a visiting priest who drove twenty kilometers every Sunday at dawn to say Mass for those who practiced the faith. We stood outside the barracks against a backdrop of pine forest and watched the sun rise as we listened to God's Word. It gave us hope."

"Hope can be elusive to some," she said in a low voice. She offered him the small jug of milk. "I'm happy you found it." She reached for a piece of the cheese. "Gütersloh. Is that a prison camp?"

How neatly she'd turned their conversation. Simon hadn't missed the flash of grief in her expression, and he ached for her. Still, he decided not to press her today. "Gütersloh was one of the POW camps I called home."

"You were in more than one camp?" Her dark brows lifted. "Please, tell me what happened after your plane went down near Liège."

He reached for her hand, and his pulse leapt when she curled her fingers around his. "I walked away from that crash unscathed, but I was captured by the Huns. I was held in a temporary prison outside the city, along with several Belgian soldiers. A week later we were sent by train to Germany."

"Was it terrible?"

"The camps at Gütersloh and Clausthal weren't as bad as the third." His muscles flinched. "Fort Nine at Ingolstadt."

"How long were you there?"

He released her hand to take the piece of bread she offered. Simon stared at the coarse food, assailed by memories of cramped quarters, lice, dysentery, and the endless months he'd spent in freezing cold cells eating half rations of black war bread and beetroot soup.

"Almost two years at Ingolstadt." His words came out rough. "I was sent to Fort Nine because it was considered the highest security prison." He put aside the bread and picked up a slice of the cheese. "I kept trying to escape, you see, and the Huns kept caging me behind bigger walls."

The sharp cheese tasted tangy against his tongue. "I didna stop trying," he said, after he swallowed. "I spent much of my time confined to a mangy stall reeking of petrol." He gazed at the walls around him, and his skin flushed. "Sometimes this wee space puts me in a fine sweat."

"When did you finally escape?"

"Six months ago." He looked back at her and smiled at her rapt attention. "My fifth attempt. I walked for eighteen days, foraging food in the woods."

Simon recalled the exhaustion and hunger of those agonizing days, the pain in every muscle and joint of his body. He'd been chased by the Huns and their dogs, and so many times he'd wanted to just lie down and die. The image of Eve had kept him going.

"I finally made it to the Swiss border," he said. "I spent two months in a hospital there before I was repatriated to Britain."

Eve stared openmouthed at her husband. "That's incredible," she whispered.

Compassion filled her as she realized the hardships he must have endured. She thought of his escape into Switzerland. How could someone survive that many days in the wild without decent food or shelter?

He made light of the experience, but she guessed there was much he hadn't told her. No wonder he'd objected so fiercely to going back.

It dawned on her then he'd spent nearly the entire war behind enemy lines.

She was a prisoner herself in terms of being trapped in Belgium; even going from one city to the next required a special pass from the Germans. Yet how could that compare with being locked away in a cramped cell stinking of fuel, surrounded by barbed wire?

"When did you finally return to London?" she asked softly.

"I got back in September. Despite my time in the Swiss hospital, Marcus sent me off to Craiglockhart in Edinburgh for evaluation." His mouth lifted. "To make certain I hadna gone daft being locked up for so long, I suppose." His amusement dimmed. "I was weak, and I'll admit, the blue devils chased me, but in time I got my strength back . . ." His gaze held hers. "And my hope."

Eve envied him his convictions even after all he'd been through. Hers lay buried beneath the ever-present guilt weighing against her heart.

He'd asked her why she didn't attend church, and she couldn't bring herself to tell him that it was because deep down she felt beyond saving, and despite her repeated attempts

172

at prayer, she couldn't seem to rid herself of this burden she carried.

It would also mean having to explain to her husband what she'd done. Eve couldn't bear to see his pain or his condemnation.

"When I returned, I asked Marcus to try to find you," he was saying. "In prison, I'd learned through the British Red Cross what had happened in Louvain. They couldna find any record of you or your family having survived the atrocities."

"What?" His words grabbed her attention. "You thought . . . *I* was dead?"

"I feared it," he said, his expression grim. "I was first able to write to you from Clausthal, months after my capture. The Huns only allowed prisoners two letters a month, and those were censored, so it took me some time to find out you'd left Britain for Belgium shortly after the war started.

"When I finally received word back from the Red Cross, I was determined to escape. I prayed to get back to Britain so I could seek you out myself. I didna want to believe you were really gone."

"I'm sorry." This time she reached for his hand. The city of Louvain had still been in a shambles when she and Mama left to come to Brussels. "How *did* you find me?" she asked, curious.

"A few weeks ago, Marcus tracked down Madeleine Arthur—"

"Maddie?" Her pulse quickened. "How is she? Where is she?"

"She was working at a casualty clearing station somewhere in France. Marcus managed to find her and learned you sent correspondence to her after Louvain."

Eve nodded. "Maddie evacuated with most of the British nurses shortly after arriving in Brussels," she said, remembering how much she'd longed for the company of her friend. "By the time Mama and I came to the city, no British mail was being allowed in or out of Belgium by order of the Germans. Since the Americans hadn't yet entered the war and were here as neutrals working with the food relief program, I wrote to Maddie in care of a very kind gentleman who promised to mail her my letter before he returned to America."

She gazed down at their joined hands. "I never heard back and could only wonder if she received my letter." She looked up at him, a smile on her lips. "It seems she did."

"Aye." His gray eyes lit with warmth. In a gentler voice, he asked, "Will you tell me now what happened to you, lass?"

Her pulse jumped, knowing he meant Louvain. She wavered. He'd been forthcoming about his own life over the past three years. She could do no less. "The Germans marched on the city soon after I arrived," she began, recalling the tide of soldiers and the boy whose gray eyes found hers in the crowd. She described the mayhem that ensued. "You know what followed," she finished, still unable to tell him her part.

He bowed his head as though in prayer. "I'm sorry I wasna there to protect you."

The regret in his voice only made her more miserable. "We cannot undo the past." Her words came out harsher than she intended. "Neither of us planned for this to happen."

"You're right. We didna choose it, nor can we change what's happened to either of us." His perceptive gray eyes met hers and his voice gentled. "But we still have the future, and it belongs to us." He smiled, squeezing her hand. "This war will not last forever."

Eve saw the love and assurance in his expression. For a moment she tried to imagine a future with him back in Britain, buying a cottage in Highbury as they'd planned.

But could she return to a normal life, burdened by the knowledge of her assault, and through that violence, the loss of their baby? Tainted by so much death?

Would Simon forgive her?

Would she ever forgive herself?

The familiar weight pressed in on her as the image of the boy's rounded cheeks and reddish-gold hair rose in her mind again, the soft gray eyes reminding her so much of Simon's. *A life for a life . . .*

Eve didn't hold out hope.

CHAPTER 18

*Z*oe! When can we eat?"

Zoe Marche stood beneath the overhang and wrung out another white shirt. "That depends, Nicholas," she called across the yard. She reached to pin the shirt to the clothesline. "Have you and Michel finished cutting up the potatoes?"

"*Oui*," he said in a plaintive voice. "And I am hungry!"

From beside the washtub she plucked up a pair of Nikki's overalls and dunked them in the soapy water. Placing them against the washboard, she noted the torn inseam and sighed. Her brother was growing faster than they could keep him in clothes. "Put the potatoes in a pot of water and boil them on the stove," she instructed him.

"Women's work," he grumbled.

Zoe hid a smile. "The faster they cook, the sooner we'll eat." She held up his dripping overalls. "Unless you'd prefer to do the washing?"

"Where is Madame Boulanger?" he said. "She knows how to boil potatoes."

"She has been in town all afternoon helping a woman deliver

176

her baby," Zoe said sharply, speaking of the young midwife who shared the cottage. "If she arrives home in time for supper, she will be very tired and should not have to cook. You and Michel, on the other hand, have spent most of your afternoon playing at war in the parlor, so you can start those potatoes right now."

"We aren't playing." Nikki's expression turned thunderous. "There is a war going on and we are preparing ourselves to fight."

"Potatoes, now!" she said.

Muttering words she couldn't make out, Nikki spun around and retreated into the house.

Zoe returned to her task of scrubbing the grime from his overalls. He was growing up fast, she realized. Soon Nikki would be fourteen, old enough to labor for the Boche. A chill tore through her as she imagined her brother working in the enemy's trenches. Already many French boys his age had been taken away.

It would still be a couple of years before he was old enough to go and fight for the French army, though he and Armand's fourteen-year-old brother, Michel, talked of nothing else. That worried her too, and she prayed the war would end before the day came.

The autumn rain continued to fall steadily from a dull sky, drumming against the metal roof above her head. The skies had poured out for days, yet she was glad for the constant *shushing* sound, filtering out the steady drone of mortar and artillery fire to the west.

Above the noisy raindrops a train whistle blew, and Zoe jumped at the sound, grabbing for the side of the tub to steady herself.

She hated the sound; it always reminded her of the nightmare she and Nikki had endured.

She closed her eyes, again hearing the screams and seeing the dead bodies in the streets while the Boche marched them toward the Louvain train station. Mama had told them to run, just before she was struck on the back of the head with a rifle.

Tears burned her eyes as she again conjured the image of her mother lying dead in the street. She and Nikki *had* run, breaking free of the queue boarding the train and pumping their legs as fast as they could toward safety. But it hadn't been fast enough; a pair of strong hands collared them both, jerking them off their feet. Zoe had let out a cry as the German barked an order she couldn't understand, then shoved them back in the direction of the station.

She and Nikki had boarded along with dozens of women and old men and crying babies. Zoe overheard some Belgians speaking and realized they were being sent into Germany to be put to work in factories and coal mines. Her heart had threatened to explode in her chest, while Nikki sat wailing beside her in the cramped seat.

She had stared out the train window at the city, their home, smoldering amid a mountain of destruction. What had happened to Eve and Uncle Eugene? Had they perished, like her mother? Or did they end up on the trains too?

Zoe never saw them again.

Her hands shook as she rinsed the overalls in rainwater, then hung them to dry. The painful memories were a stain she couldn't scrub out. Grabbing up another of Armand's white shirts, she held it to her face and breathed in his familiar scent, calm once again settling over her. She dipped the cloth into the soapy water.

He had saved them both.

Thinking back to her first impression of him, Zoe's pulse quickened. Armand Rousseau was tall and broad-shouldered, and the black patch over his right eye only enhanced his handsome dark features.

He had a kind face and a gentle voice, so when he spoke to

them on the train heading east, Zoe grasped at his words like a lifeline. He seemed so assured and capable, so intelligent. A teacher like her papa had been, though he taught history, not mathematics, at Catholic University in Louvain.

His brother, Michel, was close to Nikki's age, and as the two boys sat together on the train, Nikki regained his composure. When Armand learned they were on their own, he told her of his plan to jump from the train when it slowed at the town of Angleur, just beyond the station at Liege, and travel on foot to their childhood home in Anor.

She'd been breathless at the notion of escape. Was it possible? Yet like the notorious Blackbeard in her books, Armand seemed to be a fearless pirate, ready for any challenge. The hours passed on their journey, and soon his confidence became hers. By the time they approached Angleur, she and Nikki were ready to join them.

Others in the car had had the same plan; Zoe's heart nearly burst when the guards rushed to stop an attempted escape at the front of the car—her cue to jump. Blindly, she'd thrust open her window and leapt out, joining Armand and the two boys in their race toward freedom.

Michel had broken his wrist in the fall, and Zoe twisted an ankle, while all of them received cuts and bruises from the sharp gravel lining the tracks. But when Armand lifted her into his arms as they ran for the shelter of the nearby woods, she knew she was safe.

They hid themselves in the hollowed-out trunk of a giant oak, listening in fear to the sounds of gunfire and shouts in German, followed by cries as the other escapees were shot down or apprehended.

When the train finally moved on, the four traveled south, keeping to the woods as much as possible. Immersed in her grief and plagued by the incessant pain in her ankle, Zoe had clung to Armand's strength as he carried her, while the two boys straggled along behind. They were exhausted when they reached some loyal Belgians and French, who sheltered and fed them and provided medical attention.

Three weeks later they arrived at the Rousseaus' small cottage in Anor.

Through the rain, Zoe could see Armand coming into the yard, leading a cart drawn by a pair of the neighbor's mongrel dogs. He'd been at the railway station, loading bricks left over from a silo demolished by the Boche near the tracks.

He stopped to let the dogs out of their harnesses. They were all three soaked through, and the dogs' furry coats sprayed water as they tried to shake off the rain.

Armand approached the overhang. "*Bonjour, chère.*" His deep voice was as smooth as Belgian chocolate and made her insides flutter. He pulled off his wet cap and leaned in to kiss her. "How are you coming on my shirts?" he asked, his smile teasing.

"See for yourself." She flung the wet shirt at him, laughing. He caught it and tossed it back into the washtub before taking her in his arms. He kissed her again, more tenderly this time, and Zoe slid her soapy hands around his waist.

Warmth seeped through her, despite the chill of the dampened air. She'd found refuge in Anor three years ago; now she had a new life with this man and a reason to hope again. Her arms tightened around him.

"I love you, *mon coeur*," she whispered, and he responded with another kiss. Armand had begun to court her once she turned eighteen, and already they'd made plans to marry after the war. Another reason to pray for an end to the destruction.

"Come along," he said, smiling. "We have a shopping list to make."

Zoe met his gaze. "A long list?"

"*Non*, but a full one." His handsome features sobered. "The Boche are on the move."

A shiver tore through her and she hugged him close as they ran together toward the cottage, where inside a small fire burned in the grate to remove October's damp chill.

Her brow creased as she spied her brother and Michel at the far end of the parlor, fencing with bayonets carved from wood. They each had stick rifles, tied with old rope and slung over their skinny shoulders. The military caps they wore were stolen surplus from a supply train recently forced to stop at Anor when a tree fell onto the tracks. It was an event, she suspected, the two boys had arranged.

Near the hearth, Madame Boulanger's small auburn-haired daughter, Annette, talked with her rag dolls in the rocking chair. With so many German troops in the area, the soldiers either billeted with the French or requisitioned their homes. Madame Boulanger had been forced out of hers, so with her ten-year-old daughter and elderly father-in-law, the young midwife had found refuge with them while her husband fought in the French army.

Eyeing the little girl, Zoe remembered her own dolls when she was that age, and a sudden longing for the innocence and simplicity of that life seized her.

From the back of the cottage Monsieur Boulanger emerged, his tall, spindly frame clad in canvas overalls. White hair sprouted outward from above his ears, while the bald spot at the top of his head shone in the fire's light. The elderly man looked tired, new lines etched against his already wrinkled features.

"Monsieur, I've brought a whole cartload of bricks," Armand called to him. "We will use the dogs in the morning to take them into Trélon."

The old man nodded. "The Boche should be grateful."

He and Armand had been pressed into working for the

Germans as masons, erecting an armament storage facility near the German headquarters in Trélon, a few kilometers to the north.

Monsieur Boulanger looked at Zoe. "May I help with supper?" he asked.

"Go and visit with your granddaughter, Monsieur." She glanced at the stove, pleased to see the potatoes boiled and sitting in their broth. "I still have some tinned meat from the American Red Cross, so I'll make up a quick soup and we can eat." She paused to look questioningly at Armand.

"The list can wait," he said.

Half an hour later, six bowls of hot soup sat ready on the table. Zoe set out slices of K bread, the slimy texture made up of potatoes, rye, and flour, and palatable only after she toasted them over the brazier.

She was just putting out a few pats of the butter she'd been hoarding when Madame Boulanger entered the cottage.

"*Bonsoir*," she called to them, looking quite soaked. Strands of auburn hair lay plastered against her pretty face. She gazed hungrily toward the meager fare Zoe had prepared.

"Go and get dry while I serve you up some soup," Zoe offered.

Within minutes they were all seated at the table and saying grace. Zoe glanced around at each of them as they ate, and emotion rose in her throat. *Home*, she thought. A new life and her new family. If only Eve and Mama and Uncle could be with them, too.

During the first few months after their arrival at the cottage, Armand had tried to find out about her sister. He would slip across the border into Belgium to see his uncle who owned a small farm in Chimay. But Monsieur Duval, while sympathetic, had not been able to offer them help.

Sorrow and guilt pressed in on her as she remembered the promise she'd made to her sister, to take care of Mama and Nikki.

She hadn't been able to keep that promise. What would she do if the Boche came for her brother? Or Michel?

She continued to worry as she cleared the table of dishes after supper. The boys returned to the parlor, while Madame Boulanger went to ready her daughter for bed. Monsieur Boulanger took to the rocking chair his granddaughter had vacated.

Once the kitchen was cleaned, Zoe retrieved a small square of cigarette paper and a pencil from the drawer and sat back down at the table. Armand took a seat beside her.

Her pulse accelerated and she wet her lips. "I'm ready," she said, pencil poised.

"Five cars carrying troops," he began.

Zoe knew the code well; there were usually forty men to a car. *Two hundred cigarettes*, she wrote on the thin piece of paper.

"Three cars carrying horses."

Each car carried eight horses. Zoe wrote, *Twenty-four cans of chicory*.

"Fifteen mitrailleuse," Armand continued, and she scribbled the number of artillery guns. *Fifteen kilograms of flour.*

"Ten cars loaded with supplies," he said.

Ten kilograms of beans.

"The train was headed south."

Six o'clock. *Six sacks of potatoes*, she noted. Zoe had come up with that part of the code herself—giving direction in sacks of potatoes and correlating it with the hands of a clock.

"Take it with you in the morning," Armand said, rising from the table.

Zoe eyed him with apprehension. "More troops returning from the East every week," she said. "I wonder what it means."

Armand shook his head, his features grim. "All I know is the Boche have a plan and it probably isn't good for us."

Anxious thoughts about the boys returned as she folded the cigarette paper into a tiny wedge no bigger than a piece of straw. Leaving her chair, she grabbed the broom from a corner of the kitchen and twisted off the top section of the handle. The wood beneath had been hollowed out. She stuffed the tissue paper note inside before replacing the top.

Employed as a maid at Anor's only inn, L'Hotel Fosse, she would exchange the broom for another when she arrived to work in the morning. Their letterbox, the inn's proprietor, Monsieur Sylvan Fosse, would pass along the information in the broom to their team leader in Hirson, who would then get it into British hands.

For the past few months she, Armand, and the others had been working for the underground intelligence network La Dame Blanche. Recruited by Monsieur Fosse, they, like many other townspeople, wished to aid the Allies against Germany by train watching.

Today Armand had disguised his surveillance of the troop trains by collecting bricks from the silo next to the station. Since he would have to work in Trélon the following day, the boys would pretend to play near the tracks, keeping watch for Boche trains and the number of cars carrying men, horses, and weaponry.

From Anor, the direction of the trains was either south to Hirson or north toward Trélon and points beyond. Even the Boulangers took their turn watching trains and reporting the German troop movements.

Zoe's job was to record the information using La Dame Blanche's "shopping list," which would later be decrypted by the British. With the recent increase in troop activity, the Allies would need the information as soon as possible. "I'll go early tomorrow," she promised, replacing the broom.

They moved into the parlor and sat down on the worn divan near the fire. While she and Armand sat together and watched the flames, the two boys resumed their fencing.

Zoe turned at her brother's laughter. Nikki had thrust his stick knife toward Michel, his blue gaze narrowed, the freckled features intent.

He looked so eager, she thought, and time was passing much too quickly. Her muscles tightened as she turned back to the fire. The past three years had been a struggle, but she'd found a measure of peace in this new life.

If only her restless brother could do the same.

CHAPTER 19

old still," Eve said, "and I won't cut your throat."

Seated in a high-backed chair, Simon gazed up at her, his face lathered in shaving cream. "If you do, you'll just have to stitch me up again," he said.

A ghost of a smile touched her lips. He ached to kiss her. She'd visited him tonight using the tunnel from the laundry shop, and brought with her a bag filled with apples, a cabbage, more of the black war bread, cheese, and three tins of meat. She'd also confiscated for him a set of clean clothes, including his own boots, which she'd salvaged, and a shaving kit.

Already two weeks had passed since that night, but during his brief time at the rectory he'd made great strides, literally, using the crutches the priest had provided. He could amble across the threshold of his tiny room into Father Francois's chamber and take advantage of the brazier, as the weather had turned to a permanent chill.

"Shall we keep the moustache?" she asked, razor poised in her hand.

"What do you recommend?" He'd let her make the decision. Unwillingly, his thoughts returned to the Hun major and the thick brush above his upper lip. Had Eve developed a liking for the look?

"I say we take it off."

His muscles eased as she added lather to the area beneath his nose. His wife then began whisking away his stubble with the razor, and his skin tingled where she touched him.

"I've always thought you more handsome without one," she said.

He gazed at her, warmed by the unexpected compliment. She seemed equally surprised at her words, and an irresistible blush colored her cheeks.

He would have laughed if not for the fear of getting nicked by the blade.

"You're walking nicely with the crutches. How's your heel?"

Her prim voice made him smile. "I still canna put my full weight on the foot, but each day it gets better."

"I noticed the swelling at your ribs has gone down and the bruises are fading. Do you still have pain?"

He looked up to see concern in her gaze. She was so close he was tempted to reach for her.

"Not too much," he said easily. The razor beneath his nose wasn't the only thing keeping him still. He enjoyed the fragile bond they'd established and didn't want to press her.

She'd been coming to visit him nearly every day, bringing food, checking his wounds, and informing him of the latest German propaganda being spread around the city. During their visits he was careful to avoid talking about her leaving Brussels with him or questioning the work she and the others were doing "for the good of Belgium." Simon wanted to find common ground with her and not friction, if they were to have a chance at reclaiming the years the war had stolen from their marriage.

"I'm glad you're feeling better," she said, going back to her task. "In another week you shouldn't feel discomfort at all. A few weeks more and your ribs will have healed completely."

And hopefully by then I'll have found a way to get us out of here, he thought.

"Done," she said minutes later, wiping his face with a warm, moist towel.

"Do I pass inspection?"

She leaned back to survey her work. "I think it's quite an improvement. Most of your bruises are gone, and your cuts are healed. You've even got hair growing back where I removed your stitches."

"Is that a yes then, lass?"

She met his gaze. "Aye," she said, her eyes sparkling.

Simon grinned, his heart pounding with pleasure. Though she was still somewhat reserved, his wife was beginning to relax with him. "So what's the Hun propaganda today?" he asked, hoping to continue one of the safer topics of their conversations.

He regretted the question as the amusement in her eyes fled.

"No propaganda today." Her mouth tightened as she wiped the razor clean. "They're too busy ransacking homes again. It isn't enough they've stripped the city countless times already. Dishes, cutlery, rubber, leather, glass, it all gets sent back to Germany to use in making their war machines."

Her frown deepened as she sat on the bench across from him. "They're confiscating more dogs for the Front, too. The Boche prize Belgian shepherds, and they took most of those early in the war. Now they're going after just about any mongrel."

Simon had learned from Marcus that even Britain was training animals to be used in war. Dogs were useful for delivering messages on the battlefield or for carrying first-aid kits to the wounded. Some could even detect poisonous gas and alert the soldiers in the trenches.

"Have the Huns ever ransacked your aunt and uncle's home?" he asked.

"Once, after we first arrived in Brussels, but thankfully not since then." She grimaced. "Perhaps because they eat at my uncle's café and worry he'll poison them."

Or because of the Iron Cross you wear and the Hun major's undying gratitude, Simon thought, though he held his silence.

It struck him that she might have a pet she was worried about. "Do you have a dog?"

"No, and I'm glad of it," she said with a hint of defiance. "Otherwise the Boche would have to lock me up for refusing them."

Simon remembered her sixteenth birthday party and the kitten that had drawn blood. "And what would you do with Button?" he teased, hoping to lighten her mood.

Her eyes widened, and a faint smile touched her lips. "I would make certain he climbed the tallest tree and stayed out of harm's way."

"Have you been climbing any trees lately?" he asked. He was rewarded when her smile broadened.

"I had my fill of tree climbing the night you kept me from falling on my head."

"And then I bandaged your wound." He smiled and cast a rueful glance at his injured foot. "Little did I know, the next time it would be you bandaging me."

"I still have it, you know. Your handkerchief." Her voice was soft, and another blush lit her cheeks as she reached for her coat and fished a wad of white cloth from the pocket.

She shook it out and held it up to him.

Seeing the initials *SF* on the aged linen, Simon's chest tightened with emotion. "You've kept it all this time."

She nodded. "I hid it away in a safe place, in case our apartment got ransacked. But after you arrived, I . . ." She looked at him, clutching the handkerchief to her breast. "I wanted to keep it with me. It brings back wonderful memories."

"We have those, lass." He spoke softly, despite his pounding heart. "Flying the skies together, crossing an entire country just to have a bonny wedding in Scotland."

Her face took on a wistful expression. "It was lovely."

"And a fine Burns Night supper," he added with a wink.

Her soft laughter was like balm to his wounded soul. "I admit, even the thought of eating haggis sounds delicious," she said. "Especially after years of war bread and potato soup." Her gaze took on a faraway look. "You know what I miss most?"

His breath wavered. "Tell me, lass," he said in a low voice.

She looked at him with an impish smile. "Strawberry biscuits and a nice cup of Darjeeling."

He let out a surprised laugh, having hoped for a different answer. Still, her mood pleased him. "You remember McCrory's Tea Shop?"

"Oh yes, the best raspberry jam in London. And what about Swan's on the West End? Earl Grey tea and the most delicious buttermilk scones I've ever tasted."

She closed her eyes, the dark lashes stark against her pale skin, and his heart leapt with the old joy. Memories filled him, of those mornings he'd watched her sleep, assuring himself she was his and real, thanking God for the gift of her love.

Her eyes opened then, and a blush stained her cheeks, as if she'd read his thoughts. "We should probably stop talking about such heavenly food." She glanced down at the foodstuffs she'd brought him. "This 'earthly fare' will taste all the worse. Though I shouldn't complain when so many in this city are starving."

"Surely the café does a thriving business?"

"That's because my aunt and uncle prepare German fare for the soldiers and government staff. The Boche take a percentage of food from everyone, so Uncle Lucien receives enough to make up their menu . . ."

"And your family benefits as well." While he disliked the

Bernards' pandering to the enemy, Simon was relieved his wife and her mother received enough to eat. "Did the major arrange this?" he asked, his tone flat.

She hesitated. "Yes."

"And this food you brought is from the café?"

"No, I purchased it myself, on the black market." She raised her chin. "Any leftovers from the café, my aunt and I secretly pass on to the city's soup kitchens." Her gaze narrowed on him. "The arrangement may not meet your standards, Simon, but the café is in a position to help many who might otherwise go hungry."

"I do understand," he said. "I'm glad your family is taken care of." He was eager to change the subject. "Know what I miss most?"

Her expression eased and she shook her head.

"Sipping a good cup of coffee while reading my morning edition of the *Times*."

Her smile returned, lifting his spirits. "The *Times* is considered contraband here in Belgium, but I might locate an old copy somewhere," she said. "As for the coffee, it's poor fare these days, but I'll see if my uncle has any stashed away at the café." She checked her watch and sighed. "Which reminds me, I need to go. My aunt is probably wondering about the linen, and Monsieur Tulle will close his shop in a few minutes."

"When will you be back?" Already he missed her company, and he was getting restless cooped up inside the rectory. He'd read most of the books in Father Francois's small library and played cards with the priest several times. Simon planned to explore the tunnels once he was steady on his feet, but until then there wasn't much else to do.

His wife sensed his mood. "I'll come back tomorrow night, once I close up the café. I can stay a bit longer then. Shall I bring anything?"

"Not unless you've found a way to get me my documents."

While the plane crash precluded Simon meeting his contact, he'd decided to inspect the secret orders for himself before he destroyed them. They might offer some clue to finding the enemy agent in La Dame Blanche.

"I told you before, it's too dangerous." Her expression had turned guarded. "Not only are the secret police everywhere, but for the price of a loaf of bread some hungry Belgian will spy on his own mother, or anyone on the vampires' watch list, and report back."

"Are you on a watch list?" he demanded, realizing she took great risks simply in coming to see him.

Her features paled. "I don't know, but the possibility is reason enough for why I cannot bring them to you."

"No, of course not. I would never put your life in danger, lass," he said. Still, Simon was vexed. He wanted those orders. Whom could they trust? He thought of the priest. "What about Father Francois? Could he bring them here?"

"I don't think it's a good idea," she said slowly.

"Why not? Marcus told me he was reliable."

She sat back down on the bench. "So it was Marcus Weatherford who sent you to Brussels?"

"I volunteered for the mission, because of you," he said. "Once he'd located you through Maddie, I was determined to come here and find you."

"That would explain your Belgian passport." She wore a pensive look, before her expression softened. "I am so glad to see you," she whispered. "I'm just sorry I can't . . ."

She turned away, and his heart dropped into his stomach. He knew what she'd been about to say. She couldn't come back with him, not if it meant leaving her mother behind.

He still wasn't ready to give up. Perhaps the three of them could exit Belgium to the east, through Luxembourg, or south into France? Father Francois had said he was from Rouen, a city still in Allied hands. Simon would speak with him. He would try to learn what he could about the enemy agent and his mark.

The priest had been tight-lipped before, when Simon asked about La Dame Blanche. Simon gazed at his wife. If she was involved in the underground, Eve might know someone who could put him on the right path.

"Have you heard of a network called La Dame Blanche?" he asked.

She turned to him, and Simon caught the flash of grief and surprise in her pallid features. "I haven't heard the phrase in a long time, but I'm well aware of the White Lady," she whispered. "There are many such underground resistance groups in Belgium. Why do you ask?"

He deliberated over how much to say. "I'd like to . . . make contact."

"And you think I can help?"

"Can you?" he challenged.

Instead of answering, she rose from the bench. "I'm sorry, I have to leave now."

She started past him when he grabbed for her hand. Simon held her as their gazes locked, and he could tell by her expression she was waging some inner battle.

Finally she said, "I can try to make some inquiries." Her voice was tight. "Who is it you wish to contact?"

He stared at her, already regretting his request. His wife was clever, without a doubt, and he suspected her work for the Belgians held some risk, but the agent Marcus had sent him to investigate, this Pi, was extremely dangerous. Whether or not Eve knew someone in La Dame Blanche, he couldn't tell her about the traitor. If she started asking the wrong people questions she could end up dead.

He released her hand and leaned back. "So you'll return tomorrow?" Two could play her game of avoiding questions.

Her eyes widened slightly in surprise . . . or was it relief?

"Yes," she said. "Tomorrow night."

She leaned to brush her fingers against his smooth cheek, then turned and slipped behind the panel.

He sat in his chair, bemused at what had just occurred, and reassessed his situation.

It seemed he'd have to wait to ask questions about Pi once he left the rectory. As Albert Janssen, and with a sufficient disguise, he could move around and do some investigating on his own.

Simon gazed at the bench, toward the pile of clothes his wife had brought him. For a start he could quit his sweat-soaked hospital gown and dress like a man again.

He ran a hand over his hair, now stiff with sweat and blood. He could use a bit of cleaning up, and with more than the meager sponge baths he'd had over the past two weeks. Most importantly, he had to continue building back his strength.

Taking the crutches, he rose and went to the panel opening where the brazier burned warm in the other room. The priest hadn't yet returned from the church. Simon made his way across the threshold and began walking back and forth across the spacious room, putting as much weight on his injured heel as he could tolerate.

Once he was healed, he would see about finding Pi himself. He could show the traitor's mark to the priest, and he might then agree to help. Simon would also discuss with him the other options he'd considered for getting Eve and her mother out.

"I'm sending you to Charleroi."

Eve turned from gathering up clean bandages at the nurses' station to stare at Nurse Hoffmeyer.

"The hospital there needs an extra nurse," the matron continued in a matter-of-fact tone, notebook tucked beneath one arm as usual. "They've received an unexpected wave of casualties."

"But we have casualties." Eve looked around. While the beds in the spacious ward weren't yet filled, two trains with wounded from the Front had arrived in the past week.

"You will leave in the morning." Matron's voice brooked no argument. "They've also requested bandages and morphine, which we can spare. An orderly will take a supply truck and you will accompany him."

Eve hid her agitation as she reached for a bottle of antiseptic solution. She couldn't leave Simon for an extended period of time. "How long will I be gone?"

"Until their new nurses arrive from Berlin," the matron said. "The administrator expects them by Friday."

Eve frowned. What if they didn't arrive? A few days might not be a problem; after Simon's questions to her last night she wasn't eager to resume the discussion any time soon. She knew the White Lady and her legacy only too well; hearing the phrase on Simon's lips had jarred her.

She was keen to know whom he wished to contact in the network, but when he'd suddenly dodged her question she was afraid to pursue it. If he realized her involvement in La Dame Blanche he would never leave Brussels. For his own safety and hers, he must go.

Still, she couldn't be away from Simon for too long before his departure.

"Why must I go, Matron?" Eve gazed out at several of the kerchief-clad nurses attending patients. "We've plenty who are qualified to do the work and would love an opportunity to leave the city."

"Why *not* you, Sister Marche?" Matron's tone was sharp. With her pointed chin she indicated the rows of occupied beds. "With my changes in place, we are now running this ward efficiently. The patients are happy and well cared for. Your being here isn't necessary." Her dark eyes gleamed. "In Charleroi they have many wounded who need immediate care. They are certain to appreciate my sending a nurse with your vast experience."

Eve studied the imperious woman. Matron's anticipation was more than obvious. Aside from the fact that the ward was running much the same as it had when Eve had been acting matron, Nurse Hoffmeyer no doubt relished getting rid of her for several days—perhaps longer, if she had her way.

Surely this haughty woman wouldn't exert her influence with her brother-in-law to get Eve transferred permanently?

A knot formed in her stomach. Simon depended on her, and so did her family. Eve also had a mission to complete. "Did Herr Major approve this?"

"I am in charge of the nurses here; I do not need anyone's approval." Matron's flattened features hardened. "If you wish to continue serving the Red Cross at this hospital, Sister Marche, you will do as you're instructed."

Eve fought to control her temper. "Very well," she bit out. "Will there be anything else?"

"Herr Doktor is waiting for you in the operating theater. See that you go right away."

Which meant no stopping at Otto's office first. Eve turned so Matron wouldn't see her scowl and collected the rest of her supplies to assist Dr. Schlagel in removing Corporal Ziegler's leg cast.

Afterward she stopped by Otto's office, relieved to find he hadn't yet left for the day.

"Sister, come in." He looked up from his desk and smiled. Then as if sensing her mood, he rose from his chair. "Is there a problem?"

"I've been ordered to leave for Charleroi in the morning."

His eyes widened in alarm. "What?"

"Apparently the hospital there needs an extra nurse. I do not wish to go."

"Why wasn't I told of this?"

She stared at him, her mouth flat.

"Never mind," he muttered. "I should have known. When are you coming back?"

"On Friday . . . I hope."

His expression eased. "Well, then, it's only for a few days. You had me worried."

She'd hoped for a different reaction. "We have so many patients here that need care."

Otto's smile faded. "*Ja*, and it's going to get worse." He grabbed a folder from the stack on his desk. "Troops will be returning from the East over the next week. The wounded will flood our hospitals, while many more are given leave before they embark for the Front. That means drinking and brawling. Likely half of them will end up needing medical care."

He frowned and shook the file at her. "To make matters worse, billeting for these soldiers will be necessary, and the hotels are already full."

More troops arriving from the East? Eve stared at the stack of files on his desk. Rotterdam would certainly be interested in the information. She decided to return to Otto's office once he left for the day.

She was disheartened to learn that housing would again be at a premium. Wolfe and Kraus had left for the Front the previous week, and their room had not yet been reassigned. Eve and her family were enjoying the privacy they hadn't experienced in a long while, the freedom to simply live without the worry of being watched in their own home.

It seemed that freedom was about to end.

"If Matron had checked with me first," Otto was saying,

annoyance in his tone, "she would know we cannot spare any personnel right now."

"You could speak with her about keeping me here," Eve suggested.

He blanched. "As much as I would wish to, Sister . . . Eve, if you've already been promised to Charleroi I can hardly rescind the order." He offered a weak smile. "We'll just have to manage until your return."

Coward, Eve thought.

"While you're there," he said, tossing down the file before reaching into his desk drawer for a cigar, "I trust you'll keep an ear out for any useful information?"

Intelligence for his government friend. Eve stifled her irritation. "I'll do my best, Herr Major."

"*Gut.*" He nipped off the end of his cigar but didn't light it. Instead he gazed at her a long while, a sudden flush to his cheeks. Finally he removed from his tunic pocket a pair of tickets she recognized from Brussels's Théâtre de la Monnaie.

"I'd purchased these for Frau Reinhardt and myself," he said. "But she is not able to make the journey from Berlin after all. Saturday evening is the premier for the operetta *Schwarzwaldmädel*. If you are back in Brussels by that time, would you consider accompanying me? It would be a shame to let these tickets go to waste."

Eve blinked, too startled to speak. He was inviting her to the opera?

She didn't know whether to believe his story or not, but the theater catered to Boche officers, and occasionally members of the German High Command. It would be a diamond mine of intelligence, especially the pre-opera dinner, when colonels and generals enjoyed appetizing cuisine, fine aged cognac, and no doubt plenty of conversation about upcoming strategic plans against the Allies.

She was sorely tempted to go, but she had no innocent illusions where the major was concerned. "I . . . I don't know what to say."

"Say you'll go." He shifted, while heat suffused his face. At her continued silence, a frown formed beneath his moustache. "Well?"

"Thank you for the honor," she said. "I will consider your offer, though it will also depend upon my returning Friday . . ."

His face brightened. "Certainly, certainly," he said. "I will apprise Matron of the facts." He indicated the folders, then reached for a match and struck a light to his cigar.

"*Danke*, Herr Major," Eve said, relieved to have given him an incentive to get her back. But at what cost?

CHAPTER 20

Y ou're leaving Brussels?"

Eve heard the agitation in Simon's voice as she lit the last of several candles she'd brought from the café. "It's only for a few days, to help out at the hospital in Charleroi. I'll be back on Friday."

Warm light soon infused the small chamber. "Much better," she said and gazed toward her husband, seated on the bench. "I can see you now."

Noting his damp hair, she caught a whiff of soap and sage. "You had a bath?"

He smiled at her. "About time, don't you think?"

He was also wearing the clothes she'd brought him the night before.

"You're like a new man," she said, both surprised and heartened. "How did you manage?"

"The priest helped me with the hair washing." He raked his fingers through his curly damp locks. "I took care of the rest. I managed all right, and kept my bandage dry, but I was surely missing my nurse's tender care."

Eve's stomach fluttered at the devilish gleam in his eyes. He looked quite handsome. "Well, you smell very nice," she said softly.

She walked to the bench and began emptying her coat pockets of the tinned meat and vegetables she'd purchased from the black market. From an inside pocket she produced a small stoppered jug of hot cabbage soup. "It's not coffee, but it will warm you." She smiled. "And I admit it's left over from the *Kohlsuppe* Uncle Lucien prepared tonight."

She'd made an excuse to leave the café an hour before closing, and had entered the tunnel by way of the church. "You shouldn't starve while I'm gone, and there are enough ingredients so that Father Francois can make you both a decent stew."

Eve still worried about leaving him. She assessed him from head to toe, trying to reassure herself he would be all right. "Are you getting on with the crutches? How is your foot?"

His mouth lifted. "If I didn't know better, lass, I'd say you cared."

"You know I do," she insisted, despite his teasing.

His smile broadened. "Then I'll just have to show you."

Instead of reaching for the crutches leaning against the bench, he stood and began to pace slowly back and forth across the small space. Eve could discern only a subtle limp as he favored his injured heel.

"That's wonderful!"

"I thought so, too." He grinned, his pride in the accomplishment evident.

Her pulse quickened as she gazed at his beautiful smile and flashing white teeth, then at the strong jaw with its tiny cleft. His eyes were the color of rain, and they gleamed in the candlelight. A pang of sadness seized her. Soon he would be well enough to travel, to leave Brussels and return to Britain. Without her.

His smile faltered, as if he read her thoughts. He retraced his steps and stopped before her. Just two weeks ago he'd been lying in the hospital bed, bruised and broken, wearing bloodstained bandages. He seemed a much different man now.

"You'll be waltzing right out of here before long," she said in a throaty voice, but he didn't seem to be listening.

"You're so bonny to me, lass," he whispered, reaching to caress her cheek with the back of his hand.

She closed her eyes and leaned into his touch.

"Such skin, like Ayrshire cream," he murmured in his soft burr. "With eyes the color of heather. I used to dream about those eyes every night while I lay in my cell. And later, when I was confined for weeks and months after trying to escape, I imagined us together, like we were in those stolen weekends in Dover. We even had . . . conversations."

Eve opened her eyes to see his features had turned ruddy. "What did we talk about?"

His soft laugh was tinged with emotion. "I . . . I thought I was losing my wits," he said, his voice thick. "I was afraid I wouldna remember."

"Remember?"

"You." His eyes shone like the sea. "I didna want to forget one moment with you."

Her eyes burned and she reached for his hand, pressing it to her face. Again she imagined his fear and the pain of thinking the worst after Louvain. The years he'd spent grieving while he tried to hold on to his hope.

She knew his journey through the shadowed valley well enough; hers had been much the same—at least the grief, the emptiness of losing the one she loved. And as the months passed, in its place came the reassurance that he would never know of her sins or the pain they'd rendered. Until now . . .

Eve released his hand and took a step back. "You must be tired. Why don't you sit down?"

The light in his eyes faded, while her chest tightened with regret. Still, he moved to sit on the bench, the haggard lines in his face revealing his exhaustion after the effort.

A pitcher of water sat beside his bed. She went to pour him a cup.

"Do you love me, lass?"

She had her back to him, but his question made her stiffen, sloshing water from the glass. She turned to him. "You asked me that before, and I gave you my answer," she whispered. "I do love you."

"Then why do you keep pulling away from me?" His voice was quiet, while his gaze studied her. "What are you afraid of?"

Her laugh came out more like a sob. "So many things."

"Like what?" he said gently.

She stared at him while her heart ached. *I fear you'll come to despise me as much as I despise myself for coming to Belgium at the price of our baby. I'm terrified that once you know the truth, that your wife is a murderer, you'll never look at me again with those same loving eyes, that smile . . .*

Her vision blurred, and a hot tear tracked down her cheek.

He rose from the bench. "Sweetheart, you need to tell me what's wrong."

Still her courage failed her. "I'm afraid I'll never see my brother and sister again," she cried softly. "I'm afraid this ungodly war will never end." Then, with a tremulous breath, she managed an offering from the deepest part of her soul. "I'm afraid to have hope."

He watched her, his expression sad. Then he sighed and opened his arms. "Come here."

She hesitated a moment before rushing into his embrace. Her tears continued to fall as she laid her head against his shoulder.

He stroked her hair. "My love, you and I are living proof nothing is impossible for the Almighty. Look at us, here together. It's nothing short of a miracle."

But you must leave me. Eve knew the dangers at the border

crossing; they might never see one another again. Why would God give him back to her if it was only for a short time?

"I wish I had your faith." She raised her head to him, suddenly desperate in her desire to believe. "I wish I could trust in this miracle."

He tipped her chin. "Know what I wish for?"

She shook her head.

"Another taste of heaven." His smile was tender. "Kiss me, wife. While I still have the strength to stand up and hold you in my arms."

The love shining in his eyes crumbled the last of her resistance. She lifted her face and pressed her mouth to his, surrendering to the familiar touch and warmth of his lips. Her eyes drifted closed while he deepened the kiss, and she didn't think about the past and its pain, or the future with its uncertainty. Instead, Eve allowed herself to sink into sensation: the muscles shifting in her husband's arms as he held her, the solid warmth of his body next to hers. Breathing in the smell of fresh soap and sage and a scent she recognized as uniquely Simon.

The candles burning all around them might have been the sunlight surrounding them on their wedding day, and she vowed to remember the moment, so that later, when the danger and subterfuge of war resumed, she would have this memory with him to cherish.

"Ah, sweetheart, you feel so good in my arms," he said when their kiss ended. He continued to hold her, while his breath came in short gasps and she knew it must pain him.

"Come and lie down," she said, and helped him over to the bed.

Once she'd settled him and his breathing steadied, he gazed at her. "I could use more of that tender loving care."

He spoke in a low voice, and she smiled, while heat rose in her cheeks.

"I love that look on you. Stay with me tonight." He reached for her. "I want you here beside me, in my arms."

Eve took his hand in hers, her desire to remain warring with the need for caution. She also had work to finish for La Dame Blanche—decoding the information she'd taken from Otto's files. She would have to deliver it to Madame Bissette along with more of Mama's lace before leaving for Charleroi in the morning.

"I won't see you again for three days, maybe longer."

His gaze was so inviting, Eve couldn't help but surrender. "I'll stay until you fall asleep."

Lying down beside him, she was careful of his injuries. He grunted as he shifted onto his side, and a moment later his arm slid across her waist to pull her gently to him.

"We've the whole world to hope for, my love," he whispered, then kissed her lips. "This war won't last forever. When it's over, we'll find Nikki and Zoe together."

Eve gazed at him, her heart heavy at the reminder of what lay ahead. The war wouldn't end before she must seek out her brother and sister and then complete Simon's mission, without his knowledge.

Before that, he would leave her, without ever knowing the truth.

She nudged him onto his back, knowing he'd be more comfortable. Curling up beside him, she laid her head on his shoulder, careful of his ribs, before his arm moved to encircle her and draw her close.

"Sleep well, husband," she whispered, and pressed a kiss to his chin. Then she closed her eyes, fighting off a wave of despair. Yes, he must leave her, but for now they had these moments between them, the love they shared.

It would have to be enough.

Eve awoke with a start. A dim, flickering light met her gaze and she remembered where she was. She'd fallen asleep!

Simon still held her close, his heavy arm cradling her against him. His body was warm next to hers, his breathing soft and steady in sleep.

The fat candles were burned down to nubs. How long had she been there? Hours?

Carefully, so as not to awaken her husband, she removed his arm and slid off the mattress. Turning, she laid a hand gently against his chest, feeling his warmth, before she rose to her feet. Once she'd straightened her skirt, she patted the sides of her chignon.

She glanced at her watch. After midnight! She thought of the message she still had to prepare and almost groaned. There would be no more sleeping tonight.

She donned her coat and looked toward the open panel leading into the priest's chambers, mentally cursing her lapse.

Monsieur Tulle was long abed and the blanchisserie closed; since her bicycle was still inside the church, she had no option but to slip through Father Francois's room and enter the tunnel through his closet. She would make her way back into the church and let herself out.

With a last look at her sleeping husband, Eve turned and tiptoed into the priest's room. Silence met her ears but for the hiss of the precious coal burning in the brazier. She glanced toward the bed at the far end of the room and vaguely made out a shape beneath the covers.

With the utmost quiet she moved to the closet and opened the door with painstaking care. She was about to step inside when the priest's familiar voice stopped her.

"I think, Sister Marche, there is more between you and your patient than you would have me believe."

CHAPTER 21

*H*ow is our patient doing?"

Eve glanced at Dom as he steered the lorry south beyond Brussels toward Charleroi the following morning. "Captain Chandler is improving daily," she said. "In another week, perhaps two, he'll be well enough to make the journey into Holland."

"Does he remember why he and the pilot were flying over Brussels that night?"

"His memory is still a problem." She reminded herself the lie was for Dom's own good.

"Who's taking care of him?"

"Someone trustworthy."

"Why the secrecy?" he demanded. "You continue to keep me in the dark. I thought we were friends, comrades for the same cause."

She caught his wounded look. "We are both," she said, trying to reassure him. "You were there when I needed a friend most, and we've worked together faithfully ever since. It's because of that friendship I will not tell you. As I said before, the less you know, the safer it is for you, and for Captain Chandler."

Seeing his grim profile, she added, "Please, Dom, for now you must trust me. Soon enough I'll need your help getting the captain safely across the border."

His features relaxed. "Well, since you put it like that, *chérie*, how can I stay angry with you?" He turned and smiled. "I will be ready when you need me."

"I'm counting on it." She eased back against the seat as they neared the next checkpoint. Already they'd stopped at two guard stations, showing their passes and Red Cross credentials. Charleroi was only about fifty kilometers from Brussels, but with all of the stops in between, the city seemed leagues away. "At this rate, we may reach the hospital sometime next week," she grumbled, handing Dom her pass for the guard.

The sentry ignored them as he inspected their paperwork, then returned it before waving them through.

"It does get ridiculous," he said as they resumed their journey. "Maybe they think we'll disappear in a puff of smoke between here and Charleroi, eh?" He shook his fist. "With the entire country surrounded by fences and German troops, how could we possibly get out?"

"We must think of a way soon, Dom."

"Yes, I know. The captain."

"No, I'm talking about myself. I need to get out."

"What?" He jerked his head around, eyes wide. "You are leaving?"

She nodded. "Once we get the captain into Holland, I need to go to France."

"What?" he repeated. "Why?"

"I have an important errand," she said. "My brother and sister are there."

While she hadn't given Dom all of the details about Louvain, he was aware of how she'd lost her siblings. Now she relayed to him her recent conversation with Corporal Duval.

"*Fantastique!*" Dom glanced at her. "You and your family must be so happy."

"I've told no one else, Dom, at least not yet." She thought of Mama. "I don't want to raise my mother's hopes in case I cannot find the children. I'd much rather surprise her by bringing them back to Brussels."

"That makes sense," he agreed. "But if your brother and sister are in France and you can get through, how do you plan to bring them back?"

She sighed. "I don't know. I'm hoping you can help."

"We'll think of something," he said. "Where is this town, Anor? I have not heard of it."

"It's in the north of France, just beyond our border. Chimay is one of the closest Belgian towns."

"That's good," he said. "You won't have to go too far into occupied France." He turned to her. "The situation there is no better than here, and in some places worse."

"That's what Corporal Duval said." Shifting against the seat, Eve glanced out the window. She was excited at the prospect of finding Nikki and Zoe, but she worried about them, too. Were they well? Did they have enough food? Would she be able to find them easily enough?

How *would* she manage to get them back into Brussels?

The questions continued to occupy her thoughts as the ambulance wove along the country roads toward Charleroi. The land before them stretched out flat and green beneath heavy skies, with farms, watermills, and the occasional orange-and-yellow stand of fall beech and maple. The rain fell steadily, adding to the small ponds rimmed in marsh grass, where black coots swam placidly and a blue flutter of wings signaled a kingfisher taking flight.

Stone turrets of distant castles could be seen in the low hills, and as they neared the checkpoint at the town of Waterloo, Eve gazed toward the wonder of Butte du Lion. The conical green mound rose like a pyramid against the horizon, the lion statue at the top commemorating the famous battle with Napoleon a century before.

Eventually the fallow fields gave way to more populated areas. Cobbled streets and villages grew into the concrete buildings, roads, and factories of Charleroi.

Dom pulled up alongside the hospital's brick façade, and Eve noticed several ambulances parked out front. Uniformed soldiers and orderlies were off-loading stretchers with wounded and taking them inside the building.

Once he'd parked the truck, she leapt out and went to the nearest ambulance. "Can I help?" she called inside. "We've come from Brussels—"

"Eve Marche! Is that you?" The voice called from the shadowy recesses of the ambulance, and a nurse appeared at the back of the truck. "I never expected to see you here!"

Eve gaped, then cried, "Maddie Arthur!"

Maddie climbed over the tailgate and Eve rushed to hug her friend. "How . . . why . . . what are you doing here?" she stammered when they stepped back to gaze at one another.

Maddie's green eyes glistened. "I could ask you the same thing," she said. "A few weeks ago the Red Cross sent word to me from London, asking about you. I wondered if you had somehow managed to get home by now."

"Hardly," Eve said with a rueful smile. "The hospital in Brussels where I work sent me here on temporary assignment."

"How is your family?" Maddie asked.

Eve hesitated. "I've much to tell you . . . later."

Dom had approached, eyeing them both with curiosity. "Eve? Are you going to introduce me to your friend?"

The two women shared an amused look. Eve said, "Dominic Lesser, may I introduce my dearest friend in the world, Miss Madeleine Arthur."

Clearly intrigued, he offered a bow and extended a hand to Maddie. "My pleasure, mademoiselle."

"Please, call me Maddie. I'm delighted to meet you, Monsieur Lesser."

He grinned. "Dom is perfect."

Maddie cast another smile at Eve, then stepped back and said, "I have a few wounded here who need to get inside."

Dom wasted no time. Dropping the tailgate, he and another orderly began lifting the stretchers of men and taking them into the hospital.

"He's a big brute of a fellow," Maddie said as her gaze followed Dom toward the building.

"With an even bigger heart." Eve smiled. "And I think he's quite taken with you."

Again she assessed her friend. "You haven't changed, though you seem a bit thinner than the last time I saw you. How have you been?"

"Busy." Maddie led the way to the front of the ambulance and retrieved a satchel and her traveling valise from the cab. "I've been working at casualty clearing stations throughout northern France. Yesterday there was an attempted breakout at the POW camp in Jeumont, just across the border. French snipers attacked the German guard. Before long we had more wounded then we could care for. Charleroi was the closest facility." She sighed. "So here I am."

"And very glad we are." Dom had approached with the other orderly to collect another stretcher.

"I'll grab up the supplies we brought with us," Eve said to him.

A few minutes later she joined Maddie and Dom inside, where they began several hours of intense work in caring for the heavy influx of patients. The ambulances had started arriving the day before, when Nurse Hoffmeyer had received the call, but they continued to appear with more casualties throughout the day. Because it involved the POW prison camp, there were British, French, Australian, Belgian, and German soldiers among the wounded.

"That must have been some attack," Dom said once the three were able to take a break.

Maddie took a sip of the watered-down chicory brew and wrinkled her nose. "I think this is the worst part of being in the war," she said. "I miss having a nice cup of English tea in the afternoons."

"As do I," Eve said, her thoughts returning to those happier times in London.

Maddie's eyes sparkled. "So it's a very good thing I carry a survival kit." She produced a small tin from her nurse's apron.

Eve gasped. "Is that . . . real tea?"

"It is." Maddie beamed. "And I'm happy to share." She turned to Dom. "Would you like a cup as well?"

"I'm a coffee man, but in this case . . ." He glared into the murky contents of his cup. "I'll change sides."

Maddie put a kettle on the brazier. "So how long have you two known each another?"

"Over two years," Eve said, smiling at Dom. "We started working together at the hospital in Brussels." She eyed her friend. "Did you leave Britain to come back and work for the Red Cross in France?"

Maddie nodded. "After leaving Brussels three years ago, I returned to work as a nurse at the London Hospital, but I didn't stay long. We were receiving constant reports of heavy casualties overseas, so I rejoined the Red Cross and sailed to France. I spent two years working at hospitals in Abbeville, Étaples, and Marseilles."

She dumped the contents of their cups and poured the hot tea. Silence fell as the three inhaled the delicious, lemony fragrance of Earl Grey.

"Eventually I decided to get closer to the action," Maddie said. "I took up working in casualty clearing stations, and I've been near the front lines ever since. I was posted to a station just south of Jeumont when the attack broke out."

"That's very brave of you." For Eve, being a British nurse in German-occupied Brussels had its own set of hazards, but working as a nurse near the fighting . . . "I imagine, where you are, the mortar fire and poison gas are real threats?"

"Yes, and constant." A shadow flitted across her friend's pretty features. "Still, it's what I feel called to do." She settled back in her seat, hands cradling the cup of steaming tea. "It is good to see you again, Eve. It's been so long." Maddie's smile was warm. To Dom she said, "Your accent is lovely. What part of France?"

"Paris," he said quickly. "The City of Lights. Have you been there?"

Maddie sighed. "Yes, and I thought it beautiful. I'd like to return after the war. There is much to see."

"*Oui*," Dom agreed. "Perhaps one day I can show you my city."

Eve sipped her tea, enjoying their flirtatious banter. Longing pierced her as she realized how much she missed her husband, and she thought back to the poignancy of their time together last night—the candlelight kiss, then lying beside him as he talked of their future.

Would they have a future? She wanted to believe Simon was right, that the war would eventually come to an end and they could pick up the threads of their marriage.

But she also knew they would never have a true union unless they were honest with each other.

She took a long sip of the hot tea, letting it burn her tongue. Their time together was running out; the day would come when she must tell her husband everything about Louvain. About La

Dame Blanche. Simon needed to understand why he deserved better than half a wife, and why she must remain in Brussels: not only to protect her family, including her brother and sister, but to continue doing her part to save as many Belgian souls as possible.

Then perhaps, in the end, she could save her own.

CHAPTER 22

Simon stood, his right side leaning against one of the crutches. Cold and miserable, despite the brazier burning in the adjoining room, he stared at the dull stone walls enclosing his small sanctuary and missed his wife.

She'd left him only that morning, and he couldn't help being concerned. With the Huns everywhere, what if something happened to her?

A smile touched his lips at the irony. They'd been separated by three years and untold horrors, and she'd managed admirably without him. Still, having found her again, he was entitled to resume his role as her protector, regardless of his injuries. It was a husband's honor to be able to care for his wife's well-being, and his pleasure to hold her in his arms . . .

The memory of last night was still fresh in his mind. Once more Eve's passion had burned in their kiss. And afterward, as she lay beside him, touching her familiar softness while the scent of her rose water filled his senses, it had felt so right. Like his dreams during his years of incarceration.

He was glad he'd opened up to her. Simon could tell he'd broken through some of her barriers, though there was more behind the pain in those violet eyes. He could only hope that with time she would decide to confide in him.

"*Bonsoir*, Captain." The priest ducked his head and entered the small room carrying Simon's food tray. "I am glad to see you are putting weight on the foot."

"Have you heard from Sister Marche?"

"Ah, missing her already?" The priest's eyes twinkled as he set the tray on the bench. "She's been gone less than a day."

Simon glanced at the floor. "I just want to know if she arrived safely in Charleroi."

"I am certain she's fine. Now eat, I've warmed the soup on the brazier."

Father Francois set out a bowl and filled it from the pottery jug Eve had brought the night before. The smell of cabbage and spices permeated the room.

"If it will bring you ease, my son, I'll send someone to the hospital and inquire."

"Thank you." Simon hesitated, then said, "I suspect Sister Marche is more active in her fight for 'the good of Belgium' than what you and I discussed." He frowned. "I don't want anything to happen to her."

The priest straightened, his wise brown eyes no longer teasing. "She told me," he said. "It must be difficult . . . your wife taking such risks."

Simon stared at the priest. "You know who I am?"

Father Francois held up a hand. "Only that you are her husband," he said. "And I did not give her a choice. I returned from the church to find the two of you, eh . . ." He paused. "More intimate than nurse and patient."

"Nothing happened, man," Simon muttered, torn between laughter and resentment. "I can barely manage to walk without the use of this crutch."

"*Oui*, I understand!" Twin spots of pink appeared on the priest's rounded cheeks. "But while she is your wife, Eve is still a member of my flock. I would not let her leave until she explained." He touched his heart. "But your secret, Captain, it is safe in here."

His expression sobered, and sadness was reflected in the dark eyes. "You have both been through much," he said. "I pray that one day, after the Boche are defeated, you and Eve can resume your lives together."

"Better to pray I get her out of Belgium before then," Simon groused. Suddenly he was tired. He dropped into the ladder-backed chair in his room. "She won't leave her mother behind, not that I blame her. This place is a prison."

"Truly," the priest said. "And I know of no way to get out of Belgium other than what I have already suggested."

"What about going east to Luxembourg?" Simon asked. "Or taking them to the south of France?"

The priest shook his head. "The risk is greater in Luxembourg, where the Boche are thick. Reaching the south of France from here is impossible, too. Louise Marche would never survive such an arduous journey."

Simon propped his hands against his knees. "Eve wants me to go, but I canna leave without her. I'll risk the danger to stay and protect her."

"I don't think you understand." The priest's tone hardened. "If you remain, you put *her* in grave danger, along with the others who helped you to escape. The Boche have witnessed your death. You cannot come back to life."

Simon swiveled his head toward the priest, his mouth tight. Of course he couldn't stay. In truth, his heart had known this for some time, but his pride refused to consider the reality of his situation. Even disguised, his injuries would impede him, increasing his risk of being identified. Nothing must happen to Eve or to the others who had risked their lives to save him.

That didn't mean he had to like it. "Blasted Huns!" he ground out, infuriated at his own helplessness.

Father Francois eyed him with compassion. "I'm sorry. I wish I had an answer for you."

Simon grunted. Maybe when he returned to Britain he could come back with a plane. Land near the Sonian Forest, where he was supposed to have dropped before the crash. He could fly Eve and her mother out of Belgium.

His pulse quickened. The days were moving swiftly. Soon he'd be well enough to travel into Holland, and while he loathed leaving his wife, he *would* come back for her. And if he failed . . .

She would have to remain here in Brussels to wait out the war. How long would that be? Both sides were running out of men and the will to fight. Like the priest, Simon could only pray the end would come soon.

"She plans to go after her brother and sister," he said.

Father Francois's eyes widened. "In Germany?"

"Eve has learned that they are in northern France. They escaped the train."

"*Dieu merci!*" The priest's expression held wonder as he took a seat on the bench. "Did she say where?"

Simon shook his head. "She told me she planned to consult you for help." He stared hard at the priest. "You must make certain she stays here in Brussels, where it's safe—safer, at least, than going into occupied France."

"Eve knows her own mind," Father Francois said slowly.

"I've been told to trust you." Simon's tone turned fierce. "I want your word."

The priest tilted his head, the brown gaze steady. "I promise to do my best to look out for her."

It was all he could really expect from the man. Simon took little comfort, however, especially with an enemy agent loose in Brussels. He didn't yet understand the depth of Eve's involvement in the Belgian underground, but the possibility she could cross paths with Pi—or perhaps already had—sent a chill down his spine.

"Do you know what the symbol for Pi looks like?" he asked, in a desperate bid to salvage his mission and protect his wife.

The priest eyed him curiously and nodded.

"Have you seen the mark anywhere in Brussels, or perhaps somewhere else?" Simon leaned forward. "A piece of correspondence, anything?"

"I'm sorry, *non*." His salt-and-pepper brows drew together. "It's important?"

"Aye." Simon leaned back against the chair while his hopes plummeted.

Marcus's instructions had been clear. If anything went wrong, he was to abandon the mission and destroy the secret orders. Simon had wanted to see them for himself first, but if Eve couldn't risk delivering the documents, he'd have to ask her to burn them. Someone else would be sent to pick up where he'd left off, and hopefully would have more success.

His thoughts returned to the idea of flying a plane into Belgium, or even to an air base in France, and making his way to her. But then he thought of what he must do first: cross the border with its electric wire fences, armed guards, and dogs.

Simon grimaced. He would need to stay alive long enough to come back.

CHAPTER 23

I will return for you on Friday," Dom said, drawing the ambulance to the curb of the local hotel where Eve and Maddie would billet during their stay in Charleroi.

"I hope so," Eve said. "As much as I will enjoy spending time with Maddie, please don't let Matron keep me here indefinitely."

"I'll do what I can."

After the two women exited the truck, Dom leaned his head out and smiled at Eve's friend. "I hope we get an opportunity to meet again, *chérie*," he said with a wink.

"He is a bit full of himself, isn't he?" Maddie said, grinning as he drove off.

Eve smiled. "He's French. What do you think?"

Later that night, after they had secured a room at the hotel and eaten a simple meal of potato soup and black bread, the two women returned to their room and readied for sleep.

"All right, now we're alone and I want to know everything." Maddie sat on the bed across from Eve's. "How is your family? When I returned to Britain years ago, we heard about the awful things that happened in Louvain. I was so relieved to receive your letter, but you didn't say much. What have you been doing in Brussels for three years?"

Eve had turned back the covers of her own bed and sat facing her friend. Her one and only letter to Maddie years before had been vague and brief, a precaution in case the note fell into enemy hands. "This might take a while."

"I've got nothing but time." She leaned forward with interest. "So tell me."

Eve began her narrative, recounting what had happened in Louvain, while omitting her own ordeal. Then she told Maddie about saving Otto's life and coming to Brussels.

"Dear Lord!" Maddie's features held compassion and awe. "I cannot even imagine what you must have gone through. And your poor brother and sister . . ." She rose and moved to sit beside Eve, taking her hand. "I wish I had been here for you."

"Me too." Eve said, leaning against her. She thought of the months she'd longed for her friend's comfort. "Though Mama and I have managed to survive." She hesitated, then said, "There's more. Simon is alive."

Maddie gasped, and Eve told her friend about the plane crash in Brussels Park and Simon's admittance into the hospital.

"That would explain why London came looking for me." Maddie still looked dazed. "So whose body did the RFC spot near the crash site over Liege?"

Eve shook her head. "I only know that it wasn't my husband's."

Maddie reached over to hug her. "I'm so happy for you, that he's alive and you're back together again. Is Simon still in the hospital?"

"Not exactly." Then Eve quickly sketched for her his escape, adding, "He's safely hidden away at the moment."

"Good heavens, Eve Marche, talk about being brave. You win hands down." Maddie shook her head. "I remember hearing the stories about Nurse Cavell, but still, I'd never have the nerve to pull off something like that."

"I was terrified," Eve confessed. "I couldn't bear the thought of what might happen to Simon if I failed."

"With such frightful odds, it was nothing short of a miracle."

"Yes, I suppose it was."

Simon had said much the same thing, that their being together again, finding one another, was a miracle.

Looking back, Eve had to admit the entire situation should have been doomed from the start. By all accounts, her husband should have died, if not in the crash then when she applied the ether, or when Herr Schultz held his blade over Simon's heart, ready to plunge it through . . .

Gray eyes and rounded cheeks . . . bloody hand against the knife . . . her hand . . . his word . . .

Mother.

"Eve, you're squeezing the blood out of my hand!" Maddie said, trying to extricate her grip. "Are you all right?"

"I'm sorry." She patted Maddie's hand while heat rose in her cheeks. "Leftover memories, I'm afraid. And honestly, I'm done in."

Maddie offered a sympathetic smile. "We've had a full day of it, haven't we?" She rose as a yawn escaped her, and returned across the room to her bed. "Try and get some sleep."

Though Eve was tired, she slept fitfully, plagued by dreams of Simon running for his life, then being attacked while she, and not Herr Schultz, held a blade to her husband's chest. He stared at her, wide-eyed, blood oozing from a corner of his beautiful mouth . . .

She jerked upright in bed, blinking in the darkness. Sweat trickled down her back. She glanced over at Maddie's undisturbed sleep while tears burned her eyes. Would the nightmares never cease? Would the guilt keep her shackled the rest of her life?

Lord, please speak to me, she thought, clenching her fists to her temples. *Forgive me . . .*

Eve awoke exhausted the next morning. The day showed no mercy, however, and she and Maddie shared the burden of tending the wounded, working nonstop except for a few minutes to lunch on tinned meat, cheese, and thin slices of bread the hotel had packed for them.

Though the first day of November was chilly, the rain had abated enough that they sat outside on a bench in a small woodland area usually reserved for the hospital's recovering patients.

The park was empty.

"I didn't tell you last night, but I believe I've found my brother and sister," Eve announced, unwrapping the cheese.

"What?" Maddie froze with the jug of tea halfway to her lips. "Where are they? For goodness' sake, are Nikki and Zoe all right?"

Eve told her friend about her encounter with Corporal Duval. "I don't know *how* they are, only that they're living in Anor, at least according to the corporal," she said at length. "As soon as I get Simon safely into Holland, I plan to go after them."

"Holland?" Maddie's brow creased. "I've heard the Belgian-Holland border is a death sentence to any who try to cross. How will you manage it?"

"I know people who have the means to get him out."

"Spies?" Dawning lit in the green depths, and Maddie scanned the empty park, then turned back to Eve. "You work for the Belgian underground, don't you?"

Eve eyed her friend. She trusted Maddie with her life. She trusted Simon as well, but unlike Maddie, he would try to prevent her from taking risks, stakes that might be necessary to complete Rotterdam's mission *and* save Nikki and Zoe.

"Over a year now," she said quietly. "My small bit to help the Allies win the war."

"I'm sure it's more than a bit." Maddie looked impressed

before concern returned to her features. "Your work must be dangerous. You're taking every precaution?"

"On my honor." Eve smiled, raising her right hand to give the Girl Guides' pledge.

"Good." Maddie lifted the jug and drank some tea. "This is all so much to take in, especially your being a spy." She flashed a curious look at Eve. "I don't suppose you can talk about it?"

Eve reached for her hand and squeezed it. "I'm afraid not, for both our sakes."

"I suppose." Maddie sighed, adding, "I wish this beastly war would be done with. I hate the thought of our parting again before we even get a chance to spend time together. I'll go back to Jeumont—"

"Maddie," Eve said as a thought struck. "When do you return?"

Her friend took up a slice of bread and some of the cheese. "As soon as Charleroi gets their new nurses, I imagine."

Jeumont wasn't that far from Anor; her friend had been in France for some time and knew the country. Perhaps she could find out if Nikki and Zoe were still there.

Eve explained her thoughts.

"I'll gladly try and help," Maddie said. "But the restrictions in occupied France aren't much better than here. Even though I'm Belgian and with the Red Cross, I was only allowed to come through because of the emergency at Jeumont. I doubt they'll let me travel back and forth so easily once I return to France."

It was true. The fence around Belgium was like a tightening noose, choking off those living inside from the rest of the world.

"Still, I can try," Maddie said, looking hopeful.

Eve offered a weak smile. "That's something at least."

CHAPTER 24

Whatever Sister Marche was hiding, it must be important.

He wasn't the only one after it.

Felix leaned against the brick building across the street from Chez Bernard and reached into his jacket pocket for another cigarette. Striking a match against the brick, he stood in the shade of the alley, drawing smoke into his lungs while he observed the familiar silhouette moving back and forth upstairs in Eve's room, doubtless taking advantage of her absence to do what he planned on doing shortly—snooping around.

His stomach rumbled and he checked his watch. *1230 hours— half past lunchtime.* Normally he would be eating at the café now, since the hospital's food was abominable, but he had more pressing concerns. Like discovering why the British captain was flying over Brussels the night he and his pilot crashed.

He also wondered why Eve had taken such risks to get the man out of the hospital. Who was this Captain Chandler to her? And did it have anything to do with the leather pouch?

Felix hadn't believed her story about the blue pamphlets. She knew more than she was telling. He could see it in her expression: so beautiful, and so full of secrets . . .

Schultz or Jaeger would love to get their hands on whatever

she was hiding. As one seeking promotion, it could mean a commendation.

Or for someone on the take, a whole lot of money.

A few minutes later, his predecessor left the apartment and descended the steps. After scanning the street, the man turned to walk back in the direction of the hospital.

Felix put out his cigarette but remained where he stood. One must always anticipate the unexpected.

Just as he began to move across the street, a second man opened the apartment door and stepped outside. Slipping back into the shadows, Felix watched the familiar figure sail swiftly down the steps, then turn and walk in the same direction as the first.

A slow smile touched his lips. Eve's apartment had become a hive of activity. Had this one been looking for secrets as well?

Felix waited another minute, then strode across the street. He surveyed the area before ascending the steps to the apartment. The aunt and uncle were downstairs in the café, but he wasn't certain about Eve's mother.

Fortunately, the two before him hadn't re-locked the door, saving him the trouble of picking the lock—so he cautiously entered. All was quiet but for the faint ticking of a clock in the kitchen. He glanced into the empty room, then continued down the hall. The sound of soft, steady breathing issued from an open door on his right, and he stuck his head inside.

Eve's mother lay asleep on the bed.

Easing out a breath, he moved quickly toward a second flight of steps to the next floor. He passed another door, which was closed, and caught a whiff of cologne. Recognizing the strong pine scent, he backed up and opened the door to peer inside.

Felix frowned as understanding dawned. The day was producing all kinds of surprises. He wondered if Eve knew what was in store when she returned.

He closed the door and continued up the last flight of steps to the attic.

Reaching her door, he opened it and went inside, quickly scanning the room. He strode toward the bureau and began opening drawers, sorting through the contents with practiced care. Next he scoured the hat boxes and portmanteau beneath her bed, even inspecting the stitching on her mattress. Nothing.

He went around the room examining every inch of wallpaper, hoping to find a loose corner where Eve might have hidden messages. He searched behind the two pictures on her wall, then deftly felt around the edges of the shrine of the Madonna and Child, looking for signs of an opening.

Still nothing.

Again he checked his watch. He had to get back to work. He'd promised Dom he would return with the camera, for Chandler's new passport.

Raking a hand through his hair, he went to the closet and made a thorough search, checking skirt pockets and feeling at the hems; he examined shirt buttons, notorious for hiding tissue paper notes.

Nearing the end of his fruitless search he stood back, hands on hips, and stared around the room once more. Had his predecessor beaten him to it? Or the other one, perhaps?

No, the information had to be here, he felt certain. But time was running out.

Felix ground his teeth, sweat beading along his brow. Already Dom was becoming suspicious.

He cast a final look at the room and started to leave when light from the window reflected against a thin line of gilt on the gown of the Madonna.

Felix strode back to where the niche hung on the wall. Though he'd examined the frame for some kind of opening, he hadn't inspected the relief itself. With his fingers he traced the sculpture, first the Madonna, then the Baby Jesus.

A tiny latch released with a *snick*. Felix smiled as he opened the front panel and found the shelf. He looked past the holy water and rosary and picked up the Bible. As he opened the tome and glanced inside, his pulse pounded.

He'd discovered Eve's secret.

CHAPTER 25

They've asked me to stay on here in Charleroi," Maddie said in a dazed voice. "The new matron seems a fairly decent sort, especially considering that she's German."

Friday had arrived, and to Eve's relief, so had the train with the new nurses. She and Maddie had worked beside them all morning, and it was noon when the two finally managed a break for a cup of tea.

"Matron does seem to appreciate our work." Eve had told Maddie about the high-handed Nurse Hoffmeyer. "Still, despite my new dragon back in Brussels, I'll be glad to return."

"You have your reasons." Then Maddie offered an apologetic look. "I know I promised to try to help find your brother and sister, but it's been so long since I've worked in sanitary conditions, and slept on a real bed with clean sheets . . ."

"Of course you should stay," Eve said. "And you're right, getting word back across the border might be impossible." She gazed into her teacup. "When the time is right, I'll go myself."

"I don't like the idea of you going alone."

Eve looked up. "Don't worry, I'll have help."

"Like that charming Frenchman?"

When Eve didn't answer, Maddie said, "All right, never mind. Still, I do look forward to seeing him again. What time will he be here to pick you up?"

"The hospital telephoned and said to expect him by early afternoon."

Maddie sighed. "I know you want to return, but I do wish we'd had more time. There's still so much to catch up on."

"Why don't you come to Brussels?" Eve said, excited by the sudden idea. "If I can secure a city pass, would you like to spend the weekend? Mama would love to see you again, and I can finally introduce you to my aunt and uncle."

Her friend lifted a brow. "Do I get to say hello to anyone else?"

She meant Simon, of course. "That may be too risky for both of you." Eve scanned the empty nurses' lounge. "And please, don't speak of him, not even to Dom. I've told you more than anyone else. The less said the better."

"I understand."

"We'll have a grand time together," Eve said. "It's been so long since I've had my friend to confide in."

Maddie's eyes brightened with emotion. "Then get me that pass and I shall be there."

Someone had been in her room.

Eve's pulse pounded as she stood at her attic room door and stared at the scarlet thread on the floor. When had they entered? She'd been in Charleroi since Wednesday morning. An intruder would have had plenty of time to search . . .

Simon's papers! She rushed inside, her gaze darting around the room. Nothing seemed amiss. Still, her skin prickled with unease as she sensed a disturbance.

Closing the door, she dropped her valise on the bed and

hurried toward the shrine. She released the hidden latch and grabbed up the hollowed-out Bible and opened it.

She exhaled, leaning back against the wall. Simon's documents were as she'd left them. Her hiding place hadn't been discovered.

Eve removed his handkerchief from inside, then returned the Bible to the shelf and closed the panel. Still, the scarlet thread on the floor meant someone had trespassed. She made a quick inspection of her room and noted the slight disarray of clothing in her dresser drawers. That action ruled out her aunt or Mama, as they had no reason to comb through her things.

Rarely did she lock her door. Her family would never invade her privacy unless it was an emergency, and a locked room invited suspicion if the Boche decided to ransack the apartment.

Had it been the secret police? The chilling thought seized her. She'd been followed from Guerin's cigar shop just weeks before. She recalled Jaeger's harsh interview, and the vampire Schultz's obvious disdain for her Iron Cross.

She took a deep breath. Before jumping to conclusions, she would go downstairs to the café and ask her family. If it wasn't Mama or Aunt Marie who had entered, they could tell her if someone had been in the house while she was gone.

With the need to put her mind at rest, she searched her meager wardrobe for a change of clothes. Deciding on a clean but worn blue-and-white-striped shirtwaist and gray skirt, Eve dabbed on a bit of rose water and headed downstairs.

Halfway down the hall, she jumped back as the door to the spare room opened.

"Ah, it is you!"

Otto Reinhardt stood on the threshold facing her.

"Herr Major, wh-what are you doing here?"

He stepped out into the hall. "I am your new boarder."

Eve reached for the wall. Dear heaven, he was living under their roof. Wasn't it bad enough she must suffer his presence at work?

He smiled beneath the moustache while his gaze traveled over her with appreciation. "When you're at the hospital, or in the café, I rarely see you without an apron. The color of that skirt enhances your remarkable eyes."

Heat singed her face. "*Danke*, Herr Major." Then, "When did you arrive?"

"Yesterday morning."

Her prickle of disquiet returned. Had he been her intruder?

"Don't you remember? I told you troops were arriving in Brussels over the next week, and the hotels were already full."

Eve nodded. She'd sent Rotterdam the information from Otto's files before leaving for Charleroi.

"I was outranked when a colonel from the Eighth Army desired my suite at the hotel," he explained. "My choices were either to live here or in an apartment above the tanner's smelly shop." His mouth curled in distaste. "It wasn't a difficult decision."

"With the shortage of leather, I'm surprised the tanner has any work that would make his shop reek." Eve spoke mildly, hiding her resentment.

She glanced at the major's leather boots, then to her own wooden sabots. Because the Boche had taken the leather *and* the tooling from shoe factories for their own means, many in Belgium went barefoot or wore bits of carpet on their feet, or the wooden sabots. With winter's approach conditions would worsen, adding new cases of frostbite to the hospital.

Otto seemed oblivious to her remark. "Why would I choose to live anywhere else? The café is right downstairs, and I find the scenery here much more to my liking than the short, hairy *Wildschwein* who owns the tannery." He smiled. "Now, Sister ... Eve ... I hope you will join me in celebrating my new accommodation with a glass of cognac?" He swept a hand toward his room. "I also have sherry, if you prefer."

Eve started to refuse when she remembered the pass she needed to obtain for Maddie. "A sherry would be nice," she found herself saying. "In the parlor."

"Of course." A flush colored his cheeks. "I will bring the drinks and join you directly."

Eve continued on her way while her stomach clenched. How could she continue her clandestine work at night with Otto living just down the hall?

Wolfe and Kraus had been so easy! The young lieutenants had not only trusted her, but they enjoyed their drink and slept like the dead, allowing her privacy to carry out her duties for La Dame Blanche.

At the café, the major rarely overimbibed. She had no idea how late he stayed up at night, either. And then there was his sudden renewed interest in her. She hadn't forgotten his invitation to the operetta the following night. While the prospect of gathering intelligence among the German high echelon was tempting, she wouldn't encourage Otto's affections.

She entered the parlor, rubbing at the goose bumps along her arms. She would definitely start locking her bedroom door at night.

"Here we are." Otto appeared in the parlor doorway. He carried a silver flask, presumably the cognac, and a glass decanter of sherry and set them both on the table. Removing a glass from each of his pockets, he filled them accordingly and handed her the sherry.

As Eve had taken the only chair, the major took a seat on the worn divan. He raised his glass. "To new beginnings."

She grimaced, wondering what kind of "new beginning" Otto had in mind. Bringing the drink to her lips, she savored the sweet, smoky flavor.

He sipped his drink. "Was your trip to Charleroi productive?"

So, he intended to press her for information. Again Eve wondered if he was the one who had been in her room. Otto had been frustrated over the leaflets, to the point of tossing out threats. Did he sense she'd withheld information from him?

Taking another sip of the sherry, she scoured her thoughts to come up with an offering, some harmless tidbit she'd overheard in Charleroi. But between tending so many patients and enjoying her time with Maddie, Eve hadn't gleaned much.

She did learn from a wounded German soldier that a convoy carrying supplies and foodstuffs had been traveling through Jeumont on its way to the Front when the attempted prison break began. Apparently the French set two of the supply trucks on fire.

Otto didn't need to know that, however. "There wasn't time," she said, unable to think of anything. "The hospital kept us extremely busy."

His expression darkened. "I was counting on you. I called the hospital. They told me you were treating Allied soldiers as well as Germans."

He'd been checking on her? She observed his rigid posture as he edged forward on the divan. His expression seemed almost desperate. She wondered if his government friend had threatened him. With so many German troops being routed through Brussels on their way to the Front, did Otto worry he would be called up?

"I did speak with a young British infantryman," she said. "He told me he'd written a letter to his mother in Cheshire and told her how the Germans attacked Broodseinde a few weeks ago and 'clobbered' their regiment." She paused. "Does that help?"

"Hardly," he said, though his expression eased.

Of course the news of another German victory would please

him. Over the past several months the war had gone well for the enemy, which demoralized the Belgians and frustrated Eve and the others who worked so hard to find a chink in the Boche armor.

"If you think of anything else, you'll tell me?"

"Of course." She was relieved to have the interrogation over. "I met a friend while I was at Charleroi, a nurse, Sister Madeleine Arthur. She works with the Red Cross." Eve hesitated, then said, "I was hoping you could obtain a weekend pass for her to visit Brussels."

"You want a favor from me?" His expression soured. "When I get so little in return?"

He leaned back against the divan, sipping his cognac while he studied her. Finally he said, "Have you given any more thought to my invitation for tomorrow night?"

Eve tensed as she carefully took another sip of her sherry. It always came down to blackmail with him. Otto Reinhardt was still a Boche, through and through.

She wished she had some disinformation to offer him, but nothing had come through from La Dame Blanche in a while. Because the hospital had received few Allied patients in the past two months, and with Simon pretending amnesia, Otto hadn't really pressed her until now.

Wishes wouldn't help her at this point. Eve edged forward in her chair. "Madeleine loves operettas," she said, countering his move with one of her own.

He seemed to consider her words. "Is she Belgian?"

Eve nodded. Unlike herself, Maddie was native born, before her family moved to Britain.

"Is she pretty?"

"Very much so," she said, resisting a biting retort. "I'm certain if you find a suitable escort for my friend, we will all enjoy tomorrow night's performance."

Otto moved the glass of cognac back and forth slowly between his hands, his brow furrowed in thought.

Would he accept her terms? Attending the theater with him, unchaperoned, was unthinkable; having Maddie at her side made the outing safe enough, and she could gather choice intelligence while she was there.

"I will obtain Fräulein Arthur's pass tomorrow morning." He raised his glass to her.

She eased out a breath, lifting hers. "*Danke*, Herr Major."

"I believe my friend on Herr General's staff would enjoy accompanying us."

Even better, she thought. Eve had never met his government friend. Perhaps he would spill some secrets of his own.

Anxious to escape his company, she rose from her chair. "Thank you for your consideration for my friend and for the sherry." She set her empty glass on the table. "If you'll excuse me, I must freshen up before I go and greet my family downstairs."

"I am headed to the café myself." He smiled. "See? Already I enjoy the benefits of living here. I need only descend a flight of steps to get a decent German supper." Color touched his cheeks as he rose and sketched a bow. "I look forward to tomorrow night, Eve."

"As do I, Herr Major." *And the report I shall make to Rotterdam.*

She waited upstairs by her room until he'd exited the apartment. Then she retraced her steps and paused at his bedroom door before slipping inside.

Otto's housekeeping seemed as austere as their last boarders. His bed was made; the tightly cornered sheets and blanket looked iron-pressed. In the armoire were three uniforms, along with an extra pair of polished boots and a belt with a shiny gold buckle. Keeping alert for sounds of anyone entering the apartment, she rummaged through the pockets of his clothing and checked inside the boots, but did not find even a piece of lint.

One side of the bureau held a neatly arranged set of brushes and combs. On the other side sat a photograph. Eve picked up the frame. Otto posed in front of a painted studio background in full dress uniform. With him stood a buxom, plain-featured blonde near Aunt Marie's age, clad in a dark jacket and skirt. In front of the pair sat two small children in rocking chairs: a dark-haired boy of about ten years and a little girl with blond ringlets who couldn't have been more than five.

She studied the stoic faces. Otto didn't have a picture of his family on his desk, nor had he ever shared much about them. Eve knew only that he went home to Berlin on occasion to visit.

Gazing at his wife and children, she thought about his unwarranted attentions toward her. Did he simply want companionship or something more?

Eve considered again their strange seesaw relationship and how, despite being on opposite sides of the war, she and Otto had become indebted to one another. And while at times he treated her as if she was the enemy, at others he seemed sympathetic toward her, almost affectionate.

She sighed, thinking of the upcoming operetta, very glad Maddie would be with her.

CHAPTER 26

Zoe put the finishing touches on the cake, pleased she'd managed to set aside the extra flour and sugar they'd received from the American Food Relief, while Madame Boulanger had bartered her midwife services for a half dozen eggs and a jug of milk.

Supper would be the usual simple affair, of course—Jerusalem artichokes cooked, mashed, and salted, along with toasted slices of K bread and two tins of meat.

She sighed. She hoped the single-layer cake would make the rest of the meal more palatable and keep their bellies from grumbling tonight.

The door to the cottage suddenly burst open, and her brother and Michel entered.

"Happy birthday, Nikki!" she called out, placing the cake at the center of the table.

"What's so happy about it?"

She looked up to see his thunderous expression, and her stomach tightened. Had something happened at the railway station? She'd heard the train's whistle just an hour ago.

"Was there trouble with the Boche? Are the neighborhood children who went with you all right?"

His jaw clenched, and he breathed heavily through his nose.

"No, no problem. We all played a game of football while we waited for the train, and then we got what we needed."

"That's good." She went to retrieve the cigarette paper and pencil from the drawer, sat down, and began to write as the two boys recited the numbers of troop cars, horses, supplies, and artillery. After she'd recorded the information into a list of cigarettes, chicory, beans, and flour, she asked, "Which direction did they go?"

"North," Michel offered. "To Passchendaele, where the fighting is."

Twelve sacks of potatoes, Zoe wrote, then folded the list carefully. She retrieved the broom and placed the note inside the handle.

Again the cottage door opened, this time to admit Armand and old Monsieur Boulanger. Both men looked tired and dirty from a day of bricklaying in Trélon.

Zoe's pulse quickened as she eyed her love. He smiled at her, despite his haggard features, and she noted traces of brick dust in the dark hair peeking out beneath his cap. He held a large paper package under one arm.

"Something smells good," he said. "Birthday cake?"

She smiled, nodding, before he turned to approach her brother. "*Bon anniversaire*, Nicholas."

Nikki looked surprised as he took the package. He glanced up at Armand. "For me? *Merci*!" He darted into the parlor with Michel, and the boys sat on the divan while Nikki opened his gift.

Zoe looked at Armand, and unexpected tears brimmed at her lashes. Whatever was inside the package, he must have worked extra hours in order to afford it. She went to him and put her arms around his waist. "You are too good to us," she whispered.

Armand smiled down at her. "I think I am the fortunate one."

He bent his head and kissed her, and Zoe melted against

him, breathing in the smell of the brickworks—a combination of soil, lime, and the dampness of the air outside—and the familiar scent that was Armand.

When their kiss ended, she searched his face. "You look tired, *mon coeur*."

"Twelve hours each day is a test of strength," he said. "Poor Monsieur Boulanger can barely keep up, so I help a bit."

She lifted a hand to his cheek. Each day Armand, Monsieur Boulanger, and others were taken by truck into Trélon to slave for the Boche. "More brick buildings, I suppose," she said, bitterness rising in her tone. "So they can store their weapons to use against us."

"At least I can stay here with you, in Anor." He covered her hand with his. "They haven't yet forced me to go to Germany."

"You would only escape again." Zoe flashed him a sudden smile and reached up to straighten the collar of his shirt. "And I would miss you until you came back."

He grinned, the patch over his eye lending him a rakish look.

She hugged him again. She was glad he wasn't forced to leave, but she couldn't help being angry when she thought of his passion for teaching and what the enemy had reduced him to. When would the Allies defeat these monsters and send them back to their own country?

"Well, what is it?"

Michel's impatient voice drew Zoe and Armand's attention toward the parlor.

"It's . . . clothes," Nikki said. He held up a dark brown work jacket. Next he pulled from the paper wrapping a pair of matching trousers and a white cotton shirt.

Armand leaned toward her. "I repaired the wall in Monsieur Fosse's entryway. The clothing belonged to his son."

She nodded soberly. Sylvan Fosse, her employer at the hotel, had lost his son at the Battle of Verdun the previous year.

"You're growing up, Nicholas," Armand called to him. "It's time you wore a man's clothes, eh?"

The reminder that her brother might soon be pressed into working for the enemy made Zoe shiver. She thought of the promise she'd given to Eve, and how she'd failed their mother. Nikki was the only one left she could protect.

"Is something the matter?" Armand asked.

She lifted her head, then realized he wasn't speaking to her but to her brother.

Armand frowned. "Do you not like the clothes?"

"I thank you for the gift, Armand," Nikki said. "But I would much rather have a French uniform."

Zoe drew in a breath. "You are too young!" Leaving Armand's side, she marched toward her brother. "You cannot fight."

"I can and I will!" His boyish features turned fierce. "Have you forgotten what the Boche did to Mama, or to our uncle and sister?"

Stricken by his outburst, she paused, blinking at him. "Of course not," she whispered. She sensed Armand's approach, his solid warmth behind her. "I just don't want anything to happen to you. You're the only family I have left."

"Don't you see, Zoe?" His deep blue eyes shone suspiciously bright. "If I do nothing, I'll still be sent to the Front, to work in the enemy's trenches." His expression turned mutinous. "The Boche boys are allowed to fight. We saw them at the train station. We want to fight, too."

"We?" Armand moved around Zoe to face his brother. "Michel?"

"Nikki and I are tired of looking at trains with the women and children." Michel's olive-skinned features flushed. "We want to go and fight like men."

Zoe caught the fury in Armand's expression before he masked it.

"So, you think what we do to aid the Allies is a children's game? When every time someone watches the trains they risk being arrested as a spy?" His quiet tone held an edge.

Nikki and Michel stared at him.

"When I was a boy, a shard of glass from a broken window did this." Armand jabbed a finger toward the black patch over his eye. "So I do not fight at the Front. Does it mean that I am not a man? That I am not brave enough?"

"*Non!*" cried the boys together.

"You saved Zoe and me from the Boche," Nikki said. "You came up with a plan to escape the train and risked your life to bring us to France." He hung his head. "You are the bravest man I know."

"And I watch the trains." Armand's voice turned calm. "With the women and children." He crossed his arms, his expression stern. "You will do the same, until I decide you're old enough." His tone was implacable. "And God willing, the war will be over long before then."

CHAPTER 27

"I knew we had a reason to celebrate," Eve called from the opening of Simon's room. She'd entered through the laundry shop.

"Daughter, you are back!" Father Francois rose from his chair and lumbered toward her.

"At long last," she said, stepping into the priest's much larger chamber.

Simon stopped walking across the spacious stone floor and quickly turned to her.

Eve's heart thumped in her chest at his slow smile and his gray eyes the color of silver in the room's lamplight. "You're walking splendidly," she said, ignoring the pang at what it signified.

"I've missed you, lass."

His low Scots burr sent a tremor of excitement through her as she watched him approach. He wore the clothes she'd brought for him a few nights ago and walked using only a cane, his gait sure and steady.

"Welcome back." He reached for her, pulling her into his arms, not caring that the priest was there as he kissed her soundly.

When he released her, Eve stepped back, breathless. "I've missed you, too." She glanced toward Father Francois and

243

caught his smile. "I've brought something special for our supper tonight." She held up a linen sack.

"It's not your night for laundry, is it?" Simon glanced back toward the way she'd entered.

"No, but I thought it safer to visit the blanchisserie while hauling this bag, instead of the church. I made an excuse to leave the café. I didn't want to wait until morning."

She was rewarded with another of his beautiful smiles.

"Let's make the most of it then. Shall we sit in here?"

He looked to Father Francois, who answered by pulling over a low wooden table and two more chairs near the brazier's warmth. Eve set down her bundle.

"What kind of something special?" The priest peered inside the sack with childlike anticipation.

Eve shooed him away and withdrew a white linen cloth, which she spread onto the table. Then she began setting out the black market feast she'd purchased: cheese, real meat sausages, chocolates, apples, and a bottle of wine. It didn't matter that the delicacies had cost most of her meager earnings. They would celebrate her return and Simon's progress in style.

"A banquet for angels!" Father Francois exclaimed. He rose and disappeared for a few moments, presumably to the rectory kitchen, and returned with a knife, a corkscrew, and three glasses.

Eve opened the bottle and poured them each a measure of the dark French wine.

"To homecomings," she said, raising her glass. The others did the same.

"Aye, to homecomings," Simon murmured.

She met his gaze, knowing he meant the day when they could be together again in Britain. Her anxiety mingled with desire as she took a sip of the wine.

"To the end of the war," the priest said, raising his glass a second time.

"To the end of the war," she and Simon echoed.

Eve set down her glass and reached for a piece of the chocolate, while the two men tucked into the food.

"After days of war bread and beet soup, this is a dream come true." She picked up her glass. "To good food, when and where it can be had."

"To good food!" the two men chimed.

Several minutes of contented silence followed as they savored the repast. Eve kept casting covert glances at Simon, her pulse jumping each time he caught her look and smiled at her, his gaze full of promise. Awareness heated her face, and he seemed to know that, too, when he grinned at her over his wine.

Nervous beneath his scrutiny, she moved to replenish their glasses.

"No more for me," said Father Francois. He grabbed up a handful of the sausages and cheese, then rose from his chair. "In fact, I must take my leave." He winked at Simon. "I'm sure you two would like some time to yourselves, without this old man around. I need to go and collect a few items before returning for Compline."

To Eve he said, "Bless you for such a bountiful meal, daughter. I will relish the memory for a long time." His features sobered. "Are you able to bring a camera tomorrow?"

She nodded, a wave of sadness crashing against her buoyant mood.

"Why a camera?" Simon asked once the priest had left. He'd remained in his seat, his rugged features focused on her as he sipped his wine.

"Your new passport." Her voice was quiet. "Very soon, Father Francois will make arrangements for your crossing into Holland."

He sighed. "I confess, after three weeks of being confined,

both at the hospital and here at the rectory, I won't be sorry to leave these walls." He scanned the priest's chamber. "Not after years of being locked up. I'm ready for a bit more space in which to breathe."

He turned to her, the glass in his hand. A wealth of emotion filled his gaze.

Eve blinked back tears. Already she was missing him. She rose to collect the food containers and linens, and shoved them into the bag. "I . . . I must get back. I told Aunt Marie I'd only be an hour, and it's already long past that."

He rose from his chair. "Eve."

He held out his hand, and when she reached for him, he pulled her into his arms. They had so little time left, and she knew it was her guilt, her secrets keeping them apart.

"I understand about your brother and sister, lass, but there's more, isn't there?" He gently rubbed her back. "Will you not tell me what's in your heart? I canna bear to leave us like this."

Eve lifted her head and saw his concern, the gray eyes like dark clouds of sadness. She knew she must tell him, but the fear of his inevitable disillusionment in her, perhaps even his rejection, kept her silent.

"I only want to help—" he began, before she pressed a finger to his lips. She leaned in to kiss him, offering her love instead, and his arms tightened around her, drawing her close as if he could shield her from her own misery.

When he ended the kiss, his lips brushed along her cheeks, her lids, and more tears stung her eyes as she wrapped her arms around his waist. If they could simply remain together like this, let the world pass . . .

But the world was cold and heartless, and waited for no one.

"I have to go," she said against his shoulder, loathing the idea of leaving his arms.

"I know." Yet he seemed unwilling to let her go. "I meant

what I said. I want to share your burden, lass. Whatever troubles you, together we can bear its weight."

Love for him expanded inside her as she gazed into his face. Could he share her burden . . . or would he judge her by her own measure?

"Be patient with me, husband," she begged. Then she touched the side of his face and kissed him one last time. Gently she pulled away and took up her linen bag, despising her own cowardice. "I'll be back tomorrow," she said.

Reluctantly she turned and retraced her steps through his room toward Tulle's.

Because the laundry shop closed at six o'clock, Monsieur Tulle had already gone upstairs to his apartment. Eve entered through the cupboard panel at the back of the store and mounted the inside stairs to the family's residence. Still haunted by her husband's look of disappointment, she knocked at Tulle's door. Without question he let her and her bicycle out the back door of his shop.

Once on the street, Eve forced aside thoughts of Simon as she surveyed the area for German patrols. It was not yet dusk, so she could ride without having to use her lamp. Most Belgians had returned to their homes with the approaching curfew, but that didn't mean a stool pigeon wasn't lurking in an alleyway.

Her unknown trespasser continued to weigh on her thoughts. She'd spoken with her family, and no one save Otto had been seen coming or going from the apartment during her absence. Eve still hadn't ruled out the secret police. With Mama usually napping in the afternoons and Otto at the hospital, anyone in the vampires' pay might have come inside to search.

Tossing her linen bag into the basket, she pedaled toward Chez Bernard, and in ten minutes she arrived at the door to the café's kitchen.

She grabbed up the cloth bag and walked inside—and ran straight into Otto Reinhardt.

"Where have you been?" The major loomed over her as he checked his watch. "You've been gone almost two hours."

Eve gaped at him. "I . . . I had an errand," she managed.

He eyed her bag. "You were at the laundry shop? Why so long?" He leaned forward, sniffing the air. "And you've been drinking wine." His features registered surprise, then suspicion. "Did you have a secret liaison?"

"Of course not," she lied, alarmed. "I . . ."

"Eve, did you get those fresh tablecloths?"

She glanced past his shoulder in time to see her aunt reach for a glass of red wine on the counter and quickly dump the contents over a clean stack of linen on the shelf.

"Well?" Aunt Marie moved to stand beside them. She snatched the sack from Eve's grasp before she could speak.

Her aunt opened the bag, and with a satisfied smile quickly whisked it off to the shelf. To the major she called, "The careless girl spilled wine on the clean tablecloths Laurette fetched last night."

She pointed to the wine-stained linen stacked on the shelf, then glared at Eve. "And making poor Monsieur Tulle work late to clean and press the new linen."

Astonished, Eve could only murmur, "I am heartily ashamed, Aunt."

Otto's scowl remained. "Why were you drinking back here in the kitchen?"

"It was a new bottle, Herr Major," her aunt supplied smoothly, pulling an opened bottle from the counter. "One of us always tastes the wine first before it's served. You officers don't want vinegar with your meals." To Eve she said, "You are a clumsy girl, and shall not touch the wine in future."

"Yes, Aunt." This time Eve dutifully lowered her head, her heart pounding as she waited to see what Otto would do next.

She felt his hand on her shoulder. "Now, Frau Bernard, it's

not a crime. You have your new linen, and the laundry shop gets paid for their work, so no harm done."

Eve eased out a breath.

"I suppose."

She glanced up to see her aunt's disgruntled look and marveled at how well she played her part.

"Don't let it happen again, Evelyn," she said.

"I promise, Aunt. And thank you . . . for being so understanding." Eve didn't have to pretend at gratitude. Aunt Marie's quick thinking had saved her.

Her aunt's dark eyes shone. "You are welcome."

Eve turned to Otto. "Why are you here in the kitchen, Herr Major?"

"I was looking for you." He reached into his tunic pocket and produced an envelope. "I found someone in the pass office tonight after they'd closed. Fräulein Arthur may enter Brussels tomorrow for the weekend."

Giddy with relief, Eve beamed. "*Danke*, Herr Major."

CHAPTER 28

*E*ve!"

Maddie rushed through the front door of Chez Bernard early the following afternoon, while Dom trailed close behind, toting a small rucksack. He'd played chauffeur that morning, delivering Maddie's pass and returning with her to Brussels.

"You're here!" Eve's heart lifted at the sight of her friend. "Come and sit, I'll get you both some lunch."

She went to the kitchen and returned with a plate of bread. Aunt Marie and Uncle Lucien followed, bearing smiles and bowls of piping hot *Bibbelsche Bohnesupp.*

Eve made quick introductions, and once her aunt and uncle had delivered the potato soup and offered an effusive welcome, they left to return to their duties.

She fetched the coffee next, and since most of the lunch crowd had departed, she joined her friends at the table.

"You made quick time," she said to Dom, taking the Red Cross rucksack he offered her. She slung it over the back of her chair, knowing it held the camera she'd need for Simon later.

"*Oui*, despite the nuisance checkpoints." Dom picked up his spoon and stirred the steaming soup. "It's a good thing I had a reason to go. If Charleroi hadn't wished to repay us the

250

supplies they borrowed a few days ago, Maddie might still be waiting for her pass."

"I'm grateful, *mon ami*," Eve said.

"I was happy to do it." He winked at Maddie across the table, and her friend blushed.

"Aunt and Uncle said I could take off from work once you arrived," Eve told her. "After you finish lunch, I'll take you upstairs so you can get settled."

Maddie sighed. "I'm looking forward to our weekend." Then she took a sip of the ersatz coffee and wrinkled her nose.

"The coffee's worse here than in Charleroi," Eve said. "The food we receive is very basic and scarce. If my aunt and uncle weren't so talented in the kitchen, everything would taste bad."

"The soup is *délicieuse*," Dom said, having tucked into his meal.

"It is," Maddie agreed. "And you can hardly taste the bread if you soak it in the wonderful broth."

Eve smiled, and while they sat together she forgot about the war and its horrors for a time.

"I am off to the hospital," Dom said when she'd cleared the table. "Felix covered my shift this morning, so now I must go and relieve him." He paused, nodding toward the rucksack. "Do you have all you need?"

Eve flashed him a cool look. "We should be fine, thanks."

He reached for Maddie's hand. "Think of me while you're enjoying yourselves."

"Poor Dominic." Maddie pretended to pout, then smiled. "I wish you could join us."

"How about at three o'clock?" he said. "I'm working late, but I'll still take my break."

"We could stop by the hospital then," Eve said, pleased. Maddie could spend time with Dom while she went to visit Simon.

He grinned. "I look forward to it."

After he left, Eve snagged the rucksack while Maddie toted her valise, and the two walked arm in arm up the stairs to the apartment.

"That's a lovely dress suit." Eve admired Maddie's green skirt and jacket. "Is it new?"

Maddie laughed. "I've had these clothes since the war started. I rarely get to wear them. My only other outfit is my nurse's uniform. You learn to pack light, working in field stations." She nudged Eve. "You remember what it was like when we first crossed the channel."

"I've managed a few more things since then," Eve admitted. "But with the occupation and shortages, clothes shopping is a thing of the past. We must keep mending what we have, even our shoes, until they wear out." She stared down at her wooden sabots.

"It's been difficult here, hasn't it?" Maddie's voice held compassion. "You told me about Louvain, but in Brussels too, yes?"

Eve squeezed her arm. "You've been working close to the Front, so I imagine it's been worse for you. I get most of the wounded after you've tended and patched them up enough to send them here."

"That doesn't mean you haven't suffered."

"Of course not," Eve said, "but the battle here is more . . . insidious. The Boche have bled the country dry of funds. People are left to starve and go without heat. Crime has become epidemic with so many people desperate for food." She sighed. "The enemy creates the problem, but their answer is to take more and punish those who protest."

"Occupied France is the same," Maddie said in a disheartened tone. "Conditions in some places are intolerable."

Eve imagined her brother and sister, living oppressed, perhaps starving. "I hope Nikki and Zoe are safe," she whispered.

Maddie placed a hand over hers. "I pray you find them so."

KATE BRESLIN

Eve smiled her gratitude, and hoped God heard her own prayers for them.

They entered the apartment and found Mama in the kitchen. She clapped her hands in delight when she saw Maddie. "Welcome, *ma chère*! It has been so long, and look at you, all grown up!"

She held out birdlike arms and Maddie rushed to embrace her.

"Madame Marche, it is good to see you."

Over Mama's head, Maddie smiled, and Eve's eyes burned with tears. After years of hardship, these two people she loved so much had reunited.

"Did you eat?" Mama asked when they parted.

Maddie nodded. "I enjoyed a bowlful of Uncle Lucien's delightful potato soup."

"I'm taking her up to my room," Eve said, and Maddie gave Mama one more hug before they left to travel down the hall and climb the short set of stairs to the next landing.

Eve put a finger to her lips as they passed Otto's door. Maddie lifted a brow but kept silent as they ascended the final steps to Eve's attic room.

Once inside, Eve locked the door. "Our German boarder." She indicated the door they'd just passed. "I don't want him barging in on our time together." *At least not yet*, she thought, reminded of the upcoming operetta. She still had to discuss her arrangement with Maddie.

"I've heard of the Germans billeting with civilians," Maddie said. "It's the same in the French villages."

Did Nikki and Zoe share quarters with the Boche? The thought made Eve uneasy. With her sister now eighteen, she hoped Corporal Duval's cousins were able to protect her.

"I like this room."

Maddie had turned full circle, taking in the bed, the nightstand and bureau, and finally the small brazier. "It suits you."

253

"It's tiny, but the bed's big enough for two." Eve was relieved to change the subject.

Maddie sat down on the bed, testing the mattress. "Believe me, I've slept in worse." She looked up and said, "How is our mutual friend?"

Simon, of course. "He's better every day. He'll be leaving soon."

Maddie reached for her hand and she clasped it. Neither spoke for a moment, but Eve drew comfort in knowing her friend understood.

"I have a favor to ask." She sat down beside Maddie. "A rather large one, I'm afraid."

"Oh?" Maddie's green eyes narrowed. "Why don't I like the sound of that?"

Eve hesitated, then said, "How do you feel about the opera?"

It was midafternoon when Eve entered the church. She'd sent Maddie off to meet Dom in front of the hospital at the appointed time while she came to visit Simon.

She'd agreed to join them in a half hour's time at Fournier's patisserie on rue de Namur for coffee and the lumpy bits of mixed potato and flour that passed for biscuits.

Maddie had of course agreed to accompany her to the opera later, jokingly adding that she hoped the major's German friend was well behaved.

Eve hoped for the same thing, and she anticipated reaping valuable information for the Rotterdam office.

Aunt Marie had allowed them to rummage in her closet, and they had emerged with a black lace gown for Eve to wear and an ivory tea gown for Maddie. With a little modifying, the dresses would be presentable for this evening.

Much to her dismay, St. Magdalene's was busy for a Saturday. A line of people had already queued up waiting to enter the confessional. Eve meandered toward the front of the church while she casually surveyed the two dozen or so people scattered in the pews.

A tall, thin, dark-haired man dressed in the rough wool sweater and neckerchief of a fisherman drew her attention. He kept his head down, but he seemed to be looking more from side to side at the church patrons than he was praying.

A stool pigeon?

His gaze caught hers then, and shock rippled through her as she recognized the bristling moustache and hazel-eyed stare of Herr Schultz.

Was he there for her? Eve's heart hammered as she continued moving toward the altar. She pressed a hand to her stomach and felt the small camera hidden beneath her corset—secret contraband that if discovered would likely get her shot.

She slipped into a front pew and stared at the sacristy door. Frustration mingled with her fear. She wanted some time with her husband before she was to meet the others.

Eve turned her gaze to the image of Christ on the cross, and it occurred to her that with Simon's arrival she'd spent more time in church during the past three weeks than she had the previous three years. She also realized that amid the quiet reverence of her surroundings, she felt less alienated than she had before.

She was acutely aware that Herr Schultz sat several rows back. Kneeling, she clasped her hands in prayer. *Lord, please let me get to Simon. We haven't much time.*

"Halt!"

The shout rose from close behind her. Eve twisted around to see a small man in a brown jacket running toward the back of the church.

Herr Schultz, along with another man several pews away—a

short blond in blue coveralls and beard who looked oddly like Herr Jaeger—launched from their places and gave chase, creating a commotion that brought the priest out of the confessional.

Eve took advantage of the distraction and rushed for the sacristy door. Slipping inside, she made her way through the vestment closet and into the tunnel. Less than a minute later, she burst through the closet door leading into Father Francois's chamber.

Simon—or a man who resembled him—stood near the brazier, cane raised to strike.

He relaxed once he saw her and lowered the cane. "The way you came barreling out of that closet, I thought the Huns were attacking."

"You look so different," she said. "Your hair . . . it's black."

"Aye, the priest's idea." His eyes held a warm glint as he ambled over to her. "It's good to see you, lass."

"And you." Eve continued to stare as she rose on tiptoe and kissed him. His mood seemed lighter than when she'd left him yesterday. "How are you feeling today?"

He handed her the cane, then turned and walked several paces.

"Your limp is hardly noticeable," she said, amazed.

"I padded the inside of my shoe." He returned and came back to stand before her. "It helps with the pain."

And soon you'll be waltzing right out of here. Eve held on to her smile, refusing to let melancholy diminish their time together.

"So why did you come blasting through that door?" he said. "Trouble getting here?"

"I made it here because some poor fool panicked and ran from the church." She relayed to him what had happened. "Jaeger and Schultz were disguised in plain clothes and took chase."

"Are you in danger?" His mouth turned down as he grasped her shoulders. "Could they have been after you?"

"No, I'm sure they must have been after that man." She remembered her prayer then, and disquiet filled her. Surely God hadn't orchestrated his capture because of it?

Lord, I pray you let him slip away.

She thought of the man in the brown suit running like a frightened rabbit, enticing the two Boche hounds to chase him. Simon's words niggled at the back of her mind. Had Jaeger and Schultz been there for another reason? Were they watching her come and go from St. Magdalene's?

Eve gazed at her husband and realized her visits were becoming dangerous for both of them. He would leave soon, and once he was safely across the border she must go to France, regardless of whether or not Rotterdam sent the mission information. The sooner she left Brussels for a while, the better.

"I've brought the camera," she said, anxious to remove the concern from his features. "Did Father Francois get the necessary items?"

He continued to watch her, his gray eyes dark as slate. "I'll get them."

When he returned from his room, he said, "Since you're so talented with a razor, I thought you might help me put these on."

He held up a set of whiskers—a black moustache, goatee, and wide chopped sideburns. His other hand held a tin of adhesive paste and a pair of wire-rimmed spectacles.

He set everything on the table. "Where's the camera?"

She began to unbutton her coat. "Turn around." At his curious look, heat rose in her cheeks. "It's hidden inside my corset."

A slow smile spread across his face. "I can help with that, wife."

His soft Scots burr caressed her senses, and Eve's skin grew warmer.

He approached her, his gaze heated, intent. "With the priest over at the church for the next few hours, hearing confessions . . ."

She removed her coat while her heart raced, her mind filled with visions of sunlit mornings and the warmth of him next to her as she'd awakened in his arms. Such a tantalizing notion, she thought, to spend the rest of the afternoon with him. It had been so long since she'd been his wife in truth.

Her heart beat with a flutter of excitement. Perhaps they would even make another child . . .

Coldness crashed down on her then, shattering the dream. She wouldn't risk another child in this accursed war, or bear the horror and sadness of losing it.

She gazed into his eyes, so radiant with love. "I want to, husband." Desire and regret filled her voice. "Just not here, not now. A baby . . ." She paused. "I'm sorry. I couldn't."

His expression fell, disappointment evident in his features. For a long moment he was silent, before he said softly, "I understand, lass." His tone hardened as he added, "But I'll not turn around. You're my wife."

She lifted her chin at him, heat flooding her face. "Then I will."

Eve spun around and began lifting the hem of her skirt. The small camera lay wedged beneath the bottom of her corset, near her abdomen. As she was about to reach for the device, Simon's hands slipped around her waist. His solid presence warmed her back.

"I'll help you," he whispered, then gently kissed her nape.

Eve shivered, her skin hot then cold, while her heart pounded against her ribs. For several moments, she was reluctant to move, but with the camera in hand, she finally turned in his arms to face him. Simon's eyes shone with desire.

Eve tried to wet her lips, but her mouth had gone dry. In a hoarse whisper, she said, "You can sit down." His lips held a trace of a smile as he took a seat in the chair. Her hands shook while opening the small tin of adhesive paste. She broke off a strip, then picked up the moustache. "Maddie is here in Brussels," she said, trying to regain a sense of composure.

"Madeleine Arthur? Why is she here?"

She turned and found his attention fastened on her. "I was able to get her a pass into the city," she said, still trying to catch her breath. "I met her while working at the hospital in Charleroi."

She approached him and affixed the tape before pressing the moustache into place above his upper lip. She'd moved close enough that his hands settled against her hips, and again her pulse quickened.

"It looks natural enough," she said, glancing at the moustache.

"But you like me better without one?"

More heat rose in her cheeks, and she met his look, nodding. Another smile touched his lips. "How long is she staying?"

"Just the weekend." Eve next held up a sideburn against his cheek so that it touched the edge of the moustache. "It's good to see her again." In a quiet voice, she added, "Having you both here with me reminds me of happier times."

He pulled her onto his lap. "We'll have them again, love," he said. "Be patient with *us*."

Eve gazed at his handsome face, so determined and confident. She leaned in to kiss him, and afterward she couldn't help smiling. "I really do prefer you without that brush beneath your nose."

He waggled his brows, now black as his hair, and her laugh was tinged with emotion. How many times had he teased her like that, trying to make her blush?

She rose and continued her task. Once she'd attached the whiskers, affixed the short goatee, and had him don the spectacles, Eve hardly recognized him.

"I'll take several photographs, and we'll use the best of the lot." She readied the camera and began snapping pictures. When she'd finished, he carefully removed the set of whiskers and set them aside.

"I suppose I'll need these later," he said.

"Your new passport will be ready in a couple of days." She tucked the camera into her coat pocket and struggled against the desolation trying to claim her.

He stood and reached for her hands. "I know we haven't much time. I want you to destroy the orders," he said. "I'm certain Marcus will send someone else to finish the job."

Eve was relieved he'd at least decided to let go of the mission. "I'll burn them."

He nodded. "I know my staying here jeopardizes you and your family." His grip tightened. "I *will* come back for you, love. Promise me you'll stay safe."

If she was ever of a mind to tell him *she'd* been ordered to "finish the job," that consideration vanished. Simon had finally come to terms with the fact that he must leave. Aside from a multitude of other reasons for going, he needed to fully recover from his injuries in a safer place than Belgium or France. He would have that chance in Britain. "I'll do my best," she said.

She was bound by love to reveal one truth to him, however. Simon was her husband, after all.

"I need to tell you something." She hesitated. "It was a condition to get Maddie a pass into the city. We have to attend the theater tonight . . . with the major and another officer."

He looked thunderstruck.

"It's not what you think, Simon," she said, already regretting her forthrightness.

"You're my *wife*." Still gripping her hands, he pulled her to him so that he towered over her. "I don't want that dirty Hun touching you."

"He won't! Simon, nothing will happen." She tried to reassure him. "Maddie will be with me and—"

"I forbid you to go."

His face was a mask of anger.

"Forbid me?" Disappointment over his lack of faith in her fueled her anger. "I haven't seen you in three years," she said. "In that time I've had to live in this prison *by my wits* in order to survive, which includes wearing an Iron Cross and pandering to a self-serving, puffed-up Hun, as you call him, in order to keep my family safe."

Thinking back on what she'd been forced to endure, she added in a bitter tone, "Believe me, Simon Forrester, attending an opera in a foursome and with my fellow nurse for company is quite harmless in comparison."

"I know about prison *and* about surviving," he said, his features hard. "I wasna sitting behind a desk taking my tea, or attending Sunday cricket matches."

Her anger fled as she realized he was hurting, too. Tears sprang to her eyes. "I'm sorry," she said, leaning against him.

He sighed. "I'm sorry, too." Releasing her hands, he put his arms around her and kissed the top of her head. "I just don't want to lose you again."

"Will you trust me?" she said against his shoulder.

It was a moment before he said, "I want to."

She should have been grateful for his honesty, but it still hurt. "I didn't have to tell you about the theater," she said. "I chose to."

"Aye, but I don't like it."

When she lifted her gaze, he leaned his head against hers. "Be careful tonight?"

She answered him with a kiss, and his response was filled with such passion Eve was again tempted to stay and leave the world to its own destruction.

She lingered another few moments before leaving his arms. "I must go." Already she regretted her folly with Maddie's pass and the invitation from Otto. She would much rather remain here with her husband.

It was too late, however, and the stakes were too high. "All will be well," she said, trying to reassure him. "The major is harmless. He's a married man with a family in Berlin. And I've got Maddie to protect me."

She watched Simon's mouth lift in an effort to smile. Of course he wasn't happy about the arrangement. Eve didn't want to imagine his reaction if he found out the major had moved into their apartment. "I'll see you tomorrow."

"Watch yourself. And hide that camera." He glanced toward the priest's closet and frowned. "Can you leave through the laundry shop instead?"

"Good idea." She kissed him again, then headed through his room to the passageway leading toward Tulle's. He was right; it would be foolish to leave through the sacristy and risk being seen by the vampires.

After Monsieur Tulle had provided her exit, Eve walked along rue de Namur to meet with Maddie and Dom.

She savored the moments of intimacy with Simon, his gentle touch, his kisses. He hadn't pressed her or made demands, simply offered her the same love and understanding he'd shown whenever they were together—and the patience he displayed each time she pulled away.

He would be well enough to travel soon. The thought of his absence left her desolate, empty, as though she'd received word of his death all over again. Eve wasn't certain how she could go on living in this hellish place without him, mourning his tender smiles and the love and passion in his gaze. Having his strength to lean on in a world gone mad.

As she entered the patisserie his assurances came back to

her, his promise to return and take her out of this prison city. She wanted to believe in his words, in his hope for them to be together in the days to come.

It was because she'd found him again, and because he'd held her in his arms that she must hold on to that belief.

Otherwise, she didn't think she would survive.

CHAPTER 29

Relief flooded Simon as he watched his wife emerge from the priest's closet the following morning. Since she'd left him yesterday he'd been restless, exploring both tunnels and wearing a path across the floor, waiting for her return.

"Good morning," he said in a quiet tone, watching her expression.

"It is, isn't it?" She smiled as she approached and leaned to plant a kiss on his lips. "How are you feeling today?"

The tension in his body eased. "Better," he said, his response having nothing to do with the state of his physical injuries. "So, how was your opera?"

"I wouldn't know." Her violet eyes sparkled. "We didn't make it beyond dinner. In fact, Maddie and I walked out halfway through the soup course."

He lifted a brow, secretly pleased. "What happened?"

"Maddie's escort, Major Dietrich, arrived at the restaurant quite inebriated," she explained. "He continued to imbibe as we ordered and waited for our food. What I could manage to glean from his rather loud conversation with Major Reinhardt was that the German army suffered a great loss at the Front on Friday. He was quite upset. In fact, several of the generals dining nearby turned and gave him severe looks, but he seemed oblivious." She smiled. "I've never seen Major Reinhardt look so tense.

"When he was finally able to restore his friend to a jovial mood, and pointed out how lovely Maddie looked in her ivory gown, Major Dietrich went from being a drunkard to becoming a letch."

Simon caught the sudden ferocity in her expression, along with a flash of pain, and he wondered at it.

"In the end, poor Maddie was forced to defend herself. She gave him a good, solid push." His wife smiled with vindication. "He toppled right over the side of his chair onto the floor. We left immediately afterward."

Simon wasn't amused. "You take too many chances, wife. Baiting them like that."

"What do you mean?" Her face was now suffused with anger. "He was in the wrong, not Maddie."

"You know it makes no difference," he said, uneasy over the backlash his wife and her friend might receive. "The Huns may keep their behavior in check when it suits them, but don't ever forget they are the enemy."

Her lovely expression sobered and she seemed to consider his words. "Maddie will be on her way back to Charleroi this afternoon." She moved toward the chair near the brazier. "So I doubt she'll feel any repercussions from last night's debacle."

"What about you?" He followed her toward the brazier and took the opposite chair.

"I'll be fine." She smiled at him, but Simon wasn't reassured. "Now, I want to examine your ribs. I think they've healed enough that we can leave the binding off."

His mouth flattened as he unbuttoned his shirt. They seemed to be finished with the conversation.

As she leaned forward and began unwinding the linen from around his torso, he bent to kiss the top of her head. She paused for a heartbeat in her task, and he smiled, glad to know his touch had that effect on her.

Once she'd removed the cloth, she inspected the condition of his ribs. "The bruising and swelling are gone. Do you still have any pain?"

"Let's see." Seated in the chair with his shirt parted open, he breathed in and out deeply, hiding his discomfort. Next, he flexed his chest muscles and then almost laughed. His wife couldn't stop staring.

"Much better," he said, stretching the truth for her sake, "though I haven't done much in three weeks to make them sore . . ." He winked at her then and was rewarded with her blush. "Like tennis." He gave her an innocent look. "If I were lobbing balls across the court, things might be different."

She arched a brow at him, as if she knew what he was about. Then she smiled. "No tennis for at least three more weeks." She straightened in the seat. "You can button your shirt."

Feeling a bit of the devil, he leaned back against the seat, ignoring her request while he gazed at her in amusement.

Heat bloomed in her cheeks once more and he grinned. It did his heart good, knowing she had eyes only for him, and not the Hun.

Her face turned a brighter shade as she picked up the bandages. "Now take off your boot."

Grudgingly he removed his shoe, presenting her with his bandaged foot.

"It seems well enough," she said, inspecting his wound. "I'm sure the padding helps."

As he replaced his boot, he saw her watching him with a soft, wistful expression. "I'll have the new photograph for your passport tomorrow," she said, her voice subdued. "Father Francois will let us know when he has his people in place."

A somber silence fell between them, the only sound the low

hum of the breeze blowing outside the priest's window. Neither he nor Eve wanted to speak, and Simon's heart ached, knowing it would be merely days before they had to part.

Gazing at him with his shirt still open, his gray eyes dark and brooding, Eve was seized with a pang of longing. She had known his days in Brussels were drawing to a close, yet she'd been so focused on the mission, keeping everyone safe, including Simon. She hadn't truly realized how much his leaving would tear her apart.

They'd had just three weeks of stolen moments together, and in that time their fragile bond had strengthened. Yet it wasn't enough. "Come with me," she said softly, rising to stand in front of him. She held out her hand.

He left his chair and followed her into the smaller chamber. Eve replaced the panel, giving them privacy before she drew him over to the bed. "I want to stay with you for a while," she said. "Just hold me, husband."

As they lay down together, he wrapped her in his arms, his kisses gentle at first, then more intense. Then he leaned over her, searching her face. "I want you with me, Eve. Here"—he gently touched her forehead—"and here," he said, laying his hand over her heart. "I miss you, wife."

She wanted all of that too: to be able to love him wholeheartedly and without reservation, to live beyond the shadows of her ghosts. But that meant being honest with him about the past, about the White Lady . . .

Not yet, she told herself, *but soon*.

Then he kissed her again, and tears trailed along the sides of her face as she wrapped her arms around him, clinging to the man she loved, clinging to the hope of their future.

Advise Janssen status.

Three words. Eve sighed as she sat on the bed in her attic room the following evening and stared at the message Vincent had delivered. The brewer had been waiting at the café when she returned from her linen exchange. She'd gathered more troop information from Monsieur Tulle and made a quick visit to see her husband.

Impatience gnawed at her. Already she'd done as Simon asked and burned his orders in the brazier. Having memorized their contents, she'd hoped by now to receive final instructions for the meeting with the kaiser's assassin in France.

She needed time to prepare. German passes were only good for a few days after they were issued, and according to Simon's orders, just two weeks remained before the attack on Trélon. It would certainly help to know what was expected of her in France *before* she left to find her brother and sister.

Eve set the note on the bed, beside a pair of the special wooden bobbins she used for messages. Then she opened her lap desk, the rosewood chamber filled with crisp white sheets of stationery and her pen. The carved set had been a gift from a former patient, a British infantryman about to leave for a POW hospital in Germany. While she'd gracefully accepted his offering, she never told him that because the Germans blocked British mail, any letters she wrote would never leave Belgium.

The one letter she did manage to get through to the outside world had been her smuggled note to Maddie, correspondence that years later proved to be life-changing in bringing Simon back to her.

She removed the pen from the desk. As she reached for the hollowed-out Bible on her nightstand, her gaze fell on the tin of Earl Grey beside it.

A wistful smile touched her lips. Maddie had charged her

with taking care of the tea tin until they met the next time. They'd enjoyed their weekend together, and after a tearful good-bye yesterday her friend boarded the train back to Charleroi.

Even Dom, who had met them at the station, seemed long in the face. Eve wasn't certain when she would see Maddie again, but she hoped her friend wouldn't return to the Front.

She opened the Bible and withdrew two small squares of thin rice paper. Placing one of the squares on her lap desk, she decided to tackle the easier of her two messages first. Both would be delivered to Madame Bissette in the morning.

Despite what she'd relayed to Simon, her intelligence gathering Saturday night hadn't been a total loss. In between the odious Major Dietrich ordering more drinks and ranting about the German defeat, Eve had overheard two colonels at the next table quietly discussing a secret upcoming meeting in December, when General Ludendorff of the German High Command would be in the Belgian city of Mons. She'd grasped the words *Operation Michael* and something about a new type of poison gas—both vital information to pass along to Rotterdam.

As Eve scrawled her note with the information, she paused, reflecting on the restaurant fiasco. While she and Maddie later laughed over Major Dietrich's "fall from grace," or more aptly, his tumble onto the restaurant floor, Eve noticed today at the hospital how the incident had affected Otto.

The major's manner had been subdued, which was a relief. After her talk with Simon yesterday, she'd worried that he might try to retaliate.

Before she'd finished work, however, Otto informed her in a quiet voice that Major Dietrich had received orders to go to the Front and take command of a battalion company with the Fourth Army at Passchendaele.

Eve wondered, with his government contact gone, if Otto would still pursue her for Allied intelligence. She was relieved at the idea of ending his blackmail, but the disinformation she'd passed to him from La Dame Blanche had greatly helped the Allies.

Eve finished her missive and folded the rice paper into a tiny, straw-sized piece. Grabbing up one of the bobbins, she tugged the wooden stem from its hollowed base and stuffed her message inside before recapping it.

She took up the second square of the rice paper, placing the sheet on her lap desk beside the message she'd received from Rotterdam.

Advise Janssen status. Eve's pulse fluttered. Before she'd left Simon tonight, Father Francois informed them "Chandler" would leave on the morning of the seventh—just two days away.

Despair and a mounting sense of panic gripped her, knowing her husband was about to leave. Dom and Felix would dress as tradesmen and accompany Simon, who would pose as Albert Janssen, a Belgian telephone representative. They would take the train from Brussels to an abbey in northern Belgium. Father Francois had arranged payment for two passeurs to take Simon from there across the border into Holland.

Her friends planned to cover their shifts at the hospital so they could remain at the abbey until the following morning. By then, if he survived the night's hazardous trek, Simon should be at British headquarters in Rotterdam via a Dutch agent, and from there be sent on to Britain.

She agonized to think that in a week's time he would be across the channel—less than two hours by plane, yet a world apart from the one in which she existed.

Lying in her husband's arms yesterday at the rectory, she'd done her best to imprint forever the warmth of his body beside her, the press of his lips against her skin.

In the aftermath of those precious moments he'd promised her that one day neither of them would have to look back; they would have a fresh start, looking only ahead, making their plans and sharing their lives together.

Her eyes burned. *Hope*—it was a fire that lit the soul, a belief in both the impossible and in everything imaginable, the budding anticipation of joy, waiting with each breath.

It was a feeling that for years had eluded her, but now through Simon's love seemed finally within her reach. But she had yet to put it to the test. *Lord, please help me.*

Gripping the pen, Eve scribbled out her answer to Rotterdam:

Janssen to make Holland on the 7th. Awaiting your instructions. —Pi

CHAPTER 30

*Q*uick! Wake up, my son. You must go!"

Simon was jarred from sleep by a hand against his shoulder. He opened his eyes to see the stout figure of the priest leaning over his bed, holding a lit candle.

"What's going on?" he said. "Where's Eve?"

"She'll meet you in the tunnel." Father Francois pointed toward the passage leading to the laundry shop. "You're leaving a day early, I'm afraid. There's been another arrest, someone caught outside the church at dawn. The secret police are making a thorough search of the grounds, including the rectory."

As he spoke he was laying out Simon's disguise, including a fedora hat, on the bench. "Take these with you," he said. "Eve can help you with the whiskers. She'll also have your new passport."

Simon rose from the bed. "What time is it?"

"It's still early, seven thirty." The priest handed him a dark blue business coat and a pair of dress shoes. "I was able to contact Dominic at the hospital before he and Felix finished their shift. They will let Eve know, and she'll meet you shortly."

Simon dressed quickly, then sat down on the bench and padded the heel of the right shoe.

"I trust those will fit," the priest said. "Take good care. They might be the last leather shoes left in this country."

Simon grunted his assent as he slipped into the patent leather ankle boots and buttoned them. Next he rose and shrugged into the coat.

"The inside breast pocket contains a fountain pen and a small appointment diary with the Bell Telephone insignia." The priest scanned Simon from head to toe. "No one will question that you are a businessman with the telephone company. Now come quickly."

He handed Simon the candle and led him to the small door on the opposite wall.

"The tunnel starts just inside the passageway." The priest lifted the latch and removed the panel. "You'll travel a few hundred meters before reaching the end. There you'll find another door that leads into the back of the laundry shop."

Though Simon had already explored the tunnel, he said nothing. He extended his free hand to Father Francois. For two weeks the man had taken care of him, been his friend, and offered prayers and wisdom. "I owe you so much."

The priest ignored his hand and leaned to embrace him. "You owe me nothing, my son. Godspeed." In a quiet voice he added, "I shall continue to pray for a quick end to this war, so that you and your lovely wife may have a new beginning."

"Thank you, Father." Simon's voice came out gruff. It was his prayer as well.

The realization he was about to leave Eve behind again pierced him like a knife.

"Take care of her for me," he said, staring at the priest.

"I will do my best." Father Francois's gaze was unflinching. "Now go."

Simon held the candle aloft as he bent his head to enter the small passageway into the tunnel. He turned to raise a final hand of farewell before the priest replaced the small door.

Darkness lay thick in the cavern, but for his flame. Simon moved through the tunnel, the air cold against his face as he felt his way along the stone wall. The ground beneath him was hard and fairly even.

He reached the end and recognized the panel door to the laundry shop. He sat against the cold stone floor a few meters away. Placing the candle beside him, he withdrew the whiskers and adhesive paste strips from his coat pocket and began applying them as his wife had done. Once he'd finished, he hoped all was on straight. Eve could tell him when she arrived.

Again the thought of leaving her stabbed at his insides, colliding with the anxiety in his chest over the coming journey. In a short time, perhaps even minutes, he'd be on his way to the north and back to Britain.

Simon hadn't slept much the night before after hearing he'd be leaving so soon with the two orderlies from the hospital. Eve hadn't been able to stay long, and knowing their time was limited, he'd been glad for the few hours they spent together on Sunday.

The memory warmed him. He remembered her softness tucked up against him as she lay wrapped in his arms, her fragrance of rose water, and the sweetness of her lips—all would sustain him in the days to come. Though he'd yearned to make her his own again after so many years, she'd been right to be cautious. Things would have gone too far, and it was difficult enough for her to live in this place without the hardship of being pregnant with their child. He'd had to content himself with simply holding her, memorizing her touch and the warmth and smell of her skin.

Simon closed his eyes, leaning his head back against the wall.

274

Despite all the perfectly good reasons for leaving her here, it went against his honor, especially knowing an enemy agent hid somewhere in the city.

He'd been on the verge of telling her several times, but he always came back to the worry that she might try to investigate the matter herself, putting her directly into the traitor's path.

But Eve was her own woman, as Father Francois had said. She'd managed just fine without Simon for years, even after enduring what must have been a horrific experience in Louvain. She'd carved out a life here, "living by her wits" in the midst of the enemy and always keeping her head.

She was his equal in so many ways—more than his equal, he thought, his heart swelling with pride as he recalled her daring success in getting him out of the hospital. He'd always championed her right to decide her future, from that evening long ago when she had faced her father and told him she'd rather become a nurse than a math teacher.

A smile touched his lips. Eve had come a long way from the young woman he'd saved from falling out of a tree. She'd saved him, when he'd fallen from the sky.

He should trust her with the truth, warn her about the enemy agent. At least then she could be on her guard.

The loud, echoing *snick* of a latch drew his attention. The panel door at the laundry shop opened against a flash of daylight, and a slender silhouette appeared and stepped into the tunnel. The panel was quickly replaced, throwing him back into darkness.

"Simon?"

His pulse quickened at the sound of her voice. "I'm here," he said, raising the candle so she could see him.

Eve groped her way toward the flickering light and found her husband seated with his back to the tunnel wall.

"I hardly recognize you," she said, taking in the new clothes and his disguise. She sat down beside him. "Are you all right?"

"Aye, for someone shaken out of a sound sleep," he groused. "Have I got things on straight?"

He lifted the candle so she could see his face.

She smiled. "The chops and beard are all right, but you've got the look of a permanent smirk." She reached to straighten the bristle above his upper lip. "There. Perfect."

He set the candle at their feet. "How much time do we have?"

"Felix went home to change. He'll be back to take you to the station in twenty minutes."

Eve had raced home from the hospital herself when Dom met her at the entrance and relayed Father Francois's dire plea.

Reaching into her coat pocket, she withdrew the passport for Albert Janssen with Simon's new photograph. She also had his pass for Antwerp. Luckily, Dom had secured the three-day passes yesterday. She handed Simon the documents. "Once Felix arrives, Monsieur Tulle will rap a signal against the panel door."

He nodded, and while she couldn't see his face in the flickering candlelight, she imagined him bracing himself for the dangerous trek to come.

She pressed close to him and tried not to think about the danger awaiting him at the border. God knew thousands had already died in their failed attempts to get across.

"I'll be back for you," he said into the dark. "Marcus and I, we'll come up with a plan to get you and your mother out of Belgium. Then we can work on finding your brother and sister."

He grasped her hand, holding it tight, and a lump rose in her throat.

"After the war we'll buy one of those places in Highbury." His voice turned soft. "Not too small, so we can start our family, eleven lads and one sweet lassie just like her mum." He turned his head to hers, his breath warm against her face. "I promise, it will be grand, love."

She didn't speak as tears filled her eyes. *Tell him the truth now*, her heart whispered. If they were ever to have a future, ever to have hope, she must share her burden with him. Otherwise, when the war and the spying were over and they were once again in Britain, her past and the guilt it bore would forever remain an obstacle between them.

Her heart pumped with anxiety. What would she do if Simon rejected her? How could she go on? She'd faced so many difficulties over the past three years, but to lose this man . . .

Eve swallowed against the fear choking her. This life with him now, shrouded in so many secrets, was no life at all. She had to become whole again, for her husband's sake, if not her own.

"I need to tell you a story, Simon," she said, forcing out the words before she could change her mind. "My father used to tell you stories about his war, and now I have one to share with you as well." Eve wet her lips. "You asked me once about La Dame Blanche. Do you know the legend?"

His body tensed beside her. "Medieval folklore," he said, his voice low, cautious. "About a woman in white haunting castles in Bavaria, I think."

"That's right," she said. "It's a fourteenth-century tale about the widowed countess Kunigunde von Orlamonde."

"Tell me."

She slid her arms around his waist and hugged him to her, absorbing his strength. After she finished her story he might push her away.

"Kunigunde wanted to marry Albrecht von Hohenzollern, a Franconian prince," she began. "Albrecht told her they could marry if not for the 'four eyes between them.' He meant his parents, who would disapprove of the marriage, but Kunigunde mistakenly thought he meant her two young children."

Eve drew a steadying breath while the familiar images flashed in her mind: the soldier, his scar looming over her as she plunged the blade into his skull; then the boy, with his reddish-blond hair and soft face, his gray eyes wide as he stared at his bloodied uniform, her hand still on the knife.

"Kunigunde set out to murder her little ones," she said faintly, "piercing their heads with a golden needle so it would appear they'd died naturally. Hiding her secret."

"A murderess." Her husband's tone was grim.

Eve's chest ached, his words cutting into her like the blade itself. "In the end, Albrecht would not have her." Her voice grew thick. "It was said Kunigunde was mortified over her actions and traveled on her knees to see the Pope in Rome and beg his forgiveness. From there she was thought to enter into a monastery until her death, and since then to haunt the castles of the Hohenzollern dynasty, the kaiser's ancestors, promising their demise."

She turned to him in the darkness, pulse racing, knowing she stood on the precipice between her happiness and utter despair. "It's the reason the Belgians took the name La Dame Blanche in their fight against the kaiser and his armies," she finished in a whisper.

"And you . . . you're a part of this White Lady?" he asked hoarsely.

"I *am* the White Lady, Simon," she said in a low, tormented voice. "I am Kunigunde, the murderess."

Before he could say another word, Eve emptied her soul of the burden she'd carried for years. She told him about the soldier with the scar, the violence done to her, and the knife she'd used to kill him before slaying an innocent young boy, whose only mistake had been to put on a man's uniform.

Finally she confessed the horrible price she'd paid for having come to this country against his wishes—the death of their unborn child.

"I have not been on my knees to Rome," she finished in an anguished whisper, "but like the White Lady, I cannot find peace."

Simon was unable to speak for the tumult of emotion roiling inside of him. Helpless rage against the beast who had abused his wife. Cold satisfaction in the knowledge she'd killed him. Sorrow over the death of the boy, and compassion for Eve, haunted by the memory.

Anger that the lad was just one of tens of thousands of lads whose lives had been forfeited in the three-year struggle for power.

And the bairn . . .

His hands clenched into fists. The death of their child wounded him like nothing else, constricting his chest with a driving need to lash out against the injustice and assuage his fury. But war had been responsible for his loss, too immense for one man to conquer.

Guilt weighed heavily on him, realizing what his wife had suffered. He should have been with her, protecting her. Instead he'd been constrained in one prison after another, trying to escape with as much success as flying against a squadron of German Fokker pilots, when there was nowhere to go but down.

He turned to her, longing to take her home and keep her safe, to comfort her and make her forget the past. "Eve . . ."

Her soft sob reached his ears, and Simon rose, drawing her up with him so that they faced one other. In the dim light of the candle flame, he saw tears streaking down her cheeks.

Something hot and fierce seized him, and he pulled her close, holding her tight while his eyes began to burn. "You're right, lass," he whispered against her ear, as her thin shoulders shook. "We canna be what we were before."

She lifted her head, still trembling in his arms.

"We can be better." His smile was tender as he wiped at the

279

tracks of wetness against her face. "We can be stronger, for the rest of our bairns to come."

Simon cupped her chin and lowered his head to capture her mouth with his, the kiss filled with his unspoken promise to love her to the end of their days. No matter what happened, he would never let her go. She kissed him back with fervor, and he sensed that finally the barrier she'd erected between them had fallen. Her arms slid around his neck and she pulled him close, as though she too had no intention of letting go.

The sudden rap on the panel door made them both start.

"It's time," she whispered.

He leaned his head against hers. He had to protect his wife at all costs, even if it meant going against Marcus's instructions. "I need to tell you something, love," he whispered. "Trust no one. There is an enemy agent in Brussels, a man inside La Dame Blanche."

"What?" She pulled back from him.

He withdrew the fountain pen the priest had given him and hiked up his left sleeve. Angling his exposed arm to the candlelight, he drew the mark π against the inside of his wrist.

"This symbol is his moniker," he said. "Be careful. He'll go to any lengths to protect his cover."

Electrified by his words, Eve stared at his wrist. The symbol for Pi, her code name in La Dame Blanche. She looked up at him. "How do you know about an enemy agent?"

Then she remembered his asking her about the network, his desire to make contact. Was it the traitor he'd wanted to meet?

"One of the reasons I was sent here," he said, "was to keep an eye out for anyone using the symbol." His features grew taut beneath the disguise. "Have you seen it?"

Eve shook her head, while fear made her stomach clench. She'd never used the mark in her correspondence, having always written out her signature, "Pi." Surely it wasn't coincidence that someone was using the symbolic form of her code name to infiltrate the network in Brussels?

"Is there anything else you can tell me?" she said.

He shook his head, and she could see his frustration.

The click of a latch echoed in the tunnel. Suddenly the panel opened and Monsieur Tulle's tall, thin frame stood in the opening. "Eve?" he called into the darkness. "All is ready."

Simon bent to retrieve their candle before he reached for her hand. "Come, sweetheart," he said, before giving her a last kiss.

He led the way to the opening. Eve followed, the budding hope she'd held for their future giving way to agitation and more fear. She tried to imagine who might be the enemy among them, but there were many in the Brussels cell: Dominic, Felix, Victor, Madame Bissette, even old Monsieur Tulle. And with each agent familiar with the others' code names, it could be any one of them.

Monsieur Guerin was also a part of the network. Eve considered again the cigar shop owner's strange behavior of weeks before, and the day she thought she'd been followed back from his shop. More recently was the search of her room while she was in Charleroi, and then seeing Schultz and Jaeger disguised inside the church on the same day she went to visit Simon.

Was someone laying a trap for her?

Monsieur Tulle stepped back to allow them entrance into the cramped floor-length cabinet. All three exited into the steamy air of the laundry room, where bundles of linen lay heaped on shelves. A trio of fold-out ironing boards held irons and clothing.

"I sent my wife and daughters upstairs," Tulle explained, while Eve and Simon followed him toward the front of the shop.

Felix was at the counter, clad in a bargeman's cap and dressed as a tradesman. He eyed them both, then checked his watch. "We need to get to the station before nine."

Simon turned to her. Eve longed to rush into his arms, but she held back.

He wasn't out of Belgium yet. She glanced at Monsieur Tulle, then over at Felix, and caught his shrewd stare as he studied them. Uneasiness filled her. How well did she know the orderly?

"Remember what I said," Simon whispered, as though reading her thoughts. "Promise me you'll be careful."

She turned to him. "I promise." Then boldly she rose on tiptoe and kissed him once, twice, three times on either cheek, in the way of her mother's people. "And you as well."

From behind the spectacles his eyes shone bright. He searched her face, as if memorizing her image, before he turned and followed Felix out the door.

Eve remained where she stood, saying a silent prayer for his safety . . . and for her own.

CHAPTER 31

*H*e shouldn't have left her.

The thought hammered against Simon's conscience as he walked outside and slid onto the seat of the truck, while Felix Giroux set the throttle and went to the front to crank over the engine.

Simon glanced back at the laundry shop, the dark curtains obliterating any view inside. His disquiet remained as he remembered their last words. Was she involved with La Dame Blanche? She'd paled when he drew the symbol for Pi. Her brave smile and her kiss at the end had belied the sadness and fear in her eyes.

He thought about how badly she'd been hurt, not only physically but in her soul. The brokenness he'd sensed over the past few weeks had been revealed to him today as she described the horror and loss she'd endured at Louvain.

Eve needed his comfort and his strength. She needed his protection, yet he could do nothing but leave her in pieces while he fled the country for safety.

He ground his teeth, staring out at the street. His entire reason for coming here had been cursed by the Huns. He *should* have met with the agent and handed off the orders and been done with it. He *should* have been able to move about Brussels freely and have more time with his wife. *Time*, that ever precious resource. Perhaps he could have planned a way to rescue her mother and get them all out of Belgium together.

Instead, his presence had put his wife and her family in greater danger.

The engine roared to life, drawing him back to the task at hand. Felix slid behind the wheel.

"We should arrive at the Schaerbeek train station in about twenty minutes," he said, releasing the brake. "Dominic will meet us there."

The truck lurched forward as they headed north along rue de la Madeleine toward the district of Schaerbeek. Simon stared from the window at the city streets. He'd been cloistered in the rectory for most of his time in Brussels, and he couldn't help taking note of his surroundings.

Cold drizzle fell from the dull sky, wetting the sidewalks and sending rivulets of rainwater gushing along the outer edges of the street. Shops and stores built in Gothic style rose along either side, the mismatched reds, greens, and yellows of their multistoried façades lending color to an otherwise sullen canvas.

Above each enterprise, apartment windows were draped in dark curtains and, like the laundry shop, gave evidence to the occupation and its blackout conditions.

As the capital city of Belgium, Brussels seemed relatively quiet. Simon observed a long queue of people standing in the rain, shuffling toward a soup kitchen, bowls in hand as they awaited their turn. Eve had told him people were starving. He'd had no idea so many were in need.

The sight of gendarmes patrolling the sidewalk at the end of the street made him tense. Across the road a staff car sat motionless, its motor running. He tried to imagine the kind of existence his wife had been living here, housed in an apartment much like these, held captive by the constant awareness of being watched by the enemy. A prison-city she'd said, and he could well believe it.

"Once we reach the station we won't have another opportunity to speak," Felix said, breaking the silence. "The German patrols are positioned everywhere. Since you're posing as a businessman from Antwerp, you'll go into the station and buy your own ticket.

"Dominic and I will follow at a distance, to avoid arousing suspicion," he continued. "We'll find you on the train after you board. When we arrive in Antwerp, we'll disembark first and wait for you. Once we make eye contact, you'll follow us."

"What happens then?"

"We didn't expect to be leaving a day early. As it is, Dom and I had to scramble to get our shifts covered for tonight. So our transportation won't be waiting for us. We'll have to figure out a ride with someone on the train. Or we'll have to walk."

He glanced at Simon. "Since it's over seventy kilometers to the abbey in Postel, I'm hoping for the first option. Our passes will be useless beyond Antwerp, so we may need to use a little subterfuge to get through." A smirk flashed beneath his dark moustache. "A strategy I'm sure you're familiar with."

Simon frowned as he studied the man beside him. While Eve still hadn't admitted to working with La Dame Blanche, he began to suspect her friends did. The orderly's hands flexed repeatedly against the steering wheel. Was it anticipation . . . or was it fear?

"Have you done this before?" Simon asked. "Smuggle Allied soldiers across the border?"

Felix shrugged. "Once or twice."

"With the White Lady?"

The orderly turned and gave him a blank stare. "I just help where I can."

Simon curled his lip. "For the good of Belgium, is that it?"

Felix smiled. "Something like that."

"How well do you know Sister Marche?"

"We've worked at the same hospital over a year, though we have different shifts," the orderly said. "I usually see her in the morning as she arrives and I'm ready to leave." He turned to Simon, his amber eyes intent. "How well do *you* know Sister Marche?"

Simon gave him a guarded look. "Meaning?"

"Come now, Captain. She kept you hidden from us for weeks. And considering the risks she took getting you out of the hospital, I think there's more going on than Sister Marche doing her part to aid one Allied soldier."

"I think you've got quite the imagination." Simon turned to stare ahead. Had Felix been watching Eve? He was surprised she hadn't divulged his hiding place to the orderlies, especially since they were aiding in his escape. Was it simply out of caution . . . or was there another reason?

He wondered at Felix taking him for a spy. Unless Eve had told him about the actual contents of the leather pouch, only she knew the information it held.

He tried again. "What other work do you do for the underground?"

"No more questions." Felix pointed to the road ahead. "We've arrived."

Simon gazed at the expansive structure of white-and-orange striped brick that was Schaerbeek station. Crowds dressed in traveling clothes waited outside the terminal to enter.

"Getting their passes checked," Felix said as he parked the truck.

Simon caught sight of a military transport vehicle and a dozen German soldiers hovering at the edge of the crowd.

"They watch the station constantly," Felix said, following his gaze. "Go ahead and get in line. I'll be a few people behind you. Just show them your documents, then go inside and purchase your ticket for Antwerp." He pulled several Belgian francs from his pocket and handed them to Simon. "When they call to board, get on the train. We'll find you."

The line seemed to crawl forward. Finally Simon stood in front of a stony-faced German soldier. Sweat rolled down his back. He handed over his paperwork and forced himself to breathe as the Hun checked his passport. Without benefit of a mirror, he prayed the moustache and goatee were still on straight.

His muscles eased once his papers were returned.

"*Geh hinein*," the guard said, pointing a thumb toward the interior of the station.

The call to board the train came shortly after Simon purchased his ticket. He stepped from the platform into one of the furnished cars and found a seat.

A minute later the two orderlies walked down the aisle past him and without a backward glance took up position several seats away.

They reached Antwerp in under an hour. Felix had given him a German newspaper, the *Cologne Gazette*, which Simon pretended to read while he cast occasional glances at the German soldiers patrolling the car.

He waited until Dominic and Felix passed him and exited the train, then he casually folded the newspaper and left it on the seat before departing the car.

The train platform was a swarm of activity; clearly the Huns had claimed the city. Hundreds of German soldiers were embarking on trains marked Ghent, no doubt heading west to join the fighting at Passchendaele.

He caught sight of the orderlies and followed them at a leisurely pace through the terminal's vaulted interior, then outside to a grove of trees. The pair scanned the area before climbing into the back of a covered truck.

After surveying the area for himself, Simon joined them.

"Keep this in case you need to hide beneath it." Dominic handed Simon a folded sheet of canvas. He and Felix had similar cloths.

Three large wooden barrels stood on end up against the truck's cab, accounting for the yeasty smell of beer that filled the air. Dominic closed the tailgate curtain, then rapped twice against the truck's metal side before the vehicle lurched into motion.

"So, Captain," the big Frenchman asked in a low voice, "how do you like our accommodations?"

Simon spread out the canvas. "I take it you met someone on the train."

"*Oui*. A beer man coming in from Mechelen. He and his brother own a brewery in Mol, a few kilometers from the abbey."

"So we will be walking, just not as far," Felix said. "The Boche are avid beer drinkers, so it's usually the safest transportation. They rarely halt deliveries when they're told the beer is for some general's party."

"Relax for a while," Dominic said, leaning against one of the barrels. "It will take us two hours to reach Mol. From there we'll make our way to the abbey. Hopefully the passeurs can meet us there tonight."

Simon settled against the side of the truck and pretended to close his eyes. He observed both men and the covert glances they exchanged. While he didn't remark on the tension—after all, a venture like this would make anyone nervous, with Huns crawling all about—he was becoming more and more uneasy.

Why had Eve kept his hiding place a secret from these two, when she'd involved them both to such a degree?

Trust her instincts, he told himself. He continued watching the silent interchange between the two men. Despite his agitation, he prayed the priest would keep an eye on Eve until he could return to Brussels with a new strategy to get her out.

He was glad he'd put her on her guard. Until he returned, or until Marcus sent another to complete the mission, she and those who helped the people of Belgium ran a grave risk of capture.

By early afternoon they arrived in Mol. After thanking the Belgian brewers, the three men took to the surrounding woods and reached the abbey two hours later.

The monks welcomed their unexpected arrival with a hot meal—the fresh food a vast improvement over the stale fare Simon had eaten in Brussels. Since the abbey also brewed its own beer, the men were treated to large glasses of the amber liquid.

Afterward they were taken to the cellar, a community room with several bunks that served as a place for wayfarers to rest.

"The abbot has sent word to the passeurs to meet us tonight," Dominic said, tossing his heavy coat onto a bunk. "You'll leave for the border near Reusel after that."

Just after dusk the two men arrived, tall, strapping Belgians dressed in dark clothes and wearing bargemen's caps. They sat at the community table downstairs, and one of them held open a rucksack.

"You'll need these," the first passeur said in French as he withdrew for Simon a pair of India rubber gloves and rubber socks. "When we arrive at the border, my partner and I will wait for the right moment to advance. Once we rush the fence, we'll spread apart the barbed wire and signal you to come forward. You must get through as quickly as possible, then pass beneath the second fence, which is electrified. The rubber gloves and socks will protect you from being cooked if you brush against the wires."

"You must get through the barbed wire of the third fence on your own," the second passeur said. "All of this must happen in less than two minutes. The Boche have guard shacks positioned every one hundred meters, and each houses two guards. They patrol their distance of fence on either side of the shack, converging with the next guard down. In that way they can patrol every inch of the border."

The first man continued the instructions. "We will wait until the two guards return to their respective shacks, when they are at the farthest distance from each other, before we attempt the fence. Our speed is critical, as it won't take them long to retrace their steps. Once you get through onto Dutch soil, you must hide until they've separated again. Then move north until you reach the first road. An agent will meet you there."

Simon wiped his damp hands against his trousers as he glanced at the gloves and socks on the table. The priest had been right. Crossing the border into Holland could be a fatal endeavor. He'd been a fool to think he could get Eve or her mother across!

Once Felix had paid the two men, all was in readiness. Ascending to the main floor, Simon followed the passeurs out through the back to the grounds. When he turned, he saw that the orderlies still followed.

"You're coming with us?" he asked, surprised.

"I promised Sister Marche I would see you safely across the border," Dominic said.

"And I'll go along to keep him company," Felix added.

Simon again sensed the subtle friction between Eve's two friends.

The party of five navigated silently through fields, farms, and woodlands in near total darkness, not daring an electric torch for fear of discovery by the Germans. Fortunately, the passeurs seemed to know the terrain well and led them to their destination without incident.

It was midnight when they approached the border. Reusel lay just beyond the fence. The orderlies were directed toward a stand of Scotch pine ten meters away, while Simon was motioned to crouch alongside his paid guides in a cluster of tall grass.

He had already removed his disguise and tucked it inside his coat. He had to abandon the shoes the priest had given him and quickly donned the rubber socks and the gloves.

A pair of lights shone from electric torches ahead as two armed sentries patrolled back and forth along a strip of fence. One of them shined his light toward the Dutch side, and Simon's heart gave a lurch as he glimpsed three nine-foot-high multi-tiered fences.

Sweat beaded along his upper lip. He glanced over at the two orderlies hiding in the copse before he turned to the two passeurs beside him, poised and ready to pounce.

The light beams finally merged into one as the two sentries met at a central point along the fence. After a quiet exchange, one withdrew a pack of cigarettes and offered it to the other. The flicker of a match illuminated the night, and soon a haze of smoke crossed the beam of torchlight.

The two separated, moving away from each other back to their shacks.

Simon had a fleeting sense of relief that there were no dogs; then a nudge from the passeur on his right alerted him to follow.

Suddenly he was racing toward the fence behind the two men. They reached it just before he did and stretched apart the lowest rung of barbed wire. He dropped to the ground, rolling through the space, gritting his teeth against the pain in his ribs. Then the hum of electricity filled his ears as he glimpsed the white porcelain knobs charging the second fence. He slid his body beneath the electric wire, using the rubber gloves to protect himself.

Simon was halfway through the last fence when a shout echoed in the darkness, followed by a single shot. A barrage of gunfire ensued as the German sentries, along with the other guards at the shack, fired rounds into the night.

Time slowed while Simon lay wedged beneath the barbed

wire of the third fence. He watched the two passeurs crumple to the ground. Then he scrambled out from beneath the barbed wire, ignoring the cuts to his face as he belly-crawled to the nearest cover, a thicket of dead blackberry vines.

Pain seared his chest as he stared back at the scene on the Belgian side. He glimpsed someone running from the copse of pine. Then more gunfire erupted, and the figure stumbled but kept moving and disappeared into the woods.

The Huns moved to stand over the passeurs and fired on them again. From his hiding place Simon tried to breathe as wave after wave of shock washed over him. He'd heard the shout in French, words of indictment meant for him to hear, followed by the single shot.

He'd recognized the voice—and the shadowy figure who escaped.

Simon had found the traitor.

CHAPTER 32

Had her husband survived the crossing?

Eve left the hospital after work the next day, the knot in her stomach growing with each passing hour. Dom and Felix should have returned from the north this morning, but so far she hadn't received word from either of them.

Yesterday, after seeing Simon off, she'd struggled to keep her mind on her tasks at the hospital, imagining the danger he would face getting to Reusel. Matron had taken her to task for dropping a jar of tongue depressors, the glass shattering against the ward's tiled floor.

What if Simon had been discovered? Fear and despair settled in her chest. Eve couldn't lose him again; she'd finally found the courage to share her past with him, and he'd overwhelmed her with his tenderness, his warm reassurance as he held her. *We can be better, lass. Stronger . . .*

Simon loved her despite the awfulness she had inflicted and suffered, and for the first time in a long while hope managed to filter its way into her heart. She had begun to anticipate their future together.

Now she had no idea whether the man she loved was dead or alive. She'd sent a message through to Rotterdam yesterday morning, informing them that Albert Janssen was on his way and would cross into Holland a day earlier than planned. Did the information get through, and had they found him . . . or were they searching even now?

She smothered a cry as an image of Simon lying dead somewhere in the north rose in her mind. Surely God would not let that happen.

On her way to the café she spied the familiar spire of St. Magdalene's and changed course. Minutes later, she entered the cool, quiet interior of the church.

She hadn't been back since the evening before Simon left the rectory. Now she walked toward the front and slipped into a pew. Kneeling, she clasped her hands together and bowed her head. *Lord, please let him be safe. Please let my husband come back to me . . .*

Her eyes burned as she lifted her head to gaze at the image of Christ on the cross. The story of John 21 again rose in her mind, and she thought about Jesus' words. "*Simon son of John, do you love me?*"

Do you love me? Her husband had asked that same question, and through his gentleness, his patience, and his understanding, he'd drawn her out from behind the wall of her pain.

Jesus was Love, and love was all of those things: gentleness, patience, and understanding. By offering them to Simon Peter, He'd drawn the apostle out from the depths of his regret, offering him mercy and hope.

She had railed at God's silence; yet now she thought about the prayers He *had* answered for her. In Louvain, she'd begged Him to keep her family safe, and with Mama here in Brussels and the news that Nikki and Zoe were in France, she saw that God had watched over them. He'd also brought Simon back to her and then kept him safe inside the city.

God had offered her forgiveness, too, when three years ago

she'd gone to the priest to seek her confession. But she had continued to allow the tyrant guilt to keep her locked in the past, blinding her to the future, to *hope*.

Eve caught a movement and turned to see Father Francois entering the confessional. There were a few people queuing up to wait in line.

Perhaps God had been silent only because He waited on her to put her faith forward and trust in Him instead of sliding backward into fear and regret.

Leaving her seat, she made her way toward the line. She would take the first step, a fresh start. And she would work on putting the past behind her.

She would learn to trust in Him and accept His mercy.

Janssen received.

Eve hid in the water closet at the café the following night and read the message that Vincent had delivered. Her heart swelled, while tears dampened her lashes. Simon was alive. She thought of her prayer yesterday at the church. God had heard her.

Wiping away her tears, she read the rest of the note:

Meet Lundgren. Restaurant Hotel de Gilbert, La Bouteille, France, 13 November, 1100 hours. Look for red poppy. Provide contact name: Generaloberst Adler, Château de Mérode, Trélon, France. Acknowledge receipt.

Eve considered the timeline. The ambush was to take place on the twentieth. Once she met with Lundgren and gave him the name, he'd have less than a week to get inside the château.

Trélon wasn't far from the town of Anor, where Nikki and Zoe were supposed to be. An Allied attack would mean guns, mortars, and artillery fire; the city would swarm with soldiers shooting from both sides.

A scene much like Louvain rose in her mind, and she shivered. In all likelihood her brother and sister would be in danger, though now at least she had the exact place and time of her meeting. She could get them away beforehand.

Refolding the note, she tucked it inside her corset. She would acknowledge receipt of the message later. She left the water closet, her pulse quickening. With only five days until her meeting with Lundgren, she would need to start planning. Like getting passes and finding a way to travel south . . .

"Eve!"

"Coming, Aunt!" She hurried to the sideboard and gathered up a tray laden with steaming bowls of Thursday's special, *Zwiebelsuppe*, and began serving customers.

Otto Reinhardt sat at the far end of the café in his usual place, and Eve noted he'd barely touched his meal. Beer onion soup had always been one his favorites. She paused at his table.

"Herr Major, can I get you anything? Is there something wrong with the soup?"

"*Nein*," he said quickly, then pressed the linen napkin to his lips. "I seem to have lost my appetite." His features flushed. "My . . . my wife wrote to me. I'm taking the train to Berlin in the morning."

Eve hid her surprise. Otto hadn't been the same since the night of the operetta, and she suspected he was worried over the possibility of being sent to the Front at Passchendaele like his friend and so many others currently leaving the city. A part of her sympathized with his fear. Yet another part of her, the one suffering the daily indignities of living under the German's thumb, felt justified, and she was glad he was leaving for Berlin. It might even make her departure from Brussels easier. "I hope nothing is wrong," she said. "How long will you be away?"

296

"Only until Monday." He stared into his soup bowl. "They have so little to spare . . ."

Eve barely caught his last words, yet as she glanced at the uneaten bread, and the soup he'd barely touched, the truth dawned. His family was starving.

She'd read enough of the Belgian underground newspapers to know that over the past year German U-boats had struck Allied merchant ships carrying food to Belgium and France. Great Britain had retaliated by blockading food ships bound for Germany. Now the kaiser's people went hungry in much the same way as the Belgians.

She could find no sense of righteousness in it, however. "You should eat, Herr Major." She nudged the plate of bread in his direction. "You will do your family no good if you go hungry."

He glanced at her and offered a weak smile. She gave him one in return and nodded toward his bowl. "Please, don't let it go to waste."

Otto lifted his spoon and began to eat. As Eve drew away and headed back to the kitchen, she realized she might well be gone before he returned next week. On her way, God willing, to see her own family.

❧

"I'd like a transfer to the Red Cross hospital at Chimay."

Eve stood facing Nurse Hoffmeyer's desk the following morning, hoping the woman would embrace the idea of removing a British nurse from her staff.

The buxom matron paused from writing in her ledger to look at her in surprise. "Is there a problem, Sister Marche? You have been very unsettled lately." She glanced at the charts on her desk, and her tone turned peevish. "Our patient beds are full right now, and two orderlies have simply vanished. While I would be most happy to grant your request, it's not convenient that you leave at this time."

Eve's jaw tightened. She had this one opportunity while Otto was gone to make her escape. She needed to obtain a pass to Chimay; Corporal Duval's father had his farm there. He should be able to help her get into occupied France.

Only a few days remained before she was to meet the assassin. "I do have a problem," she said, as inspiration struck. "It involves Herr Major Reinhardt."

Matron rose from her chair, a frown curving her lips. "How so?"

"As you probably know, Herr Major asked me to accompany him to Brussels from Louvain. While he has been a fair employer, I'm beginning to feel a certain amount of . . . obligation."

The older nurse's gaze was razor sharp. "What kind of obligation?"

"His attentions, you see," Eve explained. "Recently he moved into our apartment, and already he and I are together all day at the hospital . . ." She pressed her lips tightly together, as if she couldn't go on.

"I believe I understand, Sister." Matron laid her pen down carefully against the blotter on her desk, then straightened to her full height, her blunt features suffused with anger. "That kind of behavior will not be tolerated in this hospital," she rasped. "I will contact Herr Colonel Rutgers—"

"*Nein*!" Eve held up a hand, seized by a twinge of conscience.

Otto was the enemy, true, and he'd spent years threatening her for information, but he *had* taken care of her family. Now, with his own so desperate back in Berlin, she didn't relish having him sent to the Front, which would surely happen if Nurse Hoffmeyer spoke with her power-wielding brother-in-law.

"Herr Major has not been improper toward me," she hastened to add. "I only worry that because I saved his life years ago, his favoritism toward me may take a turn . . ."

"I have noticed he favors you." Matron's tone was flat as she resettled into her chair.

"Yes, that is why I hope you feel it would be better for all concerned if I transfer out. Herr Major can remain at the apartment." As a safeguard to Otto, she added, "He has been a competent administrator here at the hospital. I know he approves of all your changes to make the ward run more efficiently."

Matron's scowl eased. "He said that?"

"He did." Eve didn't add that Otto feared to do otherwise and risk upsetting the sister-in-law of the kommandant's senior staff officer.

Matron eyed her another moment, then picked up her pen and bent to the ledger. "I will see what can be done."

"Thank you, Matron." Eve forced the words, stifling her impatience at the woman's vague answer. "I'd like to leave as soon as possible, at least before Herr Major's return to Brussels. You understand."

"I do not understand." Matron looked up, incredulous. "Today is Friday. Herr Major will return on Monday." She blinked. "You wish to leave today, Sister Marche?"

Eve hesitated, then nodded.

The older woman huffed out a breath. "Impossible!" She slammed the ledger closed. "I'll need more time. I must check my roster of nurses and request a replacement from Berlin—"

"Please, Matron," Eve said. "I must leave now. I don't wish to confront Herr Major, or have my leaving reflect on his treatment of my family."

Nurse Hoffmeyer stared at her, tapping her pen against the blotter as if weighing some decision. "If you agree to work tomorrow, so I can rotate my nurses' schedule, you may leave on Sunday." She paused, her mouth hard. "We can simply say a nurse was needed at Chimay."

Eve's shoulders eased. "Thank you, Matron."

"I'll still need to make a telephone call." She rose again from the desk, her features sour. "They may not even want you."

Biting back a retort, Eve thanked her again. On her way out, she laid a hand to her throat and tried to steady her racing pulse.

Later that night, as she entered the café to begin her shift, anxiety and excitement coursed through her. In just a few days she would see her brother and sister!

Laurette's mother was working the main floor when she arrived. Madame Fontaine had been training as a waitress for the past two weeks, and Eve was relieved that her aunt and uncle were pleased with the woman's work. It made leaving less of a burden on her conscience.

Halfway through her shift, the café quieted enough that Madame Fontaine could handle the customers. Eve went to the kitchen.

"May I have a word, Aunt?"

Aunt Marie was at the oven pulling out a tray of black bread. The smell of the coarse bread was always better than the taste. Once she'd placed the tray on the counter, she turned and wiped her reddened hands against her apron. "What is it, dear?"

With Simon's unexpected arrival, Eve had postponed telling her aunt and uncle about her siblings. Now she took a deep breath and said, "I've found them, Aunt. Nikki and Zoe."

Aunt Marie's mouth went slack. "Where are they?"

"Anor, in France. One of my patients told me they escaped the train before it ever reached Germany. His two cousins fled with them, heading south into France to the cousins' home."

Her aunt reached for the stool near the stove and sat down. "They have been nearby . . . all this time?"

"All this time," Eve whispered, and her throat tightened with bitterness. So much time lost.

"It's a miracle." Her aunt's brown eyes glistened. "Have you told Louise?"

"I cannot tell Mama until I'm certain they are still there," she said, putting voice to her worry. "Nikki is fourteen now . . ."

Anger flashed in her aunt's features. "The Boche will put him in the trenches. When will you leave?"

Eve eyed her with affection. Aunt Marie never questioned she would go after them. "I wanted to leave tomorrow, but Matron insisted I must work Saturday's shift for another nurse. I'll leave on Sunday instead, and stop and see Maddie on the way."

Matron had at least agreed to hold a supply truck until Sunday so Eve could get a ride into Charleroi. From there she could take a train to Chimay.

"I'm sorry for the short notice, Aunt," she said, taking her aunt's hands in her own.

Aunt Marie shook her head. "No, you must go as soon as possible and bring them back. I have always regretted I didn't convince them to stay with Lucien and me, instead of going to Louvain." She gave Eve's hands a returning squeeze. "We'll wait before telling your mother, *oui*? Simply say you are needed at one of the hospitals for a time."

"*Merci, Tante.*" Eve leaned to kiss her on the cheek.

"Do you have any idea when you will return?"

Between the scheduled meeting with Lundgren in La Bouteille and figuring out a plan to get her brother and sister back into Belgium, she had no idea. "A week, perhaps? Maybe longer."

"Then I wish you well, *ma chère.*" Her aunt rose from the stool and embraced her. "And be careful."

"Sister Marche, can you please come with me to the church?"

Eve walked out of the hospital the following afternoon, surprised to find Father Francois waiting for her, his face solemn.

"Is everything all right?"

"I hope so. I have a parishioner who . . . needs your help."

"Of course," she said, curious.

When they entered the church, he said, "He's in the room recently vacated."

A prickle of alarm rose along her neck. She eyed him sharply, Simon's warning ringing in her ears. Surely the priest wouldn't lead her into a trap.

He merely nodded and waved her toward the front of the church. The pews held only a handful of people seated or kneeling in prayer.

Eve took her time moving toward the altar, searching for anyone suspicious, anyone resembling Jaeger or Schultz.

Father Francois had remained at the back of the church. When she was a few feet from the sacristy door, she turned and watched the priest nod before he dropped a brass incense burner onto the stone floor.

The crash reverberated across the vaulted ceiling, and everyone present turned to stare in the direction of the noise. Eve slipped inside the sacristy door and into the vestments cabinet.

Once she'd made her way through the priest's closet into his chamber, a familiar voice called from Simon's old room, "I bow to your genius, Sister Marche."

"Dom?"

She entered the small quarters and found her friend lying on the mattress. His face was cut and scratched, and his left arm was bandaged below the cut-off sleeve of his shirt.

"I didn't know you and the priest had this kind of operation." The edge of his mouth lifted as he raised his head to greet her. "I especially like the tunnel."

"What happened to you?" she demanded, kneeling to inspect his wound. "I've been so worried."

He winced as she peeled back the bandage. Eve stared at the bullet wound. "Dear heaven, did the Boche do this at the border?" She looked into his eyes. "Where is Felix?"

"I don't know where he is." Dom tossed his head back against the pillow. "But it was his bullet that did this."

"What?" She leaned back, stunned. "But . . . you two are friends. Why would he do this?"

"He's no friend." Fury flashed in his eyes. "Once we reached the border and Chandler began to cross, Felix pulled a pistol on me. He said he was tired of pretending."

Eve sucked in a breath. Felix was the traitor! "He shot you then?"

Dom shook his head, scowling. "He fired the first round at Chandler. Then the German guards began spraying bullets everywhere, killing the two passeurs. I'd already started running for my life, but Felix put a slug in me before I could make the woods."

Pulse pounding, Eve barely heard his last words. "Did Felix hit . . . the captain, too?" she asked, trying to keep her voice steady.

Dom shrugged as he gently replaced the bandage over his arm. "I have no idea. I kept going until I reached the abbey at Postel. The monks patched me up. I stayed a few days, then got a ride as far as Antwerp, and from there I hid in the back of a utilities truck to Brussels."

He surveyed the secret room. "I hoped the priest would take me in. I didn't expect this."

"It's convenient for hiding people who don't want to be found," Eve said. "I wonder where Felix is now."

"Likely with his Boche friends," Dom ground out.

Eve struggled to grasp all Dom had told her. Felix was the

enemy agent. While she was relieved to know the identity of the infiltrator her husband had spoken of, it unnerved her that she'd been oblivious to a man who shared coffee with her at the café, and even aided her in Simon's escape.

Had he intended all along to kill her husband?

She finally rose and sat on the bench. "I had my suspicions about a saboteur," she said to Dom, and the thought flashed through her mind that Felix had probably been the one to search her room. "Still, it's hard to believe. We worked side by side with him every day, and yet he betrayed us."

"You can imagine how I feel," Dom muttered as he again touched his bandaged arm.

She eyed him with compassion. He and Felix had been friends for a long time. "Well, I'm glad you're safe now, and I hope Chandler wasn't hurt too badly."

"I don't even know if he made it out alive."

"He did."

Dom looked at her in surprise.

"I received a message that he arrived. I assume at Rotterdam."

He released a breath, his mouth curving upward. "I'm glad to hear it."

Eve nodded. "What will you do now?"

She was startled when her friend's face crumpled in despair. "I don't know, *chérie*. I cannot go back to the hospital, or show my face in Brussels. That *cochon* Felix is still out there. He will tell the secret police I aided Chandler at the border."

Eve's heart pounded in her chest, his fear contagious. Would Felix set his sights on her next? He knew she'd orchestrated Simon's escape from the hospital. Even though he had no proof, a word to Jaeger and Schultz would be enough to have her arrested and imprisoned.

"I must leave in the morning," she said. "Yesterday Matron agreed to my transfer to the hospital in Chimay and gave me a pass. Once I arrive there, I'm going into France to find my sister and brother."

She told him about Corporal Duval's father having a farm near the Belgian-French border. "I hope he can help me get across."

"Let me go with you." Dom reached for her hand. "There is nothing left for me here." When she hesitated he said, "Do you have a plan for getting them back into Belgium?"

Eve shook her head. There hadn't been time. She hoped Monsieur Duval could aid with that as well.

"I can protect you, *chérie*," Dom pleaded. "I'll help you find a way to get the children back. France is my homeland, so I can be of use to you."

Seeing his desperate look, her compassion warred with duty. No one must know of her mission to La Bouteille. "I wish I could take you, *mon ami*, but it's not possible."

"You would leave me here to die then?" His stricken gaze searched hers. "Please, I'm begging your help."

Eve sighed, knowing she couldn't possibly refuse him. "There's a supply ambulance taking me as far as Charleroi at seven o'clock tomorrow morning," she said. "Can you be ready?"

The lines in his battered face eased. "*Oui*, just tell me where to meet you."

They made a plan that Dom would remain out of sight near the side entrance into the palace, where the ambulances usually parked. Eve would distract the driver while her friend climbed into the back and hid beneath the rack of stretchers.

She rose from the bench. "Once we get into Charleroi, we'll see what Maddie can do for us. In the meantime, get some rest. I'll meet you tomorrow morning at 0700."

"I'll be there," he said, looking hopeful.

Eve was in a flurry later that night getting ready for her departure. Instead of her usual valise, she chose her rucksack, since it would be more practical for the journey ahead.

She collected her documents, including a map to Monsieur Duval's farm, a change of warm clothes, and her nurse's uniform. Eve had offered to go to Dom's apartment to get his Red Cross passport, but her friend said Father Francois could manage that and his clothing. Dom would meet her at the pre-arranged spot in the morning.

When she'd finished her packing, Eve opened the shrine of the Madonna and Child. She decided to leave the holy water, taking the rosary instead. She would need all the help from heaven she could get.

Next she picked up the Bible, and taking it over to the small brazier in her room, she removed the sheets of rice paper, tossing them into the flames. She then began ripping the hollowed-out pages from the tome. She hated the idea of burning the holy book, but she had no choice. Felix could return at any time and strip her room. She had to get rid of any evidence that might implicate her. Without proof, and with her being gone from the city, her family should be safe enough. Still, she would forewarn her aunt and uncle of the circumstances, just in case.

Would she even be able to return to Brussels? She frowned as she fed the last of the Bible's pages into the fire. The leather cover she could toss in with the café's kitchen garbage later.

She'd requested and received a transfer to Chimay, a ruse in order to get her close to Monsieur Duval's farm and the French border. But what would happen when Matron discovered she'd never arrived to work at the hospital? Or later, when Eve reappeared in Brussels in the company of her brother and sister, who had no passports or passes into the city?

She had yet to come up with a clearly formed plan. Still, she knew the only way to keep Nikki from being sent to the German trenches was to bring her brother and sister back to the city. With the help of Father Francois, Nikki would at least have a chance to get across the border into Holland.

Eve also realized that with Felix on the loose, her cover could already be blown. She wouldn't be able to accompany the children back to Brussels without putting her entire family in danger.

Anger and despair washed over her. What could she do?

Maddie. She would help. Once Eve got her brother and sister back into the country, Maddie could bring them into Brussels. Eve would put her friend in contact with the priest, and he could help her to arrange everything.

The thought gave her hope, yet she ached at the knowledge that she herself would have to remain outside the city, away from her family. She wanted so much to be there when Mama was reunited with her son and younger daughter. But it was more important to protect them.

Simon's handkerchief still lay on the bed, and Eve reached for the precious linen square that held so many memories. How much she missed her husband!

Was he already back in Britain? Again she wondered if he'd been injured in the gunfire at the border. Would he be able to keep his promise and come back for her and her family?

Eve pressed the cloth against her cheek, its soft, worn texture offering some tangible comfort. Then she prayed, both for Simon's well-being and for his promise to return.

With Otto in Berlin, the house was quiet as she left her bedroom and walked down the hall to her mother's room. Mama might be up when she left in the morning, but Eve wanted to spend time with her. It could be a very long time before they saw one another again.

She found her mother dozing in the chair at her worktable, her gnarled hands lying motionless atop the bobbins in front of her.

"Mama?" she whispered.

Her mother roused and turned toward the door. A smile touched her lips and her lashes fluttered as she straightened in the seat. "Come, *ma fifille*. I was just working on another piece of lace."

Eve entered and saw that the lace pinned against the pricking on the cushioned worktable was already a quarter of a meter long.

"You've been working since dawn, haven't you?" She touched her mother's thin shoulder. "No wonder you sleep sitting up. Come and lie down on the bed."

Her mother shook her head. "I must finish this special piece for Madame Bissette."

"I shall take it with me early in the morning," Eve said. "After that, you can rest for a time. I am going to Chimay."

"When will you return?"

Heart thumping, Eve gazed into the beloved face of her mother, seeing the years of soft words and comforting arms, quiet strength, and always, unconditional love.

She cleared her throat. "I'll be back as soon as I can, Mama." With the dangers ahead, and the possibility she might never return to Brussels, Eve was unwilling to promise more. "While I'm gone, I think Aunt Marie would appreciate your help in the café, if only to keep her company."

Her mother nodded. "You do so much work for the good of others. I know that sometimes you must leave us, but hurry back, all right?" She reached for Eve's hand on her shoulder and gave it a squeeze. "I will miss you while you are gone."

Eve closed her eyes as she bent to kiss and gently embrace her mother. Despite her courage, Mama was so fragile; already she'd lost two of her children, and now she was about to lose the third.

Only God knew how long Eve would be away. In the meantime, she must try to get Nikki and Zoe back with their mother. Even if only for a short while, they must have the chance to be a family again.

CHAPTER 33

"I found your enemy agent," Simon announced as he strode toward the desk in Marcus Weatherford's London office. "The fool almost got me killed crossing the border."

From behind the desk, Marcus's brown eyes grew intent. "Tell me."

Simon quickly outlined the events that had occurred from the time his plane went down in Brussels, including his escape from the hospital, his subsequent recovery at St. Magdalene's, and finally the night he was taken north to cross the Belgian-Holland border.

"I was sandwiched in by barbed wire when I heard one of the orderlies shout. Then a gun went off and all perdition broke loose. I managed to get past the fence and keep myself hidden until things quieted down."

"Well, which one was it?" Marcus leaned forward in his chair. "The enemy agent?"

"Dominic Lesser."

Simon began pacing the carpeted floor. "I have to get back to Brussels, Marcus. Eve is in danger. She trusts the Frenchman and has no idea what he's capable of. I've already lost five days in trying to get back here from Rotterdam."

310

"Then he's the one who contacted me right after your crash?" Marcus asked. "I thought you said Eve found you first, and you gave her your documents in the leather pouch."

Simon spun around. "That's right, it was Eve. Lesser knew nothing of the sealed orders."

"Eve." Marcus's expression turned pensive. "Did she return them to you?"

Simon shook his head. "It was too dangerous. I had her burn them when I couldna complete the mission. The passport I reused with a new photograph, to get me to the border." He stared at his friend. "Look, Marcus, I need a plane. I've got to get back to Eve."

Marcus seemed deep in thought, his dark features grim. Finally he looked up and said, "We were contacted by the suspected enemy agent after your crash. Pi was the one to apprise us of your situation in Brussels, and kept us advised as to when you would leave Belgium for Holland."

Simon stared at him, disbelief warring with a sudden, piercing stab to his middle. "No." He came back to stand facing his friend. "No, it's not her, Marcus. My wife canna be Pi."

Yet as Marcus continued to frown, Simon's doubts returned, thrusting their way into his mind. He thought of Eve's reticence, her evasive responses to his questions—especially about her involvement with the underground. Her look of utter shock when he'd drawn for her the Pi symbol on his wrist.

He didn't want to believe it, but who else could have made contact with Marcus about his situation?

"Is Pi a member of La Dame Blanche?" he asked, already knowing the answer.

Marcus nodded. "I didn't tell you before, but after La Dame Blanche's leader, Henri van Bergen, was arrested, his agents began sending information directly through to Rotterdam. That's how we first learned of Pi. We already knew from MI5 that messages using the symbol for Pi had been confiscated from known German agents here in Britain."

Simon gripped the back of the chair adjacent to the desk and stared at his friend. *My wife, a traitor?* He'd made that same assumption about her weeks ago when she handed over the pouch, but now . . .

"There's got to be another explanation, Marcus," he said in a harsh tone. "My wife would never commit treason. You're wrong about her."

"Time will tell." Rising from behind the desk, Marcus came around to perch against its edge. "We aren't certain if it was coincidence or if Pi and the agent signing with the mark are one and the same," he said. "Since we've been receiving good intelligence from the former, we decided to try to rule out the possibility we're dealing with a double agent." He paused. "The secret orders I sent with you to Brussels will offer that proof."

"What are you saying?" Simon's gnawing suspicions were playing havoc with his heart. "I told you Eve destroyed those orders."

"The orders were a ruse," Marcus said in a flat tone. "We called it Operation Behead the Snake, a fabricated ambush against German army headquarters in Trélon to assassinate the kaiser, who is often in residence. We wanted to see if Pi would alert the Germans to the upcoming attack, compelling them to pull troops from the north down into Trélon to protect their leader."

He leaned back, crossing his arms. "The imaginary ambush will take place on the twentieth, just over a week from now, when an actual surprise Allied attack is planned for Cambrai to the north."

Despite his churning gut, Simon couldn't help being impressed. Not only would the disinformation expose the double agent, but if the Germans acted on it, their weakened northern troops would be vulnerable to the real Allied attack.

"Had your plane not crashed, Simon, you would have met Pi to hand over those orders. As it is, everything still worked out in our favor, and we've been dealing with Pi up to this point."

Anger flared in him. "Say her name, Marcus."

"Eve," he said. "From what you've told me, we've been communicating with Eve."

"I still think you're wrong." Simon pushed himself away from the chair. "If she's involved with La Dame Blanche, then so was Felix Giroux, and so is Dominic Lesser. I heard Giroux's cry accusing Lesser as a traitor. I saw that hulking Frenchman run for the woods. He's your enemy agent, not my wife."

"Did Lesser have access to the secret orders?"

"I canna believe he did," Simon said with impatience. "What does it matter now? They're gone, destroyed."

"The game is already in play." Marcus eyed him steadily. "Pi has alerted the Germans. Our intelligence officer near Cambrai reports two battalions from the Second Army have begun moving south into Trélon."

Coldness seeped into Simon's bones. Reason told him Marcus was right, and all indications pointed to Eve's guilt: her safekeeping of his orders, while they'd obviously been decoded and handed over to the enemy; Eve's secrecy in working for La Dame Blanche; and her using the code name Pi.

Again he thought of the tunnel and her stunned expression when he'd shown her the enemy's mark. He had thought her reaction was fear. But was it guilt?

Had she lied to him, leading him on a merry chase?

No, his heart told him. He'd held her in his arms in that same tunnel, tears falling against her cheeks, while her shoulders shook with sobs. He'd heard the agony in her voice as she confessed to him the horrors she'd endured in Louvain, and then she'd poured out her love to him in the passion of their last kiss.

Their reunion in Brussels had been hampered by secrets and half truths, but the last days they'd spent together, the way they felt about one another—that had been real.

Eve had been real.

"Dominic Lesser has to be responsible," he said in a matter-of-fact tone. "I don't know how Eve is involved, but I won't believe she's culpable."

A knock sounded at the door. "Come," Marcus called.

A girl dressed in the uniform of a Girl Guide entered and handed his friend a large envelope.

"Thank you, Miss Walters."

"Does everyone here work on Sunday?" Simon asked once she'd gone.

"It's wartime." Marcus returned to his chair before he opened the packet and placed the contents on the desk. "No one gets a day off."

Standing across from him, Simon angled his head to eye the official MI6 report sheet, along with several large photographs.

"Dominic Lesser." Simon pointed at a picture of the over-sized Frenchman standing on a narrow street, perhaps an alley, facing a tall, broad-faced man wearing a dark coat and fedora.

"That's a German agent," Marcus said, indicating the man in the coat. "Last year MI5 had him under surveillance here in London."

Marcus flipped to the next photograph of Dominic, and Simon muttered a curse.

"He's with Jaeger and Schultz, the two Huns who gave me a thrashing in the hospital." He pointed at the white-faced Schultz. "This one stabbed me in the heel to make sure I was dead."

In the picture the three men were huddled beside a dark, nondescript car. Dominic wore the same tradesman's clothes he'd had on the morning he took Simon north to the border. He seemed to be handing Jaeger a small package.

The next photograph showed an official document in code, laid alongside a hollowed-out Bible that contained a passport and . . .

Shock rippled through Simon as he recognized the handkerchief with his initials lying beside the Bible.

"Those are the orders I gave you," Marcus remarked. "I'm not certain what the other items signify."

"That's my handkerchief." Simon's voice came out hoarse. "I gave it to Eve years ago, at the birthday party you and I attended."

His friend looked up, his dark eyes filled with compassion. "I'm sorry, Simon."

Marcus reached for the official report and scanned it. "Belgian agents from Postel were able to retrieve the body of Felix Giroux. Once they found information hidden in the buttons of his coat, they conducted a thorough search and discovered a small roll of film in the hollowed-out heel of his left shoe. The intelligence was forwarded to Rotterdam immediately, where it was processed before being sent here."

He flipped the page. "Giroux apparently suspected Lesser of being a double agent, with political ties to a pro-German movement. He surveilled him and took these photographs. He also observed Lesser searching the apartment of a fellow La Dame Blanche agent, and the photograph is included."

Simon and Marcus looked at one another. "Eve's apartment," Simon said.

"It says here the last photograph is another copy of the same intelligence, discovered in Lesser's apartment when Giroux conducted a search."

Before Marcus had a chance, Simon flipped the last photograph and stared at the image. Another copy of the orders he'd been given, or rather a photograph of the orders. Scrawled across the top was the name of a German officer, Colonel Rutgers in Brussels, while at the bottom was a scrawled note of warning in German and signed with the symbol π.

"According to this report, it was Lesser who photographed the orders in Eve's apartment, then developed them and sent a copy to this Colonel Rutgers," Marcus said.

"Meaning she was unaware of his actions," Simon concluded, and a weight lifted from his shoulders. "Eve is blameless."

"It would appear so," Marcus agreed. "It also explains why Giroux was shot. Lesser must have realized he'd been discovered. And that made him desperate."

Fear and anger surged in Simon as he leaned against the desk. "I'm going back to get my wife, Marcus," he said. "And I'll take care of Dominic Lesser while I'm there."

"It might be too late."

"What do you mean?" His pulse hammered. "What's happened?"

He eyed Simon. "Once we learned you were in Holland, we sent a message to Pi through Rotterdam with information for the 'assassin,' along with a date, time, and place she was to meet him in La Bouteille. In reality, we'd planned to send an MI6 agent to the meeting and make an arrest."

A chill ran along his spine as Simon recalled Eve's words, and he relayed to Marcus his wife's desire to find her siblings.

"She'll try to make that rendezvous and then go in search of her family," he predicted. "I need to get back into Brussels and prevent her from leaving and walking into *your* trap."

"She's probably already left for France, Simon. I can notify the agent in La Bouteille about the change in our situation, but unless you know the whereabouts of her brother and sister, I doubt you'll find her beforehand."

"But what if she's still in Brussels? When Lesser learns of your latest correspondence with her, he'll do all in his power to get it. She might even offer the intelligence to him, since they're both involved in La Dame Blanche." Simon's gut twisted, thinking of what the orderly could do to his wife. "You said yourself, Marcus, Lesser is desperate and his cover is blown. Once he gets the information from her, she'll become his liability. Look, I can parachute in tonight near the priory, the way it should have happened the last time I was there. I still have my passport and my disguise; I'll make my way into the city and find her—"

"That's foolhardy," Marcus argued. "We just got you out of there. And your ship from Rotterdam docked less than two hours ago, so you probably haven't slept. You're in no condition to jump out of a plane."

"I'm fine," Simon gritted out. His ribs were sore, but he was determined.

"What about the risk of recapture?" Marcus rose from his seat to lean his fists against the desk. "From what you've told me, your 'resurrection' in Brussels would put several people in grave danger, *including* your wife."

Simon glared at Marcus. He knew his friend was right. The miraculous reappearance of Captain Chandler in Brussels would set the vampires off on an all-out search for those who had aided in his first escape. Eve would be at the top of their list.

But if his wife was still in the city, it might be Simon's only chance to save her. The longer she remained in Dominic Lesser's company, the greater risk to her. Lesser knew about the mission; he too had been waiting for those final instructions. With only days remaining before the attack, he would know Eve had them. He might even use force . . .

"I understand the risks, Marcus," he said. "Either way, Eve's life is at stake. Waiting until she arrives at La Bouteille could be too late." His tone hardened. "If I have to steal a plane and land it myself, I'm going back."

Marcus's mouth twisted beneath his dark moustache. "And what will you do if she's already gone? The meeting in La Bouteille is set for the thirteenth. Once you're in Brussels, you'll have very little time to find her."

"If she's not there, I'll contact her mother. Louise will know where Eve's gone. The priest can get me transportation and the means to get across the border into France." Simon drew a breath. "If I don't find her before the rendezvous, then I'll meet her in La Bouteille. So you can call off your agent."

Marcus was still frowning, but Simon refused to back down. Eve needed him. One way or another, he was going after her.

At length his friend sighed. "Let's order up a plane. And pray you don't get caught."

CHAPTER 34

*I*t seemed fortune had smiled on him after all.

Dom lay beneath a canvas sheet in the back of the ambulance heading toward Charleroi. While most of the story he'd given Eve was fabrication, his fear at remaining in Brussels had been real enough. Thankfully, she'd taken pity on him, and now he was on his way toward freedom.

Chandler had witnessed what happened at the border. With electric torches shining everywhere and guns going off, Dom had glimpsed the captain beneath the barbed wire, watching the scene play out. And doubtless he'd heard Felix Giroux's shout of accusation before Dom's gun went off.

He should have killed Chandler when he had the chance, but the captain's death had never been part of Dom's plan. After seeing the documents in Eve's room, he realized the captain was a courier for MI6 and decided it was better to let him return to his superiors none the wiser, since Dom had obtained what he wanted. The last thing he needed was British agents swarming into Belgium to hunt down the murderer of one of their own.

But Felix had forced his hand, and now Dom regretted his decision. His cover was blown, and not just with the Allies. The Germans would no longer be able to use him, either.

He could still support Germany in fighting for his cause in

Belgium, but now he must use extreme caution. Perhaps when things settled down he would migrate farther west, toward Ghent.

Taking Chandler north had presented him with an opportunity to dispose of Felix, but he hadn't intended to do it so close to the border. Once the passeurs had parted ways, if they'd lived, Dom would have preferred the long, lonely trek back to the abbey—a more private gravesite for his co-worker, away from any witnesses.

He'd suspected Felix of surveilling him for some time, and had seen the man standing across the street from the café when he'd left Eve's apartment that day. His suspicions proved certain when he found evidence that his own apartment had been searched shortly thereafter. So certain, in fact, he'd packed along a pistol for the trip.

He'd made a costly assumption, however, thinking that when Felix insisted on "keeping him company" at the border he'd merely wanted to spy on him. When the two passeurs made their move with Chandler to rush the fence, Dom was surprised when Felix suddenly rose.

It was then he'd noticed the rubber gloves. Giroux was leaving with Chandler.

Knowing his cover was about to be blown, Dom had drawn his pistol. But Giroux had seen the intent and shouted his indictment before Dom got off the shot.

The border lit with gunfire, and Dom had to run for his life.

The ambulance hit a rut in the road and Dom cursed, grabbing his injured arm. He hadn't counted on getting nicked by German gunfire, but at least he was alive, and the wound had helped to lend credence to his story.

Once again the ambulance bounced along the uneven road, and with a growl he tore back the canvas. Light from the back window let him see his watch. 0900. They should be arriving at Charleroi within minutes.

The thought of seeing the lovely Maddie Arthur once more softened his mood. He'd found the pretty blond nurse to be a pleasant diversion. Maybe she'd feel sorry for him and wish to tend his injury while they were there.

His humor dimmed. What he really hoped for was a successful means to get beyond Charleroi, to Chimay, and from there into France. While he'd promised to help Eve bring her brother and sister back into Belgium, Dom suspected she had received more than the news about Chandler's arrival at Rotterdam—like the place and time to meet the assassin in La Bouteille, and the name of the German contact inside the château.

In searching her room, he'd been impressed to discover her secret niche inside the shrine of the Madonna and Child, and delighted when he'd flipped open the Bible to find Chandler's orders, along with his phony passport.

Dom still didn't understand why the captain's plane had been flying over Brussels when the mission was in France, but Eve had decrypted the orders, which told him she knew of the meeting with the assassin. Since she'd been corresponding with MI6 through Rotterdam, it was likely they had sent her the final instructions.

Her secrecy had angered him at first. Eve had lied to him about the leather pouch, and then she refused to reveal Chandler's whereabouts once they freed the captain from the hospital. Dom had actually been hurt by her mistrust.

Still, he'd refused to act on his emotions by turning her over to his German counterparts. She was much more valuable to him as an agent. While he did admire her courage and her beauty, more importantly she'd made for him the perfect scapegoat.

Pi. He thought it brilliant when she chose the code name after joining La Dame Blanche. In honor of her dead father, a math teacher, she'd said. And it provided him with opportunity. He soon took to using the Pi symbol in his communiqués with the Germans, knowing if Rotterdam intercepted the intelligence they would look to Eve Marche while leaving him free of suspicion.

Dom cursed the fact that his cover had been blown. He wondered which side had recovered Giroux's body, and what identification the Belgian had carried on his person.

Had Felix learned all of his secrets? That he was Flemish and not French, and active with *Flamenpolitik*, Germany's efforts to help his people break away from Belgium?

Dom had fooled them all, with his gift for mimicking accents making everyone believe he was from Paris, not Flanders, and that he worked solely for the Allies, when in truth he sought to aid the Germans and his cause.

Until now.

The ambulance came to a sudden halt. A moment later he heard Eve's voice near the tailgate, giving instructions to their driver to go and see the head nurse about the disposition of the supplies.

"Dom?" she called softly into the back of the truck.

When he scrambled from beneath the stretchers, she glanced around, then waved to him. "Hurry, before he comes back."

He grabbed up their rucksacks and exited the ambulance. The lorry was parked at the back of the hospital.

"Shall we go inside?" he asked. Both wore their Red Cross uniforms.

"Let's go to the front and check to see if Maddie's here. Otherwise I'll have to walk to the hotel."

He followed her around the side of the large brick structure, again wondering how they would manage to make Chimay. Eve had said there was a farmer who might help get them into France.

"Eve! Dom! What are you doing here?" Maddie Arthur rushed toward them, her green eyes wide with surprise.

Eve shot him a relieved smile. To Maddie she said, "I'd hoped you would be here today."

"Since I'm their newest hire, I pulled the Saturday overnight shift," she said. "I was just leaving to return to the hotel."

"We need to talk," Eve said.

Maddie's eyes lit with sudden interest. "Let's go out into the patients' park." She noticed the packs Dom carried. "Can I stow those somewhere?"

"Thanks, *chérie*, but they don't weigh much." He clutched the rucksack that carried his pistol. "I don't think we'll be here long anyway."

Maddie looked more intrigued. "Follow me then."

She led them around to the small park reserved for patients. The wind was cold, and no one else was outside. Dom stood while the two women sat on a bench.

"We need to get transportation to Monsieur Duval's farm in Chimay," Eve said. "I hope he knows of a way we can cross into France tonight, if possible."

"Nikki and Zoe?" Maddie asked, and Eve nodded.

"Mine was a last-minute decision to leave Brussels," Dom said vaguely. "I have my Red Cross badge, but no pass beyond the city, so I cannot take the train."

Maddie looked up at him. "I'm not certain the trains are even running today."

"Then you can see why we desperately need your help, *chérie*." He winked at her and she blushed a lovely shade of pink.

"It's hard to refuse your pretty speech." She smiled, then looked at Eve. "The trip to Chimay and back shouldn't take more than three hours. Matron isn't working today, and the motor pool clerk owes me a favor, so I can take you."

Eve grabbed Maddie's hands. "Thank you, dear friend."

Dom was pleased when less than an hour later they were back on the road. Maddie had obtained a hospital pass and an ambulance on the pretext of giving a fellow nurse a lift to the hospital in Chimay.

Unfortunately, he had been relegated to hiding in the back again. As long as he remained unobserved they expected to have no problem clearing the checkpoints along the way.

Easing onto his back, he tucked Eve's rucksack beneath his head, careful to keep his injured arm from bumping the floor. As the three had talked in the patients' park, Eve had enlisted Maddie's help in getting her brother and sister into Brussels. She'd said only that *"recent events"* prevented her from returning to the city herself and putting her family at risk.

Dom understood. Eve now believed Felix was the traitor in La Dame Blanche. He almost chuckled. Surely now she would confide in him, tell him what news Rotterdam had sent her. Perhaps then he could circumvent the rendezvous and arrive beforehand, taking on the assassin himself.

This Lundgren wouldn't leave La Bouteille alive. Instead, Operation Behead the Snake would turn and take a bite out of MI6.

CHAPTER 35

I think this is the place." Maddie turned the lorry onto a dirt driveway toward a small farm on the outskirts of Chimay. A ramshackle barn sat off to one side, and the wood siding revealed the dingy gray-black hue of age and weather.

They drew to a halt beside a cottage, and a plump black-and-white cat slunk around the corner of the porch. In the distance Eve spied a sway-backed sorrel grazing on a patch of tender grass, where it was tethered by a long piece of rope staked into the ground. The cluck of chickens and the bawling of a calf accompanied the faint smell of manure, and a cold mist fell from the sky.

The door to the cottage opened and an older man appeared on the porch. Stocky and of medium height, he wore a white collarless shirt, dark trousers, and a brown felt cap sporting a white chicken feather. His olive-skinned features were lean and lined with age. A man of about fifty, Eve guessed, with a handsome face looking so much like the young corporal she'd tended weeks ago, his hair and moustache the color of rich earth.

As he stood watching them, he tucked his thumbs around the blue suspenders holding up his trousers.

"Monsieur Duval?" Eve hailed him as she stepped from the lorry. Maddie exited on the other side.

"I am," he called out as the two women approached.

Eve hid a smile as the older man quickly reached up a hand to smooth his moustache. She introduced herself and Maddie, then said, "We have a friend with us, an orderly from the hospital in Brussels. May I get him?"

At his nod, Maddie went to the back of the truck and reappeared with Dom, who carried their rucksacks.

"I'd like to speak with you," Eve said once the three faced the farmer. "If we could go inside?"

He invited them in, his whiskey-colored eyes appraising Dom's hefty frame. They sat in his parlor, the worn divan and wooden ladder-backed chairs showing much use over the years. The room was tidy however, and the frayed dark curtains in the windows seemed clean enough.

Monsieur Duval went to the kitchen and returned with a tray of hard-boiled eggs, a round of cheese, and bread that looked as though it had been made with real flour. A slab of butter accompanied the bread. He made a second trip and returned with coffee.

Eve couldn't recall the last time she'd seen so much delicious food. Even her black market forays couldn't compare with this freshness.

They all murmured their thanks at the bounty he laid before them, and once their host sat down, Dom and Maddie began tucking into the food.

Eve was too nervous to eat, so she told the farmer how she'd met his son, Jean, at the hospital in Brussels a few weeks earlier.

Monsieur Duval leaned forward in the chair he'd taken, his work-roughened hands clutching his cup of coffee. "He is . . . all right?" the farmer asked, in the barest whisper.

Eve nodded. "He was sent to a POW hospital in Düsseldorf. From there he'll likely be transferred to one of the camps."

"*Dieu merci*," Monsieur Duval whispered. He looked up at her. "I am glad he will not be going back to the Front. I have heard of so many boys dying in France."

Eve thought of her brother, wondering for the thousandth time whether she would reach him in time.

"Monsieur, we've come here because Jean told me that my brother and sister escaped the train from Louvain three years ago. They were with Jean's cousins, Armand and Michel Rousseau."

"Ah, *oui*!" The farmer beamed. "Nikki and Zoe, I know of them. They are with my nephews in Anor, just a few kilometers from here, across the French border."

Eve fell back against the divan, her heart pounding. The children were alive and in Anor! She moistened her lips. "I need to get to them," she said. "And I'm hoping for your help."

His smile faded as concern flashed in his eyes. "France is dangerous. There is a barbed wire fence, and German guards patrol the border. My nephew, Armand, has managed to slip through every other month to check on me and to bring me any news about Jean, but I know the risk he takes."

Eve leaned forward. "Please. I have waited so long . . ." Her throat tightened. "I worry for my brother, now that he's fourteen."

The farmer tipped his head, a frown showing beneath the dark moustache. "*Oui*. Armand was a teacher in Louvain before the Boche came in and destroyed the city. Now he lays bricks for them." Disgust filled his tone. "I know Michel is fourteen as well, and I worry for him. I pray Armand can get them on his work crew, so they will not be sent into the trenches."

He took a sip of his coffee. Then he said, "There is a wood-cutter in Macon, not far from here. He has taken people across for a modest price."

"That would be wonderful!" Eve said, relieved he was willing to help. "How soon can we travel?"

"I will ride over on Leopold and ask him," the farmer said. "I imagine he could take you tonight." He smiled. "You are welcome to stay here until then."

"Thank you." Eve barely contained her excitement. She would see Nikki and Zoe in the morning!

He set down his cup, then rose and went to fetch his coat from a peg on the wall in the entryway. "I will return within the hour."

Once he'd left, Eve stood and turned to Maddie, who had finished her meal. "I suppose you should probably start back?"

"Yes." Maddie rose and came to her, taking her hands. "I pray you find Nikki and Zoe well, and I wish you both a safe return into Belgium with the children." She glanced toward Dom. "Take care of my friend?"

He smiled. "You know I will, *chérie.*" He stood also and moved to embrace Maddie. "Thank you for your service to us."

Maddie blushed. "Yes, well, I want them back as much as you do." To Eve she said, "Once you return, contact me through the hospital. I'll come straightaway."

Eve nodded, her eyes burning as they hugged each other.

"Godspeed, my friend," Maddie whispered.

Eve watched as she left the cottage. Moments later the lorry's engine roared to life, and soon the sound of the ambulance faded into the distance.

She gazed at Dom. They were on their own.

God had heard her prayer for Simon's safety. Eve prayed now for her own, and for the safety of those in her care, hoping He would hear those prayers, too.

❧

Dom wrinkled his nose at the musty smell of damp straw as he and Eve sat huddled in the barn's hayloft. The farmer had gone to bed, leaving them to make their way to the run-down building and wait for the woodcutter.

Already he missed the warmth of the cottage, though the heat from the animals helped to block out some of the November chill. He was grateful to be dry at least, since it was raining steadily outside.

He didn't relish going back out into the wet. He hoped the rain would stop before the woodcutter arrived.

"What time is it now?" Eve asked beside him. Like Dom, she'd donned a heavy sweater, trousers, and a thick coat, yet he could still hear her teeth chatter.

He reached into his rucksack for his electric torch and flipped it on, checking his watch. "One in the morning," he said, and yawned. They'd left Brussels eighteen hours ago. It had been a long day.

"He should be here anytime."

Dom grunted. The farmer had indeed arranged for their border crossing this night, though the woodcutter's "modest price" for the service was far more than what the passeurs in Postel had charged. Apparently the man's patriotism came at a price. Or the danger of being smuggled into occupied France was greater than at the Belgian-Holland border.

"What's the plan once we arrive in France?" If he was going to risk his neck, he wanted some answers.

"Monsieur Duval said there is a Red Cross hospital in Trélon. Since we have our uniforms, we might as well see about getting transportation."

"Steal an ambulance, you mean?" Dom chuckled, and his pulse quickened as he thought of how close they would be to German army headquarters at the Château de Mérode in Trélon. He wondered if the kaiser had arrived.

"Exactly," she said. "From there we can drive south to Anor. According to the map, it's just a few kilometers from Trélon."

"We'll have to be careful at the hospital," he said, baiting her. "I think the Boche army is entrenched not far from there."

She tensed beside him, and a smirk touched his lips. He'd struck a nerve.

"If that's the case, we'll be certain to avoid them," she said. "I need to get to Anor as soon as possible. With the instructions the farmer gave us and a bit of luck, we should arrive at Armand's cottage before ten o'clock in the morning."

"Shall we have the woodcutter come back for us tomorrow night then?" he asked, trying to draw her out again.

"No, I still need to take care of a few matters."

"What kind of matters, *chérie*?" Dom's heart pounded. "Can I help?"

In the darkness he felt her warm hand against his.

"You are more help to me than you know," she said, sincerity in her voice. "Just being here and giving me the courage to go through with all of this." She squeezed his hand. "I'm so grateful, *mon ami*."

It wasn't the answer he wanted; in fact, she hadn't answered his question at all. He'd learned during their years together that she excelled at prevarication. He knew little about Eve's past and even less about her relationship with Chandler. She too liked keeping secrets.

Did she really have no other agenda in France besides her brother and sister? Or was she trying to keep information from him?

A soft whistle sounded below—the woodcutter's signal. As he'd been instructed, Dom whistled back. He and Eve grabbed up their rucksacks and climbed down from the loft to face the tall, broad silhouette of a man.

"You wish to cross over into Anor?" He spoke in French, his voice rough.

"We would like to cross at a place near the Red Cross hospital in Trélon," Eve answered.

Dom heard the woodcutter exhale.

"Then we will need to backtrack to Macon and cross there," he said. "You will follow me and make no sound. Put that torch away."

Dom ground his teeth as he extinguished the light. The man was certainly full of himself.

"When we get near the crossing, I will signal you to wait. Remain close to the ground. I will tap you both when it's time to move."

"What kind of fencing?" Dom asked, dreading the answer.

"A single fence of barbed wire, six feet tall."

The news surprised him. "What about guard shacks? Dogs?"

"No dogs and no guard stations, but the German sentries carry weapons and travel in packs. The same on the French side, so make sure to follow my instructions."

The crossing sounded far easier than Dom had imagined. He eyed the bulky woodcutter and remembered how many francs this was costing them. Instead of arguing, however, he asked, "When do we leave?"

"Why, now of course." The woodcutter's gruff tone held amusement.

"Let's go then," Eve said beside him, anticipation in her voice. She took Dom's hand as they followed their guide outside into the darkness and the rain.

Dom reminded himself of why he was doing this—for the glory of Germany, and ultimately for his cause. Eve let go of his hand and walked faster, moving in directly behind their guide.

Dom stared at her, his jaw set. He would bide his time, at least until they got into France. It was obvious that seeing her siblings came first, which meant any meeting with the assassin wasn't going to happen right away. Afterward, however . . .

He slung his backpack over his shoulder, feeling the heavy weight of the Luger inside. Before leaving Brussels, he'd considered the possibility that he might have to kill her. He hated the idea of destroying a woman with such intelligence and beauty. Still, her life in exchange for the truth, the information that would save the life of the kaiser, was a small price to pay.

CHAPTER 36

E ve's rapid breath came out in steamy puffs as dawn arrived, streaking light across the sky. The clouds had parted, letting the sun's rays illuminate millions of glistening raindrops clinging to the tips of green grasses and the needles of evergreens.

They had cleared the fence, a harrowing experience she did not look forward to repeating. The three had crouched in the wet grass near the trees for nearly an hour after reaching the crossing point near Macon, watching a troop of soldiers amble past. Because the span of fence they patrolled was quite lengthy, the woodcutter had made them wait until the Boche were two hundred meters away before Eve and Dom were allowed to follow him across the fence. Getting through wasn't all that difficult, but watching for the enemy on the French side was a blind risk. They had immediately taken to a copse of fir trees, waiting several minutes before their guide ascertained the guards were well away. A few more kilometers though the forests and wooded areas finally brought them out near the hospital.

"I'll leave you here," said the woodcutter. They stood next to a small outbuilding at the edge of a field, safely beyond the fence. "You can see the hospital isn't too far."

In the light of day Eve could see that their tall, muscular guide was a middle-aged man with a kind face, his eyes the color of chocolate. She turned to where he pointed, and recognized the Red Cross symbol painted in vivid relief against the side of a building a few hundred meters away.

She turned to him and held out a hand. "*Merci.*"

His dark eyes squinted as he smiled. "If you need me again, just let Armand know. He can get word to me."

The woodcutter nodded toward Dom, then slipped back into the woods and was gone.

Dom tried the door to the outbuilding. It opened to reveal shelves piled with burlap sacks, masonry trowels, a pair of wooden sawhorses, and a wheelbarrow.

"You can change first," he said.

Heart pumping, Eve entered and quickly exchanged her coat, shirt, and trousers for her Red Cross uniform. She prayed that if they were stopped, their ruse as employees of the hospital would work. She soon emerged from the outbuilding and stood guard while Dom did the same.

Once they were properly garbed, they shouldered their rucksacks and walked in the direction of the hospital. They held their heads high, as if they were on their way to start their shift. Eve's breath caught as she observed several German soldiers loitering in front of a small café. The strong scent of coffee and freshly baked bread wafted toward them, and her stomach rumbled.

She wondered if the café's food was fresh like the meal Monsieur Duval had served them the day before, or if what she smelled was ersatz coffee and war bread.

Her muscles relaxed as they left the soldiers behind and neared the hospital. The roof of the brick-and-mortar facility was badly in need of repair.

She came to a stop and glanced further up the road. Before them was a POW camp, the four wooden towers, one at each corner, surrounded by a steel fence topped with coiled barbed wire.

Several dirty, emaciated faces watched them from behind the fence, and Eve's compassion was overpowered by anger at the Boche as she gazed back at them. She thought of her husband, how thin he'd become in the three years they'd been separated. Simon must have gone hungry, much like these men, regardless of how light he'd made of the conditions.

"There."

Eve turned, following Dom's gaze. Several ambulances stood parked near a set of bay doors behind the hospital. "Wait here," he said, then swiftly made his way toward the building and slipped in between the trucks.

She looked back to the POW camp and walked a few steps. Gazing beyond the camp, she spied a gray stone turret rising above the trees. Was it the château? To the left of the turret, she glimpsed a flash of white. Taking a few more steps, she halted, gaping.

A sea of canvas tents stood pitched on a field. Only a few soldiers were up and moving about, but she imagined the tents could house up to several hundred.

A chill curled in her belly, and she hastily returned to wait for Dom.

The back of the hospital had a run-down look. A few empty wooden crates lay strewn about, while the trash bins were overflowing. Dirt and rust lined the base of the brick building, and she wondered if the Boche were responsible for the neglect.

The minutes passed and her pulse quickened.

Where are you, Dom? She checked her watch. He'd already been gone five minutes. Had he been apprehended?

Her breathing quickened. Praying her disguise would hold, she started toward the building when the sound of an engine cut through the morning's silence.

A moment later a Red Cross ambulance pulled up beside her.

"Can I give you a lift?" Dom smiled at her from behind the wheel.

"Oh, you gave me a fright!" she scolded him, sliding onto the seat. "What took so long?"

"I had to forage for extra cans of petrol," he said. "I also checked out the area first, so I wouldn't get caught. Not too many personnel about yet, just a couple of cleaners." He turned to her. "Where to now?"

"South." She pointed to a road sign marked *Hirson*, a larger city beyond Anor.

Dom eased the ambulance forward. As they traveled the city streets of Trélon, Eve was stunned at the squalor she witnessed. Dejected, hungry faces peered out from doorways and windows of the shabby homes, watching them with large eyes as they passed. So many like those in Belgium, she thought sadly.

Were Nikki and Zoe half starved as well? Were they emaciated, like the POWs in the prison camp? Monsieur Duval had offered to provide them with a bag of food, but she and Dom had brought only what they could fit into their rucksacks. Crossing over into France without getting shot by the Germans had been difficult enough without having to carry an extra pack. Still, she would gladly surrender her block of cheese and small loaf of bread if her brother and sister needed it.

Glancing back through the window of the ambulance, Eve could still see the turret in the distance. Coldness swept through her. If that was indeed the German army headquarters, the kaiser could reside there even now . . .

She hadn't thought much about the mission in terms of her part in the assassination. She knew the kaiser was responsible for the devastation of many innocent people, as well as the death of countless soldiers from both sides, and the wounded she'd tended over the years. She knew that the sooner he was dead, the quicker the unrelenting carnage would cease.

Yet her clear perception of the righteousness of the mission blurred as the old wounds rose to haunt her. Killing him wouldn't bring anyone back to life; it wouldn't undo the damage that had already been done. And like those under his control, the kaiser had a family, a wife and children who cared about him, who would grieve at his loss, and bear the scars of his shame after the war ended. Suddenly Eve wasn't certain she'd be able to see the mission through.

Could she give Lundgren the contact name he needed in order to accomplish the kaiser's murder?

Hadn't she already enough blood on her hands?

The ambulance jerked, sliding along the muddy, rutted road, and she grabbed for the side of the cab to steady herself. Her chest was weighed down with guilt and anxiety over the coming mission as her mind warred with her soul.

Turning to stare at the dingy cottages and run-down farms along the roadside, Eve caught sight of a sign that read *Anor*, and all other thoughts fled.

The small town soon came into view. Eve leaned from the cab, scrutinizing the few people already out that morning, her pulse rapid with anticipation. She tried seeking out a familiar face in each young woman and boy she saw. Had her brother and sister changed much? Would they still recognize her?

"Turn here!" she cried as the road Monsieur Duval had described loomed directly ahead. Dom swung the ambulance onto the long, rutted drive, and soon a cottage appeared. It was in bad need of paint, but the dark roof and the immediate grounds were well maintained. A small lean-to sat off to one side.

A tall woman with auburn hair stood on the front porch holding the hand of a young child, a little girl with the same color hair.

"Is that your sister?" Dom asked.

"No," Eve said, disappointment washing over her in waves. Tears filled her eyes, and she had to force herself to breathe. Did they have the wrong house?

A small, thin woman wearing a flowered kerchief and white apron walked toward the cottage from a shed, followed by a scruffy brown-and-black dog, barking at their arrival.

"Perhaps they'll know where this Armand lives?" Dom suggested.

Despair settled like a weight on Eve's heart. She'd come so far. "I hope so."

"Where is my wife?" Simon asked the priest without preamble.

Having arrived at St. Magdalene's just after Monday morning Mass, he strode toward the altar where Father Francois was extinguishing candles.

The priest turned at the question, and his features went slack. "What are you doing here, my son?"

Simon had donned his Albert Janssen disguise at the Groenendael Priory, shortly after parachuting down near the Sonian Forest a few hours before. Suffering from lack of sleep and his aching ribs, he'd had to walk six kilometers through the woods to get into the city.

"Eve is in danger."

The priest glanced around the church. Only a few people sat in the pews. "Come with me."

He led the way outside and over to the rectory. Once they were back indoors, he said, "Now, please, tell me what's happened."

"Dominic Lesser is an enemy agent," Simon said. "MI6 has

the proof. I've come to warn my wife and stop her from going to France."

"What?" The priest's eyes widened. "But Eve left yesterday morning for the hospital in Chimay. And she took Dominic with her."

Dread and fear gripped Simon. "I need transportation at once."

"I will try, my son, but most of the vehicles in Brussels are the ambulances at the hospitals and the military staff cars driven by the Boche." He dropped his gaze. "Are you sure about Dominic? He came to the church on Saturday, bruised and bandaged, seeking a place of refuge. He said Felix Giroux had tried to kill him at the border, and he'd barely escaped with his life."

"It was the other way around," Simon retorted. "Felix was shot in the head at point blank range. I saw Lesser run after he made the shot. He was hit with a bullet from a German rifle, just before he fled into the woods."

"*Ciel!*" The priest crossed himself. "He said he had to flee Brussels, and he begged to accompany Eve." He tilted his head. "I thought she'd requested the transfer to simply get out of the city. After you left she was desolate."

Simon's chest tightened at the priest's words. "If she planned to go into France, do you know the city?"

The priest was still in shock, shaking his head at the news about Dominic. "I should have suspected," he muttered. Then he met Simon's gaze. "Her family should know. They may even be able to help with transportation. In the meantime, I'll see what I can find. You will also need a pass to Chimay."

Father Francois gave him directions to Eve's family's apartment, and Simon agreed to meet him back at the church at noon.

The morning air was cold, and a drizzle fell from the sky as he struck out walking from the church. Once he'd turned onto rue des Sols, he headed the few blocks to the café.

He'd made all kinds of plans. If Eve had still been in the city, he would have eliminated Lesser, then traveled with his wife and her mother to the abbey at Postel, where the two women could have found sanctuary until he figured out a plausible escape or until the war ended.

Since she'd left Brussels and likely headed for France, he and Marcus worked out a fallback plan: the airfield at Toul, southeast of Reims. With the French airfield controlled by the Allies, he could fly them both back to Britain.

Marcus had agreed to notify the MI6 agent in La Bouteille. If Simon arrived before Eve, he would take Lundgren's place at the rendezvous.

His friend also obtained for him a French passport and lapel pin, a red poppy, which he'd been instructed to wear at the rendezvous. Simon hoped he would find Eve before then. And he prayed he would get to her before Dominic Lesser decided she was no longer useful.

It was still early when he arrived in front of Chez Bernard, and the café was closed. He mounted the outside steps toward the apartment. Knocking lightly at the door, he touched his whiskers, making sure all was straight.

The door opened to reveal a tall, slim, middle-aged woman with honey-colored hair. Her dark brown eyes surveyed him with a hint of suspicion. Was this the aunt perhaps?

"I'm looking for Louise Marche," he said in French, offering a slight bow.

She didn't move from the door.

"Marie? Who is it?"

A thin voice rose from behind her, and Marie stepped back. In the opening Simon caught sight of a small, frail woman in a dark dress. He hardly recognized her.

"Louise?" he said softly.

Louise Marche blinked at him, hesitating, and Simon seized

the opportunity to step inside. He removed his spectacles, then the moustache and goatee. "Do you not know me, Mother?" he said.

Her breath caught as she began to weave on her feet. Simon reached to steady her.

Tears welled in her hazel eyes, and she reached up with knobby hands to cradle the sides of his face. "*Mon fils*," she said softly. "You are back from the grave."

She dropped her hands and encircled his waist with her frail arms, and Simon held her tight as his own eyes stung. Years had passed since he'd last seen her, and he remembered their many letters to one other before the war. She'd given him her blessing when he longed to marry Eve, and he knew the grief she'd suffered, losing all but her eldest daughter.

"I have missed you," he said, stifling his anger at what the war had done to her.

She pulled back to gaze up at him, and he was humbled by the joy in her expression. "May I speak with you?" he said quietly.

Her answer was to smile and take his hand, leading him deeper into the apartment. Marie followed and closed the door behind them.

They arrived at the kitchen, where a stocky man with thinning brown hair and blue eyes looked up cautiously from his coffee and toast. Marie went to stand next to him, then said, "Louise?"

"Lucien and Marie Bernard, meet my son, Simon Forrester. Eve's husband." Louise Marche gazed up at him, her eyes shining with tears. "It is a miracle."

Lucien rose from the table. "*Bonjour*, Monsieur Forrester," he said, looking startled. His wife could only stand with mouth agape.

"*Bonjour*." Simon indicated an empty chair. "May I?"

"*Oui*." Lucien gestured for him to sit, then reached for an extra coffee cup from the counter. Simon removed his heavy coat, and Eve's mother took it from him to hang on the back of a chair. She fetched more of the war bread from the cupboard and set it on the table, along with butter and a jar of black currant jam.

Marie Bernard finally spoke. "It is so wonderful to meet you."

"And you as well." Simon sat down across from her. "Eve told me you and your husband own the café downstairs?"

All three stared at him. "When did you speak with her?" Marie asked.

Then Simon told them about the crash in Brussels Park, along with his time in the hospital.

"That was you?" Eve's mother cried, pausing with the jam in her hand. "She . . . she never told us you were here."

"She wanted to protect you. All of you. She loves you very much." Simon paused. "The truth is, I've returned to Brussels because I need to find her."

"I'm afraid she has left," Eve's mother said. "Yesterday. She had to go and work at another hospital, in Chimay. I'm not certain when she'll return."

"It's important I find her."

He became aware of Marie observing him from across the table. "Louise," she said, "it's quite chilly in here, and I've left my shawl on the bed. Would you please get it for me?"

"Why . . . of course." Eve's mother glanced at Simon before she rose and hurried from the kitchen.

Marie leaned forward. "Is my niece in danger?"

Simon nodded. "I must reach her as soon as possible."

Marie raised a reddened hand to her lips before she said, "She has gone to France to get Nikki and Zoe. She took the big Frenchman with her."

Simon stilled. "Do you know where in France?"

"Anor, I think she said. She planned to stop and see her friend Madeleine at the hospital in Charleroi first."

Lucien handed Simon a cup of coffee, then sat back down at the table. "So you really are married to our niece?"

"We wed just before the war." Simon relayed how his plane had gone down at the onset of the invasion and that he spent years in POW camps before he made it back to Britain. "I came to Brussels when I learned that Eve was here."

They heard sounds in the hallway, and Marie spoke quickly and quietly. "We must not speak of this in Louise's hearing," she said.

Then a gasp tore from her throat, and she and Lucien rose from the table, staring past Simon.

Simon turned and launched from his chair. Standing in the doorway was the Hun major, wearing a greatcoat and holding his cap and a portmanteau.

He stared at Simon in shock.

Marie started around the table toward him. "Herr Major! When did you get back?"

What was the blasted Hun doing here, in Eve's apartment? Simon glared at him, while inwardly he cursed. He'd removed most of his disguise for Louise, stuffing the articles in his coat pocket—the same coat pocket in which he kept his pistol.

"Just minutes ago," the major said, never taking his eyes off Simon. "I took an early train back from Berlin."

"Would you . . . would you care for coffee and toast?"

"I am not hungry." The major dropped his portmanteau at the door and walked toward the table.

Simon turned slightly. His coat was hanging on the back of a chair, just out of his reach. If the Hun thought to pull a gun on him, he'd have to try to wrest it away. Shoot the man, if necessary. Nothing was going to stop him from saving his wife.

"You," the major said. "I know you." His scrutiny turned to recognition. "Chandler? But how . . . ?" Then he answered his own question. "Eve."

Simon's gaze held the major's. Vaguely he heard Louise's soft exclamation as she returned to the kitchen with the shawl, then slipped over toward the table.

"Is it true?" the major asked. "You are her husband?"

Simon hesitated, then nodded. "Three years," he said in German.

The major's jaw began to work, as if he couldn't decide what to do next. Finally he asked, "Was the baby yours as well?"

Anger and pain lanced through Simon. "It was."

The major looked past him then, staring toward the kitchen window. "The violence in Louvain was . . . indescribable," he said. "I was bleeding out, with shrapnel here." His hand grazed over the vein at his neck. "Eve didn't care about the color of my uniform. She kept pulling the metal pieces out of my body . . . even while she bled onto the floor. If she had stopped her work, I would have died." He looked at Simon again, his features shuttered. "Where is she?"

"She's gone to Chimay."

The man jerked his head back in surprise.

Pulse pounding, Simon decided to take a chance. "I'm here because she's in danger, Herr Major. I need a truck, and a pass to get to her."

"You fight for the Allies. Your soldiers shoot ours." The major scowled. "Why should I help *you*?"

"Because my daughter saved your life."

Both men turned to see Louise Marche's diminutive figure standing beside the table. With arms raised, she held a pistol pointed at the Hun. "And now you must save hers."

Simon drew in a sharp breath. How had she managed to filch the gun from his coat pocket?

"You owe it to her, Herr Major," Louise said, her voice shaking. "I have lost my children, my eldest brother, my grandchild." The hazel eyes glittered. "I will not lose my Evelyn, too."

Lucien and Marie stood as if frozen in place. Simon's muscles flexed, ready to attack if the major harmed his family.

But then the man seemed to deflate, his expression defeated. "I have just returned from seeing my wife and children. They too have suffered much in this war. Family is everything, madame," he said softly. "I don't know what I would do if I lost one of my precious little ones." He glanced back at Simon. "I will try to get what you need."

Simon bit back his impatience. The major's offer was the best he could expect. "What about Eve's family? Will they be all right?"

The major looked toward the Bernards. "I will do my best to look out for them, as long as I am in Brussels." To Louise, who had set the gun down on the table, he added, "I owe her that."

Then his voice took on an edge of annoyance as he turned back to Simon. "Anything else, Captain?"

Simon shook his head.

"*Gut*." His blue gaze hardened. "After today I never want to see you again."

CHAPTER 37

At the sound of the approaching car, Zoe hurried to carry her firewood back to the cottage, hoping Armand had returned with news of the boys. Nikki and Michel had been gone two days without a word, and she was haunted by the determined look in her brother's face when he'd said he wanted to go and fight in the war. Another promise broken . . .

What if they'd followed through on their threat to join the French army? Her heart wrenched as she imagined them lying in pieces in some trench. Or maybe they'd been caught by the Boche and taken off to the enemy's camp.

She approached the yard, expecting to see Monsieur Fosse behind the wheel of his shiny Delaunay-Belleville, with Armand seated alongside. Yesterday her love had said he would get Zoe's employer to give him a ride into Hirson, since it was likely the boys had gone in that direction. He promised to remain until he had some news.

It wasn't Sylvan Fosse's black limousine coming up the drive, however; instead, a lorry approached, a red cross along either side of the hood.

An ambulance? Her pulsed throbbed with fear. Were the

boys injured . . . or worse? She hurried forward, the kindling still clasped in her arms. Where was Armand?

The ambulance came to a halt just short of the yard. A large man slid out from behind the wheel, while a tall, slim woman exited from the other side. Both wore the uniforms of the Red Cross.

Her mouth went dry as dread seized her. Her feet refused to move as the pair approached. Zoe's gaze was drawn to the nurse. There was something strangely familiar about her walk, the way she carried herself . . .

Hair rose along her nape, and as she glimpsed the sable locks beneath the nurse's cap, the wood in her hands clattered onto the wet grass. She didn't need to see the woman's eyes to know they were violet.

"Eve!"

At the sound of her voice, the nurse broke into a run. Zoe rushed to meet her halfway.

"*Ma chère soeur!*" she cried in a high-pitched tone as they threw their arms around one another. Zoe began to sob, while her sister's shoulders shook as they hugged one another tightly.

Finally she pulled back, blinking away her tears as she gazed at Eve. "It's really you," she said, still unable to believe her eyes. Her sister looked older and thinner than she remembered. "How . . . how did you get here? Where have you been all this time?"

"In Brussels." Eve wiped at the wet tracks against her cheeks. "Mama and I thought you and Nikki were taken to Germany—"

"Mama?" Zoe began to shake violently. Searching her sister's face, she dared not hope. "She is . . . our mother is alive?" she whispered.

Eve nodded, and Zoe burst into fresh sobs, not knowing if they were born of relief or joy or both. Her mother was safe. "Praise God," she finally managed, before her knees buckled and she grabbed onto Eve for support.

Bursting with love, Eve held her sister. Zoe was rail thin, and a few centimeters taller than when she'd last seen her. The honey-colored hair beneath the kerchief had darkened too, matching the tilted soft brown eyes.

Eve clasped Zoe's head, grieving for her brother and sister as she imagined the two young children lost, forced onto a train bound for the enemy's labor camps, believing their mother dead. Running for their lives for days and nights through the woods, from one country into the next before finally reaching this place.

Eve knew well the pain she and Mama had endured, and it broke her heart to realize these children had suffered the same agony. "You are my brave, brave little one, *chérie*," she whispered, pressing her cheek against the warmth of her sister's. "You and Nikki both."

Zoe drew back, her brown eyes rimmed red. "I tried to keep my promise to you," she whispered, before her face crumpled again. "But now he's gone. They're both gone!"

Eve stared at her sister while a prickle of dread crept down her spine. "What do you mean?" She looked toward the cottage, seeing only the auburn-haired woman and her little daughter. She turned back to Zoe. "Where is Nikki?"

"He ran away," she said, sniffing. "He left on Saturday, with Armand's brother, Michel."

She began to cry again and Eve pulled her close, her pulse hammering. Had the Boche captured them? "Can we go inside?"

Zoe nodded, wiping away her tears. She looked past Eve toward the ambulance.

"Dom!" Eve called, and he came forward. She made the introductions, and Dom looked ill at ease with her weeping sister. They were about to head inside when a lean, broad-shouldered man wearing a dark patch over one eye rode up into the yard on a bicycle.

"Armand!"

Her little sister broke away to run to him. The man quickly dismounted the bicycle and leaned it against the overhang's post before taking Zoe into his arms. He bent his head and spoke to her in a quiet voice, then kissed her.

Stunned, Eve stood watching the couple. Neither of the Duvals had described their relative, but this must certainly be Armand Rousseau, brother to Michel.

As the pair walked arm in arm toward her, Eve took a long look at her sister.

At eighteen, Zoe was a grown woman. Eve hadn't stopped to consider the possibility that her sister might meet someone and fall in love in this Godforsaken war.

"Armand, this is my sister, Eve."

"What?" Though his expression was grave, Armand's dark brows shot up. He glanced at Zoe, then back at Eve. "We . . . thought you were lost to us," he said in a deep voice, clearly stunned. It was a moment before a smile touched his lips and he extended his hand to her. "It is very nice to finally meet Zoe's sister."

"This is Dom, my friend and co-worker from Brussels," Eve said, and the Frenchmen greeted one another.

"Armand, I told them about Nikki and Michel," her sister said in a tearful tone.

He pulled her sister in closer, his features grim. "I traveled the length of Hirson yesterday without seeing any sign of them." To Zoe he said, "Monsieur Fosse gave me a ride into town, and I stayed the night with a friend, a man who works with us in Trélon. He let me borrow his bicycle to come home. He said there was word the French have retaken La Malmaison. I think the boys took their bicycles and went in that direction."

"Through German-held territory?" Eve said.

Armand nodded, and Zoe buried her face against his chest.

He held her tight. "We will find them, *ma chère*. Do not lose hope." To Eve he said, "Zoe's employer, Monsieur Fosse, will lend us the use of his car. We can go south—"

"We'll take you in the ambulance. We're already dressed for the part." Eve glanced at Dom and caught his look of misgiving. "I think we stand a good chance of getting through, don't you, Armand?"

"It would be easier," he agreed. "There are many German checkpoints along the way, and a Red Cross truck would draw far less attention than Monsieur Fosse's limousine."

"When shall we start?" Eve was eager and anxious to go after her brother.

"*Pardon*," Armand said. "I need just a little food first."

"Of course," she said and glanced at Dom. "We've brought a bit of breakfast with us."

Dom returned to the truck for the rucksacks while Eve followed her sister and Armand to the porch, and more introductions were made. She learned that the auburn-haired woman, Madame Boulanger, and her small daughter, Annette, shared the cottage with them.

Once inside, Zoe made coffee as they all sat around the table. Dom returned and handed Eve her rucksack. She took out her small block of cheese and loaf of bread, then gazed pointedly at her friend. He flashed her a sour look before removing from his own bag the half dozen hard-boiled eggs and two winter apples that completed their meager feast.

Glancing up, Eve saw that no one had moved; they simply stared at the food before them. Little Annette had come inside with her mother, and she wiped at her mouth with her sleeve.

Recalling the POWs in Trélon, Eve was filled with compassion. "Zoe, may I please have a knife?"

When her sister complied, Eve cut the block of cheese into thin slices. She held one out to the child. Annette looked at the others around the table before she snatched the slice from Eve's hand and stuffed it into her mouth.

Eve next began to slice up the apples. To Madame Boulanger and the others, she said, "Please help yourselves. This food was a gift to us from Armand's uncle, and we are happy to share."

Armand's jaw slackened. "How do you know my uncle?"

Eve explained how she had met young Corporal Duval in the Brussels hospital weeks before.

"Our mother and I, we'd thought Nikki and Zoe dead, or working in some German coal mine. But your cousin told me how you and Michel helped them to escape the train. Jean also gave me the address for his father, your uncle in Chimay. I went to see him."

Zoe came to stand beside her, laying a hand on her shoulder. Eve reached for her while she relayed to them how Monsieur Duval helped her and Dom meet the woodcutter and cross into France at dawn.

"Your timing is perfect," Armand said as everyone began tucking into the food.

"How far is this place, La Malmaison?" Dom said, peeling one of the eggs.

"To the south, more than sixty kilometers." Armand tore off a chunk of bread. "The French army took back the fort and the village from the Boche a few weeks ago." He glanced up at Zoe. "Nicholas and my brother, Michel, have been talking nonstop about going off to be soldiers." His expression darkened. "I ordered them to remain here, but they have disobeyed."

The image of the German boy rose up to haunt Eve. Would her brother be slain, simply for wearing a uniform?

"We must go," she said, panic squeezing her chest as she rose from her chair. "I don't want to wait." She looked to Armand, who gulped down his last bite and stood.

Dom did the same. It was decided Zoe would remain at the house in case the boys returned.

"Armand, what about your work at Trélon?" her sister said. "Monsieur Boulanger left just before you returned this morning. He offered to tell them that you are ill and cannot leave your bed."

"Keep them out of the cottage, if you can," he said.

"If they come to the door, I'll get under the blankets and pretend I am contagious," Madame Boulanger offered.

Armand smiled his thanks, then moved around the table to take Zoe in his arms and kiss her. Eve realized her sister and the others survived by being clever, keeping one step ahead of the Boche, much in the same way Eve and the rest of their family had endured in Brussels.

A few minutes later, they stood outside. The weather was turning, and a light rain began falling from the sky.

"*Crotte*," Dom breathed. "The roads will be slow going once they turn into mud."

Eve hugged her sister good-bye. "We'll find them, Zoe," she said, praying she was right.

"Godspeed, *ma soeur*," Zoe said.

With Armand hidden in the back of the ambulance, Eve took her place beside Dom before he turned the lorry back down the drive. She craned around to wave at her sister, then looked ahead as Dom headed south. They must find her brother and Armand's.

On the heels of that thought came the reminder of her rendezvous with the assassin, set for tomorrow at the hotel in La Bouteille, 1100 hours.

Her jaw set as duty warred with her heart. She simply must find the boys before the meeting.

CHAPTER 38

When Simon entered the Bernard kitchen two hours later, he was surprised to find a pass for Chimay on the table. He rushed to the front door of the apartment and looked outside. An unmarked truck stood parked across the street.

A stirring of grudging gratitude mingled with his dislike for the arrogant major, and Simon had to admit perhaps the Hun was human after all.

With the Bernards already downstairs at the café, Simon went in search of Louise to say farewell. He was anxious to get on the road and locate Madeleine Arthur in Charleroi, hoping she could shed more light on his wife's plans.

He found Louise in a small bedroom off the hall, seated at her worktable making lace, much the way she'd done years before in the parlor at the Marches' Oxford home. Standing at the open door, he noted her serene expression as her fingers worked the bobbins, and marveled anew at her earlier bravery in facing off with the Hun.

Like mother, like daughter, he thought in grim amusement.

"Louise?" he called softly.

She looked up and smiled. "Did you get some rest, *cher*?"

He nodded. "I must leave now, to go and find Eve."

353

She sighed, then turned to stare at her bobbins. "While she is gone, I have no special lace to make, just this random pattern with no meaning." She cast him a sidelong glance. "She is clever, my girl."

Very clever, he thought. "You and she make special lace together?"

Louise nodded. "We help the Allies."

He caught the note of pride in her voice. "La Dame Blanche?" he said, an edge in his tone.

"*Oui,* and why not? Someone must stop the Boche." Her gaze flashed with the same hard glint he'd seen earlier when she'd held the pistol.

Then her features relaxed, and she rose from the chair and came to him, grasping his hands. "You will find my girl and take care of her, promise me."

"Or I will die trying," he said, meeting her gaze.

She searched his face. At length, as if seeing he meant every word, she embraced him. "Be safe, *mon fils.*"

Simon held her close, while in his heart he made himself another silent promise. He would find a way to get Eve's mother out of Belgium.

The hospital in Charleroi loomed ahead, and Simon gripped the wheel. Thanks to the major's pass, he was able to pose as a hospital supplier making his rounds.

He parked in front and went inside. At the matron's office, he asked for Sister Arthur by name and was told to wait inside a room adjacent to the office.

Instead of sitting on one of the straight-backed chairs, he paced, turning just as Madeleine rounded the corner and entered the room.

"May I help you?" she said.

"Hello, Madeleine."

He took off the spectacles so she could see his eyes. It was a moment before her own grew wide. "Simon?" She scanned the empty room before her gaze returned to him. "Is it really you?" She rushed to give him a hug. "I can't believe it!"

"It's good to see you, Maddie." He gestured toward one of the chairs. "Can we sit a moment?"

She took a chair, and Simon sat across from her. "I need to find Eve. She's in trouble. Is Dominic Lesser still with her?"

Alarm flitted across Maddie's features. "Yes. What's going on?"

"He's not a man to be trusted. I'm worried that when she gets into France, he'll turn on her."

"But he's so charming," Maddie blurted, her fingers twisting in obvious agitation. "Why would he try to hurt Eve?"

"I can't give you details, but we have proof he is a double agent. He has killed before, and will do it again."

"Oh my goodness!" Panic rose in her voice. "I drove them to a farmhouse in Chimay, near the French border. Monsieur Duval . . . his son is the one who told Eve about her brother and sister."

"When did you take them?"

"Yesterday," she said. "I think they were going to cross last night."

Simon ground his teeth. He was a day behind. "I have a truck. Can you give me directions?"

"I can take you if you like."

He shook his head. "I'll go alone. I just need to know the way."

Maddie left for a moment, then returned with a pen and paper and drew him a map. "It's only about an hour and a half from here," she said. "Just let Monsieur Duval know you're with Eve."

Simon tucked the note into his pocket. He thought of the upcoming meeting with Lundgren in the morning and prayed Eve hadn't revealed the details to Lesser. It was the only leverage that might save her life. He rose from the chair. "I've got to go."

She rose as well. "Take care, Simon."

With a backward wave, he moved toward the door. Outside, he cranked over the truck's engine and slid behind the wheel. As he took off for Chimay, his pulse hammered against his throat, and his hands were damp against the wheel. He had to get across tonight, or all was lost.

CHAPTER 39

The skies had opened up, turning the road ahead into mud soup.

Eve strained to see through the sheet of rain as she scanned the sparse landscape for two boys on bicycles. Beside her Dom gripped the wheel, muttering curses and struggling to keep the truck on the road, which ran parallel to the railroad tracks.

Armand lay hidden in the back by the stretchers, keeping watch for Nikki and Michel through the tailgate's open canvas.

They had already driven through the town of Vervins, and Armand estimated they had gone about thirty kilometers—halfway to La Malmaison.

Earlier they had passed a road sign marked *La Bouteille* and Eve had been jarred, realizing she would meet with Lundgren there the next day.

The roads grew increasingly difficult to traverse as the rain continued. Once they neared the town of Marle, Eve began to notice the scarred terrain, a seeming endless string of water-filled cavities, like dirty lakes, exposing the half-immersed barrel of a cannon gun, or the hindquarters of a dead horse. Once she was horrified to see what appeared to be a pair of bodies, or their parts, floating facedown in the mire.

Groups of German soldiers slogged through the muddy fields, some following behind the Red Cross trucks that were heading south, making their own presence in the area go unremarked.

The sudden screech of shellfire from the next hill made her jump, and it occurred to her they hadn't thought to bring gas masks.

"Armand!" She turned to shout through the open window separating the cab from the back of the ambulance. "Get me whatever bandages you can find!"

He passed her a wad of white cloth, and she held it out to the rain until it soaked through. "For the gas," she called to both men, separating the bandages and handing each a wet cloth.

Eve was seized with new fear as she wondered about the conditions her brother and Michel must have encountered if they'd come this far. Between the rain, the cold, and the mud, how could they have reached La Malmaison? With so many Boche milling about, it was more than likely they'd been captured.

Their ambulance halted at a fourth checkpoint as they entered the German-occupied city of Laon. Having already passed three on their way, Dom had made pleasant conversation in German with each guard, telling him they were returning for more bodies. The ambulance and their Red Cross guises had so far seemed enough to bluff their way through.

The guard at Laon, however, chose to be difficult. "Passes," he barked.

Dom quickly flipped his Red Cross badge from Belgium. "We're headed to the hospital at Laon."

When the guard left his post and went around the back to look inside the ambulance, Eve's breath froze in her lungs. *Armand!*

She glanced at Dom and saw he was ripping away the bandage on his arm. For an instant she forgot about the guard. "What are you doing?"

The guard returned a moment later. "Your truck is empty." His brow knit beneath his helmet. "Passes!"

Dom showed him the bloody bandage, and the guard reared back in distaste. "This morning I got shot while taking your wounded comrades to the hospital in Marle, Herr Corporal," he lied. "I need a new bandage, and this is the closest place."

The guard jerked his head, then stepped back and waved them through.

Eve eased out a breath. "That was quick thinking."

Dom turned to her, a strange gleam in his eyes. "Lying becomes all of us at one time or another, *chérie*," he said softly.

She wondered at his cryptic words, but then her attention quickly turned to the wet streets of Laon. The hilltop city lay almost untouched by the war. Smart-looking shops rose along either side of the avenue, with bright flags and evergreen garlands draped across several of the stone façades in anticipation of the coming holidays.

It could have been any quaint, peaceful town in Europe, but for the German armored trucks and the military staff cars and horse-drawn carts patrolling the streets. Soldiers flocked in clusters, much as in Brussels.

Beyond the town, their ambulance continued on toward more rural areas, and again the war showed itself. Pocked hills and valleys gave way to the Germans' defensive line trenches lying just outside Laon. Eve dug her nails into her palms and was reminded of Louvain as death marked the countryside.

An hour later, they finally arrived at La Malmaison, or what was left of it. The battle had ended less than three weeks ago, and the small village resembled a pile of rubble, with only a few buildings the straggling survivors of destruction.

The fort stood some distance away, its stone façade chewed away by artillery and mortar fire. Yet the French flag waving from the rampart was a comforting sight to see.

Normally the drive from Anor to La Malmaison might have taken two hours, but between the often impassable roads and several German checkpoints, they had journeyed twice as long.

Inside the shambles of the village, Dom parked the ambulance near a café, reopened for business despite its pitted-out shopfront.

The three went inside to have coffee and rest awhile.

Eve asked the proprietor if he remembered seeing two boys come through on bicycles, but the older man shook his head and said they were the first visitors he had seen in over a week.

She asked about the fort, as it was likely Nikki and Michel had gone there to try to enlist. The café owner said there was much being done to fortify and repair the structure, but they could check with the commander there.

Because it was leaning toward midafternoon, Eve asked about accommodations. Even if they left now, it would be six o'clock, possibly later, before they returned to Anor, and she had no desire to get caught in the war zone after dark.

The café owner suggested a rooming house just down the street, which had also escaped most of the artillery damage from the last siege.

Thanking him, Eve and the others finished their coffee and a small meal, then returned to the truck. Armand now sat in the cab on Eve's left as Dom headed in the direction of the fort.

"If they are not here, should we retrace our steps to Hirson?" Dom asked.

"Let's not give up hope just yet," Armand replied. "I have a feeling we'll find the boys here. They were adamant about joining the French army, and this is the closest and perhaps the safest place they could enlist."

He turned and looked at Eve, and she could tell by his grim expression what he didn't say—that the possibility was good only if the boys hadn't already been taken by the Boche.

At the crumbling fort, Armand's hopes prevailed. When he and Eve sought out the commanding officer, a Captain LeClair, and asked about the boys, the man actually smiled.

"Come with me," he said, and took them directly to where two young boys clad in blue French uniforms were digging out rubble from the rear side of the fort.

"Michel!" Armand cried, and the head of a dark-haired boy, eyes much like his brother's, shot up from a deep trench.

"Armand!" Michel's relief was almost comical as he dropped the tool he'd been holding and scrambled out of the crevice.

Behind him another boy's head popped up, the blue eyes stark against his mud-covered complexion.

Tears suddenly blurred Eve's vision. "Nicholas Marche, get over here right now!" she cried, before a sob escaped her.

The pair of blue eyes widened in shock before he vaulted from the trench. "Eve!" Despite his filthy uniform and any semblance of fourteen-year-old poise, he ran to her and threw his arms around her waist, his body shaking with sobs.

She held him close, thanking God for giving him back to her. She looked to Armand, whose lean, dark face held joy as he slung his arm around his brother's shoulders.

"I knew the boys were lying about their age," Captain LeClair said after the happy reunion. "I hoped after a few days of digging trenches and lugging stone they would tire of playing soldier and go home."

Eve resisted an urge to embrace the man. Her family was once again intact. "*Merci*, Captain," she said. "I appreciate your time and your patience in teaching them such a lesson."

Beneath his cap, the captain's dark eyes grew sad. "In the past month we have suffered heavy losses to regain this little piece of France. I am glad at least these two young fellows were spared."

To Nikki and Michel, he said, "I commend you for your bravery and your service to the French army, *mes camarades.*

But wait until you are a little older before you decide to pursue the life of full-time soldiers, eh?"

They all returned to the ambulance, where Dom waited. As the boys and Armand climbed into the back, Eve had a thought.

"Captain," she said to the French commander, "would you have any spare German uniforms?"

CHAPTER 40

*Z*oe Marche?"

Simon stood at the door of the cottage, clad in his guise as Albert Janssen.

He hardly recognized the slight, thin woman who answered the door. Eve's sister was not yet fourteen the last time he saw her, shortly after the death of her father.

With Maddie's instructions yesterday, he'd easily navigated and arrived at Monsieur Duval's home in Chimay in the afternoon. The helpful farmer had engaged a woodcutter from a nearby village to take him across into France.

"Do I know you?" Zoe said, eyeing him with a quizzical expression.

Simon was pressed for time. The meeting with Lundgren in La Bouteille was to take place in three hours. He removed the spectacles and tore off the whiskers. "Does this help?"

She gasped. "Simon?"

"Hello, Zoe." He smiled as she gaped at him. "Where is your sister?"

"She . . . she is with Armand, the man who owns this cottage, and another, Dominic. They've gone south to La Malmaison to find Nikki and Armand's brother, Michel. I expect them back soon."

Relief swept through him. Eve was still alive.

Zoe, seeming to remember her manners, stepped back from the door. "Won't you come inside?"

Simon entered the cottage, walking through the clean, sparse interior as she led him into the kitchen.

"Coffee?"

"Please." He sat at the table. "Why is Nikki in La Malmaison?"

She served up his coffee, along with a boiled egg and a slice of buttered bread, then sat down at the table across from him. She explained how the two boys had run away on Saturday, and it was believed they planned to join the French army.

"Eve arrived in an ambulance yesterday morning with the big Frenchman, and she insisted they go after Nikki and Michel. Armand is with them."

Simon sipped the coffee, then said, "How far is this place?"

"Over sixty kilometers." Her thin features were pinched with worry. "I pray they have found the boys and are on their way back."

He would never catch up with Eve if he tried to follow her to La Malmaison. He'd have to risk that she planned to stop at La Bouteille on her way back. He could meet her there.

"I need transportation," he said, setting his cup down. "Eve is in danger."

His sister-in-law paled. "What kind of danger?"

Briefly Simon explained enough to make her understand that Dominic Lesser was a threat.

"Monsieur Fosse, my employer at the hotel, has a car," she said. "As soon as you finish your breakfast, we will go and ask him."

In answer, Simon rose from the table. "Let's go now."

Walking with Zoe the kilometer into town, Simon was glad to shed his disguise, as the French passport Marcus had supplied didn't require the props.

L'Hotel Fosse was a traditional inn with white stucco walls and a red tiled roof. Zoe's employer, an older man with silver hair and a matching moustache, smiled at them from behind the desk as they entered.

"Mademoiselle Marche, what brings you here on your day off?"

Zoe made a quick introduction, then explained the circumstances. "My brother-in-law desperately needs the use of a car," she told her employer. "My sister and Armand are in the company of a man who is a threat to them."

The older gentleman looked alarmed but didn't hesitate as he came around the desk and put the *fermé* sign in the window.

"Of course I will help," he said. "Zoe and Armand have done much to help France, and so I am happy to aid her family." He paused. "Where are we going?"

Simon shot him a quick glance. "We?"

"*Mais oui*," the older man said, looking surprised. "I cannot let my automobile out of my sight; the Boche might try and steal it."

"It could be dangerous," Simon warned.

"Here we live daily among the enemy, monsieur." The old man's eyes gleamed like polished stone. "I have become much accustomed to danger."

"I'm relieved to hear it," Simon remarked as he fished the red poppy pin from his pocket. "Because you'll probably get more than you bargained for."

CHAPTER 41

"Wait here," Eve said as she moved to exit the ambulance. She'd glimpsed Dom's scowl over her sudden request to stop at the Hotel de Gilbert in La Bouteille on the way back, but she didn't explain her reason. She hoped that in the company of Armand and the boys, he wouldn't ask.

Nikki, Michel, and Armand lay in the back on stretchers, posing as wounded Boche. The ruse, flimsy at best, was all she could think of yesterday when she'd asked the French captain for the German uniforms.

"I won't be long," she said to her friend, offering him a tight smile before she turned and went inside the hotel.

The furnishings were grand, with rich carpeting and an oak-lined reception counter. A crystal chandelier hung in the lobby, high above a leather divan and a scattering of richly upholstered chairs.

She removed her nurse's kerchief and tucked it inside her coat pocket as she found her way to the restaurant. Beyond a set of leaded glass French doors sat a large green potted palm; an incongruous sight, she thought, having just traveled through vast stretches of wasteland.

Eve checked her watch. 1100 hours. Dom had made good

time after they left the rooming house at La Malmaison, as the rain had stopped last night and allowed the ground to dry a bit.

She entered the restaurant and quickly scanned the room and its occupants. Three German officers, captains by their badge ranks, sat at the bar drinking beer and eating platefuls of what looked like spaetzle. Across from them two civilians in nice suits, French businessmen, she decided, sat at a table deep in discussion as they sipped glasses of red wine.

An older couple sat at a table near the restaurant's large bay window. An elderly man in a porter's white coat was serving glasses of white wine and steaming bowls of what smelled vaguely like onion soup.

In the far corner of the restaurant, behind the potted palm, a lone figure sat facing her, his brown fedora tipped forward, apparently engrossed in reading a menu.

Eve spied the red poppy pinned to his lapel and froze. Lundgren.

Her pulse sped up as she considered again what she was about to do: give this man, this *assassin*, a name that would gain him entrance into the Château de Mérode and German army headquarters in Trélon. He would "behead the snake" by murdering the leader of the Boche.

Eve wet her lips and forced her feet to move forward, fueling her purpose with the memory of the emaciated POWs she'd seen in Trélon, the death and destruction she'd witnessed en route to La Malmaison . . . the horrors she'd endured in Louvain.

She reached the table, sat down, and waited for the man to look up. He raised his head.

"Hello, lass."

Simon! Eve swayed in her seat while joy surged through her. "Why . . . what are you doing here?"

He reached across the table for her. "Give me your hands."

She hesitated only a moment before curling her fingers with his.

"Now just play along," he said. "We're being watched."

Heart pounding, she forced a smile.

He said, "Now, tell me you're all right, love."

"I'm fine, but what . . . why—"

"Where is Dominic Lesser?"

His tone caused a chill to ripple down her back. "He's outside, waiting in the ambulance. Simon, what's going on?"

"We need to talk about what happened at the Holland border."

Eve listened, stupefied, as he quickly told her the truth about the night he'd been taken north.

"Marcus and I have proof that Lesser photographed the orders you kept for me. He forwarded the information to a German government official and signed the document with the symbol I drew for you in the tunnel." His expression turned fierce. "Dominic Lesser is the enemy agent we've been seeking."

The impact of his words suddenly registered, and Eve vaulted from the chair. "The boys . . . they're in that ambulance!"

Simon rose from the table as well. They were about to exit the restaurant when Armand, clad in the dirty German uniform, appeared in front of them.

"What's wrong?" Eve said.

Armand looked confused. "Dominic returned to the truck and said you wished to see me."

Eve and Simon shared a look. "He must have seen us together," Eve whispered. Panic bloomed in her chest. "Simon, he's taken them!"

The three rushed out to the empty street.

Armand cursed. "He's gone."

"I've got a car over here." Simon waved them toward a black limousine parked on the next block. They ran and found a surprised older man sitting behind the wheel.

"Get out, Monsieur Fosse," Simon ordered. Whether it was

the ferocity in his voice or the murderous look in his eyes, the gentleman scrambled out of the car.

Armand cranked over the engine as Simon slid behind the wheel. Eve sat beside him. "We'll come back for you," Simon called out, as Armand jumped in and the limousine took off.

The roads were still muddy, though not as bad as the war-torn landscape further south. Simon floored the accelerator, and a few minutes later they had the ambulance in their sights.

Eve clung to the door's edge and watched Dom's lorry snake back and forth along the road leading north. She vaguely noted several German military vehicles along the way, and soldiers who paused to watch the two automobiles racing past them.

She hoped they would not take chase but instead assume that the ambulance and a car racing behind it were simply headed toward a hospital. "Do you think we can catch up with them?" she asked.

Simon offered a grim smile. "Just watch."

At a slight bend in the road, Dom turned to glance behind him at the black limousine slowly closing the distance. He muttered a curse as he pressed harder on the accelerator, causing the ambulance to swerve and slide along the muddy, rutted road.

Chandler was in France! Dom had followed Eve inside and been shocked to see the captain. He'd waited at the restaurant door while he surveyed the room. When he'd finally caught sight of her seated at a corner table, she was holding hands with a man he'd assumed was Lundgren, the kaiser's planned assassin.

Only it wasn't Lundgren . . .

Confusion and panic clouded his thinking. If Chandler was the assassin, why had he been carrying the orders in the first place? It didn't make sense.

He glanced behind him again. The limousine was rapidly

gaining ground, enough that he could recognize Chandler's face behind the wheel.

What was the man's relationship to Eve? She'd risked all to make certain he escaped from the hospital, and then enlisted Dom's aid and that of Felix Giroux to ensure he safely crossed the Holland border.

Now he was back and she was with him again. *Was* Chandler the assassin after all? Had the orders been designed merely to throw him off?

Dom ground his teeth. She'd made a complete fool of him.

He had to get back to German army headquarters in Trélon and warn them. Pressing his foot hard against the fuel pedal, he gripped the wheel as the ambulance tried to zigzag across the road. Dom cursed the mud, then he cursed himself for having allowed Eve Marche to play him along this far. He'd been overly confident, allowing his pride to do his thinking.

The town of Hirson was just ahead, and he was forced to slow down in order to turn left, heading north back toward the château.

"What's going on?" a young male voice demanded from the canvas opening near his head. "Why did you leave Armand and my sister?"

Dom turned to see Eve's brother leaning out, his expression angry.

"Why are they chasing you?" the boy demanded.

"Shut up and get down," Dom snarled.

Before he'd finished the turn, he heard another voice yell, "Jump!"

With lightning speed, Dom grabbed hold of the boy's tunic as the other one jumped. Making the turn single-handedly, he saw the one they called Michel rolling along the road's shoulder.

With a growl, he pulled Nicholas Marche through the opening and pressed him against the bench seat. The boy tried to struggle, but his skinny frame was no match for Dom.

"Keep moving like that and I'll stop this truck and shoot you," he snapped.

Wide-eyed, the boy quit struggling. Dom sneered, then headed north toward Anor and Trélon, pushing the accelerator against the floor.

"Michel!"

Beside her Armand cried out, and Eve watched in shock as the boy leapt from the back of the ambulance. He rolled several meters across the muddy expanse into a ditch beside the road leading into Hirson.

Simon stopped the limousine long enough to let Armand jump out.

"Go on!" the Frenchman shouted, waving to them.

Her husband needed no prompting. He pressed down on the pedal, and the car nearly careened onto its side as he rounded the corner heading north.

"My guess is he's going to the château," Simon said as he gripped the wheel. "He thinks he's found his assassin."

Eve barely heard him over the panic roaring in her ears. She'd seen Dom jerk her brother through the opening, then watched as Michel leapt from the truck.

"Simon, go faster!" she cried as the ambulance sped farther ahead. "We have to save him!"

The limousine quickly resumed speed, and Eve glanced at her husband, his knuckles white as he steadied the wheel. They both watched the ambulance in front sliding back and forth along the rain-drenched road. A few people toting wheelbarrows or pulling dogcarts had quickly stepped off to the sides as they heard the automobiles barreling up behind them.

Soon Eve saw the sign for Anor, and a few minutes after that she recognized the row of squalid cottages lining the road into Trélon. She saw a pair of soldiers standing beside an armored truck, and her breath caught.

"What about the troops?" she said, remembering the field of white tents she'd seen the day before.

Her husband didn't answer, and Eve knew the mission could easily cost their lives.

As they passed Trélon's hospital and nearly closed the distance with Dom, Eve glimpsed again the turret of the château.

Suddenly the ambulance ahead swerved crazily, running headlong into the ditch.

"Nikki!" Eve screamed, and Simon brought the limousine to a stop. Dom emerged from the cab, dragging her brother with him.

"He's got a gun!" she cried, seeing the pistol pressed against Nikki's head. A red line of blood slashed across her brother's forehead. *Dear Lord, please don't let him die*, she prayed.

Dom began pulling him along, stumbling in the mud as they made their way toward the château less than a kilometer ahead. The rain began in earnest, rivulets streaming down fresh gullies in the direction of the hospital.

"Stay here." Simon removed a pistol from inside his coat. "I'll slip into the woods and flank him, then come out in front and head him off." He got out of the car, then turned to look at her. He reached inside for her hand. "I'll be back before you know it, love. Don't give up hope."

"Be careful," she whispered, but he'd already turned and slipped into the thicket of trees.

Eve looked ahead through the windscreen and saw Dom slip and fall, along with her brother. As the two struggled to get back on their feet, he continued to press the gun against Nikki's head.

Do you love me, daughter?

Eve heard the Voice in her heart as she stared at her brother. He wore the same uniform as the boy from long ago, the boy with wide gray eyes and freckled features, the boy whose last word had been a cry for his mother.

She found herself opening the car door, stepping outside, while the rain beat down against her face. Moving forward, struggling through the mud in her wooden sabots, she held the image as she drew closer to Dom and her brother.

"Dominic, please let him go!" she shouted through the downpour.

He glanced back at her for an instant, then jerked Nikki along as he continued up the muddy rise.

"Take me instead!" she challenged, struggling against the desperation raining on her from the sky. "I'm more valuable to you as a hostage than a boy who knows nothing!"

Dom paused again, his wet hair matted against his forehead while his gaze scanned the perimeter. "Where's Chandler?"

"You mean my husband?" she called back.

He stared at her, shock in his expression.

"He's coming for you, Dom. You should take me instead. He won't dare try to hurt you if you have me." While she spoke, Eve kept moving forward. "You know I'm right." She held out her hands. "Let him go."

He hesitated, glancing from her to Nikki, then back again.

"Imagine the glory, to be able to hand over an Allied spy to the kaiser," she said.

Her words struck their mark; in a flash Dom shoved her brother away and grabbed her wrist, jerking her to him.

"I'll kill you if he comes near me, *chérie*," he said, pressing the pistol against her neck.

Eve didn't struggle as Dom turned and began pulling her along toward the château, his gaze constantly searching the trees.

"Nikki, go home to Zoe, now!" she called back to her brother. Her sabots had filled with mud, and the fine stone cut at her feet as she stumbled forward.

A warrior's cry sounded from behind them; in the next instant, Nikki leapt onto Dom's back, trying to take him down. Dom shook him off like a leaf, though he lost his footing for a moment. He turned and aimed the pistol at Nikki's head.

"No!" Eve wrenched her arm from him and blocked his shot. An explosive *crack!* pierced the air, searing her shoulder with hot pain. Her brother shouted, and another shot rang out.

Dom froze, wet-faced, his eyes blinking, before his mouth went slack and his body crumpled to the ground.

Eve staggered, looking up in time to see Simon, his face grim as he swiftly put away his pistol. Her knees buckled, and the muddy ground rushed at her face before she sensed strong arms encircling her, lifting her up. She heard Simon's sharp voice giving instructions to her brother.

And then she heard nothing at all.

He had to get them to safety.

Amid German shouts to halt and the bursts of machine gun fire coming from the château, Simon glanced at Eve's brother, who knelt over the body of Dominic Lesser.

"Hurry!" he hissed, and Nikki scrambled to his feet. Simon strode back to the car carrying his bleeding, unconscious wife in his arms, praying to God the wound wasn't mortal.

He set her gently into the back seat, then slid behind the wheel and set the throttle while Nikki cranked the engine.

The car was moving as the boy dived in on the passenger side and hung on. Simon pushed the accelerator to the floor, trying to put as much distance as possible between them and the gunfire spraying past them.

Glass shattered as a bullet hit the back window. "Get down!"

Simon shouted. He too crouched low against the wheel while pressing the limousine forward along the sloping road, against a morass of mud, water, and floating debris.

Soon the gunfire grew faint. Simon continued on at top speed, gripping the wheel to keep the car steady on the road.

The sign for Anor loomed ahead.

"There's the cottage!" Nikki shouted.

Simon turned onto the drive and sped forward to halt in front of the entrance. Leaping from the car, its engine still running, he opened the back door and carefully lifted out his wife.

Nikki rushed ahead to open the front door. "Bring her inside. Madame Boulanger is a midwife, she can help."

Simon could only nod in anguish as he cradled Eve in his arms and made for the porch.

Zoe and a young auburn-haired woman stood back from the open door. Zoe let out a gasp, then said, "Come, we'll take her to my room." Quickly she led him to a room at the back of the cottage.

In the dim light he could see a neat row of three small beds.

"Here," Zoe said, and he set Eve down carefully. Simon gazed at her stark white face streaked with mud and rain, and he brushed a wet strand of dark hair from her closed eyes.

God, I can't lose her now, not again, he thought, his throat tight.

"Let me see."

The midwife nudged Simon aside. She'd brought bandages, hot water, and an array of instruments.

Simon stood back, hardly breathing as he waited.

"A flesh wound," she said. "The bullet went cleanly through the shoulder."

Simon sagged against the wall and closed his eyes. *Thank you, God.*

"I'll tend to her wound," the midwife was saying. "So long as there is no infection later, she should recover in good time."

Simon remained in the room as the woman expertly cleaned, stitched, and bandaged his wife. He heard someone enter the cottage and went to the door.

Armand and Michel had just returned.

"I saw the car in the yard," Armand said. "I've hidden it away in an old barn not far from here. The boys and I covered it with canvas and straw." He added, "With the broken back window, Monsieur Fosse will likely need to report it stolen to avoid casting suspicion on himself."

"Speaking of Monsieur Fosse . . ." Simon realized they'd left the man stranded in La Bouteille.

Armand chuckled. "He will be fine. Several contacts frequent the Hotel de Gilbert; they will give him a ride back to Anor."

"Contacts?"

"Obviously you work for the British," Armand said. "Rotterdam?"

Surprised, Simon hesitated, then nodded.

"We also work for the Allies," he said.

"La Dame Blanche?"

"*Oui.* The network is extensive throughout Belgium and northern France. We pass the Allies information about German troops and artillery moving through our sections by train." He paused. "Dominic Lesser, he is a traitor to the Allies?"

"Yes," Simon said. "He's also very dead."

"How is Eve?"

"Your midwife patched her up. It's a clean wound that should heal well."

"*Dieu merci.*" Armand smiled. "I will make up a bed for her down in the root cellar. You both should remain there for a time, in case the Boche come searching."

Simon agreed, and in a short time he descended into the

cramped, musty cellar with Eve in his arms. He found the make-shift bed that Armand had constructed hidden behind a large, empty potato bin.

"From the stairs you can't be seen," Armand said. "I'll bring you food later."

Simon laid Eve down gently and covered her with the quilts Armand had spread on the straw-filled mattress.

⁂

Eve awoke to darkness, fiery pain searing through her. The smell of decaying earth permeated her senses. Where was she?

Her eyes soon adjusted to the dim light, and she made out the familiar outline of her husband beside her.

"Simon?" she croaked.

The welcome warmth of his hand rested against her forehead. "How do you feel, love?" His voice was achingly sweet, filled with concern.

Eve swallowed, her mouth parched. "I hurt," she said. "And I'm thirsty."

He lifted her head slightly. "Take this. It's a morphine tablet." He laid the pill on her tongue, then touched the rim of a cup to her lips, and she drank greedily.

"It should help with the pain. The midwife gets the drug from the Trélon hospital."

"Where are we?" she said. "It's so dark."

"We're in your sister's root cellar, hiding from the Huns."

The memories rushed back: *Dom with a gun to her brother's head . . . Nikki leaping onto his back . . . a pistol firing . . .*

Her pulse hammered as panic rose. "Nikki . . . ?"

"He's here and he's fine." Simon's warm hand returned to stroke her cheek. "You took the shot, a flesh wound to the shoulder. Madame Boulanger is a midwife, and she tended you." Anger edged his voice. "You should have waited in the car."

"I had to go after Nikki," she said, remembering the Voice in her heart and the image of the young German boy. "I had to save him."

His hand stilled against her cheek. "So you've lost all confidence in my ability, lass?"

"I trust you with my life." She pressed her face into his touch. "But it was something I had to do." Her voice shook with emotion. "I couldn't let another boy lose his life because of me." Hot tears stung her eyes. "I have been lost for a long time, husband," she whispered. "I had to find my way back. Today, God gave me that chance."

"Forgiveness?" he said gently, while the back of his hand grazed along her skin.

"Mercy," she said. "God forgave me long ago for what happened in Louvain. I was just so blinded by my own guilt and despair I wouldn't allow myself to accept it. My faith wasn't strong enough." She reached for his hand. "But I've come to realize over the past few weeks, in the examples of your love and your understanding, that His mercy was always present, always within reach, just waiting on me. I had to find the courage and the conviction to reach for it. Nikki's life . . ." A sound that was part sob, part joy, rose in her throat. "I believe it was a sign."

"I'm glad you've finally found some peace," he said, before his warm lips pressed against her brow.

"It's a good start." The morphine was starting to take effect, and the pain in her shoulder eased. She was sleepy but had too many questions she wanted to ask. "Tell me about Dominic Lesser."

"He's dead. Once he laid hands on my wife that was an end to it."

She turned to him and whispered, "Did you come back to kill the kaiser, Simon?"

"No." His touch was gentle as he brushed a lock of her hair from her temple. "I came back for you."

He explained to her how Operation Behead the Snake had been no more than a ruse, disinformation purposely leaked to the suspected enemy agent in La Dame Blanche in order to flush them out.

"And you and Marcus thought I was the enemy agent." Hurt filled her voice. She'd risked her life countless times over the past year, sending valuable information to the Allies across the border.

"Love, no one had any idea it was you until I returned to Britain. After van Bergen and the others in Antwerp were arrested, and Rotterdam began receiving your messages directly, they wondered if Pi was the same agent who had been turning Allied secrets."

"So Dominic was responsible for the agent arrests?" Eve already knew the answer. For some time she'd suspected an infiltrator in La Dame Blanche had turned them in.

"Marcus and MI6 seem convinced. Lesser must have sent their names to his German government contact."

"When I returned from Charleroi, I knew someone had been in my room. I thought it was the secret police, but it was Dom."

Simon had already told her at the restaurant how Dominic had photographed the secret orders and forwarded a copy to a German official.

Resentment mingled with her confusion at the Frenchman's betrayal. "I still don't understand why he would help the very enemy besieging his own country of France."

"Dominic Lesser wasn't French at all, but Flemish," he said, to her surprise. "He was active in the German push to make Flanders a state separate from Belgium. Felix Giroux provided

MI6 with plenty of information, which he'd scavenged from Lesser's apartment."

"And now Felix is dead," she said, saddened. "I actually believed Dom's story."

"Lesser was a master spy, sweetheart. He fooled quite a few people."

"So this 'behead the snake' was all a worthless game?" Frustration filled her as she thought of how she'd been maneuvered by Marcus Weatherford, how she'd kept secrets from Simon and worried about meeting Lundgren. She'd even risked her life at the hands of Dominic Lesser because of the ruse, and none of it was true.

"Not worthless," he said, telling her that because Dom passed along the information, German troops had been moved south into Trélon to protect the kaiser—which left their army to the north weakened and vulnerable for a real planned Allied attack.

"All those white tents near the château?" she said. "Soldiers brought down from the north?"

"That's right. Before we left Trélon, I had Nikki tuck a message into Lesser's pocket. It was the same instructions you received about meeting with Lundgren and providing him an inside contact. Hopefully the Huns will suspect Dominic Lesser was the assassin and quit their hunt for us."

"But with Dom dead, won't they realize the threat is gone?"

"Not quite," he said. "Regardless of whether or not the kaiser is even in residence, the contact name you were given *is* a real German officer at Trélon headquarters. While Generaloberst Adler is interrogated, without success, of course, the Huns will remain vigilant to any attack and keep their troops in Trélon."

Eve's eyelids were drooping. It was all so much to take in. "What happens next?" she asked, yawning.

"In the next week, the real Allied offensive will begin to the north, in Cambrai," he said. "With the Germans preoccupied,

I will get another ambulance and take you and your brother and sister south to Reims, then east to an Allied airfield at Toul, where Marcus will arrange for pilots to fly us back to Britain."

Freedom, she thought. It had been such a long time since she'd experienced life without fear, or being forced to do the will of the enemy.

"What about Mama?" Eve had intended to send Nikki and Zoe back through Belgium, where they could reunite with their mother, but Simon's plan seemed a far better way to get her siblings safely out of the war. "We cannot leave her, or my aunt and uncle," she said.

"I spoke with the major before coming here," Simon said.

"Otto Reinhardt?"

"Yes, the Hun," he said, with a touch of sardonic humor.

Eve listened in disbelief as he explained how Otto had provided him with a truck and a pass into Chimay. And though Simon was somewhat cryptic, he added that Mama had been helpful in swaying Otto to promise to care for her and the Bernards as long as he was able. "He said he owed you that."

Though she was touched with gratitude, Eve still worried. "We can't simply abandon her in Brussels."

"Sweetheart, I promise to do everything in my power to get your mother out of Belgium," he said gently. "Until then, however, I know that above all she would want her children kept safe, and that includes you. Your aunt and uncle will care for her. And even though he's a Hun, I believe Otto will keep his word."

Eve knew he was right. Still, she ached at the thought of leaving her mother behind. "What about Maddie?" She worried about her friend remaining in Belgium. "Can we let her know what we're doing in case she wants to leave with us?"

"We'll get word to her through Monsieur Duval and find out."

"You've thought of everything, haven't you, husband?"

His leaned over her. "Not everything, wife," he said. "But you can help with that."

Then his warm lips touched hers, and Eve met his kiss, her heart beating a steady rhythm, a new, quiet assurance she hadn't felt since the war began. He loved her, and he believed in her.

More importantly, she thought, Simon Forrester still believed in *them*.

EPILOGUE

*E*ve stood outside Victoria Station and again observed how daily life in London differed from the three years she'd spent in Brussels.

The faint but constant drone of artillery fire she'd grown accustomed to was missing; the people milling about the station appeared lively and full of hope—even the British Tommies, home on leave from active duty. Despite the food rationing that had begun throughout Britain, most citizens fared better than those who remained in Belgium and France, less beaten down than the people still imprisoned beneath the kaiser's rule.

Several planes streaked across the sky overhead, and Eve shielded her eyes from the bright sun as she looked upward.

No leaflets falling from the sky, making rash promises of comfort and hope. Instead, the Royal Flying Corps home defense squadron remained vigilant against air raids by the German Gotha pilots who occasionally tested their luck flying over Britain.

Knowing how many husbands, fathers, and sons were still conspicuously absent from the cities in old Blighty, Eve was selfishly grateful her husband remained homebound these days, training new pilots for the RFC squadrons at the Larkhill Aerodrome in Wiltshire. She had taken a nursing position at the rehabilitation hospital near their cottage in Highbury Court, helping the wounded who had returned to try to rebuild their lives.

Still, life was far from perfect. Most of her family remained across the channel. Mama was still living in Brussels with Aunt Marie and Uncle Lucien, and Eve could only pray Otto Reinhardt was making good on his promise to watch over them.

Marcus Weatherford was working on a plan to get her mother out of Belgium even now, perhaps into France, where Zoe had chosen to remain with Armand and Michel.

When they had arrived in Toul, Eve tried to convince Zoe to come home, but her sister announced she and Armand intended to marry, if Eve and Simon would stand up for them.

It was a small yet beautiful ceremony in the local church, and Eve realized that her sister had made a new life for herself, such as it was. Understanding firsthand the pain of being separated from the one you love most, she could only wish them both well and pray that the city would remain in Allied hands.

At least Zoe could write to her now and let Eve know how they fared. Maddie had decided to remain at the hospital in Charleroi, with the promise that if she was able she would look in on Eve's family in Brussels.

A whistle shrieked loudly, and Eve heard the rumble of the train's approach. Soon people began exiting the station, and her pulse quickened at the sight of the familiar pair emerging from the throng. Simon looked so handsome in his RFC uniform, gripping a tooled leather satchel at his side. His other arm rested around Nikki's shoulders.

Her brother was home for the weekend from his classes at Bloxham, near Banbury. In a few years he would be old enough to attend Oxford, where their father once taught. By then, Eve hoped, the memory of this horrible war would be just that for him—a memory.

Seeing Nikki's boyish grin, she smiled and realized he was more precious to her now simply because he was alive. It was hard to imagine just a few months ago she'd saved him from death on that muddy road in France, when God in His all-seeing wisdom had finally offered her the means she needed to forgive herself.

She would always regret the death of the German boy who had played soldier and the senselessness of it. Yet war created abominable situations, and until the fighting ended, mothers everywhere would mourn the loss of their sons and daughters through such violence. Hadn't she lost her own child?

Eve pressed her lips together. She would always wonder what their first son or daughter might have looked like, how their child would have walked and talked, and the possibilities awaiting in life. That potential was gone now, never to be fulfilled. The pain of loss lay deep in her heart, an ache she knew would lessen with time but never altogether leave her.

The two men in her life waved at her and walked briskly in her direction. Eve waved back, a secret smile playing at her lips as she laid a protective hand gently against her abdomen.

God had not only shown her His divine wisdom that day in the mud and the rain, when He allowed her to save a boy from violence—today He'd offered her new hope for the future. Today she would present Simon with a new gift, one he'd wanted for the longest time. *A life for a life* . . .

Once Simon reached her, he dropped the satchel and swept her into his arms. Uncaring of their audience, he bent his head and kissed her deeply.

When the kiss ended, she leaned her head against his chest, reassured by the steady beating of his heart.

Do you love me, daughter?

Gazing up at the heavens, Eve knew His voice, and accepted His mercy as she counted her blessings.

AUTHOR'S NOTE

*D*ear Reader,

     I hope you've enjoyed reading Eve and Simon's story, and for those who read *Not by Sight*, perhaps you recognized a familiar face. With so much WWI-era history yet to explore, I wanted to write another novel, not only to illuminate the hardships of those who lived in occupied countries like Belgium and France, but to share with you the remarkable people of the Great War who worked behind enemy lines.

While *High as the Heavens* is a work of fiction, much of the story was inspired by real people and events. Eve Marche's character was influenced by the lives of three Belgian heroines: British nurse Edith Cavell, who helped a covert group smuggle Allied patients out of occupied Belgium; Gabrielle Petit, who started working with British Intelligence shortly after helping her fiancé, a soldier wounded in the war, to cross into the Netherlands to rejoin his regiment; and lastly, the most influential to my character, Marthe McKenna (née Cnockaert). As Tammy M. Proctor writes in her book *Female Intelligence*, "Born in Westroosebeke, Belgium, McKenna was a young woman trained as a nurse when the Germans invaded her village in 1914. Her home was burned and her family was temporarily separated. McKenna was employed almost immediately by the Germans to work among the wounded, first in her village and then . . . at the Roulers German Hospital as a nurse until late 1916, winning the Iron Cross for her service."[1] While all three women were eventually arrested after being discovered by German spies, only McKenna was saved from the firing squad. After the war she wrote a memoir about her espionage experiences, which Sir Winston Churchill hailed as "The Greatest War Story of All."[2]

Early in my story, Captain Simon Forrester describes to Eve the time he spent in German prison camps and his subsequent escape into Switzerland. Simon's narrative was inspired by British RFC pilot A. J. Evans, who published his exploits as a POW in Germany in his book *The Escaping Club*.

Germany's invasion into neutral Belgium at the start of the war was brutal. Several Belgian cities were sacked and many civilians killed. The assault on Louvain was peculiar in that it didn't occur immediately; rather, the mayhem began a week later, from what is described as mistaken friendly fire. According to a post-war report, "In the streets numerous civilian corpses lay, and in some places corpses of German soldiers, who had been killed by one another in the night. Victims of panic and obsessed by the thought of francs-tireurs [guerilla fighters], they [the Germans] had fired on every group which they met in the darkness."[3]

The spy network *La Dame Blanche* was created in 1916 when British Captain Henry Landau of MI6 at Rotterdam, Holland, received ". . . a promise of train-watching posts at Liege, Namur, and Brussels . . . [He was] informed that the organization would be called *La Dame Blanche*, after the legendary White Lady whose appearance would herald the downfall of the Hohenzollerns. The name was appropriate, for they certainly did their share in contributing to the defeat of the German army, and ultimately to the abdication of the Kaiser."[4]

A sidenote: At the time of Simon's crash in Brussels, the British hadn't yet sanctioned the use of parachutes for their pilots (the first pilot to parachute from a plane was German, in 1918). However, in chapter 9 of Landau's book *The Spy Net*, he relates a story that by his account occurs prior to mid-September of 1917, of the need to "drop a spy by parachute"[5] into enemy territory after other attempts failed to establish a train-watching post at the Hirson–Mézières railroad line.

Also, while the secret tunnels beneath the church rectory in the story are fictional, you may be interested to know that the Church of St. Mary Magdalene in Brussels was "established by the Brothers of Mercy in the 13th century. Excavations carried out when the church was last restored (1956–1958) revealed . . . a much older sanctuary built, it is believed, by the Knights Templar on the foundations of which the present church was initially built."[6]

—KB

Notes

1. Tammy M. Proctor, *Female Intelligence: Women and Espionage in the First World War* (New York: NYU Press, 2003), 137.

2. Marthe McKenna, *I Was A Spy! The Classic Account of Behind-the-Lines Espionage in the First World War* (first published in 1932; 2015 edition by The Pool of London Press). Foreword by the Rt. Hon. Winston S. Churchill PC, CH, MP, Secretary of State for War, 1918–1921.

3. Professor Leon van der Essen, "Belgian Judicial Report on the Sacking of Louvain," http://www.firstworldwar.com/source/louvain_judicialreport.htm.

4. Henry Landau, *The Spy Net: The Greatest Intelligence Operations of the First World War* (first published in 1938 by Jarrolds Ltd; 2015 edition by Biteback Publishing, Ltd, London).

5. Ibid.

6. http://www.brusselspictures.com/2008/01/28/chapelle-de-la-madeleine/.

DISCUSSION QUESTIONS

1. The story is set in German-occupied Brussels, where Eve Marche and other Allied agents must watch their every move against the enemy's secret police. Can you imagine yourself as a spy during that time? What would be your primary motivation? Patriotism, survival, compassion, thrill-seeking, faith, or something else?

2. After her ordeal in Louvain, Eve suffers enormous guilt and despair. She takes outlandish risks, hides her emotions, and harbors a most dreaded secret from Simon. The experience of trauma can take the form of shell shock (today's post-traumatic stress disorder.) Has someone you know struggled with this disorder? How did they get help?

3. Belgians living under German occupation rebelled by forming secret underground groups to thwart the enemy and aid the Allies. This clandestine activity only increased measures by the German secret police to ferret out Allied spies and recruit double agents. Did you have any early suspicions as to the identity of the alleged enemy agent, Pi? What was your reasoning?

4. In the story, Eve has received God's forgiveness for the young boy's death but cannot forgive herself. Only by His examples of love through Simon, and His allowing her to save Nikki's life does she come to realize God has always been there for her, waiting for her to accept His mercy. Guilt and shame are emotions we can all identify with. Has there ever been a time when guilt has been a stumbling block in your life? How did God help you through it?

5. Eve's mother, Louise, is a talented lace maker, using her skill to weave secret Allied information into her lace. Zoe Marche and Monsieur Tulle code enemy troop information using a "shopping list," passing the list on to the British by way of a hollowed-out broom handle or mended laundry. Can you think of a method you might employ to transmit secret information during that time? Use your imagination!

6. Nikki and Michel are determined to join the French army and fight for the Allies, despite being only fourteen years old. Throughout history, young men have gone off to war, even lying about their age in order to enlist. What do you think motivates these boys? Does today's commercial violence contribute to that factor? Technology? Do you see a possible solution?

7. Eve's character was based on several real-life heroines, brave women who risked their lives to save their countrymen. Is there a man or woman, past or present, whom you consider your hero/heroine? What qualities about them do you admire most?

8. Who was your favorite character in *High as the Heavens*? Why?

ACKNOWLEDGMENTS

There is so much that goes into creating a novel, the most important being this author's faith, and her thankfulness to God in seeing her through. I would also like to thank my husband, John, for his unwavering love and support, especially through those days of deadlines; my deepest appreciation also for my critique partners and friends, Anjali, Darlene, Elsa, Krysteen, Lois, Patty, Ramona, Rose Marie, Susan, Sheila Kay, and Sheila R., whose generosity of time and expertise helped to make this story that much better. A special thank you to Marti Stanbery and to Beth McCasland and Julie Enevoldsen with the Lacemakers of Puget Sound—your extensive knowledge and help in answering my questions about bobbin lace making were invaluable, and any errors about the craft that might exist in my story are entirely my fault.

To my agent, Linda S. Glaz, and to my editors, Raela Schoenherr, LB Norton, Elisa Tally, and all those at Bethany House who helped bring this project to fruition, I cannot express enough my thanks for your guidance, encouragement, and support.

ABOUT THE AUTHOR

A Florida girl who migrated to the Pacific Northwest, Kate Breslin was a bookseller for many years. She is a Carol Award winner and a RITA and Christy Award finalist and lives with her husband in Seattle, Washington. Find her online at www.katebreslin.com.

Sign Up for Kate's Newsletter!

Keep up to date with Kate's news on book releases and events by signing up for her email list at katebreslin.com.

More Historical Fiction From Kate

When a suffragette hands a white feather of cowardice to an English spy who is masquerading as a conscientious objector, she never imagines the chain of events—and the danger—her actions will unleash.

Not by Sight

You May Also Like...

When unfortunate circumstances leave Rosalyn penniless in 1880s London, she takes a job backstage at a theater and dreams of a career in the spotlight. Injured soldier Nate Moran is also working behind the scenes, but he can't wait to return to his regiment—until he meets Rosalyn.

The Captain's Daughter by Jennifer Delamere
LONDON BEGINNINGS #1, jenniferdelamere.com

Growing up on the streets of London, Rosemary and her friends have had to steal to survive. But as a rule, they only take from the wealthy. When, on the eve of WWI, a mysterious client contracts Rosemary to determine whether a friend of the king is loyal to Britain or Germany, she's in for the challenge of a lifetime.

A Name Unknown by Roseanna M. White
SHADOWS OVER ENGLAND, roseannawhite.com

When a financial crisis leaves orphan Elise Neumann and her sisters destitute, Elise seizes their only hope: to find work out west through the Children's Aid Society. On the rails, she meets privileged Thornton Quincy, who suddenly must work for his inheritance. From different worlds, can these two help each other find their way?

With You Always by Jody Hedlund
ORPHAN TRAIN #1, jodyhedlund.com

◊ BETHANYHOUSE